Villains By Necessity

This is the story of what happens when some of the bad guys left over from the ultimate triumph of Good and Light decide to *do something about it*.

"Evil is as necessary as good—that's the underlying premise of *Villains By Necessity.*

"This is an enjoyable read, and even thought-provoking on occasion, and one which traditional fantasy devotees should enjoy."

—L.E. Modesitt, Jr.

"This first novel performs the difficult literary hat trick of producing a good and competent novel in one of the most clichéd subgenres—the epic adventure fantasy. . . . Forward succeeds in creating a plot whereby readers cheer on the villains in their quest."

—*Hartford Courant*

Villains By Necessity

Eve Forward

A TOM DOHERTY ASSOCIATES BOOK
NEW YORK

VILLAINS BY NECESSITY

Cover art by Darrell K. Sweet

A Tor Book
Published by Tom Doherty Associates, Inc.
175 Fifth Avenue
New York, NY 10010

ISBN: 0-812-52228-1
Library of Congress Card Catalog Number: 94-47205

First edition: March 1995
First mass market edition: March 1996

Printed in the United States of America

0 9 8 7 6 5 4 3 2

For my mother, who got me started,
And my father, who got me to finish.

With thanks to Aaron, Adam, Anthony, Brian, Chris, Dan, Denny, Deryn, Donald, Dylan, Faust, Ginger, Glen, Gloria, Jame, James, Jan, Janie, Jed, Jen, Jeff, Jeremy, Jerry, Joel, John, Josh, Julie, Karl, Karsten, Kim, Kurt, Laurel, Laz, Llynda, Luke, Mark, Matt, Monique, Nathan, Pat, Paul, Philip, Rebecca, Richard, Robert, Saritha, Scott, Sharon, Skip, Sonya, Stacey, Tim, Tom, Wayne, Wei-hau, Yoav, Zack—
all the rest whose names I may have forgotten, and all those whom I know under other names.

"This is the excellent foppery of the world, that, when we are sick in fortune—often the surfeit of our own behavior—we make guilty of our disasters the sun, the moon, and the stars; as if we were villains by necessity, fools by heavenly compulsion, knaves, thieves, and treachers by spherical predominance, drunkards, liars, and adulterers by an enforced obedience of planetary influence."

William Shakespeare
King Lear (1606)

Prologue

. . . The War raged for many years. The last Elven city, Tintoriel, fell to the armies of the Dark King, and so fell many strongholds of the feudal lords of man. Hundreds of heroes died in the struggle to free the world from the death-grip of the Dark King's minions. In the end, it took a small but brave band of adventurers, who overcame their differences with each other to unite for the good of the entire world. At last the armies of darkness were dispersed, and the Gate through which the darkness had come was sealed forever. Even the deities of darkness and chaos were driven away, held back by the powerful forces of Good.

As the towns and cities began to rebuild, groups of adventurers, seeking glory and wealth, took into their hands the finishing work of scouring all the remaining holdouts of evil; dank crypts haunted by the undead, tattered temples to the weakening dark gods, clusters of brigands and monsters who preyed in an evil fashion upon good folk.

The towns and cities were rebuilt, better than ever before. The disruption of old social orders and the need to unite for a common goal had caused the old social and racial animosities to vanish. Reforms began, and the aura of goodness seeped into every facet of life. People smiled more and fought less, gave more and stole less, talked more and warred less.

And nowhere was this more evident than in the Six Lands at the heart of the world, where all that was great began. The people of the Six Lands were at last united in harmony. They worked together to make the world a better place, both in the Lands and the entire world beyond. Their goodness spread out from the Six Lands to all the far reaches of the world, from the desert lands of Shadrezar to the ice fields of K'kulbar. Swords became plowshares, mercenaries settled down and raised families. And even the adventuring parties put on weight and wrote their memoirs; for all was done, all was finished, all was well, all was Good. All was. . . .

I

"Boring!"

Sam barked the word aloud. It rang hollow in the empty room. He sat down with a thump in a chair and looked about the once-teeming hall of the Assassin's Guild. It was utterly, utterly empty. The assassins had all left months ago, turning in daggers and poison for a peaceful way of life, one that wouldn't trouble their sleep at night and, above all, one at which they could make a living. No assassin had had a contract in months. Members would go out on missions and would never return, only to be seen later, elsewhere, wearing relaxed smiles and working at peaceful professions. Finally the Guildmaster had stepped down, no one wanted to take his place, and the Guild, hundreds of years old, dissolved overnight. The building had been politely bought by the Town Council, which planned to turn it into a school for young girls. But now it was empty, except for memories and the last assassin in Bistort, possibly in all the Six Lands. Sam adjusted his collar so that it hid the small, star-shaped birthmark at the juncture of his shoulder and his neck.

Sam had "left" when the others had; it wasn't wise to defend yourself as the last remaining assassin. Not while there were still town guards. The emptiness of the room echoed at him. It made him angry, made him want to kill something. He got up and paced silently around the room. His black cloak swirled about him, despite the numerous weapons concealed in it, and his dark but rich clothing absorbed the light of the single candle that lit the wood-paneled room. He ran his fingers through his unnaturally black and greasy hair and sighed. He was in his mid-thirties, with rough-cropped neck-length hair and world-weary hazel eyes, built slender but deceptively strong. Average to attractive, without being distinctive in any way, with a lifetime of training but still unhindered by age, he was at the peak of his skills . . . but there was no call for them.

The hair on the back of his neck prickled. Old instincts, drummed into his mind and body since he was young, sang a shrill note of warning; someone was approaching from behind. Fast and silent as a shadow-slip he twisted and caught the figure, nearly as invisible as he, as it turned, too late to flee. With a grunt he lifted the struggling being out of the shadows by the neck. It was a small scruffy figure, perhaps three and a half or four feet tall. He snarled the snarl that had been the last sight of many men and was greeted with a twisted smirk and a pair of bright blue eyes that sparkled from under a mop of reddish curls, frosted here and there with silver, and a leather cap. With a faint noise of disgust Sam dropped the intruder onto a nearby table and wiped his hands fastidiously on the hem of his cloak. The intruder rubbed his neck and grinned at him.

"Now, then, Sam, such are a poor way for ye to be greeting your old friend!"

Sam glowered. "You're right, Arcie . . . I should have run you through." He paused. "Why is an old weasely thief like you poking around the forlorn yet proud halls of the Guild?"

Arcie sat himself comfortably on the table and took out a pipe. "Well, laddie, I'll tell ye. For cause that *the* Guild, in which of course I do mean *my* Guild, is now just dissolved, and I but wanted tae come over an' gloat o'er the much longer the trade o' sneakthief are outlived yer trade o' cutthroat." He grinned that infuriating grin again. "I ken ye'd be back here moping." He started to clean his pipe, using one of the blowgun needles Sam had had hidden in his sleeves. Sam ignored it.

"Right, longer by a whole, what, two months? Things have been happening, Arcie, and now they're happening fast." Sam glared, looking around the room with a hunted expression.

"What are ye going tae do, Sam? That are truly why I

comed over here . . . I ken *ye* wouldna go whitewash. Och, they used tae call ye . . . what were it? The Adder?"

"Viper," muttered Sam. "Long time ago."

Yes, he mused, a long time ago. Back when a thief would be killed instantly if he dared step foot inside an Assassin's Guild, and vice versa . . . animosity between the two trades was . . . *was* quite fierce. Then the Victory came, and things slowly fell apart. He knew Arcie from those days, when on the occasional job some small crawling was required that his own five-foot-eleven height couldn't fold to. It was a breach of protocol to ask another assassin for help on an assignment, so he'd turned to a thief who was not only one of the shortest people around, but one of the few who could be bribed by an assassin. They'd been a sort of team, when Sam had needed him; Sam would plot the route and get the target, hunting in his cold, methodical, superhumanly unstoppable way, and Arcie would cheerfully loot the target's house. It was all still a tremendous embarrassment to the assassin, and the other man's incorrigible attitude had never helped.

Arcie was one of the many folk of Bariga to leave his rural home and seek his fortune in the cities of the Six Lands. In the harsh cold and scouring winds of the northern province of Bariga, humans had adapted and were small, dexterous, and well-insulated. Even so, Arcie was small among his people, who more normally stood at around five feet. Short, clever, and with a certain bloody-minded selfishness, he would smile even as he robbed you blind or slit your throat. He'd done well in the big city and had become the Guildmaster of the Guild of Thieves, and actually managed to survive the office. He was older than Sam, how much he'd never said; Sam would judge him, physically, to be in his mid-to-late forties, and mentally, to be about twenty summers; far removed from the stoic, responsible inhabitants of Bariga. The black sheep of his family, no doubt. He'd lived as a thief much of his life and never really had to grow up. It made him extremely annoying at times.

"D'ye think as we're the only ones?" asked Arcie after a moment, sounding almost plaintive. Though he was pushing fifty, he still kept that certain innocence of appearance, useful in his trade. Sam took a chair and sat down.

"The only ones of what?" he asked.

"As haven't whitewashed. What haven't become good folks, law-abiding folks, little-old-lady-helping decent folks." Arcie spat on the floor for emphasis.

"I don't know . . . " Sam pulled his cloak around himself defensively. "Well, of course not. I mean, there's been evil ever since there's been sapience . . . "

"Och, laddie! I wouldna call us evil . . . " interrupted Arcie, his eyes wide and offended. "Self-sufficient, aye, lacking in a compassion, perhaps . . . "

"I wouldn't either. But you realize that that's how we're seen. Just because a fellow takes pride in his work he's branded as a villain." He threw up his hands in exasperation. "I'm an assassin! It's what I do! It's all I know!" He sighed. "I don't know if we're the only ones, Arcie. I don't really care. Let's just get out of here. This place is getting me depressed."

"More so than as usual?"

Sam ignored him. "Let's go," he said, standing up, black silk billowing.

"Go? Go where?" Arcie tapped out his pipe and pocketed it.

"Where else?"

"Och, aye. A tavern."

The Frothing Otter was a good tavern, with fine tables and clean straw on the floor. Arcie and Sam sat in the far table in the shadowy corner. Of course. Merchants and townsfolk eyed Sam's assassin blacks and whispered nervously among themselves. Happy bar noises drifted through the scent and smoke of the room. Arcie chugged his third pint of ale and peered at his sullen companion, who was nursing a goblet of dark red wine. The Barigan furrowed his red curly eyebrows at Sam, making his face crinkle up into its numerous small wrinkles.

"Ye really ought tae change clothes, Sammy. Folk are talking."

Sam snorted softly. "Let 'em talk. Not going to change clothes. Only thing I've got left. Everything I own in these clothes. And . . . " he hiccupped. "Everything I am." His black hair was dull in the lamplight. "I snuff, therefore I am." He giggled.

Arcie looked exasperated. Sam never could hold his liquor. Fragile Sixlanders. True, the past few weeks had been disappointing. All the news that had drifted their way showed a virtual mirroring of what had been happening in their own city. Guilds of smugglers, thieves, assassins, bands of robbers, ships of pirates, all were coming clean, turning honest. It had been happening for months, years, but he'd been too wrapped up in his own problems to notice. He had watched as his last members had come to him, dropped their last dues on his desk along with their papers of departure, and walked out. Most had simply vanished earlier without even that formality. Many had left town. Some became locksmiths, or craftsmen. Sam's peers he had seen as chemists or butchers. Some had become merchants, or farmers, or fishermen. It was disgusting. Years of training . . . The slide and crawl of wall-scaling, the feather-touch of pickpocketing, the snick and click of locks and traps to thwart, the silent footsteps and melting merging of stealth . . . all abandoned. He looked again at his companion. Look at him. He hasn't touched liquor in years. Why? So that his hands are steady and strong, strong enough to snap a spine. So that his eyes are clear and can pick out the motion of a moth in the darkness. So that his step is sure and silent. So that his health will allow him to endure doses of venom that would kill a normal man ten times over, and his reflexes so trained he could cut off his own arm without a whimper.

And now, thought Arcie, *now he's as useless as the tits on a boar hog, giggling his way through his second glass of wine. I gives him a year, p'raps two, before he joins his victims in the everafter. He'll die before he whitewashes.*

Sam was starting to sing softly. Pitiful. "Come along, laddie. Let's go."

They stood up and walked out, Sam owlishly counting out a handful of coins to the barkeeper. Arcie resolved to get the fellow back to the ex-Guild before his drunk reached the angry stage. As they stood by the group of merchants and caravaners sitting at the bar itself, Arcie noticed a fat purse slung on the waist of one of the men, conveniently hidden from others' view by the edge of the bartop. Being short has many advantages, he mused, as, almost without thinking about it, he employed a Ferret-foot's Brush-Cut and slit the strings of the pouch with the sharpened edge of a silver coin. His short but nimble fingers raised the flap to slip the pouch off the belt without spilling its contents onto the floor . . .

CRACK!

Arcie yelped as a complex mechanical device snapped on his fingers, immediately attracting the rather unwelcome attention of the entire bar.

I'll be baked! the Barigan thought. *Fizarian pouch-trap! I must be losing me touch.* He rubbed his sore fingers ruefully and the bar reacted to the incident by closing around them. *Haven't seen one of them in ages . . .*

He looked up at Sam, grinned, and shrugged. Sam had his hand over his face. There was no point in trying to make a break for it, not in this crowd of good citizens. Arcie felt a firm, gloved hand descend on his shoulder. He craned his neck to look up into the stern face of a town guard. He grinned cheerfully and tipped his cap.

"This is another fine mess you've gotten me into, Arcie."

"They wouldna have picked ye up as well if ye hadna been wearing the blacks."

"Can you get out?"

"Och, I'm fair skilled, laddie, but I'm surely not this good."

Sam peered through the gloom of the dungeon cell to the far wall, where the Barigan was chained. Not only was the small man virtually nailed to the wall with iron clasps on his neck, waist, wrists and ankles, but his hands had been encased in gauntlet mittens. The guard had taken all his clothing but his breeches, rather than bothering to simply search and seize his weapons and lockpicks, as they had done to Sam, and now Arcie's bare toes wiggled by way of a wave. "They must have built that specially for you," commented Sam. The wine had made his mind feel fuzzy and sleepy and depressed.

"Mayhaps. One o' yon guardsmen do have a sort of a pet peeve against me. They did swore did they ever catch me . . . " He tried to shrug in his bonds and gave his twisted grin.

Despite changes on the outside world, the cell was almost reassuringly traditional. It was dark and gloomy and had moldy straw on the floor. A flickering torch outside cast strange shadows into the cell. Sam saw these things from his own manacled roost on the wall. Echoes of dripping water drifted down the corridors now and then, and now he heard the unmistakable sounds of footsteps.

"Someone's coming."

A moment later, with a ringing of keys and clanking of a lock, the door creaked open. Into the cramped cell stepped Oarf, the Captain of the Guard, and Mizzamir, the most famous and powerful wizard in the entire world. Sam and Arcie stared.

Oarf, a burly warrior with maybe a few too many years of cozy living, looked Sam and Arcie over and gave a chuckle that made his chain mail jingle musically. Sam noted that the Captain's sword was secured in its scabbard by a peace knot. *Things must be getting really bad . . . or rather, really good,* he thought.

"Ho!" chortled the Captain, poking at Arcie's midriff with a mailed finger and patting Sam on the head, then with a tinge of disgust wiping a bit of black grease off on Sam's tunic. "What have we here, then? Looks to me like a couple of social miscreants. Poor fellows, it's not much of a life for you, is it? Always on the run, sleeping with one eye open, fighting for your life in dark alleys . . . "

Sam tried to shrug, but his bonds made it difficult. "It's a living."

Arcie piped up. "Aye, though rather, he can really make a killing in his line of work."

Sam was watching the wizard. Mizzamir was a figure held in great respect, the last surviving Hero. Bistort, like all the towns of Dous, was run by a mayor who was part of a Council made up of other mayors that made decisions for the whole of Dous. Sam knew Mizzamir would occasionally make an appearance here, Dous being short of mages, but he had never thought to see the great wizard.

Mizzamir was an Elf, one of the very few left in the world. After the Victory, that fairest race had vanished into some land beyond man's knowing, saying that their work was done. Only a few, Mizzamir among them, had remained, sacrificing that eternal Elven paradise to devote their lives to educating and aiding the humans of this world. Mizzamir had been one of the small band of Heroes that had fought the conclusive battle that ended in the Victory, about a century and a half ago. Mizzamir was head and founder of the Thaumocracy of Natodik. He was handsome despite his years, with long silver-white hair and a beardless, delicate face that showed the grace of the long-living Elvenkind. He wore pure white robes embroidered with mystic symbols in silver and gold thread, with a collar that came up to fit snugly around his neck. His fingers sparkled with rings, and chains around his neck held several important looking pendants. He held a staff so carved and inlaid it looked like a rolled-up rood screen. The wizard was fairly crackling with magic significance. Mizzamir caught Sam looking at him and gave him that high-huff yet kindly and infinitely patronizing look that Elves were so good at; Sam countered with his best silent snarl and a glare.

Meanwhile, Oarf was going on, talking to Arcie, as he seemed to be the friendlier of the two criminals. "Well, fortunately we're going to be able to help you there. No more will you have to live in darkness and evil."

"Ye are going to kill us?" Arcie looked like a hurt puppy, his bright blue eyes pure frightened innocence, while his toes stealthily worked at the loop of keys on Oarf's belt. Oarf chuckled again.

"No, of course not, little fellow," (Arcie hated that term.) "We've got something much better . . . "

Mizzamir turned his back to Sam and spoke. "Perhaps you've heard of the spell of Attitude Adjustment?"

"Attitude . . . are that like how one measures how high a mountain are?" asked Arcie. Mizzamir smiled.

"No, little one . . . " Arcie tried not to wince. "We who understand the workings of the universe realize that our world is influenced by the forces of Good, of Light, and by the Evil forces of Darkness. This is because our world, Chiaroscuro—"

"Chiar-wha?" exclaimed Arcie.

"Chiaroscuro. It is the name of this world that we live on," Mizzamir explained.

"And what's it need a name for?" demanded Arcie. " 'Tis not like there be a whole lot of others for us tae mix it up with." He was hoping if he acted dangerous enough, Oarf might step a little closer to toe-range. Mizzamir decided to ignore his comment and press on.

"Our world, with its magic used by both mages and monsters, draws the energy for that magic from two alternate dimensions, one of pure evil force, and one of pure good . . . "

While Mizzamir went rambling on about gates and portals and power flows, the two captives paid little attention. Arcie smiled and nodded while plotting his escape, and Sam was feeling the effects of wine and stress and wondering muzzily if he could manage to vomit on Oarf from this distance.

"And, you see," Mizzamir went on, "because of the way that these two forces affect everything in this world, so do they affect persons as well. The forces that dominate a person's beliefs control their actions, and vice-versa. People themselves are either good or evil, to one extent or another . . . For example, myself and Captain

Oarf here are followers of the way of Light and Good . . . "

Here Oarf nodded proudly. Arcie looked impressed and carefully worked his big toe through the metal ring of keys. Mizzamir shifted slightly and put his back to the door. He didn't like the itchy feeling Sam's dark gaze was making between his shoulder blades.

"Yes, ourselves and other right-thinking persons, as most all persons are these days, follow the path of Good. Yet some poor, misguided folk, who either through ignorance of the effect of their actions or through deliberate callousness live . . . in . . . the darkness . . . of . . . evil . . . " He turned his gimlet gaze on Sam. The assassin resisted the urge to stick his tongue out.

I wish he'd get to the point, Sam thought. *I want to go back to my hole in the wall and go to sleep.*

Arcie apparently was of the same opinion.

"So what are yer point, Mizzy?" he asked. Oarf had shifted out of range, and Arcie took a break from his clandestine efforts. Mizzamir glared over his fine handsome nose at the man with the wiggling toes.

"The point is, that no longer do we have to go about our old, brutal, nasty ways of punishing criminals like yourselves. Instead we have a simple, painless, magical process that will free you from the evil and darkness that holds you and will let you take your place in society as a decent member of the community." Sam and Arcie exchanged glances. They didn't like the sound of that.

The Elven wizard rolled up his sleeves and flexed his fingers. Oarf stepped back respectfully as Mizzamir continued, "Yes, a simple magical process, to cleanse the soul and spirit of evil and fill it with goodness and light. A process that I have perfected, and passed on to all the great wizards of all the cities and towns of this fair world, so that darkness need never threaten our ways of peace and light again. Common criminals, evildoers, who for once the only option was death, are now living happy, productive lives . . . many of your peers among them," he added, looking from one shocked face to another.

Sam moved abruptly and now seemed to be vibrating softly. In fact he had thrown every ounce of wiry muscle against his bonds and was pulling himself taut as a bowstring with the effort of trying to rip the iron cuffs free from the mortar. The mage's words threw him into panic. He knew with cold terror what Mizzamir was saying, and he didn't want it. His mind was his own, his thoughts his own, his will his own. The thought of losing his identity sent adrenalin pumping through his veins, reacting with the wine . . . The dungeon seemed to go darker, and little spots and sparks flashed in front of his eyes. The cuffs on his wrists felt red-hot as he strained every muscle against them. But it seemed no use. His back ached and his chest burned, but his hands remained chained fast.

Without relaxing a muscle, Sam hissed through his teeth, "He's going to turn us into farmers, Arcie."

The reality suddenly dawned on the Barigan. His jaw dropped and banged on the iron collar. "But but but but . . . that's not just whitewashing . . . that's brainwashing! I like being the way I am!"

"Oh, you'll like being a good person," assured Oarf. "Everyone does. All the other evil crooks and killers we've caught and done this to thanked us afterwards."

"Yes, and you'll soon forget I even did this, once it's over . . . your past of darkness and fear will just seem like a bad dream, long ago . . . " Mizzamir smiled a complacent, patronizing smile. Arcie caught his breath. Grains of sand were starting to fall away from the wall bolts of Sam's right-hand manacle. Beads of sweat stood out on the assassin's forehead, and streaks of black sweat (black?) were running in little rivers down his neck as he strained, trembling ever so faintly. Arcie spoke again to keep attention away from the assassin.

"Ye canna do this! Don't we have but any right to say as we want to live our lives? Aren't ye being twice as bad as ever we were by *forcing* us into this?"

"No, silly fellow! This is for your own good," chuckled Oarf with an encouraging wink.

"And for the good of all," added Mizzamir, reaching

for his spell-focusing components. Sam knew with sick certainty that despite Mizzamir's kindly appearance, he wasn't a wizard who forgot his spells. Arcie stammered incoherent protests.

"Now then . . . " Mizzamir opened one of his many belt pouches and took out two small squares of mirror and two small scraps of spotted fur. Putting one of each aside, he turned to Sam. "I shall cast upon you first, since you seem calmer than your chubby friend . . . " Arcie drew in his breath angrily. Sure, maybe he was a little short for his weight, but "chubby"! As Mizzamir held up the fur and mirror and took on that inward look of a mage in the process of spellcasting, Arcie had an idea. As the wizard began to chant, soft gold and lilac tendrils of magic floated from his fingers and reached for Sam, like insidious vines.

"Aletha mainaria t'thuluck . . . "

The chant echoed in Sam's ears. His wrists, hands, back, and fingers screamed in agony, but his voice was silent. In the power of the mage's spell, a dark haze, shot through with crimson flames, seemed to hover around Sam; the strands of gold and violet strove to unweave the dark haze, but the crimson singed them, held them back . . . but the flames were dying . . .

Arcie peered over the mage's shoulder at Sam. The assassin would probably be furious with him later, but there was no other choice.

He caught Sam's gaze, and whispered, "A thousand in gold fer the head of the Arch-Mage Mizzamir."

Arcie's words flew like arrows into Sam's brain and exploded at the core of his being, ignited by drunken anger. He opened his eyes, but his vision twisted inward. His mouth formed a word.

"Accepted."

Time slowed to a crawl. The chant was a dull, slow dissonance in his ears. Down within was the fire, beyond magic, beyond training, the dark seductive glimmer of onyx and ruby that had kept him alive as a bastard child in the slums of the city, that had made him feared as a young man working his way up the ladder of the Guild, that had ended the lives of many men. The deep fire that knows no good nor evil but only the target and the path to it. Sam looked outward and saw the white figure of the wizard. Then he opened his veins, and the fire flared in his blood and lit his eyes and filled his brain with a roar. The crimson flames in the darkness of his aura, seen only by the wizard, roared forth like the bitter flares from an ancient sun going nova. Mizzamir faltered, surprised.

To Arcie, watching on his wall, it seemed Sam muttered something, his pupils dilated for an instant, then there was a sudden sharp crack.

Sam's wrist snapped the cuff out of the wall and too fast to follow swung about and slammed it into the side of the Elven wizard's head. Mizzamir flew halfway across the cell and landed in the doorway, very still. His spell, uncompleted, sparked and gave off a smell of burning lemons. Oarf gave a cry of surprise and went for his sword, tugging at it in anger when he discovered he still had his peace-knot tied. He fumbled with it as Sam in silent hunting fury grabbed his other shackled wrist and yanked. Mortar shivered, but this cuff held. He yanked again, and this time his wrist actually pulled free of the cuff, almost the entire surface layer of the skin scraped away, pure white for an instant before every pore began welling scarlet.

Sam lunged for the mage on the floor, but his ankle cuffs held and he fell on his face, narrowly dodging the sword Oarf had finally managed to unsheathe. As Sam clawed at the straw on the floor, Oarf tried to club him with the sword's pommel, but Sam grabbed the guard's heavy leather boot and gave a powerful pull. Losing his balance, Oarf staggered back. Arcie made a grab with his toes and snagged the keys off the belt, as the guard recovered and switched to using the blade of his weapon. Sam was now pulling at the cuffs on his legs, his efforts scattering drops of blood from his scraped hand. Oarf slashed again, this time coming closer; the blade drew a line of crimson from Sam's side. Oarf was about to strike again when he heard the groan of the metal cuffs under strain, and one of Sam's arms almost broke his kneecap. Deciding at once that a blood-maddened assassin was not someone to cross in a small cell, Oarf scooped up the limp form of Mizzamir, and dashed out the door, slamming it behind him. Sam thrashed in his bonds in a silent fury.

"Sam! Sam! Ho up there a second, my fellow . . . here, I've got the keys . . . " Arcie jingled the keys in his toes.

Sam lay on his side in the straw, his legs twisted up from his struggles. He looked up at Arcie.

"Give them here," he rasped, holding out his gory hand. Arcie gave a flick of his foot and tossed the keys to him. Sam caught them and bent himself double working at his bonds while Arcie fidgeted. Sam's hunting was normally cold and methodical, the result of the rigid discipline of the Guild. This berserk rage must be the fault of the wine. Had the Barigan known it, he would have realized it was also due to something not normally part of the assassin's contract: emotion. Sam's anger at the loss of the only home and family he had and his fear at the prospect of what the wizard had attempted.

The last lock clicked free, and Sam lunged for the door, slamming his shoulder into it once, then thrusting one long arm through the tiny window to scrabble for the lock. Arcie piped up.

"Here, laddie, wait a tic . . . aren't ye forgetting something?"

Sam glanced over his shoulder at Arcie, who squirmed in his bonds. "You'll be safe," he said shortly.

"I don't wants to be safe, blast your eyes, I wants to be free. Let me out or I canna pay your fee and ye canna take it out of my hide, either."

Sam relented and quickly undid the cuffs that held the Barigan. Arcie dropped to the floor with a thump, pulling off his gauntlets. Sam returned to the door, as Arcie rubbed his neck and said, "We aren't going to be far popular around here shortly . . . I'll see if I can't borrow some horses, well enough?"

The door snicked open. "Whatever. He's still alive, Arcie. I saw him breathing. While he lives, neither we nor anyone like us is safe." The assassin was gone in a stagger of black cotton and silk. Arcie sighed, and followed at a more dignified pace. A quick stop at the empty guardroom yielded him his clothes and equipment and Sam's weapons. He paused to shudder a moment wondering how Sam was going to be able to carry out his instructions with only his bare hands, and then swiftly went down the dingy halls, keeping to the shadows and wielding a morning-star he'd picked up just in case. Not a real thief's weapon, but impressive looking.

The stable hand, dozing with a jug of cheap wine, was jerked wide awake by a *thock* right next to his ear, and the accompanying pain as a sliver of his earlobe parted company from the rest of him. He jerked up with a cry, and saw a small shadowy figure leaning against a wall across the room. The light hid the figure's features, but a small shaft of late afternoon sun glinted off a dagger blade held loosely in its hand, twin to the one in the wall next to his bleeding ear. A voice spoke softly.

"Well, well, laddie. I think we'll be taking yon gray gelding there, and that nice sorrel pony, with tack and saddlebags, if ye dinna mind. And no yelling, thank ye . . . or the next one's through your skinny neck." The stablehand gurgled in fear.

Sam ran through halls, gray halls with red air. Speed took priority over stealth and his footsteps slapped on the flagstones. He ran out of the dungeons, up into the castle that served as the center of the rule of the city. A guard stepped out from an annex, surprise evident on his face. "Here, you can't go . . . Awwk!" he said as Sam wordlessly rammed his bloody fist into the man's gut. The guard crumpled, and Sam ran on, hunting.

It was more than an assignment now. It was both survival and revenge. He remembered the tales he'd heard about Mizzamir. Mizzamir was one of the greatest Heroes. He'd located the forces of the enemy, he'd supplied the other Heroes with guidance and magic. He'd set out to defeat one of the main wizards of the Dark and had hunted him for many months before the final confrontation in which he had emerged triumphant. It was said of him that, as a matter of pride, he never let a job go half-finished. Well, Sam thought, neither do I. He's destroyed all my friends, the only family I ever had. Old Miffer and Tich and Cata and Black Fox and Darkblade . . . I thought they were just being stupid . . . but they were dead, their brains and souls turned to vanilla pudding by this white-robe's magic.

He passed a doorway, then with a flip turned and leaped in. Something other than logic sent him crashing through a door and there, sitting up in horror with an ice-pack on his head, was the impressive silvery figure of the arch-wizard. Mizzamir grabbed one of his rings and shouted a strange word, and Sam stumbled as the air around him suddenly turned thick and heavy, as though he were trying to run through neck-deep honey. The magic effectively halted his rush, losing him his one advantage of speed.

Both men froze. Sam knew better than to rush a wizard in this state. They faced each other, the black-clad assassin, his face bloody and stained with sweat, dirt, and sooty grease, his clothes torn and filthy, bleeding heavily from a sword-wound in his side, his eyes burning with frozen fire, and the stately old Elven wizard, in his flowing silver-white robes, his silver hair falling gently around his shoulders, his green eyes wide in surprise, the afternoon sun pouring in a window and making him shine like a star. They faced each other warily, each waiting to see what his opponent would do before moving.

Mizzamir spoke first. "You are a villain, but I see in you the potential for goodness. I will save you from the darkness, as I have saved many others."

"Save yourself first, wizard," Sam answered softly, and leaped, a burst of will giving him the strength to counteract the mage's spell for an instant. But he was still not fast enough. As he lunged, Mizzamir stepped back and, with a gesture as of parting curtains, a phrase of magic and a flash of indigo light, he wrapped the very fabric of reality around himself and vanished, the air rushing in with a *whumpf* where he had been. Sam had to twist himself in midair to keep from crashing into a table, and only partly succeeded. He rebounded and collapsed against the wall, panting, his energy draining fast now that his target was out of range. A whistle sounded outside the window.

He craned his head around to look. Down in the castle courtyard, Arcie, mounted on a swaybacked pony, held the reins of a Troisian riding horse and beckoned impatiently. With the last ounces of his strength, Sam climbed out the window and slid down the trellis, climbed heavily aboard the gray horse and clung tight as it galloped after Arcie's mount.

The two riders charged through a clustering mass of guards and ran through the town, through the gates, out into the fields and farms beyond, then vanished with the blood-red sun into the forested hills of the wilderness.

"How are ye doing, Sammy?"

Sam opened his eyes to a bleary sky filled with red curls and blue eyes and white teeth. He gasped and tried to roll away, but suppressed pain flared in his side and hands, bringing him back to the present. He shook his head and groaned.

"Pooka piss, Arcie, where are we? What happened?"

Satisfied as to the well-being of his companion, Arcie sat back on a hillock and commenced filling his pipe. "Have a look around, old chap."

Sam looked. They were in what he supposed was called a glen, or maybe a meadow; he wasn't sure of the proper term. Woods on all sides, the two horses grazing a short way off, and a glossy black raven watching him from a dead tree to see if he was going to die or not. He thought about throwing something at it, but with the way his hands felt he didn't think he could. He looked at them. They were a rich blue-purple all around the wrists in a six-inch spread, and one hand was almost black with dried blood. Dried blood also caked a gash in his side, bound inexpertly with shreds torn from his cloak. As he summed up his wounds, recent events slowly returned to his memory, and he sank back in the grass with a groan.

"Arcie, you overweight son of a tomato, how could you do this to me? How could you set me into blood-fever when I was already four-thirds drunk and after an arch-mage at that?" He looked at his raw hand. "And you don't even bother to bind my wounds."

"I'm a thief, not a healer, Sam," Arcie reminded him, lighting his pipe. "I did the one on yer side, though. Ye bled all over the horse, had to stop ye from leaving a trail. Careless of ye. Ye slept all night." The Barigan grinned at Sam over clouds of blue smoke. "It was your wrists and hangover or both of our souls, Sam . . . Ye were great, though, really fierce. Snap wham crash! Did ye kill him?"

Sam stood and shook his aching head. The sun beat down, bright and unseasonably warm. They must be about a day's normal ride out of the city. "No. He got away."

"Och, well." Arcie shrugged philosophically. "Forget it then. Urk!"

Sam picked the thief up by the front of his cloak, and raised him up to eye level. The lank black hair around his face made him look almost supernatural. His voice was dangerously soft.

"Backing out of a deal, little man?" he asked kindly. Arcie wriggled to clear his windpipe enough to speak.

"Urk, uhg, no, no, course not. 'is 'ead. T'ousand gold. Paid on deli'vry . . . " He grimaced ingratiatingly. Sam set him down gently and flexed his sore fingers.

"I thought not. One doesn't hire an assassin lightly. I want a deposit. Five hundred."

"Two hundred," retorted the Barigan.

"Three or I rip *your* head off."

"Dinna get so vicious." Arcie tossed him a small emerald. "I've had that valued at three-fifty . . . gives ye a margin for not trusting me."

Sam pocketed the stone. "You don't bother to carry paste, I know that much." Indeed, the thief carried quite a sizable sum of wealth with him at all times, in the form of gold and platinum buckles and buttons on his clothing, and gems contained in various pouches, always ready for a quick bribe or getaway to safer cities.

Arcie adjusted his clothes and his dignity. "There's a brook over yonder if ye want to wash up . . . I would, if I were you. Ye look a fair grunge-worm."

Sam went to look. The brook was clean, bubbling softly over a lot of little pebbles. Arcie followed him and sat down to finish his pipe.

Sam dipped his hands into the water where it swirled in a clear deep pool. His scrapes stung painfully at first, but the cold water soon numbed them. He began working at the caked blood.

"Are ye going to go back and kill him, then?" Arcie asked after a moment.

"No . . . " replied Sam thoughtfully. "I'm certainly not going to go berserk again, no matter how entertaining it may be for you. It's time for calm, cool, collected action." His blood swirled red in the clear water. "He's going to come to me. He's going to come looking for me. And you. He's going to get friends and they're all going to come looking for us, to save us from ourselves. They're all going to come after us."

"Will they bring food, d'ye think?" wondered Arcie, looking up at the sun. "I'm half-famined."

Sam noticed that he too was getting hungry. "We're in a forest . . . aren't there supposed to be berries or mushrooms or rabbits or something like that around?"

"We could perhaps eat that big black bird," suggested Arcie, looking up at the raven. It clicked its beak at them and shuffled farther down the branch.

"I think, before you go eating anyone, you should explain what you are doing, polluting my stream with your blood," a powerful female voice said, not three feet from Sam's ear as a figure stepped inexplicably from the trunk of a solid tree. Arcie was so startled he dropped his pipe, and Sam fell neatly into the pool. The raven flew off, croaking.

* * *

"Never would have thought of ye as a blond, Sammy."

"Shut up."

The two refugees were huddled in the strange home of their equally strange hostess. After an initial bit of suspicion on all sides she had apparently decided to apprehend them, but the promise of food made the idea not unwelcome to the pair. The young woman had led them through the tangled forest, Arcie ducking under branches, and Sam bruised, sore, soggy, and covered with mud, as well as leafmold and twigs, by the time he had clumsily scrabbled through the thick vegetation.

They had arrived at a stone hill that thrust through the leaf-covered forest floor, and their hostess had pushed aside a lethal-looking thorn bush to reveal an open doorway. Arcie was allowed to enter, but she gave Sam a scathing glance and directed him frostily to a nearby well, with instructions to wash himself thoroughly. Sam, chastened, weakened by loss of blood and a hangover, had gone to comply.

Arcie mused what sort of woman had to be so foolish as to think she could stand up to a pair of city-hardened criminals, and what sort of treasure such a woman might carry. His speculations were cut short as he walked into the softly lit cave in the stone and came face to face with a pair of yellow-green eyes looking down at him.

He quickly decided that any woman who kept a wildcat twice his size was not someone he was going to bother. A quick professional inspection of the room revealed nothing of interest to him other than food, so he had submitted to accepting instead a huge wooden bowl of some kind of vegetable stew. It was delicious, and his hostess seemed mildly pleased at his enthusiastic response to her cooking. He was on his third bowl when the sounds of footsteps were heard at the door. He looked up cheerily and reacted in surprise as Sam finally entered, dripping but clean and was told to shut up as the assassin looked warily around. Arcie followed his gaze.

The place looked like it had been hollowed out from the living rock and quite suited his traditional Barigan preferences for warm sturdy shelter. The wildcat watched him from a corner near a small cooking fire that exited through a hole in the roof. Shelves were stacked with baskets, firewood, wooden and battered metal cookware, and a few old, tattered leather books. Bunches of dried herbs and wild tubers and dried fruit hung from hooks in the ceiling. Birds flew in the window and landed on the shelves now and then, would twitter around the room awhile, sometimes picking a few crumbs off the floor, and then fly out.

Sam himself was looking different. A check of his reflection in the mirrored surface of the well had given him cause to abandon his protective camouflage of grease and coal-dust hair mixture. A scrub with some viciously harsh herbal soap left by the well and a few buckets of water had left him with his old innocent-looking sandy-blond locks. A few more splashes took a good portion of the mud and blood and debris off his skin and clothing, a quick shave with a dagger, and then he'd caught himself, wondering what the hell he was doing washing up under the orders of some strange woman who walked through trees. He'd stomped back to the cave, following an aroma of vegetable stew and wondering what kind of assassin he was supposed to be, acting like this.

Arcie had been wondering the same thing. He turned from Sam to take another glance at the woman. Was she pretty? he wondered. A moment's reflection decided that yes, probably by Sam's standards, she was. She was too tall for Arcie's tastes and stretched-out thin looking, but she did have a few qualities he recalled were attractive to others. She looked about Sam's age, maybe a bit younger, but with a strange wisdom in her leaf-green eyes that made her seem older. She had long red hair, rather tangled and unkempt, pulled out of her eyes by a headband of cloth. She wore some kind of simple robe, tied with a cord and hung with cloth pouches. She held a gnarled oak staff with a crook on the end, a bit taller than herself, and was watching them warily. He glanced again at Sam, then shrugged and went back to eating.

Sam wordlessly took a bowl of stew from the woman and sat on another log. The woman leaned against the wall and watched them, finally speaking in her strong, cold voice.

"Well, you eat, so you must be living beings enough. Have you names?"

Arcie set his bowl down and tipped his cap. "Most certainly, dear lady. I be Fredly Mirtin, of Shiredale, and this here be a friend of mine, named Eithin Frazpot, he's with a theater company . . . " He smiled widely, settling his cap back on his curls. The woman regarded him coolly.

"You lie," she replied calmly. "I heard you call this man 'Sammy' as he walked in here."

Sam and Arcie exchanged glances, and Arcie shrugged.

"Och, right then. I'm called many things, but most of them are Arcie. That yonder are Sam. I'm a freelance tax collector, and Sam is . . . "

" . . . An assassin," Sam stated bluntly.

"Ah yes," replied the woman, as if she had known all along anyway. "You are what they call criminals. On the outskirts of this forest, to the west, a company of five men in armor are searching for you and getting quite lost." Arcie chortled and reached for the water jug. "So, you are criminals, then? You lie, cheat, steal, break into the homes of innocent people and murder them and their families in their beds, spy, rape, incite riots, torture, loan-shark, and similar?"

The water jug clattered on the floor, and Sam and Arcie stared at her in blank shock. The wildcat slowly unfolded itself from the corner and stood in front of her, watching them and twitching its tail. The two men checked the door. It was still open. With the way out thus assured, Arcie spoke up again hurriedly.

"Uh, nay, miss, I dinna think you've got it quite clear . . . I mean, lying, aye, but that be just a survival tactic . . . "

Sam helped him out, while keeping an eye on the wildcat. "Cheat, well, we don't cheat much. We don't play that many games worth cheating over, mostly."

"And steal, aye. I steal things. But how else am I supposed to make a living? There bein't many options open to people my size, and my talents don't lie in any other direction." Arcie tried his best innocent eyes at her. She met them with frost. "As for breaking into houses . . . "

"And murder . . . " Sam mumbled the word distastefully.

"Myself, I dinna usually kill people. I steal things so well that I surely dinna need to beat someone over the head to take his wealth away. Myself, I've only killed once or twice, p'raps, and that fully in self-defense . . . well, mostly," Arcie shrugged.

"And neither I nor any of my compatriots has ever murdered an entire family in their beds," said Sam. "We kill whom we must, whom we are hired to, and we do it well and mercifully. Torture is not a service we provide. We never kill on a whim or for fun. We are hired, just as mercenaries are. If you are not strong enough or skilled enough to build your own barn, you hire someone to build a barn for you. If you lack the will and strength and training needed to kill someone whom you need to kill, you hire someone to kill him for you."

Arcie continued, "Spying and riots and loan-sharking, miss, them's not our trade . . . not usually, anyway. Not many people exists as trusts a thief to spy without robbing the place blind and so gets noticed. Assassins are too stuck up tae do anything but what as they're trained for, and even if ye can convince them, they charge far too dear." Arcie glanced over at the assassin as he spoke.

Sam ignored the comment. He was noticing that his boot dagger, his three specialized throwing knives, his two cuff blades and his carnelian-pommeled dagger seemed to be missing. **Damn you, Arcie, you thief,** he thought. He'd deal with this later.

The thief continued. "And no one's loan-sharked since the Victory, not with the government's handing out welfare to get everyone back on their feet . . . everyone except those of us what can't claim a legitimate occupation."

Sam's voice was cold and distant, his eyes flashing a strange anger and bitterness as he spoke.

"And neither of us has ever raped anyone or anything, at least I assume Arcie hasn't been . . . " He glanced at the Barigan, who shook his head.

"I'm only insistent about money and meals. Besides, women are nothing but trouble. My father always did say . . . "

"Rape and brutal murder and mugging and other violent, unprofessional acts . . . those are unorganized crime," interrupted Sam. "Crimes of insanity, or rage. The people who do that sort of thing often aren't criminals beforehand. Just jealous spouses, angry young men, and people who aren't quite swimming in the same river as the rest of us. They give us criminals a bad name."

"Sometimes us has to weed them out, ye ken . . . "

"Yes," nodded Sam.

" . . . if they persists. Our Guilds dinna put up with that kind of dangerous action from their members, and we don't like getting the blame for actions o' non-members." Arcie managed to look noble.

"Admittedly," added Arcie, "we've had less work for ourselfs since the Victory. The system are breaking apart, and we're becoming obsolete."

The woman's eyes watching them widened slightly. "You are speaking the truth," she noticed, seeming somewhat surprised. "More or less, anyway . . . "

Sam relaxed a little, and concluded, "In the society in which we evolved, we were a vital part, somehow . . . law and crime and disorganized anger, and the civilians milling through it all. It was a sort of balance."

"Yes. A balance." The wildcat curled up again, and Sam and Arcie breathed deep sighs of relief.

The woman pulled up a log and sat at the table. "I had hoped you were such ones, a dark element but not to the extent that you would not comprehend what I must tell you. Continue your meal, and I will explain." The Barigan grinned and snagged a loaf of bread from a nearby shelf and began sawing it in half with a knife that Sam recognized as one of his own, but the assassin was feeling too tired to bother with it now. Sam sipped his stew and watched the woman warily as she began to speak.

"My name, if you wish to know it, is Kaylana. I am what in the olden days was known as a Druid, though now the best I can explain myself is as one who understands and can utilize the power of nature."

"Really?" exclaimed Arcie. "Och, I might have guessed . . . the mistletoe, the pets, the vegetarian stew . . . "

"The way you walk through trees," muttered Sam. Kaylana ignored them and continued.

"There are no more Druids existing in the world now, as you may know . . . all were slain in the last bloody wars before the Victory."

"Seems to me I remember hearing of something like that. I were just a wee lad at the time, of course . . . "

"You weren't even born," scoffed Sam. "Neither was I. That was over a hundred and fifty years ago." Arcie grinned apologetically at him, and went on talking to Kaylana.

" . . . dinna they all get snuffed by the forces of Darkness?"

"*I* heard that they joined the Darkness, there at the end, and the forces of good had to destroy them," put in Sam.

"You are both correct. We—they, fought on the side of Light when the Darkness threatened to overthrow the world, in the winter of the Wars. Then when the Darkness was in retreat, and the Light had pulled back to reform as well, the Druids stood away. They refused to help the Light any farther, to heal their wounded or guide them to the foe or turn the weather in their favor. We hoped the war would end in stalemate. Our old allies grew angry, but soon had the strength to push home their attack on the Dark. As the Darkness began to retreat, we joined its forces and fought against the armies we had once served. Though we tried to aid them, the Darkness did not trust us, for we had helped the Light; they called us spies, and killed us. The Light called us traitors, and killed us. The armies ran through our forests, shot our animals, pulled our plants, burned our forests, and turned our plains into blood-soaked battlefields."

Her voice had softened with remembered sorrow, and the wildcat padded silently over to sit near her. She stroked its huge head gently.

"But why did yer Druids do such? Turncoat as that, I mean?" asked Arcie, wide-eyed.

"It has to do with what we believe, and what we are, as keepers of the Balance. What do you know of Light and Darkness, Barigan?" asked Kaylana, watching him. He shrugged. He'd never thought about it much.

"Only of what I've heard," he answered, and told her of Mizzamir's explanation of . . .

"Lime mints, he called them," finished the Barigan dubiously. "I weren't paying much attention . . . "

Sam shook his head. "No, it was something else . . . "

"I know what the Barigan means," inserted Kaylana. "Your Elf mage is typical. What he does not realize is that light and goodness overtaking the world is just as terrible as evil and darkness engulfing it."

The two looked at her curiously. She picked up an empty wooden bowl and demonstrated. "Imagine that this bowl represents the existence of this world. Good and Evil, as your mage supposed, act as forces on the world." She rested the fingertips of a hand on the rim of each side of the bowl and wobbled it in gentle circles on the tabletop. "The forces are in conflict and harmony at once. You may not understand this, nor does the mage. But we of nature do. For birth, there must be death. For night, there must be dawn. For one man to be good, another must be evil. For someone to win, another must lose. This is the cycle of nature, the seasons . . . This is the way of life, the way of balance, and this is why we do not follow your philosophy of choosing the extremes of Light and Darkness as the attitude that guides our path of life. We are standing in balance, in neutrality, and we strive to keep the world this way. The magic and power of nature take their strength from the mingling and dilution of the forces of life and death, Good and Evil, as they are poured into this world from the dimensions of magic and react to each other.

"That is why we fought on both sides, in struggle to maintain the balance. If darkness prevails . . . " she pushed down on one side of the wobbling bowl. It tilted up, its wobbling halted. " . . . the world is unbalanced. Death outruns life, night is forever, even the creatures of evil finally slip into death in their own darkness." She righted the bowl, set it wobbling again. "This did not happen. The Victory saved us from the evil . . . but something just as bad has happened. Light conquered, and drove the darkness away, far, too far away." Her fingers pushed slowly harder down on the other side of the bowl with each turn of her fingers. Its wobbling slowed, grew unsteady, began tilting under the gradual pressure. "This is what happens now. We are unbalanced. Nature is affected; the nights grow shorter, and the stars are brighter at night. The animals reproduce more, and the weak and ill do not die as they should, to make room for the new life. The vegetation runs riot. The people are slowing, drifting into ennui of constant prosperity. Every day, the balance is upset further, as more of the creatures of darkness die in the light, and people such as you vanish. You are not servants of darkness, but you represent it, wittingly or not. Your existence is a facet of darkness . . . but though the people curse you, and your darkness makes you alone, you are as necessary to the survival of the world as predators are to an environment. If everyone and everything were evil, the world would be plunged into eternal darkness. If everyone and everything were good, the world would be sublimated in a dazzling brilliance."

"I wouldn't want to be sublimated," commented Sam. He still felt weak, dizzy. Arcie looked up at Kaylana with a quizzical expression.

"What if everyone were neutral, like ye, then?" he asked.

Kaylana looked at him, and pressed her fingertips into

the center of the bottom of the bowl. It stilled. "Stasis. Everything would slow to a stop. Neither light nor day would come, so the world would be in perpetual twilight. The world would not move, nothing would grow, no wind would blow, no animals would run, no water would flow. Nothing would die, nothing would be born. Nothing would change. That is why good and evil are necessary. It is the conflict that allows change that allows existence to continue."

"So what's yer point of all this, then?" inquired Arcie.

"The point is, the world is in danger of being, as I said, sublimated. The balance is distorted, the world is slipping over. Soon, it will pass the point of no return, and there will be no way we can bring the scales back to level. It will be the end, but for the final flash of light."

"But don't the mages and other wise men know this? If the world's going to be destroyed, surely they wouldn't want that to happen?" Sam looked startled. He wasn't sure quite why, but he believed this so-called Druid. He himself had felt that the increasing goodness wasn't right, somehow . . . like icing on a cake that was too sweet, so that you couldn't eat it . . .

Kaylana put the bowl away wearily. "If they know, they do not believe. They cannot. They are Good, you see. They cannot tolerate evil. It goes against what they believe. Even if you could convince them that evil, that monsters, Nathauan, dark dragons and trolls and thieves and assassins were necessary for the existence of the world, they could not allow such creatures to exist and move in their evil ways. They have to fight them; it is what makes them good, and in the past that conflict was the motion that drove the world . . . as long as neither side won. They do not realize that by destroying their opposites, they undercut their own existence." She looked at them. "I feel you are among the last of those who once were the necessary dark forces of counterbalance. You are indeed evil . . . " Arcie started to protest, but Sam hushed him. Kaylana looked at him sternly. "Yes, thief. But understand it is not an insult. You know that what you do is wrong, but you do it anyway, for your own reasons, and simply because, though you do not realize it, somebody must."

Sam realized what she was saying, though his head was still feeling fuzzy. A chill shook him briefly.

"In a game of chess, someone has to take the black pieces."

"Exactly."

"So how do we keep from sublimating?" asked Arcie.

"I know not, Barigan. The world is in danger that it does not realize. It thinks it has won and need never worry again. It is a strange thing, when good is so powerful that it is evil that must save the world. Sometimes the world was too evil, and then needed purifying. And now, the world is too pure . . . it needs corrupting."

"How are ye supposed to go about that?" wondered Arcie.

"We, Barigan. I will need your help, you two villains. I have not been out into the Six Lands in many years, and their ways are strange."

"Why should we help you?" asked Sam. Kaylana shrugged.

"It is your choice. Come with me, and help save your world and travel under my powers of concealment. Or, if you prefer, wander out and face the search parties looking for you . . . assaulting a Hero is a very bad move, assassin."

There was a pause. Then the two villains nodded.

"Aye, well enough . . . where do we start, then?" sighed Arcie.

"We start by assessing the situation. We will seek the wisdom of the Gypsies. They travel far, and will know of the situation in other kingdoms."

Gypsies, Sam thought to himself. He nodded sleepily. Something on the floor by his log caught his attention. A puddle. Hmph. Well, if the wench was going to make him wash then she'd just have to put up with him dripping onto her floor. Nice red puddles . . .

"Sam?" said Arcie, as the assassin slid slowly off onto

the floor. Kaylana stood up in consternation. Blood was slowly welling out of his tattered tunic from the sword wound Oarf had given him.

"He bleeds on my floor. Why did you not tell me he was wounded?"

Arcie shrugged. "You didn't ask."

Sam awoke to a sea of yellow light, the sweet smell of Barigan tobacco, and a rumbling noise. A heavy weight was on his legs. He opened his eyes to see Kaylana kneeling near him with a swatch of cloth that looked to be covered with crushed plants in an acrid-smelling green paste. The wildcat lay across his legs, purring and watching him with slitted green eyes. Kaylana skillfully removed a similar swatch from his side and replaced it with the new one. Raising his head to look, Sam noticed the wound was almost healed. His hands felt better too. He looked at them, folded on his chest. They were all bound up in cloth and weeds, and one of his fingers was immobilized in a wooden splint.

"You're a healer?" he asked the woman in surprise, as she removed the bandages and he flexed his hands and fingers.

"Not as you know it," she replied, "but I do have healing powers." Sam turned his head and saw Arcie, sitting on an upturned bucket and smoking his small curved pipe. The Barigan grinned at him.

"Ye're getting a lot of sleep these days, blondie," Arcie greeted him.

"It's morning already . . . seven or so. We've got to be getting on." Sam tried to sit up. Kaylana gave him a light shove in the chest and he fell back with a grunt.

"My magic weakens as the balance is destroyed, but fortunately most of the forest herbs retain their potency, and positive healing magic is easy in this Light-filled world. Still, you have lost some blood and needed the sleep."

"We must be moving, Sam. Kaylana here says as the town guards be coming closer. She's got all yon birds and things working as spies for her . . . "

"Is Mizzamir among those approaching?" inquired Sam, sitting up again, this time more carefully. Kaylana lashed a final binding around his side and let him regain a semi-upright position. He noticed she was wearing armor of some sort, made out of some kind of stiff woven cord, over a shirt and pants. The dun-colored robe hung loose over her clothing and armor.

"The Hero? No," answered Kaylana, getting up and starting to pack herbs, cloth, and bundles of food into woven canvas sacks. Sam nodded wearily. Somehow he'd figured that. Mizzamir was an archmage, after all . . . he'd come for Sam in his own time. And then Sam would do his best to kill him; for pride, for self-defense, for revenge . . . for that inexplicable perversity of what he could assume now was his dark nature. And for a thousand gold tellins, too, of course.

"We have collected your horses and packed them with supplies for the journey. We awaited only your return to consciousness." Kaylana took down a wooden shield from an alcove in the wall and slung it over her back. "Come. We must leave." She took her staff from where she had leaned it briefly against the wall and walked out the door. Arcie trotted after her, stuffing a few rolls from a shelf into his pocket, and Sam slowly rose and followed.

Outside, Kaylana made a trilling noise and clicked her tongue a few times. On silent padding feet, the wildcat trotted out and vanished into the woods, followed by a few birds, and, a short while later, a young weasel and a family of dormice. Kaylana nodded and pushed the thorn bush back over the entry. Then she touched her staff to its roots, closed her eyes in concentration, and murmured softly under her breath for a moment, using her ancient magic to persuade, hasten, encourage . . .

At first, nothing happened. Then, suddenly, the thorn bush writhed, its branches curling and snaking as they lengthened, the dirt bubbling as the rapidly spreading bush thrust thick roots into the soil. Sam and Arcie stepped back from the cracking plant, and Kaylana gave it a look of satisfaction and moved away. Within minutes the whole of the huge rock that was Kaylana's home was covered three feet thick in a snarl of thorns and leaves. A gnarled trunk and roots blocked the entry as effectively as an iron portcullis.

Sam shook his head and turned to pat his horse. It sniffed at him and tried to eat his hair. Standing with the horses, Sam noted, was a large stag, his antlers still velvety. As he looked at it, Kaylana went up to it and patted its neck lightly, and then gracefully vaulted onto its broad back as it stood calmly. It wore no saddle or bridle, but Kaylana looked like she knew what she was doing with it.

Wondering what he was getting into, riding out to save the world with a half-pint thief and a strange Druid who rode a deer, he heaved himself up into the saddle. The horse tossed its head, but he steadied it and settled back to watch the comical process of Arcie mounting his pony.

As a rule, Barigans distrusted any animals much larger than the diminutive shaggy ponies native to their chilled and rocky land. This pony was of Troisian–Einian stock, and just barely qualified for the title of "pony." In Sam's opinion, Arcie would have fitted better on a large sheep (or, for the assassin's own preference, the end of a spear), but the Barigan, irrepressible as always, took the long reins in his teeth and grabbed hold of the dangling stirrup. With an agility surprising in a man of his build and stature, he climbed hand over hand up the stirrup leather. As soon as he could, he swung around and planted his feet carefully on the pony's side, and used the additional leverage to struggle up to the seat of the saddle. The pony bore this ridiculous treatment with a lowered head and laid back ears. Arcie knew what he was doing when he'd chosen this horse; he'd seen it around town, taking small clusters of the children of the worthies around on its back. Compared to their trick-riding and wild yells, the Barigan's clumsy scramble was commonplace. Arcie heaved himself into the seat and sat panting. Sam applauded him silently, and then added, in a gentle yet venomous voice, "By the way, old chum, I'd like my things, if you don't mind."

"Things?" Arcie was pure innocence.

"Come on, you cheating thief! Nobody falls asleep in your presence who doesn't wake up about ten pounds lighter. You and I both know I haven't had a cent on me since those guards finished searching me and shackling me. But you and I also know that I'm nowhere near as efficient without a few daggers and knives: seven to be precise. Also my blowgun, forty needles for same, two rolls of wire, nine vials of various interesting chemical substances, my shortsword, my lockpicks, my tiger claws, my throwing blades, my other articles of the trade, and my small folding grappling hook with the silk rope. Hand them over, Arcie. You're not going to get out of our contract that easy."

With a sigh, the Barigan complied, pulling the items one by one from various pouches and pockets. Sam and Kaylana looked increasingly interested as various items seemingly too large or long for the confines of the pockets emerged. Sam took the items and slipped them into their sheaths concealed about his person, his confidence slowly returning. True, he knew eighty-four different ways of killing someone without a single tool, but it did feel nice to be back in uniform again. He glanced at the last pouch Arcie was tucking back into his belt sulkily. "By the dead gods, Arcie . . . how much of that chub of yours is Barigan and how much is ill-gotten loot?"

Arcie glanced at the tall assassin. "None of your damn business, blondie."

Sam inspected him a long moment. Then with a smile and a shake of his head, said, "True . . . my business is to take the most precious of possessions, and you just take everything else." Arcie grinned at him, and Kaylana's stag started forward, picking its way carefully through the forest. The assassin and thief followed on their mounts, and birds alighted in the still-twitching thornbush to watch them go. They scattered a moment later, as a glossy black raven swooped low overhead and glided on ebony wings down the path.

* * *

In a crystal tower, Mizzamir drummed his long fingers pensively on the edge of the font. Within the swirling silver waters, three tiny figures were visible: one on a horse, one on a large deer, and one on a pony. They emerged from a blurred green forest of trees and headed across the heath. Southeast. Mizzamir's fingertips touched the silvery runes decorating the rim of the white marble font in sequence. The picture increased, showing the three riders in silent progression, a tattered black-clad man, a scruffy, shorter man, and a young woman with red hair. To Mizzamir's magical sight, the faint greenish-white wisps of nature energy were dimly visible about her and the staff she carried. He raised an eyebrow in mild surprise as the image swiftly grew fuzzy and blurred, as the nature magic wisps obscured his scrying spell.

"A Druid. Hmm. That may complicate things a bit." Mizzamir sighed and scattered the image with a flick of his fingers.

"Was that her, with the red hair?" asked Fenwick, who had been looking over the mage's shoulder. He was a sharp-jawed young man, skilled at the hunt and the duties of heroes, with handsome features and brave eyes, and a prince in his own right. His great-grandfather had been one of the Heroes, the Forest Lord Fen-Alaran, and had ruled Trois, the southernmost of the Six Lands, graciously until his peaceful death before Fenwick was born. Fenwick was a man known for his defeat of the Trollish Legions at Halfast and the annihilation of the evil Nathauans. Mizzamir smiled benevolently at the young champion of good. *Just like his great-grandfather,* the mage thought.

"Yes, that was her. It could cause some problems. I had thought the Druids and their foolish ideas gone, but apparently one remains." He began to pace the crystalline floor of his conjuring room, his robes billowing in the shafts of sunlight. The light poured in through the stained-glass windows and flashed off the polished and faceted crystal of his tower room, blindingly bright, even for midmorning.

"She is very beautiful," commented Fenwick. "I had

not thought of Druids as beautiful young women." He rubbed his small, neat beard thoughtfully.

"Caution, lad. She's older than she looks, if I'm any judge," said Mizzamir gently, his eyes troubled. "A problem . . . I did not wish for bloodshed. But if they are allied with a Druid, she will not surrender, no more than her kinsmen did. We must move cautiously now. Her powers protect the rogues, so that I cannot hear their thoughts, nor see their motives, their plans."

"Cannot you simply appear magically where they are and subdue them with your mighty magic?" inquired Fenwick.

"Yes, I could," answered the wizard thoughtfully. "But it stirs my curiosity, to wonder where the Druid leads them, to discover what plans they may have, what they intend to do. I am concerned, lest they may know of something that may threaten the rule of peace and goodness for which we have worked so hard. Perhaps they journey to meet with other of their ilk, perhaps they seek a lost artifact that might give them power to threaten us." He looked at the prince from under his arched silver eyebrows. Fenwick felt something was expected of him.

"And you feel that the potential reward of whatever it is they seek is greater than the small victory of capturing the villains and the Druid. Very good, sir!" Fenwick said, admiringly. Mizzamir smiled and looked out the window.

"The forces of evil are scattered, Fenwick. They drift, lost in a sea of light, dying, confused. But like calls to like, Fenwick. These two and their Druid will be like a lodestone dragged through sand in which are hidden iron filings. If we wait, sooner or later they will pick up others of their ilk, and thus we may save those as well or, failing that, eliminate the threat they pose to Light."

"And their plans?" asked Fenwick.

"Yes, we must know of those as well." He sighed a sigh of regret. "Though it pains me, the necessity is there, and it is the most peaceful way. We shall need an agent, Fenwick . . ."

"I volunteer, sir." Fenwick stepped forward proudly.

Smiling apologetically, Mizzamir shook his silver-maned head.

"Of course you do, Sir Fenwick, but I am afraid your face and fame would reveal you to their cunning villainy. We need someone who is not so pure that the light would reveal itself to these villains, yet not dark, of course, else how could we deal with him, how could we trust him? We need someone who will be our agent, but not obviously so . . . can you find me such a one, Fenwick?"

Fenwick drew himself up nobly. "I will do my best, arch-mage."

Mizzamir smiled, pleased. "Good, lad. Very good."

The three rode on across the hills. A road going the same way could be seen winding in the distance to their left, but they did not dare to take it . . . wanted for theft, jail-breaking, attempted murder . . . Maybe Mizzamir was right, thought Arcie. It is a hard life, it does involve a lot of running away . . . but I wouldn't trade it for all the security in the world. Rather a free and hungry hawk than a stuffed and caged turkey. But caution was an important part of that life. With a subtle gesture Arcie indicated to Sam to drop back a bit, letting the Druid move ahead. Sam and Arcie walked their mounts side by side and spoke in the silent tongue of those who prowl the alleyways at night. It was a language taught by both the rival Guilds, but had many gestures used by both, so that they could understand each other. An observer watching them would have seen only slight gestures of body and fingers and facial expression, would not even have heard the few softly muttered monosyllabic words.

"Her there not normal," implied Arcie. Sam looked at the red-haired figure on the stag, then back at Arcie.

"No, but she understand. I trust for now," insinuated the assassin. Arcie let exasperation creep into his gestures.

"You trust anything in skirt? You hear her talk. She talk of old like she there."

"So? She want to kill us, she do while I sleep, set cat on

you all food-sleepy. Didn't," he added pointedly.

"But why she help us?"

"She believe what she say," Sam shrugged.

"Come on there, you two. We have a long way to go," called Kaylana. The two spurred their mounts and rode to catch up. A raven blinked a bright eye at them from a treetop and glided after them.

The day was warm and bright as they rode along and the sun slowly followed them across the sky. The hills were extremely grassy and thick with wildflowers, buttercups, daisies, and lots of little red and blue and purple blooms that Sam couldn't identify. The influx of positive power did indeed seem to be having its effect on the land. Sam realized with a start that it was already the autumn of the year; he didn't know much about when flowers and things grew, but he had a hunch that they weren't supposed to be doing it now. He hadn't noticed before, living in the heart of the city; the increasingly mild winters for the past several years had just represented a savings in heating fuel.

They stopped at noon, had a short lunch of bread dipped in the cold leftover stew, and then continued. The grass began to be interspersed with trees and bushes, often arching over strange, overgrown ditches in the earth that made no sense for drainage. Puzzled, Sam pointed them out to Arcie, who agreed that they were odd, but he didn't know what they were. Kaylana heard them talking and told them that these hills had been the site of one of the great battles before the Victory. The gouges had been made by the wheels of great war machines and the fighting and dying of men and horses. Arcie was intrigued.

"I'm going to ride ahead, just a short ways, to be sure there bein't any pitfalls or like," he called back over his shoulder as he took the lead. Sam shook his head and looked at Kaylana.

"He means he's going to go ahead and see if the ancient warriors left anything around worth picking up, like magic daggers or somesuch."

Kaylana looked puzzled. "But the wars were many many years ago. Any such things would be beneath the soil by now."

"That won't stop him," Sam sighed. He looked at the trees putting out wide green leaves that turned in the sun and heard the birdsong. Violets clustered in the shade, and bluebells trembled in the sunshine. Waving innocently among a riot of flowers along a hedgerow he spotted an old friend and patted the white florets atop the tall spotted stalks as he rode past. Good old sharnlock, or sagebane, ingestive toxin class four, crush well and render juice, distill through Mufwort's process for maximum potency.

A squadron of bright yellow butterflies flashed up from his horse's hooves, and he watched them go dancing and spinning among the leaves like a lost contingent of autumn aspens. Somewhere, a bird called a liquid, two-toned note, then fell silent. He turned, and saw Kaylana watching him.

"I thought that assassins took pleasure only in blood and darkness and death, and had no concept of beauty," she said with a hint of humor in her deep eyes. Sam turned away.

"There's beauty in many things. The balance of good blade, a well-executed plan of attack . . . But you don't have to be a whitewash or a Druid to admire a place like this. There is color, and grace, and pleasing lines. There is music, which bridges the dark and the light. Sometimes it hurts us, but we know beauty when we see it." He glanced at her, then looked away. He was about to speak again when Arcie's voice echoed down from the top of the next hill.

"Ho, you two, come along! Ye can see the next town from here!" They crested the hill and looked down into the valley to see the dark smudge of buildings on the banks of a river. As they watched, the sun dipped behind the mountains, and the valley darkened. Lights in the buildings twinkled in the twilight and on the outskirts of the city walls they could just glimpse the dark orange-red flicker of campfires. Kaylana indicated them with the point of her staff.

"Gypsies," she said. "We will need . . . what do you call it? Money."

As they stared down into the valley, a raven that had been sitting in a tree just behind them gave a satisfied croak and took to the air, winging over their heads and down into the city.

Kaylana slid off her stag and rubbed its muzzle gently, then with a shooing motion sent it bounding back into the cover of the trees. Sam debated a long moment, then after some inner wrestling dismounted as well and silently offered Kaylana his horse, which, after some thought on the ride, he had named Damazcus, after the wavy-patterned Shadrezarian steel that was so good for dagger blades.

"I do not need to ride. You are injured and need it more than I," was her calm reply.

Sam waved irritably at Damazcus. The horse took the opportunity to rub its itching forehead on his shoulder, almost knocking him over, then snorted moistly into his hair. He wiped his cheek off in disgust. "You are of course correct, but I'm not walking into that town and have everyone seeing me sitting pretty while a lady walks through the mud. Nothing points out a bad character like lack of chivalry. Half-pint is excused because we'd leave him behind if he wasn't riding." Arcie grinned and tipped his hat at mention of his nickname, one of the few comments about his height he had come to tolerate. "So get on, or I will start to get cross and ill-tempered as my nature is so famous for."

Kaylana looked sternly at him. "I will not be treated like some delicate noblewoman. I am Kaylana, and by Oak, Ash and Thorn, I will not let a scamp like you . . . "

"I've been kicking around for thirty-some summers, ma'am," replied Sam tersely. Kaylana drew herself up haughtily and rapped her staff on the ground. Arcie drummed his fingers on his saddlehorn impatiently, and the horse in question sighed.

"And I have seen times and places you will never . . ."

Her sentence was cut short as Sam sighed, and in one lightning motion scooped her up off the ground, staff and all, and tossed her into the horse's saddle. She glared furiously down at him, too outraged to speak. He looked back at her tiredly. "All right. Do it as a favor to me, then? I don't want to get hounded in this town any more than I will anyway, and I'm tired of standing on this hill arguing." He started walking down the slope. Arcie followed, and after fuming in silence a moment, so did the Druid.

As they approached the gates, it was Arcie who spoke first. "You said we'd need money? How much, and what for?"

"For the Gypsies," said Kaylana, a bit sulkily, Arcie thought. "They travel the wide world over and will know of the state of things in towns and cities. Thus we may discover how far the domination of Light has progressed, and where its weak spots may be, that we can begin to undermine and with luck turn the tide back to balance. But the information of Gypsies is not free . . . I imagine we will need the worth of three horses to pay them, but you will need the horses. So somehow we must get the money another way."

"Horses," mused Arcie, "average about forty gold, say . . . three of us, then. We each need to come up with forty gold tellins." He grinned. "No problem!"

Sam thought a moment. Of course the Barigan could; he probably was carrying at least ten times that much anyway. On a sudden thought, he checked his pocket where he'd tucked Arcie's deposit. It was gone, of course. Sam decided not to press the issue now: they were almost to the gates. But later . . . and Sam would collect in full when he could hand Mizzamir's bloody twitching head to Arcie. At the moment, Sam was broke, but he knew a trick or two himself. "I can do it." The two rogues looked at the Druid.

Kaylana looked back at them haughtily. "Good."

"Spiffywell," the Barigan said, rubbing his hands together gleefully as they rode through the open gates (unguarded, as was so common in these peaceful times). "We'll split up then, and meet back at yon inn over there." He indicated a swinging tavern sign. "I've got wee bit of spare change already on me, as it just happens . . . I'll find a place to stable the horses."

"We'll go with you, old chum, just to be sure you find one so that you don't have to take them to another town, or sell them, or something," said Sam pleasantly.

"Och, they're my horses! I did stole them fair and . . . mmmph!" Arcie exclaimed loudly, then sputtered as Sam reached up and clapped a hand over his mouth. A few townsfolk, wandering about and chatting pleasantly, watched them curiously and laughed. They found stabling for Damazcus and the pony, which Arcie had taken to calling Puddock, then they set out on their separate ways.

Arcie walked cheerfully through the warm early evening. He stopped to pass the time of day idly with a Barigan greengrocer. He wandered down into what must have been the bad side of the town, all undergoing renewal and renovation. His trained eyes spotted thief signs here and there, faded with age and painted over in a few places. One series of marks led him to what must have been the local Guild. Most of the larger towns had a Guild of some size, though the thieves of a few looser cities ran instead in competing gangs. Assassin's Guilds were far rarer. Sam's had been the only one he'd known of in the Six Lands. The Thieves' Guild here in Mertensia was disguised of course, in this case as a bakery. His own Guild had run under the cheerful cover of a milliner's shop, before all his members had left and he'd had to scrape his losses together and turn everything into easily portable items. At any rate, might as well see if RISE AND SHINE BAKED GOODS had done any better. He wandered in. A small bell announced his arrival, and the aroma of warm bread drifted around him.

Kaylana was in difficulties. She put on a brave front, but she hated cities. The cobblestones were rough under her feet, and the air was smoky and hard to breathe. Eyes stared at her, in her homespun armor and dun robes, but she would not look at them. The eyes made her feel itchy, tense, panicky. She had to stop at the small park in the center of town to try to recover herself. She sat on the small patch of grass and waited until she stopped shaking.

How long since she'd been in a city? Many, many seasons . . . last time she had stepped foot inside a large town such as this, she had sat in an alleyway and watched with burning eyes as a huge crowd roared the praises of the Heroes. She knew little of them, or of what they had done, only of the results. She had seen them then; a warrior, a wizard, a healer, a scout, a woodsman, and a knight in silver armor. News of the Victory had spread to all corners of the world, and the people laughed and wept for joy wherever the Heroes appeared. Time had gone on, there were other, local, heroes. The original Heroes, and those who had fought on their side but not gained quite the fame, settled down and took up the burden of repairing the war-torn land. Many of their children went on to become heroes as well. But the swallows had not brought any news of heroes for many months, reflected Kaylana. Perhaps the heroes were running out of heroic things to do.

Kaylana didn't like this. She didn't like trusting either the short fellow or his impertinent tall friend, especially if it led her to cities like this one. But she had no choice. How far they trusted her, she was still not certain. They'd come this far, true, but would it be as the others had said, that they would not work, would squabble over meaningless things rather than do what must be done, whatever it was? "Come away, young one," her kinsmen had said to her, the last ones, on the day of the Victory. "You can do nothing here." The spirits of her past, dancing in the trees. She had turned away, refused, and had gone back to her woods, vowing that she must do something. With the death of the other Druids her powers had increased little by little, as their dying spirits passed strength to her that she might survive. Her body had transformed so that she hardly seemed to age from that day onward . . . but she had realized long ago that she would have rather died when they did. She watched, in bitter sorrow, as the world tilted to its inevitable searing end in white light, unable to do anything but wait. Following her instincts, learning to control her strange gifts and knowledge, waiting, doing what she could, here and there. Until these two had appeared. She had met the two men and had not been surprised to hear they were of darkness. Now, she led them where her instincts led her, where strange dreams of past and future guided her. But though her voice was strong as her will, and her powers and instincts and eerie inner wisdom were those of a thousand long-dead Druids, her mind sometimes shivered in fear like a young girl's—a girl who had seen all she ever knew and loved cut down in blood while she hid trembling in the hollow of an old oak tree.

Sam wandered about in the increasing twilight. He thought he glimpsed Kaylana striding past in the distance, but didn't do anything about it. Fair was fair, they all had to earn their own money.

"What am I doing here, anyway?" he asked himself. "I'm no hero. Let the world blow itself up. It's its own fault." But he knew. He, and he was sure Arcie felt the same, would much have preferred to hide, lay low somewhere until the problem had passed on. But when the whole world is in danger, where is there to hide? He believed Kaylana, with the inner sense that had saved his life many times before. Besides, she'd spoken of corrupting the world. Well, she was right, it needed it. He'd do it out of spite, dammit, that was a perfectly dark reason. Spite and sheer evil nastiness, you big bad assassin, he said to himself. He skulked off among the shadows with an evil leer on his face, his golden hair somewhat spoiling the effect by shining in the torchlight every now and again.

* * *

Across town, Arcie was getting frustrated.

"Look, can ye bake me a cake with a file in it?" he asked, giving the portly man behind the roll-strewn counter his best If-you-know-what-I-mean look.

"A file, sir?" asked the baker, perplexed. Arcie tried again.

"This all looks so good, I could *steal* it, man," he offered, searching the man's face for some kind of acknowledgment that the baker was a fellow sneakthief. He encountered only bovine confusion.

"We've the best prices in town, sir . . . "

Arcie looked around, saw there was only one other customer in the shop, who was about to leave. He glanced again at the baker, and said, "Look, I . . . run the Bonny Bonnets Shoppe in Bistort." Most Thieves' Guilds knew of each other's existences and covers, simply because one needed to obtain a license to thieve in another Guild's territory anyway and it was impossible to keep out spies in the process.

"That's nice for you, sir. Now then, do you wish to buy anything or not? My shop closes soon." Arcie stared at him.

"This really are a bakery?" he whispered. The man nodded, obviously thinking the short foreigner was quite mad. Arcie sighed. "Well enough. A dozen jelly doughnuts, please."

Arcie walked down the street, trailing powdered sugar. The sounds of drunken singing reached his ears, and with a shrug he ducked into the shadows of an alleyway and waited. A group of three young merchants' sons staggered past, passing a skin of wine between them. Arcie paced them silently down the alley, now soft as a shadow at their side, now a silent padding behind them, now a drifting breeze on the other side, lastly a swirl of vague form that melted into the shadow of a building and was gone like a dream, leaving only a small sprinkling of white sugar behind.

The youths emerged at the other end of the alley and slowed in muddled surprise, their song of revelry drifting away. Not only was the wineskin gone, which was what had alerted them, but so were their belts, pouches, rings, necklaces, ornamental rapiers and lefthand Kwartan daggers, the eldest one's feathered cap, and the youngest one's brand-new silver spurs. They turned and peered down the alley, but it was empty.

Elsewhere, Kaylana sighed, and decided to take care of the unpleasant business of gathering money. She was of course not skilled in theft and had nothing to sell and no services to trade, so she would simply have to ask for the forty tellins. She was glad the Barigan had figured out the exchange and the currency used; the last time she'd seen money it was a handful of rough bronze lozenges with the face of an ancient ruler stamped into them. She knew what to ask for. The trick was asking in a certain way.

She selected a gentleman who looked very likely to have coin in excess of the worth of a single horse on his person, and enough to not miss it too much. A merchant-lord, by his garb, or at least whatever passed for one these days. Bustling, well-fed, in rich clothing of velvets and silks, he was hurrying home after a good dinner with friends, lubricated with fine wine. The scruffy Druid caught his sleeve as he passed, pulling him about. He turned with a snort to give her a good telling-off . . . and met a pair of green eyes, expertly lit in the glow of the street-lantern.

It is doubtful if he saw anything about the woman other than the eyes, or if he even realized they belonged to a woman at all. All he knew was that they bored into his brain, as a questing root drives through the soil. Kaylana reached through the man's mind, easier even than calming a wild animal; noting with interest the slightly over-smoothed texture of his thoughts, evidence of magical adjustment. Perhaps this fellow had been something much less than an honest trader before a mage with the skill for light-minding had found him. Her will wrapped around his easily, not forcing, just suggesting in a way that was so sensible and simple, and yet absolutely irrefutable, as she said calmly:

"Sir, you wish to give me forty tellin coins as a gesture

of charity." The green eyes were as unstoppable as spring.

The merchant nodded dumbly and reached into his pouch, fingers counting as his eyes never left hers. Forty thin gold coins, the size of small aspen leaves and marked with the seal of the Six Lands united under the Six Heroes were dropped into her hands. Kaylana closed her hands on the coins and stepped back. Only then did she release the man from her gaze. He shook his head, glanced around, but saw only a scruffy woman standing there. Such people were beneath his station. He didn't quite recall what he had been doing, but it was perfectly right and sensible, whatever it was. He adjusted his waist-coat and, ignoring the common woman, set off down the street again. He had important things to do. Kaylana didn't bother to watch him go, but tucked the coins into a fold of her robe and went off to find the others. She disliked having to touch the minds of humans; it was risky with anyone more willful than a lazy, half-drunk merchant, and difficult unless she had the opportunity of surprise. And their minds . . . she shook her head. So much ignorance.

Sam had seen some low dives in his time, and this wasn't one of them. The tavern was well-lit, with a warm fire burning in the huge fireplace at one end, over which some serving lads were making mulled wine and tea. Plates clattered and voices chattered. He wandered over to where a group was playing at darts and watched with an expression of shy interest on his face. At last one of the men noticed him.

"Well, hello there, lad! Fancy the darts, do you?" The man's eyes twinkled pleasantly. Sam wondered again why everyone thought he was so young . . . though it was true that he looked almost ten years younger than his approximate age. That had always been a lucky mystery and might help him here by making the players think he was even more inexperienced. The man seemed patronizing and smiled out of his thick curly brown beard. Sam fought down a retch at the easiness of it all, and at the Beard Man's complacency. He made himself smile back in easygoing innocence.

"Oh, I play a bit now and then . . . " he said. The man gave his cronies a wink, and they grinned and laughed and nodded. The cheerful fellow turned back to Sam.

"Well then, my black-garbed fellow, you're welcome to join the game! We play for stakes here, you know," he added, his eyes showing a joking concern. Sam returned it.

"I'm afraid I have no stakes, nor roasts, nor even chops or brisket, but . . . " he let the good-natured laughter at the old joke die down, then continued with a smile, "But I do have this to wager." Upon the table he set an intricate gold ring with a single red stone. If the truth were to be known, the gold was gilded brass, the stone merely colored glass, the whole having the purpose of flipping open when pressed in a certain way so that the contents of the tiny compartment within could be poured into a glass. It was empty now, of course, but still glinted richly in the warm light. It held many memories for Sam—a gift from Cata, way back when; he'd never used it professionally except once to carry willowbark and mayweed powder in, sovereign against the headaches that plagued him one year during a particularly bad pollen harvest.

Cata, Cat-a-Crags, sapphire eyes, seductive and deadly as the fey black panther she took her name from, that would call like a crying woman in mountain passes and would lead brave men to a bloody death. Cata would call the men in a different way, but the death was just the same . . . Cata, beautiful dark dancer . . . who had vanished one day and was never heard from, until years later when Blarin received reports of her—living in a small provincial village, a farmer's fat wife, cleaning and cooking and tending two small chubby brats. Sam had been in a vicious mood for days, feeling betrayed without knowing why, unable to understand what had happened, and why. *Mizzamir, you're going to hurt for that one,* he vowed. His reverie was broken as the jovial Beard roared:

"A fine wager!" and clapped Sam on the back. "Come, my fellows, put up your gold, we will play at darts with Blackie here." Sam looked flushed and pleased at being allowed into their circle, and the game was on.

As the others made their tosses, Sam inspected the darts. Not everyone's weapon, to be sure, but then, an assassin was trained in just about every weapon that could easily be concealed under a suit of normal clothes. Darts were one of Sam's favorites. Sharp needles perfect for a sticky coat of poison, with no annoying twang or puff sounds such as you got with a crossbow or blowgun. Easier to aim than a blowgun, too. Daggers were his specialty, but darts were a good second choice. They had made some lovely darts in the Guild workshop, he remembered fondly: clear glass ones that could be filled with acid or poison or the potion of your choice, silver rune-worked ones that could be enchanted (if one could find a sorcerer to do so), ones with tiny tiny barbs in the break-off needle, so that the sharp point would continue to work its way inward with every breath of its victim until . . . He shook his head. These were simple, cheap, and common darts, and had seen much use. The points were dull, the fletching tattered. He lifted them one by one, testing the balance, smoothing the feathers. His hand finally closed on a set of three, blue and white, with brass tips. Good enough for now, he decided, until I've gotten the hang of it again. Just in time, too.

"Your turn, Blackie!" crowed the bearded man, and Sam pretended to look worried as he studied the board.

Darts as a pastime was an old sport, taken from archery practice in the reign of the Mage-King Verurand, long before the Victory, even long before the War, back when the Six Lands were a mass of feudal struggles and border disputes, and the rest of the world little more than savages. Variants of the game were so numerous Sam didn't bother to brush up on the rules, but had watched this group long enough to recognize the scoring system. They were starting with two hundred and one points and going to exactly zero. The others hadn't done too bad for their first toss, he decided. His only problem would be looking clumsy enough that they didn't get suspicious. He selected one of his darts and managed to stick himself lightly in the finger with a small yelp, which brought good-natured laughter from his new friends. He scanned the board. Nothing too showy for a first shot, he decided, and squinted until he couldn't see and his eyebrows hurt, then threw.

The missile thwoked into an outer single score ring, subtracting a nice fifteen points from his base. He grinned myopically. He tossed his next two shots off in similar casualness and then collected his darts and inspected the pool. Not quite twenty gold, he noted, after translating the pile of gold tellins, silver lunins and copper stellins, and sighed. He'd have to show off for the rest. The game progressed. Sam watched, threw, watched, trying not to yawn, and then at last made his move.

He stepped up to throw, hefting his darts. He'd gotten to know them well over the short game. This one had a bit of a lean to the left, this one was point-heavy, and this one was the best, having only a slight downward drift. Good enough. He took the left-leaner in fingers, and looked at the board. Thank fates his hand was healed, he thought. Fifty-five points. Might as well make it look good.

The world narrowed until all that remained was the dingy, pock-marked dartboard, and all that was clear within it was the single-score outer space labeled "2" by its rim. His hand moved. The center of the space sprouted a fletching.

His gaze shifted ever so slightly. All was silent, or at least he heard nothing, though the vibrations of voices shivered on his skin. His eyes caught the tiny wedge of yellow that was the narrow triple-score ring, held in the triangle labeled "1." A small spot, true, like the barest chink of pale flesh that shows through a man's armor. Throw. Blue and white feathers obscured the square. The last one was easy. He didn't even hesitate, but tossed, putting a bit more force on it just in case . . .

Thunk!

He came out of his self and looked around, remembering to look amazed at his "luck." Bull's-eye, of course. "Fifty-five!" Around him the fellows had noted the same. Cheers of laughter and congratulations pealed out, and his bearded buddy dropped a mug of ale in front of him. He looked embarrassed and modest as he shyly took the coins from the pool and slipped them into his pouch, while the others encouraged him to drink up. Two of them were over at the dartboard exclaiming over the last dart, sunk to the end of its needle in the elm-wood. Sam looked a little disconcertedly at the ale.

"Oh no, I couldn't . . . " he began, but caught the looks of puzzlement as he did so. Beard pushed the mug closer to him with a chuckle.

"Come on, Blackie, 'tis good for you. After you've beaten us at our own game the least you can do is drink with us." He eyed Sam carefully.

"Well, all right then," he replied and raised the mug to the fellows. As they went back to their hearty laughter and cheers he tipped the drink down his throat with a mental sigh, keeping up appearances.

Arcie lurked. He'd had to ditch the ungainly long rapiers in a garbage pile, after removing the gold-plated hilts with gems in them, but the rest fitted nicely into his various packs and pouches, cunningly designed and possibly even slightly magical as well. The Barigan thief had always been well-off enough to afford the best, both for business and pleasure. Sound, useful, and concealing pouches and clothing were a wise investment, as was his cloak, so drab and shadow-colored he could walk into a bar like this one and, while perhaps he might be seen, he would not be noticed.

There was Sam all right. He was holding an empty ale mug, several others of which were scattered around the table near him, also some plates with the remains of a dinner on them. Sam was looking at a large fellow with a beard and a gold tooth. Arcie was momentarily intrigued, wondering how one might go about stealing such a gold tooth. Sam probably hadn't even noticed it. But what was Sam up to?

"Two tellins," said the Beard, "says you can't do it."

"F-four tellins," replied Sam, holding up three unsteady fingers, "shays I can." The Beard laughed and slapped four coins down on the table. Sam, after a moment to lift his head again, picked a dart up off a side table. Beard yelled merrily to a cluster of patrons and a serving maid to get out of the way. Sam turned around in his chair, looking over his shoulder, then turned back, and, keeping his dreamy weary eyes semi-focused on Beard, tossed the dart over his shoulder. Arcie whipped his head to follow it. It went *thunk* into the center of the bull's eye. Beard roared in laughter and amazement and went for more ale as Sam owlishly tried to pick up the tellins. Arcie padded over to him.

"Sam!" he hissed.

"Wazzat?" came the reply, and Sam peered over the edge of the table at the Barigan. "Oh, it's you. Whasit?"

"No thanks," replied Arcie. "Have ye made yer quota?"

Sam thought a moment. "Yep. Wher . . . 's the girl?"

"I dinna ken," replied Arcie. "Give it up for today, Sam. Ye've had a long day, and besides which this person coming over to our table looks a fearsome lot as one of your old instructors. Bye!" Arcie vanished among the crowd, just another Barigan lost in a sea of knees. Sam looked up to see a figure that made his blood shiver as past memories collided with present reality.

"Hello, young fellow," said the older man, pulling up a seat across from him. "I've been watching you. Some very nice tossing, there."

Sam murmured "Thanks," trying not to stare at the fellow, with the red-brown hair all washed clean and shining, the clothes with the mark of the shipwrights on one sleeve, and—gods!—a small but promising potbelly.

"I used to be quite good at the darts myself," the man said conversationally, "but I lost it after awhile . . . lack of practice, I guess . . . kind of hard to remember." He shrugged, smiled. "My name's Reynardin, by the way," he added. Sam tried not to whimper. *It's Black Fox,* he thought to himself. *Black Fox with the gleaming eyes, who once walked the wire between High Temple Street and the clock tower in a high wind. Who taught me seventeen different ways of breaking bones without breaking the skin. And now he's probably sewing up rips in sailcloth all day.*

"Uh, they call me Blackie here," spoke up Sam, trying not to look like an assassin. The alcohol was fizzing in his brain.

"Fair enough," replied Reynardin. "You don't have relatives in Bistort, by any chance, do you? Your face seems familiar . . . "

"Oh, yes, I have a brother there," Sam lied quickly. *He really doesn't remember! Like Mizzamir said . . . What must it be like for them? Living in a pink fog, not knowing what you've lost . . .* "We look a lot alike."

"Thought so," exclaimed the shipwright. "Well, it was a good show of darts, lad. Have a nice evening." With a grin the ex-assassin clapped Sam on the arm and moved off into the crowd. Sam reflexively checked his arm for needle punctures; Black Fox had, like most of his teachers, taught him caution the hard way. Looking around, he saw his bearded buddy kibitzing a card game in the far corner, and thought he glimpsed Arcie over at a table of tradesmen. He got up and headed over to them.

A moment later, the door of the tavern swung open, and Kaylana strode in, fiercely ignoring the whistles and exclamations she attracted. Locating Sam and Arcie, she approached them.

"Well, we have met, then," she said as soon as she was in speaking range. "I have the coins required. Now then, you may get rooms or not as you wish, I am going to stay in the relative peace and sanity of the stables away from the cluster of this town. I will see you at dawn, on the east outskirts of town." She turned to go, but Sam tapped her on the shoulder, the drink and laughter and praise and noise dancing in his eyes. She wheeled suspiciously on him.

"If you're saying you can't afford a room, lady, I've already rented one, you're welcome to share mine," Sam began with a grin, but there was a flash of furious green eyes, a blur, he jumped back too late and a heavy oak staff whapped him smartly upside the head. He dropped like a stone. Arcie laughed and raised his mug of stout to Kaylana, who was already storming out the door, to riffles of applause from giggling barmaids. The door slammed as Sam raised his head woozily. Arcie grinned down at him.

"Och, I think that means nay, laddie," said the thief.

Dawn was pinking the sky outside his window when Arcie awoke. He bounded out of bed and with brisk efficiency washed, combed his hair, shaved, got dressed, checked all his equipment, counted his wealth, and padded out into the hall. He knew Sam would still be asleep, after getting so soused last night. He'd best wake him up. Down a few doors to Sam's room—the only one with a locked door. With a happy smile he extracted a thin piece of stiff copper wire and clicked the lock open. A spurt of oil at the hinges, and he inched open the door and peered into the room.

Sparse but tidy, with Sam's clothes folded over a chair; a torn black tunic, black silk shirt, black leggings, black socks, tattered black cloak lined in mottled dark gray and black, and scuffed black boots. Sam himself was a pile of tousled blond hair on the pillow of the rumpled bed. The faint sounds of peaceful breathing drifted through the room. Just then, a draft blew the locks of blond hair, stirring them slightly.

The bed exploded. The covers went across the room, the pillow flew out and knocked over a jug on the washstand, and in the midst of it all Sam leaped to an alert crouch, hazel eyes staring about wildly, and brandishing a sharp dagger he'd had under his pillow. His eyes found

Arcie, and he sank back onto the bed with a whimper as his hangover caught up with him. Arcie bounded cheerfully over to make sure he didn't go back to sleep.

"Rise and shine, blondie! Interesting, I mean, I ken yer ways about assassin uniforms, but black underwears, Sam?"

Sam was indeed wearing black cotton shorts. "Shut up, Arcie. If you must know, it's so we don't show a white bunnytail if we are so unfortunate to rip our seams on a mission. Now go away and let me die in peace."

"Sorry, laddie. The Druid said we were to meet her at dawn, recall ye?"

Sam replied with a few choice and not terribly kind words about Kaylana, finishing with, "I'll be dammed if I'll follow some treewalking wench on any crazy hallucination of hers anymore. I'm going to go back and track down Mizzamir and then . . . then . . . "

"Then what, Sam?" There was no answer. "If ye think of summat, let me know, and I'll join ye. We're men without a place, without a life, without a cause. Kaylana's the only one as is offered us any hope for restoration of our old ways, and revenge on them what took them from us. Whether anything else she says about the world being in danger is pooka piss, it's given us something to do, someplace to go. Ye were bored stiff hanging around that abandoned Guild in Bistort. Now, ye're at the least doing something. 'Tis an adventure, as heroes used to go on all the time . . . Though for us, it's either go on and keep hoping, or go back, and either whitewash or die. And as for the being damned . . . we both are already. So quit feeling sorry for yerself and get on yer feets and out."

A muffled groan escaped as Sam tried to scrape some of the fluff off his tongue, then a sigh.

"Arcie, one of these days I'm going to throttle you. Luckily for you, I'm already on an assignment. All right. I'll meet you downstairs."

Arcie padded out, shaking his head.

It was well after dawn when the three mismatched persons assembled at the eastern wall of the city. Kaylana was waiting with barely disguised impatience, reminding Arcie of a wren, as the two rogues walked up. Kaylana greeted Arcie coolly and did not even look at Sam.

"We must not delay any longer," she said. "The Gypsies even now prepare to move on. We must speak with them before they go." She turned and strode briskly down the dirt road toward the Gypsy encampment, her oak staff tap-tapping on the hard ground as she went. Arcie nudged Sam as they followed.

"Secure your pouches, Sammy," he cautioned. The Barigan had already tucked his main coin pouch down inside his shirt. Sam began carefully transferring his few pouches to inner loops inside his tunic and cloak. He looked ahead at the marching figure of the Druid.

"Should we tell her as well?" he wondered. Arcie shook his head.

"She's the one as suggested it, she must know what she's about."

Out of curiosity, Sam left one of his pouches, empty, on the outside of his clothes, hung snugly from his belt in a way that would have been normal and safe in any city. Arcie shook his head. The assassin would find out, soon enough.

And, in fact, Kaylana knew very well what she was doing. The Gypsies were one of the few groups of people she'd had any contact with in her long self-imposed hermitage. They would sometimes stop by her forest, and she would emerge to speak with them. Their ancestors had known the power of the Druids, and they did not wish to cross her.

They walked into the Gypsy encampment—the two men warily, Kaylana with her usual cool confidence. All around them were the exotic wooden wagons, with their painted trim and windows, and fringes of tiny bells along the edges that tinkled in the early morning breeze. Horses and ponies, fat and well cared-for, cropped the sparse grass of the hollow that sheltered the encampment or nickered at the sense of excitement in the air. The Gypsies themselves moved among the wagons and horses; handsome, fox-faced people, with brilliant white teeth that flashed in smiles across their dark skin. They chattered in a strange language among themselves, with a rich, rhythmic cadence. The children, swift and nimble as swallows, ran about with bundles of packing, or chased each other, laughing. The adults watched the newcomers with bright eyes that learned all and told nothing.

Kaylana moved on, and spoke in the strange language to an old man who sat on the tail of his wagon smoking a long curved pipe. He flashed his teeth at her, then at Sam and Arcie. Sam had decided he liked the Gypsies. They were as happy as the whitewashed townsfolk, but they were not whitewashed . . . he could see that in the sharpness of their eyes, the quick restlessness of their children, and the fact that Arcie had told him to secure his pouches. As if hearing his thoughts, Arcie spoke to him in a low voice.

"They move around so much, and are so wary . . . they've escaped the fate that our comrades met with. Aren't it fine?"

Sam agreed silently. He watched the children playing in the light of a new day and felt a thrill in his heart to see them so wild and free, growing up to follow their spirits, free of the shackles of law and other people's standards of right and wrong. But if Kaylana spoke truth, these youngsters might not live to adulthood . . . At that moment one of the grinning children, a little boy, surely not more than five summers old, tugged on his cloak. Sam looked down into the mischievous face and was surprised to be handed his own leather pouch back. He took it, with a look of surprise, and murmured a confused thanks. The boy's smile flashed, and he gave a low bow before springing off on some other pursuit. Sam watched him go, and no longer questioned why he was trying to undo the imbalance of the Victory; it was for the sake of that boy, and others like him, including a young assassin who once had to fight for his life and his living every waking moment. Darkness, he realized, takes courage, whether you fight it or live it.

Meanwhile Arcie had moved ahead and was beckoning him.

"Come along, laddie! We're to talk with their wise-woman."

Sam glanced at the lettering on the side of the wagon Arcie indicated and stifled a groan.

"A fortune teller?"

Inside the wagon was cramped and dim, but scrupulously clean and tidy. Tapestries and rugs covered the walls and floor, a bead curtain separating this half of the wagon from the other, which, Sam assumed, probably was the sleeping quarters of the ancient woman who sat before them now. She seemed lost in her embroidered robes and hiding in her black and gray hair, which was braided and plaited over and around a pair of polished black cow's horns, holding the odd decoration in place. She nodded silently to Arcie and Sam as they walked in; Kaylana was already seated on one of the tattered cushions on the floor before the woman's low five-legged table. The smells of incense and game stew lingered in the air. The Druid looked up at the two as they entered. Her face was grim.

"Ill news, villains. The Gypsies have wandered for all this year and report that nowhere have they found any further trace of members of the populace such as you."

"Madame Shorla sees many strange things ahead for you," cackled the old woman, peering into her crystal ball. Her voice was heavily accented, and her bright eyes glittered. "A long journey, a dark stranger . . . "

"And for this we paid all that gold?" whispered Arcie to Sam. Sam hushed him.

"A great river, gold light in a dark place . . . blue water and sandfire." Madame Shorla looked up at Arcie. "With you, small one, I see red blood in a swamp, and a lifeline from darkness by light that you must not trust."

"Spiffywell," said Arcie, looking over the fortune teller's shoulder to see if the wagon had anything interesting worth taking. The woman turned to Kaylana.

"And you, Druid . . . I see a man on horseback, and the sign of the Dragon. Hold fast and you may survive." Kaylana nodded respectfully. Then Madame Shorla glanced at Sam, then back to her crystal ball, and cackled.

"Yes, this is very clear. I see one who searches for you, a wizard of great power . . . " said Madame Shorla, running her wrinkled fingertips over the surface of the crystal ball. Sam nodded. *So what else is new?* he thought.

"Yesss . . . a wielder of magic, seeking, planning . . . great magic . . . "

Suddenly the room grew dark. Three heads snapped up, stared at a figure posed in the doorway, leaning against the frame. The figure smiled. White teeth, terminating in delicate points, shone out of the depths of a cowled hood.

"Somebody mention me?" The voice was female, dark and rich as old honey. On the figure's shoulder, a familiar glossy raven clucked to itself contentedly and fluffed its feathers.

Sam was on his feet before he realized it, sending cushions flying. Arcie, ever-stalwart in a crisis, melted like summer snow into the shadows and vanished. Kaylana got to her feet with regal dignity and glared at the stranger. Madame Shorla looked up at the figure, then back to her crystal ball, puzzled. She tapped the globe with a ringing sound, saying thoughtfully,

"No, that's not the one . . . "

"Too bad," replied the figure, stepping into the wagon. "I see you have the sense enough to stand in my presence . . . that's very clever. I can see we'll get along, provided you keep this up."

As she stepped out of silhouette, the dark outline resolved itself into the figure of a woman. Young?—Old? Impossible to tell. She was certainly strikingly beautiful, wearing a black clinging garment that showed off her shapely form. The black cloak she wore, lined with crimson, was cut along the edges to resemble bat-wings. She lifted up a long-fingered hand at the end of a very pale arm and pulled back her hood. A wave of midnight blue-black hair fell down about her shoulders and around a perfectly sculptured face, pale as marble, and almost as hard, her beautiful features set in a cold smile. Her eyes were unusually large, and the irises glowed an eerie violet. Her eyebrows arched like an Elf's, and her facial structure echoed those fairest of folk, but those sharp pointed teeth . . .

"Nathauan," hissed Sam in surprise, angry at being startled. The raven hissed back at him, and the woman turned and regarded him from beneath one arched eyebrow.

"Something wrong with that, assassin? You've got good taste in clothing, but it looks like you don't take very good care of it. Really should do something about your hair, too." She turned away from him to face Kaylana. The fortune teller was watching them all with glittering eyes, her gaze not shifting as she reached behind her with her cane to whap Arcie's hand sharply as he reached for a chest of drawers.

The Nathauan extended her hand to Kaylana, saying in her honeyed poison tones, "You must be the clever girl who's keeping these two rapscallions in line. Well done, dear. I am Valeriana Ebonstar, Sorceress, and I've been watching your progress with considerable amusement and interest."

Kaylana looked at the proffered hand. The pointed fingernails were long and lacquered black and shiny. She didn't move. Valeriana drew her hand back with grace and used it to scratch her raven, continuing, "You've a good grasp of the sense of things, dear, but no concept of the physics of how to go about anything. I'll attribute it to living in a briar patch." She turned away from the fuming Kaylana and flashed an icy smile around the cluttered room. "I know how you can accomplish what you seek, and for my own personal reasons it suits me that you do so."

Arcie appeared in a corner of the room, his hand on his morning-star. "Oh aye?" he retorted. "And what about our *own* personal reasons? We don't even ken who ye are . . . Why should we even bother to listen to ye?"

For an answer, Valeriana extended one of her hands

and pointed an ebony fingernail out the open doorway of the wagon. Her eyes flashed, and she spoke a harsh phrase. There was the faintest sense of a sudden painful warping chill in the air as the sorceress bent the very fabric of reality to her will for an instant.

A blip of something too fast to see shot from her fingertip, out the doorway, and hit a gnarled apple tree to which was tied a sleepy bay horse. There was a rocking explosion as the tree burst into fragments of splintering, burning wood and droplets of molten sap. The horse screamed and bolted, and shouts erupted throughout the encampment. The fortune teller, shrieking angrily, leaped spryly out the door in pursuit of her horse. Kaylana muttered an oath and followed her, her Druidic instincts fearing for the animal. Arcie and Sam, hands on their weapons, stared at Valeriana in shock. She blew a puff of smoke from her fingertip and smiled like a shark.

"I'm sure you'll find it wise to listen to me notwithstanding, gentlemen," she said.

II

The two rogues, one Druid, and one sorceress rode south, away from the little town. Valeriana kept her cloak pulled close around her and the hood pulled over her face, protecting her fair skin from the climbing sun. A disgruntled band of Gypsies could barely be seen, heading north. Kaylana had seen to the horse; it had only been frightened, but she still glowered in silent fury at the new addition to their party, who was riding on a liver-chestnut gelding tacked in fine black leather with silver trim.

Kaylana knew that this "Valeriana" person was certainly an agent of darkness, far more so than the two insufferable men, and thus Kaylana was bound to ally with her against the imbalance . . . but that didn't mean she had to like her. She was also angry at the assassin for his remark of the previous night, and she didn't trust the Barigan any farther than she could throw him, which was probably about five feet, six maybe, with a good footing. All in all, she felt, it would be a miracle if they could manage to keep the group together long enough to do anything. At least the threat of suffering the same fate as that poor tree seemed to be keeping the two males compliant, but she didn't like to think what they must be plotting in the dark reaches of their minds.

In fact, Sam was brooding over what Mizzamir might be up to now. He knew he couldn't run from the white wizard's magic and had no idea where to find him so as to get the first strike, so he was just waiting, waiting, always ready. He'd let himself get careless in the town, getting drunk and then hung over, so he hadn't noticed Valeriana's approach. Never again, he vowed, his head still sore and his mouth still tasting poorly. He wondered why it was that he, an assassin, could consume rue and bee agaric and dimondfish oil and other poisons that would kill a strong man and yet still fall so easily under the spell of the grape, or the hop, or whatever it was. His body would move in the ways he'd trained it, just as it had with his fancy dart shots last night, but the fire was dimmed, dulled. If drunk or hung over, he'd stand no chance against Mizzamir.

Arcie, for his part, hadn't decided what to think about this sorceress. A mage was certainly useful to have around, he decided, even if she had more or less threatened to blow them into tiny, tiny bits if they crossed her. He felt sure he could outsneak her and get away, though, if it came to that. Sam and Kaylana would have to take care of themselves. Sam had accosted him earlier and demanded the return of the large emerald Arcie had given him as a deposit on the contract, and after a few harsh words about thieves and people who couldn't look after their property, and Sam doing the annoying thing of picking one up by one's neck, Arcie had relented and given back the stone. Now, as they rode away from the abandoned Gypsy encampment, he tallied up the newcomer's apparent possessions and their relative worth after fencing costs. All still in her possession, of course; his few covert theft activities had been instantly detected by some means he was not sure of and after a warning shot of magic from the sorceress's finger put a smoking hole through his cap, he had chosen to leave her alone. But it helped to pass the time to silently evaluate what might be a fairly profitable haul if he could ever get it.

He'd gotten as far as the silver-and-ruby dragon-motif dagger on her belt: *Probably ceremonial, she doesn't seem the type to do much hand-fighting. I'd guess it's modern Shadrezarian, nice gems, make it about forty gold, fifty if the blade's any good* . . . when she turned around, looked back at the party, apparently judging they were far enough from town now, and called a halt.

"I suppose you're wondering why I've got you all here today . . . ," she began.

"Yes!" Arcie snapped.

"Not really," Sam commented drily. Kaylana was silent, mounted on her stag, which had met them in the hills outside town as the Gypsies departed.

Valeriana drummed her shiny long fingernails on the pommel of her expensive saddle. The raven, sitting on her shoulder, hissed. "All right. I suppose I'll have to explain everything to you peasants. Might as well do it now and save time." She indicated a copse of dark trees not far off, with a wave of a black-gloved hand through which the nails emerged like claws. "We'll go there and be able to talk out of this beastly sun."

They made their way to the copse and stopped their mounts in the shade of the trees. "Make yourselves comfy, sunlanders, I'll speak slowly so you can perhaps get the sense of my words through your thick skulls." Valeriana's teeth flashed in the darkness of her hood, and her three fuming captives dropped their reins and sat back, keeping a wary eye on the sorceress as she began speaking.

"Nightshade here," she said, scratching the raven on

her shoulder, as it blinked sleepily at them, "told me that this dear Druid has told you of the imbalance, and how it threatens the lives of everyone, good as well as evil. What she obviously doesn't realize is how far things have gotten already, how long it will be before the imbalance is irreversible, and what to do about it before that happens. Well, I know those things, and that's why I went through all the tedious bother of looking you up.

"You see, I'm a sorceress, not a backwoods grubber. I don't believe in all of this nonsense about light and darkness needing each other. I'd personally love to see this world taken over and suppressed by hordes of trolls. But that didn't happen, and when everyone else had the Victory, we lost. The Heroes found the legendary artifacts that allowed the forces of Light to win the war. The armies of darkness were routed right royally. Why? Because the Heroes had also destroyed many of the Darkportals through which the energies of darkness flowed."

"What's a Darkportal?" interrupted Arcie. Valeriana glared at him.

"I was coming to that, Barigan. Outside our world exist dimensions of power, of matter and antimatter, light magic and dark magic respectively. The Darkportals, you see, were gateways to the plane of darkness and evil. There are Lightportals, too, linking this world with the plane of goodness and light, positive energy against the dark's negative energy. When all was working normally, the portals' conflicting charges kept life balanced, as your Druid might say. The magic of the world was fed by these portals, with the white wizards, good dragons, benevolent spirits, and the like drawing energy, directly or indirectly, from the forces of the Lightportals, and the black sorcerers, evil dragons, undead, and suchlike drawing on the Darkportals.

"But with all the Darkportals closed or destroyed by the Heroes or those that came after them, most of the evil creatures died or were easily slain, creating a vacuum in the world. The only thing that could fill that vacuum was Light, and Light energy, for most of the Lightportals were still functioning. With their source of existence cut off, the armies of darkness were easy prey. The few that survived the Wars, the once great and powerful but now weakened and wounded, were driven by the forces of Light to the DarkGate."

Valeriana paused and wove her hands in mystic patterns through the air. The others tensed, in case she was about to cast some devastation spell. But it was only a shimmering image in midair of a windswept summit of barren dark rock. Like a mirror of night, a slightly slanted black pit was visible in the image of rocks, a circle of darkness unlike anything natural.

"This Gate was the greatest Darkportal, an artifact of strange power and great age. While the minor portals only allowed the passage of energy, the Gate was, as it sounds, a Gate into the dark plane from whence the powers flowed. It, like the LightGate, had remained unthought of for eons, only remembered in rumors and tales. The gradually increasing forces of Light were able to bring the DarkGate from its place in the under-fabric of the world . . . "

"What?" demanded Sam. Valeriana scowled.

"The DarkGate and LightGate, unlike the Darkportals and Lightportals, do not exist here as we know it. Rather, they are everywhere and nowhere, like threads that run through the underside of a fabric rather than across the surface. The Heroes figured out how to pull the DarkGate to the surface. They managed to open it as the Heroes drove the last of the forces of Darkness toward it. The last of the dark forces fell into that Gate, vanishing, and the Gate was sealed by means of mighty magics and hidden from the knowledge of men. By the Labyrinth, which became another thread hidden in the under-fabric."

In the image between her hands, a shimmering field wove itself over the top of the pit, and then the image vanished in a swirl of golden fog. Valeriana let the fog disperse, and rubbed her hands together.

"Then the forces of Light went on to track down all of

the remaining Darkportals and destroyed them. Their world was cut free of evil, and all that remained was to clear up the evil still remaining in their monsters, in their criminals. Heroes and adventurers sprung up like weeds, raiding dungeons, destroying monsters, attacking cities . . . "

Her voice trembled a moment, and she halted. For a moment all was silent, then she continued, strong again.

"Meanwhile, the wizards had developed ways to dissolve the evil in the minds and spirits of men and women who followed that path, burning the darkness away with a pure white magic that left the victim what they never wished to be: a good citizen. And thus more goodness flowed into the world. Without the Darkportals to provide a release, a counter, the world becomes like an inflating bubble, stretched thinner and thinner, until finally, 'Pop!' " She folded her hands and looked at them from within her hood.

Arcie spoke up. "Kaylana here says we'll be sublimated."

Sam broke in. "Yes, I mean, both of you ladies seem to know your stuff, but I don't know which one of you to believe . . . what is really going to happen?"

Kaylana shook her head and spoke. "Though our sharp-toothed escort has a few of her theories crossed, she is basically confirming me. There is too much light, not enough darkness to counteract it."

Valeriana's voice had a bit of a snarl in it. "If that is how you can make sense of it in your common little minds, yes."

Kaylana continued. "And as for what is going to happen at the end of the world . . . I cannot say for certain. I have never seen it before, and I do not think I shall see it more than once." She looked over at Valeriana. "At any rate, sorceress, I think you have given us enough background, and now likely you mean to inform us as to what you are going to force us to do."

"Fair enough," replied Valeriana in a dark voice from the depths of her hood.

"Unfortunately, the only way to save our own skins will also save the skins of a bunch of worthless fools whose fault the whole mess is in the first place. But, for what's at stake here—ourselves and our way of life—it's justified. No one else will help us. We're among the last of the people of darkness in the world—excepting you, Druid—and the only ones among those who know what's going on."

"So what do we have to do?" sighed Sam.

"I should think it would be obvious. We've got to open the DarkGate. To do so we will need the Key that has been scattered and hidden across the Six Lands, by the power of the Six Heroes of the Victory and guarded by unknown wards. And, should we succeed in that, we will face the most difficult task . . . The way to the Labyrinth of Dreams will be opened, that much my research has shown, but beyond that . . . " She shook her head. "I will go with you, because, somehow," she smiled at them, "I do not think you would go voluntarily."

That evening, they camped in a small dell at the edge of a forest. They were well into the southern wilderness of Dous by now, some days from the next inhabited area. They sat around a small fire while the horses and stag cropped the grass nearby, and watched each other warily. Though all were tired, no one wanted to be the first to fall asleep in this company.

Kaylana heated up the last of the stew in a pot and ate her share, while Sam and Arcie appropriated the rest and supplemented it a bit with meat from squirrel Arcie had managed to kill with a handmade sling when Kaylana wasn't looking. Valeriana watched them with mild amusement, as she pulled out a silver bowl, filled it with dark wine from a wineskin in her saddlebags, added some dried chunks of meat, and dipped a finger into the mixture, murmuring a few words. In an instant the food in the bowl was simmering and steaming slightly. With an evil grin at Sam, who seemed to have lost interest in his squirrel, she casually licked off her fingernail and took out a silver fork from a pouch and began eating. Sam turned away. Arcie was puzzled, but since Sam didn't seem to be in the mood to talk, he decided to strike up a conversation with the sorceress.

"Here, how come, if you're a dark sorceress and all the power supplies for dark magic are gone, can you do magic?" he asked brightly. Valeriana looked at him coldly.

"I have my methods, gnome."

Arcie shrugged. "All right, be that way. My name's Arcie, by the by. And I'm a human, not a gnome." Valeriana glowered at him. She'd taken off her cloak and lain it on the grass and was sitting on it. The firelight flickered around her face, and Arcie wasn't sure he liked her expression. He decided to introduce the other two, in hopes of diverting her attention. "And that's Sam and that's Kaylana."

"Sam?" Valeriana's voice carried the sneer that turned her dark lips and transformed the name into a scoff. "An assassin, by his clothing and his manner, and his name is Sam? What sort of name is that for a hired killer? It sounds like the name of a farmhorse."

The idea intrigued Arcie. "Aye, blondie, how come your name are Sam?" Always better to side with the stronger party. Kaylana watched the exchange silently.

Sam didn't turn around, just stared out into the dimness around them. It was awfully light out for this late at night. He answered after a moment.

"It's short for Samalander."

The name, the flickering light on the trees, the heat at his back, the crackle of the fire, plunged him into reverie.

**Smoke in the eyes, legs too weak to move, fire everywhere . . . Sorrow and anger and pain ringing in the ears . . . hands, slippery, scrapes, splinters on the palm . . . ash and cinders, loud ripping noise and things falling, me falling, tumbling, spilled out among charred timber and coals and a black leather boot in front of my eyes as my sight fails. Voices echoing, male voices but not frightening . . . "Well, what's this?" "Some kid, looks like . . . " "Can't* *be more than five summers. Crawled right out of the burning building there, just like a samalander out of a Wintertide log." "Blood on him, look . . . " "Not his, though. Come on, little samalander, something tells me you're one of us . . . " Hands lifting up, gently, as consciousness falls away . . .*

"Really?" said Arcie. "Hmm, I can see why you prefer Sam." Sam shrugged. There was a pause, then Kaylana asked cautiously,

"Do you not mean 'Salamander'?"

"No," Sam retorted firmly. "Samalander." And that seemed to end conversation for the evening.

Night was clustering on. Though it wasn't getting very dark, the company felt slumber coming on. Kaylana silently drew a wide circle in the soft grass with the end of her staff, speaking softly to herself. Then she looked at the others pointedly and lay down inside it, curling up in her armor and robes like a dormouse, and fell asleep. No one bothered to ask her what she'd done or risked finding out if the circle was a bluff or not. Shortly thereafter, Valeriana pulled a black fur coverlet out of her saddlebags and curled up in it in the softest hollow in the turf. The raven, Nightshade, seemed to be waking up. It sat on her arm as she lay there, fluffing out its feathers against the night's chill, and clucked to itself. Sam got the distinct impression it was watching him. In an effort to be friendly he tossed a crust of bread at it, but it had already shared Valeriana's meal and regarded the offering with withering scorn. Sam gave up and curled up in his cloak, setting his instincts to wake him in the event of any danger. Arcie had fitted himself inside a nearby hollow log they'd broken pieces off for kindling, after checking to be sure it held nothing more fearsome than some woodlice and a few mushrooms. He lay on his stomach with his head propped up in his hands and looked at Sam.

"Laddie? Be you asleep?" he whispered after a moment. Valeriana's breathing was even and deep. Sam opened one eye and looked at the Barigan.

"Yes. What is it?" he asked.

"What are a Nathauan?" the Barigan inquired softly. Sam rolled over to face him and rubbed his eyes sleepily.

"They're a race of evil people that used to live in the Underrealm, below where the Dwarves used to tunnel, in mountains and hills and fens. You probably didn't hear much about them in Bariga. Some say they used to be Elves once, others say they're of demon blood. They used to raid the surface world and take slaves and prisoners and such, and no one who was captured ever returned. They torture people as a form of beauty and art, they hate everything sunlit, they're fearsome sorcerers but not very good at fighting, so they raised some of the dark monsters from the tunnels to serve as their guards. They're also gourmands. They especially like eating the sapient races, like humans and Elves and such, and they eat each other, too. They were all wiped out years ago by the Verdant Company, under Sir Fenwick of Trois. I was about twelve at the time. Right after that we caught one skulking around Bistort, and the Guild brought him in. He told us what I've just told you, adding that he was the last one of his community. The Company had moved on and were wiping out the rest of them that year. He was a nasty fellow, almost as bad as Sharkbreath over there. No one would hire him for a normal job, so we tried to train him. He wasn't a very good character for the craft, too messy, no real talent . . . and not very stable." Sam's voice trailed off.

"What happened to him?" asked Arcie. "Did he get whitewashed?"

"No," said Sam, with a sudden coldness in his voice. "Quite the contrary. He did something stupid and got himself killed. By the Guild."

Arcie was quiet a moment. "What are we to do about her?"

Sam glanced over at the dark figure of the sorceress. "I'm already on an assignment, you cheap-donkey."

"We canna let her threaten us around like this, yet."

"True . . . all right." Sam switched to the silent rogue's language. "I will incapacitate her, leave tied up in ditch somewhere, how's that? No charge," he added magnanimously.

"Fine," replied Arcie, in the same code.

Sam rolled to his knees stealthily and slipped the sections of his eighteen-inch blowgun out of his sleeve. He fitted them together swiftly and silently. A brush of his collar yielded a two-inch thin steel needle, while his other hand felt in a pouch and ran a finger along the lids of several secured vials, feeling the code of raised dots that were the labels. The hand found and brought out a small ceramic tube of thrice-distilled bluewort leaf, blended with rasophar oil for consistency. His thumb popped the flip cork, his fingers dipped the point of the needle, the lid thumbed shut, vial set aside as blowgun raised, leveled, needle inserted, vision contracting, nothing but the target . . .

"Craaawwow!" Sam was knocked backwards by a furiously squawking heavy ball of black feathers. He lashed up with one arm and batted the angry raven to one side, but it kept yelling. Valeriana and Kaylana awoke, looking about in confusion. Through the flailing jet feathers Sam saw the pale sorceress slowly rising from the black fur like a poisonous snake in lethal anger, her long-fingered hand pulling her gown close about her . . . but not before he'd had a glimpse of the strange pendant she wore. It was like an oval the size of a hen's egg, a flat cabochon made of some stone so black it reflected none of the bright starlight, set in a ring of gold. Her gown covered it, and she called to her raven as she sat up.

Nightshade flew back to her shoulder and glared, as did its mistress, at Sam, who was silent. Kaylana started to speak, but hesitated. Instead she held her staff across her knees and waited to see where the confrontation would lead.

For a moment they faced each other. Then Valeriana smiled. "I suspected as much. Yes, it is not surprising you have lasted . . . you will be useful. But—" and her eyes turned a deadly purple in the light, the smile vanishing. "Do not try this again, or I will turn your bones to ice and your blood to molten lead, and you will die."

With that she curled up again. Sam turned away with a shiver and looked around for Arcie.

"So much for your bright ideas, Arcie . . . Arcie?"

A soft snoring emanated from the hollow log. Sam looked and saw the Barigan flat on his face, blissfully asleep, with Sam's blowgun needle hanging from his left earlobe like an odd bit of jewelry. Sam smiled, reached out and pulled the needle free. Arcie didn't even snort.

"One way to shut him up," muttered Sam. "I'll have to remember that."

Kaylana, secure in her circle, shook her head. "Hopeless," she muttered and went back to sleep.

The next morning, they continued westward. The air was bright and warm, the birds were singing, the flowers were blooming, the bees were buzzing, and Sam was plotting.

Arcie had awakened at the smell of breakfast being heated and had wriggled out of his hollow log with no ill effects. He was surprised to see both Sam and Valeriana still with the group, and with a shrug passed the whole incident off as a dream.

As they rode, Sam looped Damazcus's reins around the saddlehorn and let the animal follow placidly behind Arcie's. The ground was dry and even, and the animals spread about and shifted position as they walked along. The sun rose in the sky, becoming a burning on Sam's face and arms, and he suffered in his black garb. Valeriana had her hood up again, he noticed, to protect her precious face. The raven, sleepy from its night vigil, rode her shoulder in silence with its head under its wing. Good. He took up the end of his cloak and inspected it. Dirty from prison and mud and blood, torn by sword and thorn and wear, the whole thing was altogether too long and hot for this weather. It carried too many items to simply discard, however. Ah well, he would trim it. He flipped out his fourth-best dagger, the one with the pearl set in the pommel, and went to work.

The odd sound of tearing cloth prompted first Arcie,

then Valeriana, to look around. Sam, busy at his tailoring, glanced up and gave them a bored look. "Too long," he commented, by way of explanation. After a last suspicious glance, Valeriana turned back, as did Arcie . . . but a moment later the Barigan turned to look at him quizzically and Sam winked. Arcie grinned and looked away, but continued to watch the assassin out of the corner of his eye.

The assassin was tearing strips off of the edge of his cloak; cutting, checking the line of the cut, cutting again to even the edge, checking, cutting . . . and collecting variously sized strips of black fabric, which he was knotting together stealthily. He worked fast but innocently, whistling softly through his teeth. No one trusts an assassin who's being very quiet. At last he dropped his shortened cloak to fall down behind his back and picked up his reins again. Valeriana rode her liver-chestnut horse to the side and a little ahead. Arcie's was only a few paces away. He urged Damazcus forward a little and caught up with the pony. Wordlessly he handed Arcie a double handful of black strips, tied into an untidy but strong net, about three feet in diameter. As he did so, he signed in the silent language:

"Get bird. Hold. Listen me." He looked ahead. Valeriana was just heading down the other side of a hill. "Go!"

The two criminals whomped the sides of their horses in unison. The horses leaped forward in surprise, bolted up and over the hill in a few strides, and came scrambling down upon Valeriana, one on each side. Her horse shied and reared, and then there was chaos.

Arcie made an astonishingly quick and dexterous lunge, tossing the folds of the net out over the startled raven just as it was spreading its wings. He yanked, tangling its head and wings in the mesh and ripping the taloned black feet from Valeriana's hooded cloak. It cawed and squawked in fury.

Even as the bird was snatched from its perch, Sam was standing in the saddle. A flash of the fire that came with sudden action sprung him out of the seat like an arrow, and he crashed into Valeriana in midair as she turned to grab her torn shoulder. The force of his leap threw them both off the horse and sent them crashing onto the grass. A struggle, then Sam held the sorceress pinned on the ground, one hand holding both her wrists painfully tight, the other holding a dagger to her throat. Valeriana, her impressive chest heaving theatrically, her eyes almost magenta with rage, opened her mouth to call words of power that would blast the assassin into oblivion. Then she saw over his shoulder the figure of Arcie, cockily sitting on his pony with her beloved Nightshade in his grubby paws, his hands around her poor darling's throat! The raven was frozen in fear as the fingers held almost too tightly to its feathered neck.

Sam saw her expression change, from livid rage, to fear and livid rage, and smiled nastily.

"One false move, sorceress, and your familiar gets it," he whispered. She glared at him in fury but said nothing.

Without taking his gaze off his deadly captive, Sam said, "Good job, Arcie. Have a care now and don't let it go. If she moves, rip the blasted crow's head off." The raven gurgled in terror.

Sam shifted the point of his dagger and pushed aside a corner of the Nathauan's collar. There, like a hole into nothingness against white skin, gleamed the stone. Valeriana gasped in fear, panic and anger and started to speak, but a muffled croak from her raven froze her again. With the point of his weapon, Sam hooked the heavy gold chain that held the pendant and lifted it free of her neck. It revolved slowly in the sun, the gold frame glinting in the light, but the black stone was featureless as a midnight lake. Sam glanced from it to the sorceress.

"This must be quite important to you. You take off all your other jewelry when you sleep, to keep it from marring your fair skin, but not this heavy thing. You hide it under your gown that hides nothing else. And you reach involuntarily for it in moments of stress . . . just a twitch, perhaps, but it's there. You said you had means of wielding power in a world lost to Light . . . could this perhaps be it?" Sam's hand jerked the dagger up, snapping the chain and sending the pendant hurtling into the air. With a shriek Valeriana lunged for it, her panicky strength breaking Sam's grasp. But Sam was quicker. He leaped up to the side and caught the stone neatly in his palm. As Valeriana sprang, teeth bared, he raised it over a boulder, preparing to smash it. She stopped dead. At the same instant, Nightshade gave a strangled gurgle as Arcie's fingers closed on its throat. The peril of her familiar and the loss of her amulet were too much for the sorceress. She turned and collapsed onto the grass, shoulders shaking, with anger or tears, they couldn't tell.

After a tense moment, Sam and Arcie looked at each other. Arcie's fingers slowly relaxed, and the raven gave what might have been a sigh of relief. Kaylana, unhurried, ever collected, stepped down into the hollow leading Sam's and Valeriana's horses. She handed their reins to Sam, who took them in embarrassed silence; Damazcus wiped his nose on Sam's shoulder. Kaylana stepped softly over to the huddled figure of Valeriana.

As the Druid approached, Valeriana whirled on her, her hood falling away. She cringed in the sunlight, her sensitive eyes squinting tight, but her voice was strong and proud.

"All right then, you've won! Kill me now, as I would have killed you! You'll die in the end yourselves when the Light overflows."

Kaylana spoke. "We will not kill you." She looked at Sam and Arcie as she said this, and somehow they had a feeling it would be as she said. "To do so is to build our own coffin. The Light threatens us all equally. The rest of us will not kill a one . . . but nor will one of us rule the rest. Bear that in mind, Sorceress." She glanced over at where Sam was holding the horses and amulet, then back to Valeriana, who was replacing her hood, her arms already reddening from the sun. "Valeriana, is what Sam suspects true, do you draw your power from that amulet?"

"Yes," muttered Valeriana. "As you may have guessed, it's a Darkportal. The last one I know of. Very small. Very weak. But enough."

"And," pressed Kaylana, "can you do magic without the amulet in your possession?"

"No," said Valeriana weakly. "Without it I'm as helpless as a child."

Kaylana sighed. "You are lying," she said resignedly.

"All right, all right! Your powers outfathom mine without my Darkportal. I can do some magic, so long as the amulet is nearby . . . I am weakened, yes, but I can still manage." Valeriana, hood restored, stood up, brushing the grass and dirt off her skirt. Kaylana nodded, satisfied.

Sam spoke up. "I vote we keep the amulet hostage, to prevent the lady from attempting to command us with fear again. That way she can still serve our mutual cause, yet not be so great a threat to us."

Arcie nodded, and Kaylana did the same. Valeriana gave in with bad grace.

"All right then, I'll accept. Let Nightshade go."

Kaylana nodded to Arcie, who took his hands away and pulled the cloth net off the bird. Nightshade fluffed his feathers and glared at Arcie. Suddenly, his thick black beak lashed out, lightning-fast, slashing the Barigan on the back of his hand. Arcie swore. Smugly, the raven flew back to Valeriana's shoulder and began to preen. Kaylana looked around the party.

"Very well. We must be under new leadership, then; that of necessity. Though our motives may be different . . . " she looked pointedly at them all " . . . as I know they are, the end result . . . the restoration of darkness to its place in the world . . . is our common goal. Valeriana has told us of a way in which this goal may be achieved. We have no other way known to us. I say we shall continue on. Any opposed?"

Not a hand was raised. Kaylana nodded.

"As I hoped. We move on."

"So where are we going, then?" Sam asked.

Valeriana swung up into her saddle again. "Well, obviously the knowledge of the Gypsies was of little help. To find the locations of the segments of the Key, we must seek different help. Even the Heroes themselves do not know the true locations . . . the sections of the Key were hidden by the gods themselves."

"Well, then, there's not much we can do, is there?" scoffed Arcie.

"Not quite, you impudent thief. If it is gods that have hid it, it is gods we must ask."

"Are you out of your mind?" cried Sam. "Gods? Any gods that would even notice us would turn us into slugs sooner than look at us. All the gods that ever might have been on our side are long gone."

"Not all," said Valeriana mysteriously.

When they stopped that evening, Sam took out the amulet and inspected it. He'd carried it in his pouch, not really trusting the strange stone from which Valeriana drew her power; Sam felt sure she'd wreak fearsome vengeance upon him if she recovered it. He turned the amulet by its edge in his fingers. The back was flat and resembled a mirror of hematite. He caught his own eye looking back at him from within it and was startled by the cold predatory viciousness he saw there. He flipped the stone back to face him. The dark cabochon intrigued him. He picked up a twig and poked it. It didn't seem to touch any surface, just gave a vague resistance like one feels when touching opposite ends of a lodestone to each other, until he couldn't press the twig any farther and it snapped. A cautious prod with a finger revealed much the same sensation, only as his finger encountered greater resistance he felt a chill, like an icy wind.

Arcie was coming up behind him, Sam noted with mild interest. Sneaking up on his fat booted feet, going to talk right in my ear and see if he can make me jump.

"Be you having fun, Sam?"

Sam didn't twitch. After a finely judged moment he glanced over his shoulder.

"Yes indeed, half-pint. How goes it?"

Arcie, only mildly disappointed at not having been able to make Sam jump, plopped down on the turf across from him, and pulled out his pipe.

"You've been here," he said. "What do you think, then? Are this an adventure or no?"

"It's certainly different." Sam palmed the amulet and tucked it inside one of his secret pouches. "Cut off from my past, thrust out into hostile wilderness with a couple of weird women and a thief, camping out at night, tromping around under blazing sun all day . . . I can still feel it on my face."

Arcie peered at his face a moment. "Looks to me as you got sunburned."

"Oh great," muttered Sam. "An assassin with freckles and a peeling nose."

"No one will suspect you, at least," Arcie pointed out. Sam nodded. Arcie went on.

"But see you, we should travel by night. Dark times for dark business, as they says. No sun to bother Valeriana or you; Kaylana's surely is no' disadvantaged, and I know *I* work better in darkness. Anybody looking for us will have a harder time of it. Besides, marching in daylight is for the heroes. If we're going to do this, we may as well go all out."

"That's a fine idea," agreed Sam. "Especially as it hasn't been getting very dark at night lately anyway."

"You noticed that too?" asked Arcie. "I thought that were odd . . . something with the weather?"

"Maybe . . . " replied Sam doubtfully. "Or something with the world."

The decision was reached to travel by night. As time was pressing (or so Valeriana implied), they broke camp after just a short rest and rode on into the odd dim twilight.

It was nearly dawn when they started into the far edge of the Windarm Mountains. Only a minor range, fortunately, and the party's path had intersected at a pass.

They started up into the rocky foothills, searching for a secure place to rest, for they were now very weary. As they walked their mounts into a narrow side canyon, they met their first great challenge.

It began as a slow reek as of rotting flowers that drifted through the air, making their horses stamp with nervousness. Kaylana's stag pranced with anxiety, and she had to lean along its neck in an attempt to calm it. Meanwhile, the others glanced around uneasily for the source of the distress.

The canyon was long and twisty, but narrow, a floodwater outlet that had been formed long ago. A faint breeze echoed around them. Polished pink stone curved in strange shapes from the rippled walls, and the sky was a pale strip of slowly brightening light overhead, and the changing light sent shifting shadows through the canyon. The ground was perfectly level and covered with fine gravel that crunched under the animals' hooves.

"This place doesn't half willie me," whispered Arcie. "Can't we go back?"

"This is the only pass through these mountains for two weeks' journey, Barigan," retorted Valeriana, her voice tense.

Just then, one of the oddly shaped rock formations opened a huge golden eye and then jerked itself up on a long serpentine neck. A fang-filled mouth cracked open, glowing flame, and a shrill piercing trumpet of a voice cried, "Villains!"

Sam was aware of an explosion of animal panic underneath him, and then he was flying through the air. He landed on his feet with a jarring crunch in the gravel and spun to see his horse bolting out of the valley, hotly followed by another horse, a pony, and a stag. His companions were getting to their feet, their faces masks of shock—the faces of people facing certain death.

It was a dragon, just as the legends told of them: golden eyed, gaping mouth filled with sword-long teeth, breath a flickering flame of fire, and, as it heaved itself over the outcropping, great folded bat wings, vicious curved claws, a huge bulk of a body and a long lashing tail. It was a soft faded-rose color, flecked with gray and gold, like the very walls of the canyon. It drew in a deep breath.

The group scattered, lunging for the safety of the sculptured walls as a blast of flame blew two inches of gravel off the ground where they had stood and melted the rock beneath. Sam rolled to a halt behind the comparative shelter of a large boulder and winced as shards of superheated gravel clattered around him. A few feet over, crouched in an overhang, was Kaylana.

Valeriana and Arcie found themselves pressed into the space behind a whorled stone column. The dragon screeched again.

"Villains! Come out and fight, you nasty people!" Arcie looked up at Valeriana in puzzlement.

"Dragon of Light," she whispered. "If only I had my amulet!"

"Can't you do something?" hissed Arcie, wincing as the dragon's heavy feet came nearer. "We can't get out through the canyon without it flaming us!"

Valeriana snarled to herself and pulled out a few items from her pouch. Hoping her amulet hadn't gone far, or worse, been destroyed, she gathered together her concentration, softly chanting, then thrust her head around the corner of rock and with a final harsh word threw a bolt of black fire at the creature's huge pink stomach. It hit with a flash. The dragon roared, more in anger than in pain, and flame washed over their hiding place.

The moment was all Sam needed. A thin paper pouch of dust arced through the air and burst open on the dragon's muzzle. The dragon blinked, sneezed, then began pawing at its eyes and nose furiously and lashing about wildly with its tail. Kaylana gave the assassin a startled look. He was hefting a dagger. "Blinding and sneezing powder," he whispered, "only thing I had enough of. Won't last long." So saying, he hurled the dagger. It flashed in the air, spinning madly, missed the dragon's thrashing head by an inch, rebounded off the far wall, and thunked instead into the fine pink membrane of a wing. He cursed as the dragon roared and leaped out of shelter again to try another throw. The dragon, hearing the crunch of his feet on the gravel, lashed out furiously with a taloned paw. Sam dodged the claws, but the reptile's palm smacked him off his feet, sending him crashing into a pile of loaf-sized stones, where he lay stunned.

Arcie, meanwhile, was creeping up the canyon wall with surprising ease. From this raised vantage point, he swung at the dragon with his morning-star, thinking as he did so that he was being extremely foolish and would have been better off staying at home. The blow caught the blinded dragon a nice clip on the side of the face, and the creature's head whipped around, its muzzle crashing into the stone wall. The jarring blow shook the Barigan from his perch, causing him to lose his weapon, and dropped him neatly onto the top of the dragon's head, just behind the horns. He had only a second to reflect on the novelty of this when the dragon tossed its head violently. He slid, scrambled, and ended up hanging from one of the great fan-like ears, clutching the leathery skin as the dragon shook its head, trying to rid itself of the effects of the powder and the weight of the fat thief on its delicate ear.

Kaylana gripped her staff and smashed at the dragon's hind toes, the only part of it she could reach. The staff missed, smacking into the gravel, as the dragon lifted its foot to change position. Kaylana struck again, but her aim was off, and the staff crashed into one of the diamond-hard talons. The resulting ringing shook Kaylana's teeth and the staff trembled, but the dragon yelped as a bruise flowered under the nail. The dragon's foot kicked as its head whipped down to deal with this sneak attack. Kaylana sprang away, wooden shield raised in defense.

Valeriana, meanwhile, was edging over to where Sam lay motionless. If she could recover her amulet from the fool's body . . . but suddenly something heavy hit her between the shoulder blades, and she went down like a poleaxed hippogriff. Arcie made a mental note to thank the sorceress later for breaking his fall. He jumped to his feet and staggered—one of his ankles seemed to be sprained, or broken.

The dragon at last sneezed flame prodigiously and opened its eyes, red and streaming, but focused. Seeing the only threats still standing were a young woman and an unarmed Barigan, he opened his gaping jaws wide to flame and bite and tear the dreadful creatures of evil that had disturbed his peaceful nap . . . when the sound of hoofbeats made him freeze in surprise. Kaylana and Arcie turned, and even Sam and Valeriana managed to raise their dazed heads.

Walking calmly into the battlefield was a large, glossy black warhorse. Its great hooves crunched the gravel, sounding loud in the now-silent canyon. Dark plate and chain barding glittered and rang, echoing the armor of its rider—a tall, massively built figure, encased from head to toe in black plate armor. It, a man, likely, by build and armor, looked neither right nor left, but faced the dragon. He wore a black-plumed full helmet, with the visor down. No chink of flesh or fold of clothing showed anywhere. At his side hung a huge black-hilted sword. One arm held a solid black shield on which there was no device. The other hand held a lance, raised, tattered black pennant flapping in the wind. The dragon hissed.

The four companions scrambled out of the way as the great horse snorted and pawed the ground, and the dragon growled, visibly unnerved. It shrilled out in a trumpet voice.

"Who is this dark knight in black armor, who dares to challenge me?"

Slowly the lance lowered, until it pointed at the dragon's chest. The only sound was the faint creaking of the knight's armor. The warhorse snorted and stomped, like a bull. The dragon was visibly unnerved. He had met villains and wicked fighters before; he, Lumathix the Rose-Gold and his kin were the dragons of Goodness and Light and had fought in the War against the creatures of Darkness. And all those creatures were full of curses and wicked words, or the occasional plea for mercy. But the small villains that had awakened him, and this newcomer, did neither. He decided to get it over with and not worry about it.

"Die, spawn of darkness! Feel the wrath of Lumathix!" he roared shrilly and blasted out a tongue of flame.

The knight's horse turned broadside to the fire as the knight raised his shield. The center of the cone of fire struck the shield and spread out and away, leaving rider and horse unharmed. In a moment the stream stopped, and the dragon was left staring at an undamaged knight on horseback with a smoking shield, who was now turning to face him, that nasty looking sharp lance pointed at his soft underbelly. Wordlessly, the knight—his lance lowered and couched—clapped his heels to his horse, and the animal lunged forward eagerly into a galloping charge.

Lumathix squeaked faintly. He was too large to turn around in the narrow canyon, too bulky to fly straight up, and far too heavy to jump. He turned to meet the attack in true dragon offensive, with teeth and claws and fire. He was so intent upon the charging knight he didn't see the other villains moving to either side of him.

As the dragon lunged to meet the knight's charge, pain seared at his foreleg, as three poisoned daggers, in rapid succession, sunk into the tender, delicate skin below his armpit. Simultaneously, a pebble struck his shoulder and exploded, bruising him. Another followed, and another, ordinary stones enchanted by Valeriana and fired with professional accuracy by Arcie's pocket-sling. Kaylana struck the ground with her staff and called out a phrase of power, coaxing the very nature of the rocks themselves, and the gravel on which the dragon footed his lunge turned to shallow, slippery mud. He toppled forward, roaring, as the knight reached him. The knight with his horse at full gallop splashed into the mud, dodged a claw swipe with a sideways swerve, and slammed the shield up into the face of a ferocious bite, crashing sparks from the dragon's mouth and sending a tooth chip flying. The blow knocked the knight's aim off, however, and the lance, instead of plunging into its heart, drove deep into the dragon's uninjured foreleg and snapped. The knight then drew the huge sword, but Lumathix had had enough. Battered, bruised, limping on both legs and his beautiful rosy scales all covered in mud, he scrambled around the knight and down to the exit of the canyon, a last lash of his tail barely missing the knight. They heard his heavy clawing feet scuttling down the passageway and then heard heavy wingbeats as the dragon took to the air. All was tense for a moment, as they feared it would appear over the canyon to roast them, but the sound died away in the distance. The four adventurers turned to look at their unlikely rescuer.

The knight swung down from the saddle and gave them a nod. Then he turned to his horse, and tenderly picked up its huge hooves one by one, making sure the animal had not been injured in the combat.

The party was in something of a quandary. People in plate armor were generally champions of good and justice. Nothing was more irritating to the hard-working evildoer than a knight in shining armor. But this fellow looked to be cut from a different cloth.

Sam staggered up to the knight, who stood to face him. Sam was looking his most evil: gasping, and frothing just a bit, a trickle of blood at the corner of his mouth. He spoke in a harsh rasp.

"I'm an assassin, and behind me are a Druid, a thief, and a black sorceress." Sam heard a faint scrambling noise to his rear. "We're nasty. If you don't like it, you can either get back on your horse and ride out of here, or you can try to fight us, and we'll snuff you."

The knight raised his helmeted head to peer over Sam's shoulder. Fates, the fellow was huge. His black plumes stirred in the air a good bit more than a foot and a half over Sam's head. Risking a sideways glance, Sam saw that the only one of his companions who had remained "behind" him was Kaylana, leaning against a rock and looking heavenward in disgruntlement. The knight looked at Sam, looked out the way the dragon had gone, and extended a gauntleted hand. Sam froze. With mailed fingers the knight touched a tattered fold of Sam's black cloak, then slapped the palm of his hand lightly into the face of his black shield. Then he patted Sam's shoulder.

Sam straightened up and wiped the blood from his mouth. "Oh, all right then," he said, in his normal voice, wondering why he understood. The knight swung up into his saddle. Sam turned and walked back to where his companions had been. "It's all right! He's one of us."

Valeriana and Arcie stepped out of concealment, regarding the knight curiously. Arcie hopped up on a boulder to speak on a level with the newcomer.

"Ho there, stranger! T'were some pretty fancy jousting there," he spoke, grinning wide. This fellow didn't seem to have much worth stealing, unfortunately; no gems on the sword or armor, a dagger there, yes, but not a particularly fine one. No pouches. The horse would fetch quite a bit, but Arcie didn't think it would be worth the trouble of stealing. The knight inclined his head slightly in acknowledgment of the compliment, but said nothing. This intrigued Arcie. "You're a quiet fellow. You don't talk?"

The helmet turned slowly from side to side.

"Guess you can't tell us your handle then, aye, silent knight? What are we to call you?"

The mailed shoulders moved in a gesture of noncommittance.

"You don't care? Aye well then, I'll think of something . . . " Arcie inspected the knight. "Take off your helmet so's we can see what as you look like, then."

The helmet moved again in negative. "No? Why nay? Oh, I forgot, you really can't explain . . . Put the visor up?"

Again a negative. Arcie frowned in frustrated curiosity. Kaylana, who had been listening, called up to the Barigan.

"Leave the knight alone, Arcie. He has just saved our skins. It is not civil to go prying into his personal habits in return."

"But, Kaylana," argued Arcie, and then gave up. He gave the knight a parting glance. "You are a fellow in there, aren't you?"

A nod. Arcie looked relieved. "Thank the fates. There's getting to be far too many pushy women around here." He hopped down from the rock and scampered over to where the others were gathered in conference. The knight followed on his horse. The others looked up as the mounted knight approached. Valeriana spoke, addressing him.

"You have been following us, have you not?" A nod. "You know what we seek?" A nod. "You wish to help us?" Another nod.

"Agreeable chap," commented Sam. Kaylana elbowed him in the ribs.

"Well, that saves a lot of tedious explanation on our part," said Valeriana. "What about on yours?"

"He canna speak," piped up Arcie. The knight confirmed this with a nod. "He won't take off his helmet, neither."

"And yet," mused Valeriana, "I pride myself on knowing things. I cannot see his thoughts, nor can I see what manner of man—or monster—it is that dwells within that armor."

Kaylana added, "He speaks not. Thus I cannot say if his words are true."

"But his armor shows he is of darkness and had he wished us dead, he would have left us to the dragon. He is obviously a skilled warrior. We may well have need of such. I think we should allow him to accompany us."

"Sounds all right," consented Sam.

"Well enough," from Arcie.

"Very well," allowed Kaylana. The knight bowed from his waist graciously. The horse whickered, and Nightshade gave a rasping croak.

"Unless anyone has any objections, we may as well camp here. I do not think the dragon will return," said

Kaylana, kicking thoughtfully at the pebbles.

"Are you sure?" asked Sam, looking up at the sky uncertainly.

"Fairly so," replied Kaylana. "I think it was just napping here. See, there are no bones, no fewmets, no old claw-marks. Its lair must be elsewhere."

"Oh. That means no horde of dragon gold, then?" asked a disappointed Barigan voice. Valeriana scoffed.

"Small fool. If the dragon's hoard were here, we wouldn't have driven it off with such relative ease."

"I shall call the stag and horses back," announced Kaylana. "It may take a while for them to arrive, however . . . I hope they have not fled out of range." She began gesturing in midair with her staff, eyes narrowed in concentration, as her magic searched for the auras of their mounts among the many animals in the area.

The knight tethered his horse to an outcropping of stone and began untacking it as the animal cropped the sprigs of wildflowers growing out of the wall. After a moment, a bag of oats was unslung from the saddlebags and placed before it. Kaylana quickly tended the Barigan's sprained ankle and the others' cuts and bruises. Arcie and Sam then set out to scavenge for deadwood to build a fire, and something to cook on that fire.

They wandered up the canyon. Twigs were scarce, and it was not long until their search took them out of earshot of the others.

"I don't feel proper about yon knight, Sam," mused Arcie, picking up a small branch.

"I'd rather have him on my side than not, that's for sure," replied the assassin, debating whether a bird's nest high up the wall was worth the climb.

"But see you well, we dinna even know what he looks like! He could be a horrible skellyton . . . "

"Not very likely," responded Sam. He decided to climb. The twigs would be useful, if nothing else. "Not in this world, if what the two ladies say is true."

"Or a monster or just all hollow inside! One o' these days," plotted the Barigan, tugging at a small branch wedged into a crack, "I'm going to knock his helmet off, accidentally of course."

"Good luck," scoffed Sam's voice from somewhere above him. The Barigan looked up at the assassin crawling along the rock face about twenty feet from the ground.

"What do you mean?" he inquired.

Sam grabbed the bird's nest; it was empty, a couple years old at least. He took it anyway and began climbing back down. "I got a good look at him when I went and talked to him," he said shortly. He jumped lightly to the ground, and looked away as he stuffed the nest into their wood-gathering sack. "His helmet's one of those that has hinges, so it opens up in the back in two halves so that you can put it on and it doesn't fall off if you turn upside down in a joust."

"So?" asked Arcie, looking up curiously at the assassin.

"His is welded shut."

They filled the sack and made their way back to the group in silence. A fire was lit, and Kaylana began making something that looked like porridge.

"There is not much," she apologized. "The horses with the provisions have not yet returned."

"No game about, either," Sam apologized. "The dragon's smell must have scared everything off."

They sat in the shade as the sun moved overhead, feeling weary from their day and night march and life-or-death battle. All were sleepy, but once again no one wanted to be the first to slumber. Valeriana looked around them in mild amusement.

"We will be journeying through terrible dangers, where the survival of all will hinge upon the strength of all. And yet we cannot stand sleep in the same company. We will have to forget our differences and plan our goals. What are our goals?"

"Kill Mizzamir the wizard and put the world back the way it was," came from Sam. Their silent, armored companion turned his blank visor to look at Sam, but made no other comment.

"Restore the balance." Kaylana watched them from green eyes.

"Get rich!" Everyone looked at Arcie, and he hastily added, "Aye, and of course put the world back the way it was, as Sam said."

The knight nodded, seconding Arcie's last statement.

Valeriana's beautiful face turned stern and sad within the shadows of her cloak.

"And mine is to wreak vengeance upon those who destroyed my people. Unable to do that, however, I must settle instead for preventing their rule from becoming absolute, preventing them from winning the final battle. Nothing would upset them more now than seeing the world 'put back the way it was,' as you so quaintly put it. There, then, we are of a common cause. We will strive together."

A moment of silence, then Arcie asked the question that was on everybody's mind.

"Yet can we trust each other?"

They looked around at themselves, tired, sleepy in the morning sun: an indiscriminate thief who would cheerfully abandon even his close friend at any sign of danger; a cold, merciless assassin with the reflexes of a panther and the strength of will and body to kill at the slightest need; a Druid who had implied that she would abandon them and fight against them if the tide ever turned their way; a black sorceress whose race dined upon theirs and who, if she ever regained her amulet, would likely visit great and terrible punishment and pain upon them; and a strange, dark, silent figure in plate mail about whom they knew nothing more than his superb skill as a warrior and the fact that he had not eaten any porridge at dinner.

Sam gave a matter-of-fact shrug. "Who else is there?"

Sam took the first watch that day, and the rest slept. They would have far to go tomorrow, and a strange and dangerous task to perform. The knight sat with his back to the wall, unmoving. Sam assumed he was asleep, at any rate, though the dark steel breastplate showed no signs of a rise and fall. Sam settled down in the dusty gravel, splotched with drying mud, and watched, and thought about gods, the Mad Godling in particular.

In days of legend, gods would oft walk the earth and meddle in the affairs of men. Now, in these days of Light, the evil gods were all vanished, and, as if bored by the lack of conflict, the good gods remained in their lofty high dimensions, unseen by mortals and unknown except for the words and powers of their respective priests—who used their divine magic to benefit the people and interpret the will of the gods. The last great miracle had occurred in the days following the Victory. The DarkGate had been locked by means of a great artifact created by the powers of the Six Heroes and the gods. This treasure, the Spectrum Key, had been shattered into six Segments, and the Segments hidden and guarded, as no power known could destroy them, and to leave the Key whole was to risk the opening of the DarkGate should the Key ever fall into the wrong hands. The wards placed on these Segments were such that, should the need ever arise, a true hero could pass the Test set up in magical fields around each Segment, and thus retrieve it. The Tests were designed by the Six Heroes, and then the gods of Light themselves hid the Tests and the Segments with them, concealing them from the eyes of foolish mortals and even from the Heroes themselves.

Now, not long before all this, according to the priests, there was, or rather, had been, a demigod, the offspring of a deity and a lesser immortal being. This offspring, not yet a demigod, was Bhazo, the son of Rhinka, the goddess of wisdom, and Cwellyn, the patron saint of the bards, symbolizing knowledge. Cwellyn, being only a lesser power, actually went to fight at the side of the last few true bards in the battle against the Light, in alliance with the Druids. He tried to win his former lover Rhinka to his side, but she was enraged by his impudence for the attempt and struck him dead with a large meteorite.

With his father's death, Bhazo came into the picture, claiming that, now that there was a celestial vacancy, he should be promoted to godhood. He claimed that, as his father had been a divinity of knowledge and his mother of wisdom, he now be granted the powers of a deity of knowledge and be privy to all the wisdom and secrets of the gods, even those that the gods kept from each other. But the gods could see into his semi-divine heart and saw there the flickering of greed. Bhazo knew that knowledge is power and knew also that with all the knowledge in existence he could become the most powerful of gods. The gods were angry, but instead of smiting him into dust, they visited an even more terrible punishment upon him: they gave him what he desired.

Bhazo was only a semi-divine being; his mind could not hold all the knowledge of all the omnipotent beings. He went utterly mad, his mind constantly aflood with that which no one mind was meant to know. He was banished to the heavy surface of the material world, to wander forever in mad semi-immortality. Insane, he sought relief from the torment that plagued him, and went to end his life. He fashioned a cord of dragon's breath and built a gallows above the burning light of a chasm that led to the fires at the center of the world. But as he stepped from the platform, feeling the noose jerk tight about his neck, he saw his action through the eyes of the gods and knew that he had only doomed himself still further. For the gods suddenly appeared, binding his spirit back into his flesh even as it struggled to leave, and made him fully immortal, that he might not slip out of his punishment. And thus Bhazo was left to shriek and gibber the unfathomable knowledge of all creation to an echoing chasm, the dragonfire noose ever-burning around his neck.

And Valeriana wanted the band of renegades to go and talk to him, for no other being on the world would know the location of the six Segments of the Key.

The morning sun shone into the window of the Silver Tower of the Castle of Diamond Magic in Natodik.

Rainbow color spilled about the walls from the stained-glass border, depicting the glorious triumphs of the Victory. Mizzamir, resplendent in his silver-white robes, sat at his carved goldenwood desk, reading from an ancient leather-bound tome, the very picture of sophisticated wizardry. Birds alighted on the windowsill and sang a good-morning chorus to him, their eyes glazed with the happiness of it all. He smiled at them with his hazel-green eyes.

A light tap sounded at the door. Mizzamir closed the book, and looked toward the door. "Enter, Sir Fenwick," he said kindly.

The door opened, and the handsome young hero entered, bowing his respects to the great wizard. He was garbed as usual in his fine chain mail, over his shirt and pants of forest green, the color of the nobility of Trois, with the fringed vest and gloves that were the fashion in that country. From his shining leather boots to his peaked hat with its pheasant feather, he was an impressive sight. "Arch-Mage Mizzamir, I have located an agent, such as you requested."

"Oh, good! Very good . . . " said Mizzamir, but then noticed something seemed to be troubling the man. He raised his finely arched silver eyebrows in question. "Fenwick? Something troubles you this fine day?"

"Sir . . . " the human paused a moment, unsure, then continued strongly. "Are you certain 'tis better to do nothing but follow these villains? Would it not be simpler and safer if I were to lead the Verdant Company in pursuit of them? We could track them with ease, and catch up with them in a matter of days, even faster with your help. Then, we could subdue them, or slay those beyond saving . . . "

"No one is beyond saving, young Fenwick," admonished Mizzamir gently.

"Subdue them then. I do not like to leave such people running loose, especially to gather together. It is like leaving a viper in one's garden."

Mizzamir shook his head in amusement at the impetuosity of youth.

"Dear Fenwick, I'll not have you or your men risk their lives nor waste their time riding after a troupe of ruffians who will very likely end up killing each other soon anyway. Nothing they do can hurt us."

The mage rose from his chair, and went to stand in the window, looking out at the sun burning its way through a few scattered pink clouds. His voice continued, deep and majestic.

"The Gate is sealed forever, guarded by the Labyrinth I helped build. Our forces hold peace secure. The world is purged of evil as Light assumes its rightful benevolent rule! They can do nothing! The Light shall rule forever!"

He flung his hands wide and upward in a gesture of ecstasy as the sun burst through the clouds and illuminated his silver robes and hair with dazzling light. The magic of his aura spun about him in a shining blur as the radiance cascaded around him and rainbows danced flickering on the walls and ceiling. Showers of light shot from the mage's fingertips and flashed purest white. Fenwick watched in awe. The moment broke as the sun moved back behind the clouds, and Mizzamir turned to look at him with a benevolent smile, the radiance shifting back to its normal gentle warmth.

"Ah, I do get carried away at times. You said you had found an agent for us, Fenwick? Please, bring him in, I do wish to meet him and advise him of his mission."

"Uh, yes, of course," stammered Fenwick, then recovered. "I'll tell you a bit about him first. He wishes to be a minstrel, but has only started his career . . . "

"A minstrel, eh?" Mizzamir looked thoughtful. "Not a bard, I hope?"

"No, no . . . " assured Fenwick. Bards had been a mixed problem. For one thing they shared too many talents with thieves. For another, quite a number had been allied with the Druids. After the Victory, most of the bards had vanished. The rest had been exterminated, just to be safe. Now, the place of the bards had been taken by the more normal sort of strolling minstrel and storyteller. These good folk lacked the strange ancient ways of the bards and their mystical powers as well, but they were thus that much more comfortable to have around.

"No, he's to be a minstrel, right enough. He was born good, but not so stridently as you or I, Arch-Mage . . . thus I think, with a bit of your magic to conceal his true goodness, he will be able to join the renegades without arousing their suspicions. I will warn you, though, he is fairly naive in the ways of wickedness. His name's Robin. I'll fetch him now."

He walked out of the room, reappearing a moment later, saying, "Arch-Mage Mizzamir, I bring you the aspiring minstrel, Robin of Avensdale."

Hoofbeats rang on the flagstones outside. Mizzamir's eyebrow arched. Was the prince playing a joke on him and sending someone in on horseback?

His concerns were allayed as Robin stepped into the room. The fellow was a centaur. A young male, with wide, innocent eyes and fair skin. He wore clothing, a mark of civilization: a loose-sleeved white shirt and deep blue vest on his human torso, cut and fringed in imitation of the Troisian fashion and clasped at his human waist with a leather belt. A centaur of the Commots, no less, noted the mage, pleased. The Commots were the only civilized group of the wild but good horse-folk and were of far higher intellect and distinction than their hairy, merry, carousing brethren, with a finer, lighter build. This young one held a plumed white hat in his hands and looked awe-struck at being in the presence of one of the great wizards. He had long gray hair that matched a horse-body of dark dappled gray, with four white socks over pink hooves, and a gray waterfall of a tail. The centaur saw Mizzamir and instantly dropped his eyes and bowed low, both from the waist and down on one forefoot. Mizzamir smiled.

"Rise, Robin, and do not fear. So, has Fenwick told you of what you are to do?"

The centaur hoisted himself erect. His horselike, gray-furred ears, set high on his head, flicked forward attentively. "Only to a small extent, your greatness . . . " His voice was an uncertain tenor, only newly changed with adolescence.

"Well enough, then. I will elaborate.

"The people you are going to travel with are evil, vicious, cruel, heartless, wicked in all ways. They may seem clever, but it is cunning. They have no friends and are friends to none. They are villains, the antithesis of heroes. They are weak, because they do not stand together. They fight as much with each other as they do with their enemies, for they are too self-centered to work together coherently, and will abandon each other in trouble. They are thus always fearful of being betrayed by their companions, insisting that others take all the risks that they themselves might survive danger. They twist all happenings to suit themselves. Their lives now, trying to survive in each other's company, are ruled by disharmony and squabbling."

"You have heard them? Seen them?" asked the centaur, eyes wide with awe. Mizzamir shook his head regretfully.

"The powers of two of the members have hindered my scrying which is why your job is so important. Some brief, unclear scrying has succeeded here and there. Only hours after they escaped from prison, the one we believe to be an assassin tried to strangle his companion. Then the Druid pushed him into a pool. Later, the same Druid hit the assassin a cruel blow with her staff. They met with a dark sorceress, how one has survived I know not, and she threatened their lives by blowing up a tree as an example. Her powers, added to those of the Druid, have decreased my ability to focus my scrying, so we have only had vague images of what they have done since. Later, the two men attacked this sorceress and clubbed her off her horse. They subdued her and moved on and, since then, have been keeping their defensive magics strong. Images have been so poor we have not bothered to scry for them. I will try now, just to be certain they are where we thought they were headed, if we can make them out from their surroundings."

The mage walked to the center of the room, into the center of a circle of ivory-white tiles inset in the floor, and gestured with a hand. In a dazzling shower of light, a hole irised open in the center of the tiles, and a crystal scrying font slowly rose from the radiant depths. Beams of white light shot forth and splashed in rainbows along the walls. Mizzamir moved to the font and motioned the centaur to approach. As Robin did so, one tentative hoof at a time, he watched the mage gesture over the font, his fingertips now and then brushing the multishaded gems set into its rim. Slowly, within the font's light-filled waters, a swirl of color and form began to be visible. Curiosity overcoming fear, he moved forward to look.

Within the bowl was a distorted and blurred image. Mizzamir tapped it irritably, sending ripples through the water. "Hmm . . . well, it was worth trying. The last we saw of them they were headed for Guthright's Pass; we will send you there, and you will intercept them." He stepped away from the font and clapped his hands. Light flashed, and the font sank slowly into the floor as the mage paced toward the window, the uneasy centaur following.

"It will be dangerous. The wild forces of good that roam the land will know these wicked folk for what they are and will seek to defend themselves. If the villains die in this sort of encounter, it will be a shame . . . but you must get yourself to safety, for those wild forces may not know you for one of us. And do not think your companions will help you if you get into trouble. If you are near death, you will be left to die. Evil despises weakness. And of course, if they find out that you are of the Light, they will kill you without fail."

He gave the centaur a stern look. "Be careful. These people are darkness and death, all that is base and wicked and spiteful in existence. Do not become fooled by their casual ways, their seemingly normal existence . . . for they are just as deadly and evil as any bat-winged demonic fiend from the blackest hell, seeking only to wreak fear, chaos, death, destruction, war, and pain wherever they go." The centaur looked nervous, but resolved.

"I will go, Arch-Mage Mizzamir. What shall I do, and how?"

The mage smiled. "I'll ask Fenwick to have someone get your things . . . Fenwick? Sir Fenwick?"

The two looked around the conjuring room. The young champion was gone.

"Hmm," sniffed Mizzamir. "Well, we'll get them in a minute. Now then, you will be posing as a wandering minstrel, wishing to learn the ways of the trade, and of course you seek to record the travels of this band of adventurers for a ballad, what with questing heroes being uncommon these days, and *then* . . . "

Robin leaned close, absorbing every word, eyes wide and ears pricked.

III

Sir Fenwick strode down the hall. The wizard was old, yes, and wise, true, and good, of course, but he didn't have much field experience in dealing with small bands of villains. He was a powerful figure who worked from afar, he didn't actually get down into the hand-to-hand sort of combating evil, like Fenwick did. Fenwick knew in his bold, free, hero's heart that he could not remain in safety while a troupe of evil people roamed free. He was a skilled hunter and woodsman and could tell what those villains' situation was. Outnumbered, on the run, no one to trust, desperate, panicking, fearful, like wounded beasts. They were so strung-out they'd go berserk at the slightest provocation, like the one who'd attacked Mizzamir. They were heading into wilderness now, but on the other side of that wilderness were peaceful towns, lying in sleepy contentment. If they happened into one of those . . . He shuddered at the imagined resulting destruction. He had no choice.

Mizzamir's advice or no, he was going to call out the

Verdant Company and put an end to these rampaging villains once and for all. He stopped to collect his close companion, Towser, a wizard of intermediate powers and leader of the wizards of the Company. Towser easily folded the fabric of reality to let himself and Fenwick step through to a place many miles distant, on the continent of Trois: the home of Clairlune Castle and the Verdant Company.

Fenwick ran up the winding stairs to the top of the signal tower and took a key from around his neck to unlock one of the cabinets in the tiny guardroom. He took out and unfurled a flag, and climbed up the trapdoor to the signal platform with its high, empty flagpole.

With a creaking of pulley ropes, a square of rich green emblazoned with a pair of crossed swords in gold slowly unfurled against the blue morning sky. All over the city, the members who wore that device looked up, saw, and responded.

Kaylana, on watch, was alerted by the sound of approaching hooves. Well, she thought, finally. She rummaged in her pouches for bandages in case any of their mounts had been injured in that mad dash of dragon-induced terror. Abruptly her head snapped up. Wait a minute. There was the light sound of the stag's hooves, but they'd only had three horses, and she heard the hoofbeats of four . . . she glanced at the knight's horse to be sure it was still there and then gripped her staff and moved to a defensive position, nudging those of the party she could reach with her foot.

A young tenor voice called uncertainly, "Ah, hello? Is there anyone here? I've found your horses . . . Hello?" The words echoed around the walls.

Kaylana peered from her hiding place. From the direction of the canyon exit came the sound, and a moment later so too came their horses, being led placidly by the reins in the hand of . . . Kaylana's eyebrows raised in surprise. *Well*, she thought. *A centaur. Haven't seen one of those for awhile.* Her stag followed warily behind them.

The centaur, a gray one, with a nervous air about him, walked further into the canyon. He looked about, at the remains of their campfire, at the knight's horse standing quietly in a corner, and flicked his tail uncertainly. Kaylana glanced behind her and saw that the others had wakened and had hidden behind the same outcropping. She motioned to them to be still and watched carefully. The centaur walked forward uneasily, letting the horses' reins slip. As the animals moved over to greet the black warhorse, the centaur stepped down the way a bit, his hooves sinking into the sticky mud left from their encounter with the dragon. He clopped forward a pace, then pawed at the mud with a confused air. Kaylana gripped her staff and whispered a phrase of power. As before she had coaxed the stuff of the stones to take water from the air and fragment themselves into clay, so now she reversed the process, from erosion to fossilization.

Robin gave a shrill whinny of fear as the soft mud around his fetlocks gave an ominous crackling sound and then hardened into black rock. He tugged at his feet, managed to get one forehoof loose, but the rest were caught fast in the unearthly stone. He was trapped! Trapped with the villains nearby, for how else could this have occurred . . . He tugged at his hooves and gave a faint squeal of terror, his one free hoof pounding frantically on the stone.

"Stop that, or you shall soon injure yourself," snapped a voice, and a woman in dun robes stepped up from where there had been only strange stone before. He tried to shy, found himself unable to move, and almost fell over. He grabbed for the bracelet Mizzamir had given him . . .

"Be calm, centaur . . . we shall not hurt you if you mean us no harm." The woman held her hands wide to show that she carried no weapons, only a wooden staff. Robin recovered what courage he could and turned his head to face her. Her eyes were deep gray, he noted distractedly, the same shade of gray as oak leaves.

He felt his shivering calming, his equine instinct to flee

dissipating. He recovered his resolve and steadied himself, trying to ignore the cold tightness around his hooves. He almost lost himself again, when from behind the same rock came a man all in plate mail and another one with blond hair and a small slim woman, dressed all in black, and a very small, older human with a leather cap. He glanced at the first woman again. By the verse, he thought, I really have found them. This must be the Druid who hits people. The expressions of the others approaching made him uneasy.

In fact they were just miffed, at being woken out of a very sound sleep. They inspected Kaylana's captive with mild interest.

"Fine work," enthused Valeriana at once, showing her sharp teeth in a cheery smile. "Very well done. He'll make a lovely breakfast this evening. Centaur is really one of the finer meats, especially if you use a bit of red wine and . . ."

"Cease your mockery, Valeriana," admonished Kaylana as Robin's eyes rolled in fear and he struggled in his stony bonds. "Do not worry, centaur, we shall not eat you."

"Red wine, and what else, did you say?" Arcie inquired of Valeriana, taking out a scrap of paper and a stub of inkwood. Sam looked aghast at the Barigan, who looked offended. "I were only jesting! Fates! A fellow gets pretty sick of oatmeal day after day!"

Kaylana faced the centaur. "Pay them no heed, centaur. Tell us, why have you come here?"

Robin swept off his plumed hat and held it over his chest. "Good lady, I am a wandering minstrel, seeking to improve myself in the trade. To do so I must learn and record events in song and story . . . but I have been born too late, and all the deeds of heroes have been recorded already, and the more experienced minstrels get all the breaks. I happened to come across your horses, and they resembled those such as an adventuring party might use, with filled saddlebags as for a long journey ahead, and already weary from a long journey past. They led me to this canyon . . . and it does indeed seem to me you are a party of adventurers. I wish to journey with you and record the events of your quest to delight my audiences when I move on to become a full minstrel. Please, allow me to come with you. I can run and I can fight and I can entertain you with music and song. See, I show you the proof of my profession." The centaur reached awkwardly into a saddlebag on his withers and drew out a graceful seventeen-string harp made of pale golden wood. It had a dolphin carved on the neck, and the pillar was smooth from much use. He gave it a quick strum and looked at them.

The party exchanged glances. "Excuse us a moment, won't you, while we discuss this?" said Sam pleasantly. "Don't go anywhere," he added, as the party moved out of earshot.

"I won't," muttered Robin, looking down at his trapped hooves.

The group formed a vague huddle.

"He's a wimp," decided Arcie.

"Look who's talking," scoffed Valeriana.

"His words are true though, despite the fact I think he is leaving some things unsaid," replied Kaylana. Valeriana nodded.

"And he's not a victim of Mizzamir's light-minding process, either. The aura characteristic is distinctive, and he lacks it," she added.

"He'll slow us down, if we come to someplace we can't take horses," reasoned Sam.

"The race is fairly adept," commented Kaylana. "He could probably make it through any terrain passable by mule or donkey."

"He'll eat too much," muttered Arcie.

"No, didn't you notice, sneakthief? He's got saddlebags with oats," retorted Sam.

"Aye, I noticed. But he'll still eat too much."

"We could eat *him.*"

"No, Valeriana."

"Writing songs about us? I don't know if I like *that* idea," replied the sorceress.

"D'you think he knows who or what we be?" wondered Arcie.

Kaylana glanced over at the centaur, who was scraping the stone with his free hoof. "If he does not, he will probably figure it out sooner or later."

"Then what?"

"We lose him," shrugged Sam.

"He's large. Awkward," commented Arcie.

"We could use him as a shield, if the need arose, though," Sam said.

"Or as bait, if the need arose," replied Valeriana drily.

"It might be a fair thing to have music to break the monotony of travel," mused Kaylana.

Sam looked up at the silent knight.

"What do you think, dark one?" he asked.

The knight glanced deliberately over at the centaur, debated for a long moment, then gave a thumbs-up.

"Yeah, thumbs-up here too," agreed Sam. The rest concurred.

"We can always eat him later, if he fouls up," commented Valeriana, as they moved back to where the centaur stood. Kaylana muttered and rapped the ground with her staff; the stone turned back into soft mud, freeing Robin's hooves. She smiled slightly at the minstrel.

"Congratulations, centaur, we have decided to allow you to accompany us. What is your name?"

"Robin of Avensdale, lady," said the centaur, his ears flicking in relief as he got away from the treacherous mud and back onto the gravel. "And yours?"

"I am called Kaylana. There stand Sam, Arcie, Valeriana, and . . . " Kaylana wavered as she indicated the knight, who shrugged slightly. Arcie grinned. He had thought of a name.

"We calls him Blackmail," he said. The knight's armor rattled slightly. They looked at him. But for the lack of a voice, it seemed, the knight was laughing. After a moment, he spread his gauntleted hands in amused acceptance of the name, and nodded his head to the centaur.

* * *

As cool night fell, they started on again. Though the shadows of the canyon should have made the pass dangerously unsafe in darkness, the odd half-light of the night sky, combined with the brilliant stars and moon, were enough to cast a pale silvery glow over everything, and even the deep shadows were a milky indigo rather than black. It made them uneasy, Kaylana and Valeriana noting how the increase in Light was becoming even more literal, and Sam and Arcie, members of professions to whom shadows were friend and sanctuary, felt like rabbits caught aboveground with their burrows covered. The pass soon wound out of the floodwater canyon and led upward along winding rock-strewn trails and twisted scrambles of scree. They went on foot, leading the mounts, climbing into the thinning air, searching among the forgotten passes for a crevice like a stab wound into the heart of the earth, that legends said would echo with the sounds of screams and ravings enough to freeze the very blood. For here, Valeriana's research had indicated, was where the lost cavern of the Mad Godling could be found.

They climbed higher and higher, the footing getting ever more treacherous. Robin soon grew weary and frightened by the rough footing, and seemed to be terrified by the few glimpses they had of the ground far below. At last he stopped, and refused to budge.

"I'm sorry, brave adventurers, but I simply can't go any further," he whickered apologetically. "My hooves weren't made for this sort of thing . . . I'll just head down, and see you at the bottom . . . ?"

"Och, I would guess as much," scoffed Arcie. Kaylana nodded, and said, "Yes, centaur, I understand. Then, will you lead our mounts down as well? They seem to trust you."

"Probably something in the smell," Sam muttered to Arcie.

They tied the horses together in a line, except for the newcomer knight's great black warhorse, which stood placidly by its master as the knight adjusted the animal's bitless bridle. As Robin led the other horses back down the pass, the warhorse trotted down after them, finding its way carefully along the rocks. Then the two-legged members of the expedition started off again.

For several hours, they climbed higher into the hills. Sam was beginning to have doubts about these legends, and the others too seemed to be getting footsore and tired from the long steep climb. But Valeriana kept checking landmarks and viewpoints, muttering under her breath, and at last suddenly turned down a small pass that the others would never have seen, so cunningly was it concealed by a double-bend of two large stones.

As soon as they began down this path they knew that it was the right one. Not by any demi-godly screams—the air was still and quiet but for the wind—yet the ground under their feet was crunchy with pumice and obsidian, and the rocks were warm, as though heated from within. A feeling of oldness, and strangeness hung in the air; perhaps others, seeking the legendary advice of the Mad Godling, had come this way, but they had changed nothing.

At last they rounded the corner and came to the end of the pass: a blank wall of rock marred by a deep cleft, wide enough at its base for a man to walk through with his arms extended. Smoke, faint puffs of sulfurous fumes, drifted slowly out of the top of the cleft. The air was very warm now, and tense. The little band of renegades exchanged glances.

"Is this what we seek, Valeriana?" Kaylana asked, gripping her staff tight. The dark sorceress nodded.

"It must be, you tree-planter. You, thief, assassin, go in and examine the place."

"I'll *not* go alone," retorted Arcie.

Sam put in, with a lazy, dangerous smile, "No, rather, I think we'd best all go in together. This is, after all, supposed to be a group effort."

Blackmail, the knight, seemed to agree, and so, squaring their shoulders, they walked into the dark cleft in the stone.

Though dark and dim compared to the bright moonlight outside, the rough and twisting tunnel within was faintly lit by a reddish glow. The hot air was thick with the sulfur smell, and a distant roaring could be heard. They crept along the passage, each not wishing to be the first to encounter what they had come to seek.

When the tunnel at last opened abruptly into a large, round, high-ceilinged room, they were stunned. The cavern was lit with a hellish light. The roaring sound had its source here, in a pit at the center of the room, a flickering, boiling pool of fire that sent clouds of sulfurous fumes belching upward to circle around . . .

But wait, there was something above that, from the ceiling, tied fast around a stalactite: a rope, a stream of burning, shifting fire, bright golden-orange and crackling with brilliant fury without ever changing shape from its long length that dropped down to form a noose around the neck of . . .

It was hard to see, in the strange firelight of pit and rope, but it was a human figure, taller than normal, perhaps, dressed only in charred and tattered rags, swinging ever so slightly in the drifting air currents. His face was turned toward them, a face wracked and hideous by long years of pure anguish and madness, streaked by decades of soot, the hair lank and ugly around the face, the eyes . . .

The eyes were closed. Feverish twitches animated the eyelids as even in dreams the unfathomable knowledge of the gods raced across his bleeding brain. Bhazo, the Mad Godling, was asleep.

"Looks as we came at a poor time," whispered Arcie, as he began backing up rapidly. His incautious foot loosened a rock, making a loud clatter. They all froze as the echoes bounced around the cavern.

The figure, hanging suspended over the pit of flame, stirred, and yawned slowly, then stretched. Lanky battered limbs extended, and the figure revolved grotesquely, his head lolling in the fiery noose. His lips smacked thoughtfully, the eyes squeezing tight though they had not yet opened. The figure sighed and took a deep breath, as the five watched in fear from the half-cover of the entrance. Then one eye opened and saw them.

They were too far away to see clearly, but all instinctively looked away from that mad glitter. A slow smile spread across Bhazo's face, wild and twisted, showing broken teeth. Then he screamed.

"EEEEEEEEEEEEEEEEEYAAAAAAAHAAAAHAAAAAAAHAAA-AAAHAAAAAYAAA!!!"

The sound ripped through the cavern like a storm, refracting and magnifying as the figure danced on its gibbet, spinning. They stumbled back, hands to their ears. Arcie immediately turned and ran, heading for the safety of outside, but Kaylana jerked out with her staff, the crook catching through his belt and jerking him to an abrupt halt. The noise went on and on and on . . .

"EEEEEEEEEYAH! YAH YAH YAH! THE AVERAGE RAINFALL IN THE SHADREZARIAN PLAINS IS DETERMINED ENTIRELY BY THE NUMBER OF KUNDA FRUITS THAT FALL UNATTENDED IN THE CALIPH'S PALACE GARDENS! YEEEEEE-EEEEE YAAAAAAAAAAAAA!!!! YAH YAH YAH YAH YAH . . . "

The voice had slowly trailed off, and now stopped, the echoes dying away. When they looked up, Bhazo had swung around so that he now had his back to them and was dangling, muttering something about turnips. Arcie untangled himself from the Druid's staff and, now that the noise had stopped, crept up to where the knight, Druid, assassin, and sorceress were huddled at the edge of the cavern.

Bhazo's slow rotation continued, and he soon faced them again. He seemed to react in surprise, eyebrows raising slightly and unevenly.

"You're still here," he commented, then fell to muttering to himself, swinging back and forth gently.

Valeriana managed the courage to step forward, raising her hands to begin weaving a spell. There was a smell of melting butter as her magic began to work. "Oh fearsome spirit of the semi-divine, I seek your counsel, and do with the powers of mine hereby abjure and demand . . . "

"Demands demands demands! Ha! Valeriana Ebonstar, Widow of Talar, you are far more mad than I if you think your powers will work on me." Bhazo laughed, an eerie, tortured cackle that ran down their spines. **"Fish and small frogs, all left to blow away in the wind. Flowing water, that's the way. Always has been, ever so it may."**

Valeriana fumed and her fist clenched tightly around the piece of parchment and inkwood twig she had brought out in the hope of having to take notes. Sam, however, was frowning for a different cause. The figure seemed confined to its rope above the fire-pit, and his danger sense warned him of nothing. So he stepped forward, out of the shadows.

Bhazo, meanwhile, had noticed Blackmail. His expression, fluid as sun on the leaves, changed again, to a kind of admiring amusement. He stared at the black knight, who returned his mad gaze silently. Arcie had already crept off into the shadows of the walls to explore the room.

"Oh, that's clever. That's very clever," Bhazo was saying softly, as he stared at the dark knight. **"That is so clever it is funny, so foolish it is brilliant. I heartily approve."** He giggled. **"And people say *I'm* crazy . . . "**

"Bhazo," Sam spoke, "people do say you are mad and that this cavern rings day and night to the sounds of your wild gibberings and shrieks . . . why then are you now so calm?" He used the stilted, ancient form of the language, which seemed more appropriate to address a godling.

It took a moment, as Kaylana quickly shushed the assassin, but the Mad Godling did seem to hear the question. **"Ah, yes . . . people expect so much of one, like five by south winds. I usually give a few yells to satisfy them, scare them off. True, I bellowed and gibbered like a trout for a few decades, but after awhile even chaos becomes boring, even agonizing pain—"** He indicated, with a limp, disjointed hand, the burning noose around his neck, **"becomes monotonous."**

"Enough idle prattle on all your parts," snapped Valeriana. "We want to know the locations of the Segments of the Spectrum Key."

Wild, chilling laughter rose up again, and Bhazo revolved in his noose once more. Arcie, who had already made it halfway round the cavern, searching for hidden treasures, beat a hasty retreat back to the rear of his fellow villains.

"The Segments! Oh, such a wild lark, and when May leaves are cold in the morning, rain is sure to follow and Artelis is *still* angry about that incident with Ellhan's longbow. Right, I'll sing you a song, it's not very long, but it's jolly!" He stopped suddenly, and peered out from under his lank hair at them, the dragonfire noose making his eyes glitter.

"Not so fast . . . what's in it for me?"

"What do you want?" hissed Valeriana. The others had stepped back; Valeriana seemed willing to take the initiative here, no sense in the rest of them getting involved and, perhaps, killed. Sam mentally ran through his list of weapons; none, he was sure, would be suitable against a god, even a minor one.

"Freedom! You, Nathauan, own a Darkportal, though the assassin lurking there carries it. It is the last seen in many years by any sight of man or gods. The magic-sink of a Darkportal, even one so small, may be enough to break this blasted fire-rope." Bhazo's eyes glittered, cold and calculating and mad. **"I shall give you your answer in the only form the gods have ever let themselves think it, if you will sacrifice that Darkportal and free me."**

"It's not hers to sacrifice anymore," put in Sam, feeling the cold weight of the amulet in his concealed pouch. Valeriana turned on him, was about to speak when the rasping voice of the godling poured over them.

"No, but only she could wield it correctly to break the noose. Noose noose, chocolate moose . . . that is my price, cheaper than linen in T'Patak, and I'm staying by it." He folded his arms on his emaciated chest and rocked back and forth stubbornly.

The villains exchanged glances, and Valeriana, after a long moment, nodded. Sam, after a glare from Kaylana, withdrew the pouch with the amulet and held it in his hand. But Valeriana held up a hand.

"Wait. The answer first."

Her question struck just as Bhazo was slowly swinging down into another of his fits of madness. With a grin he looked up.

"Fair enough! Ahem, ahem . . . " there was a brief pause, and Valeriana scrambled to get her notes. Then Bhazo began, chanting in a singsong voice that rambled from a high squeak to a low growl and back again. It seemed to Sam that he'd heard the words before, long ago, but had forgotten them until now . . .

In the town where first they met,
The center of the smuggler's net,
Seek and climb the flowing stair,
Spin and see what's hidden there.

Magic's heart of southern skein,
In russet vault of constant green,
Deep within the eldest wood,
Touch tip to earth where Heroes stood.

Golden griffin's homeward path,
He who questioned, risked our wrath,
Where he came to doubt, his shrine
Measures slow, eternal time.

Diamond spire spears the sky,
Focus of the wizard's eye.
Lead, Light, and Sand, the Test define,
When washed in ancient magic's brine.

Walk now the line twixt Mula's sign,
And the path her tears define.
Here Fate will take you like a wave,
The hardest Test of all to brave.

T'krung-Tabak, in eagle's claws,
Where warm blood outlines stony flaws,

If dare to face the inner eye,
Go to thy knees 'neath moonlit sky.

Coils of the Labyrinth loop below,
They are not here, but do not go,
The Key is that which fits the Lock
But also on the door will knock.

"I threw in the last verse gratis," Bhazo explained proudly. **"That one refers to the Labyrinth itself, and there's another line about about about about about. What with all the elements needed, but that's pretty obvious . . . "**

"I'd figured that out before I left the caverns," retorted Valeriana. "I just needed the Segment locations . . . but if there is one Segment on each of the Six Lands, then which of your riddles refers to which?

"They're all in order, perfectly clear as the Sacred Mirror of Pikasaho that hangs five miles below the earth below the two hundred-fifth duth-duth bush east of Mount Skoo," retorted Bhazo impatiently. **"You'll be racing around, against the clock, starting yesterday! The Darkportal!"** The godling writhed, holding out his hands beseechingly. **"Set me free, and I'll even try and kill myself right this time! You've no idea how uckle uckle uckle ga fooney . . . "** Bhazo lapsed into some heathen language in his mad ramblings, while still pleading, until at last he slipped back into Sixlandish: **"The Darkportal! All you have to do is . . . "**

"Actually, I rather think not," replied Valeriana, and before any of them could do anything she had turned and darted back down the way they had came. Bhazo froze for a moment, and then, rage suddenly exploding in his face, screamed.

"AAAAAAAAAAAHHHHHHHRRRRRRRRRRRRRRRGG!"

The scream shook the walls and made the stone tremble. The cavernous pit belched forth fire, and the heat wave blasted into them as they turned and ran after Valeriana. From behind came the continuing echoing screams and the sounds of a cavern partially collapsing.

"An' what did you have to go an' piss him off for?" demanded Arcie, when they finally caught up with Valeriana halfway down the mountain. She was inspecting the sheet of notes, with Bhazo's words hastily copied down.

"She didn't want to lose her amulet, I'll wager," retorted Sam. Kaylana and Blackmail were looking up the mountainside, to where puffs of smoke could be seen in the dim evening light and screams still faintly heard.

"Of course not. What do you think I am, mad?" replied the sorceress, calmly rolling her priceless scrap of notes into a scrollcase.

They collected Robin, who was full of questions, but his eagerness made them suspicious, and they told him nothing, preferring to play mysterious for now. The group neared the end of the pass just as dawn was starting to coat the sky in shades of pink and lilac. Valeriana looked up and frowned, drawing her hood up over her face. "It gets worse," she said to them. "Already the very nature of the world shows signs of the influx of Light. The problem is escalating . . . we must open the Gate soon, or else it will be too late."

They proceeded in silence out of the pass, having seen nothing in their crossing other than a few animals and the long-dead remains of campfires of the notorious Ruddyleg bandits of the area, now long gone.

Far away and above, a smoking, screaming crack in the side of the mountain fell silent. No one was there to hear, but had someone been, he would have heard a soft dry sound, like a chuckle, and a voice, hoarse with shouting, say,

"I knew that would happen . . . "

The Verdant Company was a group of past heroes and adventurers who had found kinship in their love of combating evil. The longest-standing members had been Fenwick's companions in his youth. Then those had persuaded their friends to join, and, as the Company grew it had attracted young hopefuls, who, if they proved worthy, would be admitted. Now the Company numbered some one hundred fifty—a minor army of elite archers, warriors, white wizards, and a few priests. They were arguably the best small fighting force still in existence in these peaceful times. Their numbers had been diminished, true, in the wars with the Nathauan and rock trolls, as well as one or two evil dragons, but there were plenty of eager replacements. The members lived civilian lives in the city of Glinabar, the capital city of Trois. But when the green flag flew above the signal tower at Clairlune Castle, they would pick up their weapons, don their armor, and gather at the fortified stone castle tucked into the shelter of the wooded hills. It was here that Fenwick himself addressed them now.

The Prince stood on the low balcony, dressed in shining chain-mail over his deep green tunic and leggings. His traditional woodsman's hat sported a new bright golden sun-pheasant feather. His brave eyes burned with destiny. Despite a long adventuring career, he still showed himself to be a young man of perhaps barely thirty summers. His great-grandfather, the Hero, the Forest-Lord Fen-Alaran, who had ruled the Land of Trois for many years, was rumored to have been of the stock of Elves. Whether this was true or not, Fenwick would have made his grandfather proud this day, determination burning in his eyes as he surveyed the assembled Company.

After many days of travel, down from the mountains and through peaceful countryside, the renegades had reached the southern coast of Dous, and the fabled city of Taillerand. They had gradually become used to the silent presence of Blackmail; he seemed content to care for his horse and travel, standing his turn at guard but never seeming to need sleep or food. Robin too proved useful, picking the best path for the horses through the occasionally rough terrain. They wandered through the occasional sleepy hamlet for food, rest, and care for the mounts, but for the most part saw nothing more of interest than scenery and wildlife, all overflowing in profusion with wildflowers and birdsong, even in the twilight hours they traveled in.

"Y'know," Arcie commented to Sam at one point, "even if what Kaylana and Valerie-Anna say aren't true, I'd still go on this quest. This whole world is too disgustingly cute."

Sam nodded thoughtfully. He agreed, actually. It was all too . . . *nice.* Dawn had broken while they were still on the road to Tailerand, and the land was at its most flamboyant in these early hours. A twinge of contempt from his evil nature made him steer Damazcus through a patch of purple clover, trampling several mating butterflies and crushing the blossoms. A whistle from up ahead brought his attention back, and he and Arcie spurred their mounts to catch up to the others on the broad road into the city.

Tailerand was a seaport city, about half the size of Sam's native city but more sprawling and open. The sea air mingled with the scents of human habitation, the faint roar of the surf with the rounded noise of the large trading river that emptied into the sea here. For several miles outside of the city were fields and orchards taking advantage of the last of this continent's mild climate. The sea winds helped protect against frost, and the produce of this area, both grown from the soil and harvested from the sea, was taken upriver or sent out on ships to the rich but wild Land of Trois, to trade for wood, pelts, precious ores, and horses.

Most of the renegades had visited here one time or another; Blackmail silently led them to a small livery stable, which looked poor and out of the way, but was spotless and well-kept within, all the horses stabled there well-fed and shining. Kaylana, having sent her stag to run free back to the woods it had come from, examined the horses for sale and finally picked out a young piebald gelding, purchased by a loan at ruinous interest from Arcie. They boarded their mounts there for a token fee, and prepared to set out on foot. Blackmail himself insisted on untacking and stabling his huge black stallion, who showed high spirits by stealing the feed bag and occasionally pushing his master playfully against the wall. As the ancient stableman watched, the horse used its lips to stealthily work open the buckles on one of the saddlebags, the one containing the sweet grain with which the knight fed the horse.

"That's a fine clever beast you've got there," said the fellow. "Looks like a Kwartan warhorse." Blackmail nodded absently, too busy currying to reply further, as the others waited impatiently.

At last they managed to drag the knight away from his companion, and they set off through the town, enjoying the tang of ocean in the air. Arcie was marching proudly down the main street, pointing out landmarks; Robin had been here not too many months before, when he had first left his home and came by ship to this port, ready to start a new life in the fabled Six Lands. The very air here seemed to have a hint of that excitement, of beginnings and expectation, where anything was possible.

Kaylana said, "This is where it all started. Where it all starts," as though she had read Robin's thoughts. It made him a little uneasy.

"Where 'they' first met, then?" Arcie asked. "Och! I thought so. Where the warrior Hero Tamarne caught Jasper Dunthwittle trying to steal from him, and the two became fast friends, and met with their other companions, and decided tae stomp out evilness, and so forth." He shook his head. "Supposedly were the first and last time Jasper tried to steal anything. Pah! Some thief. Typical Wilderkin though, aye. No sense of self-preservation."

Sam was looking about. He'd been here once before on an assignment. Tailerand, last he'd seen it, had made him nervous. Of course there was no Assassin's Guild; the one he had come from was the only one in the Six Lands, though there were rumors that such institutions had existed in distant lands such as Shadrezar and Kono. Tailerand hadn't had a Thieves' Guild either; that population had lived in small, free-roaming, competitive gangs. Sam had run afoul, briefly, of such a gang back then. The conflict had resulted in several broken bones, a minor concussion, and several missing teeth for the thieves, who were very wary of anyone wearing black for many weeks after. It occurred to Sam, much later, that they likely would never have attacked him if they hadn't been desperate. And desperate they must have been, for now there was no trace of their activity.

Arcie had noticed this too. Here, as in Mertensia, the town where they had sought out the Gypsies, the subtle graffiti of thiefsigns scratched on walls and posts were faded or missing. These had once marked the territories of the rival gangs, showed threat or warning, or marked neutral turf for the occasional rare truce. He stopped to trace one with his short fingers thoughtfully. "What is it, gnome?" asked the sorceress impatiently. She had been nervous since entering the city, its air of cheerful expectation making her skin itch.

Arcie glowered. " 'Tis a sort of 'help wanted' sign, Valerie."

"Valeri*ana,*" corrected the Nathauan with a glare. But Sam and the others knew that she was probably going to be stuck with the nickname, what with her amulet held captive so that she could not enforce her desires.

Kaylana, also not approving of the crowded city, was watching the citizens apprehensively. Their small group, three of whom were garbed mostly in black and containing such rare sights as a centaur and a huge man in full armor, was attracting a lot of stares. Two members of this crew wanted by the very nobility of the land of Dous, and a mage involved . . . it was probably a good idea to get out of sight. She said as much to Arcie.

"I agrees," he said immediately. "And, I think I know of a place where we can find both a hidey-hole and an ally. Follow me." He set off down the road, occasionally pausing at thiefsigns to touch them lightly, frowning as he translated the faint rough markings.

They passed through the waterfront district. Sam noticed the familiar name of one of the most popular taverns. The Frothing Otter, he thought, looking at it. In a bar of the same name back in Bistort this had all begun. The sign at this establishment showed one of the thick-pelted sea otters that were once quite prolific on this coast, lying on its back in the water with its whiskers full of foam and a half-full tankard of sea ale balanced on its chest. He pointed it out to Arcie, who nodded, saying nothing. It was a common name for a tavern in the Six Lands, no one knew why. Probably if they'd looked they could have found one in Mertensia.

At last, down a back alley, Arcie found a small door, half-covered in old rotting fishing nets hung with dead starfish. The air had a fishy smell and a strong hint of dust and drains, warm in the growing sunlight. Arcie rapped a soft, complicated tattoo on the rough wood, and sucked his knuckles silently because of the splinters. A moment later, he tapped again, and the door burst open, and a whirl of multicolored cloth swirled them in.

As the door closed and a lamp was turned up, their host was illuminated, a woman, younger than Kaylana, wearing the flouncy colorful skirts of a Gypsy, topped with a dark blue tunic, the standard item of dress in Dous, and fitted with a brown leather bodice. Her hair was blond, lighter than the assassin's, and hung in soft waves around her face, accenting blue eyes. She shook Arcie's hand in delight.

"Mr. MacRory!" she cried. "So good to see another friendly face after all these years!"

"MacRory?" Sam exclaimed in surprise. Arcie shot him a glare.

"Perfectly good family name, Sam. My father's quite a respected gentleman in the Old Country. Kimi, this bounder are called Sam, the ladies are Valerie . . . " The sorceress rolled her amethyst eyes, but said nothing, "and Kaylana, the knight by the door we call Blackmail, and the centaur goes by the handle of Robin. Fellows, this is Kimi, who were quite a promising student at my Guild before she ran off here with some rapscallion from a street gang. Whatever happened to him, anyway?"

"Knifed by the Sharks five summers past," Kimi said

with a sigh. "Things were crazy for the longest time there. All the gangs sort of dissolved. Most of them lost their leaders to mysterious disappearances. Then, of course, discipline fell apart, there was murder and warfare for a few weeks, and when the smoke all cleared I was the only one left. At least it's easy pickings now, but I was hoping to get another gang under way . . . that's why the thief-sign. You and these fellows interested in joining? Of course, you'd have seniority, sir, being a Guildmaster and all . . ."

"No, Kimi, that's not what we're about today." He glanced around, and his eyes lighted on the centaur. Something would have to be done about that; he still didn't quite trust the minstrel. As Kimi bustled around the room, dumping books, plates, ropes, candles, pouches and other objects off various surfaces in order to clear a space for them to sit, he motioned to the centaur.

"Robin," he said, looking up at the tall being, "do us a great favor and stand watch outside, will you? There's a good fellow," he added, as he gently but forcibly shoved the centaur's back toward the hidden door. The centaur, despite his bulk, was not very large or strong; built more like the delicate, deer-like racing horses of the desert folk of Shadrezar than the large, familiar Troisian breed. Robin had barely begun to stammer a protest when his haunches bumped open the door and he stumbled out into the daylight, the concealed door shutting in front of him.

"Was that necessary, Northerner?" Kaylana asked, as Arcie stepped back from locking the door. Arcie sighed and scratched his head.

"Call it a hunch, lady. Now then, Valerie, Kaylana, will you explain to Kimi what brings us all here? For 'truth I'm not able to keep straight all this business of portals and keys and suchlike."

As the two women explained to the young thief, Arcie lay back and lit up his pipe from a pouch of tobacco he'd found on a small table. Kimi didn't smoke, but loved all kinds of clever tricks and distractions—the harsh smoky herb could be used in numerous ways for this. Blackmail remained standing in a corner, looking like, well, like a suit of armor, oddly out-of-place in Kimi's mish-mash den. The cluttered, shadowy room, smelling of candle wax, paprika, and mildew, was barely big enough for them, but passages twisted off into the darkness beyond. For a moment, Arcie thought Sam had vanished again, but then saw him, a slightly different patch among the shadows, looking at what appeared to be a large, cracked, round-bottomed bowl on a tottering pile of sea crates.

Outside, Robin breathed a sigh of relief, chest and sides giving a deep heave, and twitched his beloved, beautiful tail thoughtfully. He was glad to be out of that cramped thieves' den and away from the staring eyes of the villains. Time to do some long-overdue reporting. He rolled up one white sleeve to show the delicate silver filigree bracelet set with two cloudy gemstones, the gift and token of Mizzamir. With thumb and forefinger he pressed the gemstones, tensing himself for the transition.

It was more unnerving than Mizzamir had said: a sensation of the ground wiggling under his hooves, a brief moment of speed, and a smell like cedar that faded into the familiar scent of lavender and ozone so characteristic of the Silver Tower, in the Castle of Diamond Magic. He opened his eyes and saw Mizzamir look up from his desk.

"Why, Robin of Avensdale! I was beginning to become concerned! How have you fared?"

"With some difficulty, your Greatness," stammered Robin, quickly doffing his hat in respect. He related the happenings thus far, including the party's secretive visits to the cavern of the Mad Godling and the thieves' den in Tailerand. Mizzamir listened thoughtfully, drumming his fingers on a pile of parchment on his desk. The sunlight made the dust motes in the room shine like tiny suns.

"Interesting," Mizzamir said when he had finished. "Excellent reporting, your minstrel training has served you well. We have done well in choosing you as our agent." Robin blushed deeply and scuffed his forehooves on the floor, looking down bashfully. Mizzamir smiled at his discomfiture, then his face grew thoughtful again. "Hmm . . . it would almost seem . . . but surely they cannot have that in mind. Stay here awhile, Robin, and rest yourself, until you can meet with the villains tomorrow. One of the servants will show you to a spare room . . . your aura indicates weariness." He smiled and rang a summoning bell. Robin allowed himself to be led off to a small room with a floor-corner bed, as the centaurs used, and curled himself up on it with a yawn, and was asleep before the last strands of his waterfall tail had finished settling.

Back in the thieves' den in Tailerand, Kimi and Arcie were poring over the parchment with the prophecy of the Mad Godling written upon it in Valerie's sharp liquid handwriting. They had partaken of a late meal and had a nap, while the young thief herself went out on her various rounds, dressed in her becoming clothes to lull the unwary while she harvested a living from picking their pockets. In the early afternoon, they made their plans. Valerie stood looking over their shoulders, while her raven hopped about among the clutter, snapping up spiders and the occasional young mouse, croaking softly. Sam had returned to inspecting the bowl. He thought he could almost make out words in the bird's noises; it sounded like a gruff old man muttering to himself. He watched it as it picked up a knitting needle to winkle a beetle out of a crack and wondered exactly how intelligent the creature was. It winked at him and snapped up the beetle with a tiny disgusting scrunchy noise, its throat feathers puffing. Kaylana wandered over, gave the bowl he was examining a brief glance, and muttered, "Wyvern eggshell."

Kimi chewed on the end of the inkstick she was using to make notes. "Town where they first met . . . that's Tailerand, we're assuming, 'They' being the Heroes. Then . . . 'The center of the smuggler's net' . . . net, net . . . smuggler's net. Let me think . . . smugglers, Heroes, Tailerand . . . there's no place I know of *called* Smuggler's Net, but it would make sense that everything in these riddles would have something to do with the Heroes . . . "

"A net, used to catch smugglers?" suggested Arcie. "Did the Heroes . . . "

"Yes!" cried Kimi suddenly. "That has to be it! Mr. MacRory, I'm with you and your friends. Let's bring the world back to the way it was, when we all were free. I admit I don't see any signs of the world being, uh, sublimated, but if there's any chance to return the world to the good old days, I'm all for it. And I know exactly where the net for smugglers must be."

A short while later, after Kimi had changed from her skirts into a sensible set of leggings and tunic and armed herself with a long rapier and several daggers, they gathered a few candle lanterns from the clutter and set off down into the dark back passages. Kimi led the way, Arcie following alongside, then Valerie, Sam, and Kaylana, with Blackmail bringing up the rear, trying to walk quietly and occasionally having to duck because of the low ceiling. Kimi explained as they travelled:

"Back just before the War proper, supposedly, there was an evil trade of smugglers in Tailerand, and one of the first things the Heroes did, when they had all met here, was decide to rid the town of this menace. The smugglers, hundreds of them, operated in a series of catacombs under the sewers, and the Heroes won by trapping them in there and then rerouting the floodwater systems through those tunnels. A lot of the place gave way, sunk and settled. One of my gang's initiation rituals was to spend the night down in there; it's supposedly haunted."

"Did you see anything?" inquired Arcie. The idea of ghosts had always intrigued him; being able to walk through walls! That would be quite useful. Kimi shook her head.

"Ghosts would be unlikely, of course," Valerie added, as she walked along the dim flickering tunnel gracefully, her huge purple eyes dark with their pupils dilated. "The undead require negative energy to function, and these days there's not much of it about."

They wandered on through the tunnels. The air was

cold and close, with a definite pong of sewage. Kimi led them in detours from the main sewer pipes and drains, but soon they had to extinguish their lanterns because, Kimi explained, of the danger of pockets of explosive gas that sometimes collected at these levels. The tunnels now, however, were lit with the faint iridescent glow of the mossy slime that covered walls and ceiling, while the floor was a dark slup of mud and slurry. The smell was less noticeable after awhile, and soon the only one bothered by it was Valerie, who fastidiously kept a fold of her cloak over her nose and mouth.

"And about a flowing stair . . ." Kimi shook her head. "That I've never heard of or seen. I guess we'll have to just get to the 'center of the smuggler's net' and look for it."

They were now already in what appeared to have been a more habitable part of the underground. Though piles of rubble and rotting supports jammed every corner, and the moss grew thickly, the tunnels looked more like corridors, and occasionally broken-in rooms, full of decay and rats, could be seen. Kimi stepped quickly and silently through the passages, counting corridors under her breath. Occasionally, she'd make a wrong guess, and they would backtrack, nevertheless it was impressive how well she found her way about. Kaylana noticed that she and Arcie both moved with the same kind of careful, light grace, especially surprising in the short and seemingly ungainly Barigan. Sam moved in a similar fashion, but his gait was ever so slightly smoother, less predictable, and more predatory. Kimi called back to the others from where she and Arcie were leading the way. "We should be getting close to the center about now . . . keep an eye out."

They wandered through the small maze of broken rooms and passages that marked the center of the ancient smuggler's den, and wandered back through them again, but saw nothing. At last they stopped to rest.

"No sign of a stair, flowing or otherwise," Sam remarked, knocking dottle from his boots.

"You mean we've gone through all this *filth* for nothing?" snarled Valerie in disgust. Blackmail leaned back against the wall, and Kaylana sighed and stooped to pat a small rat that had wandered out of a crack to sniff at her sandals. Kimi looked around, and Arcie took off his cap and scratched his head in thought.

"Flowing stair . . . wait a tic. Kimi, what time is high tide here?"

"Around four, this time of month . . . why?" Kimi looked at him.

"What time are it now?"

"Close to it," said Sam from the shadows. "Half-past three or so, I'd say." He'd always had a good timesense.

"Then wait," said Arcie. "Just sit here and wait."

They waited. Kaylana fed the rat a few scraps of bread from the pockets of her robe, and Arcie lit up his pipe again, despite warnings from the others about the flammable gas pockets. Valerie, bored, carved sigils in the moss with her fingernail, and Blackmail just stood against a wall, unmoving. Sam decided to strike up a conversation with Kimi.

"Kaylana said that was a piece of wyvern eggshell you had back in your room," he began. "How did you happen to come by that? I've never seen such a thing before."

Kimi sighed, and took out a dagger (she drew it left-handed, Sam noted, and the weapon was in fairly poor condition; it obviously had not seen much use) and began to pry up bits off moss from the floor with it absently. "That's a long story . . . but, seeing as we don't have much to do here anyway, I'll tell it. Back a couple years ago, after I was on my own, I was in a tavern and I heard a group of men talking about how they were going to go kill the wyvern. This wyvern, it used to live out on the sea-islands you can just see from the docks. The fishermen and traders had learned to avoid coming within about fifty ship-lengths of the island, or the wyvern would attack them. It was pretty simple, as they didn't need to go that close to get to the fishing waters or the trade routes. Sometimes it was even considered lucky to see it, if you were far away."

"I should think that would be one of the qualifications,

certainly," Sam put in with a smile. Kimi nodded.

"But these men got the town very upset about it, accusing them of cowardice that they let the evil thing survive out there, and bully them away from better fishing waters and whatever treasure it had stolen from the sunken ships, that it must be keeping out on that island. Finally one of the fishermen volunteered to take them out there on his boat, under cover of night, so that they could kill it, for a share of the treasure.

"Well, as I said, I just happened to be listening, and I thought, 'Treasure, that would be a nice thing to have around the place.' I found the ship the fisherman spoke of, and when they set sail that night I was hidden in one of the cargo holds, which they really should put better locks on. By the way, I don't suppose you have any use for a couple pounds of elgerite, do you?"

"Nope, sorry . . . I'm not much of a cook. Ask the nasty with the raven."

"Didn't think so. You're an assassin, aren't you?" Kimi inquired cautiously.

Sam nodded. "Don't worry though. We're . . . I'm, not quite as insane as people would have you think."

"I was going to say, you don't seem so, except for that you're running around on this weird quest of yours. Anyway, where was I?"

"In the cargo hold, with the elgerite."

"Right. So anyway, the boat pulls up into the shallows, and the men, all armored and all, slip off into the water, and I follow them. It's pre-dawn dark, no moon, and we climb ashore. They head off inland, talking about spoor and lairs, and I follow, mousey quiet, behind them. It's getting paler up dawn when we get to a big cliffside, with a ledge and a sort of scraped-out hollow in it. I can't really see anything yet, but the men are all excited and there's this smell in the air . . . we're working our way closer, sort of up and along the cliffside; it was really rough and easy to climb, but high; I guess the wyvern needed the drop in order to take off. Anyway, just as we're coming in closer, the sun comes over the horizon, and we see it. It's all curled up at the mouth of the hollow; that's what made it look so dark. It's a shiny, blue-black color, like a beetle, all tiny little round beady scales, about so big—" She indicated a size about twice that of a tellin, about the circumference of a circle formed by the thumb and forefinger. "The men all grab for weapons, I don't notice because I'm looking at the wyvern. I didn't even notice if it had any treasure visible. It looked so unreal . . . but just then, the wind changed, in the wyvern's favor.

"It woke up with a noise like a huge snake. It looked huge . . . later they said it was only twenty-three feet, twice with the tail . . . but it was like this mass of black scales and spines and wings that kept uncoiling and unfolding, making a noise more angry and evil than anything I had ever heard. I was terrified, but all I could think of was how deadly beautiful it was. The men were all expecting it to fly, but it didn't . . . it just sat there, wings puffed out, coiled up like a snake to strike, with a crest of spines all around its head that it rattled, and its eyes were orange. I thought it didn't have legs at first, but then I saw them, tucked up in the coils; just rear legs, like a hawk's. I thought: It's scared, it wants us to go away, to go away and leave it alone. The men had all been expecting it to charge, I know, and they were all ready for it, but it just sat there, hissing and swaying. Once it spat at them, a spray of yellow mist, poison I guess, but it was too far away, while the men talked amongst themselves. Then they all unslung bows and crossbows and started shooting.

"They were good shots, I'll admit that. That wyvern was spattered; some of the arrows bounced off the scales, but most of them, at medium range, went into the wings and neck. The wyvern hissed, almost more a scream than a hiss, backed up, and struck, spitting again. The men all dodged and fired again. The wyvern thrashed around, trying to defend its lair and attack at the same time . . . and that was when it saw me. I was hiding a little behind the men, higher up the cliff, behind a rock, watching, and suddenly its eyes met mine." Kimi paused. "I never want to look into eyes like those again. That creature was so evil, so dark, and yet had a spirit and pride and will so many times greater than mine . . . " She shivered. Sam nodded sympathetically, and Kimi continued.

"Then one of the crossbow bolts took it in the throat. It was gurgling and hissing, and when it tried to spit poison again, it only spat a cloud of blood. They charged at it, waving swords and axes, and it met them head on, blocking the entrance to its lair. There was chaos and blood and shouts and hisses flying, and I crept closer, to see if there was any treasure. From out of the battle I suddenly saw its head come up, and look at me again, looking at my very soul. Then it turned, and seemed to try to fly; it leaped, but as its wings came up one of the men chopped into its shoulder with a huge sword, and it jerked and tumbled down the cliff, taking half the men, shouting and cursing, down with it. The others, yelling encouragement, ran down the slope after their comrades, where they were all pounding and slashing at the poor beast.

"I ran into the cave, of course; it must have been a pretty amazing treasure to have had the wyvern so intent on defending it. But when I got there, it was only a hollow about half the wyvern's length in depth, lined with palm fronds. As for treasure; there was stuff there, but it was all junk! Bits of brass from ship parts, bottles, lumps of quartz, some pieces of a mirror . . . shiny things. And in the middle of the shiny things was an egg.

"I don't know why I wanted something so bulky and useless, but I grabbed it. You saw the shell, it was about the size and weight of a watermelon. I came out of the hollow and looked down to where the battle was just ending. The wyvern was so battered and bloody you could hardly tell what it was. One of the men had its head pinned with a spear while another was slowly chopping through its neck with a war-axe. I saw its eyes turn, ever so slightly, and look up at me a last time, as they slowly glazed and unfocused. I ran down the far side of the cliff, the men too busy in their butchery to notice me.

"I couldn't swim back to the boat with the egg, so I hid away from the cave and the shore with it. I found some gull's chicks and brought down a seccerbird with my sling, and was cooking them when the egg started to hatch.

"It happened so fast I wasn't sure what was happening. It rocked, making clicking noises, and then I saw a tiny hole in it. The hole suddenly split into a crack, and then the egg broke in two, and this tiny wyvern, about as big as a cat, fell out. It was like soft leather, no scales yet, all slate-gray colored, spines and wings all floppy and soft, its eyes closed. But I could see it was in trouble. It flopped on the sand and rolled over, kicking weakly and wriggling like a lizard. I picked it up, tried to help it somehow. It tried to bite me, but its jaws didn't seem to want to function. Its breathing was all bubbly and weak. I tore off bits of the seccerbird, and tried the chicks too, but even when I got the food to go down its mouth it would just puke it up all over me again. It was so limp, so weak, and I could feel its heart going, too fast and too faint."

Kimi stabbed at the moss with the dagger. "I tried everything I could think of. But it died before sunset, just stopped moving. It opened its eyes right before it died. They were blue, but they had the same look in them as the mother wyvern's."

She was quiet a moment. "After the wyvern was dead, ships started coming over the next day to explore the island. I met up with one of the explorer parties and said the wyvern had captured me and brought me there last year, but I had escaped. They took me home, and I brought that piece of shell with me."

"Listen!" Arcie said suddenly, holding up a hand for silence. "D'you hear it?"

They were all quiet a moment. Past four, Sam noted. And in the silence, along with the occasional drip of the moss, there was now a faint noise, a soft muted rush of flowing water, combined with a faint cold breeze that smelled of the sea.

It took them some time to locate the direction the

breeze came from; from a tunnel blocked by fallen rubble and mud, which collapsed away when a blocking wooden beam was removed. They went down the passage, the sound of flowing water growing louder, when at last they turned a corner and saw.

In the center of a half-round room, a wide stone staircase led up into the darkness. The smell of the sea was strong here, and the phosphorescence was thick. The stairs shone brilliantly with fresh seawater running down them from above to vanish into cracks in the floor. The slimy algae that covered the stair glowed like fireflies. The rushing of the water echoed in their ears.

"That's a flowing stair, all right," admitted Valerie.

"Yes, and if it weren't flowing, we would not be able to climb yon," pointed out Arcie, indicating the top of the stairs. A rusted coil of wire was attached to a plank of mossy wood that the flood of the water kept propped open. It was designed to pull the door closed when there was no pressure from the other side. Valerie frowned, sensing something.

"There is magic nearby," she commented.

"That would likely be the Test, then," said Kaylana. "Come, let us find it. We climb the flowing stair."

Easier said than done to scramble up the slippery, ice-cold steps, but they managed. They went through the opened door, Kimi leading, and came out into the center of another half-circle, moss-covered room, with no other openings except the tiny vents in the floor that allowed the tide to pour in and down the stairs. The room was dimly lit by the moss and cold.

And empty.

"Empty!" cried Arcie. "Well, now what?"

"It said spin and see," offered Sam. Arcie responded by revolving rapidly until he resembled a small rotund tornado, then collapsed, shaking his head.

"Nowt, just the room going in circles."

"The magic is strong here," said Valerie with a frown. "I can't pinpoint it though."

"Maybe we found the wrong stair?" suggested Kimi.

"Unlikely that anyone would go through this much trouble for a false lead," answered Kaylana.

"Spin," said Arcie thoughtfully. Barigans loved mental puzzles in the form of riddles and the like, and Arcie was no exception. "Spin from coming up yon stairs . . . " He stood at the head of the stairs, turned around, and walked straight to the wall there, the diameter of the half-circle. The wall was covered with soft moss. "Kimi, come here a sec . . . "

The two thieves inspected the wall, then began tapping it, searching for hidden caches. Kimi felt along the faint cracks in the moss as Arcie tapped along the wall.

Tap tap tap tap tuk—

"Heh, Kimi, lemme borrow that dagger a moment . . . "

Arcie took the dagger and made a cut along the wall. Suddenly, with a soft sliding noise, a huge carpet of moss fell away from where it had been loosely growing and clinging to an intricate mosaic of tiles.

The mural they stood before depicted faraway lands, forests, wolves, clockwork, and treasure. The central figure was the Wilderkin Hero, Jasper Dunthwittle, who had died in service to his kin in the resettling days after the Victory. He had long hair and pointed features with a fairly serious and matter-of-fact expression. He stood next to a half-opened door, with a key in his hand.

The Wilderkin in their own society were a fierce, proud people, staunch defenders of their territory, with trained foxdogs as their companions. But let them wander from that society and move in the cities and ways of humans and the other sentient races, and they soon degenerated, or evolved, into a cheerful, friendly, fairly naive little people.

"What does that inscription say?" inquired Kimi, pointing to the angular, ancient runes over the pictures.

"Hmm . . . " Valerie inspected them. "Here is Jasper's Test of skill, for Scout and Locksmith's . . . "

"That means 'sneakthief,' basically," opined Arcie.

"Hush, Barigan! This translation is difficult. '—Locksmith's place to fill. Stealth and quick of hand and eye, you alone this Test must try.' "

"That means only one of us?" Sam asked. Kaylana nodded.

"It would make sense. One of us, of the . . . locksmith profession." A faint smile hovered around her mouth.

"Well, there's two of us . . . Mr. MacRory, do you want to do it?" asked Kimi. Something in the eagerness of her stance hinted to Arcie that the young thief was rather interested in daring the legendary quest herself; he was well content with that.

"I'm too old for such things, Kimi . . . why don't you give it a go?" he said with a smile.

"Right!" she said, drawing her rapier. "What do I do? How does it open?" She walked up to the mural, tapped it, and then pushed on the key in the hand of the figure of Jasper. There was a shimmer, and she vanished into the mural, as though she had walked right through it.

"She's gone!" exclaimed Arcie. "Now what?"

"Now we wait, I suppose," said Sam.

They had rested only a few minutes when something happened. A sudden brilliant explosion of light from the mural, and a figure, moving impossibly fast, crashed into the floor in front of it, as though fallen from midair. The eyes of those watching recovered to see Kimi lying twisted on the watery ground, eyes staring sightlessly at the ceiling. They ran to her, but there was nothing they could do. Her body was already stiffening.

"She is dead," pronounced Kaylana. "As though fallen from a great height."

"Dead . . . " Arcie whispered, staring.

Sam had seen death many times, but he never enjoyed it. Blackmail patted Arcie's shoulder in consolation.

"This is a bother," grumbled Valerie. "Well, you're next, Barigan."

"What?! Me? Nay!" cried Arcie, jumping away from Kimi's body and the Test mural. "No one said anything about—death!"

"Arcie," said Sam, taking him gently by the shoulder,

"Kimi was barely a journeyman . . . used to street thieving. You, on the other hand, are a Guildmaster."

"*Was* a Guildmaster," retorted Arcie.

"Now, I know you don't have any obligations regarding Kimi, but this Test needs to be done. You're the only one who can; I'm not much good with lockpicks or traps. But you, you're the best."

"Can, mayhap. Won't, definitely." Arcie folded up his arms over his broad chest and looked away.

"Arcie. Do you want Kimi to have died in vain? For all those years of thievery to vanish forever, for a whole way of life to die, Fates! A whole *world* to die . . . all because you wouldn't do a simple test of your skills?"

"Better them than me, I always says. You want heroics, you ask a hero!" Arcie did feel saddened by Kimi's death, but his own immediate danger was far more important.

"Argh!" fumed Valerie in impatience. "Regardless of this Test and the time we are wasting here, the thought of all those magical relics and treasures lying unclaimed within the Test makes me itch!"

"Magic treasures?" Arcie asked, turning around slightly. Sam noticed a faint twinkle in Kaylana's eyes. Meanwhile, Blackmail gently stooped and picked up Kimi's still form from the floor, holding her in his arms, out of the water. Valerie ranted on.

"Drat! All the ancient magical gemstones and weapons, too powerful for the new worlds, so the Heroes thought! Sealed up in the Tests! If I could only get my hands on one of those super-powerful magical daggers or something . . . "

"I'll do yon Test," said Arcie, decisively. He struck a noble pose. "For poor departed Kimi. Borrow one of your daggers, Sammy?" the Barigan asked, flipping the birch-handled one the assassin had had in his boot, up and down in his palm. Sam rolled his eyes.

"*Borrow,* yes. Good luck, you rotund sneakthief."

"Thanks, ye spindle-shanked maniac," answered Arcie with a cheerful grin.

Arcie stepped up and tapped the key in the mural with his finger and vanished.

"Are there really all kinds of magical treasure in the Test?" Sam asked. Valerie smiled her famous shark smile.

"Would I lie, my dear little assassin?"

"Yes," put in Kaylana, bluntly. "But in this case, well done."

"Of course, any minute I expect the little twerp to splat out of nowhere. I suggest we move," added Valerie.

"Hey, give him a chance. He's a pain, I'll admit that," said Sam, "but he is a pretty fair thief."

"Enough that you trust his fat self not to land on your head with terminal velocity?" retorted Valerie.

"Well, I didn't say that, did I?" replied Sam, following her and the others to a safe distance.

Arcie found himself in a small room, just about his size, and stopped to wonder a moment whether a full-sized human encountering this Test might not have a bit of trouble, then noticed a piece of ancient parchment on the floor, with thin spidery writing on it. He scooped it up, and read:

> *The object of this test is for you to steal the Citrine stone and escape. I've drawn you a map.*

Therewith followed a tangle of lines, arrows, passageways, doors, circles, and crosses. It made Arcie's eyebrows hurt just to look at it. He shook his head and started to pocket the note, then thought better of it and left it on the floor.

"Citrine stone, huhm?" he mused. "I wonder if that's one of them magical treasures? Well, best start off then." It was the work of a moment to locate the secret door hidden in the panel before him and slip through.

He stepped out into a dim passageway and heard footsteps. He ducked back into the shadows, hiding in the small recess of the doorway. The passageways he had come into were of dark granite, rough-hewn into tunnels and bolstered by wood supports—a welcome relief from the mossy dampness of the catacombs. Where he was, or what the nature was of where he was, assuming he was anywhere anyway, he didn't bother to wonder about.

Two heavy squat creatures flapped past his hiding place, ugly brute-faced humanoids with tusks and battered leather armor. They carried pikes and rusty shields.

Groinks! thought the thief. He'd never actually seen any before; he'd thought they'd been extinct for some time. But he did recall his father telling him about them. Strong, evil, vicious, keen sense of hearing and smell, but not terribly bright. As they passed, he reached out a careful hand and gently lifted a ring of jingling keys from the belt of one of them. The Groinks went on to the end of the passageway before one of them noticed the silence of his keyring.

The Groink turned around with a suspicious snort, but Arcie had already padded silently forward and was lurking in the shadows nearby, birchwood dagger in hand, hardly daring to breathe. A moment passed, then the Groink began retracing its steps, looking back and forth in the shadows and along the walls while the other stood by a small wooden door, belching to itself thoughtfully and picking its nose.

Arcie gave a mental sigh. He didn't like having to do this, it really was sort of infringing on Sam's territory, but the Groink was between him and that door. He shifted position slightly and threw the dagger with all his strength into the back of the Groink's neck. His aim and strength were nowhere close to Sam's, but at this range it was hard to miss. The Groink gurgled and fell over, and the one at the far end of the hall pricked up its hairy ears in suspicion.

One gone down, thought Arcie, ducking back into the shadows after retrieving the dagger. **But now yon other knows as something's amiss.**

The Groink padded back up the hallway and inspected its dead comrade, then took the pike from the dead body, as well as the helmet that seemed to be some mark of rank. Quickly exchanging these for his own, it began peering about into the shadows, poking around with its pike. Arcie slipped past the back of the creature, ducked into the doorway, and swiftly unlocked it with one of the keys.

As the Groink turned with a snort toward the sound, Arcie shoved open the door and ducked in, slamming it behind him and locking it.

He noticed his hand was sore as the scene shifted around him. There was a small hole in the heel of his palm, with a stain around it. He tsked thoughtfully. There must have been a needle trap on the door . . . Behind him, the barred door had vanished. His hand was hurting pretty bad now, and he felt a bit weak. The room seemed to be spinning.

Damn, he thought to himself, as he sank to his knees. *I didn't even get as far as Kimi did. Will mine dead corpse just materialize outside? Will they be upset? Will they bury me? Will Sam notice I've gotten Groink blood all over one o' his favorite daggers?*

The Groinks must have known about the trap on the door. The trap was fairly complex and hard to see. Groinks were stupid. The Groinks probably ran the risk of getting tagged by such a trap, even if they only had existence when someone came to take the Test. Therefore, they must have taken some measures to protect themselves. An antidote. They'd had no pouches, no pockets, just the dirty clothing and weapons . . .

And a ring of keys.

Arcie felt his throat starting to close up and the humming tingle that was spreading up his arm reaching for his heart. With his good hand he fumbled with the keyring, hardly daring to hope . . . keys all too heavy, solid, but . . . he struggled, collapsing, and managed to pull the thick brass ring in half. A fine gray powder poured from the hollow therein, onto the floor. He just barely had the strength to roll over and press his tongue to it, as the room filled with red spots and a loud buzzing . . .

When he came to, every muscle ached, and his tongue

was still coated with a layer of fine power. The rest that had spilled was gone . . . he could only assume he'd eaten it. At least he could move, and as he stood, he violently and colorfully expressed his unhappiness with the nausea and agony that ran through his body. That finished, he found a wall to sit against, shaking and occasionally dry-heaving, to wait for his insides to calm down.

His current visible means of support was a wall ascending into shadow. The discomfort seemed to be subsiding, and he silently thanked whatever dead gods once looked out for thieves and villains. He could continue on now, though he didn't much want to. No other passages . . . the only way out was up. About forty feet up, the wall became smooth; at forty-five feet a rope hung a short distance from the wall.

"Climbing," he groaned. "This must be where Kimi fell. I hates climbing. So undignified." But he sighed, and rubbed his hands and flexed his toes. "Best get it over with, then."

He scanned the walls. They were mortared stone, easy enough. He set his fingers and stretched up, then got back down again, and took his boots off. He gagged again, made a mental note to wash his feet, and then once again grabbed fingerholds, dug his nimble toes into lower cracks, and began climbing.

"The trick in wall climbing," he muttered to himself, as he used a catclaw, a small metal hook and loop that was part of every thief's tools, "is not to lose yer momentum. If ye pause and hang, yer fingers get sore, rocks work loose, and ye falls, thump. Or splat." His dislike of walls wasn't just for reasons of dignity . . . he often wasn't tall enough to reach handholds, and his body was a bit dense for this sort of thing. Sam was the best wall-crawler he knew of alive today, but there had been some far better in his old Guild. He reached the edge of the rough part of the wall without too many stumbles and saw the rope hanging nearby. He had to hammer the catclaw deep into the smooth part of the stone, pull himself up, trust his weight to it while he hand-walked his height up the smooth wall, reached for the rope . . . then suddenly drew back.

Kimi, he thought to himself.

Something in that Wilderkin's expression on the mural warned him against grabbing for the safety of that convenient rope. He instead crawled up the smooth wall with extreme difficulty, fingernails and toenails bending in tiny cracks of stone, using a spare set of picks as pitons, every muscle straining. At last a suspicious outline in the stone offered itself. With a sigh of relief he triggered a hidden mechanism, ducked as a crossbow bolt whizzed out of the far wall and shattered near his ear, then pulled a latch and tumbled into a hidden passageway set in the wall.

He sat on the ledge of it, flexing his stiff fingers and toes and getting his breath back. Then he took out a candle, lit it with his tinderbox, and shone it up into the shadows from which the rope dangled.

High up in the shaft were wooden rafters. The rope hung from a large block of stone precariously balanced on one of these; a firm tug would send the block and rope and anyone climbing it crashing to the floor below. It must reset magically each time someone tried the Test . . . and Kimi, while unlucky enough to fall, had at least not been pulped under that stone.

"Seeing *that* would have sent me running all the way back to Bariga," muttered Arcie. "Magical treasures or no. Pretty sneaky, Jasper," he said to himself, and turned and headed down the passageway, locating and disarming traps in the floor, walls, and ceiling as he went. They were difficult, but not impossible, and traps were Arcie's forte.

He came to the end of the passageway and found a small door. The door was very thoroughly locked, with so much brass, iron, and steep keeping it shut it looked like there was more metal than wood to it. There was another note pinned to it, in the strange, almost coded handwriting. It said: "Through here, but keep your ears open."

"Silly thing," snorted Arcie. "Mine ears are always

open." He set to work on unlocking the door. There was a series of locks, padlocks, finesse combo locks, and even some concealed keyholes and sliding panels. It would have been an ideal thing to have in the Guild for the apprentices to practice on. Arcie poured fast glue on a few spring-loaded traps, dissolved a few catch mechanisms with a few drops of strong acid, and then set to work with picks and hooks to get the numerous locks to release their hold on the doorframe.

At last the final tumbler clicked into place, and he stepped cautiously into a small room. On a pedestal in the center was an orange chunk of crystal. It was about the size and shape of a slice of grapefruit, perfectly smooth and clear.

He walked over to it, inspected the pedestal for traps, and disarmed the pressure plate in the base with the use of a well-placed iron spike. The trap clicked, and he scooped the stone off its cushion and started to walk away when the faintest of sounds reached his ears. A faint rumbling noise, coming from . . .

He threw himself flat as a huge block of stone whistled over his head, thrust with breakneck force from the wall by a huge spring trap. It shattered with a tremendous crash against the far wall, smashing itself and the wall into great piles of rubble.

Arcie got up shakily. There was a faint funny feeling about the top of his head. He reached up, uncertain, patted his hair, and looked. The corner of his leather cap was just visible underneath the rubble. The collision had revealed a secret passageway, maybe leading out. He stopped a moment to uncover the cap, now much the worse for wear, then turned to the passageway and crept down it cautiously.

It turned into a narrow squeeze tunnel, a tight tube of stone with light dimly visible at the end. He tried to go down it, but it closed in tight, and he backed out. He judged the width and paused.

He couldn't fit through it. It was like a drainpipe. But then what was he to do? Wait here until he grew so skinny he could slip through, while the world likely sublimated in the meantime? Or . . . wait. He *could* fit through it, maybe, if he got rid of everything but his clothes. As Sam had speculated, a good portion of his bulk was equipment and money hidden in interior pockets. He could get rid of some of that excess girth. There was even a small niche in the wall as if for the purpose of keeping his belongings.

Arcie sat and thought. This, he felt, was unfair. He wondered how long it would take him to slim enough, and whether the hunger would be worth it. He was already recovered from his nausea, and his empty stomach ached. He'd collected his possessions over years and years of a very profitable thieving career. Give it all up now, just for the sake of a rock, not even any magical treasures? No way.

Maybe he could make it with the loss of only a few things. He took off his morning-star, and set it in the niche. Then his cloak, and Sam's dagger, stained with Groink residue. He tried to sneak down the passageway again, nearly got stuck too tight to escape, and backed out with difficulty. He inspected his pouches again.

After much inner struggle he relinquished a sling, a pouch of miscellaneous objects, and an empty waterskin.

He thought for awhile, and divested himself of his rations and smoking paraphernalia, and another couple of pouches. All he had left now was his moneypouches, his thieves' tools, his pockets of coins and various knickknacks, a waterskin partly full of excellent Barigan whiskey, and the Citrine. He tried to stuff the other items into a pocket, but it was too full already with the various bulky loot he'd accumulated. And he was still too encumbered to pass through the far end of the squeeze tunnel.

"Bother," he muttered to himself.

With a sigh, he added the waterskin, pouches, tools and detachable pockets, and all his other knickknacks and treasures and paraphernalia to the pile in the niche. Then, with a regretful nod, he held the stone in one hand and squirmed through the tunnel, on his belly, pushing his way along with his toes and free hand.

He came to the end and tumbled out in a bright flash of light, into a stink of fish and moss. The others of his party looked up in surprise from where they had been pacing around the room.

The others saw the mural flash, saw Arcie stumble out, looking noticeably thinner. "Here!" Arcie greeted them angrily, holding the stone aloft. It was cold and heavy and icy smooth. "There weren't no magical treasures at all! Just this stupid rock! And I losted all my stuff!"

"That's no stupid rock, fool," retorted Valerie. "That is a Segment of the Key." Sam and Kaylana exchanged glances, and Blackmail gave Arcie silent applause as the Barigan looked at the Segment, stunned.

Just then, the mural flashed again, and an outline opened in it. Arcie gave a pleased exclamation and padded over to the niche in the mural. His things were piled safely inside.

"Och! I knew that Wilderkin were too much of a Hero to take all of a fellow thief's possessions," he told Sam smugly, "he were just too nice a guy."

Arcie reached into the niche, took hold of his belt of pouches—and jerked his hands back with lightning speed as a razor-sharp steel blade fell suddenly across the opening with a metallic clang.

Arcie's eyes were wide. He looked at his hands. They bled from where the skin on the backs of his fingers had been neatly sliced away, showing little white knobs of knuckle.

"Ye sneaky little bastard, Jasper," whispered Arcie. "There *is* no honor among thieves." He curled up, cursing, as the pain hit.

"I'll get Kaylana over here to heal you," Sam said, and Arcie nodded weakly as he worked the chopper blade aside with shaking, bleeding hands to recover his possessions from the niche.

"She cared. She tried. In wyvern's blood she is remembered. May the sun warm you, may the moon be your pathway, and the wind at your back. Spirit of fire, freedom of air, strength of earth and immortality of water go with you." Kaylana gently set the eggshell down next to Kimi's chest, where the young thief lay on the seacliff, eyes closed, hands folded. Seagulls mewled overhead, and Sam stepped forward.

"She was a strong young woman. She lasted when all the others gave out, and she gave her life in service to the cause of evil and freedom of the night. Tharzak, keep her blades ever keen. Hruul, hold her safe and hidden in your shadows." Sam paused, then added softly, "Azal . . . carry her gently."

The name of the God of Death sent a faint chill through the air, which lingered even as Sam gently lay her rapier and dagger on her chest, and placed her cold hand over them. Sam stepped back, and Blackmail stepped forward. The dark silent knight did not speak, but gently touched the young woman's forehead with his gauntleted fingers, brushing the hair away. Then he too stepped back.

Valerie, feeling out of place, stood where she was. The others looked at her. "She had guts, I'll admit that. A pity." Nightshade croaked in agreement.

Arcie then stepped forward. "She were my student. She were talented and cunning, but she left the Guild, not for greed, but for love. She lived a life that were free and her own, and she died trying to preserve that way of life what we all stand for. May all rogues now and forever remember Kimi Quelustan of Tailerand. May Baris and Bella keep ye cunning and quick, and may ye dance free forever beyond the final lock." Arcie gently set Kimi's lockpicks next to the dagger and rapier, and lay her other hand over them, then stepped back.

Kaylana leaned on her staff and spoke softly. Slowly the ground rippled like water, and parted as gently as a sigh, easing the body down into the warm soil. The ground closed over, still rippling softly, and grass and wildflowers raced back across the brown scar of the earth. In a moment there was nothing to be seen but a profusion of tiny blue-green prilla blossoms, smelling faintly of lemon. Without a word, the villains turned and walked down the hill, toward the setting sun and the town of Tailerand.

The next morning, Mizzamir graciously teleported Robin back to the city of Tailerand. The centaur trotted about until at last he located the rogues breakfasting in one of the public houses. His questions about what had occurred in his absence gathered no useful information, the party being wrapped up in their own thoughts. Arcie had found a ship sailing for Troïs in a few hours, and booked passage for the six of them, with their horses. Blackmail and Kaylana took care of loading the horses, and Sam clandestinely settled Kaylana's loan from Arcie by a few decisive arguments that involved Sam's annoyance at the stinking and discolored state of his birchwood dagger, and the fact that he, Sam, could still pick up Arcie by his neck and if Arcie wanted to be forgiven he could jolly well give Kaylana the horse-loan as a gift.

At last, the sails unfurled, the dock slipped away, and the villains, on their way once more, took the time to rest and sleep the day away again, ignoring Robin's questions and attempts at ballads. But Arcie stayed awake a long time, looking at the strange orange wedge of crystal and thinking.

IV

Crossing the channel was uneventful and peaceful. The villains spent their time in various ways: Sam sharpened all of his weapons; Kaylana talked to sea gulls and dolphins; Arcie trolled for "whatever's out there" with a hand line; Valerie avoided the sunlit deck, but at night could be found up on the prow, with a serene smile, sending magical bolts of black death-energy causing bloody agony and death to the occasional frolicking dolphin or jumping fish; Blackmail spent much of his time in the hold, grooming his stallion or exercising it up and down the aisle provided for that purpose. Sometimes Sam and Blackmail would spar on the large open deck, much to the entertainment of the crew; Sam's speed and reflexes kept in practice, but his hardest blows and sharpest blades never made the slightest impression on that dark armor. At one point he attempted a deliberate shattering strike to the back of the knight's helmet; the force of the blow sent his hand into tingling numbness, and Blackmail, helmet undamaged, slowly waggled a reproachful finger at him. Sam blushed and did not try again.

Robin's strange appearance and large size at first made the crew wary, but as soon as they discovered he was not only timid but infinitely gullible, Robin became the favorite target of various practical jokes. The crew invited him to a deck party, and were even willing to supply the half-keg of rum that it took to get the centaur soused. Robin clopped around unsteadily on deck, singing one of the interminable ballads of the Victory in a quavery tenor, and occasionally even managing to hit one of the strings on his harp. Due to healthy bulk and constitution, however, the crew was disappointed to see him bright and chipper the next day, his only side-effect being a few gaps in his memory.

One night the crew recounted terrifying tales to the minstrel, of the swift, aggressive, deadly sea-snakes of the channel, that would leap right up onto a ship to sink their dripping fangs into some hapless fool, the poison rotting the victim in agony and gruesome death. At the climax of the tale, one of the men gave a shout and threw a dripping rope over the centaur's withers. Robin's scream of terror and panicked galloping awakened the entire craft, and the captain sternly reprimanded the men responsible. After that, the voyage proceeded uneventfully, until at last they docked at the port of Pithcar, and once again felt the good solid ground beneath their feet.

They rested in Pithcar through the day, waiting for nightfall before moving on. They had a pleasant meal at a tavern—another Frothing Otter. The keeper was quite pleasant and even allowed Robin into the main dining area. Then, as night at last descended, they moved on, out through the countryside and into the hills, the wild green magical forested lands of Trois, under the combined rule of aging Lord Fendalis and his famous and heroic son Sir Fenwick.

Sir Fenwick, at the moment, could not believe his luck. His sources reported a group of people had landed in Pithcar a few days ago who exactly matched the description of the villains. They had since been seen moving inland.

"It hardly seems possible!" he exulted. "They're coming right for us! What a fine hunt this will be, the likes of which the company has not seen in ages! Now then . . ." He rummaged about in his workroom, a long hall filled with texts and maps, decorated with his many hunting trophies and various medals of honor given to him for his heroic service to the cause of good. On the balcony his mews of prized messenger swifts twittered and fluttered, and one of his many Feyhounds, the red-eared white hunting dogs of the royal house, slept on its back, snoring softly. Fenwick pulled out a rolled map, sending the others in the stack crashing down with a noise loud enough to make the Feyhound twitch one ear and yawn. Ignoring the mess, Fenwick unrolled the map. The green and blue and brown of his kingdom spread out across the table, all rich forests and rolling hills and shining rivers, with a small range of mountains in the northern coast like a crown. He inspected the view thoughtfully.

"Now then, if I were a villain, where would I go in Trois?" he mused. "Perhaps I should ask Mizzamir if he's learned anything from the centaur? No," he decided. "The Arch-Mage might want to know what I was planning, and I don't want to bother him with it. Besides, they're in my jurisdiction now and my responsibility. I will deal with them myself." He pored over the map a bit more, frowning. "Drat . . . there are any number of fine places they might choose to despoil. The High Temple here in Glinabar, the green horse-fields of Trebitha, the gold mines in Malain. I'll have to send scouts out." He looked out the window thoughtfully. Here he had called out the Company, bid them train and prepare for a hunt . . . and he could not find where the hunt was to begin. It was most discomfiting. He would make the villains pay for this. He wondered if Mizzamir's agent was doing any better.

"So," Robin asked, as they trekked across the lush countryside, filmed with silver moonlight and cool breezes, "where are we going?"

"To the Glina Forest, beyond the Falorin Lands," replied Valerie tersely. "Which unfortunately happen to be the haunt of that despicable do-gooder Sir Fenwick."

"Sir Fenwick?" inquired Kaylana, looking at the sorceress.

"A hunter of sorts. An adventurer hero. A royal bastard who I would much like to see impaled on a bolt of dark flame for eternity," was the response. Robin shivered.

"Any particular reason, or just general dislike for the opposite side?" Sam asked casually, looking over his horse's neck. Blackmail on his huge warhorse clomped along beside him, a single deep shadow in the night, the horse snorting and prancing in the fresh breeze.

"None of your business."

"Whush!" exclaimed Arcie. "What's the matter, Valerie? That time o' decade?"

"Please be quiet," insisted Kaylana, riding ahead on her piebald. "The creatures of Trois are much influenced by loyalty to the Forest Lord, and I would not have our presence so advertised. Even the trees themselves seem to be listening."

"Be there still Wilderkin in these parts?" inquired Arcie, thinking of his Test at the hands of the long-dead Jasper Dunthwittle.

"Oh yes," Robin answered. "Living the wild free life, at harmony with nature and the woods, in company with their trusted foxdog companions . . . "

". . . Occasionally ripping apart the chance bandit or other evil marauder," added Sam ruefully. "Let's be careful. I don't feel like taking on a berserk pack of feral Wilderkin anytime soon."

As they rode out into the wilderness, the countryside was filled with broadleaf forests that spread over the rise and fall of low hills. To the party, the trees in the moonlight looked like green foam on lighter green water, thin in some places, a green canopy in others. This was the Falorin Lands, the haunt of feral Wilderkin and stranger creatures.

Several days passed, peacefully slept through, and nights of long travel as they moved steadily toward their destination. But it was not to stay peaceful long. It was early one evening, lit by the faintest sliver of a new moon, when they were spotted.

Large watchful eyes in the treetops followed them.

"Did you get a good look at them, Sunglade?"

"No, my chief."

"Then we will hope Leafwind has done better than we." The hidden figure raised his head and sent a coded whistle sweeping into the night. *"Leafwind!"* The whistle was answered.

"I see them, my chief. On the Western road."

He looks, and sees. Sharp eyes focus on . . .

A coldly beautiful, pale-skinned woman, with large dark eyes. The others in the group are of no consequence. His whistling call rings with ancient anger as he calls to his tribe.

"There rides tonight a dark one, if not the same then surely kin to the serpent woman who tormented our ancestors and the Great One Jasper so many years ago. She is darkness. She must be slain before she comes for us and our children!"

Robin started as a terrifying, eerie sound rose from the shadows of the forest. A strange whistling, mingled with yaps and barks. Valerie, her cowl pushed back from her face, seemed to grow even paler as she tried to work out where the sound came from.

"The Wilderkin," she whispered. "I hoped we had avoided them."

"Sounds like just animals to me," said Arcie. "Wasn't Jasper the Hero from this same area?"

"Yes," replied Kaylana.

"He died here too," put in Sam. "The Wilderkin Hero, I mean."

"Yes," confirmed Robin, looking around nervously. The sounds came again, closer now.

"Yes indeed," confirmed Valerie, drawing up her reins. The sound was definitely behind and to the left. "He was killed fighting with a Nathauan who kidnapped some Wilderkin for a magical experiment. Now his descendants make their home here, and they'll kill any Nathauan they see, and probably you too for good measure. Run!"

She spurred her horse and tore off through the forest as the whistles erupted again.

Sam looked back in concern at the knight, who remained steadfast even as the others glanced from side to side, looking for a way to run. "Come on!"

The knight ignored him scornfully. Sam rolled his eyes. "Look, I'm sure you'd far prefer to die nobly than run from a fight, but you're all in armor. Your horse still has a soft underbelly and will likely get it torn out by foxdogs and Wilderkin if you don't move it!"

Robin was prancing with eagerness to flee. His ears had picked up a shift in sounds. "Come on! Valerie's led them off to the side! We can make it to the Clawrip Canyon!" He set off at a canter, and Sam, Kaylana, and Arcie did the same. After a long pause, so did Blackmail, a clanking shadow in dark armor.

They came to the edge of a wide, steep-sided chasm, with a faint trail of river glimmering in its depths, downstream of a large wooden bridge across the top. Valerie emerged from the forest farther upstream and almost fell into the torrent, but wheeled her mount around and galloped toward them, the dark span of the bridge between them visible in the moonlight. They headed for it, the whistles of the Wilderkin erupting all around them.

As the horses ran for the bridge, the shadowing rocks of the canyontop were alive with the flickering motion of small long-haired figures accompanied by long-legged foxdogs. Further figures seemed to come leaping out of the forest. The whistles and yaps echoed across and around and down the chasm, magnified a hundred times. A whirring flight of arrows spattered around them, a pony squealed and there was a gasp and a muffled curse. Then they felt the ground change to the drumming wood of the bridge. Valerie galloped up to them and, without hesitating, spurred her gelding across the span. The others followed, the sound of horses' hooves rolling like thunder. Shouts of rage erupted around them as the Wilderkin saw their quarry escaping.

Valerie wheeled her mount around the instant its hooves touched the stone of the far edge, and then waited fuming until Sam, bent low over his charging horse, thundered to safety. Instantly drawing on the dark magic from the amulet concealed in Sam's pocket, she fired off blast after blast of dark energy at the supports of the bridge. The centaur, Arcie, and Kaylana scrambled to safety. Blackmail came galloping up just as the bridge supports failed. Sam saw the bridge crack and buckle, giving way under the knight. But the valiant black warhorse slammed its huge back feet into the last of the falling bridge and leaped. Like a huge black cat, it soared up, stretching its forelegs desperately, the dark knight hanging on tightly, letting the horse do what it must. The huge plate-feet scrabbled on the crumbling bank, and the hind legs came up and under again to bound away from the failing slope. In the distance, howls and screams told them that the falling bridge had taken several of the Wilderkin and their foxdogs with it.

The stallion came to a stop, panting, and Blackmail dismounted instantly, checking the animal's hooves. The others turned in fury on Valerie, while on the far side of the bank, the vague shadows of Wilderkin flickered in frustrated rage, and the faint voices cried revenge.

"You almost killed us, you stupid wench!" shouted Arcie. "Blowing up the bridge whilst we was still on it!"

Robin stood trembling a moment. He had only made it across the bridge by shutting his eyes and running by sound, but as the bridge had buckled he had unfortunately looked down. The sickening plunge, the thinness of the air . . . his legs slowly folded, and he collapsed in an ungainly heap. Kaylana, after a burning glare at the sorceress, turned to attend to the centaur.

"Of course, foolish short one. I am, after all, a dark sorceress." She smiled. "I wouldn't have waited for your blond friend either, but that he has my amulet in his possession."

"Lucky for me," muttered Sam, trying to get his breath. Damazcus snorted, and the smell of equine sweat was thick.

"We must move on," insisted Kaylana, as Robin rose unsteadily under the influence of sourweed waved under his nose. "The Wilderkin will have every living thing up in arms for miles around before dawn."

Shaken and chilled from drying sweat and adrenaline, they moved on through the dark woods, until dawn lightened the sky and they judged themselves far enough away from the Wilderkin territory. They found shelter beneath a grove of oak trees Kaylana proclaimed safe and fell into exhausted slumber.

The sun shone on the golden feathers of the sun-eagle perched on Fenwick's wrist. The young hero stroked the bird's head gently, as he looked into its dark, intelligent eyes. He spoke to it, half with his mind, and half with his strong voice.

"Fly, my friend, hunt-brother. Ride the winds to the west, to seek and find the foe. Search for them, my friend, seek out the dark ones, and bring the news to me."

With a shrill cry the eagle leapt from his wrist and flew powerfully out the open window, into the clear sky. Its mighty, six-foot wingspan flashed like a golden star, then it was gone.

* * *

The villains were still sound asleep under the trees when the golden bird soared high overhead. Seeking movement, as its instincts had always instructed it, it did not notice the still, dark-colored shadows, and the horses standing aimlessly about were just large animals to its hunter's brain, not matching the mental image Fenwick had given it of the ones it was meant to locate. It flew on, its shadow racing below across the treetops, as the sun dappled the forest, and the small band of renegades dreamed.

Kaylana stirred uneasily. The drifting of the leaves sounded in her head like rushing water. There was water, a torrent, it foamed before her. She gripped her staff and peered into the water. It flowed over white stones . . . a chill wind swept through her as she saw the strangely shaped rocks were in fact bleached bones . . .

Arcie dreamed of his old home, the snug crofter's cottage built low and thick like the men and women of the land itself, back in the cool, rainy, peaceful hills and dells of Bariga, so far away to the North now. As he had when he was just a lad, he sat in front of the fire, watching his father smoke a pipe, reading from an old book. A knock sounded at the front door. Arcie went and opened it, and a gigantic Sam reached into the hall and grabbed him by the collar, hauling him out like a rabbit . . .

Robin slept uneasily, not used to the change from diurnal to nocturnal. His dreams were fitful, involving terrifying sea-snakes that took their evil hissing noise from the sound of the wind in the leaves. A roaring growl came from a horrible demon-beast in his dream, frightening him awake; when he heard the sound again, in waking, he almost bolted, but turned to see it was just the Barigan thief, lying on his back and snoring loudly. The centaur calmed himself by taking time to brush out his long beautiful tail, a hundred strokes with a comb he kept for the purpose, and then did his mane as well. Then with a sigh he readjusted his position against a tree and slept again.

Valerie dreamed the confused tangle of the mind of the

Nathauan, lost not in fantasy and illusion, but in remembering. Her husband Talar, tall, dark-eyed, hair streaked in silver, the way he smiled, the warmth of his arms, the love in his voice when he spoke. Her daughter, quick as a deer, learning to play the intricate lacy dulcimer of the Underrealm, her childish seriousness as she sternly reprimanded her dolls for their imaginary disobedience. The joyous grin of her husband when she'd told him she carried his son. And then, and then, the shouts, the smoke, waking them in the middle of the night. Talar on his feet, eyes bright with anger and fear, grabbing his staff of power, opening the door and staggering back with a bolt in his chest. Nightshade cawing and flapping as he tried to get his mistress to safety. A ball of magical fire sweeping into the house that was formed from living rock, igniting the wooden furniture and transforming the building into an oven. Fighting through the flames to her daughter's room, hearing the strangled cries. An armored figure in green leaping into the room and cutting down the still struggling Talar, then lunging at her as she tried to raise her hands in defense, a blade flashing down, a blow that struck pain and fire all the way through her body, the wordless death-cry in her mind of her unborn son, and then darkness, left for dead in the ruined tunnels.

Sam dreamed of Mizzamir. He saw the mage at the end of a long room and drew both daggers, throwing himself to attack. But what was wrong with the floor? It threw him into the air, and he drifted through the air in slow motion. In midair the old Gypsy woman appeared beside him, smiling and shaking her head. "One searches for you, assassin . . . one waits," she cautioned, and vanished. As he drifted toward the mage, who stood still in confident power, he saw the mage had the same expression, smiling in amusement. "Silly boy," the wizard scolded him gently. "Always jumping into things." The wizard stepped back and revealed a pit of razor-edged spears aimed to receive Sam's helplessly drifting form, set in a pattern like an extended star . . .

Blackmail did not sleep. His horse slept while the knight sat watch, gauntleted fingers covered by soft gloves, gently massaging the horse's strained legs in the warm sunshine.

At last the cool of evening drifted through the woods. Sam woke with a snurfle, early dew beading on his nose. The moon and stars and setting sun still lit the area well, but in a different set of shades as the light of day—grays and whites and soft washed colors, pools of blue-purple shadows. Nearby was the knight, still fussing silently over his horse. The stallion was resting its head contentedly on the tall armored shoulder. Sam had never ridden a horse for long periods and had always sort of regarded them as mere transport. But he admitted he was already rather fond of Damazcus, who would carry him without complaint and had a friendly way of whickering when he approached. Still, it seemed odd that the knight would fuss over his warhorse to such an extent.

Kaylana was awake, stirring up the ashes of the fire and adding some more wood to prepare breakfast. She glanced at Sam as he sat up.

"Evening," she greeted. "I think tonight you shall cook breakfast. And do not tell me it is women's work, either."

"I'm not arguing," grumbled Sam, rolling to his feet and walking over to tend the fire. "It's just not usual for someone to ask an assassin to do the cooking."

"I am asking. The others will have to take their turns as well. This evening, you are awake, and you do eat breakfast, unlike our silent friend. I will trust you with the chore." Kaylana moved over to see how the other horses were.

"Thanks," said Sam softly. "For trusting me." He went to work on the fire, and soon was heating up some of the food. "Kaylana?"

"What is it?" muttered the Druid, checking for burrs in her pony's ear.

"I . . . I want to apologize for that remark I made, back in the bar . . . in Mertensia." Sam looked very interested in something in the bottom of one of the cookpots.

"Very well. Your apology is accepted. You were drunk, and not perhaps in full possession of yourself." Kaylana patted Valerie's gelding on the flank and moved on to Arcie's pony, Puddock, who was standing near Damazcus.

"I forgot to thank you for healing me, before, too . . . Thanks."

"It is nothing. You are assisting me in the salvation of the world. But do make my efforts worthwhile."

"Sure," replied Sam. He stirred the pot on the fire. "Um . . . "

"Well!" Arcie sprang up onto his feet. "I'm starved! Sammy, you're cooking? Oh, bugger."

"Don't eat it if you don't like it, Arcie," retorted the assassin.

Awakened by Arcie's outburst, Valerie and Robin soon came over. Robin self-consciously unpacked a bag of the strange wrinkled high-energy oats the centaurs raised, and ate these in addition to his share of the food. He might have, as Arcie had feared, eaten more than any of them, but as the silent knight ate nothing, it seemed to balance out well enough. Sam wondered about that as he saddled his own horse afterwards. Did Blackmail ever eat? Not in their presence, certainly, but perhaps while they all slept? Perhaps by some magic he had no need for food? It was very puzzling . . . but the knight seemed to mean them no harm, whatever his nature might be. *I wouldn't like to come between him and that horse, though,* thought Sam.

They traveled on through the moonlit forests and glades, making good time through the wilderness. Sometimes in the distance they could see the lights of cities and towns, but they strictly avoided these.

"Couldn't we stop at a town just once?" pleaded Robin, after several days of travel. "I'm getting really tired of pine-sap in my tail every morning."

"Aye, and I'm hungry," complained Arcie. "Gruel and wild roots may be all right for you, Druid, but us Barigans like a bit more substantial fare."

"We cannot risk being seen here," insisted Kaylana.

"For once, she's right," Valerie agreed. "I hate Fenwick more than anything, but I will admit he is a clever bastard. We can't afford to attract his attention."

"Time enough for that later," muttered Sam.

"What do you mean?" Kaylana asked.

"You've said we're going to the Glina forest?" Sam looked at her. She nodded.

"It is a legendary place of ancient magic and legend . . . it is surely the 'eldest wood' of the Mad Godling's prophecy," the Druid explained.

The assassin sighed. "I don't know how much you know of geography . . ."

"Oh blast," swore Valerie suddenly. "The blond misfit is right. The Glina forest, of course . . . surrounds the city of Glinabar." Her raven, sitting on her shoulder, cawed derisively.

"Capital city of Trois, and home and hearth to the Fenwickster himself," finished Arcie. "Great."

The Fenwickster, or, as he certainly preferred to be called, Sir Fenwick, was finally getting to exercise his cramped commanding muscles. Though the sun-eagle had returned without having seen the villains, it reported the destruction of the Clawrip bridge and the mourning of the Wilderkin. The villains had to be responsible. And now he knew where they were headed.

"Straight toward us, it seems," said the clever woodsman to himself. "But why? Well, no sense puzzling over it when there's work to be done. I and my Feyhounds can track anything. Today the company and I will ride forth to intercept them."

He rolled his maps up, snatched his hunting hat from its peg, and went to gather his men. Tucked safe in his pack was his finest suit of rich green embellished with gold. When at last the villains were captured and dealt with, he would want to make a good impression upon the poor, misguided, but oh so lovely red-haired woman who traveled with them. Many women had fallen to Fenwick's charms in the past, and this one, he was sure, would be no exception.

In addition, he went to the royal armory and took down his enchanted sword from its jeweled rest. This was the magical sword Truelight, Slayer of Darkness, a silver longsword that burned with its own pure light and had a strange, semi-intelligence of its own. He had wielded this sword against trolls and dragons and Nathauan in the past . . . it would serve him well once again. The diamonds and rubies set into its hilt glittered as he grasped it, and he smiled.

They were approaching the western boundaries of the kingdoms proper, still a wild land, of rocky crags and valleys, the everpresent forests, and swelling hills. The weather had grown hotter, sultry and heavy in daytime with sunlight and beesong, warm and still in the evenings. They were pestered by mosquitoes.

All seemed well, however, until one day, as they slept, Nightshade the raven decided to explore. He took wing and soared above the crowding woods, above the mugginess of the ground. The cool air refreshed his feathers. Far in the distance, he saw a sparkle of something other than water. His raven curiosity and interest in bright objects pulled him closer, sweeping across the miles to see what it was that could twinkle from so far away.

Valerie was awakened by a frantic croaking in her ear. Startled to her feet, she comforted the raven on her wrist until he recovered his breath enough to be coherent to her. While the others could not understand his croaks, mutterings, and hissings, Valerie listened intently.

"He says the Verdant Company is approaching," she said after a moment, her voice tense. "He saw something shiny and went to look and found it was the polished swords and armor of Fenwick's men, in two hunting parties. They have many men, and hounds, and seem to be headed this way."

"Can your raven describe the terrain well enough to draw a map?" Kaylana asked. Valerie conversed with the raven a moment.

"I think so," she answered.

The map, scratched in the dirt, was crude and out of scale, but showed clearly what Kaylana wanted to know. Here was their position, and the city of Glinabar in the distance. Between the two were the forces of the Verdant Company, in two groups quickly advancing down either side of a narrow river that flowed from the city itself. Kaylana studied the scratchings seriously.

"So what do we do?" inquired Sam, looking over her shoulder at the map.

"We are hunted, so we go as the hunted fox goes." She drew a line with a stick directly up the winding path of the river. "Leaving no scent, and in directions unexpected . . . in this case, directly toward the enemy."

Branching out into two parties had been a good idea, Fenwick decided. They could scout through twice the area and still make good time to his estimated location of the villains. He fully expected to be noticed, of course; stealth and trickery were not a part of *this* hero, by Artelis! He judged that the dark sorceress and the lovely Druid would have mystical means of locating his party and took that into accord easily. He would drive the villains back from the golden heart of Glinabar, and chivvy them cross-country, using his superb knowledge of his territory to at last lead them back to the Clawrip Chasm. There they would be cornered by the very impasse they had created, and his Wilderkin allies would be avenged. An elegant poetic justice, he felt.

One afternoon on the trail a raven was sighted, swooping over the camp. Fenwick called to it in the language all the animals of Trois shared, but it ignored him. He watched as it flapped about, circling over the camp, and his eyes narrowed. Such a bird he had seen before, through Mizzamir's crying font, in the company of the dark sorceress. A young member of the company took a lazy potshot at the bird with his longbow; the raven dodged easily and then retreated to just out of bowshot range, then soared away to the west. Fenwick turned to one of his officers standing nearby.

"We have been spotted," he declared. "The enemy will turn tail now. We ride double time, in pursuit!"

Horns sounded, and the Company, a gallant pattern of green and gold and flashing steel ringing through the trees, rode to the hunt.

And thus it was, that as the Verdant Company, men, women, horses and hounds, slept peacefully beneath a sky full of stars in a glen near the rushing cold Silverwend River, a company of six dark shadows quickly but carefully splashed their way upstream through the shallows.

A young warrior in service to the company had awakened to a call of nature and ambled to the riverside to attend to it. As he stood in the idle preoccupation that accompanies such moments, his sleepy eyes saw large shapes moving up the river, the outlines of people on horseback clear in the moonlight. An exclamation came from them.

As he stumbled back, quickly trying to tie up his codpiece and grab his signaling horn at the same time, one of the riders detached itself and came charging toward him. He turned to run, but the figure exploded into two shadows, the horse racing past him as the rider pounced on him with predatory silence, striking and pinning his arms back in a powerful grip while the other hand threw a gag around his mouth. The attack was so sudden he barely had time to breathe two breaths of forest air before his mouth and nostrils were filled with the reek of old sock.

"Good work, assassin," a cold female voice said, as the other figures came riding up. One detached itself from the others and caught the loose horse by the reins. In the moonlight, the warrior's eyes widened in surprise. The very villains they had been hunting had hunted him!

"A guard or a spy? Doesn't matter," said another female voice, with a faint accent. The warrior was too young to have been present at the great battle against the Nathauan, but still the voice chilled him, even as much as when it continued, "Kill him, dump him in the river, and let's be off."

"You want him dead, you do it," retorted a voice by his ear. "I'm already hired."

"No! Don't kill him!" exclaimed a trembling tenor voice.

"The minstrel is right," said the first cold voice. "He may be useful. And I am sure his commander would know if he went missing. He can provide us with information, if nothing else."

"Well enough," said a new voice, as a small shape dismounted and bounded up to him. He felt a dagger prick his ribs, and the voice hissed in his ear, "Talk! Where's yer commander, where are you headed, where are yon guards, how much money are you carrying and do you have any of those little cheesy oatcakes in yer food supplies? Och," the figure added, in a different tone, "and did you know as your codpiece are open?"

"He can't talk, Arcie, I've got him gagged," the voice by his ear said. The warrior tried to struggle, but his invisible captor's grip was like iron. "You could at least do something useful like get me some rope."

"We can't trust him for information," said the accented voice. "These bastard Verdants are totally loyal. He'll cry for help as soon as you take your sock out of his mouth."

"It is not necessary that he speak," said the cold female voice. He saw a robed figure carrying a staff dismount and approach. The largest mounted figure stood nearby, eerily silent. A soft light flared, like a cluster of glowworms, in the approaching figure's hand as it kneeled by him. The light illuminated a female face, smooth and young and fair, framed by long hair. But it was the eyes that caught and held his gaze, eyes of pure emerald, deep and pure and ancient as the eldest forest . . .

The warrior felt his thoughts swimming in a sea of green, as a strange wind ruffled through his memories like autumn leaves, light and unstoppable. The voice, low and strong as oak roots, drifted through his mind. *You will not remember. You came to the river, slipped on a stone, and bumped your head. But you are uninjured, and you will return to your Company to continue as you were.* And then he was falling, drifting away on a sea of green . . .

"Let him go," Kaylana commanded, and Sam let the limp warrior slip to the mossy ground. Arcie looked at Kaylana with respect. The Druid was rubbing the bridge of her nose and wincing as if in pain.

"By Baris and Bella!" exclaimed the Barigan. "I dinna know you could do that."

"It is not something I like to do," she retorted. "The minds of men are complex and strong, and it is difficult. We must leave now. He will wake in a few minutes. When we are clear of this place I will tell you what I have learned."

They quickly remounted and splashed up the river at a brisk trot, the sounds of their movement concealed by the roaring of the river.

"So them will have run right past us?" exclaimed Arcie, when Kaylana had explained what she had read in the young Verdant's mind. "Spiffywell!"

"Saves us a lot of trouble, anyway," agreed Sam.

"And the path to Glinabar should be clear," said Valerie.

"Why are we going there anyway?" put in Robin, still trying to do his duty to the great Mizzamir.

"Don't concern yourself with it, centaur," said Valerie. "Though I admit it would have been nice to go ashore and find that blasted Fenwick and murder him horribly, at least this way we are making good time and staying out of his way."

"At least until he figures us out and turns around," Sam put in gloomily. "And when he finds out what we've done . . ."

" . . . He's going to be very *put out,*" finished Arcie, sobering.

But they traveled uneventfully, and at last they crested a hill and saw below them a vast valley filled with thick woods: the Glina Forest, lusher and deeper and darker and greener than any they had yet seen. Far in the distance, nestled like a pile of jewels in the center of this was the twinkling of the lights of a city, the starlike street-lamps and shining windows of Glinabar, the city that lived in harmony with the forest and its ancient magics.

"We must be extremely cautious," warned Kaylana, as they started down to the woods. "The forces of good are afoot and likely no more so than here."

"Aye, it do have that sort of a look about it," commented Arcie. "But it's just about dawn now . . . We should camp soon."

Sam looked around. "The ground here's pretty rough . . . " Indeed it was, ragged with rocks and gravel that had fallen from the walls of the hills and rolled onto the sparse rabbit-chewed grass.

"And if Fenwick has discovered our move, he will have sent word back to Glinabar," added Valerie. "It will be safer, I think, if we camp in the shelter of the trees. You three," she indicated Sam, Arcie, and Robin, "make yourselves useful and hunt something." Nightshade croaked mockingly at them.

"I'm a sneakthief, not a woodsman, dammit," Arcie muttered under his breath. Sam looked resigned and took out a throwing knife.

"Fine. Kaylana and Valerie and Blackmail go set up camp, we'll catch up with you."

The party split in half, one half remaining on the shorn slopes while the other vanished into the trees. Robin soon proved himself useless as a rabbit-hunter, his hooves startling the animals down into their holes. When one of them, flushed out by Arcie, bolted straight toward his legs, he shied and stomped at it, missing completely and sending it shooting down another hole. Arcie, his hands smeared with dirt, looked up at the centaur in disgust.

"Thought you said you could fight," he scoffed. "You canna even stomp a bunny rabbit."

"I can fight!" insisted Robin. "I trained under Mercala the Mercenary himself."

"Trained! How many battles have ye been in? How many times have ye had to fight for yer life? How many times have ye killed anything larger than a horsefly?"

"He's never killed anything," commented Sam, as he examined a rabbit he'd caught neatly and dispatched with a snap. "Obviously."

"All right, so I've not much experience in the field," snapped Robin defensively. "But killing isn't everything to *me*. How many people have *you* killed, assassin?" asked the centaur, his pale cheeks flushed, his ears laid back in nervousness.

"About a dozen," answered Sam shortly. "Permanents, anyway."

"Permanents?" inquired the centaur.

"Aye, see," broke in Arcie, "You know as powerful healers can bring the dead back to life . . . yet only if the body's fairly intact. You want someone dead and stayin' so, you must needs decapitate 'em, or burn the body, or sometimes cut out the heart, I've heard . . . "

"That's messy, though," muttered Sam.

"Assassinatin' someone that way's a 'permanent.' Baris only knows how many he's killed in other ways . . . Speaking of which," Arcie said, "I wonder whatever happened to Mizzamir?" Robin almost dropped the rabbit, but Arcie didn't notice.

"I'm working on it, you deposit-stealing feeb," retorted Sam. "Give it back, by the way."

"Here, I paid ye. It's not my fault if ye can't look after yer money."

"Be that way for now, but next time I need to buy something, I'll get it from you if I have to turn you upside down and shake it out of you."

"Hrmph. Such a rude attitude to yer employer. Last time I hire you," Arcie grumped.

"And last time I take an assignment from you, welsher," Sam retorted.

He lunged suddenly, and there was a soft crunching sound. Robin paled slightly. "Got another one, Arcie. I think this is enough. Let's go find the others," Sam said. He looked over at Robin, who tried to smile. "You're looking a little woozy there, minstrel," Sam commented, handing him the rabbit.

They found the rest of their party without difficulty, and after a tough but filling meal they rested on the outskirts of the ancient wood and pondered their next move.

"Well, Glina is certainly 'magic's heart,' and Trois is the southernmost of the Six. We figured that out before. Does 'oldest wood' refer to Glina too?" Sam asked.

"I rather think it is more specific than that," answered Kaylana. "And I think I know what it means. In the memories of the young man you captured on the riverbank was a prominent vision of an important time in his life, his recent initiation into the Verdant Company. This ceremony took place in the woods, before a huge tree like none I have ever seen. Its bark was rust-colored and shaggy, and yet its leaves were like those of a conifer. It was so tall it seemed as though it could not exist, and wide enough at the base that five horses could have ridden through it. It must surely be the oldest tree in the woods, if not the world."

"Sounds like it would be important enough to merit the attention of gods," agreed Arcie. Kaylana nodded.

"From what I learned from that Verdant, it is where the Elven King who once ruled Trois gave the Crown of Oak to the Hero Fen-Alaran, charging that he and his descendants should rule the land forever, when the Elves had vanished from the world. It is a place of great importance. The Elves named the tree the *Fa'halee.*"

"That translates roughly into 'blood guardsman,' " Valerie commented.

Robin listened intently. He wondered what they were talking about. Were the villains planning to cut down the tree? It would be a terrible act, but such things were not beyond these people. But why?

He was still wondering when he fell asleep, the others slumbering peacefully around him, except for the dark and silent knight, who kept watch, his hand resting on his great black sword.

About nine o'clock that evening, they wandered through the forest searching for the *Fa'halee.* The forest seemed oddly peaceful at night, Sam noticed. There were the occasional faint noises of animals, but the alert, intense goodness of the day was dispelled in the cool of night, as many of the noble creatures of the wood settled down to slumber. Fireflies startled the group at first, but the insects did nothing more than contribute to the unearthly beauty of the night forest. Tiny moths glimmered momentarily in the light of the fireflies, or stopped to land upon the dimly luminescent fungi that sprang in fairy shapes from fallen log and mosscover. The ferns whispered amongst themselves as the party's mounts walked past, and Arcie thought more than once he spotted strange tiny faces watching him from the cover of leaf or tree hollow. Overhead, the leaves riffled in the night breeze, making the too-bright stars flash and the moonlight dance in streaks through the branches and splash in rippling puddles across the forest floor.

As they moved through the thickest part of the woods, ducking to avoid low, moss-covered branches and easing their mounts around tangles of bramble, they entered a tiny clearing in which there appeared at first to be both fireflies and large toadstools growing in abundance. They were in the midst of them before they suddenly realized that the glowing points of light were not fireflies, but lights shining from tiny windows cut into the sides of the milking-stool-sized mushrooms. Little crooked chimneys emerged from the red and white tops of the strange fungus, and Arcie shivered with inexplicable emotion when he saw that in some of the tiny windows were hung tidy spotted curtains. The others looked about in surprise, stopping their horses to avoid crushing any of the tiny houses.

"Oh, no . . . " groaned Sam in dread as he looked about him. "I don't like this . . . let's get out—"

"Eeeek!" squealed a little voice by Damazcus's hooves. "Humans!"

His horse snorted and stepped back in dismay . . . and Kaylana winced as its hind hoof tore a large hunk out of a mushroom house with a crunkling sound, like someone biting into a hollow watermelon.

"Hey!" piped another voice from the house angrily. "That's not a very nifty thing to do!"

In a matter of instants the clearing swarmed with tiny figures that came boiling out of the little houses and ran around in panic. There were yells, cries of "Humans!" "Humans in the Village!" "Horses!" "Get Daddy Nifty!" and "My house!" The figures all seemed to be identical, Sam noticed; they were perhaps six or seven inches tall, built rather like tiny dwarves, but unbearded. They looked like any of the pictures he had seen of the semi-mythical "wee folk" of magical forests, more on the order of gnomes or leprechauns than fairies. Some of them were wearing tiny nightshirts, but many wore simple clothing of breeches and shirt for the males, skirt and bodice for the females, and each head was covered by either a loose white cap, or a tall conical hat in some bright color. The horses, upset at suddenly finding all available footing covered with a swirling sea of unpleasant soft squashy objects, refused to move.

The squeaking of the creatures was getting on Kaylana's nerves. She gripped her staff, and yelled, "SHUT UP, by Rowan!"

There was a universal squeak of terror from the tiny creatures, then the swirling aimless running stopped as a slightly deeper squeaky voice piped up from the crowd. The creatures turned to face one of their number, a member with a white beard. The little fellow climbed up on a table and cheerfully addressed the crowd.

"Yes indeedy, let's not have all this running around, shall we? That's not very nifty, you know. Let's talk to the nifty humans! Talking is a very nifty thing. It is by talking that we make friends!"

"Hey yeah! Nifty! What a nifty idea!" chorused the little gnomes, and immediately began talking to each other and the group animatedly and incomprehensibly.

"Gnomes," muttered Valerie in disgust. "Gnifty Gnomes."

Blackmail was looking down. A cluster of tiny Gnomes was piping up at him and trying to sit on his horse's hooves, but kept sliding off.

"One at a time, my Gnifty Gnomes!" clarified their bearded leader in a loud voice. The inane chatter stopped, and they all looked expectantly at him. He cleared his throat, and addressed the renegades in a cheerful voice.

"My goodness! Humans and a centaur! It certainly is nifty of you to come and visit us! We don't get many nifty visitors these days! But now you're here, and we'll have a big nifty party!"

"Yeaayyyy!" chorused the Gnomes.

"We'll have nifty music, we'll do the Nifty Dance, we can eat Niftyberry pie and Niftymuffins and drink Niftyapple juice . . ."

"Yay! Niftyparty with the humans!" cried the gnomes. They fetched firefly lanterns and festive paper and began stringing them from house to house. From somewhere a bouncy cheerful tune piped up. The decorating Gnomes began to sing merrily.

Valerie and Kaylana exchanged pained glances and kicked their mounts again. Nightshade gurgled in throaty nausea. Arcie was petrified by a female Gnome, who had managed to scramble up his pony's loose reins and was sitting on the animal's neck and batting her impossibly long eyelashes at him.

"Gee, you're pretty nifty for a human," she squeaked. "Nifty hat! Wanna dance?"

"Uhg, no thanks," stammered Arcie, and after a quick check to see who was watching, swatted her off her perch. She sailed through the air with a squeal but landed safely in a tiny pond.

"You look like you've seen some un-nifty times, humans," piped up the bearded Gnome again. "But that's all right! We'll get you new clothes, all nifty and bright and happy, and we'll be your nifty friends, and pretty soon you'll be nifty just like us!" He beamed at the stricken party, which abruptly clapped panicked heels to its mounts' flanks. Except for Blackmail, of course, who rode out of the clearing with greatest dignity, even in his disgust, his warhorse's huge hooves completely annihilating several mushroom houses. The renegades raced out of the clearing, little cries echoing behind them of, "Hey! Come back, nifty humans! We haven't even had the nifty party games yet! There's pin the tail on the Nifty and bobbing for Niftyfruits . . . " The terrible, sickly music followed, ringing in their ears.

Sam halted a few feet away from the clearing, staring at a huge half-rotted dead tree. Blackmail, on his horse, stomped up to him and stopped. They looked at each other. They looked at the tree. Then, with a gesture, Blackmail dismounted, pushed Sam on his horse aside, and unslung the massive black sword. He hefted it, then swung with mighty force at the trunk, cleaving it off its base.

It creaked and fell, slow and unstoppable, crashing down with a thunderous noise upon the village. The disgusting piping of music stopped. With a satisfied nod, the two men headed off on their horses into the night forest.

In the nighttime camp of Sir Fenwick and the Verdant Company, Fenwick's friend and officer, the journeyman wizard named Towser, was running.

He ran across the camp, his green coat-robes flapping, leaped over a couple of dozing Verdants, and charged up to Fenwick, who was sitting and taking the burrs out of a Feyhound's fur. They had traveled all day, but no sign of the villains' trail yet. Fenwick looked up as Towser stopped.

"Slow down, old friend! What is it?" he asked, standing.

"Sir!" exclaimed Towser. "Young Arnold, sir, the warrior. He was gathering firewood with the others and banged his head on a limb!"

"Why is that so worrisome?" interrupted Fenwick. "Have one of the healers see to him; surely a bump on the head can't be so serious?"

"It's not that, sir!" Towser explained frantically. "The bump knocked out some kind of mind lock he'd had on him. He saw them, sir! They're going the opposite way!"

* * *

The next evening they skirted around the lights of Glinabar, stopping only a moment on a high hill to admire the city. The city, built with Elven influence and that of humans who could not bear to harm the rich ancient trees of the forest, was fascinating. Straddling the Silverwend River, it was a metropolis that sprawled both up and out, weaving around the great trees, as well as ascending up their immense trunks so buildings and streets continued up among the branches, over swaying bridges and great arches of wood and stone. All was elegantly crafted and, in the dim night, lit up like a Yuletide tree with shining lights strung along the bridges and streets to keep travelers from falling. The houses, shops, and inns twinkled like tiny suns, and the faint smells of food and soft drifts of music and revelry could be heard.

"It's beautiful," sighed Robin.

"Roast venison," whimpered Arcie, sniffing the air. "Can't we . . . "

"No," sighed Sam. "This isn't Dous, Arcie, where people like you and I were the first to settle and the last to leave. This is real Good territory, heroes aplenty. We walk in there, me and Blackmail and Valerie all looking like the villains from a historical play, and we'll be like mice in a den of cats."

"It would be nice to just slip in there and set a few things ablaze," said Valerie wistfully. "I bet all that dry wood would go up like a—"

"Save the world first, my fellows, and you can come back to enjoy it later," interrupted Kaylana. "We must not waste so much time. Valerie, can you send Nightshade up to scout? The *Fa'halee* must stand out among the other trees, and we must know which way to go from here."

With bad grace Valerie sent the raven winging into the air. A few minutes later it returned, and the two conversed. Valerie looked up, then, and pointed northeast. "That way. Half a night's ride, as the crow flies."

"We're not flying like a crow, though," grumbled

Arcie, as they set off again, the lights of Glinabar becoming lost in the trees behind them.

It was a lot farther than half a night's ride by horseback and through unknown terrain. They did not reach their destination that night. When they camped at dawn, they did not know that miles away, a *very* put-out Sir Fenwick was urging men and horses and hounds to ride like the wind. No one, especially no villains, could be allowed to pull a stunt like that on him and survive. This was more than just heroism . . . this was a matter of pride. Fenwick fumed as he led the way, bent low over his blood-bay stallion's neck, the thunder and belling of riders and hounds behind him.

Cool dusk fell, and the villains moved on hurriedly through the thick woods. The ground was uneven here, and the horses stumbled often. Robin volunteered once again to lead, after the crack of hoof on stone had made him wince too often, and with his combined sapience and knowledge of horse-travel managed to pick out the best path over the jutting rocks and twisting roots.

"He's pretty good at getting about in a forest," Sam commented quietly to Arcie. The stout thief, who had been noticing the same thing, nodded thoughtfully to himself.

"Sam," he muttered softly, "You know, about these Test things . . . "

Valerie sent Nightshade wheeling up into the sky every so often to help guide their progress. The deeper shadows of near midnight had just turned when they burst out of the thick woods into a small clearing, and the object of their search lay before them.

In the center of a circular clearing, perhaps thirty paces wide, stood a monolith that could only be the *Fa'halee.* A vast trunk, wider than the span of the arms of ten men, loomed up from a knotwork of ponderous roots. The bark, shaggy and dusty, glowered like old dried blood in the moonlight. The tree went up and up and up, branches and limbs garbed in brushlike clusters of flat needles unlike any leaves they had ever seen . . . they tilted their heads back almost in unison to follow the height, Arcie unable to see the top until his head smacked into the cantle of his saddle. It seemed as though the tiny distant summit must stab the moon itself. Kaylana was the first to recover.

"Well, this is it, obviously. Now we must locate the Test."

Valerie extended her hand, concentrating, spreading her fingers before her face. Sparks of green and blue crackled around her fingers and discharged with faint popping noises off the tips of her black pointed nails. "Powerful," she reported, "Just as before . . . except this time I'm also getting a lot of interference from the tree itself."

"Robin!" cried a cheery voice. The centaur minstrel turned, and saw Arcie, grinning broadly, motioning him over. He trotted up, ears pricked forward curiously, as the Barigan dismounted and tethered his pony.

"The girls'll be messing about with yon old tree for some fair time," confided the thief. "No telling what they want with it, really. Let's us just get comfy whilst we waits . . . Sam! Blackmail!" he called, motioning them over. " 'Tis been a long ride. Let's rest and refresh ourselves, and give our minstrel friend here a chance to show off his talents!"

Confused but compliant, Sam dismounted and secured his horse, as Blackmail did the same and Arcie queried Robin about his repertoire of music.

"Arcie, are you sure it's a good idea to be making a lot of noise here?" Sam asked, looking around. "After all, this is Fenwick's woods . . . "

"Bah! Fenwick!" scoffed Arcie, making a dismissive gesture with the wineskin he was holding, and subtly winking at Sam, the old code for I'm-doing-something-here-just-play-along-and-help-me-out. "Fenwick could not find his own rump with both hands."

It was unusual for the Verdant Company to travel by night, but they had done so in the past, and would do so again. Fenwick had long ago learned the limits of his army and knew just how far to push; several hours of forced march, a period of rest, and then on again. Slowly the Company ate up the distance, and even had the energy for a cheer when they saw the valley of Glina spread out below them . . .

"A tune, minstrel, a tune," insisted Arcie. "Give us . . . oh, I dinna . . . do ye know 'Jack and the Dryad,' perhaps?" He pulled out his pipe and began stuffing it, as the four of them relaxed at the edge of the clearing. The centaur flushed nervously and took out his harp.

Valerie and Kaylana, at the base of the *Fa'halee,* looked over at them as the first strains of music began. Valerie frowned.

"What are those sunlight-crawlers up to now?" she muttered. Kaylana shook her head.

"We have not the time to deal with it. We must find the entrance to the Test, if it is indeed hidden by this tree. 'Touch tip to root where Hero stood.' But where is that?"

"I would suppose there." Valerie pointed to a small slab of marble stone set into the deep moss near the base of the tree. They walked over to it and read the inscription, as the sounds of centaur and human voices raised in loud bawdy song belted across the grove.

"Here in the First Year of Light, Triumph of the Victory, The Elven Lord Tiratillais Pallindarthinar Fallinnamir—" Kaylana sputtered with difficulty over the ringing Elven name, "did pass his Lands and Kingship into the Hands of the great Hero Fen-Alaran, witnessed for all eternity by the Blood Guardsman, Ancient Spirit Tree, the *Fa'halee.* May all the Children of Man in Trois keep this Grove sacred."

"Sacred groves, isn't that one of your Druidical things?" Valerie looked at the Druid, who frowned.

"Yes and no. All Druidic practice was lost with the Victory. Elves worshiped trees as symbols without understanding them, or knowing what the trees themselves worshiped. Elves knew the dance of life, but they followed Light, rather than walking the balance. But, both they and my people are gone now, and there remains this puzzle to solve. To touch the tip to the root . . ."

"Looks like a job for you, Druid. Bend this tree and let's get this under way."

Off to the side, she could hear the Barigan complimenting the centaur on his playing, and plying him with "A drink to soothe yer golden throat, my lad." An explosion of equine coughing followed, and the voice saying merrily, "Good stuff, aye! Finest Barigan whiskey, that are! Have some more, 'tis better after yer throat go numb."

Kaylana looked up again, at the immense span towering over her. The marble marker was directly at the base of the tree. She admittedly had quite a bit of power over plants, but to coax such a giant to fold itself double, wood and fibers snapping and straining . . . She set her brow, and sunk the end of her staff into the soft soil at the base of the tree, until she felt the shivering roots of the tree's life beneath it. Her green eyes closed, and she concentrated.

Sweat beaded her brow, unfelt as her mind dived into the roots and struggled with the tree. She tried coaxing, but the tree seemed to ignore her, its thoughts too ancient and slow even for her methodical magic. It was too . . . Elven, she realized. Its aura pattern was unlike any tree she had ever known. It was a plant that did not belong to the Six Lands, and possibly not even to this world. But what other world was there? Where the Elves had gone? Somewhere, beyond the stars or behind the sun, was there a land full of these huge red trees?

She tried then to force the tree to bend, attempting to wrest control of its life-force, to shrink half its cells while expanding the others, to pull it around as a blossom follows the sun, but the tree resisted like a rock. When she persisted, it seemed to lash out, a slap of powerful Elven magic that made her stumble, concentration slipping. She was barely able to channel the excess power away through her staff. All around her, the moss and tiny plants instantly folded themselves over obediently, as Kaylana slumped against her staff, panting. It would take a whole circle of Druids to bend this giant. As her burning eyes opened, she saw by the shadows that perhaps a quarter hour had elapsed. Sam and Blackmail and Valerie watched her curiously, Arcie seemed to be mournfully regarding an empty wineskin, and the centaur was trotting back and forth, hiccuping and singing a bit. He blinked at the grass as it folded up under his hooves and stumbled over to them.

"Whatcha doin'?" he asked, smiling lopsidedly.

"Trying to touch the tip of the tree to its roots," replied Valerie, impatiently, "and obviously not succeeding."

"If it was a younger tree," began Kaylana defensively.

"Why don' you jush cut the tip off and put it there?" asked Robin, looking up and swaying.

"How are we supposed to cut it off?" retorted Sam, feeling he ought to defend the Druid somehow. "Not even I want to climb up this thing, especially that last twenty feet where it's no thicker than rope. And I certainly can't fly up there."

There was silence a moment, and then everyone turned to look at Nightshade, who stuck his black pointed tongue out at them.

"Oh, come on, cutting yon tip off willna work," exclaimed Arcie. "That's *cheating.*"

"What else do you expect from villains?" Valerie said, a smile starting to form.

"If you cut the tip off, the tree will never grow any taller," Kaylana put in, but without much protest.

"It *can't* work," insisted Arcie. "That's, I mean, it *are* cheating. No magic Test are going to work that way."

"You never know 'til you try," hiccuped Robin sagely.

There was a pause.

The Verdant Company swept through Glinabar, horns blowing. The remainder of the Company, staying on call in the city, leaped to horse. Fenwick shouted orders, and in a moment a great net of skilled warriors, mages, and woodsmen swept out into the night, curling around over many miles. It was not long before the hunting horns blew the triumphant signal—a trail.

"Fine work, my feather-wether darlingkins," cooed Valerie, as the raven swooped down with a triumphant croak, a pointed sprig of bushy green needles in his beak. He had easily flown to the top of the great tree and nipped the last foot or so free, noticing to himself the sharp taste of sap. Now Valerie carefully lay the sprig upon the marble slab and stood back. Nothing happened.

"See, I told you so—" Arcie began, when suddenly a green light burned from the trunk of the *Fa'halee.* With a flash it resolved itself into delicate swirling carvings in the wood, done in colors that glowed from within, unfaded by moonlight.

It was like a mural of an archway, definitely reminiscent of the one they had encountered in the Smuggler's Net. Surrounding the archway was a mural of trees, through which scenes of hunting and archery could be seen. On the archway itself was the figure of a man, a woodsman by gear and garb, with a familiar look about him. He wore a green jerkin, fringed vest and boots, brown leggings, and carried a longbow and sword. One hand held the collar of a Feyhound, white and red as birch and cedar, and the other was extended towards them, palm out.

"Fenwick!" exclaimed Arcie. "Why did thems put Fenwick's picture down here?"

"It is not Fenwick," answered Kaylana. "See, the pointed features, and an older face."

"It's the Hero Fen-Alaran," said Robin, wonder filling his voice despite the alcoholic haze. "Grandfather of Lord Fendalis, who ish the father of Sir Fenwick. Am I dreaming?"

"Yes," replied Sam seriously, looking at him. Robin nodded thoughtfully.

"I thought sho," he said.

"Fenwick's grandfather?" Arcie asked meanwhile,

looking at the mural. He felt a terrible urge to draw a big hairy mustache on the figure.

"It makes sense," said the assassin. "What does that inscription say?"

Sharp runes were cut into the stone over the archway. Sam could pick out a letter here and there, but ancient languages hadn't been a big part of his training.

"It says," translated Valerie, "This is the Test of the Strider . . . "

"Spider?!" yelped Arcie, looking around.

"*Strider,* Barigan," corrected Kaylana gently. "That is the name once given to those we now call woodsmen."

"Ah," Arcie relaxed. "Go ahead, Valerie."

"Thank you," said Valerie coldly. "Test of the Strider, 'for the Emerald Stone. Let you who are keen of eye and ear, quick of foot and bowsight clear, enter this test by pressing here.' "

"Rhymes," commented Sam. "Sort of. Well, we've been in this dilemma before . . . Who's to go?"

Blackmail raised his head, as though listening to something, and then walked quickly to the edge of the clearing, where their horses were tethered.

"Here, Robin," Arcie spoke up, "what kind of wood d'you suppose that are?" He carefully pointed to the carving's outstretched palm, carved from some golden-pink wood. "It looks to me as it has the same texture as your harp!"

"Really?" hiccuped the centaur, trotting forward. "Let me see . . . "

He reached out a hand . . .

"Stop!" called out Kaylana, but too late.

Robin, hiccuping, curiously pressed his hand to the wood . . . and vanished, in a brilliant flash of green light.

"Got him!" crowed Arcie, and he and Sam triumphantly exchanged an enthusiastic ritual rogue's Partners Handshake.

"How could you do that!" exclaimed Kaylana. "He does not even know what he is doing! He had done nothing to you!"

"Miss, remember, we're evil!" replied Arcie, with a grin. "Them Tests kills people. When ponyboy appears out here, dead of some weird occurrence, it'll give us a clue as to what to expect in there, the better for one o' us to survive, whoever's stupid enough to go in there next."

Seeing Kaylana still fuming, Sam tried to comfort her. "You never know," he said. "He may even succeed. All centaurs are traditionally taught how to use a bow, certainly, and the Test asks for someone quick of foot and keen of ear . . . he's got more in the way of feet and ears than any of us."

There was a clatter, suddenly, and Blackmail reappeared, motioning them urgently. Distracted from the glowing Test mural, they followed him to the lip of the bowl-shaped clearing. The dark knight motioned for silence, and they listened.

On the night breeze, faint but getting closer, came the distant sound of hunting horns.

Robin found himself in an open forest glade. There was no sign of his companions, or of the huge tree, the one with the reddish bark and the deep gray-black needles. Indeed, the whole area seemed misty and dreamlike.

Dream, he thought through a slight alcoholic haze that was slowly clearing. *The dream-Sam I spoke to said I was dreaming, so I must be dreaming still. I wonder what happens in this part of the dream? I feel like there's something I'm supposed to do . . .* The hazy images of trees drifted around him, and the faint sounds of birds, animals, and wind in leaves tickled his ears. The smells of the forest reached him, leafmold and moss and pollen. Leaves of dark gray whispered overhead, against a sky of paler gray, with white clouds. Piles of dead leaves, some orange and red and yellow from autumn, drifted under the illusion trees. A faint path seemed to stretch before him.

He started forward, stepping across the muddy ground . . . and then jerked back as a pair of snapping blades just missed his left forehoof. He froze.

It's like a trap! he thought. *A trap in a forest? How do I get out of here?*

The area was probably a very carefully prepared set of traps, with perhaps a single safe path through it . . . that was the way dreams usually went. The trees undoubtedly hid all kinds of fatal and intricate devices.

It's a dream, he told himself sharply. *I'm going to wake up now. Now!* But the forest remained there. Like it or not, he was going to have to play by the rules. He examined the ground in front of him. It was muddy and soft for a few paces, then led into moss, leafmold, and finally stone. At the end of his field of vision, bounded by the ghost trees, he could see a large standing stone archway. That must be what he'd have to get to. In the mud were various tracks.

Tracks, thought Robin. *I remember . . . something about a test? Like, maybe, a woodsman test? Tracking something?* But tracking what? There were all kinds of prints here . . .

He cast his mind back to the mural in desperation. The woodsman, standing there, the hunting of stags, bears . . . He looked at the mud. Stag prints! He knew a bit about tracking; the Commots were bounded by some fairly wild lands, and any young colt who wandered in had better know his way around or risk becoming a meal for a wood-tiger or hulah. If herbivores traveled a path, it might also be known to predators.

He stepped on one of the stag prints cautiously. There was the faintest of faint sounds, and he ducked as an arrow whistled over his head. Not the stag, then. But what?

The Feyhound. It was the only animal in the central image of the mural he had seen . . . That had to be it. He looked at the tracks again, and finally found one that looked like that of a large dog. He put his hoof on it. Nothing happened. His hoof rested firmly.

He looked around. There were other dog-like footprints around, but only one set of the size and angular shape of the Feyhound. He stepped into another, and then another. He was making progress.

The Feyhound, he noted, had a strange loping gait, if these indeed were its tracks. It had a kind of rhythm to it, like that old song they had used to dance to at festivals in the Commots.

The connection with music made him secure, and his four legs swiftly adapted to the loping gait, constricted slightly because his body was much longer than that of a Feyhound. *Left* **hind,** *right* **fore,** *right* **hind,** *left* **fore. . . .**

So natural was it to the music that he hardly needed to see where the tracks were. His hooves dropped one after the other into the safe areas marked by the prints of the Feyhound. It was not until he reached the hard earth where the tracks finally petered out that he noticed the tracks had been getting fainter and fainter . . .

Robin lost the rhythm and stopped. He looked behind him, but the way he had come had dissolved in flowing mist. Ahead the earth shifted into bare stone, with no tracks visible.

He hiccuped mournfully to himself, the whiskey making his thoughts woozy.

Best stay with what I know, he told himself. *I had the rhythm there, same beats and pace as the Dawn-Summer Dance. Just go forward, keep moving, and hope I hit enough safe spots to make it.*

With that, he took out his harp, and strummed a few quick notes to recall the music to his memory. Then he put it back safely, and started his feet into the steps, in place.

Centaurs and their kindred, fauns and satyrs and suchlike creatures of the mystic woodlands, seem to be built for dancing. With the swift angular grace of a fine horse, and two extra legs, centaurs in particular are noted for their incredibly complex dances of celebration and religious ritual. Robin could almost hear the shing-shing of the dancing bells on his hooves as he pranced in place. He'd left the Commots to live a life of music, and gone into Mizzamir's offer with the hopes of seeing the world.

Well, he had seen the world, and now parts of it were trying to kill him, even in his dreams. He caught the cadence, and stepped out at a brisk pace, moving his legs in the lope of a running Feyhound and heading as fast as he could.

A section of floor slid away under one hoof, but his threelegged stance held him up and let him move on without a pause where a human would have stumbled and fell. He ducked as a spear whistled by, and pranced away as the two sections under his alternate feet gave out at once, and dodged the strike from a hissing snake that darted out of a crack at his legs. Then with a final leap, he landed on the moss in front of the standing stone archway, and was safe.

He caught his breath and looked around. The dream scene dissolved in mist, and he was left standing at the far end of a long hallway. The archway had turned into a pedestal, on which rested a strung longbow and a single silver arrow. Across the hall, at the far end, he could dimly make out a target, a fuzzy blur in the distance, rings not even distinguishable. His jaw dropped.

"Hoofrot!" he exclaimed. His voice echoed in the huge empty room. "I can barely see that thing, let alone hit it." He picked up the bow. It was very fine, of dark wood ringed with bands of dark gray, about the same shade as the leaves in the illusion. It seemed to be in perfect shape, but then, why should it not? A dream bow was not bound by the problems of being left strung. He took up the arrow, fitted it, and looked at the target again.

"Well, I've played this dream so far," he said, wondering who he was talking to in this dream world. The last of the Barigan whiskey was bubbling out of his system through his sweat, and he felt strangely clear-headed for one dreaming, despite his confusion as to where he was. "But I'm a minstrel. I haven't practiced the longbow in years. I'm going to even the odds."

He stepped down from the shooting post and started to walk closer to the target. He intended to get as close as he needed, then fire the arrow, but it seemed the forces of his strange dream didn't hold with cheating.

The target shimmered, and transformed into a huge scaly creature with great fangs and hairy limbs like a bear; it charged at him with a roaring howl, great claws striking sparks from the floor.

Robin's instant instinct was to flee. The familiar thickening of the air, so common in dreams of being pursued, flooded in around him. Death stared him in the face. Even though he knew he couldn't outrun the monster, his limbs ached to try. He fought his equine instincts and stood his ground, drawing the longbow, forcing himself to think calmly, to aim. Fletchings tickling his cheek, the beast so close he could see its burning eyes and smell the terrifying reek of its carnivore breath. His arms trembled with the effort of pulling the heavy bow. One shot, one shot only . . . There, where the leg met the chest . . . he fired as the beast leaped into the air with a triumphant snarl.

The beast somersaulted and tumbled crashing toward him. He dodged as it rolled past him from the force of its charge, coming to a halt on the smooth floor in a pool of dark blood. Robin stared in astonishment at the silver arrow sticking from its throat. An instant later, the body shimmered and vanished, and in its place lay a large sparkling gray stone.

"Fenwick!" cursed Valerie, as she scrambled up on her gelding. "How could he have gotten here so fast?"

"Never mind!" shouted Sam. "We've got to move! Come *on,* Kaylana!"

The Druid stood firm. "We must get the Emerald Segment from the Test!" she replied firmly. "It is no use running now to have the world be destroyed around us soon after!"

Just then, a brilliant flash of green light made them turn.

Robin had picked up the stone, a wedge of crystal. Light flashed from it, and he found himself suddenly back in the glade, the shapes of the villains visible at the edge of the clearing, as they turned in surprise toward him. The shock of sudden air and the rushing adrenaline that flooded him from his near-escape took over.

Thud.

"He made it!" exclaimed Arcie in blank amazement, as they ran forward to where the centaur lay unconscious on the moss. Sam scooped up the chunk of brilliant emerald crystal that had fallen from the minstrel's hand and concealed it in the largest pocket of his black tunic. Kaylana quickly began to revive the unfortunate centaur, slapping his face gently and waving acrid-smelling herbs under his nose. Blackmail and Valerie, already on their mounts, fidgeted impatiently to be off. The horns sounded again, closer. Robin staggered to his feet, saying, "Kaylana, you know, I had the strangest dream . . . " in a puzzled tone. The Druid vaulted onto her piebald gelding and cried, "No time, minstrel! We must ride!"

The renegades spurred their horses and galloped from the clearing, Kaylana leading the way, not from cowardice, but trusting her knowledge of woodlore to lead the others through the tangled night maze of forest at the fastest pace possible. Robin, still shaking his head dizzily, followed last, beginning to question his dream . . .

"Where be we heading for?" shouted Arcie, crouched low on his pony to avoid the lashing branches.

"Keep to the northwest!" called Valerie. "If memory serves me, we may be able to reach the Saltangum!"

"Cross the Saltangum?!" whinnied Robin. "Why?"

"Would you rather have your underbelly torn open by Feyhounds?" snapped Sam. Robin fell silent. Of course, he knew the gallant woodsman Fenwick and his men would not harm him, but his duty to Mizzamir was to follow these villains, follow and report. And if they were going to run, then he must run also.

It was like a nightmare, Sam thought. The whipping of sharp branches across the face and shoulders, the labored breathing of Damazcus. Occasionally there would be the brief horror of running into a spiderweb with one's face. Sam shuddered in revulsion and scrubbed his face with the edge of his cloak. And still the horns and hounds could be heard, growing ever louder. A high scream overhead made him look up; a great hawklike shape wheeling across the sky. Not the swift sculling form of Valerie's familiar, but a huge soaring bird, like an eagle . . .

* * *

Fenwick had called a five-minute break, in the secure shadow of the sacred *Fa'halee.* He had forgotten the Company was somewhat out-of-shape, despite his best efforts to keep them in fighting trim. After all, they had not had any great evil to combat for several years. The night air was cloudy with the fog of panting horses and dogs, and the smell of sweat was thick.

The sun-eagle, brittle-minded from being flown at night, skree'd out of the sky to land on Fenwick's upheld wrist, and perched there, wings pounding, keening frantically as it tried to convey what it had seen. He had to calm the bird before he could make out coherent words in the avian language. What he heard gave him a splendid idea.

"So, they're heading for the Saltangum?" he said to himself, stroking the eagle's proud head. "To cross Saltangum Ford, and they think I won't follow?" He motioned to Towser, who sat by his horse, his elegant robecoat of deep green in disarray from the ride. Towser stood up, wincing at his saddlesores, and hastened over.

"Towser, old friend, I'm sorry for this exertion. But now I have something you can use your magic for. How are the other wizards faring?"

"Zanithir fell off a half-hour ago, and bruised his arm," reported the lead wizard ruefully, "but he's all right. Sir . . . " he paused, uncertain, then handed the young prince something. "Mella found this on the Inscription Stone when we arrived."

Fenwick examined the token. It was a sprig of green needles, of a strangely pointed shape. "I don't understand. What use is this?"

"Sir . . . " Towser braced himself. "We were suspicious, and Marcus cast a Seeing . . . it . . . it's the tip of the *Fa'halee,* sir."

There was silence a moment. Then the ranger's hand slowly folded around the sprig, crushing it. There was the smell of fresh sap.

"Towser," said Fenwick, his voice cold as the slopes of night. "Towser, take your mages, and Team B of the

Company. Use your magic. Teleport yourselves to the Ford. Divide into two. Take up positions distant but within sight on either side of the Ford. When we reach the Ford, I want you to be ready in case the villains should attempt to cross. I want the mages on each side to cast that lovely spell of yours, Waithain's Wracking Waves, into the Saltangum Ford."

"Sir . . . " Towser was wide-eyed. "At this time of year the Ford is filled with river debris . . . logs and mud and branches. It will be like a liquid avalanche."

"I know." Fenwick whistled for the hunt to begin again, and swung up onto his stallion. "The Druid alone would have the power to save herself from the waves. The natural elements are under her command . . . and I know Mizzamir has given the centaur minstrel some means to save himself. But the villains who have desecrated the *Fa'halee* will be slain, and their corpses washed into the Saltangum at our feet."

"What if they survive the flood?" Towser asked.

"They'll wish they hadn't."

Though the renegades traveled as fast as they could, the Company was far more skilled at moving through the forest; they knew all the terrain, and the paths to avoid that cost the villains precious time. The air was now illuminated with the gray pre-light of dawn. Horns sounded as the trail grew steadily warmer.

"This is insane," panted Sam, "trying to escape the greatest hunter in the Six Lands, in the middle of the night, on his own terrain, without rest . . . "

"Why are they chasing you anyway?" exclaimed Robin, curiosity and frustration getting the better of subtlety and caution. His query went unanswered as they galloped down a crumbling hill and were met with a breeze of salt and mud.

"The Saltangum is just ahead!" cried Kaylana.

"And with Fenwick just behind," replied Arcie tersely, holding his cap atop his red and silver curls as the pursuit came so close they could hear the shouts of the men.

Valerie risked a glance back, to see the shapes of white hounds and mounted riders come flooding out of the trees and down the hills in pursuit. As they ran into the first tangled grasses and twisted trees of the sea-marsh called Saltangum, there was a strange high whistling, and suddenly the air was raining arrows. Kaylana's horse squealed as an arrow took it in the leg, and stumbled.

An explosion came out of the villains' ranks, a black knight on a black warhorse that had wheeled in the mud and turned back, and now headed straight for the charging Verdant Company. With greatsword held high and helm-plumes whipping in the bitter air, his great horse steaming like a dragon, his silence held more menace than the fiercest war cry. The leading men of the Company faltered, unsure despite themselves.

Far down the banks of the Saltangum to either side, two groups of wizards watched through spyglasses . . .

Blackmail tore into the ranks of the Company like a scythe. The lightly armored men had no defense other than to run. Those who did not, ended their lives quickly, and in several pieces. Weapons clanged off his armor without effect. Fenwick's command held firm; he quickly directed his men around and past the knight to continue pursuit, while he and his officers approached the knight.

"Knight he may be, and his armor may be magical," Fenwick muttered under his breath, pain in his heart to see the bodies of several of his men, "but I have magic the equal of his." So saying, he reached around into the special scabbard on his back and withdrew the sword Truelight, slayer of darkness. He spurred his mount to catch up to the knight, the sword glimmering magical light. So great was its power that, while the knight was busy fighting, his great black warhorse saw the shining blade and spooked, running away from the combat.

The knight allowed his horse to run. Apparently seeing the rest of the Company wash around him and continue their pursuit, he sped after them, and after his companions. For such a huge animal, the warhorse moved surprisingly fast. Fenwick had to content himself with swiftly drawing his bow and firing an arrow into the unprotected knee-joint of the animal. The horse barely faltered, and kept running, plowing through the forces of the Company and the finest horses of Trois, outdistancing them, and catching up to the fleeing villains.

The black knight's attack had bought the villains some time. The marsh of the Saltangum was treacherous, and pools of the legendary quick-mud sucked at their horses' hooves. They had to slow themselves to avoid the deeper of these, that could engulf a man in minutes, leaving no trace.

Blackmail, galloping over the crest of a sand dune, apparently didn't realize this until too late. His horse swerved to try to avoid a pool, but its injured leg tweaked under the stress and it stumbled, throwing its rider into the mud. The knight's armor, his invincible defense, was now about to be his silent doom as the thick, greedy quick-mud pulled him down.

The other villains, too concerned with running away, didn't notice, except for Sam. He saw the knight fall, and stopped his horse, steeling his nerves against the sounds of approaching pursuit, and turned back, to try to help. Thus it was that he was witness to a strange occurrence.

As soon as Blackmail fell, his horse stopped, turning, limping on its leg, and whinnied anxiously. Blackmail made shooing motions at it, as he groped in the mud for his sword. But the stallion instead came up to the edge of the pool, stepping into the shallows to reach closer, then tossed its head in a very deliberate way. The thick black scalloped-leather reins flew over its head and landed next to the knight, who saw them but ignored them as he tried to keep himself from sinking. He made the shooing motion at the horse again. With a snort the horse jerked back its head and whipped back the reins, then tossed them again. This time they landed over the knight's head and shoulders, and, as he lifted his arms free of the mud to remove them, shaking his head emphatically, the stallion jerked again, and got the reins beneath his arms. Then the huge beast set its four legs firmly in the mud and pulled, bent awkwardly in the slope of the pool, blood spattering from its injured leg.

The horse pulled and backed, and with a drawn-out squelching sound, the knight was pulled free. As he scrambled up the bank he saw his mount's injury and gave the horse a shove in the direction the others had gone, while he turned to face the charging Company, barely a hundred yards away. The horse buckled its legs, and slammed itself into the side of the knight. As he stumbled, it shoved its broad shoulders underneath him, and, staggering slightly, stood up, the knight falling into the saddle from his own weight. Then, before he could dismount again, the stallion ran after the others, stumbling and limping. Sam wheeled his horse around and ran as the knight followed, the Company hard at his heels. Again came the rain of arrows, as Kaylana led them to the Ford, and plunged in without hesitating.

With this second archery attack Robin decided he had had enough. He ducked around behind a grass covered sand dune and hunkered down, hiding, as the sounds of pursuit swept past.

The villains plunged into the Ford. The sea-channel between the lands of Trois and Kwart was at its narrowest here, a slow-rocking span the width of several rivers, made passable by a land bridge that kept the water, at its deepest point, at the height of a horse's neck. During high tide, though, it was impassable by all but boats. The marshy ground of the Saltangum and the tides prevented bridges or settlements being built. Even now as they crossed, the tide was only just beginning to recede, and they realized their horses were going to have to swim out in the deepest part of the channel. The water was cold and muddy, brackish and full of floating logs and branches, but the shouts and arrows of the Company urged them on. Though Blackmail struggled with his stallion's reins, trying to get the injured animal to shore. The stallion's bridle had no bit to enforce its rider's commands, and the horse forged grimly on. Sam, looking back at this, saw Fenwick halt his men at the edge of the Ford.

Strange, he thought. *Why aren't they following? They shouldn't give up this easy . . .*

Then he heard the water.

Two muddy-green walls of water loomed in the distance on either side—flowing leaping lions, roaring with manes of white foam, that whorled up out of nowhere and came rushing down upon them as they floundered into the deepest part of the channel . . . Their shadows fell over Sam, vision of tumbling waves, the wrench of the current as it yanked at his mount, Damazcus's last, terrified squeal, and then . . .

The impact was so powerful it almost knocked him senseless. He was helplessly swept off his horse, his ankle twisting as it was wrenched from the stirrup. The water pushed him down through its depths, smashing him with heavy sodden logs caught up in the flood, and bounced him off the rocky bottom of the Ford, making him gasp; inhaling water. Sam choked and spun, pinned below the water by the rushing force as he felt consciousness and life begin to slip away . . .

Kaylana was dashed from her horse as the water hit and her staff was torn from her grasp. The water pulled at her, clinging, drowning, and she was battered by debris, sogged, helpless . . . then one of the chunks of wood that struck her felt of familiar. She grabbed it and felt her power returning. She clung to her staff, concentrating her will. An eddy of calm surrounded her, and she spun to the surface, gasping. But the water was under another's magic, strong with the power of light, and she could not regain control of it to calm the flood and save her companions.

Someone surfaced near her, a gasp of breath that was answered by anxious cawing, as the raven tried to grasp Valerie's cloak and hold her head above water. The sorceress had a gash on her pale forehead, and she seemed to have surfaced more by luck than by skill. Kaylana kicked over to her, the eddy surrounding her like a halo.

"Give me your hand!" she shouted.

The black-nailed hand flailed desperately out of the

froth, and Kaylana grabbed it, pulling Valerie into the eddy, holding her head above water.

"Where is that stupid assassin?" were the sorceress's first words, as she found she could breathe again. "I can't cast magic enough to save us without my Darkportal!" Kaylana looked, then lunged out with her staff. A sudden weight rewarded her as the crook on the end of her staff caught a dark shadow that had gone spinning past underwater.

"He is on the end of my staff! I will channel the energy to you!"

"Think *cold,* then, and help me!"

Valerie gasped a phrase of harsh, prickly words, bitter as the killing frosts of winter. Kaylana felt the evil magic flow from the Darkportal on the assassin, up through her staff, and down her arm into the sorceress. Her own magical powers, woven through her soul and through the staff, strained and trembled at the imbalance of the power they were containing, but Kaylana closed her eyes, thought of cold, balanced cold power, and concentrated on making herself a perfect, neutral channel.

Something bumped against their legs, a huge, smooth, cold, slippery something. They slid and tumbled as a large ice-floe, swirled and sculpted from the spinning waters on the bottom of the river, surfaced. Whorling columns and sweeps rose from the surface and around the edges. Draped over one of these was the huge form of Blackmail, struggling feebly. Sam, unmoving and waterlogged as a drowned rat, lay sprawled on the ice, the hood of his cloak still caught in Kaylana's staff. Valerie rolled over, coughing and gagging as she tried to clear her lungs. A feeble splash next to them, and Kaylana lunged forward to grab a struggling Arcie out of the roaring water with her other hand. The Barigan was heaved up onto the ice, where he lay gasping. The floe rushed along the water, spinning.

"What happened to that idiot centaur?" coughed Valerie. Kaylana shook her head.

Sam's consciousness returned in a rush, and he rolled

over, coughed up what seemed to him to be about half the river, and crawled over to Blackmail. The knight was clinging to a rapidly melting whorl of ice, staring mutely out into the crashing water, holding in his hands the torn-away ends of the black leather reins.

"Come on," wheezed Sam, tugging at him. "Come on."

After a long moment the knight turned and allowed the assassin to help him up onto the ice, where they moved away from the treacherous edge and collapsed near the center. As Sam slipped into unconsciousness once more, he saw the knight sitting with his back against a column, unmoving, and, far beyond, the bank of the Saltangum with the tiny figures of the Verdant Company watching them go. The ice raft floated swiftly as they passed out of the area affected by the spell and the water carried them away from their enemies.

"Blast!" snarled Fenwick, throwing his spyglass down on the ground. "I don't know how they did it, but somehow they managed to raise an ice raft and get away! I saw them! Towser!" he barked. The mage hurried up.

"Yes, Sir Fenwick?"

"Lower the water! We must cross at once!"

"Umm," Towser looked decidedly uncomfortable. "We, uh, can't, sir. We expended all our magic to get the flood . . ."

"Well, when is it going to go down, then?" asked the prince.

"Not 'til this time tomorrow, sir." Towser looked miserable. "And we can't teleport until our power returns . . ."

"Blast," muttered Fenwick, staring at the waters.

The waves had washed up the useless part of their quarry on shore. The bodies of a few horses, drowned, broken, and battered to death by the water and waves, necks and legs in a tangle of wrong angles. Even the tack was useless, water-sogged and ruined, and any saddlebags gone or emptied. The vultures and mud-crabs could have it all.

"Well . . . at least we got their horses. They won't be too hard to catch now." Fenwick sighed and signaled to his men for rest call.

V

As the Verdant Company broke down into a comfortable hunting camp at the dry, wooded inland edge of the Saltangum, a long, four-legged figure stepped gingerly up out of the marshes, calling,

"Sir Fenwick? It's me, sir! Don't shoot! Me, Robin of Avensdale . . . "

With a sigh Fenwick went to meet the exhausted centaur, who managed, nonetheless, to doff his battered hat and perform his characteristic double-bow.

"Why didn't you go back to Mizzamir?" demanded Fenwick. "You could have been killed! A battle zone with the forces of evil is no place for games! Lucky for you I instructed my men to keep their shots far away from you. But the marshes are full of quick-mud, and, if you had chosen to go into the Ford . . . !"

"I know, sir, I'm sorry, sir," Robin whickered, lopping his furry ears down in humiliation. "I . . . I just got carried away, that's all . . . "

"Well, exuberance of youth and all that," Fenwick said cheerfully, patting him on his shoulder. "You'd best go report to Mizzamir now; you'll be seeing us again. I calculate that the villains will wash up somewhere in the Fens of Friat this afternoon, and we will be teleporting there tomorrow morning. Go to Mizzamir, report, and get cleaned off and rest . . . it's coming on to rain today, you'd best stay warm and dry."

The ice floe, made by magic and unnatural in these places, was melting rapidly in the strong sea waters off the Kwartan coast. The villains passed the time in uncomfortable misery, falling asleep from exhaustion and then waking again when the cold of the floe began to bite through the skin. Kaylana mixed strong medicinal tea, heated by Valerie's cantrips, to stave off the lung-clog that followed the experience of being half-drowned. Most of their provisions had been lost with the horses, and they ate what few rations they had and were still hungry. They kept to the very center of the melting raft, not speaking, as the waves splashed burning salt in their eyes and the gulls mewed mockingly overhead.

Robin returned to the shining halls of the Castle of Diamond Magic and made a full report to Mizzamir, as instructed. The great Elven Arch-Mage sat back in his chair, and steepled his fingers.

"Very interesting, Robin . . . was there anything else?"

Robin paused a moment, then blurted, "I had a strange dream, sir . . ."

The minstrel recounted the tale of the strange mural in the *Fa'halee,* and his unusual dream that followed. Mizzamir sat straight up in his carved wooden chair and listened intently. When the centaur had finished, twisting his hat in his hands, the wizard sat back again, rubbing his chin in a thoughtful wizardly way.

"Most, most unprecedented," said he at last. "To try to recover the Spectrum Key? To defy the gods? To dare the Tests and the Labyrinth?" For the wizard had seen in Robin's description a pattern and form similar to those he himself had followed in preparing his own Test, as all the Heroes had done by instruction of the gods themselves.

He sat in thought, as Robin stood nervously swishing his tail and flicking his ears. Mizzamir had long ago learned the folly of blindly chasing after things, as Sir Fenwick was still wont to do. The news of Fenwick's attack on the rogues was troubling, but the Prince had been within his jurisdiction. Mizzamir, however, preferred to observe, learn, and think, and then find some way to turn his enemy's actions to his own advantage.

The Test of the Wizard, which he himself had designed, was the extent of his knowledge of the concealment of the Spectrum Key. He did not even know where the Test he had designed had been hidden; the gods had kept that information to themselves. They had shattered and hid the Key because it was an artifact of such power that it could not be destroyed; the very nature of Fate demanded a loophole. Legend had it that the segments of the Key were hidden in the Six Lands, to be guarded by the descendants of the Heroes.

A most unsatisfactory situation, Mizzamir had always felt. The DarkGate must remain closed forever, any chance of it ever opening again should have been removed . . . but with the Key indestructible, what was there to do? Now, after years of research in the boundaries of existence, he had found the solution.

The commoners of this world did not call it "Chiaroscuro," a word that Mizzamir had invented. For after all, there was only one "world," just as there was only one "sun." Or so they thought.

Mizzamir knew otherwise.

By magical folding of the fabric of reality, he had discovered other worlds. To one of these distant worlds had his Elven kin migrated long ago. The border to the lands now walked by his kin were closed fast, but in other lands . . . lands of eternal fire, vacuum, or just wild terrain, or of great steel cities with smoking air . . . in such a land a small thing such as the Spectrum Key could be hidden, and then the border from that land to this sealed forever . . . the DarkGate could never be opened, and Light would rule eternal.

A brilliant idea. His problem had been that he did not have the Key, nor did he know how to get it . . . but now, if someone else might get it for him . . .

Impossible, he realized. The young centaur, by luck and courage and goodness of heart, might have managed to win Fen-Alaran's Test, but the villains he traveled with would never be successful. They were dark, cowardly, evil . . . they would be killed by the Tests. A pity, but that was the way of Fate and gods.

"Do you have the green stone you took from the . . . dream, Robin?" asked Mizzamir gently. Robin shook his head.

"When I woke up, it was gone . . . I didn't even know what kind it was . . . A Greenstone? I thought it was just a lump of gray crystal, sir."

"Gray?" Mizzamir asked, arching an eyebrow. Robin nodded, yawning in spite of himself. He was so weary. His legs were aching from the long run.

"Gray, sir . . . a little bit darker than grass in springtime."

Mizzamir saw the minstrel beginning to sway. "Forgive me, Robin. Rest yourself again in my castle, and tonight, if you will, you shall return to your mission. And when you do, continue to ask what it is that they seek to do. Whatever it may be, say that you will follow along and not interfere, because you wish to record their actions. Be careful! Say whatever you must to convince them to let you accompany them, but do not lie; for if you do, the Druid will know of your falsehood. But that is later. Take your rest now, Robin of Avensdale. You have done well." As the centaur clopped out backwards, bowing respectfully, Mizzamir turned to the stained-glass window and stared out through the tinted panes at the climbing sun.

Late in the afternoon, after a good rest and a meal, Robin was teleported to the coast of Kwart, near where the villains had been expected to land. Robin thought for a moment, then waded into the waters of the channel, and soaked and muddied himself thoroughly before trotting along the shore until he found the remains of an ice-floe, and footprints in the marshy ground. He followed them, and at last caught up with the staggering villains as they struggled to higher ground. Wary of the Druid's ability to tell truth from lie, he explained to the suspicious and short-tempered group that he had hidden behind when the others went into the Ford, escaped being captured by Sir Fenwick, and followed them later. The villains were suspicious, but too exhausted to care much. They climbed on up into the Fens proper, seeking a hilltop free of mud and brackish water. By the time they stopped, unsuccessful, they were all in rather dangerous moods . . .

Dusk fell over the Fens of Friat. Gray and white wisps of fog drifted over the scraggly moorland, ancient site of death and battles. It was a place of sorrows, desolate and tragic with its past. Even so, tiny wildflowers that had never been seen here before were scattered among the tufts of damp grass, their petals closed now against a faint mist of rain. The long-gone ghosts of the War seemed to gather here in the sad damp of an acrid bog, with the faint scents of marsh-gas and moss blowing in the wind, carrying the faint call of spindle-legged mudwalkers and the sound of bitter voices. The rain fell softly at first, then began to strengthen, drumming into the pools and drenching the battered and demoralized figures huddled around a small pile of blackened and smoking wood. It was here that the bitter voices had their origin.

"Well, this be just fine, aren't it? Just great," snapped Arcie, trying without success to get mud out of his boots. "No horses. Only heroes would walk everywhere! And on top of that, mine tobacco's all sogged. Some adventure."

"Oh, to hell with your lung-rot," snarled Sam, drawing his tattered cloak around him, trying to arrange his torn hood as the rain plastered his fair hair to his scalp.

"I could give you a cheerful tune," offered Robin, taking out his harp. Its strings hung limply in the damp.

"You just try it, horse, and I'll send you to the bottom of the bog," hissed Valerie. "I'm in no mood for cheerful tunes."

"Well, that's right, you shouldn't be," muttered Sam. "After all, you might have hurt yourself running away and leaving us to Fenwick."

"I saved your stupid hide, sun-crawler!"

"Yeah, sure. You saved this, right?" he reached into a pocket and took out the amulet. It spun gently. "Despite the fact that you gave me third degree frostbite all over my chest doing it?"

"Toss it, Sam," muttered Arcie. "We all knew do she ever get hold of it she'll have our heads for stew meat. Even without it she's more trouble than she's worth."

"You do that," hissed Valerie, "and I will tear your throat out." She bared her sharp teeth.

"And just where do you get off ordering me around, Arcie?" Sam asked, tucking the amulet back into its hiding place and turning cold hazel eyes on the Barigan, who glared back at him.

"Somebody has to. Ye're too cow-headed to do anything for yerself!" Arcie gripped the hilt of his morning star.

"Cow-headed, eh?" Sam's hand went for one of the daggers. "You little sack of nightsoil, you haven't been worth a rat's ass since you were a maggot. You've been an annoyance all my life; blowing my cover, liquidizing my profits, and now getting me thrown into prison, robbing me blind, and more than once running off, just like sharkbreath, and leaving me to be killed!"

Robin cleared his throat, and started to say something, but was interrupted by Valerie's interjection into the argument.

"Sharkbreath, hm? I'll have you know it makes a hell of a lot more sense to run away than to back a suicidal idiot like you, and as for you, you fat little—" she rounded on Arcie.

"Um, my fellows, we *are* supposed to be saving the world . . . " interjected Kaylana.

"This whole thing is stupid!" barked Sam. "The biggest mistake I ever made . . . "

"Other than being an assassin," sneered Valerie. "For all your boasting you've done nothing but bungle this whole enterprise."

"Aye, some adventure," snapped Arcie.

"Adventure?!" Sam shouted incredulously. "Where do

you get the idea that this is anything more than a wild goose-chase through the most hellish parts of the world with everything in existence trying to kill us! I don't know why I ever went along with this! You, Druid, are an idealistic dreamer with your mind in the past, and you, Valerie, are an insane bitch."

"Silence, you asinine bastard!" she snapped. The rain poured, and thunder rumbled. They had to shout to be heard over the storm.

"This would ne'er have happened if we had just decided to enjoy the laxity of the law 'stead of trying to change things," grumbled Arcie. "We could all be rich now if you lot had not insisted on tromping off after dreams."

"I think . . . " began Robin, and Arcie shut him up with a tirade.

"Quiet, you rabbit-headed pansy! We've had nothing but trouble since you showed up. You're a nuisance!"

"Almost as bad as this ominously quiet fellow," interjected Valerie, casting her gimlet eye on Blackmail. The knight sat unmoving on a tussock, head lowered in grief over his lost horse. "He's as weak as the donkey there, seeming so tough and then goes to mush when his pet horsie dies," she scoffed. The knight raised his head and seemed to glare in silent rage and sorrow at them. "Let's get rid of both of them." The knight stood up warily, the rainfall drumming on his armor.

"What's this let's business?!" hissed Sam. "It's all let-us-do-the-work-while-Valerie-sits-and-plots. And Arcie only does that because he knows that without us to coddle him he'd be dead in five minutes! I'm not going to do a damn thing any of you suggest or say!"

"You are all a cluster of fools," growled Valerie. "I would be better off killing you all now, while you are battered and sick, and taking my amulet and going it on my own." Thunder rumbled in the distance, and the rain lashed in icy sheets.

"I think if it's a question of taking over you'd better not talk too casually of killing," snarled Sam, slowly rising to his feet, a glistening blade appearing in his hand.

"And I'm not going to go under so easy either, to Valerie or you, Sam," said Arcie with quiet menace, swinging his morning star. Kaylana stepped back from the open hostility radiating from the small circle as Blackmail drew his sword and stood ready. Robin gave a squeal and galloped away.

Kaylana cleared her throat. "Stop it, all of you," she said with strange calmness.

"Shut up, Kaylana," came the terse reply simultaneously from the combatants, who were watching each other like cobras in a too-small pit. Kaylana knew she couldn't pull them together again. They'd have to do it for themselves.

"Then, while you are sizing each other up," asked Kaylana, "why do you not take a moment's thought ahead, to what the future holds for you; if you, any one of you, survives this battle and kills the rest of us?"

Such was Kaylana's persuasiveness that they did begin to think ahead. There was silence, broken only by the drumming of rain and roll of thunder and the faint hissing of angry breath.

Robin ducked behind a bank and pressed the two gems on his bracelet. In an instant he stood before Mizzamir. The wizard looked at him with mild surprise. Robin, soaking wet and muddy, bowed, embarrassed at his quick return but glad to be away from the angry evildoers.

"Yes, Robin of Avensdale? What brings you back so soon?" asked Mizzamir. Robin stood and looked at him in respect and confusion.

"Sir, it is as you predicted when this all began . . . they are at each other's throats in the Fens . . . I do not think any will survive."

It was Arcie who spoke first, his voice somewhere between a man's anger and a child's fear as he looked at Sam. "We'll none of us survive, if we kill each other . . . " he said slowly.

Sam looked at Valerie. "We're only cutting our own throats, fighting like this."

Valerie looked at Blackmail. "That is true . . . it is a waste of energy and time."

"I'd thought we was friends, Sam . . . " said Arcie. "But I don't guess as we ever were, really."

"I don't know if evil people can have friends," replied Sam, straightening from his alert crouch. "That's what Mizzamir said."

"They say we cannot have friends, or trust anyone, or love anyone, either," answered Valerie, looking into the mist and rain. "But I trusted. I loved. And I am perhaps the most dark-souled person here." There was a pause.

"When you think on it," piped Arcie, "when ye're of darkness, on yer own, all society hates you, and even other people of darkness will want to kill or betray you to get ahead . . . "

"Who could need people to trust and rely on more?" finished Sam. "No wonder evil went down the gutters . . ."

"For large-scale success," said Valerie, "There must be some laxity somewhere . . . in the days of the War, the forces of evil were strong . . . how did they manage that, if they fought constantly as we do?"

"I heard somewhere as evil people dinna work well together because they're too self-centered," offered Arcie.

"Perhaps that is true," said Valerie. "But it's also said we work together in order to use our companions. But isn't that what any group does? The strengths of the party are varied, and the different work of different members allows the group as a whole to survive."

"The only thing lacking is trust and perhaps friendship," mused Sam, sheathing his dagger.

"We don't need those," said Valerie, "if we have the solid knowledge that we all need each other to survive." Perhaps, she thought, it was not a wise idea to attempt to gain control of the party, despite it being what would please her the most . . . it would be very foolish, for not only would her position be constantly in danger, but she could not rely upon getting the full effort that the party only put out when working unfettered.

"We do need each other to survive," Sam decided, looking around. "We need Kaylana for healing, for a voice of reason, for her magic. We need Valerie for her knowledge, her power. We need Arcie, as I needed him in the past, to go where we cannot and use his talents to help us survive. We need Blackmail, for he has demonstrated his strength to us, and his loyalty . . . a valuable asset." The knight drew himself up and sheathed his sword. Sam looked around for Robin, didn't see him, and left him out. "And I think you need me, because one of our main enemies, I feel, is the wizard Mizzamir . . . and I will wager I'm the only one here who can kill him when we meet him."

The others digested this and nodded. The fate of the world, now that their minds were cleared of anger, was as clear as it had ever been, their goals as destined as ever. It has been said that it would take circumstances that were drastic and strange in the extreme to ever allow a group of people of darkness to work together . . . but perhaps the otherwise inevitable destruction of the entire world was just enough.

As the rain slowly drizzled off, there could be seen through the mist in the moonlight a string of figures making its way to higher ground, walking in each other's footsteps.

"I'm sorry about your horse," Sam said quietly to Blackmail, who nodded in silent thanks.

When Robin returned early the next morning, he trotted to where he expected to find a pile of broken bodies. Instead, there was nothing but the remains of the failed fire, and what might have been footprints heading east.

He at last caught up with them on top of a rocky tor. The rain had vanished, replaced by a bright sun scattering clouds. They were sitting about on the sparsely grassed flat top of the plateau, with a small fire of twigs and grass burning off to one side. They looked up as he trotted up to them.

"Ho hi, Robin," greeted Sam. His clothes were dry, his hair flipped a little in the faint breeze. "We figured you'd catch up sooner or later." He had a look of calm complacency that seemed somewhat familiar to the centaur. The assassin's collar was loose, and a faint brown mark showed in a star-shape against pale skin near his shoulder.

"You . . . you didn't fight?" asked the centaur, looking around at the members of the company.

"Nay," said Arcie, warming his toes in front of the fire. "Just a tad o' grouchiness was all."

"There is some rushroot soup in that pot over there," Kaylana said. "Help yourself. Since you have just arrived, I think you should take the first watch."

"Um, all right." Robin folded his legs up under himself and lay down by the fire as the others drifted into slumber one by one. He got the impression that Valerie's raven was watching him from its perch on a stone. With extreme puzzlement, he ate his soup and set his beloved harp out to dry in front of the fire.

"I say, Arcie, do you get the impression we're being followed?"

The Barigan looked over his shoulder. It was night now, and in the dimness he looked out over the Fens, back the way they had come, to the moonlit glisten of the sea in the distance. They had slept through the day, breakfasted that sunset, and had been marching on through the darkening twilight. The mist was thin and low, and in the odd half-light of the new night you could see quite far. At the outlet of one of the slow rivers that emptied into the channel was the faint flicker of campfires. The others had noticed it too.

"Looks as it," said Arcie. Kaylana shook her head in annoyance.

"Of course. Who would venture into this forsaken place but to follow us?"

"They seem to have camped for the night," wavered Robin uncertainly.

"Naturally," replied Valerie. "Only a bunch of lunatics would try to cross the Fens of Friat in darkness."

There was silence a moment, broken only by the soft whispers of the night wind.

"Let's get moving, then," said Sam at last, with a sigh. The company turned and slogged off through the boggy, festering land.

"I don't see campfires, sir," said Jeffries, the young scout posted at watch in the Verdant Company. They had crossed the water when it had fallen to manageable level that evening, and now were pausing to dry clothes and equipment. Fenwick thought for a moment.

"They must be moving by night," he decided at length. "Trying to put distance between us as best they can without horses. We'll have to go after them."

"Into the Fens, sir?" quavered Jeffries. "B-but . . . "

"Teams of three, with horses and hounds," decided Fenwick. "We'll spread out, keep in contact with horns. Just like the old chases, eh, Jeffries?" Fenwick flashed his white teeth and clapped the young scout on the back. Jeffries still looked doubtful.

"But sir . . . what about the barrow-beasts?"

"All defunct now, my friend," answered Fenwick cheerfully, whistling for his horse-captain. "The Light has driven those creatures of shadow into non-existence."

"And the Orthamotch?" asked Jeffries, nervously.

Fenwick laughed. "The Orthamotch! Don't tell me you're jumping at children's stories now! Come! You shall ride with me." The young hero sprang down from his post and began dividing men into teams, still chuckling. "I'll protect you from the nasty Orthamotch."

Soon the night was torn by the drumming of hooves.

"I don't think I like this very much," decided Robin. His hooves sloshed in the mud, and he had to pick them up like a hacking pony to keep from getting them tangled in the swamp-weeds.

"Well, it's no picnic, that's certain," agreed Sam.

"Why don't you give us a jangle on that harp-thingy of yours, if no one objects?"

The others made various noises of non-objection, as they stumbled their way through the mud. Robin shivered, conscious of Mizzamir's words that a single false note might earn him a dagger in his neck, but took out his harp, and tuning it as he walked along. The darkness and danger seemed to fall away as he worked, the carved dolphin on its head gleaming in the moonlight, the notes of the strings sounding first dull, discordant, then slowly adjusting to perfection as he tuned them with the silver key. Ears pricked as he bent over the instrument, feet left to find their own way, until at last every note sang true.

He rested the instrument in the crook of his shoulder, resting against his human side so that it was not shifted by the motion of his walking. He had built the instrument himself, as the son of one of the finest woodcarvers in the Commots and with the aid of a genuine minstrel. It fitted his form and style of playing perfectly. He watched the renegades walk for a moment, running mentally through his repertoire, and finally decided upon "The Ballad of Tirsat Lam" as being of good cheer and with a nice sort of marching rhythm. With calloused fingers striking notes from the strings, he began to sing:

Long ago in the land of Phrin
Roamed the Seeker, Tirsat Lam,
His heart was light though his boots were thin
The wandering warrior, Tirsat Lam.

The others seemed to cheer up a bit, lifting their feet with more enthusiasm. "Not bad, centaur," acknowledged Kaylana. "You might possibly have made a bard, back in the old days."

"What's a bard?" asked Robin, pausing in his singing while his fingers carried on through the refrain. Kaylana looked a little surprised and sad, and shook her head.

"Perhaps I shall tell you later. In the meantime, please continue."

"Aye, do that," added Arcie, hopping from tussock to tussock in an effort to keep out of the deeper puddles. Robin blushed a little, and went on.

He had come from the War at Galor
At the ancient Hippogryph's lair
When the trumpets sang of valor
Tirsat Lam was surely there.

"That's very interesting how you did that," interrupted Sam. "One can almost hear the trumpets blowing in the distance."

"I . . . " began Robin, but abruptly the party froze. Robin's fingers fumbled and the last notes of the harp died away, replaced by a distant sound—the call of a hunting horn drifting softly across the Fens, answered a moment later by another, closer.

"Fight or flight?" asked Kaylana, tersely. "I make it about three horses and some dogs, going to be here in a few minutes. The dogs have our scent. And I cannot do anything with the dogs . . . they sound to me like Fey-hounds, creatures of Elven-bred stock immune to my powers."

"Fight," opted Sam, flipping out a pair of daggers.

"Well enough," muttered Arcie, climbing out of a pot-hole and unhooking his morning star.

"There isn't much choice," decided Valerie. Blackmail silently unsheathed his sword, and stood ready. A moment later a crash of hurtling figures broke out of the misty shadows, and the renegades had to fight for their lives.

Sam dodged a whistling sword blow that would have separated his head from his shoulders and looked up at a figure in warrior's gear, wearing a green and gold tabard over his chain mail and under his fringed vest. The fellow grunted as his sword missed and jerked a curved hunting horn to his lips. Sam flickered, and the form fell with a slow gurgle, a pair of vertical slits in his neck.

Kaylana had lost her wooden shield in the flood, and

was now almost the unfortunate recipient of a hefty whack to the side of the head with a mace from what looked to be an enthusiastic woodsman-priest of some sort, followers of the hunters' deity Artelis. She jumped back, the mace barely missing, and fell with a splash into a pool. A cry of "I got one!" rang out. Kaylana shook her head in the water, then noticed something squirming underneath her fingertips. She could feel her staff channeling natural energy safely away from her as it touched her. With a grip of her staff and a faint whispered word, her hand closed on it.

Arcie danced around another fellow trying to hit him, sending the man's horse spinning in circles. The armored warrior cursed. Arcie abruptly yelped and leaped away as three white, red-eared hounds lunged at him. The warrior turned and found himself confronting a huge, dark-armored figure wielding a massive sword. The sword whistled through the air, and he fell off his horse in avoiding the blow.

Valerie looked over to where the Barigan stood at bay. Her eyes narrowed in anger. She remembered Fey-hounds, the vicious white tracking and hunting dogs of the people who had destroyed her life. Her dark-clawed hand lashed out with a crackle of power, her voice hissing words of magic. Arcie whopped one of the dogs on the side of the head with his morning star, and then stared in shock as all three burst into brilliant flame, yelping and running about.

Meanwhile, in a lightning motion Kaylana threw the large, smooth shock-worm she had found at her attacker, who was dismounting, preparing to come finish her off. It wrapped around his neck like a wriggling scarf, discharging several thousand volts of sky-fire into his body. He gave a gurgling shriek and fell, twitching, purple sparks flashing over his chain mail.

Sam saw the last warrior faced off with Blackmail, the two circling each other, blades clashing and clanging. He whipped out a dagger, and as he threw it a large dog, somewhat on fire, crashed into the back of his knees, spoiling his aim. He fell face first into the mud and had to contend with snarling, snapping jaws as the maddened beast tore at him.

"Ha!" cried the last man, as the silent knight closed on him. "You may kill me, but you'll all perish in the firestorm I shall unleash with my magical crystal . . . " He grabbed for the rune-inscribed pouch that had held it, and scrabbled at where it should have been. As the great black sword descended, his last sight was of a grinning Barigan sitting on a tuffet behind the dark knight, holding the pouch aloft and waving it slightly.

There was a snap and hiss and Sam shoved the hound into a puddle, breaking its neck as he did so, and then tense silence reigned, broken only by the drum of horses' hooves retreating. Three men and three hounds lay scattered about. Sam saw Blackmail wiping off his sword, Kaylana emerging from a pool, rubbing her head, Valerie dusting her hands off with a faint smile, Arcie tucking a pouch into his belt . . . and Robin standing stricken, some distance off, stock still and white as a snowbank in the moonlight. Sam coughed.

"All right . . . does anyone have a seven-inch piece of steel inside them that doesn't belong there?" he asked apologetically.

There was a chorus of confused no's, except for Robin.

"You just killed all those people . . . " the minstrel quavered.

Sam walked up to him, beckoning Kaylana to follow. He looked up at the centaur with a tolerant smile. "Never seen battle before, have you?"

The centaur shook his head.

"I thought not . . . well, if you'd been in here doing your share, I don't think you'd have caught this so easily . . . and you might have noticed if you had."

Robin looked down to where the assassin was gently tapping his equine chest. An ebony-hilted dagger set with a piece of carnelian was stuck sideways in the thick muscle there, letting a slow trickle of blood slide down his foreleg. Robin trembled all over, his ears pinned back, and then his large brown eyes rolled up in his head and he collapsed into a dead faint. His heavy body fell with a soggy noise into the muddy marsh.

Kaylana rushed to remove the dagger and pack the wound with healing herbs. "Poison?" she asked tersely.

"No . . . " replied Sam softly. "Just scared of his own blood, I think."

"You knew you'd hit one of us?" Valerie asked, coming up and inspecting the fallen centaur. Sam nodded and looked away. He thought he saw torches in the distance.

"I never miss."

"Aye come on," scoffed Arcie. "That's just yer advertizmints."

"Really," said Sam. "I may not always hit what I aim at, when I fire or throw a weapon . . . but I always hit something. Always."

"Inborn magic, perhaps," commented Valerie, her voice still showing disbelief. "Were your parents magically talented?" Sam shook his head slightly, not answering, as old wounds stung. He coughed roughly.

Robin's eyes fluttered, and he tried to roll to his feet. He got to his knees and shook his head. Sam looked down at him.

"Sorry," the assassin said. Robin goggled at him. Sam walked away, saying, "We'd better get a move on . . . these people's friends will be here soon, I think . . . I can hear the horns." He coughed again. His jerkin was torn, scorched, and bloodstained by his grapple with the hound.

Kaylana looked around the party; wounded from battle, still sore from the bruising in the Ford, coming on sickening from the air of the Fens.

"We may not survive another attack," she said slowly. "We must move away from here, quietly and without trace. Valerie, if you can summon a magical fog, I can hide our tracks from their hounds."

The searching men of the Verdant Company looked at each other in puzzlement as a slow, oily fog began to drift through the night. The hounds wandered in circles, confused, and the calls of the horns grew fainter and fewer as the strange fog muffled the noise.

In the fog, a battered string of renegades headed northeast. The men of the Verdant Company lit lanterns and held them aloft so that they could see the way, not wishing to stumble into a ditch or bog or pool. It was this that proved their undoing, however.

The three men in group D were becoming uneasy.

"This place is creepy," said the healer of Artelis, whose fellow brothers had served the Verdant Company as long as it had existed. Though his faith in his goddess was strong, the Fens seemed literally godsforsaken, and his eyes darted about nervously. The woodsman in the group nodded.

"Yes it is . . . Fenwick didn't take this fog into account when he sent us out . . . I think we'd better find some of the others and form larger groups."

"Good idea," said the warrior, and raised his horn to his lips. The sound pealed out and then died away. There was no reply. The light of the lanterns attracted flickering, midge-like insects, and all was quiet but for the snuffling of the hounds and the soggy sounds of the horses' hooves in the mud.

"Ho! Look there!" exclaimed the woodsman in delight, pointing to their left. The others turned, and saw three dim, flickering lights, softly yellow, close together but far away, surely the lanterns of three of their companions in another group.

"What a relief," sighed the warrior, and they turned their horses toward the distant lights, riding at a brisk trot to reach the safety and security of companionship. The dogs whimpered slightly, and the horses seemed less willing to follow the lights, but the riders ignored them.

They barely had time to gasp in terror as the ground suddenly fell away beneath them, plunging them into an inky morass of quicksand, kin to the quick-mud but much worse, for in the liquid muddy sand one could feel slimy things moving against one's skin. As they floundered, a clawed hand lunged up from the muck, gripping a man's face and pulling it down. There was the flash of crocodile teeth. The lights, hovering and dancing over the pool, flashed down like large, eerie fireflies to feed. They drained away the fading life essences of the dying men, leaving them shriveled and pale, stricken faces wide in frozen terror.

All across the marsh, lights real and imagined flickered, and death once more stalked the Fens.

"What's that?" asked Arcie, peering at a dim light bobbing in the distance. Valerie looked up and turned away quickly.

"Ignore it, Barigan."

"But . . . "

"Don't look at it!" snapped Valerie, stepping in front of him. She looked up at the others. "Don't any of you look at them. I'm not certain how, but there are darker things than we afoot tonight. If you see those lights, ignore them, do not look at them, and above all do not follow them!"

Sam was glancing about, trying to keep an eye on the lights without looking at them. Valerie's fog boiled around him. "They look like lanterns."

"What are they?" asked Robin, on his feet now and moving, but shaky.

"In the Underrealms, we called them *fihilin* . . . here I think they are called Willowisp. Very, very dangerous." Valerie moved on, holding her robes up so as not to get them too muddy. The raven on her shoulder closed its eyes and ruffled its feathers against the chill of the fog. The rest followed. The lights did not approach to be inspected, and the party did not seek them out.

"It will be dawn soon, Sir Fenwick." Towser sat on his horse and looked about the glooming fog. He pulled his green robes tight and arranged the hood over his close-cropped brown hair.

Sir Fenwick halted his horse a moment. The warrior-scout Jeffries, Towser, and a healer named Mella who rode with them all stopped as well. They had ceased to sound the horns, finding them useless in the fog. They stood on a lumpy hill, looked down into the plain of the Fens, and saw something that gave their hearts the courage of battle.

Straggling across the open space was a line of figures on foot, with one horse? No, a centaur. And coming up to them from behind in a haphazard sort of way, was another party of three, with lanterns lit. With silent exaltation Fenwick raised his horn and sounded the charge. His party raced down the hill as the other group of mounted men galloped forward, and they met in the middle of the dark figures.

The renegades had of course heard the horns and the hoofbeats, and thus were not totally unprepared for the attack. The horses of Fenwick's party skidded and collided as they reached the bottom of the hill, a powerful blast of the Druid's power almost knocking them over as they tried to obey her and retreat. They splashed into a ditch at the foot of the hill, on top of the three floundering hounds. Two of the men, Fenwick not being one of them, were unhorsed. Upon the group approaching behind them, Valerie, drawing on her magic powers, threw a spell of slumber. The three horses fell unconscious in mid-stride; They awoke again almost instantly, but not before spilling their riders and crashing down upon the suddenly somnolent hounds. Fenwick spurred his horse and met a well-aimed morning star with his kneecap. He slashed down in fury, the sword Truelight gleaming like frozen lightning, and something yelped.

Towser, meanwhile, had quickly gotten to his feet and cast a spell. A plume of light shot into the air and burst with a flare, illuminating the scene in garish gold light. Valerie cringed away, blinded. Two of the hounds lunged at her, teeth snapping, and she shouted another spell that sent them yipping as black darts buzzed about them. The Feyhounds snapped and growled, trying to bite her in between the attacks. Nightshade croaked loudly at them, slashing at tender muzzles with his beak while he shielded his mistress from the light as best he could with his wings.

Sudden searing pain shot through Towser's chest, and he fell, eyes glazing. Sam wheeled from the fallen mage with his dagger still dripping and saw Fenwick's horse rearing, about to come down on a small huddled figure on the moss. He threw the dagger without thinking. It spun through the air and clipped the horse's tail, making the animal lunge forward and over the prone Barigan. At that moment, the other woodsman sprang behind him, and Sam dodged away, still getting a slash on the leg from the fellow's drawn sword. He cursed and kicked the man into a deep puddle, then ran to Arcie.

There was a crash behind him, and a nasty meaty sound. Something flew through the air and landed near Robin's feet; the head of a startled looking warrior, eyes still blinking in reflex, severed by a powerful blow from a black sword. The centaur turned away, retching helplessly, closing his eyes as the huge silent knight sent the healer from the second party face-first into the mud, skewered on the great sword. Sam snapped him out of it by throwing a heavy Barigan over onto his withers.

"Come on, Robin! We've got to make a run for it!"

Kaylana and Fenwick suddenly found themselves squared off, she clutching her staff, not as a weapon, but in anger, and he on horseback, glowing sword raised. He lowered his sword and smiled his most charming smile, as the clash of blade against blade marked Blackmail's progress in the background.

"What's a nice girl like you doing in a place like this?" asked Fenwick. "Why don't you come with me, instead? Such a beauty belongs to light, not to darkness."

Kaylana glared at him. "You are far too much like your grandfather, royal fool."

"Forsake this silly Druidism, lovely flower."

"Death first, you simpering toad!" She swung her staff with such sudden speed it took the hero unawares, and across the temples.

>Crack!<

Fenwick rocked unsteadily, then fell off his horse.

"I like a girl with spirit," he said indistinctly through the mud. Kaylana grabbed Valerie and called for Blackmail.

"Come! We must retreat!"

They ran, pursued by the survivors and their limping, yelping hounds, while one of the healers stayed to aid their fallen leader and the others. The renegades ran out of the circle of light and stumbled in the sudden darkness. They were sent rolling down a moss-covered hill that suddenly opened up a dark mouth and swallowed them, from the sandal-footed Druid to the centaur carrying the Barigan. The remaining men of the Verdant Company halted, milling around, confused.

"Where did they go?" asked one.

Jeffries shuddered.

"Maybe the Orthamotch got them," he whispered. The other man looked about doubtfully, but something of his childhood fears sent a shiver down his spine.

"They've gone. It'll be dawn soon. Let's go back to the others."

They hastened back to their comrades as the last of the fog blew away and the sun of a new day began to pink the sky.

"So, oo is dis den?" asked a voice.

Sam opened bleary eyes. The voice belonged to some large hunched bipedal creature, dimly seen as a faint outline of shadows. He shut his eyes in despair.

I'm dead, he thought, *and I've gone straight to Hades, just as everyone always said I would.*

"Eh? Eh? You wake up, you." A clawed finger rapped on Sam's chest. He opened his eyes again.

The party was lying in a tangle on a large mat of something that felt like dried grass. They seemed to be in an underground burrow of sorts, with damp walls of earth, by the echoes. It was very dark. But Sam, trained to prowl the night, could extrapolate shapes from the faintest shadows and feel presences by warmth and sound.

The fire, the assassin's hunting flame, flickered in his blood and wakened the ancient senses, ancient instincts that told the hunter all he could know about his surroundings. His danger sense was humming softly, but not with immediacy. He was warned to be cautious.

The walls were cool and muffling, and his companions were patches of warm breathing. The figure before him was cold as the walls and reeked of mud and blood and a reptilian musk. As his vision adjusted further, he could make out more. Robin was groaning and trying to stand, all four legs quivering. Sam shivered faintly when he noticed that Blackmail emitted no sense of warmth, but reasoned that this was probably normal, because of the armor. The knight was standing up and rubbing his helmet.

Kaylana got to her feet and spoke. "Hello?"

"Alloo!" said the strange voice, padding over to her.

She can't see it, Sam thought suddenly. *She's normal, she doesn't have the fire, the fire in the blood that gives the night-sight . . . what if the creature is dangerous?* He tensed himself to spring, watching it. It was speaking.

"Hurt people, yes . . . blood in Fens again! Woke up old Orthamotch, and little pets too," gurgled the voice gleefully.

Sam gulped silently. Orthamotch! The life-stealing demon of the Fens! Orthamotch was the bogeyman of the entire Six Lands, said to be able to pop up out of the ground wherever he chose, particularly where little children were bad . . .

"Day now," went on Orthamotch in disgust. Then, more cheerfully, "Little pets come home. See?"

Suddenly there was a twinkle in the darkness, and then another, and another. Through a tunnel in the wall came a stream of the strange golden lights Valerie had warned them not to look at. Sam tried not to look at them now, but had no choice.

The Willowisps poured into the room like living marshlights, spinning about with a green-gold radiance and filling the room with a cold light. Sam saw his companions clearly now, slowly getting to their feet, except for Arcie, who lay where he had fallen from the centaur's back. And Sam saw Orthamotch.

The figure was an apparition out of nightmares, a strange conglomeration of reptile and human, scaly skin dripping from human flesh, with powerful clawed hands, a tall but hunched figure, and a thick, muscular tail like an alligator's. The face was a half-crocodile's snout, with large, mis-set eyes, one blood red, the other a deep yellow. The pupils were like a cat's, but doubled and crossed over each other, forming an X. The figure wore a tattered, patchwork tunic made of some sort of fur . . . if the legends were to be believed, the scalps of naughty boys and girls, as well as careless travelers. The apparition winked at Sam from its red eye. "Old Orthamotch ugly, yes? Bite your head off in a minute, he would."

Sam believed it. The figure's muscles rippled like a snake's under the wrinkled skin that looked like scale armor. Hunched almost double, Orthamotch's eyes stared into his from the same height. He tensed. Orthamotch gave a kind of sputtering hiss. Sam was startled to hear it was a laugh.

"We shall fight you, if you give us cause," came bravely from Kaylana. Valerie and Blackmail stared in silence, and Robin was shivering with pain from his chest and fear. He had glanced over his shoulder, and his back was stained with blood. He wondered how he'd gotten himself hurt this time.

"No, not going to bite today. Little pets had good hunting, yes?" Orthamotch asked, looking up at the lights. There was a thrill of sound, so high it was barely on the edge of hearing.

"Ah yes. Clutter up swamp pools, make plenty work for poor old Orthamotch." Shaking its head, it turned to the party and addressed them. "Hunters running around upstairs today. Lookie for you. Rest here?" Its voice chuckled muddily.

"For what payment?" asked Valerie coldly. "The head of one of our party for each hour?"

"No, no," answered Orthamotch with a gurgle. "Plenty heads upstairs. Got some already." It padded over to where Arcie lay unmoving and looked down at the Barigan.

Arcie's still form was abruptly flanked by an assassin, a Druid, a knight, and a sorceress.

"He's with us," explained Sam quietly. "Some woodsman tried to stomp him."

"That was Sir Fenwick," said Kaylana coldly. She knelt by the Barigan and turned his body over gently, biting her lip. A gaping wound had spilled gouts of blood from the broad chest, and the thief's face was deathly pale. Blood continued to ooze thickly through the once cheerfully yellow jerkin. Barigans are small people, without a whole lot of blood to spare, and Arcie looked like he'd lost a lot of his.

"Melibrech," cursed Kaylana under her breath. "This is beyond my skill . . . he is dying."

Orthamotch peered at the Barigan and gave a chirping whistle. One of the Willowisps detached itself from the ceiling and hovered over the Barigan. Sam snarled and drew his dagger to stab at it.

"Don't you dare feed him to your pets, Orthamotch," he hissed. He had to admit that Arcie got on his nerves at times, but this was no way for a man to die . . . Orthamotch grinned toothily at him.

" 'Course not. Giving, not taking."

The light of the Willowisp hovered over Arcie and seemed to expand its radiance to shine about him in a faint cloud that swirled into his skin. His form began to shine, and slowly the gaping wound closed, the color returned to his face, and his breathing strengthened. The light-cloud withdrew into the 'wisp, and Arcie snored loudly, then startled and opened his bright blue eyes.

The Willowisp, slightly dimmer now, returned to the ceiling with its fellows as Arcie sat up and looked around.

"Wha?" he said. "Where am I?"

"That is amazing," said Kaylana, looking at Orthamotch. The monstrous creature shrugged. "Why did you do that? You are . . . "

"Evil?" Orthamotch cackled slurpily, his tail lashing on the muddy floor with a terrifying sound. "Yes, yes!" He seemed to sober. "Hard times for poor Orthamotch. Bright days, old darkness fading . . . he sleeps in Fens, dying, dying . . . 'til suddenly blood! Blood in Fenwater! He wakes, sees, sees people, dark people hiding, running, from light people . . . "

"Not running," coughed Sam, a little embarrassed, "more a sort of strategic retreat . . . " Orthamotch ignored him.

"And so decided to take advantage of situation . . . then thought, and decided to help, even! Orthamotch very old," he added, looking around at them. "Remembers when Druids everywhere, Nathauan lived in caverns where pets hunted sometimes. Remembers War! Good hunting then, in Fens," he said wistfully. "But now all gone. Pets used to fly everywhere, told Orthamotch of many things. Told of darkness fading, of Gate closed . . . "

"You know of the Gate?" interrupted Valerie, her large eyes burning. Nightshade, on her shoulder, croaked. Orthamotch waggled a taloned finger at her.

"Yes, long since, but know. Since you know, too, Old Orthamotch guessed right! You going to fix!"

"Um . . . " began Kaylana, uncertain as to how much they should tell this creature. It shook its misshapen head.

"No need explain! You rest here, get well, then go out by tunnel to Jogrel Forest. Avoid hunters, sneak ahead!" It clapped its taloned hands and peered up at the Willowisps about the ceiling. "Pets take care of you." It whistled again. Six of the glowing creatures came down from the ceiling.

Each one hovered over the head of a member of the group, and though they were decidedly uneasy, nothing more happened than a warm radiance showering down upon them, easing aches and bruises, soothing wearing muscles. Robin felt his nausea and weakness easing, Kaylana her head clearing, all felt warmth as wounds, fatigue, and contusions healed. The radiance shone on Blackmail's armor like distilled sunlight. Sam was amazed.

"Valerie, I thought you said these things were dangerous! How do they do this?"

Valerie was about to speak when Orthamotch answered with a cheerful gurgle.

"Pets take life energy from people dying in Fens! Pets greedy, not need all . . . give some to you."

"You mean . . . ," Sam stammered, staring at his Willowisp in horror, "that this is . . . "

"Oh do hush, assassin," said Valerie cheerfully, smiling in the glow of the healing, her raven basking like a cormorant. "Don't be such a prude."

"But the people," protested Sam, trying to edge out from under the 'wisp. It followed him.

"They not need it anymore!" Orthamotch insisted, obviously proud of his pets.

"That is true enough, Sam," agreed Kaylana. "We might as well take the opportunity."

"I don't know . . . What do you think about it, Robin? Robin?"

The centaur had listened in horror and had collapsed in a faint. The Willowisp attending him finished its work and returned to the ceiling; the other 'wisps soon joined it.

Orthamotch, meanwhile, was beckoning the party to follow. They did so, minds still full of surprise and confusion over what they had just seen. Kaylana shook Robin awake, and he followed on shaky legs.

Orthamotch led them through a tangle of tunnels until at last he found one that curved away into darkness. He indicated it.

"You follow this, you soon end up in Jogrel Forest. Go now! Hunters looking for you in Fens, not catch up soon. Go!"

The group exchanged looks, but decided that they might as well follow the nightmare's advice. Ahead, the tunnel was dimly lit with faintly glowing mosses, enough to see dimly by. They hastened down the passage. Sam was the last to go. He ducked into the passage, then back out again to face the hideous creature. "Thanks," he said. Orthamotch cracked a toothy smile, and waved a shooing hand at the tunnel.

"Silly! Go. Do not think Orthamotch will be so nice a second time . . . especially if you are naughty," gurgled the creature, fearsome eyes twinkling. Sam ducked back down the tunnel after the others, and they marched along the soggy floor, rested and healthy, with a gurgling laugh ringing distantly in their ears as Orthamotch contemplated the novelty of a polite assassin.

It was dusk in the Jogrel Forest. The day had passed with the sighing of the roundtip pines and faint rustling of beech, the plash-splashing of the sparkling brook, the business of birds and animals. An emaciated tawny owl sat on a branch, drawn up into itself; unable to kill, yet unable to die. The evening sun slipped away behind gold and red clouds, bathing the woods in lavender light.

An old, dead tree stump in the middle of a small clearing shook slightly. It wiggled, and then fell over, its roots pulling up a plug of earth and weeds from the face of the clearing, revealing a dark hole and a small, red-polled head that inspected the landscape with bright interest. The head then peered down the hole in which it stood, and called softly.

"All clear, fellows," said Arcie.

"Good. Get up there, then," grunted Robin. With a light spring the Barigan jumped off the centaur's shoulders and scrambled out into the grass.

The passage they had come through had stretched for miles of twisting, dim-dark tunnels. Following the main pathway, they had occasionally availed themselves of the spy-holes to the surface to track their progress. When beneath the forest—they could tell from the thick tree roots that extended into the tunnel—they had found the main exit here beneath this stump. The passage continued on into darkness, past the shaft that extended straight up from it.

Within the hole, Kaylana peered up at the five foot tall shaft. It was barely four feet in diameter. She drummed her fingers on her staff thoughtfully. She edged aside to let Sam pass, and the assassin scrambled up the narrow chimney like a Father Yule in reverse. She and Valerie could make the climb, she felt sure, especially with the others to help, and probably even the armored knight could reach the top . . . but the centaur . . .

"Fellows, I see a problem here," she commented.

"Hmmn, yes, I see what you mean," replied Valerie, looking from shaft to centaur. "Oh well, nothing else for it then."

Robin shivered, ears twitching. "You're not going to leave me down here, are you?" he asked, trying to sound indignant rather than plaintive and not quite succeeding. He shifted uneasily. He swished his beautiful tail as he contemplated a march back down that long dark low tunnel, with the terrible figure of Orthamotch waiting at the other end. He'd barely been able to keep himself from bolting before, feeling the press of earth all around him, crushing him . . . Kaylana saw his fear and shook her head.

"No, I do not think we shall. Do not faint on us again, Robin. Have you anything to suggest, Valerie?"

The sorceress flashed her cruel teeth in an evil smile. "Well, of course we won't leave the poor dear . . . if he's too big to fit through the opening, well, we could cut him up into smaller chunks—" Nightshade clacked his beak appreciatively.

"Valerie!"

"Oh all right," amended the Nathauan crossly. "If you can widen that shaft a bit, Druid, I shall endeavor to levitate him with my magic. He'll fit if he stands on his silly hind legs."

"Does that meet with your approval, Robin?" asked Kaylana. Robin was wide-eyed.

"L-l-levitate?"

"Good, I hoped you would agree," asserted Kaylana. She looked up the shaft. "Ho there, the two of you!"

A pair of heads appeared in the circle of dim light above, peering down at them.

"Yes?" asked Sam.

"Move back from the edge, you rogues. I am going to make the sides cave in."

"Won't that be kind of hard on you down there?" asked Arcie.

"I should hope you all have more respect for me than that by now," Kaylana retorted haughtily. "Step back, you on top, and the rest of you, back the way we came."

The two heads vanished from the view above, and the knight, sorceress, and centaur backed down the dark passage. Kaylana gripped her staff, calling to mind the ancient powers. She was still rankled over her failure to save the Barigan's life by her own skill, as well as the fiascoes in Ford and Fens. Rowan roots, this was supposed to have been her original quest, and she was making a right pigeon nest of it. Around her she felt the living earth, thrumming with root and worm and beetle, seeds germinating out-of-season in the strange ever-present Lightness. The dirt of the tunnel and shaft was held in place by a thousand thousand tiny fibers and a hundred thicker roots. Fierce Druidic pride in her spirit, she drew her power together, the staff warm under her hand, and struck the far side of the shaft a light tap with the crooked knob, sending a wave of force through the soil.

Arcie and Sam were sitting by a tree, idly watching the hole. Suddenly there was a noise like a huge featherbed being shaken, and a great swath of clearing plunged downward in a cloud of dry dust. The far side of the hole and a good section of the farther passage beyond it seemed to have fallen in. They hastened over to get a better view.

Peering down what seemed to have become a low, sloping ramp into a tunnel, they saw a dirty, khaki-robed figure striding forward, staff in hand. Kaylana looked out of the tunnel at them. Arcie waved. Kaylana turned around and called back down the burrow.

"I do not believe we shall need the levitation, after all.

Come along, Robin, you can get out this way." The Druid led the way up and out of the collapsed tunnel, followed by the centaur, the knight, and the sorceress. Valerie inspected the collapsed tunnel thoughtfully.

"I suppose you could call that widening the shaft," she said doubtfully. Kaylana adjusted a strap on her woven armor and looked coolly at Valerie.

"I meant to do that," she informed the sorceress and strode out into the dim evening air. The renegades trailed after her, glad of the cool twilight air after the stuffiness of the long tunnel march.

They walked on through the dim light, tired but still vitalized from the Willowisps' unusual benevolence. Birds sang twilight songs, and a small silvery brook wound around and about their path as they followed the dim light of the setting sun. Night-blooming flowers filled the air with fragrance, lilac and violet and jasmine mingling with the cool scent of the roundtip blue pines. A low mist hung over the ground, the legendary mists of Kwart. The moon rose into the sky, and its light shafted through the trees in ghostly bands.

"A complete and utter fiasco," said Sir Fenwick crossly. He and his remnant of men were gathered on the far side of the Fens, in the shelter of rolling hills. The green smudge of the Jogrel Forest was dimly visible. He looked about the campsite thoughtfully. Six men had been lost to direct confrontation with the renegades and ten more to the Fens. Fenwick didn't like Fens at all, now. Only three of the lost men had been found; drowned in marsh pools, pale and shriveled . . . the horses and Feyhounds who had lived had come back alone. Towser and the others killed in direct confrontation had been sent home to be resurrected by powerful healers, in accordance with the Company's policy. But nothing could be done for those lost to the swamp, nor for the decapitated warrior. Decapitation was one of the few ways to slay a person beyond the call of resurrection . . . that was why, it was said, that assassins completed their contracts by delivering the head of their victim to their employer. Such violent, evil death was abhorrent to the noble Sir Fenwick, and he was much troubled. The Verdant Company rested and recovered and moved on in the light of early morning.

The Company journeyed through the woods. Though they were out of their jurisdiction—the villains had passed out of the no-man's-land of the Fens and into the territory of the feudal states of Kwart proper—they were reluctant to leave without some victory. The discovery that afternoon of a strange tunnel plunging into the earth gave them the chance for glory they had been searching for. Drawing weapons and chanting spells, they plunged into it and ran along it, following back the trails left by the renegades. It was not often the Company had the chance to rid the world of yet another evil force, and they made the best of it. Enchanted blades and powerful spells filled the tunnels, and before the night was out Fenwick's lost men were avenged and the terror of the children of an entire continent was nothing more than a pile of gristly, scaly meat. In the aftermath, the Company didn't notice the almost imperceptible lightening of the sky, the feeling of goodness and perfection increased by yet another measure. But elsewhere, a red-haired Druid felt the tremor in the fabric of reality and frowned.

"So what should we be looking for now?" Sam asked when they camped that morning. Robin was still asleep, and they could discuss their plans freely. They were rightly wary of trusting anyone other than criminals like themselves with their full intentions. "If the Tests, as they seem to be, are each linked with the leading Hero of the respective land, we should be looking for something involving what's-his-name, Prawns."

"Pryse," corrected Kaylana. "The paladin."

"So where's his castle, then?" asked Arcie. "The Test thingy's prob'ly holed up in his wine cellar or some such."

"He didn't have a castle, fool," retorted Valerie. "Everybody with any learning knows he died soon after the Victory, supposedly something to do with somehow dishonoring himself. So Kwart's still divided up into feudal states, the way it always has been, only more peaceful."

"Well, I knew he were dead," snapped Arcie. "He went hunting sea-worms in them far west oceans and got eaten."

"I always heard he'd gone in search of some holy relic and never returned," put in Sam. Blackmail had been listening to the conversation, and Sam now turned to him.

"You look like you might be from these parts, stranger-companion," he said. "Feudal states, armor, tall . . . know any local legends that might point us in the direction of . . . what was it? What was the verse we figured belonged to Kwart?"

"Let me check . . . " Valerie unfolded her sheaf of notes. "The one that goes 'Golden griffin's homeward path/He who questioned, risked our wrath/Where he came to doubt, his shrine/Measures slow eternal time.' "

"Aye, because the Golden Griffin were the device of the Hero of Kwart, Sir Pryse," put in Arcie. "But what's all this about questions and doubting?"

"Maybe Sir Pryse was doubting something, and then vanished in his quest to prove it," suggested Kaylana.

"Maybe he was doubting something of the gods," Sam speculated, not really paying attention to the discussion. He was noticing the way the sun shone on Kaylana's hair, turning it into waves of copper-crimson that flashed when she moved her head, so gracefully.

"Well, that's no help," grumbled Valerie. "Knights are always going off on stupid vigils and secret quests . . . No offense, Blackmail . . . "

The large dark-gauntleted hand waved a dismissive gesture. The knight had been more withdrawn since the death of his horse, and his stride lacked its previous proud tread. But slowly he had begun to respond to them again, and they were coming to know him better; a person of silent, deliberate wisdom, calm action, and with a keen sense of humor shown occasionally in a clattering tremble of armor, a laugh without breath. Fortunately Blackmail had no trouble keeping up with them in the march; despite his heavy armor he walked tirelessly and still seemed to have no need of sleep. Sam had seen him sometimes when he woke from his slumber mid-day; often the knight would be standing, staring back the way they had come, as he was doing now. They had seen no further sign of Fenwick and the Verdant Company, so the assassin could only assume he was remembering his lost equine companion, and perhaps hoping against hope to see it come galloping across the fields after them . . .

But now Valerie was going on. " . . . How are we supposed to know where this Hero went to complain to the gods? There must be any number of little shrines and wooded glens and sacred fonts in this chessboard of a feudal country."

"The sorceress is right," Kaylana spoke up. "Does anyone have any ideas for where we might look?"

There was a long, awkward silence. Then, with a slow clanking, Blackmail raised one gauntleted hand. The Druid nodded.

"Very well then. Tonight, we shall follow your lead."

Night brought a cool fog, typical of Kwart, and a sprinkling of stars. Sam did a few exercises to work the kinks out of sore muscles. The exertion flared the fire in his blood, and he let it flow; rich wild power and strength, predator-fire, stalk, kill . . . he scrambled up a tree at top speed and then flipped himself down and around the branches 'til he landed, crouched on the ground, and carefully stilled his heart, his breathing. The fire slowly dimmed, flickered, wound itself back into the glowing embers of his soul, and rested. Though the fire ritual was not immediately necessary, he had to keep in trim, in training. He was on an assignment, against a target that could appear and disappear at will, with many mighty magics at its disposal. An assassin must be prepared at all times while on assignment. Not much of an assignment, he had reflected; a thousand gold tellins was a pitiful price for the life of anyone, much less a Hero; but, then, prices had gone down drastically when the demand for assassination began to fall off. In the heyday of the trade, Mizzamir's head would have been worth more than five hundred times that amount, with of course the gratis blood-coin—the traditional oval-shaped disk of red-gold that was supposed to ward off the evil stigma of assassination, transferring it completely to the assassin rather than the employer. No assassin Sam had ever heard of had been cursed by taking a blood-coin; but such a large chunk of rare red-gold was a tidy retirement nest egg. That and a few more missions would buy you a nice room near the Guild, with a featherbed and a full-length mirror, maybe even a set of real dishes to eat from.

As planned, Blackmail marched ahead, cautiously finding his way out of the forest, across a few hills, and then suddenly out onto a fair road. Satisfied, he started down along it.

"Be you sure this are a good idea?" Arcie said nervously, as they walked along. "We're pretty obviously evil . . . wouldn't it be better to keep out of sight and off the roads, like we has been?"

Blackmail waved a dismissive hand once again, and by a few gestures indicated that to travel the road rather than across country would cut their travel time down drastically.

"You do seem to know your way around," Robin spoke up, from where he was idly strumming "The Flowers of Thaulara" on his harp. "Are you from Kwart originally?" The helmeted head nodded assent.

That explained a lot. Kwart was a land of magic far more subtle than any other; a land primarily concerned with keeping to itself. Any non-native who tried to find their way in Kwart would soon become lost in the mysterious fogs and similar terrain.

They traveled uneventfully 'til dawn, when Blackmail led them to a small wayside inn. Though the tall, handsome proprietor was uncertain of his new guests, as most Kwartans were of outsiders, Blackmail's regal presence and generous tipping made him more accepting. Many was the questing knight and retinue he had served in the past; perhaps the dark garb of these was due to some tragedy—the death of the knight's lady or lord, perhaps. So, he simply took the knight's tellins and served the retinue their meals, and watched as they wandered upstairs to fall asleep, missing the best hours of morning. Perhaps a forced march, he thought. The young redhaired woman was quite attractive, but the tall blond fellow had given him a look of death when he'd noticed him admiring her. The strange group left after dinner that evening, and the proprietor never saw them again.

As they set out, Sam held a silent, rogue's cant conference with Arcie. He was concerned about how long they could keep the secret of their mission from Robin. It might be better, not necessarily to let him in on the secret, but to continue with their quest and hope that the minstrel would not decide to do anything more than write songs and pass out occasionally.

"What do about horse-man?" Sam began. "Continue secret?"

"Should," was Arcie's response.

"How long?" retorted Sam. "Soon will notice."

"All right, not try. Not tell, not try." Arcie sighed. "Should kill him."

"Not self. Working." An assassin was loath to kill in cold blood when a target was already fixed in mind. Random killing diluted and confused the fire and dulled the edge.

"Self will, then," replied Arcie. "Suggestions?"

"While sleeping. Cut throat," the assassin recommended. He thought a moment. "Two hearts, can't stab. Throat."

"Right."

Blackmail's lead took them out into the wilderness once more. The darkness, coupled with the dramatic fog that seemed to infest this country, made it nearly impossible to tell where they might be going, and even more difficult to speculate how they would get back. It was as if the countryside itself—tiny woods, rocky hills, and tiny twisty streams that all looked alike—was being deliberately confusing. But Blackmail plodded on, sometimes stopping atop the crest of a hill to look around or staring silently upward at the stars.

Finally, in a small woods at the base of a steep rocky hill, they came upon a miniature grotto, a glen dominated by the gentle rushing sounds of water. The sound came from a waterfall in the hillside, about ten feet tall, silver in the moonlight. The water flowed round in a shallow pool at the base, then hurried off to join with the myriad of tiny streams elsewhere. Blackmail walked up to this waterfall and beckoned them forward.

As they approached, the knight raised up his shield and held it over his head, and stepped into the waterfall. The cascade was broken and fell widely around his shield, wider than logical physics should have dictated, in the same way that Lumathix's breath had spread out and away. Revealed behind the waterfall was a dark opening, a faint glimmer shining inside. Cautiously they walked in.

A short passage and then the tunnel opened out into a round chamber, a ceiling twice Sam's height and walls worn smooth by centuries. A small altar stood against one corner, now almost worn away by a steady drip, drip, drip; a stream of pure water that fell from a spire on the ceiling and landed in a worn pool on the altar. The drops were soothingly regular. Sam noticed with a start that they came at exactly one-second intervals; slowly measuring time for all eternity.

Blackmail strode forward and splashed his gauntlet into the pool, then roughly broke the tip off the spire. The drops and water splattered everywhere, losing count, losing time. The group startled as a sudden change in the air swelled forth.

A purple glow suffused the walls and water, and there came a clattering sound, as of stones dropping. In the wall behind the small altar a mosaic of tiles spun into place, tile by tile flipping around from its smooth back side to a colorful glossy front, scattering rock chips as it happened. They stepped back from the noise and chips; all but Blackmail, who stood and stared silently at the mural revealed.

When at last it clicked into stillness, the mural depicted a scene of dragons and battles, castles and fields. The famous battles of the War were shown, with vast clouds of swarming, bat-winged demonic fiends being driven by the shining armies of Light. The central figure in this case was a paladin, a human man in shining silver armor. The man had light brown hair and a regal mustache, just beginning to silver. His face was stern, with piercing gray eyes. His helmet, decorated with purple plumes, was tucked under his arm, and in one hand he held a shining sword, with a shield on his arm that depicted a golden griffin on a field of crimson.

"I guess this is one you're to do, knight," said Valerie, examining it.

"That looks like the one I had in my dream!" exclaimed Robin. "With the tracks and . . . but this is . . . wait a moment!"

"Uh-oh," Arcie muttered, looking at the centaur and stealthily drawing his dagger.

"What are you doing!?" exclaimed Robin. "What is this?"

Arcie readied his dagger, but felt a strong hand descend upon his shoulder. He looked up, and up, to see Blackmail lift his hand again and motion a negative. Arcie looked exasperated, but Blackmail signaled a request for trust. Arcie sulkily put away the dagger; Kaylana sighed and turned to the centaur.

"I suppose we should have explained to you earlier, Robin. Our quest is a strange one, and one that many would not approve of. I shall explain it to you, and hope that you will be as wise as my companions and can grasp it."

Kaylana briefly explained the situation to the centaur: of the world's increasing imbalance, of the danger of such an influx; of the DarkGate and the Key. Robin listened with increasing horror. Undo the actions of the Heroes? Release darkness and evil? This must not be! But at the same time, he felt a faint unease; these people he journeyed with did not seem like evil demons. They were certainly very nasty, it was true, but still they seemed so human at times; he had watched Sam's bumbling attempts to attract the attention of the Druid, heard Arcie whistling along to the music of his harp, Blackmail's obvious sorrow at the loss of his steed . . . These things showed something more than a mindless evil . . .

But that was no concern of his. He absorbed all the information Kaylana gave to him, and then steeled his thoughts. He could feel the deep gray eyes of the Druid boring into his own, but made his will stern and secret, controlling his thoughts instinctively so that her gaze did not go past his retinas, and then answered as Mizzamir had instructed him.

"Oh! Well, you should have said so. How fascinating! I won't interfere at all. What a ballad this will make, whether you succeed or fail. Please, let me continue with you . . . I may not be much help, other than as an entertainer, but this is so . . . unusual, that my curiosity, among other things, drives me to know more . . . " he stammered nervously, head swimming from the weight of this news but careful to speak only the truth. It wasn't hard. Centaurs by nature were an honest people; only Robin's poet training gave him the ability to fudge and exaggerate and delude slightly.

"Look, minstrel," Sam put in. "If you want to come along you're going to have to start pulling more of your own considerable weight. When we fight, you fight. When we run, you run. No more fainting or skipping out. Do you understand?"

"Yes, I understand," Robin answered firmly. That was true enough, anyway. He understood every word. Whether he would have to obey was another matter.

"Right, then," retorted Valerie. "Blackmail?"

The knight nodded and stepped up to the mural. Pausing a moment to trace the golden griffin device on the shield in the mural, he then pressed his gauntlet into it. There was a flash of brilliant light that left purple after-images dancing around the room, and he vanished.

"I hope he makes it," worried Kaylana. "We are running out of time and are probably being pursued even now. I wonder if we will be killed by the likes of Sir Fenwick before the entire world sublimates in light."

"How do you spell 'sublimates'? One b or two?" asked Robin, taking out a roll of parchment and scribbling furiously, to cover his shakey relief that the villains had bought his story. Now for a few convincing ballads to let them think he really was interested in their insane plot, which would also serve as notes for his report to Mizzamir . . .

"I never likes speculating on how I'm going to die," Arcie retorted, pulling out his pipe. "The only thing to do right now is wait. Smoke 'em if ye has 'em."

"There ought to be a way to get around this," Valerie said in annoyance, tapping the floor. "It irks me no end to have my own survival hang on the actions of cretins like yourselves, no offense."

"None taken I'm sure," Sam retorted sweetly.

"I am not worried," Kaylana put in thoughtfully. "It seems to me the dark knight knows what is going on better than any of us."

"Unusual fellow, him," Arcie said. "Not a word this whole trip . . . Doesn't eat, doesn't sleep . . . "

They continued to inspect the mural, while the drops of water spattered about in a random dripping chorus. "The Hero Sir Pryse," commented Valerie, looking at the mosaic. "A powerful man."

"What does the inscription say?" inquired Arcie, as they waited. Valerie studied it.

"Here is the Test of Honor," she read. "You who hold to what is right, ploys of others all despite, are the true champions of the light."

"Sort of rhymes," said Sam grudgingly.

"Who says they have to rhyme?" asked Robin. Sam shrugged.

"Well, I think it's a nice touch. I hope when you write a song about us, that is assuming we survive . . . "

"And that you can remember anything worth writing about," put in Arcie.

" . . . I hope you manage to make it rhyme, or at least try . . . too many of your modern ballads are just a collection of disjointed sentences."

"That's true," agreed Arcie. "Damned hard to remember them words after the first seven beers, some of them. Not *real* songs."

"No," admitted Kaylana. "Those were all lost with the bards."

"What—" began Robin, rather crossly.

There was a sudden popping sound, and Blackmail appeared in the room, apparently unharmed. He was holding a deep purple chunk of crystal and beckoning to them, as it flashed light and then settled into stillness. He hastened to the opening and parted the waterfall, as a low groaning grating sound began to thrum through the stone.

As they hurried out of the cave, a sudden rumble shook the earth. On the safety of the edge of the grotto, they turned. The hidden shrine caved in, rocks and water splashing, as outside the waterfall collapsed, sinking in on itself. Valerie raised an eyebrow.

"Sir Pryse was a rather crafty fellow," she commented. Next to her, Blackmail nodded, looking at the destruction. "One almost has to admire it."

VI

They passed through the rest of the sullen Kwartan countryside without incident, avoiding the looming castles of the feudal lords. Early morning, and with the sight of human habitation in the distance, the little band of renegades put aside thought of dinner and sleeping the new day away. Instead they pressed onward, heading for the large town in the distance, looking forward to recovering some of their strength and replenishing some of their provisions. Sam made a vow under his breath not to touch even the merest drop of alcohol. They passed through the front gates of Martogon, along with oxcarts of goods and chatting pedestrians, shortly before noon. Martogon was near the coast, a neutral city established here somewhat against the wishes of the local lords. Inhabited mainly by other outlanders, it was probably one of the few cities that strangers like themselves could find decent treatment.

"Fenwick's men are probably still dredging the Fens for us," chuckled Sam.

"I believe we can rest here today and tonight," suggested Kaylana, "and then move on early tomorrow evening."

"Sounds well enough to me," said Arcie. The rest concurred, and they drifted off on their own errands.

In Sam's opinion, of course, the first thing to do was buy some new clothes. He knew he looked like a villain, and a fairly scruffy looking one at that. He felt terribly conspicuous as he walked down the street, and at the first opportunity he ducked into the shadows of the buildings and inched his way invisibly toward a haberdasher's.

Within the shop at last, and free to inspect what the establishment had to offer, he found himself torn. The shop's owner, busily taking the measurement of a portly local merchant, merely gave him a look that one might reserve for a dead mouse found in one's breakfast, and left Sam to his thoughts.

Back at the Guild, of course, all one's clothes were not only tailor-made, but *specially* tailor-made, with hidden pockets and loops and slits in which to hide various tools of the trade. The average assassin didn't feel really dressed unless he was carrying at least fourteen different lethal weapons about his person. And of course, back in those days, he'd had plenty of money. He could afford the very best. People had once asked for his services in particular, hearing of his reputation, asking for the blade that never missed. He'd had a whole wardrobe then, lots of clothes and costumes for wear in the outside world so that none would know him for his trade. Merchant, soldier, beggar, prince, thief—he could appear as anyone if it helped him come within reach of his target. But one by one, the clothes had been sold away, for the money he now needed for food; his profession, the only one he knew, was no longer in demand. At the end he'd had nothing more than his "working" clothes; the uniform of matte black that allowed him to blend with the shadows. Sheer stupid stubborn pride had made him keep them this long, knowing the risks he ran in this new Light world . . . but that same pride now gnawed at his heart as he debated the clothes before him. He couldn't afford a tailor. His old outfit would have to go, there was no choice in the matter, he insisted with himself; faded, torn, tattered, it barely kept him warm. What to take its place? Within the confines of the shop's stock, clothes of a similar color were conspicuous by their absence. He couldn't have anything of bright hues; it would cut his efficiency by half, at least, besides making his eyes hurt. He rubbed his face on the soft sandwashed silk of his sleeve absentmindedly, lost in distraction. Perhaps . . . he winced. It was shameful, bitter, unpleasant . . . but unavoidable. He was going to have to charge Arcie expenses.

Arcie, meanwhile, was busy. He had followed Sam's example and padded his way to the lower merchant quarter of town, where some of his Barigan kinfolk looked up from their honest work in surprise at seeing a stranger in town. They had greeted him cheerfully, with that comradeship held between those of a country people in a world of city folk, and he had responded in kind, giving compliments on the condition of the houses and gardens. By the time he'd gotten to the store he was after, he'd already been gifted with a couple of ripe apples and a biscuit. Munching these, he padded into a different tailor's shop, exchanged words of good cheer with the seamstress, and emerged attired in a clean new overshirt of dark green and a pair of natty brown breeches with a touch of yellow braid around the cuffs, nicely setting off his newly polished brown boots. A few more stops gained him a pouch of tobacco, a new tinderbox, and a brand new hat to replace his battered leather cap lost to the recent chaos. It was soft brown, with a bright blue plume. Plumes were *the* thing to wear in Kwart; as Dous had its tunics and Trois its fringed vest, so did the people of Kwart mark themselves by plumes, in gentlemen's hats or helmets and ladies' headdress. He adjusted his new headgear in the mirror with a grin, and tipped his new hat to himself several times. Then he set off for the main part of town, to make back something of the funds expended in his little outing.

As Arcie lounged on the corner, watching the early morning crowd go past, his visual hunting was interrupted by a hiss from the shadows.

"Arcie!"

Arcie turned around to see Sam lurking in an alleyway and motioning to him. He left the corner and padded over.

"Hello laddie," he said softly, as soon as he was close enough. "What are ye about?"

"Expenses, Arcie. I need my clothes repaired or replaced . . . otherwise I may not be able to complete the job." Sam flapped his ragged sleeves like a disheveled crow.

"Job?" asked Arcie, eyebrows curling in confusion.

"Mizzamir, you feeb!" Sam hissed.

"Oh aye, so you're right. Nay problems." The Barigan shrugged and fumbled among his pouches until he came up with a small one that clinked. A twitch of the drawstrings, and he peered into it. "Aye, yon's about forty-five in tellins and stellins . . . enough?"

Sam's eyes widened. "Uh, yes, plenty . . . "

Arcie tossed him the pouch with a grin. "Take it, then . . . keep ye the change."

Sam looked worriedly at his small companion. He

hadn't expected this. Arcie hadn't become the Guildmaster of Thieves back in Bistort for handing out largess. He was the most notorious kind of thief, the kind that would steal the buttons off your shoes. The thought of him casually handing over forty-five tellins in mixed coins to an out-of-luck assassin to buy clothes was unthinkable.

Arcie watched Sam's confusion a moment. He was recalling a dark night in fog and swamp, in agony, dying, when sudden hands had pulled him free of the mud's clutch and thrown him over a centaur's withers. *Mayhaps we were ne'er really friends, before, laddie,* he thought, *but we must by rights be now . . . though I'd never dream to embarrass ye by saying so.*

"Get yerself something nice," encouraged Arcie, with a tip of his new hat, "and by Bella's breasts, my hired death-dealer, get a haircut and shave." With that, the thief turned on his bare heel and ambled off down the street. Sam was left holding the pouch of coins, standing there a long moment. Then he whispered after the departing figure a silent, "Thanks."

"You really are conspicuous, you know that, do you not?" Kaylana said sternly, looking up at the tall dark figure of the knight, who made no comment.

"Are you still insistent that you will not come out of that armor?" she inquired.

The helmet nodded. Kaylana sighed.

"You have me right confused, dark knight. You do not eat, you do not sleep, you do not drink, you do not speak. But you fight and you reason, apparently, and you hear my words. And you are dammed conspicuous in that black plate-mail."

Blackmail folded his mailed arms over his breastplate adamantly. Kaylana drummed her fingers on her staff.

"We cannot have you walking around town like that, you understand," she said. "People will notice."

The helmeted head raised in a gesture of aloof dismissal. Kaylana gave him her best exasperated look. "All right, then. You seem to be able to take care of yourself. But try not to cause any trouble."

Kaylana made her way boldly toward the local dry goods shop. She didn't need to buy anything much for herself, and Blackmail needed nothing, so she took the liberty of purchasing such traveling necessities as waterskins, haversacks, and provisions.

Valerie had taken a look about the town and given up. She risked the sun a brief moment, to remove her cloak and shake it, reversing it. She replaced it hurriedly, as the hot sun burned her fair skin, adjusting its folds over her arms and face. That was better. The crimson took in less of the heat, and would not be so noticeable in the well-populated town, but she didn't want to spend any more time out here than she had to. She hastened to the inn they had chosen, with the sign of the Frothing Otter creaking in the wind. Nightshade peered about from her shoulder.

Robin left town altogether the instant the others had wandered from sight. The few people that saw him stared and pointed, and children ran away. Centaurs were not common in Kwart, and old prejudices were still around. Ducking into a livery stable, he grabbed at the silver bracelet on his wrist. With a flash and twist of magic he appeared within the Silver Tower, in Mizzamir's magical working room.

The room was empty, but his arrival was announced by the soft chime of a bell. Robin quickly ran his fingers through his mane and tail, and straightened his collar as the rune-worked door to the room opened and admitted the radiant figure of the silver-haired Elf. Robin bowed respectfully, and the arch-mage nodded acknowledgment.

"So, young Robin, how are you getting on?" asked the mage with a raise of his elegant eyebrow. "I'd thought you had said they were killing each other."

"Sir, I had thought they were . . . but when I returned to confirm it, I found them in good health and spirits, and there was no trace of the earlier harsh words." Robin fidgeted as the mage looked surprised.

"Hmm, quite odd. Have you found out where they're headed?"

"Yes sir, I have." Robin squared his shoulders and took out his notes. To his surprise, the mage did not seem overly shocked by the news that the villains intended to recover the Spectrum Key and open the DarkGate. Mizzamir simply nodded sagely and, when Robin was through, said,

"Yes, it is as I suspected. Well, there is no harm in letting them try . . . though I wish there was some safe way of stopping them before the Tests kill them all. Or, for that matter, before Fenwick goes after them once more." He sighed. "What are they doing at the moment?"

"The villains, sir? They've stopped to rest, sir, in a town called Martogon. They've split up, running errands."

"Split up, eh?" Mizzamir looked out the window at the clear blue sky. "Well, that is convenient. If Fenwick is going to rush in like this, it leaves me no choice but to cut him off at the pass, as it were. Else he will quickly catch up to your little band of villains and put them to a nasty sticky end. Return to Martogon, Robin . . . I shall be following shortly. Do not wait for me."

Robin nodded respectfully, and with a low bow, pressed the two gray stones on his bracelet. With a whoosh and whirl of magic, he found himself once more in the warm stables of Martogon. He shook his head. The mage's face, particularly in annoyance, had seemed oddly familiar somehow. Must have been a trick of the light.

He settled down to try to get some sleep in an empty loose box, but a horse in the next stall over was making noises of distress that bothered him.

Sam had quickly changed into an inexpensive dark brown tunic and pair of green leggings, and tenderly handed his folded assassin blacks to the tailor. "I want you to mend these," he said. "Don't alter them. Don't decorate them or anything. Just mend them." The tailor took the clothes with a wrinkled nose, the plumes on his hat fluttering, and lifted a corner of the tunic. Light showed through numerous holes, making the garment appear to be made of inept lace. "Sir," began the tailor, "are you sure you wouldn't want to purchase . . . "

"I've purchased quite enough, thank you," retorted Sam. "Can you mend them or not?"

"Sir," replied the tailor huffily, "you have lost much of the original fabric. I'll need to do quite a bit of patching."

Sam ground his teeth silently. "And I suppose you don't have any matching fabric."

"There really is no call for it, sir," explained the fellow; Sam forced himself to stay calm.

"Look," he said. "I'm a member of a group of theater performers."

"Ah yes, in town for market day, are you?" asked the fellow with a raised eyebrow.

"Yes," answered Sam. "We're doing . . . " his mind raced, " 'The Tragedy of Oswald, Prince of Volinar.' You know, the one where the fellow's uncle kills his father and marries his mother? It's a very good play," he added. He'd seen it performed once, in his younger years . . . He'd taken Cata to see the performers when they came to Bistort one year. Sam had been very amused by some of the complicated poisoning scenes, since they were incredibly inept by assassin standards.

"Ah yes, sir . . . and this is your costume, then?" The tailor poked at the heap of faded blacks.

"Yes indeed," Sam nodded. "I've got the lead this year . . . only when we were rehearsing this morning one of the fellows bumped into me and knocked me off the stage into a bramble patch . . . tore my costume right up. I was furious, of course."

"Hmm, I imagine so," retorted the tailor, scratching at some of the darker reddish stains on the fabric. Sam dismissed them with a wave of his hand.

"Stage blood," he said curtly. "Didn't get a chance to wash it out. Take care of it for me, will you? I'll need them by tonight . . . Here's a deposit," he added, clinking down a gold tellin on the countertop. "There's more if you get them done in a hurry." The tailor took it with a disdainful look.

"Very well, sir," he said. "They should be ready at

about five this afternoon." He vanished into the back room. Sam dithered about for a moment and then with fretting heart took himself back to the Frothing Otter for a meal and some sleep. Valerie's amulet was nestled in a pouch around his neck. All was well, but something in the air made him uneasy.

One by one, the companions returned to their rooms at the inn and slept the sunny hours away.

Sam's time sense awoke him at precisely half-past five that same day. Lying flat on his back on the hard inn bed, his eyes suddenly flew open, staring at the cracked and faded ceiling. He slid out of the bed and peered out the window. Night was falling. A cool breeze ruffled his hair and brought a smile to his face. Five hours of intense sleep had sent sparks fizzing in his blood. He could have gotten by on two or three hours, but now he felt fully recharged and ready for just about anything. It was good to be back in a city, full of buildings to hide in and around, people to not be seen by, and the gentle flowing tide of humanity all around that had once been his livelihood. He sniffed the night air, scenting dinners being cooked, drinks being poured, buildings releasing their heat, and the presence of people going about their business. It was a beautiful night, even if it wasn't as dark as it should have been. Clouds drifted over the moon and streetlamps cast stark pools of golden light and blue shadow. The night sent shivers down his spine, so glad was he to have it to himself. He felt in very high spirits.

First things first. He snatched his moneypouch from its hiding place in his pillow and donned his hated green and brown clothes. Then he drifted swiftly downstairs and out the inn door, making his way back through town to the tailor's, forcing himself to walk normally.

He walked to the shop with tension in his limbs. Had the fellow made a mess of his clothes? Was he going to be doomed to wander the streets like a failed peasant? He ignored the "Closed" sign on the door and walked in. The tailor looked up from finishing a hem on a green silk dress and gave a twitch of his nose when he saw who it was.

"Oh, it's you again. I told you five o'clock. You're late."

Sam was in too good a mood to let the fellow get to him. "Well, I was otherwise occupied . . . got the costume?"

The tailor sniffed. "Yes, here . . . " He fumbled underneath the counter and tossed a paper-wrapped package to Sam. "I had to make a few substitutions here and there, depending upon what I could find lying around . . . I don't think your audience will notice."

Sam, meanwhile, was tearing open the packet. He unfolded black cloth, faded, yes, but clean now, and pressed. Patched, he noticed in horror, with a few scraps of black and dark gray, and elsewhere dark blue, dark green, deep purple, dark browns, and dark red. He clicked his teeth in annoyance.

"This is silly," he stated. "I'll look like a right jester in this garb." The tailor shrugged.

"See if your company has any ink or stage ichor around, then, and dye it. I can do no more."

"That's not a bad idea," replied Sam. "Here, this should cover it . . . " He tossed a handful of silver at the man. The tailor started to protest, and Sam added, "Especially since you've done an inadequate job on matching the colors and putting me through the trouble of dyeing it." He put just a touch of coldness into his voice as he spoke, and the tailor reluctantly conceded. Sam paused a moment and scooped up a pair of dark brown leather gloves and a long indigo scarf. "I'll take these too."

Arcie was enjoying the first good meal he'd had in what seemed like years. He'd scanned the inn's menu, deliberated a moment, and then ordered half of it. He was just tucking into his second plate of roast pork with apples and mushrooms when Sam came darting through the door, crossed the crowded dining hall, and leaped up the stairs that led to the private rooms. Arcie noticed an expression of glee on the assassin's face, and resolved to investigate just as soon as he'd finished dessert.

A platter of mashed potatoes, two puddings, and a slice of chocolate cake later, the Barigan padded heavily up the stairs, puffing contentedly on his pipe. He found the door to Sam's room by careful listening, choosing the one that had a sort of soft whistling coming from it, the noise Sam made when he was working on something but not being stealthy about it. Arcie knocked, and called, "Ho, laddie! what's are you about now?"

From within came the reply; "Go away, Arcie, I'm dyeing."

"What?" snorted Arcie. He opened the door; Sam had locked it, of course, antisocial fellow that he was, but Arcie wasn't an exGuildmaster for nothing. He peered inside, and chuckled at the sight.

Sam was sitting cross-legged on the floor, wearing only his black shorts and the numerous network of scars that decorated his skin. He was surrounded by wet black articles of clothing spread out on the floor. In front of him was a bowl filled with black liquid. Empty ink bottles were scattered about. Sam, the clothes, and the floor were liberally bespattered with black. Sam looked up at Arcie and sighed. "Come on in, then, and shut the door," he sighed. At some point he'd run his stained hands through his hair, and his gold-blond tufts were now half-toned and spiky, making him look as though he had a large hedgehog on his head.

"What *are* you up to, Sam?" asked Arcie. Sam had a birthmark on his shoulder, the size of a coin and star-shaped, Arcie noted. This too was ink-stained. Oddly, none of the assassin's numerous scars intersected it.

"It should be obvious. I'm dyeing my clothes," stated Sam, dipping a blue scarf into the bowl and then squeezing the moisture out of it, spreading it out to dry next to a pair of leather gloves. His other clothes, Arcie noticed, had been patched, and the patches were dark and wet. The much-abused black cloak had been hemmed neatly, and now looked something more along the lines of a patchwork quilt. Arcie shook his head in amusement.

"Well, as long as ye're having a fun time," he said, and with a final grin backed out of the room and left the assassin to his work.

A few more splotches and Sam was done. He spread the clothes in front of the open window so the cool night air would dry them. Rummaging among his accoutrements, he unearthed a small hand mirror used for distracting people and signaling other assassins. He checked his reflection. He did need a shave. He'd done what he could to maintain his appearance on the trail; Kaylana's presence was a wonderful incentive, but only so much could be done with little time and cold water. The first and last time he'd tried to grow a beard had been back in the wild days of his teenage years. He'd planned to use his beard as a place to store blowgun needles and such, but when his stubble finally had grown long enough to distinguish, he'd discovered to his horror that it was a brilliant red-gold, pitifully sparse, and downy soft. He'd tried the soot and grease on it, the same mixture he used on his hair, but then everything he'd tried to eat had tasted of rancid butter and chimneys. He'd finally shaved it off with a dagger.

His hair was a mess. He palmed a dagger off the bedside table and trimmed the longer locks. Then he debated a long moment, his eyes resting on the bowl of ink and water mixture. He rubbed the birthmark on his shoulder as was his occasional habit. That birthmark had always annoyed him, because he could just barely see it out of the corner of his eye. It was also a distinctive sort of identification his assassin training distrusted, and he kept trying unconsciously to wipe it away. His hair, too, was distinctive, and most unfitting for an assassin. But he could fix that.

A short while later, a dark-haired assassin treated himself to a thorough wash with clean water and soap and a good shave, then donned his now-dry clothing. Black leggings, tucked into black leather boots, black silk shirt, black tunic, black cloak draped elegantly over the shoulders, clipped with an ebony pin. Finally, a snug pair of black leather gloves, and a black silk scarf wound expertly around face and head until only his eyes, glinting dark hazel, showed. Into the sleeves went the sections of blowgun, dagger down the right shoulderstrap, dagger in left hip pocket, dagger in right calf innerstrap, folded tiger-claws clipped onto back of belt, garrote tucked into chest pocket, set of needles in right cuff, set in collar, vial of poison tucked into fold of cloth behind ear, yet more blades and more items. At last, as night deepened about the dreamy town of Martogon, a midnight figure slipped from an upstairs window and slid silently down the wall like an onyx raindrop.

Sam wasn't hunting tonight. He was merely enjoying being what he was, a predator, with the flow of night as his territory. He clung to the shadows and moved without a sound, enjoying the way people would walk right past him, so close he could hear their hearts beating, and never even notice him.

He stopped once and saw himself in the large window of an empty store. He paused to admire his full-length reflection, slim, sleek, deadly. He was missing something though, the touch of richness and glamour. He thought for a moment, and then reached around and found the pouch with Valerie's amulet in it. He weighed it in his hand, considering. At last puckishness overcame caution. He slipped the gold chain with its large, heavy stone from the pouch and hung it around his neck. It rested on his tunic like a deep black eye, or a hole in the world. He admired his reflection again, pleased with the utter black of the stone and the faintest glint of gold on the chain, and then slipped away into the night of the city.

He slid up to the top of a high block of flats and ran along the rooftops with the ease of a cat. It was glory, glory and pure joy, freedom to do as he pleased, free to kill, free to live, free to hunt as he chose and was born to do, as the brilliant fire in his blood sang. And because he was free to do so, he did not. In silence, he stalked passers-by in the street, people about their business in their homes as he watched from windows, men and women chatting as they dismantled their stalls in the common outdoor market. He stalked, but nothing more; crept up to them, to where an instant of movement could have meant a sudden death in the twilight, but then darted away in a joyous invisibility. Never had he felt so at one with the darkness, never before had the shadows welcomed him with such graceful ease.

As he ducked around a corner and stopped to catch his breath in silence, words drifted down to his ears and froze his delight cold.

"Please, don't, I want to go home . . . " a voice, female, young and unfamiliar, pleading. Answered by another, rough, male, heavy, slurred with drink.

"Yeah, we'll let you go home, after we've had a bit of fun . . . you like a bit of fun, girlie?" A hoarse laugh.

"No! Stop it! Let go!" A scuffle.

"Quit that, girlie, you know you want it," slurred the voice. A slap, a male snarl, and a much louder slap, a female cry of pain and fear.

"Stop! No! Help!"

The night stirred the air where Sam had been. He leaped straight up, catlike, and alighted on a window ledge. This building must be the headquarters of the town guard, grown fat and sleepy in these days of Light . . . Sam knew the type well. His brain was full of old cold anger, the fire flickering in his blood, his personal anger that was darker and colder than he ever met assignments with. The window was open. He ducked in without a sound, sprinted silently down a hall, glancing in the rooms as he flitted past. Empty, empty, barracks, storeroom . . . In this, six burly men drunk to the point of aggressiveness, in guard's uniforms. They didn't see him, he moved too fast. The last one, at the end of the hall, door closed, sounds of scuffle and sobbing. Sam went through the door without slowing down, and leaped through the air, crashing into a heavy, strong human guard, stinking of sweat and drink, who roared in surprise. A flit of someone in a blue dress ran screaming out the door as assassin and guard fell to the floor. A lantern fell over and extinguished, plunging the room into shadow. A dagger flashed like Sam's white teeth bared in fury, and blood fountained. The guard's death throes tossed the slim assassin away; he landed on his feet, looking for exits as boots pounded in the hall and angry voices came closer. Damn it, windows too small, no other doors, one door leading only into path of danger . . . only place to hide was under a large bed. No choice. He slipped into the dusty darkness beneath like a weasel going to earth.

Under the bed it was stuffy, dusty, and cramped . . . but it was also very, very dark. The unlit room was a mass of blackness, and the tiny space beneath the heavy bed was in deep shadow. He crouched in the space beneath, nervous, shaking with the afterglow of adrenalin that followed a kill and tried his best to become invisible.

Thieves and assassins share a set of skills that facilitates their business. The wearing of dark clothing, a certain way of walking, a certain way of breathing, and even a certain way of thinking combine to allow one to seem to disappear into the shadows of a scene, not so much invisible as unnoticeable, a protective camouflage with roots older and stranger than most knew. Sam had been using this skill consistently this night, and on nights past, when he walked unnoticed through busy streets.

Huddled in the darkness, Sam felt cool flatness against his chest. Valerie's amulet must've slipped down inside his tunic, against his skin. Sam ignored it and concentrated on feeling the depth of the shadows around him, stilling himself to their stillness, willing his dark-garbed clothing to melt into the darkness of the absence of light. Feet drummed into the room, loud voices called for a lantern.

Sam was silent, breathing in soft slow breaths, shaking stilled, lost in forcing himself deeper and deeper into the darkness. An assassin was a match for any man, Sam judged he was a match for any three or four with surprise and terrain in his favor, but six in a room with only one exit was suicide. A strange cold tingle swept up his chest as his will pulled at the shadows, suddenly finding them of a strangely pliable softness, wrapping deeper and deeper around him, ever more at one with the blackness under the bed . . . his mind swirled, drifting into the shadows, into instincts he'd never known he had, into magic and ancient knowledge, his thoughts moving in strange patterns like the blending of shadows, deeper, stronger. Then suddenly he *saw* the way the shadow *was,* and without thinking, moved *through* it, like a dive into cool water, even as strong hands gripped the edge of the bed . . .

A crash as heavy hands flung the bed aside, and a lantern flared at the same moment, filling the room with golden light. Shouts of victory died away in confusion as the eyes of six puzzled guards searched the room. It revealed only the gory body of their dead comrade in one corner. The man's heart had been torn out, and lay scattered in gory chunks around the room. Also . . . a bed on its side, a square of dust disturbed with a blurred humanoid outline showing where someone had been. Whatever had made the outline had vanished.

Sam had Shadowslipped.

Sam fell *up* and landed lightly on his feet in front of a square of blackness that vanished instantly, leaving only the soft gray of a background behind. His heart pounded as he raised his head and looked about. He caught his breath in wonder.

Around him, on all sides, was a landscape of unearthly beauty. He stood in a soft gray nothingness, swirling with possibility. All around him, as far as he could see, were irregular patches of black. Some lay flat on the ground, others slanted like strange walls, some were mere slivers of black smaller than his fingernail, others were great slabs of darkness that stretched into forbidding cubes or sheets. There were a few above him and a few below him, and, he noted in sudden surprise, some right near the area of where he stood, and these were moving! Six blobby shapes, flickering and twisting about, flat under his feet, like shadows cast by persons who were not there . . .

Sam realized with a flash that such was exactly what they were. Shadows, nothing more, of the six guards who had come into the room after him. Sometimes the shadows would slant up vertically, as a guard moved closer to a wall. Sam watched a moment, and marked with his eye where the walls were. Then he walked through one.

It felt like nothing, and it was nothing. He stepped into one of the solid patches of blackness. At once he noticed a difference, a strange subtle feeling, like the difference between a room with an open window and one with the window closed. The shadows swirled with that same wonderful fluidity about him, but he stepped back out of the patch of darkness.

Sam's eyes were getting used to the landscape. He found he could distinguish differences in depth between the shadows. Some were a dim, shallow black . . . Sam guessed they were too well-lit to be true gateways and were only dimmer possibilities of the deepest shadows. He also noted several very dark shadows, thick and deep, like those he would have preferred to hide in, in the sun-light world.

No doubt that was the way to leave, if there was one . . . just step back into the shadows and will yourself out? The shadows seemed to be the gateway from the world he had been born into and this strange two-toned twilight world.

Two-toned twilight world . . . where had he heard that before? He wondered as he looked down to where the street would be if his theory of the nature of this place was correct. There it was, a grayness where many moving shadows moved back and forth along a flat plane.

Two-toned twilight . . . Sam's mind had finally calmed down enough from his near escape and his sudden change of surroundings to remember an old, old song Black Fox had used to sing when he was drunk on red wine . . .

There is a land on the edge of night
A shiver in the shadow's shade
Haunted by the ones who stayed
In the realm of two-toned twilight.

Taken out of time and space
Lost in a deeper darken,

Going to another Place,
Sliding as your spirits harken,
Shadowslipping, Shadowslipping.

Those of the fire, those of the night
Those of the blood who turn from the light
Here is your safety, and here is your death,
The seduction of Shadow that takes your last breath.

Black Fox had sung it in a cold, slow, eerie voice that had made the young Samalander's flesh crawl with nameless fear, and the other assassins would throw things at Black Fox and tell him to shut up. Black Fox would laugh and sing something else, and the others would return to their wine with only a faint shiver or two. There were times, long ago, when Sam was learning the trade, that he was reminded of the old song; hiding deeply in shadows, sometimes he'd felt a faint shiver on his skin, as though the shadows were something more than just dark spots in corners . . . he'd put it off to superstition. And when he'd asked Miffer once about Black Fox's song, the master assassin had snorted softly. "Don't trouble your head with such things, boy. Black Fox doesn't know what he sings about, and nor does any assassin alive today. It's an old song left over from the old days, old even before the War." When Sam had pressed the matter, Miffer had said, "Well, a long time ago, there were certain folks who could sort of walk *through* the shadows . . . like ghosts. But they grew strange, and changed. One by one they'd walk into the shadows and never come out. So they stopped teaching it, and we're all a lot better off today. Now let's see that grapple again." And Sam had forgotten the matter . . . until now.

On the other side of town, Arcie was plying his dishonest trade. Easy pickings tonight, so he decided not to do anything extensive like burglary, that always made him feel a bit guilty; it seemed to upset people more than just having lost a pouch or a bracelet or two. Now, of course, he was on an adventure of sorts and was going to have to "rough it" anyway. His father was always very extensive in his reminiscences of "roughing it" on adventures. *"Laddie, when I done explored the icy cold of Huthor's Ruins in midwinter, I were nay older than ye, and I sleeped out in snow up to my chin and ate lichens fer my meals. Aye, no biscuits nor tea for me, laddie. I was Roughing It."* What with being chased, drowned, bogged, stabbed, chased some more, and in general kept from creature comforts, Arcie had lost some of the rose-colored haze he'd had over his idea of adventures. But still, it was better than hanging around Bistort and being bored. There was not that much that one could buy out in the wilderness, and he remembered his father's talk of "traveling light." So instead of thieving pouches of coins, which were bulky and heavy, he stuck to lighter items of greater value, such as gemstones and rings and suchlike. This was harder, of course, and you ran more risks . . . but well, that was the fun part.

Arcie was a master thief, but occasionally, even the greatest find the odds stacked against them. Right outside the inn, Arcie was leaning inconspicuously in the shadows, back against a wall, near a pair of wealthy looking fellows who were chatting up a giggling courtesan. Arcie's fingers held a light strong silver pick, and he was loosening the gems set in one fellow's sword pommel and catching them silently as they fell like multicolored drops. All was going well, when suddenly the shadowed wall *pushed* him.

He fell forward onto his stomach, scattering gems from his hand. One of the men shouted, "Thief!" and grabbed at the Barigan. Arcie promptly fetched him a smart blow on the shin with a booted foot. This was the signal for both of them to go after him with fists and swords.

Valerie was in her room with the lights out, brushing her long black hair. Nightshade sat perched on the bedside table, preening his glossy feathers. Valerie touched her throat where the amulet used to hang, and sighed.

Just then she heard a cry of "Thief!" and sounds of a scuffle. Curious, she opened her window.

In the darkness below she observed a pair of men swatting ineffectually at a small figure that seemed to be trying to escape. A henna-haired woman watched from a safe distance. Valerie knew that almost certainly only one figure of that size in this town would qualify for the exclamation she had just heard. Well, we can't have that, she mused. A quick bit of induced somnolence should do the trick. She raised her hand, called up words of power from her memory . . . and faltered. There was no power! The spell she was attempting was very minor and should have been well within her capabilities if her amulet was anywhere in town. Had that fool assassin destroyed it? She raged in silent fury while the men struggled below her. At last she recovered her thoughts and picked up the water basin from the dressing table.

Arcie started as a sudden crash erupted near him, and one of the men folded slowly onto his knees, surrounded by white china splinters. The second man paused to look to his stricken companion. "Thomas?" he said, giving Arcie just enough time to jump as high as he could with a swing of the morning star, catching the man a nice clip on the back of his head with the ball. The man fell peacefully beside his friend, and the woman gave a squeak and scampered off into the safety of the more open streets. Arcie mopped his brow with the back of his hand and peered up at the dark open window where Valerie's pale face was outlined. He tipped his hat.

"Thankee kindly, Valerie."

"Never mind that, you curlypolled idiot. Where's that fool assassin?" Valerie's voice was angry, and her purple eyes burned.

"Sam?" Arcie looked around and secured his morning star with a shrug. "I have not seen yon since he were in his room covering everything with ink. 'Round sixish."

"Well, he's not there now . . . or at least my amulet isn't," fumed the sorceress. "If you do see him, Arcie . . . tell him I'd like a *word* with him." Her shark teeth flashed in the darkness, not in a smile, and the window shut. Arcie shook his head and, out of force of habit, looted the unconscious bodies. No sense letting an involuntary mugging go to waste. He started to leave, hesitated a moment, and then went to the wall that had thrust him so rudely from its safety. He reached out, patted the shadowed surface. It was solid brick, cool in the night air, with no moving parts or anything.

"Me foot must've slipped," muttered Arcie, doubtfully. He paused a moment in thought, then tossed a pebble at Valerie's window. It rattled off the pane, and a moment later the window opened, and Valerie looked out.

"What is it now, thief?" she asked wearily. Arcie grinned up at her and tipped his new hat.

"Might I offer to buy you a spot of breakfast, lady Valerie?" he inquired. Valerie hesitated a moment, then raised an eyebrow.

Sam sat back in the dim grayness, a little startled. He'd come close to walking through that shadow just then, but his cautious boot had met with something solid that jerked like a living thing, and he'd retreated back into the safety of this strange world. He was getting more and more accustomed to his surroundings and began to wonder why the place had seemed to have such a fearsome image. It was an assassin's paradise.

It was wonderful to be able to move so freely through space, completely unseen, not even *there.* And yet, at almost any point he chose, he could appear again, untrackable, untraceable . . . it was the ultimate assassin's tool. He wondered why he'd never been able to do it before; it felt like second nature to him now. It must be a combination of his utterly black attire, his solitude as the world's last assassin . . . and probably a bit of the dark cool gem resting on his chest, he admitted to himself. But this was a better use to put the amulet to than Valerie had ever thought of, he'd wager. He would keep it, he decided. He stepped into another patch of shadow and willed himself through it, his mind parting the stuff of darkness like velvet curtain folds. He emerged into an empty storeroom. A rat squealed and skittered away. Sam smiled beneath his scarf and melted back with ease into the twilight world.

He wandered about, appearing in alleys, rooms, cellars, attics, anywhere with deep enough shadows. The night of Outside seemed pale and dry in comparison to the solitary glory of the shadows. Solitary indeed, for though Miffer had implied there were others, perhaps trapped in this world, Sam found himself alone in the shadows here. He peeped in at children sleeping, at a drunk in an alleyway, at an old woman reading by the light of a candle in a dark room. It was a world of infinite possibilities.

But only so long as there were shadows. Sam, musing on his strange discovery, felt that if indeed the world were to be plunged into eternal light, that light would close the borders forever, and this rich and fascinating realm would become nothing more than a dull gray void. Already there were fewer thick shadows than he would have supposed . . . shadows that were only dim . . . well, shadows of themselves now. But while it lasted, Sam reveled, rejoicing in the return of his earlier euphoria, the bitter pride of a kill, the ego-boost of his superhuman powers with the realm of Shadow at his disposal.

He walked among the shadows of people going up and down the street, and suddenly noticed one in particular. It was hard to be precise, of course, looking at the rough flickering blobs, but in the silhouette he could easily distinguish long hair blowing in a faint breeze, a long, flapping robe-like garment, and most important, a long object held upright in the hand—a staff. Kaylana, beautiful red-haired Kaylana . . . wouldn't she be surprised to see what he could do! Wouldn't she be impressed! He glanced around; no other people-shadows were nearby. He followed the shadow a few paces until it crossed a block of darkness on the gray ground, deepening to passable shadowdepth, and jumped through it.

He sprang up into the real world from the floor like a demon through a trap door, with a cheery cry of exuberant glee, arms wide in dramatic entrance . . . and found himself face to face with the awesome silver-white figure of the Arch-Mage Mizzamir.

The actual Kaylana, meanwhile, was rapping on the door of one of the rooms at the inn. After a moment, the door opened, and Blackmail peered silently down at her. She grabbed him by the gauntlet. Her khaki robes were smeared with mud and blood.

"Come, silent one. I need your help." She marched off down the hall, towing the unprotesting knight.

Kaylana led the way down to the stables, to a mare lying down in the straw of a loose box. Robin was huddled nearby. Kaylana explained the situation tersely.

"The mare is foaling, and she is having problems. I need someone strong to help pull the foal's head around whilst I retract the rest of it. I attempted to get Robin to help, but before I knew what had happened he went thudding down into the straw. That is surely the most squeamish centaur I have ever seen."

"I don't know nothing about birthing no foals," muttered Robin, ashen faced, from his corner. The mare whickered. Kaylana ignored Robin and patted the horse's neck soothingly, then rolled up her sleeve, looking up at Blackmail.

"I hope you will be able to assist more capably, knight. When I hand you the end of this rope and tell you to pull, I want you to pull, is that understood? Slow, steady, not too hard. We wish to deliver this foal, not whip it across the stable, is that understood?"

The helmet nodded slowly. "Excellent," said the Druid, splashing home-distilled disinfectant on her arms from a waterproofed pouch. "Let us begin, then."

"Very gentlemanly of you, Barigan."

"Well, you as good as saved me hide back yon. The least I can do," replied Arcie modestly. Valerie raised her glass of red wine to him, and he responded with his tankard of ale. The Silver Leaf Restaurant wasn't too sure what to make of the odd pair. Certainly the waiter had never heard of a few of the dishes requested, and the cook hadn't before had the experience of being called out to have his soup recipe corrected. It was a strange night in Martogon.

If Sam were a hero, tracking down a villain, he would, at this point, have said a few choice dramatic words along the lines of Mizzamir being his now, or perhaps a suggestion for the mage to make preparations to meet whatever deities he favored. But as it was, Sam was a villain and didn't mess about with such things. He stared into the mage's handsome yet terrible face for an instant, found his stare returned. The fire flared with the sighting of the target, and Sam lost himself in an instant as the channeled darkness in his soul turned him into a single-minded killer. A flip of his arm caused a dagger to fall into his hand, and he attacked.

But Mizzamir was a hero, and not just any normal hero; he was a *Hero.* And your average backwater assassin cannot kill a Hero as easily as he might kill a lesser man. An Elf of Mizzamir's age and experience has quite a bit of raw survival power. Mizzamir twisted and took the dagger in his shoulder instead of through his ribs where it was headed, and came back instantly with a spell drawn from the power of his staff.

Sam heard a word of magic and leaped like a hare to one side. A shower of golden arrow-like missiles rained around and past him, a handful striking him with flashes of searing pain and vanishing. He landed on his feet, another dagger already in his hand. With this one he took a split second to slide it through the seal on a vial of poison, giving the mage time to ready another spell. Dagger and spell then hurtled through the space between the two combatants simultaneously.

The dagger hit home with a soft thunk, biting deep into the mage's gut. Mizzamir winced in pain and gripped at the hilt as blood stained his white robes. Hopefully the preventative antidotes and magic he'd taken would last long enough . . .

Sam felt a cloud of magic envelop him. It wrenched through his body, and the air smelled of lightning and orange blossoms. His eyes squeezed closed, his skin prickling, limbs heavy, slowing . . . his dulling ears heard the mage's gasping voice,

"Don't worry . . . I'll come back for you."

Then all was silence. The white-robed hunched figure vanished in a flash of gold light, leaving the street empty, deserted but for a man-sized figure in the dim moonlight.

At the far end of the street, a door opened in a well-lit restaurant, spilling a shaft of light and noise and smells of food into the late night air. From this portal stepped a pair of figures, one quite small and stout, another taller and willowy. They passed out into the street, conversing in contented voices.

"I recall, back in Bistort," said Arcie, settling his hat on his head, "there were a wee shop as made the finest meat pies I think I ever did come across. Light, flaky, lots o' gravy . . . "

"Ah," replied Valerie, nodding. "Yes . . . we had something similar in the Underrealms as a tradition on holidays; slices of venison and . . . other meats, in a pastry crust decorated with little cut-out mushrooms . . . Great caverns! What is that?"

Arcie looked up to where Valerie indicated a large stone object in the middle of the road. The moonlight made things a little mazy, but it was fairly clear what the object was.

" 'Tis a statue of somebody. See, yon's a arm, and there's a hand, and that must be the head there, though it look like it's all wrapped up in bandages of some such." He was suddenly struck by realization. "Here! It's a statue of Sam! See, them are Sam's clothes as he was fixin', you can almost make out the lines o' the patches."

Valerie walked around the statue. "He doesn't look very happy," she commented. Indeed, the figure had one knee buckled, one arm extended as if hurling something away, and the other pressed against his brow. His body was twisted awkwardly to the side as though in the middle of a dodge.

" 'Tis no' a very good likeness," mused Arcie. "Who might have carved it? And why? And what are it doing out in the middle of the road like this? It weren't here when we come by before."

Valerie's brow furrowed. She reached out with her black fingernails and lightly touched the statue. Pale green sparks crawled around her fingers as she concentrated. Then she stepped back, dusting off her hands.

"Well, Arcie, that explains that. This *is* Sam. He's been turned to stone."

"But how?" gaped Arcie, rapping his knuckles on the rocky form. "Who?"

"My guess would be some white magician," replied Valerie. "Typical. Puts your enemies in cold storage, keeps them safe and unaware until you figure out what you want to do with them . . . very humane. Myself, I've always preferred a good disintegration or ball of fire, or if one needs to keep them around, there's always the convenient option of transformation into frogs or slugs . . . much more easily portable than massive blocks of granite." She frowned at the stony figure of the assassin. "We'd better do something before whoever did this comes back for him. Let's see, where has he got my amulet under all this ridiculous costume . . . " she passed her hands thoughtfully over the gray surface. Arcie began to fidget.

"I think you better hurry, Valerie . . . We dinna want whoever did this tae come back and find us . . . "

"Hush, Barigan. Ah, here . . . " she rested a palm over the general area of the statue assassin's chest and looked puzzled. "I thought you said he wasn't wearing it . . . he shouldn't be."

"I dinna ken," replied the Barigan. "Come on, do somewhat, change him back, whatever, he can tell us about it later."

"Pish-tosh, Barigan. I can't change him back. Have you a chisel or some such tool? We'll have to get my amulet out of there."

"What if ye slips and breaks his arm off, or take a big chunk of his chest out?" retorted Arcie. "Either change him back or let's us get out of here and kiss yer amulet goodbye. We have no got time to play sculptor."

The sorceress sighed. "I told you, I can't change him back."

"Och aye, I'd forgot. Excuse me. I'd thought you were a sorceress." The thief's voice was heavy with sarcasm.

Valerie bridled.

"I *am* a sorceress."

"Yet ye canna undo a wee spell? Call that as power?" Arcie snorted.

"I could change him back, if I wished. I just don't want to."

"Nay, I heard ye. Ye said ye couldna do it."

"I could so."

"Nay, ye couldn't."

"Yes I could!"

"Nay, nay, never ye could."

"I can and I will, Barigan!" She rolled up her sleeves. "Stand back and kill anyone who comes near." She rested her palm over where she detected her amulet, drawing power from it through the layers of gray stone. This was going to call for the undoing of another's magic, someone quite likely more powerful than she . . . and thus demanded a bit more finesse.

She sang the Words of Unbinding, her voice weaving into the magic of the stone and unraveling the enchantment upon it. She could see the threads of silver-white magic bound round the atoms of the changed stone; her voice and power had to carefully spin wires of black undoing that would lift and twist and dissolve the white power, without cutting; cutting the threads would cause the spells to collapse and leave the assassin a pile of meat and pebbles. Thank Kuluna that some Weaver training was part of every Nathauan's magical education! The concentration, the tight power of the white mage's magic was stronger than she had ever encountered, stronger than she had expected. Her mind hummed with pain as her voice sang, trying desperately to keep her power steady.

Feldspar, quartz, bones of earth,
Mica, limestone, fall away,
Return to flesh of life's given birth,
Blood from sand, and skin from gray.

Purple-black light glowed and shimmered around the statue, and then suddenly vanished. The dim gray object fluxed into black cloth and fell with a groan on its side. Arcie hopped over and shook the assassin's shoulders.

"Sam! Come on! Valerie, help . . . Valerie?"

Arcie turned and lunged just in time to catch the sorceress before she collapsed onto the cobblestones. He looked over to where Sam was unsteadily getting to his feet. "Sam! Come on, help me with Valerie here . . . I think as she strained something."

Sam looked around. Mizzamir was gone. With trembling heart he went and scooped up the unconscious sorceress and then, Arcie pelting along behind him, he ran for it.

Silence reigned as the footsteps faded away. Then, with a flash, Mizzamir appeared, wounds and poison cured with a potion of godly healing he'd had stored back at the Silver Tower . . . and found his captive vanished.

"Oh dear," he muttered. Mizzamir's plan to capture the renegades one by one as they wandered about town seemed to have failed. One of them had seen him, and, despite his best efforts, had escaped. That one might have warned the others. He'd have to rethink.

"Well, perhaps another time." He vanished again.

Sam, carrying the unconscious Valerie, and Arcie hastened through the back streets.

"We've got tae find the others and get out of here,"

panted Arcie. "The guards are going to be coming out after me pretty soon . . . I got into a bit o' trouble with a couple of locals."

"Guards," scoffed Sam coldly. Arcie looked up at him in concern.

"Sam . . . I heard a couple of them as they walked past . . . they're out looking for someone that sounds like ye, unless there be another person about dressed all in black who wields daggers . . . what'd you do?"

"Assassinated one." Sam peered around a corner. It was safe. He hastened on.

"Assassinated one?!" exclaimed Arcie. "What did ye go and do a stupid thing like that for? And on *my* time, no less! Fer shame!"

"He was trying to rape some girl. Now shut up, Arcie, and let me think."

Sam rubbed his brow. His mind was still muddled from being turned to stone, but he remembered Mizzamir's parting words . . . *"I'll come back for you."* Now that the Barigan and sorceress were safely away, he'd have to go back to that street and hope to meet the mage when he returned. And do it swiftly, and stealthily, and with a quick exit nearby in case he failed again. He looked at Arcie. The Barigan was fidgeting.

"Arcie, Robin'll be sleeping in the stable. They won't have let him have a room. Valerie . . . " he dropped the Nathauan to her feet and held her up. She blinked blearily at him with large purple eyes. "Valerie, can you walk? Just a little way?" She nodded weakly. "All right. Arcie, get Valerie to the stable. They won't think to look for us there. Then go find Blackmail and Kaylana. Tell them to help Valerie, and get everybody to the north edge of town. We've got to leave early. I'll meet you there if I can . . . If I don't show up in one hour, go on without me, as fast as you can."

Arcie was looking at him in confusion. "Sam? Are you all right?"

"Go!" The assassin gave him a slap on the shoulder and ran back down the street. His soft footfalls ceased abruptly as he turned a corner and vanished into the darkness. Arcie shook his head in puzzlement, and led the woozy Valerie across the street. The night made everything seem strange . . . happenings, people, colors . . . in the dim moonlight, peering out from the folds of his scarf, Sam's eyes had seemed to have faded from their whimsical hazel to a strange cold gray.

He got to the stable, and found a strange but very peaceful scene. Kaylana was washing her arms off in a bucket of water, Robin was lying down in a corner, eyes wide, and Blackmail was on his armored knees in the straw of a loose box, rubbing down a wobbly brown foal with a twist of straw. The foal's mother was standing and assisting him with her tongue. Out of breath, Arcie hurriedly explained the events of the evening and Sam's message. There was a scramble to collect gear from rooms, and then the party headed out into the night.

The shadows welcomed Sam like an old friend. He fluxed with a twinge of relief into the blessed coolness of the Shadowrealm, and ran in a straight line back to where he estimated he'd last seen Mizzamir. A quick scan of the area turned up no mage-shadows, so he slipped through a dark corner with some reluctance and concentrated on waiting. He hadn't been prepared to meet the Arch-mage before . . . an assassin generally preferred to hunt a target, choosing the time and moment, and with a bit of preparation such an assassin was almost unstoppable. Cunning, with reactions and strength built to an inhuman level by the skilled focusing of the fire in the blood—cold, merciless, swift, silent and deadly. It was this way with Sam now, as he waited.

After about forty-five minutes, he gave up. The mage must have shown himself, found Sam gone, and vanished. Sam felt a twinge of irritation at having wasted time by getting Valerie and Arcie out of the way. It was their fault he'd missed his kill. With a sulk, he stepped back into the shadows, sliding through into the twilight.

As he hastened through his strange new kingdom, he

noticed the available shadows growing dimmer, less passable. It must be coming on to dawn Outside. Sam wrinkled his nose in disgust. The thought of dull, bright daylight irked him. It would be faster and safer if he were to follow the others by their shadows and emerge to catch up with them when the lovely night came again. He made his wraithlike way through the gray world to what he judged would be the north side of town.

"He does not come," muttered Kaylana suspiciously. "Did he say who it was that had petrified him?"

"Nay," Arcie shook his head. "Just gave us a shove in yer direction and went running back."

"There's something strange going on with that assassin," Valerie muttered. "A while ago, I tried to use my magic, and it was as though my amulet had passed beyond the boundaries of the world. And yet when we found him again, it was secure under his stone clothing. And now?" She wrinkled her brow, and concentrated a moment, then frowned. "And now it's gone again. I find that very disturbing."

"Ye said he shouldn't be wearing it?" inquired Arcie. "Could it hurt him?"

Valerie sighed. "The Darkportal is pure distilled evil. Only a faint source, as I said, and harmless so long as its power is not used . . . but if he is wearing it, and if he is somehow using it, it will begin to affect him . . . I have trained for many years to control it, and even so it makes me the dark, cruel, evil person that I am." She smiled with her shark teeth. "What it may do to your foolish little blond friend one can only speculate."

Robin fidgeted. He didn't like the thought of anyone else as evil as Valerie coming with them. He felt it would be best to move on.

"It's been an hour, and more so. We'd better do as he suggested, and move on," he offered.

Arcie looked at the sky. It was getting lighter. "It'll be dawn soon," he muttered. "Far too early, though. The nights really are getting shorter," he said, then glanced up at the tall figure of Blackmail. "With some exceptions, of course." The helmet nodded graciously.

Kaylana sighed. "Yes, perhaps we should leave. If he is able, he will catch up with us later . . . and if he is not able, then we are at great risk every moment we remain inside this city. We will move on."

"And leave my amulet behind?" snapped Valerie. Kaylana regarded her from cool green eyes.

"Would you prefer to wait and explain your position to the city watch when they arrive, helpless as you supposedly are without your Darkportal?"

Valerie seethed a moment, then conceded sulkily. "Well, if you put it that way . . . but he'd better catch up to us." The group turned to go . . . and paused. The tall dark figure of the knight did not move.

"Blackmail? Come on," urged Arcie. The knight drew his sword and stuck it into the earth in front of him. He folded his mailed hands over the top of it, set his legs apart, and stood, like a steel colossus, unmoving. The company watched in silence a moment. Then Kaylana said softly,

"He tires of running away, I think."

"Damned knightly types," snorted Valerie. "Come along, you plated ass."

The dark figure of the knight was utterly still, except for the faint whispering of the wind in the ragged black plumes that adorned the helmet. After a moment, Valerie sighed.

"We could leave one, but not two."

"We must wait a bit longer," agreed Kaylana. Robin and Arcie exchanged the glances of those who would much rather be elsewhere and settled down to wait impatiently.

Sam found five shadows on the relevant space that signified the edge of town. Two medium sized ones, one large one, one small one, and one with four legs.

"That's them, all right," muttered Sam crossly, walking around and over them. "Why aren't they moving?

Why are they just sitting there? It's been over an hour by now. Idiots." He kicked at the black splotches. "Get up, get on with it, you scum!" he yelled. How wonderful to be able to yell that way at them, no more than a shadow's width away, and have them take no notice. Stupid people. He was better than all of them put together, and all they did was use him for a convenient way of snuffing enemies. They didn't trust him, obviously, still lurking here after he'd told them to shove off, and he didn't trust them. No doubt the first chance they got they'd trade him to Mizzamir for their own benefit. That was part of why it was so important to kill the mage.

But maybe . . . maybe he should kill these people first, before they could betray him. Then he'd be free to track down the mage without all this stupid tromping around the countryside after some mythical goal. Arcie was a little wretch who'd stolen his things several times and constantly was abandoning him in times of danger. Let's see, if he came out of shadow *there,* a quick, well-placed kick to the solar plexus should finish the Barigan *there* off quite nicely. Then next to him was that simpering centaur . . . well, his throat probably cut open as easy as anybody's. Valerie was there, that dark bitch who wanted his amulet! He clutched at the stone under his shirt. It was cool on his skin and tingled. It was his, his, and she couldn't have it. It gave him power over twilight and shadow, and he'd kill her for no other reason than to keep it. He could easily throw a poisoned dagger through her chest while the centaur was still falling. The knight was there, he'd be a bit harder, but Sam had never trusted him; he was strange, and things that Sam didn't understand were dangerous. Armored, yes, but a bag of poison dust through that dark viewslit in the visor should do the trick . . . and Kaylana, who hit him with sticks and had gotten him into this whole damned mess in the first place! It was all her fault! And she was probably the most powerful member of the party right now, with Valerie incapacitated and Sam the Invincible wise to their treachery . . . she would have to die first.

Sam didn't even bother to use his assassin skill of summoning his latent fire-energy. Vermin like these didn't need or deserve that sort of special treatment. He quickly checked his equipment, armed himself with a blade in each hand, and Shadowslipped.

He stepped out of the darkness behind a wall, and unluckily met the first rays of the morning sun and Kaylana's piercing green eyes at the same time.

He flinched away from the biting sharp light, struggling to maintain his purpose but having trouble sinking a knife into the heart of the owner of those impossible green eyes. If the fire had been leaping in his blood he wouldn't have hesitated, but he hadn't summoned it . . .

Kaylana, though she did not know its origin, saw the killing intent in a pair of strange gray eyes that squinted from a wrapped mask of silk cloth. She did not question, only countered. A will strong enough to face down a starving beast, a gaze older than the steel and cities of men bored into Sam's brain.

Though only an instant passed for the other companions, as they startled at the assassin's sudden appearance, it seemed to the two combatants an eternity; Kaylana cold and still as a mountain glacier, Sam trembling with pent-up killing force and fighting his shrinking agony of the growing sunlight.

At last he withdrew, fighting himself back, forcing himself to be calm, to act normal. *This is not the time . . . wait, wait, until later in the darkness, or when they sleep and the eyes cannot see . . .*

The daggers slipped back into their sheaths, and Sam slumped limply, tugging his mask down to shade his eyes.

"Um, sorry," he heard himself mutter. "I thought you were someone else."

"Indeed," said Kaylana coldly. "I felt much the same. Are you wearing Valerie's amulet, Sam?"

Sam stiffened, paranoia flashing anew in his brain. *Kill them! Kill them now!* "Amulet? What amulet? Oh, that. No, of course I'm not wearing it. Don't be stupid. Come on, let's get out of here." He set off at a brisk pace down the road, the others exchanging glances as they followed, except for the dark knight, who turned his helmet to give the assassin a long look. Then he sheathed his great black sword and followed. Kaylana felt the lies and strangeness in the assassin's words and mind, but kept back, and did nothing; caution must be her watchword.

They marched out into the sunshine, down a dusty road with fields of grain growing gold on either side, despite it being still the autumn of the year. At last they passed the edge of the cultivated lands, and a short ways later, came to the edge of Cranch Sealake Channel. There was a little shipping and fishing town there, not much more than a harbor for the city of Martogon further up a northflowing river. They spoke to the dockmaster, and booked passage on a small craft that would take them to the far side of the water, to the land of Natodik and the next leg of their journey.

"This are a nice change," commented Arcie. The others were inclined to agree. After long days of travel and being hunted, it was a relief to let someone else worry about where they were going.

Cranch Sealake was not actually a lake, but rather a wide, rounded channel separating the lands of Natodik and Kwart. The deep blue waters rose and fell in a strange tidal pattern that seemed to have little or no connection with tides elsewhere. Rumor had it that this strange tidal behavior was caused by the slow breathing of a huge behemoth that dwelt on the channel floor. In these enlightened times, of course, the whole thing was regarded as a foolish superstition . . . but that didn't stop the captain of the *Roslilia* from surreptitiously tossing a basket of sweet loaves and flowers overboard as they neared the center of the lake, to appease the monster and hopefully keep it in slumber.

The *Roslilia* was a small, well-built ship, two-masted, with white sails and a water-nixie carved into her prow. Fouse, the captain, ran the route from the lakeport near Martogon, across the water north to the seaport of Star-hold. He normally took few or no passengers, but these folk had paid a nice sum to be taken there immediately, instead of waiting for one of the other ships that left at different hours.

The party had a pair of small rooms below deck, although Robin found the cargo hold better suited to his needs. His four legs enabled him to balance quite well on the rolling deck, and he got the impression of really traveling, seeing new things, new lands. He spent much of his time up on deck, tuning his harp as it reacted to the salt spray, and trying to write verses—both for his own use and to convince the villains that he really was interested in their adventures. Right now, though, these villains had dragged up cushions from one of the cabins and were sitting about, enjoying a bottle of wine chilled in the ocean, off-handedly playing a game of cards, and talking.

"I dinna know," said Arcie to Sam, peering over his cards at Blackmail, who delicately held a fan of cards in his huge dark gauntlets. "Are that cheating? It truly are impossible to tell if he's bluffing or nay." Arcie glanced over at the assassin, who was still wrapped in his black mask, gray eyes glinting out from the folds. "O' course, you aren't much different."

"Don't complain, Arcie . . . " muttered Sam, his voice muffled. He tossed a silver stellin into the pot. "I'm in."

"I as well," replied Valerie from within her hood, adding a small gold spangle. She looked different, Sam noticed . . . then realized that the black raven that was so much a part of her costume was missing. A quick glance around located it perched behind the Barigan's chair, peering over his shoulder with intense interest. Sam smiled to himself in his mask, despite his cold loathing. A very clever trick, that. The ship's crew had fixed the sails and the ship was heading along at a good clip, while the crew cast confused glances at the strange group playing Bunker's Aces on the deck, using wineglasses to keep the cards from blowing away in the wind.

Valerie watched Sam try to take a sip of his wine, fumble with the scarf, then set the glass down untasted.

"Why don't you take that thing off, assassin? It's not like you're going to be working on board ship," she asked. Sam stiffened imperceptibly and answered coldly.

"I happen to like it, thank you. It keeps the sun out of my eyes." Kaylana, who could not begin to fathom the many and varied rules of Bunker's Aces and instead was amusing herself by peering over the deck and counting porpoises, turned around at this.

"You know, Sam, I suspect something is the matter with your eyes, a touch of cataract perhaps. I noticed it the other day."

"Aye, the lassie's right," agreed Arcie, casually palming a card out of his sleeve. "I noticed it too . . . yer eyes look a tad cloudy." Actually, he thought to himself, they look like they're made of lead, but no sense worrying the man.

"Nothing wrong with me," muttered Sam. "I can see just fine."

"Oh?" asked Kaylana. "Can you tell me what you see over there?" She indicated a general area of water off the forward port side. Sam stood up and looked.

"Of course," he scoffed. "It's a fair-sized white boat. Now quit bothering me, Kaylana," he growled, and sat back down. Kaylana tapped her staff thoughtfully. This was a far change from the assassin of only last week who had been one of the first to pull out of the near-certain intergroup conflict in the Fens. She decided to let it pass for now. Arcie too seemed to notice his friend's discomfiture and decided to try and bring him out with a bit of conversation. Sam had always liked to give long melancholy monologues about the justification for his profession . . . maybe the chance to do so now would cheer him. He looked around. The sailors for the most part had gone down into the galley for their evening meal, leaving a skeleton crew on deck who were watching wind and weather and not paying attention to the group of card players. Safe enough. Valerie folded with a shrug and sat back as Arcie cleared his throat and addressed the sullen assassin.

"Sam, you got us into a bit of trouble back there, with the guards, ye know . . . just for mine own curiosity, as your employer, would you mind explaining why you did something so stupid?"

For a moment, Arcie thought the assassin wasn't going to answer. But then a cold, soft voice spoke up from the shadowy folds of black silk.

"When I was young, five years old or so, I don't really know how old I was, or even how old I am now. The Guild was never really sure . . . but anyway, I lived with my mother in one of the scrappiest firetraps in Bistort. You know, over down in Turglin Street? Near the corner of Tanner's Alley."

"But there's nowt there now," said Arcie. "It all burned down a long time ago, and the mayor were going to put up lots of new buildings, but was busy with other things for so long that eventually it just sort of were cleared away and added to the open market area."

Sam nodded. "That's right. But when we lived there, it was a tottering collection of termite-and-rat-infested timber. The mayor was going to tear it down anyway, and build new houses and shops and things . . . we were afraid, because if he did we'd be out on the streets in the cold. He never got around to it, though . . . that was old Felspot, of course, not quite like the new folks and all the whitewashing and whatnot." Sam sighed, and toyed with his wineglass. He wasn't sure why he was bothering to tell them all this. Perhaps simply to take his mind away from the driveling stupidity of the card game, or perhaps because it didn't matter anyway; if things worked out correctly, as they were sure to, every one of those listening here would be dead and floating to the bottom of the sea before dawn tomorrow. He went on.

"My mother was always weak, always sick . . . I don't think she ever recovered from the strain of having me, probably some cold winter when she'd likely been starving for weeks. She wasn't quite clear in her head sometimes, either. She could never remember who my father was, nor where he'd gone, nor what he looked like. But she loved me, and took care of me as best she could. I had to grow up fast, there, and as soon as I was able to I helped out—scrounging for food in the gutters, begging for coins in the streets . . . you know the usual sob story."

Arcie nodded. He'd given more than one thin waif wandering the twilight alleys a couple of coins out of sympathy, a weak spot based in his rather domestic Barigan nature that the other parts of him snickered at. Valerie rolled her eyes and looked away, but Blackmail had set his cards aside and listened in silence. The assassin's quiet voice seemed to cut through the rush and slap of water against the hull like a cold breeze, a mist from the paths of time, tinged with his new strange bitter coldness and also an older, softer sorrow that had always earned him a reputation for melancholy. The voice and its words seemed to reach back into their own pasts, touching on tragedies long buried in the darkness, long forgotten but still as deep as tears.

"My father, whoever he was, left us penniless. Mother couldn't get a job; she was too weak for most labor and too . . . confused a lot of the time to do any intellectual work. So I brought home the bread, or cheese rinds, or whatever, especially when she took a turn for the worse one winter." Sam stretched out his long black-clad legs and peered up at the dim blue evening sky.

"I came home one evening and found her and some out-of-town drunk in the back room. He'd beaten her nearly senseless and raped her half dead. The place was a shambles. He was still . . . slapping her, yelling, naked, and she was bloody all over, bruised, and making the most terrible sound I'd ever heard, like a drowning puppy. It was quite a shock to a five-year-old boy. I suppose the smart thing to do would have been to run away . . . but I didn't feel scared, just cold, standing in the shadows by the doorway. And then . . . then I felt something, I can't describe it. No one who's not an assassin can really understand the feeling of fire in the blood. I moved, I grabbed the leg of a stool that had broken off, all jagged, and then I just sprang. I don't know how it happened, how a little underfed boy could get the better of a man seven times his age and a dozen times more his weight and skill . . . but all there was, was cold fire and thrashing and blood and shouting, and we fell down . . . he thrashed, and knocked over our one clay lamp, and it hit the floor and burst into flames as we fought. Then he went limp, blood pouring out of this hole the sharp end of the stick had made in his throat. I was shaking, tried to get my mother to get up, to get out of the house, because the flames were leaping up the walls. But she just lay there, making that terrible, despairing noise, that noise that tore into my chest like jagged ice and left huge rips in my heart . . . and I heard her sobbing, 'Not again, not again . . . ' and then she made a choking sound, her eyes not seeing me, glazing over, still . . .

"The flames were roaring then, burning the tinder-dry wood, and smoke was everywhere. I staggered away, the heat was blistering my skin, the dead man on the floor smelling like a funeral pyre. I tried to lift my mother's body, thinking in that stupid way kids have that I could save her . . . but it wasn't any use, and I finally had to stumble out of the room. I'd just made it to the front hall when the whole building collapsed, burning timbers falling all around me, dropping with me two floors down to the street level."

Sam paused, and sighed. "Obviously, I survived. I was half-buried under burning rubble, blinded, choked with smoke. I'd probably have died in the rest of the blaze except for the fact that Miffer and Fradagar happened to be heading back to the Guild and, seeing the flames, went to watch. They saw me fall out of the building and pulled me out of the burning logs. They took me back to the Guild, dressed my wounds, fed me, and then trained me as one of their own. They said later they saw in me the potential and the cold fire that makes us what we are and felt they could do no less. They felt it unsafe to let someone with the makings of an assassin walk the streets without the training and discipline of the trade." Sam clicked his tongue in idle thought. "So, that's the basis of the reason . . . ever since, when I think of that night, and of that sound my mother made as she lay there dying . . . When the circumstances occur, I allow myself one kill without a client, without payment . . . an assassin is quick and sure, and the most merciful death there is when he chooses. But no one, and no lady in particular, should have to suffer as my mother did that night."

There was silence a long moment. Sam felt mildly conspicuous. He decided to change the subject.

"That white boat's closer," he commented, looking over the rail at it. "But it's not moving. Is it anchored?"

"It is certainly still," agreed Kaylana, watching it. "But this is very deep water here, in almost the center of the channel . . . They would need to have an extremely long chain to anchor here."

"Puzzling," said Valerie. "Perhaps one of the crew knows of it." The sorceress stood up and beckoned over the first mate, who had come up on deck for his shift. He walked over politely.

"Yes'm?" he inquired. Valerie resisted the urge to smile at him. Dinner had been nothing more appetizing than salted meats, bread, cheese, and fish. She found herself wondering if men of the sea would have that same tang of salt about their flesh, but quickly pushed those thoughts to the back of her mind.

"Yonder white ship," she began, waving one graceful black-clawed hand in the craft's general direction. "Do you know of it?"

The first mate nodded respectfully. "Aye, m'm, 'tis the craft of a fine wizard. His peaceful retreat, I have heard it rumored. 'Tis by his magic that she stays in place despite the deep water and the pull of the tides."

"Wizard?" Sam's black-wrapped head snapped up. "It belongs to a wizard?"

"Aye, sir," confirmed the fellow. "A most ancient and noble mage, with hair of silver white, robes the same, and a staff of great power, set with a shining gemstone." He shuffled his feet a moment, then added, "Or so I have heard it said . . . I myself have not laid eyes upon this mage. He is most secretive."

Sam was very still for a moment. Then he nodded, and got up, stretched, and walked to the hold. The first mate noticed a rope flapping loose, and went to tie it as the companions looked at each other.

"Do ye think he's going to . . . " began Arcie. Valerie shook her head.

"Of course not. It's hundreds of yards away through choppy, cold, shark-infested waters. Besides which, it probably isn't even Mizzamir, and Sam no doubt realizes this. It would be folly to try to swim to that craft, and if it is Mizzamir, Sam will be so worn out from the swim he'd likely be killed."

"Yes, I do not think he will do anything," agreed Kaylana. "The assassin is not stupid."

"I suppose . . . " said Arcie doubtfully, looking the way Sam had gone. "But he *are* persistent." He got up and padded out the way Sam had gone, down into the hold, arriving just in time to see the assassin come out of his cabin, walk down the gangway a short step, and duck into another door, closing it behind him. Arcie followed, puzzled. Where was Sam going? Arcie had inspected the ship quite thoroughly earlier, and if memory served him right, that door wasn't anything more than . . . He hurried forward and opened it.

Within was a small storage closet, with shelves stacked with sailcloth, ropes hung on hooks, buckets, brooms and belaying pins. The light from the corridor lanterns illuminated the closet clearly. It was very small, and tightly packed . . . but otherwise, empty.

Arcie's mouth hung open in surprise a long moment, his bright blue eyes wide. Then he slammed the closet door and scampered back to the others as fast as his feet would carry him.

Sam had been quite curious to see what the lake looked like in Shadowrealm, as well as nearly desperate to get away from the glaring outlines and colors of Outside. He Shadowslipped through the darkness of the supply closet with a sigh of relief, the Darkportal amulet cool and tingling on the skin of his chest. As comforting grayness surrounded him and soothed his aching eyes, he looked about. A collection of shadows around him marked the *Roslilia,* the large block of darkness he'd stepped out of was the closet. Below his feet were the shadows of the cargo hold, and, farther down, a great mass of blackness that was the darkness at the depths of the lake. Looking out, he could just make out a collection of dark scraps on an otherwise empty gray plain. That would be the mage's ship. He broke into a run, long legs covering the distance across the invisible, intangible water as easily as flying. He noticed, as he left the "boundaries" of the *Roslilia,* that the collection of shadows moved away from him at a steady pace in another direction. But he could easily catch her up later. He would return and kill those who sought to betray him and steal his amulet, safe in the darkness.

At last he reached the shadow markings of the unseen white ship. With an effortless thrust of his will he jumped to deck level and investigated the available shadows. Most were useless for passage—too faded or too small. But at last he found a splotch of blackness large enough and deep enough to admit him, and he Shadowslipped through, the cool fire of the hunt flashing in his blood.

He emerged in the corner of a darkened room, apparently the mage's study. Books, candles, herbs, and much glassware covered the available space. He took a few interesting objects, out of curiosity, securing them in his pockets as he went to a door and listened. A rod set in a sconce in one wall glowed faintly, and, as there seemed to be no way to extinguish it, he pocketed it to blot out its light. The soft sounds of slumber drifted to his keen ears. A silent oiling of the hinges, a trip of the latch, and he eased open the door.

Sam peered in and saw a richly furnished bedroom, dominated by a magnificent four-poster, with tapestries and paintings hung about the walls and magnificent carpets on the floor. In the center of the bed was a figure in eiderdown comforters and rich silken sheets. The figure breathed the deep sleep of the good, and Sam caught sight of long, silver-white hair spread across the pillow, glinting in the moonlight that came through the round cabin window. Sam raised his blowgun, aimed, and fired.

Thap

The needle struck through the hair, sinking into the skin at the base of the skull. The sounds of breathing deepened, slowing abruptly as the sleep/paralysis toxin took effect. All that remained to collect the rest of the thousand gold was to carry out Arcie's orders . . . and those orders were to bring him the mage's head. *Then, of course,* thought Sam, as he reached into his back scabbard for his largest blade, a small black-hilted shortsword, *Then I'll kill that Barigan too, and take* **all** *his money.* Sam drew the long, sharp blade, raising it above his head with single-minded determination, the cold fire guiding his hand for one powerful, deadly blow . . .

Sam froze. Something was wrong.

He didn't know why he did it, but his other hand reached out and took hold of the coverlet, pulling it aside from the sleeping figure's face. A lined, aged face, with patchy human skin, a large blobby sort of nose, reddened by good drink and garnished with a long silver beard, stained here and there by tobacco and wine.

Sam stood for a long moment. Then he gently replaced the covers around the sleeping form, sheathing his sword. The training he'd had in the Assassin's Guild, awakened by the fire of a hunt, had brought him for the moment out of the blackness that Valerie's amulet pulled him into. To kill *the wrong person* . . . that was a shame greater than failure. The blowgun toxin would wear off in a few hours. Sam carefully pulled his needle free of the man's skin and walked out of the room, closing the door behind him. His gut was in turmoil with his near-escape from a shameful accident, fear of Mizzamir still being at large, and sudden doubt about the feasibility of killing his companions. Lost in thought, he returned to the dark study, and Shadowslipped.

As he unknowingly drew upon the amulet's power to make the passage, the darkness flooded up again inside him, filling him with new resolve. Best to get back to the *Roslilia* right away and kill the others before they could do anything. In the dim Shadowrealm things were simpler. He would kill the others, in case they had learned of his ability, and then he would return to Shadow forever. Mizzamir could never find him there, but if Sam ever found the Arch-Mage's shadow, victory would go to the assassin. It was a good plan. He jumped away from the shadows of the white ship and ran on silent feet toward the retreating collection of shadows that marked the place of the other ship, dark magic lending speed to his strides.

He leaped to be within the boundaries of the craft and was carried along as she sailed while his eyes scanned the shadows. The dark closet he had come through before was now too faded. Someone must have opened it. He looked around some more. At last a convenient patch was discovered, in what he reckoned to be one of the cabins. Very convenient indeed. Dim, with a splotch in a corner dark enough to pass through . . . and even better, two shadow-figures he recognized as Kaylana and Valerie. Very tidy, he'd be able to take those two out, then find the others and dispatch them at his leisure. He stepped into the darkest corner and leaped forward, Shadowslipping.

Valerie shouted a command as the shadows of the corner suddenly seemed to swirl and thicken, visible only to her Nathauan sight. Light flashed from the now-unshuttered lanterns held by the others, hurting her eyes, but it was not her choked-off gasp of agony that sounded in the room. A dagger shot into the room and made a metallic noise as it slid under one of the plates of Blackmail's armor. The knight, lying cramped in the bunk so that his shadow was confused with that of bed and bulkhead, took no notice. Another blade bounced off the far wall and hit Kaylana in the leg. The Druid winced, but the pain was minor compared to the shock of what she saw before her.

At the now brightly lit wall was a gruesome sight. Sam,

or rather half of him, protruded from it. His arms flailed and struggled as he pushed at the unyielding surface, eyes shut with the agony of light and the solid wall around his waist. He was silent—all assassins were trained to be absolutely silent even in the throes of agony—but his tortured face showed more pain than any scream. He thrashed like a grotesque puppet of a hunter's trophy, dying, dying, torn in two between two worlds . . .

"O caverns," swore Valerie, eyes wide in horror. "Too soon."

"Sam!" gurgled Arcie, from his concealed position on another bunk. His blue eyes stared in shock at the macabre sight.

Valerie lunged forward as a black and gold object flashed out of Sam's tunic. She caught the amulet in her hand, felt its power, the power that was the only thing keeping Sam alive right now. The chain was weak, she could easily snap it from his neck and let his lifeless torso fall bloody and twitching to the floor . . . But instead she drew upon the Darkportal's power, and spoke words of magic as the others stood frozen in shock . . . except for one. Blackmail got to his feet, sensing what the sorceress was doing, and came forward. As she shouted the final word of the spell he grabbed the assassin's shoulders and yanked him through the wall with incredible strength.

Sam fell full length on the floor and lay there gasping. His scarf had fallen off, revealing his ink-black hair and dark gray eyes that seemed to be whirling. He choked and grabbed at his neck, gripping the amulet. He looked around, panting, saw Archie frozen in fear and shock, Valerie shivering from the effort of the spell, Blackmail standing silently, ready in case of another attack, and Kaylana, watching him with deep green eyes as blood ran down her leg, over her sandal, and pooled slowly on the floor.

Sam yanked. The chain snapped, and the amulet was free in his hand. He tossed it to Valerie without a word, and collapsed.

* * *

"We figured you might come after us eventually," explained Arcie, "especially after Valerie guessed what you might be doing. She'd heard about the shadow-travel . . . it was something some of her people used to be able to do."

"We were going to confront you in a lighted room so you couldn't escape and take the amulet from you, by force if need be," added Valerie with a sigh. The Darkportal amulet, secure once more on its gold chain, hung from her neck like a black hole against pale skin. "That's why we were all there . . . except for the minstrel, who wouldn't have fit in the room and likely wouldn't have been any use anyway."

"That's for certain sure," laughed Arcie. Now that the scare was over, they had moved into that state of near hysterical relief that makes the smallest things seem humorous. "One look at you and he would have fell over like a poleaxed hippogryph." Arcie grinned. "Especially with your hair like that."

Sam smiled. He was lying on a cot, eating some soup Kaylana had brought him. "Oh, I don't know . . . is it really that bad?" he asked. He was feeling much better now. The lamplight felt warm and gentle on his face.

"Worse," Kaylana said sternly. "I shall make you a soapwort salve to get it off with, if you will do that as a favor to me."

"Of course," said Sam with a smile. His eyes were a soft hazel once more. "The least I can do after hurting you."

"Believe me, I think you hurt yourself more than you hurt me," she replied solemnly.

"True . . . if Valerie hadn't saved me I'd have been cut in half . . . and half of an assassin is just an ass." Sam smiled.

Robin, outside on deck, trying to think of a rhyme for "Orthamotch" was suddenly startled to hear an odd sound, like a group of friends laughing together. Robin looked up at the brilliant stars and wondered.

VII

They completed the crossing without further incident, and docked in Natodik with the morning tide. As they disembarked, yawning and blinking in the bright new sun, they were swept up into the brilliant dance of the land of magic.

Here at the main seaport, anything and everything could be traded. Stalls and shops everywhere overflowed out into the streets with rich merchandise: silks and spices, glassware and jewelry. In addition, Natodik, being a thaumocracy, did not simply tolerate magic, but actively encouraged it. Stores sold windservant bottles and wonderful magic potions promising everything from instant love to eternal youth; young magicians practiced their art, weaving beautiful illusions for the entertainment of passers-by. In secure stores, magic weapons could be found for the discriminating collector; no one would dream of being *violent* in the new Lightness of the world, and especially not here, in Natodik . . . where the soft ocher of weathered walls was the same golden sandstone that built the high sweeping walls of Thaulara itself! Although that fair city was far inland, its ruler was rumored to be able to see everything that happened in his domain. The eyes of Mizzamir, it was said, kept watch over all the people of Natodik . . . and even, some said, the rest of the world.

Every citizen here wore the fashionable item of clothing associated with its patron Hero; even more rigidly than other lands did, since they were the only one among the Six whose patron was still alive. The standard garment here, from toddlers to matriarchs, was the traditional mage's working robe-coat, with the full sleeves and cords for fastening tight around the waist; but only true mages were allowed to wear their robes closed. Symbolically, each and every citizen of Natodik shared in the power of magic generated by their patron, but only those who learned and practiced it would buckle their robes to symbolize their control over and containment of magic.

In addition, the robes of wizards had another, more subtle difference; they were usually one solid color, with perhaps some trim at the collar, cuffs, and hem. Sam spotted numerous young wizards, male and female, garbed in red, some others in orange or yellow, and even a few in green, as Fenwick's companion wizard had worn. The robes were marks of rank and power among the wizards themselves, increasing in the order of the spectrum; red for novices to blue or violet for the high wizards. Most of the higher orders were too busy or important to come down and mingle in the common streets; they sent their lesser-hued assistants and apprentices to run down and pick up a half-pound of dried toad spawn, or what have you. As Valerie explained the ranking system quietly to them, Sam shook his head in realization of Mizzamir's power: *He's so mighty he's right off the scale. White robes . . .*

The robes of the normal citizens swirled past in all colors—embroidered and embellished for the wealthy; worn and homespun, with big, roomy pockets, for the commoners. Men wore their robes over a suit of clothing, while women wore them over gowns, and small children often wore little else.

Kaylana's dun robes, while lacking the fullness and fineness of cut favored by most of the citizens, could pass fairly well for common peasant dress. The other renegades and Robin, however, were plainly marked as tourists. At the first opportunity Arcie motioned the others aside into a small alley, and called a conference.

"We'll be wantin' to get shent of town as soon as we might," he explained, "and set ourselfs going toward yon next doodad we're meaning to snag. Where'll we be looking?"

Valerie sighed and leaned back against a wall, taking out her scroll case with its hastily scribbled notes. "Well, by process of elimination and a few fairly obvious deductions, the verse referring to Natodik must be the one that reads: 'Diamond spire spears the sky/Focus of the wizard's eye/Lead, light and sand the Test define/When washed in ancient magic's brine.' That seems to refer to magic and wizards enough to make me think that's the one relevant to Natodik."

"Diamond spire . . . the Castle of Diamond Magic . . . ," muttered Robin to himself. Sam snapped his fingers, and Blackmail nodded.

"That must be it," Kaylana agreed. "After all, most of the past Tests have been located in places of significance . . . "

"Aye, grand head-work, centaur," Arcie chirped up. "Spiffywell!"

Robin, startled at his unwitting contribution to the villains, stammered unintelligible disclaimers that went unheeded.

"Maybe we should buy horses while we're here," mused Valerie, looking around. "I'm not looking forward to walking to the end of the world."

"Och! Buy horseflesh? In Natodik?" Arcie scoffed. "Natodik's known for having the worst horses at the highest price of any of these Six Lands. Here's Troisian imports way too muckle expensive and rare, and yon local beasts are peely-wally and so high-strung ye could be having them for Robin's harp strings."

"Well, I guess that's out then," grumbled Valerie. "The only thing I hate worse than walking is riding an insane horse."

"We'd best get on our way," said Sam. "I don't think it would be a good idea to hang around here, looking the way we do . . . we'd better get out of town now, even if it is daylight, and put as much distance as we can between cities. Kaylana," he turned to the Druid, "can you tell how much time we have before . . . "

"The end?" Kaylana shook her head. "Not precisely. It seems to fluctuate . . . but I would estimate less than another phase of the moon."

"Ee! Nowt but a month?" exclaimed Arcie in dismay.

"But lassie, things dinna *seem* as they're sublimating so fast!"

"It is subtle now, Barigan . . . the long days, the bright sun, the overabundance of life, the strength of light magic—these are the curls of smoke and heat that arise before the sudden flame. When the light has increased enough, that flame will sweep up in all its purifying brightness . . . "

"Och, I see your idea," Arcie interrupted. "We'll leave, then. If my wits still serves me, Thaulara be north of here . . . there ought to be a major road wending yonder."

"No major roads," insisted Valerie. Blackmail shook his head in agreement, and the sorceress continued, "We're deep in the enemy's territory now, small fool . . . We don't want to be seen any more than we have to. And with all this Light magic about, I don't know how well my spells will hold up. I had placed a sort of camouflaging spell on our group to get us through the city fairly unnoticed, but I can't be sure of its strength or duration."

"Well, we'll head out the north gates, at least," replied Sam, "and then angle around the north road . . . Kaylana, can you keep us from getting lost?"

"I should think so," came the calm reply.

"Then let's go."

They left that city of magic and commerce and headed out along the main road, then left its broad path and began a wide sweep northward. When Kaylana judged they were far enough away, a halt was called and they rested for the remainder of the daylight hours, then moved on by night, brilliantly lit by moonshine and high cold stars. The occasional glimmer of a small town could be seen, but once again they avoided these, skulking through the night, keeping to the darkness, like rats, like superstitions, like villains.

At least the terrain was pleasant. Natodik was primarily flatlands with some low hills and plateaus. It had once been a far harsher place; a land of burning desert sands and hard stone, with wars constantly scarring its surface. But then Mizzamir had taken it under his wing, and, after winning the trust of the local wizards, he had gone to work on the land. Spells and science had combined to irrigate the desert and plant grass and crops; the hot climate was ideally suited for citrus and other tropical fruits imported from Shadrezar and Monguna. Now, a century and a half later, the desert was blooming wildly, flowers that only opened in moonlight stretching their milky petals up to the dew. The terrain was fairly gentle, the highest raised area on the continent was a series of gentle hills crowned by the city of Thaulara. Small scattered tropical oases could be found around the occasional unnaturally clean streams and rivers, and they went through these when possible. Occasionally Valerie would send Nightshade aloft, to spy out what lay ahead. Wildflowers and sweet grasses were everywhere, and Robin ate some of these as he walked, ripping up handfuls, breaking the dirt off, and chewing on them. Arcie made a few jesting comments on his grazing, but he was secretly glad that the centaur could find some way to appease his hunger without resorting to their communal stores of food. Blackmail led the way, with Kaylana's direction, occasionally using his huge sword to clear a way through vines or tall grass. Sleeping butterflies exploded up around him as he walked.

The land was full of mystery and magic. Several times they saw ancient stone rings, of arches and monoliths arranged in symmetrical patterns now worn and disarrayed. Once they were treated to a meteor shower shortly after midnight, watching the tiny lights streak across the heavens and die. And, as they came out of a cluster of wild lemon trees into a moonlit glade, they viewed a sight that few had ever seen.

A splashing of water had its source in a magical spring that shot straight up from a tumble of white rocks, thickly covered with hundreds of tiny, sweet-scented flowers and herbs. Drinking here, its wispy beard sparkling with drops, was a unicorn.

A wild stallion unicorn, in all its glory: coat of purest white, mane and tail silver as the moonlight, cloven hooves of gold, and a long, spiraled, magical horn of ivory. Its huge eyes held beautiful wisdom. No frail and dainty unicorn, this animal powerfully muscled as a lion, strength rippling like waves under its perfect coat, hooves like cymbals of thunder. It lifted its majestic head even as their eyes fell upon it, and its glorious nostrils flared.

"Arg, bugger," muttered Arcie. The unicorn bugled a cry of ancient anger, and spoke in tones like a golden bell of war.

"What! What Ho! My Keen Senses Espy The Presence of Evil!" The great fringed hooves stomped, the horn flashing down like a star. The company stirred uneasily, gripping weapons. Sam found himself far preferring the hideous company of Orthamotch to this beautiful creature of Light.

"Aroint Thee, Foul Beings!" bugled the unicorn and charged like a wave of silver, before which the company parted like grass.

The unicorn charged past, its horn aiming for Valerie. She shouted a Word, and threw something at its feet that exploded. It leaped away, unharmed.

"Blast," snarled Valerie. She called to the party. "I can't help you! It's resistant to my magic!" The unicorn snorted. It suddenly whipped its head around, the magnificent horn easily deflecting a dagger thrown from the shadows.

"Thou Workest Dark Magic! I Shall Smite Thee!" It spied Arcie trying to sneak up on it with his morning star and lunged at him.

"Wups!" cried Arcie, and dodged. As the Barigan rolled away to safety, the unicorn spun and aimed a kick at Blackmail. The knight raised his shield, and the blow rebounded with such force the unicorn flipped over completely, landing with nimble grace on its feet. It threw its head back in anger, as a dark flashing dagger passed beneath its chin. The knight's shield suddenly jerked up again as the dagger whizzed past the unicorn. It bounced off the shield with a *spang*, and went flashing back like a mad pinwheel, bouncing off the branches of the trees.

"Spawn of Darkness, I Shall Slay Thee!" it roared, and charged again at Valerie. Blackmail stepped into its path. The knight raised his shield again, and swung his great sword as the unicorn came at him. Giving a casual toss of his proud head, the unicorn parried the blow with his long horn, the shock of the blow breaking the knight's grip. The sword went flying. Valerie saw Robin hovering near.

"Robin, do something!" she yelled, as the unicorn spun on its heels and kicked at the weaponless knight, who got his shield up just in time. The unicorn, seeing Arcie moving behind the centaur, charged Robin. Kaylana whapped it over the withers with her staff as it went past, but it didn't even slow down.

Robin lashed out at the silver-white glory with his hooves, gingerly, as though he was chasing rabbits. Arcie dived under a pile of kiwifruit vines as the unicorn galloped over where he'd been, and rolled his eyes.

"Use yer fool sword, minstrel!" he yelled in annoyance. Robin gaped uncomprehendingly. Arcie peered about the glade. Why wasn't it attacking Kaylana? And where was Sam?

"Kaylana! Duck!" yelled Sam's voice. The Druid did so, as the dagger whizzed over her head. It went *spang* off the fountain and soared through the air again, abruptly landing with a *thunk* into the meaty white hindquarters of the unicorn as the huge beast turned.

The unicorn bugled in pain and pure rage, the ringing noise making the party clap their hands to their ears. The unicorn reared in fury, its flaming eyes burning into the shadows . . . and then it saw! Saw a villain all in black, holding another dagger and looking insolent! It leaped into a charge. Sam watched the thundering hooves, saw the horn pointing straight at his chest. He forced himself to stay still, wait, wait . . . now!

Sam leaped straight up, grabbing at the branches of the ancient lemon tree as it shook with sudden, tremendous impact. Lemons thundered around him as the tree shook, and there came an equine bugle of fury. The assassin swung down, landing on his feet, and heard Kaylana mutter a spell. The tree creaked with sudden growth.

The unicorn was trapped, its long ivory horn thrust almost clear through a thick, gnarled lemon tree, that even now grew and expanded, holding the horn tightly as if it were a nail driven into the bark. The unicorn set all four golden hooves into the turf, and tugged mightily, snorting in rage. The tree shook and showered lemons and leaves down on them again. The citrus smell filled the air.

"Villains! What Is This Foul Trick! I Shall Smite Thee To Smithereens For This!" raged the unicorn.

"Amain fine job, laddie," said Arcie, coming up. "Now what are we to do with yon great beast?"

Sam looked uncertain, thinking, while Blackmail and Valerie and Robin approached. The party looked at the trapped, struggling beast, as it raged and snorted. Sam finally took out his shortsword. "I guess we'd better kill it," he said, with a shrug. "We can't leave it here to starve, and it'll kill us if it gets loose."

"I Shall Slay Thee! I Shall Scatter Thy Bloody Bones To The Four Winds, Thou Foul And Evil Beings Of . . . "

"Aye aye, aye and we ken, old horsie," said Arcie. Blackmail nodded solemnly to Sam's comment, having recovered his long heavy sword, and now moved to the creature's head, preparing to deliver the final blow. But Valerie, hastening up to where they stood, stopped him.

"Hold your blade, knight," she cautioned. Kaylana looked at her in surprise.

"Valerie? I would have thought you in particular would be all for the death of this unicorn. It is beautiful, true, but with the imbalance of Light as it is . . . "

"Yes, I know. But one life, even that of a unicorn, will make no difference now. And tell me," she said, looking about them, "In tales and stories, what is the usual fate of those who slay unicorns? Evilness is one thing, but the blood of a unicorn brings swift and sure vengeance from the forces of good . . . with whom we already have far too much troubles."

There was a pause while they digested this, and then Sam and Blackmail lowered their blades.

"The sorceress is right," agreed Sam. "But what can we do? It will die just as surely here if we leave it."

"I Shall Rip Thy Skin From Thy Poxy Form, Villain, And Crush Thy Skull Like . . . "

"Yes, all right," said the assassin hurriedly. Kaylana sighed.

"I shall slow the tree's growth, then, and induce it to release the horn. It will take it some time to comply, however . . . trees are not known for being swift to action. We should have a few hours to escape in."

"All right, then," agreed Valerie. "A pity we are not in a more secure position . . . There's quite a good bit of meat on a unicorn, and with a blackberry and mushroom sauce . . . "

"You mean you've actually eaten one of these things before?" asked Robin, horrified. Valerie shrugged.

"No, not me personally . . . but I have it on good authority they taste just like chicken."

"Chicken!! Why, Thou Foul, Black, And Evil Hag . . ."

"Watch it, horse," snapped Valerie. "Work your magic, Kaylana, and let's get out of here."

"Certes," said the Druid, resting one hand on the trembling tree and closing her eyes. Sam carefully inched around to the rear of the struggling animal, and with a lightning move yanked his dagger free of the unicorn's rump. The creature roared in fury and hammered at him with its hind hooves, but he dodged away and wiped his dagger on the grass. The area immediately sprouted with lush clover and wildflowers. He shook his head in puzzlement.

"Get yourself along, laddie," called Arcie, as the party moved away through the shadows. Sam sheathed his dagger and hastened after them.

As he caught up, Kaylana turned to him in cold anger.

"Why the Oak were you throwing all those daggers around back there?" she demanded. "I watched; you nearly struck us several times and were not even coming close to the unicorn!"

"I only threw it twice," Sam muttered. "It hit the unicorn the second time."

"Ah, is this perhaps your I-never-miss excuse?" inquired Kaylana coldly, folding her arms skeptically. "Then what, pray tell, did you hit after you threw it the first time?"

Sam held out an arm. Blood trickled from his biceps. "Could I have a bandage, please?"

Robin was nervous and fidgety the entire time they traveled. The evil villains were heading straight for Mizzamir, and he, Robin, had sent them there! The wizard had to be told! He fretted until late morning, when at last the group stopped to rest in the shade by a river, near a small town. Kaylana had been given a pouch of small coin, and went into the settlement to buy common traveling robes for the rest of the party. Soon they would need to enter the gates of Thaulara, and it would be a good idea to try and blend in somewhat. When she had left and the others had settled down to rest, Robin offered to take the first watch, and waited patiently until they had all fallen still, and sounds of slumber drifted through the bright air. Slowly, Robin stood up, propping himself up on his forelegs and then working his hindlegs up into a standing position. Shaking slightly with the effort of making no noise, he slowly began to back out of the small campsite, to get far enough away to safely activate the bracelet and report to Mizzamir . . . but a faint metallic scraping stopped him. Blackmail's helmet had raised up from the knight's chest and turned to face him in silent watchfulness. The young centaur's blood ran cold, and, ears flicking in anxiety, he settled himself back down onto the grass.

"Just stretching my legs," he stammered by way of explanation. But the dark helmet remained upright and watchful, and at last Robin dropped into fitful, guilty sleep, awakening only when Kaylana returned, bearing common peasant robes for the bipedal members of the party.

When time came to don these, at the beginning of their travel that evening, a slight hitch developed.

"He willna wear it," complained Arcie to Sam, holding the huge rough hooded robe out to Blackmail, who stood impassively.

"Have you tried reasoning with him?" asked the assassin, who was busy securing his weapons around the inside of his own dark brown robe. They were going to possibly find Mizzamir . . . and if they should encounter him, Sam was going to be ready.

" 'Tis fair hard work to reason with a feller who will not give you words to argue with," retorted Arcie.

"He would look ridiculous in a robe anyway," said Valerie dismissively. "Even if we put his hood up. A seven-foot tall clanking robed figure?"

"He is conspicuous enough as it is," sighed Kaylana. "We had better go into the city under cover of night, and leave before the sun rises. Valerie, I suggest you concentrate your camouflage magic upon the knight and the centaur, as they are the most distinctive members of our party."

"Right enough," Valerie agreed, adjusting her own ocher lady's robe. She examined the cords, then shrugged and worked her fingers over the fabric a moment, muttering the words of a spell. The color of the robe shifted into a deep blue, trimmed lightly with black and silver at the hems. Valerie somehow managed to make the garment look menacing. Sam felt that if the silver embroidery was closely examined it would show horrible scenes of death and torture. Valerie smiled in satisfaction.

"Be you a blue-ranking wizard, then?" inquired Arcie from the sidelines, where he was sitting in his too-big robes and smoking a pipe. The Nathauan shook her head as she tied up the cords of the robe. Nightshade perched on her shoulder, preening.

"The magic of the Underrealm works differently than that of the shallow surface folk . . . suffice to say, I am capable enough to wear these robes."

"Don't cause any trouble, please, Valerie," Sam asked, without much hope.

"Who, me?" she asked, smiling with a mouthful of sharp teeth. Sam shook his head.

"Innocence looks ridiculous on a Nathauan," he replied.

Mizzamir currently had far more important concerns than the approach of a few minor villains. It was the holiday of the annual Thaumatic Convergence, when wizards and sages and soothsayers and spellweavers from all over the Six Lands and the rest of Chiaroscuro would come together. This year they met in his own mighty halls, in the Castle of Diamond Magic. The events would last for three full days—contests, banquets, speeches, seminars, meetings, greetings, presentations, and panels. Young novices would flaunt their skills in performance and competitions to impress the visiting higher mages in hopes of winning an apprenticeship. Experts from the different fields of Light magic, from the geomancers to timespinners, would be in attendance to present the results of their latest studies, to win honor and prestige as well as share their knowledge freely, for the Good of all. Some of Mizzamir's compatriots had been leery of this aspect of the Convergence, but a few talks in private with the Arch-Mage had turned them around. There would be trades and sales of potions and components and new devices, and familiars of a thousand species fluttering and hissing at each other. There would be games for the apprentices and dignified dialogue for the senior wizards. A thousand things to organize, plan, arrange . . . Mizzamir had no time to hunt scoundrels at the moment. He'd had word that Sir Fenwick had landed in Natodik recently; he could only assume that the young hero was going to continue his pursuit of the villains. This bothered him a bit, but he knew Fenwick was a man of his word, a man of Good. Mizzamir had instructed that the villains not be killed, only observed; and while Fenwick might do what he liked in his own land of Trois, while on the golden fields of Natodik he would have to abide by Mizzamir's wishes.

I think it should be all for the best, Mizzamir thought as he marked off a list of guests already arrived. By horse and foot and cart, by teleport and magic carpet and winged drake and firesteed they came. *Fenwick can keep an eye on those deviants and make sure they don't cause any problems. I am simply far too busy. There are limits to even a Hero, after all . . .*

He sighed in satisfaction, his graceful Elven hands sprinkling sand over the drying ink. He looked up from his golden desk, stretching stiffened joints, and looked peacefully up at the stained-glass window in this, his private tower, the highest in the Castle. The large arched frame held a portrait of himself in glowing light, surrounded by scenes of his magical triumphs from the War and the Victory. Some of the pictures showed him in his younger years, with the golden hair he had once had before the War and powerful magics had taken their toll. The colors gleamed in the sunlight: from the brilliant color-golden hues of the Light Dragons he had called to the aid of the Heroes, to the dark, lurking shape of the Thur-Uisgie, evil demon guardian of the vaults of Putak-Azum whom he had defeated so long ago. Even now, the dark shape gave him a faint shadow of a shudder; his good nature sometimes troubled him, when he thought of how he had used that terrible creature later, in fashioning his Test; his kind heart hoped no one should ever have to face that Test. With luck, no one would . . . the gods had hidden it away, of course, so well and so far he could never know its location, and thus, no one else would ever find it. He smiled up at his image in the window, his own face beaming radiantly down upon him in soft hues.

The Verdant Company had continued its pursuit. Reduced drastically in size to spare the gentle fields of Natodik from the havoc caused by a small army on the move, the active Company now consisted of Fenwick and about a dozen of his top officers. Their mission, as Mizzamir had surmised, was nothing more than to follow, watch, and learn of the movement of the renegades, and to keep innocent people free from harm at the hands of the evil ones. They rode through the countryside at a leisurely pace, Fenwick's excellent tracking skills deftly locating and following the evasive route of their quarry.

As they approached a small forest, an odd sight met their eyes. A large, rose-gold dragon sat on the greensward at the edge of the woods, wings folded. Nearby stood a proud unicorn, white with flowing silver mane and tail. Fenwick had never seen the unicorn before, but the dragon was another matter. He exclaimed in surprise and rode forward, motioning to his company to stay back.

"Lumathix, noble dragon! Ho!" called Fenwick. The dragon's head turned, and the golden eyes widened in pleased surprise. It shrilled a greeting.

"Why, hello there, young Sir Fenwick!" Lumathix called. The unicorn snorted uneasily. The dragon raised a huge paw reassuringly. "It's all right, he's a friend of mine."

The unicorn snorted and held its ground. It had had quite enough to do with human and their ilk lately, and it still had a terrible headache from working its horn loose from the tree.

"What brings you here, Lumathix?" asked Fenwick, as he reached the two. His magnificent bay horse was made nervous by the dragon, but Fenwick was a master horseman, and the animal soon calmed. The dragon sniffed.

"I got into a bit of a scrape awhile ago, and took a few nasty wounds that started to get worse . . . so I sought out this good unicorn for healing." The unicorn bobbed its head in acknowledgment. "And *he* was just telling me about some dirty villains that did him a bad turn, didn't they?"

"Most Certain," snorted the unicorn. "Foul Fiends, Evil To The Core, Black-Garbed . . . "

"Really?" exclaimed Fenwick, "Six of them? A centaur, and a black knight, and a young woman, red hair . . ."

"Red Hair . . . Ah Yes, The Maiden," remembered the unicorn, its eyes getting slightly misty.

"Yes! And a rotten little Barigan, and a Nathauan, and an assassin!" shrilled Lumathix. "The same ones! You know of them?"

"They're the reason the Company is called out," asserted Fenwick.

"Well, something should definitely be done," sniffed Lumathix. "Nasty people, woke me up from my nap and then cut me all about."

"Something will be done," assured Fenwick. His eyes sparkled suddenly. "In fact, I have an idea . . . Lumathix, listen . . . "

The massive rose-gold dragon bent his swanlike neck and spread his great ears wide, and the unicorn tilted its head to one side as they listened to Fenwick's plan . . .

"We shall need some form of plan," said Kaylana, as they walked up the sloping roads to the walled city of Thaulara. The city glimmered like a dragon's horde in the twilight, the Castle of Diamond Magic a glittering crown of gold set with gems, stained-glass windows lit from within.

"If we be after finding a 'spire that spears the sky,' t'would make sense that such would be the tallest of towers in yon castle," suggested Arcie. " 'Tis plain as the legs on a donkey."

"Then we just have to climb up that tower and get in through a window, search the place, find the Test, and then go from there, depending on whether or not Valerie survives it," muttered Sam, as the sight of the home of his quarry sent the fire running in his blood.

"Why me?" exclaimed Valerie indignantly. "I'm the brains behind this quest, not some grunt swordfodder."

"Because you are, of course, the only one among us to have mastered the arts of the thaumatic magic," replied Kaylana coldly. "I doubt my 'backwoods peasant magic,' as you so frequently refer to it, would be of much use against a wizard's Test."

"How are you going to get up the wall?" Robin asked. They passed through the open bronze gates and were met with a rush of warm air—the sandstone buildings were releasing their heat into the night. Accompanying the breeze were smells of spicy food and sounds of merriment. Colorful bunting fluttered from buildings, adding to the general air of celebration. As if on cue, an explosion in the night made them all look up. Against the darkness over the Castle, magical fireworks were beginning; fountains of green and blue, bursts of white stars and red flames and flowers, orange and yellow and turquoise pinwheels and sparks, and huge purple fireballs that burst with the sound of bass drums.

"Looks to be as the wizards are having a party," Arcie commented. Blackmail nodded assent.

"The place is going to be lit up like midsummer," growled Sam under his breath. "It's going to be risky to climb that wall in all this."

"I can't climb at all," Robin pointed out, hoping to be left behind . . . He had to warn Mizzamir! Sam just nodded.

"I know that . . . I don't think Blackmail would like to shinny up a silk rope either . . . " he added, looking at the dark armored figure. The knight shook his head.

"In that case, we might as well split up . . . Robin and Blackmail, you had better stay in town . . . try to be inconspicuous. If Mizzamir has been keeping track of us he'll know what you look like. Valerie and I will go to the tower wall, I'll climb it and pull her up on the rope . . . Kaylana, Arcie, do you think you could sneak inside? We may need you for distraction in case things get difficult."

"A piece of cake," answered the thief, with a grin. "Belike there'll be all kinds servants and hired wenches for yon great merry bash."

"Are you expecting trouble?" Kaylana asked, looking sidelong at Sam.

"I always do . . . that way it's less likely to surprise me." He didn't add that there might be all kinds of trouble when he finally killed Mizzamir; he doubted the other mages of the Castle would be very pleased.

They split up as they entered town; Sam and Valerie, robes rustling, headed off in the general direction of the

Castle by an indirect route, while Arcie and Kaylana managed to mingle with a group of chatting robed townsfolk carrying several large casks of wine up the winding street to the Castle grounds. Robin and Blackmail wandered off among the crowds, keeping some distance apart so that their presences seemed unrelated, but staying within sight of each other.

The knight and centaur drifted through the streets. Though it was evening, the city was lit up like a ballroom chandelier; glowing magical wizard-lights, product of a simple, low-powered spell, danced and hung trembling from cornices and signposts, adding their many colors to the warm glow of regular street lanterns that shed golden radiance across the mortared yellow bricks. Robin noticed that the road beneath his hooves was cobbled in multicolored river stones; the effect was mystical by night and would no doubt be stunning by day. Mizzamir had taken care to see that the Land under his care was as fair and fine as any Elven city of old. People thronged the streets; in addition to whatever the Castle itself might be celebrating, some local festival seemed to be going on as well. Robin turned and gawked and occasionally stumbled as his eyes lost track of his hooves on the cobblestones. There were dancers and vendors and showmen, actors and poets . . . and musicians.

So much music! Music everywhere! His ears ached from turning, trying to follow every rollicking melody; fiddles and mandolins and lutes reeled out dance tunes, flutes of many different shapes trilled through the air. Drums throbbed a hundred heartbeats, and harps, some small as his own, some so huge it took two men to lift them, dropped their golden notes into the chanting night. The air was full of spicy smoke and dust and food and wine and song . . . Robin was entranced.

Blackmail seemed immune to the festivities; if anything, they seemed to make him more sober, almost angry. He stomped along relentlessly, incongruous in his dark hard armor amongst the soft colorful robes of the Thaularan townsfolk. Several people, made curious by his strangeness, tried to get him to cheer up, or at least buy something, but he shouldered winesellers and sausage vendors out of the way. It was only as he skirted the main square, glorious with its fountains of illuminated water splashing over statues of unicorns, Heroes, dolphins, sun-eagles and other people and creatures, that he suddenly stopped. This caused the dazed Robin, who was forgetting himself and following too closely, to run into him from behind. There was a brief, mutual stumble. Robin looked up to see what had caught the dark knight's attention.

The main fountain was, predictably, devoted to Mizzamir. In wrought brass kept forever golden by magic, and bedazzled by sparkling streams of shining water, was an abbreviated pictorial history of the great Elven Arch-Mage's exploits. From his first encounters with the forces of darkness to his final triumphant restoration of the city Thaulara, sculpture and mural relief chronicled the history.

The knight seemed particularly interested in the earlier scenes. Here, Mizzamir seemed somewhat younger; his face unworn by the hardships and tragedies of the war. His handsome, elegant Elven features held an expression of gentle self-assurance; in the scenes partway through the War, the face was tinged with the beginnings of sorrow, showing the heartbreak of friends lost and lives destroyed by the horrors of the Dark. Something in that face caused an eerie itch to prick at Robin's mind and withers; something familiar but frightening . . .

Blackmail turned to inspect a post-Victory scene, very small and insignificant, where a calm Mizzamir faced a scowling paladin, the Hero Sir Pryse. In the Restoration after the Victory, the two had had some difficulty in agreement upon how to restore the feudal land of Kwart, long the most strife-torn of the Six. Mizzamir had wanted democratic councils and parliaments such as the other Lands favored, while the paladin, a staunch traditionalist, had opted for the old system and resented the wizard's good-natured help with his rule. Soon after, the paladin had ridden off on his famous last quest, to die in parts unknown. After Mizzamir's newly perfected light-minding process began to eliminate the competitive urge among the various kingdoms, Kwart, in honor of its departed Hero, had opted for and been allowed to keep its feudal system. Robin remembered all this from all the endless ballads of the Victory he had learned; it was one of the few about Sir Pryse. Blackmail must have felt some kinship for the long-dead Hero who had worn plate-mail as did he; perhaps taking the paladin's Test, in the hidden shrine of Kwart, had given him some new insight into that most mysterious of Heroes? Robin made a mental note—if the knight were ever to speak, that would be one of the things to ask him. Blackmail shook his head at the carvings, motioned to Robin, and continued on, heading for the edge of the Castle grounds, where they could be nearby and ready to help their companions should the need arise.

Meanwhile, Arcie and Kaylana were trying to find their way out of the sculleries under the great halls of the Castle. Getting in had been no problem; in their simple peasant robes they had easily slipped into the kitchens and there were even a number of Barigan cooks and scullions so that Arcie's presence and accent were unremarkable. At one point a stout woman handed Kaylana a huge steaming platter of roast doves, with instructions to "Be takin' that upstairs, dearie, 'at's a girl." Kaylana had wrinkled her nose in disgust at the strong gamy smell, and as soon as the woman had passed out of sight was about to dump the entire platter down a dumbwaiter shaft, when Arcie halted her.

"Wait a tic there, lassie, I'm all about famished!" he exclaimed, grabbing one of the birds from the platter and tucking into it with gusto. "By the sides, we've a far piece to go, yet, and what could be more a better camouflage than genuine food to be servin'?" He winked at her, offering her a crispy golden wing. Kaylana made a face, and turned away, but gripped her staff tighter in her hand and balanced the tray carefully.

"Can you not get rid of yon great muckle stick, Kaylana?" asked the Barigan, watching. "It's not the sort o' thing a young serving lass should be dragging about."

"No," she replied firmly. "This staff is mine, a part of me. It is what I am. It stays in my hand."

"Well enough, have it as you would," sighed the thief. "But dinna blame me if them mages will be asking after who you took it from."

Cautiously but ever so servantly, they headed to what they hoped would be upstairs into the main rooms, and the full conglomeration of hundreds of the world's most skilled wizards.

Sam and Valerie crept cautiously through the castle gardens, keeping to the walls and the shadows. Sam was no more noticeable than a cloud on a moonless night, and Valerie's natural dark-loving tendencies let her keep to the shadows gracefully. Her footsteps were not as silent as the assassin's, however, and he had to caution her several times.

"What are you so paranoid about?" she hissed, as they crunched softly through a well-kept herb bed. The scents of marjoram, coriander, and sage drifted about them. The only other sounds were those of distant music and a droning voice drawing to a close. There was the rushing of distant applause, echoed next to them by Nightshade adjusting his ebony plumage. "No one can hear us inside with all that racket."

"You never know," Sam murmured under his breath, soft and inconspicuous. "They might have guards posted . . . perhaps magical warding beasts of some sort."

"I don't think so," came the whispered reply as they moved on cautiously. "Light mages are so smug and self-confident . . . guards are far too plebeian for them. A place like this would have some magical scrying system, to focus in on intruders . . . "

Unseen, in the Tower that loomed above them, Mizzamir's crystal scrying font dimmed and swirled of its own accord. Shown rippling in its depths were the figures of a man and a Nathauan, creeping along the dim walls and coming nearer . . . the gemstones set around the edge of the font flashed agitatedly, but the room remained silent and empty. Mizzamir was currently two floors below, heading a panel on The Cause and Effect of Spontaneous Manifestation.

They reached the base of the Tower, and Sam swore softly under his breath. Valerie came up beside him, and looked up.

A new problem had presented itself. Though the tower in the darkness had seemed to be of the same rough golden-ocher sandstone as the rest of the Castle, indeed most of the buildings in Thaulara, it was actually made of some sterner stuff. Something that felt like marble, in fact, yellow-gold and smooth as ice, without crack or seam where blocks might have been joined. Sam ran his hands over it, looking up.

"This is impossible," he hissed. "Slick as a greased eel and straight up, with a wide sloping overhang up there at the top. Not even any cracks or ivy . . . how could something like this have been built?"

"By magic, fool," replied Valerie in the same volume. "It's quite obvious. Your surface wizards like to build towers, and they build them as well as they can. Mizzamir must have shaped this tower by raw magic and then had the rest of the Castle built around it."

"If it was so obvious why didn't you mention it before we came out here?" came the reply. Valerie half-lowered her eyelids, glaring, and Nightshade the raven stuck his tongue out again.

"Can't you just use magic to fly up to the window?" asked Sam, wearily contemplating the prospect of finding a more indirect route to the Tower chamber. Valerie scoffed.

"If I were to draw on the powers of my Darkportal here, with this many Light mages about, there would be far more trouble than we could deal with; we who use magic are sensitive to it, especially to the opposite form of the sort we use . . . my power would scream out to every mage's senses through this entire castle." Sam sighed and moved back along the wall, the way they had come. Valerie followed.

"What are you doing now?" she asked. Sam took out his tiger-claws and slipped them onto his hands. Moonlight gleamed on the open-fingered gloves with the strong steel hooked blades projecting from the knuckles. A fearsome and flashy weapon that Sam seldom used for that purpose; Cata had taught him how to fight with them, he remembered now, seeing the shine of the blades in the moonlight. To use them in combat brought back too many memories, but if you had the knack, they were excellent climbing gear.

"I'm going to climb up to that window there," he explained, indicating a circle of yellow light high above, "and then pull you up as planned. We'll have to try to get to the Tower from the inside."

"What if there's somebody inside?" whispered Valerie. Sam shrugged. Valerie frowned. "Blast it, your lack of planning will be our downfall yet, blond sunlander. I'd better send Nightshade up."

She took the black raven from her shoulder and cooed softly to it. It fluffed itself, then cocked a bright intelligent eye up at the window, and took off. It flapped up into the air, past the window, up further, and then began to spiral down, pausing in mid-air to drop a smear of stinking white excrement with pin-point accuracy on Sam's shoulder. As the assassin snarled and wiped in disgust at his tunic, the raven returned to his perch on his mistress's shoulder with a definitely smug expression.

"Fluffykins says the room is empty . . . and do shut your foul mouth, assassin, the mages are likely to hear you."

Sam recovered himself and began to climb, stealthily hooking the tiger-claws into cracks, then pushing himself up until his feet had just enough purchase for a stretch, drag, hook, then pull up again. He flattened himself against the wall as another burst of fireworks exploded overhead; fewer and less showy this time; the efforts of a couple of half-drunken red-robed apprentices on the upper parapets. A few sparks nevertheless drifted past him, and the faint smell of sulfur wafted down. Talking animatedly about pyrotechnics control, the wizards staggered back inside, and Sam resumed his slow climb. The freeze had cost him; keeping his weight supported only by the strength of his knuckles (for his boots were too slippery to hold him steady and the tiger-claws had to be held at the proper angle to grip firmly) had sent slow shooting pains up his tendons. But he climbed on with spider-slowness until at last he could peer into the round open window.

The room inside was indeed empty, a small sitting room of sorts lit by a single magical lamp. The door was slightly ajar, and couches settled against the walls and around the window. A few paintings of pastoral Elven scenes shared the walls with the stuffed head of a cockatrice, whose impressive chicken-lizard head and peacock coloring did not fully dim the effect created by the expression of whimsical stupidity on its face. Sam unslung his silk rope and lashed one end to a thick oaken bench set into the stone of the windowseat, and tied the other end into a rough harness. He dropped this down to Valerie, and a few moments later hauled the sorceress up to the window. She stepped out of the rope with an expression of distaste at the undignified means of travel, and the two of them went to the door and peered cautiously around it.

The hallway was brightly lit by the now-familiar magical lamps, here shining in a soft rosy sunset color. Long carpets, richly woven, muffled their footsteps as they paced down the hall. A sudden tattoo of footsteps sounded from a corner, accompanied by talking voices; Sam swirled and seemed to vanish instantly behind an ornamental display case, but Valerie was not so quick; she had barely taken a step back when two red-robed apprentices, male and female, turned the corner and almost ran into her. They startled, then seeing only her blue robes and shocked expression, immediately dropped their eyes and began making obsequious apologies.

"Oh dear, so sorry mistress, a thousand pardons, please forgive us . . . " They backed away hurriedly, bowing respectfully, then turned down a side passage and fled. Valerie had half-raised her hand with the intent of following old instincts to leave no witnesses, but a hand from behind the case grabbed hers and pulled it back.

"No magic, remember?" hissed Sam, coming out of his hiding place. "And if I'm seen and anyone asks, I'm your personal bodyguard . . . I think Shadrezarian mercenaries still wear black."

"You're far too pale to ever pass yourself off as a Shadrezarian," scoffed Valerie softly as they continued swiftly down the hall. "But we'll hope that any more young apprentices will be just as foolish as you."

"And if we meet any high mages?" Sam led the way, counting doors, then listened intently at one. Valerie kept watch down the hallway. From all sides came constant random pulses of all sorts of Light magic as various mages demonstrated their skills or just used magic as they were accustomed to.

"We'll have to be sure we don't."

Sam tried the door and jumped back. A fat blue spark had popped silently off the handle, shocking him. Valerie brushed past him, eyes narrowed.

"A magical ward of sorts," she muttered, "designed to scare off inquisitive students and the like. But it shouldn't have discharged like that . . . not on a non-magical person. Any history of wizardry in your family?"

"No," Sam snapped softly. "None. It's probably residual from your blasted Darkportal."

"Perhaps. I'd better see if I can unweave it." She began to close her eyes, but the assassin again caught her arm.

"Wait," he insisted. "Is it on the lock, the door, or the whole portal?"

"The latching mechanism," Valerie reported, after a moment's concentration, using not her magic, but instead the innate Nathauan spell-sight.

"All right . . . keep watch." He drew out a set of seldom-used lockpicks, and, with the occasional angry indigo spark popping out around his knuckles, set to work.

Kaylana and Arcie wandered through the convention halls with that wonderful invisibility that the servant class enjoys in the company of those it serves. Kaylana's plate of doves had been apprehended by a group of yellow-robed young journeymen from one of the southeastern provinces who were playing some magical game in one of the large open activities halls. Arcie kibitzed for a moment, as Kaylana, growing claustrophobic from the stuffy warmth of the halls and the chattering crowds of mages, pinned herself against a wall near a large water cask. The game played by the journeymen seemed at first to be some complex variant of chess; an intricate board was set up, and scattered with pieces that represented various long extinct monsters and some human types. Dice seemed to determine how the figures would move, and whether a dark dragon could take out a violet mage and three knights. After a moment of watching, Arcie shook his head and walked away; it was far too confusing for his liking. One of the players had a very elaborate set of pieces, and dice made from semi-precious stones—gifts, he had proudly stated, from his master. His figures were so finely carved and painted they seemed almost to move. Arcie, unable to help himself, helped himself; to one that caught his fancy, a beautiful rendering of a hell-beast, with its blue-black scales and flowing fur, all wings and fangs and spiky talons. He slipped the miniature out of the wizard's pouch and into his own pocket, then went to peel Kaylana off the wall.

" 'Tis dangerous wandering through all these mages," he confided to her as they ducked out of the room. "We'd best try to find the other two."

"How are we to do that?" replied the Druid. "We don't even know where *we* are, much less where they might be."

"Och, lass, trust ol' Arcie. We rogues have many and

secret talents what few ever ken." He laid a finger alongside his nose and grinned, and scooped a tray of filled glasses off of a passing buffet table. Then he turned to a butler who was walking past.

" 'Ere, guv, t'mages give me an order for drink to go to the high tower," he chirped, grinning winsomely. "But blasted iffen I ken where yon be. Give us a point, please, sahr."

The butler sighed. "I suppose that means someone will have to be dispatched to clean up those rooms as well, after the festivities," he said. "We hoped they would all stay in the lower rooms, but each must have his own private conferences . . . follow this hall, take the first left and then the staircase at the end, turn left and go down the hall at the top. It'll be the last door on your right."

"Thankee kindly, guv," replied Arcie, tugging his forelock respectfully. As the butler moved on among the crowds of mages (who were eagerly heading to a presentation on Realistic Illusions presented by the famous High Wizard Lorem), he grabbed Kaylana by the arm and steered her down the hall, his tray of clinking wineglasses held high.

Sam wrestled with the lock for what seemed like ages. Not only was it well-made and stiff with disuse, but the sparks would cause his fingers to involuntarily flinch when crucial delicacy was vital. He'd never been that good at locks anyway; that was partly why he'd always had Arcie along on his missions that required such tasks. He sat back, shaking his tingling fingertips as Valerie radiated impatience.

"It's no use," he whispered. "If only we had Arcie here . . . "

" 'Allo 'allo, did I hear someone asking after me?" piped a familiar voice. Sam and Valerie turned to see Arcie, followed by Kaylana, turn the corner and approach.

"Great vanished Hruul, Arcie, I'm almost glad to see you," Sam exclaimed in a soft whisper. "Got a lock that needs your attention."

"Oho, does it now?" chortled the Barigan softly. "Let's have at it." He shook out a couple of picks from his sleeves and went to work. For whatever reason, the blue sparks seemed to leave him alone.

Valerie turned to Kaylana. "How did you find us?" she asked. The Druid shrugged, her composure returning now that she was away from the crowded lower halls.

"We asked someone."

Robin and Blackmail had drifted to the far gates closest to the Castle. Here a circle of musicians and dancers sang and danced around a roaring bonfire, while smaller fires around the perimeter roasted chickens and suckling pigs. Apples peeled, coated in brown sugar and cinnamon, and baked in the coals, were handed out freely to children, and Robin managed to obtain one from a cheerful gentleman who was impressed by the novelty of a centaur in the city. He bit gingerly at the hot confection and carefully watched Blackmail. The preoccupied knight was staring up at the Castle, his hand on his sword. Robin looked around. Crowds, noise, smoke from the fires . . . perfect. Slowly he stepped back into the crowds, letting a marching parade of drunken singers stagger between him and the knight. Then he bolted. When Blackmail looked around, searching, there was no sign of the centaur.

Robin ducked behind a stall selling festive scarves and wasted no time in pressing the two gems on his bracelet. The magic of the talisman would transport him immediately to within a few yards of Mizzamir's presence. He could only hope that immediately would be soon enough.

As the sickening feeling of strange transport faded, it was replaced by a rush of warm, stuffy air, and the droning of voices. Robin found himself in a darkened room with many other people, at the edge of many rows of seats. His hindquarters brushed tapestries on a wall. Mizzamir was seated at the center of a table of mages in front of the audience. One of the other mages was explaining something. A few of the mages seated near where Robin had materialized turned to look in surprise. Attracted by the change, Mizzamir looked up suddenly, and saw

Robin standing in the shadows, twisting his hat nervously. The Arch-Mage excused himself and came down from the panel, taking Robin aside.

"I trust this is important?" he inquired gently, as soon as they were out of earshot of the others. Robin nodded so violently that his mane flopped.

"Sir, the villains are here! In your castle, sir! They plan to enter the Silver Tower!"

"The Silver Tower?" exclaimed Mizzamir. "Whatever for?" But before the centaur could reply, he continued, "No matter. Assuming they have found the way there, I can make it extremely difficult for them to leave. Much as their escapades have proved interesting, this is too good an opportunity to end the matter without bloodshed."

Meanwhile, Arcie pushed the door open and stepped back with a flourish. "There ya be, all in a night's work for Arcie MacRory, Guildmaster of Bistort and too likely the rest of yon world as well. Best burglar in existence."

"And the most modest," came from Sam. He noticed Kaylana was looking nervous; it was strange to see her composure shaken. He wondered, as he so often had, if there was anything he could do to help her, to comfort her . . .

"We had better get back down to the lower levels," Kaylana said, looking around. "We are too conspicuous in this large group."

"The bunny-hugger is right," Valerie said coldly. "The assassin and I will continue from here . . . you two had better return."

"Right enough," agreed Arcie with a sigh. "Well and it seems we always be missing the exciting parts . . . Come along, lassie." He and Kaylana started for the hall, while Sam and Valerie slipped into the opened stairwell and up the well-worn spiral steps beyond.

"You must return to whence you came, minstrel," cautioned Mizzamir, "Lest the dark knight suspect. I shall deal with these."

Before Robin could utter a word of protest, the Arch Mage cast the spell that sent him snapping back like a rubber band to his point of departure. The whuff of the smoky night air and music swelled around him, and he stepped out just in time to catch Blackmail's arm as the knight went marching rapidly past, looking for him. The knight gripped his shoulders, as if glad to see him, and then glanced up at the Silver Tower. Robin followed his gaze.

Valerie and Sam went through the elaborately carved door at the top of the stairs without difficulty. The room they stepped out into seemed to Valerie to pulse softly with waves of magical goodness that nauseated her. Nightshade gurgled in sympathy. Sam, unaffected but still uneasy, scanned the room.

It was like a typical mage's study, only far richer. Somewhat oblong in shape, and made of silver-white marble, it held everything a mage would need, without being cluttered; a fine goldenwood desk at one end, racks of scrolls and shelves of books, as well as some tables with magical accoutrements arranged on them. But the focal point of the room was near the center, where the floor fanned out in a dais set with chips of semiprecious stones. Glittering and blinking softly in the center of this was a font, made of marble and decorated with cabochons of gemstones. The gemstones were lit up as if from the inside and sparkled like agitated stars.

"Test, Test, where's the blasted *Test!?*" exclaimed Valerie, looking frantically around the room. *"Lead, light, and sand the Test define* . . . Assassin! Search through the drawers in that desk for lead, sand, anything . . . "

Sam wasn't listening. Though the room was fairly dim, lit only by a diffuse glow without any visible source, he had noticed the windows. Stained-glass images, made eerie by their colors muted and darkened by the outside night, looked down at him. One in particular caught his attention and froze it; an image of Mizzamir, in all his silver robed glory, looking down at him, his expression mutated by the night into something old, slow, cold . . .

not darkness, but beyond it; a strange, uncaring expression that knew nothing of right or wrong, but only of good or evil . . .

Valerie stopped her frantic scrambling among the tables to see what had stopped him. She followed his gaze, and then halted herself.

A silent moment passed, then she whispered; "Of course. How could I have been so stupid? Lead and sand . . . glass. Stained glass held in a lead matrix . . . "

Her voice tore Sam out of his reverie. "But it also required light, didn't it? There's no lamps in here . . . and it won't be dawn for hours yet," he whispered back.

"And we can't wait here until it is," Valerie replied with determination. "We'll just have to hope that isn't important."

"You're right . . . that has to be the Test . . . But how do you activate it?" Sam moved back toward the door, not from fear, but from caution; his danger sense was beginning to prickle, and the fire was starting to rush and burn in his blood. He could actually smell Mizzamir in the air of this room, a faint sickly smell like lavender and cedar.

"Should be fairly obvious," retorted Valerie. "Ancient magic's brine. That font has to be at least as old as this tower, and the best liquid for scrying is a saline solution . . . we used to collect the tears of tortured slaves, back in the Underrealm."

So saying, she grabbed a glass beaker off a handy table and plunged it into the font. The gemstones flashed painfully bright, and a crackle of familiar blue sparks exploded around her. Nightshade flew straight up, cawing. The sorceress, taken off guard, was unable to keep herself from flinging the brimming beaker up and away, sending it crashing, contents and all, over the suspected Test window. The noise was like the shattering of the ice-gates of doom. The lights on the font vanished, leaving the room full of dim shadows and ringing afterimages. Nightshade perched on a bookcase, wings trembling.

It took a few seconds for them to recover. Then Valerie

said, "Of course, many mages chose to guard their fonts with various spells. I admit to a lack of caution on my part."

"Nothing's happening to the window," reported Sam, "except that it's wet." Valerie came over and gently touched the glass. It was indeed wet and cold. But there was the faintest crackle of powerful magic under her fingertips . . .

"It's the right window, the right actions . . . it just needs something else . . . " she said, frowning in concentration.

"How about light?" suggested Sam. Then wished he hadn't.

The room exploded into brilliant white radiance. Sam's assassin fires flared like lightning as sudden shock hit him. With a soft warm blast of displaced air, and a swirl of golden smoke, the Arch-Mage Mizzamir appeared in the center of the room, near the font. His ornate staff was shining like the sun, and in the brief conscious glance Sam had, before the fire filled his vision, he looked more upset than Sam had ever seen; which is to say, he looked mildly annoyed.

"Now then, this has gone far enough," he began . . .

But the light from his staff filled the room. It blasted the shadows away and rebounded, filling and spilling like liquid silver . . . it lit up the windows bright as noonday, shining out through them and back inside so that they glowed like jewels aflame. Valerie, her hand resting on the window, barely had time to notice the sudden surge of magic under her hand before powerful forces swept her up and sent her spinning down inside a whirlpool of rainbow light.

Mizzamir himself flinched from the sudden burst of light that exploded from the main window. And before he could look back again to see the Nathauan sorceress vanish, a dark, heavy shape had crashed into him, daggers flashing. Nightshade flew out the door, croaking at the top of his lungs.

* * *

Down in the city, Robin and Blackmail, still looking up at the Tower, saw it explode with brilliant light. Several other people saw, and pointed and exclaimed in amazement. But Blackmail grabbed Robin's arm and yanked him along, running at a clanking trot along toward the Castle. After a few paces, he stopped at a light two-horse carriage, near which was tethered a riding palfrey, saddled and bridled. He swung himself up on the palfrey and grabbed the leading reins of the carriage, and, beckoning Robin to follow, set off for the Castle at a brisk trot, the horse and carriage rumbling obediently alongside. Robin, not wanting to go but unsure if he could refuse, followed behind.

Mizzamir had not gone into this confrontation unprepared. Sam's daggers flashed but were repelled by a blast of force that sent him flying backward. He crashed into a wall, but staggered to his feet as he saw the mage begin to ready a spell. Suddenly, a thought sprang into his firestormed brain: *Got to get him out of here! If Valerie returns successful he can take the Segment of the Key and then he's won!* The door was still open. He dodged a bolt of paralyzing blue energy, then faced Mizzamir.

"You want me, wizard, you'll have to catch me," he hissed, and ran for it.

Valerie found herself in a large cavern, lit with a dim green-purple light that made the true size of the vast echoing area impossible to determine. It might once have had pillars in it, for she saw piles of broken columns lying about in disarray on the floor. The stone, air, dim light, and craftsmanship were certainly not that of the Castle . . . nor was the creature that raised itself up from behind a pile of broken stone.

Valerie's fine black eyebrows flew up in shock as she recognized a creature from the window panels of the Test, a strange beast that the wizard Mizzamir himself had fought and destroyed in the furthest depths of Putak-Azum, a battle matched only in fame by his confrontation, in the higher vaults of the same catacombs, with the

Dark dragon Kazikuckla. Valerie felt she would far have preferred to meet a clean, simple dragon rather than the monstrosity which reared before her now.

It was the Thur-Uisgie, a demon spawn from the early days of the world, a terrible, powerful creature. She could not recall if Mizzamir had fought the beast singlehandedly then, her mind wandering in distraction and shock. It obviously couldn't be the same one . . . could it? It seemed horribly real. Even its smell, a stink like rotting corpses, was authentic enough to make even her Nathauan stomach retch.

It had a dragon's head, topping a human torso, and sprouted shriveled vestigial batwings from the shoulders. A mane of fine black quills hung down around its head, and its three red eyes gleamed as it saw her. Its mouth showed small sucking fangs, and its three spindly arms terminated in long thin fingers. It stood upright on hind legs like a horse's, covered in fine scales. It had a scaly tail barbed with more quills, and it rattled these together now as it spoke in a hissing voice.

"So, someone comes to take the Tessst?" Valerie stood her ground. Too often had a mage been overtaken in the preliminaries of battle by an illusion.

"You can't exist," she stated firmly, forcing her voice to remain steady as she bent her will to believe what she was saying. "And even if you do, you don't have any magic. You are evil, your magic would be evil . . . and I hold the last of the Darkportals."

The Thur snapped its fangs at her. "Excellent reasoning, small Nathauan . . . but you forget I am now but a created creature in the service of Arch-Mage Mizzamir, and thus can draw my energy from the forces of Light . . . which as you know out-powers your own consssiderably. Prepare to die!" Its mouth snapped suddenly, and it began weaving the air with its hands as it cast a spell.

"Thuckssisam maleesta fn'ura . . . "

Valerie was taken off guard, but the first few words of the spell were familiar, and she instantly began chanting the appropriate counterspell.

"Kiliani marusha prethanus . . . "

Valerie had fought something similar to this wizards' duel time and time again with young upstart sorcerers in the depths of the Underrealm. Her Darkportal, in fact, had been won from a higher sorceress whom Valerie had defeated, long, long ago. But circumstances had been different; the ranges had been closer, the spells had conflicted and interfered with each other so that each one had more or less bounced off the other as they manifested (a common problem in mages' duels when both sides were using spells at close range, without room to dodge). But here, in this maze of pillars and rubble, facing the alien demon-thing, the battle would be different. Now it was spellcast and resist and counter, dodge and chase and retaliate. And what with this much rubble to interfere with full volley and this much distance to play with, the outcome was likely to be far from stalemate.

Valerie barely finished her defense in time. In the moment before it manifested, a glowing golden dart shot from the Thur's scaly fingertip. The bolt struck her in the shoulder, causing searing pain and blistering damage as it vanished, but the next seven hit and vanished against an invisible shield of magic force.

"Haass . . . " snarled the Thur. "So you do know some magic, then . . . well, perhaps I shall crush you with my bare hands!" It began to cast once more, a personal spell, Valerie judged, from the gestures.

"Maximus porenthus atalus . . . "

She decided to attack while it was thus preoccupied. She chanted rapidly and fired a bolt of devastating red-black energy. It struck the monster full in the chest, causing it to keen in rage and tremble with sudden weakness, its spell of magical strength gone.

Looks like I'm going to need a bit of a backup, Valerie thought. She took from her components pouch a pair of tiny representative items, and began to chant once more. The Thur hissed and began spellcasting as well.

Valerie wasn't hoping for much when she cast her summoning spell. The incantation would bring a few minor beings of this world to fight for her, regardless of how they might feel; but with the world as it was there weren't a whole lot of usefully dangerous things left.

In fact, as the air in front of her shimmered, she was startled to see three red-robed apprentice wizards from the convention appear, holding stacks of notes. They gaped at her in blank astonishment, until the Thur completed its spell with a flourish and blew them away in a wash of gore. They screamed as they fell, oozing, then exploded.

The blast knocked the sorceress behind a pillar, and she quickly began chanting an offensive spell while the Thur blinked. It licked the spattered gore away from its eyes and dispatched one of the still-squirming apprentices with a stomp of its heavy hoof. Valerie then jumped up from shelter and fired her spell.

Sharp sparks began to pelt down upon the Thur, and it hissed in anger, fangs snapping as it shouted a counterspell. It seemed to burst into violet flames that formed a shield around it, smothering the sparks. Using this momentary protection, it cast a lethal spell with a snarling hiss. Valerie cursed as a cloud of billowing, poisonous yellow gas erupted from the monster's hooves and began rolling toward her. An acrid stench began to fill the room as the flickering, fire-shielded Thur cackled in triumph. Valerie hastily muttered a spell.

"Palonius teletrasin portula . . . "

She knew of this magic, it was one that the Verdants had used to slay the Nathauan in their tunnels; the gas would not move back to its caster. She used a powerful shot of her energy to teleport herself *behind* the Thur.

Then she immediately began an attack spell. The Thur startled at her vanishing, spun around, saw her, recognized the words she was chanting, and, panic stricken, spun a dome of shimmering light around itself to protect it from the spell. Valerie finished the spell, and instead of aiming the sudden beam of green light at the protected Thur, she aimed it at the creature's feet. Her Darkportal throbbed against her neck, sending an icy burning through her bones as she drew dangerously powerful amounts of raw negative energy from it, to combine matter with its exact opposite . . .

The stone beneath the Thur suddenly vanished with an explosive roar, and the monster fell with a shriek and a clatter into a deep pit. A volley of sharp quills rattled up, but Valerie dodged behind a pillar and hid herself in the rubble.

A sudden phrase of power emanated from the pit, and it smote the sorceress through her ears, making her mind reel. She fell, shaking. The Nathauan lay, limp and unmoving, unable to think or act, while the creature dragged its bruised body out of the pit and came looking for her, its tiny round nostrils whiffing as it poked about in the rubble.

She had not known that Mizzamir's mimic creation could so precisely follow its original that it would even know the ancient words of Dark Power, and have the strength to use them . . . The magic of the Test was too great, too unfathomable. She was done for. She heard the sucking sounds, the Thur-Uisgie's teeth dripping digestive venom as it slowly approached.

Naturally it was far beyond Mizzamir's dignity to go running around the halls like some errant apprentice. And dangerous as well. He would no sooner chase after an assassin than follow a cobra into its hole. His scrying font was ruined; no help there, but he'd lived in this Castle for over a century, and he knew his way around *quite* well. He stopped a moment to grab a magical ice-wand from its case on one shelf, and then teleported himself with a sweep of magic.

Sam, running lightly down the second set of steps, dodged more by instinct than by skill as he felt the sudden sharpness in the air that heralded Mizzamir's sudden appearance on the steps below him. A bolt of energy flashed from a wand and struck a small wall lamp where the assassin had been. Instantly the lamp was encased in a rough block of blue-green ice, with its magical flame still glowing within. Sam had time for one thought: *Still trying to catch me without hurting me. No wonder I've survived this long.* He threw a dagger. The mage ducked, too late; but his protective spells held, and the blade rebounded off an invisible force field and went clattering back up the stairs, rebounding from the walls. Sam dived straight at the tall mage, and smashed into him. They went tumbling down the stairs, Sam trying to find some weapon that would break the wizard's magical field, and Mizzamir desperately trying to get a clear shot at the assassin with his ice-wand.

They broke apart as they crashed into the hall at the foot of the stairs, accompanied by exclamations of shock from the numerous passing mages. Sam used the impact to his advantage, kicking away from the mage by a good foothold on the wizard's chest. Mizzamir staggered back, robes in disarray, and Sam leaped down the hall. A pair of mages moved to intercept him, but he yanked a tapestry down over them, and ducked as an ice-bolt shot over his head and froze the tangled mages. As he turned a corner he heard a scream—an apprentice pierced by a mysterious flying dagger that had worked its way back down the stairwell.

Kaylana and Arcie, heading back to the kitchens, heard the commotion and ran toward it. Sam rounded a corner, shoving mages out of the way, just as they emerged. He saw them and skidded to a stop.

"ArciegohelpValerie, KaylanagetoutofherefindBlackmail," he panted, then jumped away again, running. The Druid and rogue flung themselves to either side of the hall as a shouting group of mages pursued the assassin. Down the hall, there was a sudden rush of air, and Mizzamir's unmistakable form appeared, firing rapid blasts from a wand at Sam. Sam ducked, dodged, and finally rolled as the blasts flashed around him, then he came up running and vanished again. Kaylana and Arcie exchanged glances, then ran in opposite directions, Kaylana toward the scullery exit, and Arcie back the way Sam had come.

Sam was running on pure fire now. His sensible means

of thought-reaction couldn't act fast enough, couldn't work accurately enough to dodge the sudden blasts from Mizzamir's weapon. The mage seemed to know where he was going before he did; and Sam was becoming rapidly lost in this twisting castle of corridors and rooms, all crowded with decorations and lesser mages. In addition to Mizzamir's efforts he now had to parry the other mages' offensive or restraining spells, familiars in the shapes of cats, owls, tiny dragons and stranger things all snarling and snapping at him as he pushed past their owners. His own nature, too, struggled against his consciousness, which knew he had to run, to decoy, when the fire was shouting in his blood: *Don't run away! That's the* **target**! *You aren't supposed to* **run away** *from the target!*

Arcie hurried along, and emerged into one of the large convention halls. This was all in disarray; several mages stood in surprise, encased in blocks of blue-green ice, and a number of others who had not gotten out of Sam's way quickly enough were lying on the floor, groaning and holding stab wounds or bruises from fists and feet. Near the ceiling, on a huge ornamental chandelier lit by magical lights, was a mob scene. A solitary black raven perched there, and was being mobbed by small owls and falcons, a few exotic singing birds, two tiny jewel-dragons, and the High Vizier of Shadrezar's own six-foot long winged serpent. Nightshade croaked and ducked as the creatures swarmed and swooped at him, and lashed out with his thick, razor-sharp beak as one came too close. Arcie, having been at the wrong end of that beak before, winced as a delicate star-finch shrieked and plummeted earthward. Its cry was echoed by an elegant lady wizard in one corner, who screamed and sank unconscious, perhaps lifeless, to the floor. Arcie nodded to himself. So the stories about wizards and their life-bonds to their familiar were true . . . it was a pity that Mizzamir had never decided to obtain one.

Nightshade spotted Arcie in the doorway. With a relieved caw he swept down, trailing the familiars, and hovered in front of the Barigan a moment. Then, with a cock of his head, he flew off down the passageway. Arcie ran after him, the other familiars finally retreating to their masters' shoulders as the evil intruder departed.

Though he might be short of leg and stature, Arcie could move quite fast . . . a useful trait for a thief. He came to the door he had opened for Sam and hurried up the stairs. He reached the room at the top and stopped to marvel a moment at all the open wealth. Valerie was nowhere to be seen. Nightshade flew in circles in front of a huge stained-glass window of Mizzamir, croaking mournfully. Arcie shrugged. Well, he hadn't found Valerie, but this was the last place the raven had led him to. Maybe she could find her own way back here. In the meantime, many wonderful fiscal opportunities presented themselves. He extracted a strong sharp pick and went to work on the dim font, carefully chipping the rich gemstones out of their sockets. The panels of the stained-glass window glowed eerily behind him . . .

The Thur-Uisgie didn't seem to see well and the still-diffusing clouds of gas confused its senses. Valerie slowly felt her head begin to clear as the Thur turned over chunks of pillars, looking for her, hissing to itself. She began a spell, as quietly as she could. This one was tricky, a lot of mages didn't bother to learn it; but her teacher, might the shadows lie gentle on his blasted bones that she'd left strewn in the Underrealm, had insisted that she study it . . . She was struggling through the final words when she saw the Thur looking in at her. She forced herself to finish the spell even as with a swipe of a paw it pried away a protective chunk of rubble and reached for her. Its fangs were snapping in expectation of biting into her pale flesh.

Valerie completed the spell with a gasp, and with a sudden hiss of surprise the creature flew upward to the ceiling, along with all of the rubble and pillars in that area of the room. Valerie remained safely on the floor as the Thur crashed into the ceiling and was half-buried under a pile of rock and rubble.

The gravity-reversal spell didn't last long, and Valerie ran to safety. Suddenly the magic gave out and dumped Thur and rocks back on top of each other to the floor once more, sending up a cloud of dust and quills. Groaning in pain, the Thur struggled to free itself from the rocks, and Valerie took a chance and cast one of the more powerful spells she knew. The Thur hissed as it felt its skin began to peel away from its flesh and snarled a chant of dispelling.

The Thur burst free of the stones, its skin re-forming, and with a hiss of magic words suddenly began shifting form. Huge taloned claws scraped into the stone, striking sparks. Three great dragon's heads swelled from its bulging body, breathing gouts of fire, and a powerful tentacle lashed out and wrapped tightly around Valerie's body, crushing her with terrible force as the hideous creature continued to grow.

Bones creaking, breath failing, Valerie had barely enough strength to utter a single spell, a single word . . . a Word of Disjunction, that might be enough if she could cast it properly while the creature was still in-between forms . . .

"*Portalanthankalcuzux,*" she gasped, the power cracking through her body, burning her flesh from inside . . .

There was a shrieking, tormented howl, and suddenly she was falling . . .

Kaylana emerged into the cool air with a sigh of relief. Within the building she could still hear commotion. She hoped the assassin would manage to escape . . . brave or foolhardy, she wasn't certain, but if he could keep things in a state of confusion long enough . . . a sudden clattering interrupted her reverie. She hastened to the side gates and saw Blackmail on a horse and Robin leading a small two-horse carriage. She waved and they turned toward her. She quickly recounted what had occurred, and together they headed for the base of the Tower.

Arcie's diligent efforts were cut short by a brilliant burst of golden light erupting behind him; he leaped into the air, sending tools and gemstones scattering. He turned to see Valerie stumble out of a glowing nimbus in the center of the stained-glass window. Nightshade, clucking softly, flew to her shoulder and began fanning her with his wings. Arcie quickly stuffed the gemstones into his pockets, and said,

"Valerie, lass! 'Tis surprised I am to see you . . . have you gone and won the Test, then?"

The sorceress nodded, holding up a segment of yellow-gold crystal that glowed from within. "Mizzamir . . . is . . . a . . . bastard," she panted. "Where did he go?"

"Go?" echoed the thief, stealthily appropriating a few items from shelves and tabletops as he recovered his scattered tools. "When I come to find ye, yon place were empty as ye see it. Last I seen Mizzy, he were chasing Sam through the Castle."

"Well, he was here, and that means he'll be back," said Valerie firmly. "Cease your thieving gutterhabits, Barigan, and let's get out of here."

Valerie led the way back to the room that she and Sam had entered through, and Arcie chuckled as he saw the black silk rope tied there. "Oho! Is that how ye got in . . . More fool ye, Sam, to leave yer rope behind . . . " They descended quickly. Once they stood safe on the ground below, Arcie gave the rope a complicated flip and twist. The knot slipped, and the rope fell down at their feet.

"What did you do that for?" hissed Valerie. Arcie quickly began coiling the rope.

"Old thief's skills, lass. Ne'er be leaving yer tools behind, especially ropes as shows what way ye left . . . "

"But how is Sam supposed to get out?" she demanded. He shrugged.

"Och, he'll find a way, ye mark my words . . . he always does . . . "

The sound of approaching hoofbeats made them turn, Arcie gripping the hilt of his morning star and Valerie trying to call to mind a spell, any spell . . . next to impossible in her magic-exhausted state. They relaxed when they saw the approaching figures were Kaylana, driving a small carriage, and Robin, accompanied by Blackmail on a horse.

"Well, we have found the two of you, then," said Kaylana as they came up. "Now all that remains is to find Sam."

From the Castle above came the sound of a distant crash and a few screams. Arcie wrinkled his forehead in consternation.

"Mightn't it be wiser to get out now, and hope the long-legged bounder will catch us up later?" he asked anxiously.

Sam had no real idea where he was headed, but now he was beginning to get the distinct feeling of being herded. He'd managed to grab his lost dagger, stained in blood, from the carpet at the base of the lower stairs, and now, as he raced up a familiar flight of stairs and emerged into a hallway, he suddenly knew where he was. At the end of that hall should be the door with stairs leading up to the Tower. As he stopped for a moment, Mizzamir appeared behind him and took careful aim. Sam overturned a bookcase into the path of the ice-bolts and then ran down the hall. What the mage didn't know was the other room that he and Valerie had entered through was just a few doors down, with a rope leading down to escape and freedom . . .

Bursting into that room, he jumped to the window—no rope. How—not important. He could hear the footsteps of the Arch-Mage hurrying closer.

Well, Mizzamir, he thought, *time to see how strong your protective spells really are.* With that, he grabbed up a heavy oak chair, the blood fire lending adrenal strength to his muscles, and when the wizard turned through the doorway Sam let him have it full in the chest.

Mizzamir tumbled backwards in a shower of splinters and blue sparks. Sharp shards of wood showered Sam like arrows, sinking into flesh through thick clothing. Ignoring the pain, he jumped over the struggling figure and ran out, down to the Tower door, and up the stairs.

Got to see if Valerie and Arcie made it out, he thought frantically. *Last stand . . . he knows! He knows!*

He burst into the Silver Tower, droplets of blood spattering behind him. The room was dark and empty. The font looked chewed on; most of its larger gems were gone. He squinted hard at the big stained-glass window . . . was it just his imagination, or were its colors slowly fading, its outlines melting? A sound in the doorway made him turn. Mizzamir was entering and closing and locking the door behind him.

"Well, here we are again," said the Arch-Mage, turning the wand around in his hands. He was smiling slightly. Sam cursed mentally. The Elf didn't have a mark on him, wasn't even winded. "Such a pity that you misguided souls of darkness tend to make such trouble for yourselves . . . "

"I was doing just fine until you decided you had to interfere with my life," Sam retorted. His hands were slowly reaching for a pair of his cheaper throwing daggers . . . the mage's protective spell had been overloaded by the impact of the chair . . . he had to be vulnerable now.

"Not interfere, dear boy . . . Help. Assist. Benefit. That's what I do. If you will surrender, and tell your friends that I will not hurt them, I promise you, you will come to no harm and will be given a far better life than that which you now lead . . . "

Sam was watching the Arch-Mage's hands. Were they moving also, the fingers stealthily knitting a spell?

"I don't want your help. I don't want your magic. I don't want your interference . . . " Sam hissed softly, his hands closing around his pair of matched throwing daggers. "All I want from you . . . is your head."

In a lightning-strike motion he hurled the two daggers simultaneously. Mizzamir reacted instantly, his hands leaping up and making a sudden, breaking motion. Fire exploded, a sheet of solid flame that sent out a blast of heat and force away from the wizard. The daggers glowed for an instant, then exploded like twin stars. The blast caught Sam like a wave, sending him hurtling backward.

He crashed through the window, the sound of shattering glass echoing and echoing. Melting rainbow shards burst around him, and he was falling . . . As he tried to spread himself out, he heard a distant cry, it sounded like Kaylana's voice, and the sound of hoofbeats . . .

He landed with a clatter as though he had fallen into a pile of cookware, cookware that caught him and broke his fall. He looked up into the expressionless helmet of Blackmail, who then tossed him unceremoniously into a carriage. As Valerie and Arcie hauled him inside, the knight swung back up into the saddle of a large palfrey and gave a signal. Kaylana's voice barked a harsh imperative, and the coach lurched forward.

Robin ran alongside the carriage as it thundered through the yards of the Castle and then out the northern road. Blackmail trotted beside them, looking back over his shoulder. Suddenly he wheeled his horse around and stopped.

Robin, cantering beside the carriage, looked back. On a balcony of the Castle, his hand raised as if about to cast a spell, stood Mizzamir. The evening wind whipped his robes and hair about. The beginnings of a spell were already crackling around his fingertips . . . Blackmail placed himself in the road between the wizard and the retreating carriage, standing firm with shield raised.

Mizzamir froze, staring down at the dark knight, whose black plumes fluttered in the breeze. The flickering sparks on Mizzamir's fingers died away, and the mage slowly dropped his hand. Blackmail stood his ground for a moment more, until the carriage was out of range. Then he turned the champing horse around and rode after the others. Robin did not see Mizzamir vanish, but when he looked back again, the silver-white figure was gone.

The story and rumors of how the villains had managed to infiltrate the very seat of magic authority spread like wildfire, even to the slowly following Verdant Company.

This news upset Fenwick and he shook his head sadly. He *had* tried to warn the wizard . . .

Fenwick desperately needed to know where the villains might strike next. He did have a few ideas.

"It seems to me," mused Fenwick, "that they are going to have to cross the Plains sooner or later." He was in the safe haven of the Frothing Otter, in the seaport town Panzin on the western shores of Natodik. "The dock-master tells me that they boarded a ship heading west yesterday at dawn. And nothing is west of here but the barbarian land of Sei'cks. What they can hope to find there in those peaceful wild lands is beyond me. Perhaps they have overstepped themselves with this last attack and are seeking a bolt-hole." The broken, dying ramblings of the legendary Orthamotch had been full of strange hints but no coherent information. Fenwick brushed the feather in his hat thoughtfully. "But I don't think I'll tell the Arch-Mage. No sense in his risking himself . . . besides, I think now these miscreants have become my responsibility. I will take the risk and gain the glory."

The Verdant Company had moved into Panzin that afternoon. The news of the attack in the Castle of Diamond Magic gave Fenwick new resolve. It was vital now that the villains be captured and put to death without delay. Yet he had learned his lesson in the Fens. It was too easy to damage innocent people in a direct confrontation, especially with many under your command . . . The centaur, a foolish but innocent soul, might have been slain in that battle, and the lovely red-haired Druid might have come to harm just as easily. He'd heard of Druids; they were not evil, just misguided. And he felt it would be well worth the effort to save the lady from the company of darkness and guide her around to the right way of thinking, particularly with regards to himself. He peered down at the map before him, as he rested in the inn where not too long ago the villains themselves had rested. A glass of white wine was at his elbow.

"They should reach the Plains fairly soon . . . and when

they do, there will be quite a surprise waiting for them." He smiled, and looked at the map. Its faded colors seemed to glow with promise. He took out a sheaf of paper and a quill pen, and, after a moment's thought, began to write.

A short while later, he folded up the letter, sealed it with a drop of wax from a nearby candle and marked it with his signet ring, then went in search of Towser, now much recovered from his temporary death. The resurrected mage would teleport the letter faster than any messenger could run . . . and the trap would be set.

VIII

"I believe this is your stop," said the captain of the *Sea Arrow,* somewhat gruffly. They had pulled into a large sandy-bottomed bay of clear blue water, with a small seaport arranged like a jumble of children's blocks along the shore. This was Pila'Mab, trading city of the land of Sei'cks. Cities in Sei'cks were few and far apart, settled around a few suitable ports and rivershores as centers of trade and commerce. Most of the population would have little to do with crowds and buildings, the congestion of even such small towns. They lived their lives as free-roaming hunters of the plains, living off the land and pursuing their ancient ways and traditions without any government more stringent than clan leaders, no buildings more permanent than leather tents. It was here that the Hero, or Heroine, Ki'Kartha Springdance, had been raised and trained as a priestess to the goddess Mula, Lady of Healing and Fresh Water. Though originally a simple barbarian deity, through the faith and fame of her disciple the goddess had become one of the more important and widely worshiped deities in the Six Lands. The barbarian people of the Plains of Sei'cks were a proud and independent race, still strong and fierce even though

Mizzamir's post-Victory guidance had curbed their tendency to have long blood feuds with their neighbors over who stole whose Tantelopes and when. They allowed the presence of the towns to provide trade for goods they needed, such as wrought metal and Barigan whiskey. But strangers in their sacred lands were frowned upon, and the townsfolk, most of them from other Lands, did not venture far into the wilderness for any cause.

Kaylana had been awakened and had gotten the others up to prepare to disembark. A low, small boat was lowered to the surface of the sea to carry them to shore. They had been forced to sell the carriage and horses, as the captain had been sailing with a full cargo and had no room for livestock. So cramped was the journey that they almost had to leave Robin behind as well, but the minstrel's pleading eyes were too much for Sam, and he joined Blackmail's mute insistence that the centaur accompany them. In gratitude, Robin had played and sang throughout the three days' voyage, and by the time land was sighted all the villains had learned more than they ever wanted to know about the glory of the Heroes, recorded in the greatest free verse of the minstrels of the Days of Light. Free verse canticles were the common form among minstrels, as opposed, Kaylana explained to them, to the style of bards. Their music wove through the fabric of time, and even the webs of reality, the notes and words able to draw magic from music. Robin had been first affronted, then curious, and pressed to hear more about the long-extinct bards, but Kaylana just shook her head sadly and would say no more.

They made the shore safely, pulled the boat up onto the sands, and wandered up the beach and through the small town. They could not dally here, the community was too small, and they were too conspicuous. They would have to leave at once and get into the wilderness before too much attention was paid to them. A few hills, the remnants of old dunes and buried fishing settlements before the dawn of history, slowly rolled away under their feet and hooves, until at last the countryside opened out like a huge green-gold ocean, under a high dome of clear blue sky. They had entered the Plains of Sei'cks.

"Och, 'tis as vast as me grandpa always did say," commented Arcie. The others silently agreed.

"We'd better stick to nocturnal travel," suggested Sam. "Everything is too easily visible here in daylight, and at night campfires would be seen clearly."

Valerie adjusted her hood against the bright sun. "Besides which, it's hot out here." Blackmail, in his unremovable dark armor, nodded silent agreement.

"We shall take a rest for the day, then," decided Kaylana. "And head on when evening falls. Let us see if we can find a defensible position."

"Ye dinna think Fenwick and his lot be after us yet, do ye?" asked Arcie worriedly. "He canna possibly ken where we be after . . . we scarce ken ourselves!"

"That's a good point," agreed Sam. "We'd better decide that before we go further."

"Let us see of we can find a suitable place to make camp," decided Kaylana, "and there we shall discuss the matter."

They moved off over the dunes, parallel to the sea, until they finally reached the last one, a tall hill of waving grass. Behind them, the dunes rolled down to the distant smudge of the town and the sea beyond, and ahead, the prairies stretched, flat and sunlit, a green-gold plain extending unbroken to the horizon.

"This are a fair enough place," said Arcie, looking about. "Ye can spy just about all ye can spy from this great height, and with a fine sea breeze as well."

"But then, a molehill's a pretty great height to you, Arcie," Sam joked; the Barigan glowered up from his minus-five feet.

"Does the altitude addle yer brain, laddie, or were ye born a blatherin' nitwit?"

"Here, then," decided Kaylana, interrupting the ensuing argument. The rest agreed, and began setting up camp.

As they were doing a quick search of the area to make sure there were no hostile creatures lurking nearby, Sam noticed great quantities of wildflowers hidden in the tall grasses. All shapes and colors, with thin stems and variously shaped leaves. Wildflowers were becoming more and more common all over the Six Lands this autumn, but they seemed extra-plentiful here. Looking at them, he said absentmindedly, "I'll take first watch."

"Spiffywell, then," agreed Arcie. The company settled down to rest for the remainder of the day. The sun was hot, and Valerie had appropriated the only small patch of shade formed by a lump in the hillside. Her raven hopped about in the grass, snapping up crickets. Blackmail sat leaning against the back of the hill; Arcie flopped down in a patch of soft grass and put his hat over his face and was soon snoring like a bullfrog. Kaylana had removed her heavy outer robe and woven cord armor and lay curled up on top of them wearing her simple homespun tunic and leggings, one hand firmly gripping her staff. Robin stayed awake, lying with his long legs underneath him as he watched Sam. The assassin appeared to be picking flowers.

"I'm afraid I am still not used to this night marching," the centaur ventured apologetically after a moment.

Sam looked up, his fingers holding a cluster of pale pink blooms. "Don't worry about it . . . you're doing fine. It just takes practice. Pass me that blue one there, will you?" Sam asked, waving a hand vaguely at a section of flower-covered hill.

"Blue?" Robin asked, looking at the ground.

"Yes, that one, the blue one," Sam replied impatiently. Robin looked puzzled, until Sam finally reached over and plucked the forget-me-not. "See? This one."

"Oh," said Robin, ears twitching. "I'm sorry, I don't know much about flowers. So that's what you call a Blue, is it? We call them Never-Forget-Me's in the Commots."

"Um . . . " Sam looked thoughtfully at the centaur. "What color does it look like to you?"

"Color? It's gray, of course. About the same shade as

that patch of grass there, next to those orange and yellow flowers with red tips."

"Ah, yes, of course . . . " Sam nodded and filed the bit of information away. *He can't see either green or blue . . . and doesn't even know the names of the colors, so it must be a common centaur trait.* He braided a few stems together, whistling softly through his teeth. Robin sat watching, nervously grooming a few burrs out of his long silky tail.

"This . . . quest of yours," he said after a moment. "Is it really true what you told me? That the world's going to be destroyed?"

"That's what I've been told," Sam replied. He admitted to himself that, to someone not attuned to life on the dark side, the world seemed beautiful, happy, more full of life and light than it had ever been . . . he knew the young centaur couldn't sense the sickliness of it, the boredom, the inertia that flowed over everything.

"Who told you all this?" Robin asked at length. Sam smiled wryly.

"Well, not normal sources of influence to send me halfway around the Six Lands . . . but Kaylana and Valerie both believe it."

A flash of Robin's centaur upbringing showed itself.

"Women? You come all this way on the advice of women?" he said incredulously. The advice of mares and fillies was generally held in low regard in his society. Sam pulled up a red shaggy flower and looked at him sternly.

"Well, centaur, I like to think I'm as much of a man as the next fellow . . . " They both looked at the flower in Sam's hand. Sam coughed, and threw it away, continuing hurriedly, "but what they say makes sense. You don't need to go to a wise man on a mountain to see things aren't right. I wouldn't believe it if you or Arcie or ha! even the knight told me something like that . . . but I don't think Kaylana or even Valerie is lying about this." Sam scooped up his collection of wildflowers and sat down on a tussock. "I trust them. Arcie trusts something . . . or maybe he's just along for the ride. I don't know why Blackmail is with us. And as for you," Sam shrugged, "if you aren't sleepy, you can earn your keep and play a soothing tune to calm my hurting heart. Let me hear what you have so far about us," he suggested.

Robin sighed, took out his harp, and began tuning it. "There isn't very much," he began. "We've been kind of busy . . ."

"Yes," said Sam with a smile. "Those of us that have stayed awake when we were busy, at any rate."

Robin blushed, his ears flipping backwards and forwards in consternation. "Just because I don't lust for blood and violence . . . " he began crossly. Sam waved a hand airily.

"Don't get defensive, Robin. I understand. You're young yet, if I'm any judge of centaurs. Play a song, anything you like, provided it doesn't wake up the others." Sam leaned back and began fooling with his flower collection. Robin tuned his harp in silence. Sam was apparently weaving the flowers together, whistling softly between his teeth as his nimble fingers worked the thin stems. The profusion of blooms triggered a memory in Robin, and he ran his fingers down his harp, then began an old song.

Summer's blooms blow into winter once more,
Speaking of things that have gone long before.
Maybe once when our childhood was young, we were free.
But now we are moved into ways we can't see.

He fumbled for the next line, how did it go? Caught in . . . what? As his fingers began the tune again, he was startled to hear another voice come in with the words.

Caught up in a game of daring and chance,
Moving in step though we don't know the dance.
What now is a slave, a crime, or a war?
What does a death that was not done before?

Sam sang with a soft, clear voice that added a bittersweet sound to the music, giving the ancient, cynical words a strange poignancy. Robin kept silent but continued to play. Even as the assassin's voice drifted away, the next verse was begun by a beautiful voice that made both assassin and minstrel look up in surprise. Kaylana was sitting up, eyes closed, holding her staff. Her voice was changed, different, ringing with an ancient magic and music long lost.

We are but the flashes of sun on the sea,
Nothing will change for all we may be,
Heroes and gods may far wander their ways,
But lost and forgotten shall we end our days.

Kaylana finished the song and looked at them, her eyes and voice returning to normal. "That, minstrel," she said softly, "is similar to how the old bards used to sing, long ago. They went the way of my ancestors."

"Bards?" spoke Robin. "Tell me more?"

"Later, centaur. I suggest you sleep now. I shall take the next watch in about an hour, assassin," she added to Sam.

Kaylana gave Robin a smile, and the centaur nodded. He was tired. He sighed, packed his harp away, and shifted to a softer part of the grass to lie at a comfortable angle against the slope of the hill. Kaylana drifted back to sleep, until Sam woke her up about an hour later.

She woke with a start, feeling something on her hair. She shook her head, and a wreath made of tiny flowers woven together by their stems fell into her lap. She looked up sternly to see Sam lying a ways off, watching her. He'd had to take off his tunic because of the heat, and his black silk shirt was open to reveal a muscular chest, skin that would have been smooth if not for the network of scars that crisscrossed it from a thousand old wounds. A small birthmark, like a star with thin rays, showed on his left shoulder.

"Your watch, I believe," he said softly.

Kaylana looked at the flower wreath and picked it up.

"Yes. Fine weaving, by the way. It is very pretty." The assassin had certainly got a wide range of rare flowers worked together. Some of them, she was surprised to note, even seemed to be . . . She tucked it into her cord-belt.

"Thank you," replied the gentle voice. "But it is not as pretty as you."

Without moving a muscle, Kaylana debated. Was that a remark worth hitting him again for? Or was it just an innocent bit of chat he probably was regretting even now? Innuendo translation wasn't one of her strongest skills . . . she decided, in order to keep the peace, to ignore it. She stood and dusted off her clothes. "Sleep well, assassin. We have a long journey ahead tonight."

Sam sighed, and stretched like a sleek black cat. "True enough. Wake Arcie up when you're tired. He loves all this adventuring stuff." The assassin rolled over and was soon drifting into slumber. Kaylana watched, and thought.

When she woke Arcie, the Barigan peered out from under his hat, then got up. Noticing the wreath hanging from Kaylana's belt, he swatted at it.

"Here! What's this then?" he asked. Kaylana sat down.

"It is a wreath that Sam made," she explained. The cutpurse looked at the wreath, then at Kaylana, then his face split in a wide leer.

"Oho, he did, did he? Aye, I might have been guessing! All the gossip in Bistort says how fair skilled he is with his hands." Arcie yelped as a dirt-clod struck him in the middle of the back. Sam was awake, eyes open and glaring. Arcie rubbed his back, still smirking. "Aye, yon's the man as never misses . . . heard of that before too! Izzit pretty-pansy fwuppy flowers, Sam? Ouch!" he cried again, as a hail of dirt-clods pelted him. Laughing, he hid behind the Druid, forcing the fuming assassin to hold fire and with a final glare curl up again with his back to the party. Kaylana shook her head in puzzlement.

"It is your watch, Arcie," she informed the Barigan.

"Aye, well enough . . . Be seeing ye in the gloaming, then," he said with a grin.

When evening fell, they consumed a quick breakfast and consulted Valerie's notes.

Walk the line twixt Mula's sign,
And the path her tears define.
Here fate will take you like a wave
The hardest Test of all to brave.

"The blasted riddles be harder than yer Tests," complained Arcie, scratching his head.

"There are few landmarks in this wild land," commented Kaylana. "The gods, in these puzzles, have always referred either to landmarks or historical events."

"So it must be a historical event?" hazarded Sam. "I'm afraid I don't know much history . . . "

"Well, that's what the minstrel is for," said Valerie, with an evil smile. "It's about time the four-legged fumble started earning his keep."

"I-I-I," stammered Robin, his mind racing. He hadn't yet had time to report the villains' new location to Mizzamir and was almost afraid to . . . the Arch-Mage was probably very upset by all the chaos the evildoers had wrought in his own home. Now it seemed he might have to aid them still further, in order to save his mission and possibly his life.

"That's not a bad idea, Valerie . . . Robin lad, have you any ballads of Mula's tears or the suchlike?" Arcie looked up at him from where he sat on a hillock. Blackmail sat nearby, his dark brooding presence seeming larger by the dim shadows of night.

"No . . . " he said miserably, "I can't think of any really good ones . . . religion wasn't one of my main fields of study . . . " That at least was true.

"However," Kaylana put in, "we still sit here discussing this within dim sight of civilized land. It would be wise, I feel, to move farther inland, away from those who might pursue us."

"I suppose," agreed Valerie. "If the Test is anywhere on Sei'cks it is probably inland . . . or at least not here."

So, the renegades set out, with the objective of putting some distance between them and the potential enemy. The moon hung high in a wide clear sky, and the prairie was full of sounds.

Above them, clearly visible here with no clouds or city lights to dim or obscure, the stars shone brilliantly. The long veil-like river of stars and shining dust stretched overhead from west to east. The shining band, that Sam and Arcie knew as the Scarf, Valerie would have called Moonblood. Kaylana's ancestors had named it Fors Mor, the Great Waterfall, and Robin's childhood teachings marked it as Selkin's Tail. None of them knew what Ki'Kartha believed: the shimmering band was formed from the free-flowing tears of the Goddess of Healing and Fresh Water at the creation of the world, when she wept for the sorrows of pain and wars to come.

What luck or gods could ever have guided the group of five villains and their uneasy spy? What allies might darkness have, in the world so overflowing with light that the stars themselves could fill the sky with a light that rivalled the moon? None, surely . . . the ragtag band wandered under the infinite sky, their path heading between the shining avenue of stars and the course of the constellation the Water-Giver, representative of and sacred to the worship of Mula. The people of Sei'cks had landmarks . . . they were just placed higher and farther than most.

When dawn finally broke, the company were all footsore and exhausted, and it was all they could do to scramble to the top of a small bluff. The raised ground would make a good vantage point. The horizon was now obscured in a shimmering mist, the last traces of dew-bearing fog settling down onto the plains for the morning. Birds were already caroling in the silver light. Kaylana watched the lightening sky with unease; surely night should have gone on for a few hours longer?

"Why, why, *why* did we nay buy horses in Thaulara?" groaned Arcie, as he flopped over onto his back in the short grass.

"We were going to," sighed Sam, sinking down beside him, "but you said not to."

"This, you see," said Kaylana, who did not seem to be affected at all by the long march and was observing Arcie's panting with thin scorn, "this is what comes of the continual consumption of red meat."

"Food!" whimpered Arcie. "Don't be speakin' of food less you intend to serve some straight quick. I'm not half perished and famined!"

The fog had climbed taller as it warmed, obscuring visibility past fifty yards. "Much as I hate to admit it," said Valerie, sitting down on the soft turf, "The short one has a point. Why don't you cook this time, Barigan?"

"Och, if only so can I be fed . . . I'll be at finishing me dying first, tho," wheezed the cutpurse.

"Also, that filthy pipe of yours," added Kaylana sternly. "You are a liability to us all if you insist upon weakening yourself with these bad habits."

"Och, lassie, I'm just a Barigan, not a habbit," chuffed Arcie, unable to resist the old joke.

"I don't like the looks of all this mist," Sam said, looking about. Beside him, Blackmail nodded solemnly, his gauntleted hand on the pommel of his sword. "Is this sort of thing normal, Kaylana?"

"Perhaps not a daily occurrence, but well within the range of climactic variations for this ecosystem, I believe," came the calm reply.

"That means yes, fool," snapped Valerie, noticing Arcie's puzzled expression. He shook his head and held up a hand.

"Na, curb tha tongue, vixen. 'Tis something other I'm hearing . . . Robin? Can ye hear it, laddie?"

Robin's ears flicked and turned as his eyes widened. "Hoofbeats? But . . . wrong . . . and . . . "

Sam suddenly jumped forward, pushing Arcie out of the way and knocking Kaylana to the ground, as a spattering of arrows flew out of the fog and rattled around them. Simultaneously, a disembodied voice, accented as rich and dark as cake, seemed to come from somewhere high in the air, spoke stern words.

"Stay where you are. You are surrounded, and our arrows have missed only by our choice."

The villains froze, staring, as out of the fog great looming shapes appeared. Dark angular shapes, moving with a strange stepping grace, shapes that seemed born of the fog and the green-gold grasses. As they approached, they resolved themselves into beasts; three times as tall as a man at their shoulders, with long, thin necks stretching yet again as high into the fog. Their legs were strong yet graceful, their bodies not much larger than a warhorse's and sloped to balance the weight. Their heads were like those of the Shadrezarian creature called "camels."

There were six of these Tantelopes, in soft shades of greeny-gold and shadow-brown, rippled and striped with pale white and cream like sunlight on water, and they had riders. To each sloping back was fastened a leather saddle bedecked with tassels and fringe and strings of beads, matching the elaborate pulley system that formed bridle and reins. Reins that lay loose on the knees of six fierce warrior scouts of the plains, strong, noble savages suntanned and muscled by the wild life, bundled in leather and furs and each prominently displaying a string of beads woven round and through hair-braids. The last bead of each string was a round stone of pure turquoise, symbolizing that they were of the truest Clan of the Healing Blue Water, the clan from which, so long ago, the Healer Ki'Kartha had ventured out into the world to fight the War in the service to her goddess, Mula.

The apparent leader, a dark-haired man with eagle-sharp eyes and a series of red, orange, and blue beads, nudged his Tantelope forward as his companions stood back, powerful longbows drawn and ready. Sam sized him up as he approached; he might make an attack, and even succeed, but he knew that before the dead barbarian toppled off his high mount that he and his companions would be shot through. The barbarian stopped and inspected the villains scornfully from the top of his high vantage point.

"You wander into the sacred lands without permission of my Clan," he intoned. "You are fortunate. In years past you would have been put to death instantly. Now, we are a kinder and gentler nation. You shall be taken captive and remain thus until your people make claim for your release."

"Wha . . . what people?" Robin asked nervously. The bowmen, never having seen a centaur before, were keeping an especially cautious eye on him. His voice seemed to surprise them; possibly they had thought him to be some unusual beast of burden.

"The folk of Pila'Mab will be notified; they shall know who to contact. Only fools or criminals would dare to wander into our sacred lands uninvited. We shall soon learn which you are." The barbarian made some gesture behind him, and one of the other riders gave some complicated signal to his mount.

The great Tantelope began to sink down, its legs slowly folding up in a complex arrangement of joints, until it was kneeling on the grass. The leader's did likewise, and the two men dismounted and approached the silent renegades. The villains did not dare to move; perhaps if they all scattered in opposite directions, one or two of them might escape into the fog; but none wanted to be one of the unlucky four or five. And how long could they hope to elude the pursuit of these skilled plainsmen and their stealthy mounts, who had crept up on them so unseen and unheard? Though they had fought and fled before rather than face capture, here they had no choice—surprised, tired, surrounded, and outnumbered, any villain could see the time for violence was later, and now was the time for plotting.

They remained still and allowed themselves to be briefly checked for weapons; Blackmail's and Robin's swords were taken, as were the more obvious of Sam's daggers and Arcie's morning star. A few attempts to remove Blackmail's helmet were quickly abandoned as futile, despite the knight's lack of resistance. Valerie attempted a last flash of rebellion; a quick spell sent a black explosive bolt towards one of the men, but he knocked the energy away scornfully with a flick of a strange wand he carried, and ordered the sorceress to be gagged as well. He then approached her, his wand held aloft, and murmured strange chants under his breath. His eyes suddenly widened, and his hand jerked out to grab Valerie's Darkportal pendant. There was an explosive flash, and the two flew apart, landing heavily on the grass. Snarling and flexing his scorched fingers, the shaman looked up to the leader for guidance, who made a dismissive gesture. Apparently, as long as Valerie stayed gagged and bound, he felt she was no threat. The shaman's powerful goodness, channeled through a divine force, made even the touch of the Darkportal anathema to him. Nightshade fluttered about, too concerned for the safety of his mistress to attack those who had her in their power.

Kaylana leaned heavily on her staff and backed away with a limp when the men approached; they thus assumed the staff to be a support, rather than a weapon. Finally, they bound the villains together, hands tied, with a long rope, leaving their feet free to walk. Kaylana they left unbound, and unhindered; obviously she must be a captive of these criminals, and barely able to march as it was.

And march they did. It was exhausting, after having traveled all night, and now in the growing light and heat of the day. The Tantelopes kept up a quick pace, fast as a man might walk briskly, and the villains stumbled from time to time. Requests for rest and food were ignored; the villains were prisoners, trespassers, and criminals—and criminals were to be punished.

When Valerie and Arcie began to stagger, Blackmail made a hand signal to Robin, in the lead, and the centaur, uncertain, stopped in his tracks at the same time the knight set his feet in and halted. The rope jerked, but held, and reluctantly the barbarians granted them time to sit and rest, and eat a miserable meal of dry rations and stale water. Arcie fell into a deep sleep, and when they awoke him about a half hour later to move on he awoke coughing and complaining bitterly. Yet no rest was further forthcoming, so he squared his small shoulders and trudged on, like a pit-pony so long away from the sun of freedom that it is past caring. When he finally collapsed they stopped long enough to drape him over Robin's withers and secure him, then moved on.

How long or far they traveled was uncertain, but the sun had not dipped far past its zenith, when they stopped at a section of plain not obviously different from any other. Here one of the riders dismounted, the one who had earlier defied Valerie's magic so easily. Among his leathers and beads was a necklace of turquoise and his wand, a twisted, Y-shaped stick decorated with feathers and shells and more turquoise. He held this by the forks and wandered about, chanting to himself, while the other riders watched, occasionally echoing a particularly emphasized phrase in the barbarian language.

Finally the shaman rapped the ground sharply with the stick, and a fountain of clear water burst up from the ground, swiftly flowing and pooling in a small hollow. The barbarians intoned a last set of phrases and swiftly dismounted, leading their Tantelopes to drink. The animals bent their long necks down, legs spread wide, and lapped at the water, while the exhausted and thirsty villains watched. The pool continued to flow. When the Tantelopes were finished, the barbarians moved in to drink their fill as the flow slowed to a trickle and stopped. Finally, the villains were shoved forward to drink of the shallow, muddy remains, well-mixed with Tantelope slobber.

Valerie watched the procedure of the water-summoning with interest, despite her exhaustion. "A High Priest of Mula," she grumbled, her gag unbound just long enough to let her drink. "I should have known. Powerful healing magic could easily beat my harming magic in this world . . . curse the imbalance!"

"Hush!" chided Kaylana.

They were moved on again, across the unchanging plains, Arcie, somewhat recovered, now able to stumble along with them.

As dusk fell they looked down into a wide bowl in the plains, marked around with carved stone pillars set here and there with chips of turquoise. Nestled in the bottom of the bowl was a jumble of leather tents surrounding an open stone structure, formed of slate walls and more of the carved pillars. The tents seemed to be the typical barbarian encampment, but the stone structure was obviously permanent and even majestic in a certain rugged way. Arranged in concentric circles, the stone structure had at its center an open plaza, with a large, perfectly round pool of bright blue water. At the east side of this pool was an altar dedicated to Mula, with a stone statue of the goddess carved of what looked from this distance like solid turquoise. The outer rings of the structure seemed to hold various roofed and unroofed rooms, and wandering through could be seen the various forms of turquoise-garbed figures. The barbarian rider who had captured them gave a jerk on the rope, and the party and their captors staggered down into the settlement. Folk came to assist them, or just watched, looking up from their chores at the pen where the Tantelopes were tethered, from cooking fires, from repairing hunting arrows and tanning leathers of prongbuck, ornyx, wheeumps, and bison.

Kaylana saw all this only dimly. Her mind was filled with the image of the pool, of the deep turquoise colors . . . Of Druids cut down by townspeople they once had helped; the heathen worship of indistinct forces, of nature and balance, the sun and the moon, life and death, came to be seen as evil under the teachings of a powerful religion that worshiped one goddess, had one creed, that promised only healing and water and sought to rid the world of night and death. The pool's image glowed in her mind, like blue crystal.

Their captors forced them, still bound, into a small, circular hut made of animal skins, near the edge of the encampment. Another barbarian, this one even taller and broader than the Tantelope riders, came to stand in the doorway and glared at them. In addition to his leathers and furs, he wore a rough tunic of heat-hardened leather armor, and carried a "Plainsman's Sword"—sharpened chips of obsidian set at right angles into a stout wooden club. Sam noted this, as well as the numerous chinks in the armor where a well-flung dagger would do the most good.

Arcie had landed in their new situation rather heavily; the barbarian community had always been fond of being able to pick up and bodily throw smaller people, and Arcie had sailed so well he'd rebounded off the back wall. He'd hit the ground with a thump and a curse, and rolled a short way. His snores had started almost before he came to a stop. Sam inched his way over to make sure the Barigan was all right, then looked at the others. Valerie had her back against the wall, the gag still in her mouth. Were her eyes closed in exhaustion . . . or narrowed in cunning? It was hard to tell. Kaylana sat serene and thoughtful, her staff across her lap; the barbarians had not bothered to tie her once they had reached the village. Robin, sweat-streaked and exhausted, gave the tent the slight pong of hot horse. Blackmail had walked into the tent under his own power, calm and strong and silent as ever, and now stood in front of their guard. The guard scowled and flexed his grip on his sword. Sam saw a confrontation coming, and said,

"Blackmail, please, sit down . . . when he finds out he can't do any damage to you he'll just take it out on one of us, the cowardly bastard."

Blackmail turned to look at him, then nodded, and backed away. The jailer had listened to Sam's speech with blank incomprehension. Sam's deliberate insult had been useful; it seemed their guard could not speak the common language of the Six Lands. It was not unusual; the Plainsmen felt such strong pride for their own culture that other influences were often seen as corrupting.

With a helpless, strangled sigh, Valerie slumped down to lie prone on the floor, her hair and cloak falling over her face as she turned her back on the guard. Nightshade sat on her arm, glaring up at the barbarian. She seemed to fall asleep, but a moment later Sam heard the faintest of sounds, like a set of sharp shark-teeth chewing their way through a simple leather gag.

Kaylana looked at the assembled company. "Apparently the fates would have us rest here," she said calmly. "Thus we shall rest. There will be time for discussing . . . our circumstances when we all waken once again."

They lay down on the floor of trampled grass and earth, and fell into various slumbers. But just before the dream-shadows claimed him, Sam heard a faint snap; the soft sounds of chewing stopped.

A trio of the Plainsmen had been sent to ride to the town of Pila'Mab, to notify the authorities of the capture of the suspected criminals. The Tantelopes, loosed to their full loping gait, covered the miles swiftly. Upon their arrival, they spoke with the mayor and the town guard captain about the capture, but the captives had no criminal records in that city.

A handsome man garbed in green and gold, newly arrived by ship that day, overheard the conversation. When the barbarian emissary's audience was over, Sir Fenwick approached them, smiling.

"Forgive me, but I overheard you that you have captured some criminals," he said. "And criminals they are, though the officials of this town do not know it. They are wanted across half the Lands for various evil crimes too numerous to mention."

"We thought as much," grunted one of the barbarians, the speaker for the group, who had spent much time learning the common language. "We of the Plains know such things, and these we have caught are like the black spider-viper under the cold rocks of Pit'zkah, that do creep and sting like ice."

"Er, right, yes," affirmed the young prince. "I wish to claim them, that they may be taken back and tried for their crimes in the places where they have committed them."

"Hhhrg," replied the speaker. "In your civilized, weakened laws I suppose that is what you must do, and we in our pact with your wizard Mizzamir have said we shall allow your justice to your criminals. But be warned! These are fearsome serpents, waiting to poison and kill . . . do not let them fly free lightly. We ourselves caught them only at the point of many arrows."

"I will not, o noble son of the Plains," replied Fenwick, with a courteous bow. His spirit rankled, however, at the thought that these grunting primitives had succeeded where he had failed.

He also had no intention of taking the villains back to Mizzamir. He and the choice members of his Company had brought with them many arrows as well. All he had to do was to collect the villains, take them along out of sight, and shoot them dead. It was a just punishment for their crimes, he was just taking the shortcut. He was a *prince,* after all, he did have some authority. The villains were too slippery to handle any other way . . . He could not risk any more noble lives trying to bring them back for Mizzamir. It might have surprised him to know that, given the choice between death at the points of his arrows and enlightenment at the magic of Mizzamir, every villain in the group would have gladly chosen the arrows.

The villains woke some hours later when their captors brought them a few bowls of thin cold soup and some bread. Kaylana took these and, since she was the only one unbound, began to distribute them. At a nod from the guard she loosened their bonds enough for them to feed themselves. The guard, she noticed, had two friends with him as back-up; another male warrior and a woman in the same garb, with a wicked-looking longbow at the ready.

Blackmail, as usual, ate nothing. Valerie took her share weakly, still not turning toward the guard. Sam took a quick glance, and saw that the fine skin of her mouth and lips was raw and scraped, but the leather gag was chewed to fragments and hung limp and sodden around her neck. It was night again; Sam judged it must be about two in the morning. The cool darkness outside called to him. Valerie seemed to feel it too. He could sense the faint prickly feeling of magic as her long-nailed fingers slowly closed about her Darkportal. Almost hidden under her long black hair, one large violet eye winked at him.

Sam sneaked a glance at Blackmail, who nodded ever so slightly. The assassin casually slid his hand into his boot and withdrew a slim, balanced shaft with a needle point and a flared end, the whole about six inches long, along with a wafer-thin fletching that fitted at right angles into the flare. He rubbed the needle against a small glob of resinous toxin under the flap of his boot, and then abruptly sent the dart zipping through the darkness, easy as any pub-toss.

The second male warrior gripped his biceps and gasped, and a swirl of darkness courtesy of Valerie flashed across the tent and enveloped the woman archer. She stumbled, her longbow falling from her hands. Before their guard could raise his club, a heavy mailed fist came down on his head. He staggered, and glared at Blackmail, who seemed almost surprised. Then the dark knight shrugged, and hit him again, and this time the guard folded over to join his unconscious friends. Sam and Blackmail quickly dragged the unconscious bodies into the tent. Kaylana and Robin watched in surprise, while Arcie took advantage of the distraction to grab another loaf of bread.

"We must move fast," hissed Valerie, as she climbed to her feet and pulled off the remains of her gag. "They'll be bound to check up on us soon."

"Where do you propose we go?" replied Kaylana. "If we flee into the wilderness they shall only catch us again."

"Not if we were to get rid of their longneck beasties for them," mumbled Arcie through a mouthful.

"No! We should just stay here," whinnied Robin, his ears flicking. "They haven't hurt us yet, but if we try to escape they may shoot us!"

"Robin, you have a lot to learn about survival," retorted Sam, from where he was ripping the more accessible clothes from the fallen warrior. Blackmail was doing the same for the tall guard he had felled.

A short while later, the tent flap opened slowly. A tall figure, clad in leather and a voluminous fur cloak with the hood pulled over its face, stepped out, clanking slightly. It was followed by another leather-wrapped figure, somewhat smaller, and then Kaylana, Valerie, Arcie, and Robin. The shorter figure turned to whisper to them, as Kaylana quickly donned the female barbarian's hooded cloak.

"Blackmail and I will go and let the Tantelopes out. Kaylana, we'll need you along to help handle them . . . Valerie, can you make some explosive distractions if they seem to start to notice us? Arcie, you and Robin and Valerie all get out of town as fast as you can."

"What?" hissed Valerie. "You mean I have to pin my escape upon the actions of the short one and horse-boy?"

"Valerie," Kaylana broke in gently over Arcie's and Robin's protests, "we need you to take care of the thief and the centaur. They may need your magic to allow them to escape."

"I dinna need no—" began Arcie indignantly, but Sam nudged him and he fell silent.

"Better yet, Arcie," he said, "can you sneak around and get our weapons? That would be useful."

"And how, by Baris and Bella, am I meant to carry all yer swords and daggers and the like?" retorted the Barigan. "Specially yon knight's great meat cleaver? I can't so much as lift it!"

"I gather, then, that you've tried?" said Valerie, with an arched eyebrow.

"Well, just find them then, and tell us where they are," snapped Sam in exasperation. "We can't stand here talking all night. Go!"

They split up, the three cloaked figures making their cautious way into the encampment, the centaur and sorceress swiftly heading out of the area as stealthily as they could, and a small, stout figure vanishing into the shadows of the surrounding tents.

Robin and Valerie made their way along the rough path they had been brought down before. A guard, all in leathers, rose up out of the darkness to challenge them; Valerie fired off a blast of negative energy, and sent the watchman tumbling silently down the far side of the hill. The sorceress and centaur scrambled up the hills until they reached the edge of the gully. The night was dark, but the stars and campfires illuminated the encampment with a silver-gold light. The leather-hide buildings, flapping softly in the night breeze, made the camp resemble a nest of huge, sleeping beasts. Arcie could not be seen, but after a moment they did see the three hurrying figures of their companions moving toward the Tantelope pens.

"Can you do something, I don't know, with the weather or animals or something like that, to make a cover for our getaway? To hide our tracks, and that sort of thing?" Sam asked Kaylana.

"Yes," came the soft reply. "I will need a moment, however . . . and it may take awhile for the effect to manifest."

They turned a corner, following a strong animal smell, and came within sight of the Tantelope pens; an area fenced in with high barriers made of leather ropes tied between tall poles. The Plains barbarians were nomadic, each taking their turn with the seasons to visit the holy Temple of Mula here in this gully. All the tents and enclosures could be folded and packed away for travel at a moment's notice. When Sam saw the few guards by the animals' pen, he quickly pulled himself and his companions into hiding behind a tent used for storing the saddles and tack of the beasts.

"You'd better take your time now to do that distraction and hide our trail," he whispered to Kaylana.

"Very well," agreed Kaylana, and, gripping her staff, she closed her eyes in concentration. Her head tilted back, and her hair fell like copper fire in the flickering light of campfires, the same light that shone on her cheekbones and highlighted a face of such beauty and sorrow and wisdom, and the faint aura of ancient, natural, primal power floated in the air around her. . . .

Blackmail tapped Sam on the shoulder, interrupting the assassin's thoughts. Sam returned self-consciously to the matter at hand.

"Right," he whispered sternly. "Now, we'll need to take out those guards . . . how many did you count?"

A gauntlet held up three fingers. Sam said, "Three, yes, and there's one more at the far edge, looking out across the plain. You take the two closest, I'll get the others."

Sam pulled a length of stiff cord from the seams of his shirt, silently wishing for his blowgun, or a dagger, or even another dart. He slipped out into the shadows and a moment later heard Blackmail move as well.

The first guard was sitting facing away from Sam. Sam decided that a large rock by his feet would do as a weapon. He scooped it up and brought it down heavily on the man's head. The barbarian grunted and folded over. The other two inner guards got up and cautiously approached the nearby clanking sounds, their spears at the ready. As Sam crept up on the outermost guard, he heard a sound like weapons rebounding off invulnerable armor, and then a noise like two thick heads being knocked together, then a double thump. The Tantelopes snorted and began to move about.

Unfortunately, this was enough to attract his target's attention. The barbarian stood up, saw his companions missing, and shouted a warning. Sam was astounded at the roaring power of the man's voice. His sudden bellow not only brought answering shouts from the camp but spooked the Tantelopes, who added their low, honking voices to the din. Sam saw the barbarian heading toward him and did not hesitate to lash out with the cord and quickly loop it around the barbarian's thick neck.

Sam was used to the lighter folk of the southern and western Six Lands, and this man's bull-thick neck was almost too broad for the cord. The barbarian roared and flipped the slight assassin over his head, slamming him into the dirt. Sam leapt up before the man could jump on him, and dodged a wild roundhouse swing. He brought his own hand up, blindingly fast, to slam with what should have been disabling force to the solar plexus. He might as well have tried to hit a stone wall. The barbarian didn't even grunt, just let loose a blow that caught Sam on the side of the head, sending him flying. The night exploded, and Sam experienced a brief sensation of weightlessness and numbness, then scrambled to his feet as the fire flowed into his blood . . .

The barbarian approached; the fire danced in Sam's muscles and washed the pain and weariness away, drove away the concern for stealth, and replaced it with the double force of the urge to kill and the urge to survive. The night became a red and black blur.

The next thing he noticed was a thundering of hooves. The fence had been torn open, and Blackmail had found a long whip and was cracking it loudly. The panicked Tantelopes galloped out into the night, honking and wheeling into the darkness. Sam looked down at the still form of the barbarian he had fought. There was a large hole in the man's neck.

Well, he thought, *Tirrik's Bite. And Miffer said I'd never master that attack. What would he say if he could see me now?* And then, remembering how Miffer was now an honest, good citizen, thought wryly, *He'd probably vomit.*

He had no chance to speculate further, because just then somebody hit him.

Kaylana had sent her mind sailing out into the night. The weather was clear and vast, no storms would be brewing for months, so a good bit of rain was out of the question.

She paused to stir the soft, nervous minds of the Tantelopes in the pen, enhancing their natural fear and flight instincts. Then she moved on, out into the wilds, into the minds of a thousand living things. Her Druidic spirit could sail far along the winds of nature . . . it was bringing it back that was the problem. This was similar to a magical spell of Seeking . . . both required the caster to slip their spirits from their bodies, a dangerous and unnatural thing to do.

The Plains contained many minds, abounding in excess in the times of Light and life. She reached out with all her power, as far as she could, miles away, her arms opening up in a huge embrace, to gather them all . . . and then behind them, she placed Fear.

First one, then another, then more, began to run. As they ran, they gathered others, who did not know why they were running but only that they must run. Bound together by herd instinct and ancient fears, they ran.

She wanted to run with them, to let her mind fly free in the double feeling of pursuit and flight, to leave the poor, simple human shell behind her and ride forever on the wind of a thousand minds, minds that knew no good or evil but only the endless chains of life and death, linked for all eternity. She could see how easy it would be, to pull her spirit free of woman and staff and just be, a wild dancer on the winds of nature.

She had stretched herself far to call the animals, far out past where any mortal should go from their own self. It was not worth the trouble and pain to return . . . but . . . her dim memories sang a warning, the slow twisting torque of a world slipping out of balance; the animals felt it, the grass knew it, the earth ached with it. And with regret she recalled, dimly, that it was her duty and trust to stop. She had no choice but to return, return and continue. She left the minds running free as water and pulled herself back, slowly, painfully, her spirit crying and fighting as she forced it once again back into its prison of flesh.

As she did so, she had a sudden vision. Her mind, still open from its journey, sensed a force. The pool at the center of the stone temple burned like a jewel in her mind. It shone in endless threat but with irresistible attraction. It dared her and seduced her and hypnotized her all at once.

As her spirit settled into her body, she opened her eyes: the image and challenge still hovered in her brain. Around her she sensed motion, light, and shadows; the dim echoes of noise fluttered on her skin. But all seemed to have no more meaning than a world of ghosts; all that existed was the blue crystal pool. She walked forward, more awake than asleep, and the barbarians crowded around and past and by her, neither noticing the other.

Arcie heard the commotion begin, and sighed to himself in the shadows of yet another tent. "Och, I did fear as much," he said softly to himself. "No' more'n some few minutes before the place is falling about our ears." He scratched his curly head. "And none of yon hulking savages speaks the language . . . no interrogation for me this day." He looked around. "I must have searched full all yon tents times over . . . where might a load of leather-bound clodpolls keep foreign weapons?" He thought a moment, then sighed. "O' course. They would be giving them to their chief. And his tent will be yon great fancy one in the center. Surrounded by guards, I doubt not." He settled his cap on his head and stood up, yawning. The discovery of a food storage had provided a few good mouthfuls of some jerky and a good swig of Barigan whiskey from a hidden cask, but he could do with a good sit-down meal and another few days of sleep. His limbs ached from the long march. "Well, if that be the case, then 'tis a job for Sammy, not myself. I'd best be at finding him."

The short, pudgy shadow slipped off into the increasing chaos of the night.

Up on the hill, Valerie and Robin watched the Tantelopes wheel away into the plains, and then heard the commotion begin in the village. Valerie sighed and stood up.

"The fools can't do anything without creating a fuss,"

she grumbled to herself. "Well, if distraction they want, then distraction they get."

"What are you going to do?" Robin asked nervously, shifting from one hoof to the other and swishing his tail. Valerie treated him to a toothy smile, made somewhat worse by the few flecks of blood that still marred her lips from the gag.

"Wait and watch and learn, boy. And be sure you spell vengeance correctly in your ballad."

She drew her right hand back, while her left hand closed around her Darkportal amulet. Her fingers flexed slightly, and a slow, swirling ball of darkness laced with glowing red began to form in her hand. It swelled into the size of an apple, and with a final bitter word of magic, the sorceress hurled it down into the camp.

It fell like a meteor, vanishing behind a tent. There was an explosive blast, and a gout of red-black flame bloomed up. The leather huts began to burn with a black, stinking smoke and sullen red flames, and the shouting and chaos increased.

"You might have hit one of your friends!" Robin exclaimed, watching in horror.

"They aren't my friends. And it should serve them right if they are stupid enough to get in the way," came the retort. Valerie was already spinning another flame-ball. This one she hurled away to the left of the first, nearer to the stone temple, and more evil fires started up. The smoke, instead of rising into the sky, clung and slunk along the ground in heavy clouds and coils.

"I give you smoke, chaos, and panic, you incompetent rogues," Valerie hissed softly down to her unseen allies below. "Use them."

Kaylana was almost at the impact point of the second blast. It erupted before her, causing screams and panic and a searing blast of heat. She was dimly conscious of blue-robed figures flooding out of the temple, carrying things. They swarmed past her as she walked slowly on, her staff measuring her steps in gentle beats. Before her loomed the stone entryway into the temple area. It seemed to be set with murals, depicting a female shape in barbarian clothing . . . sometimes it seemed to be Ki'Kartha, the Heroine, shining with the power of her goddess . . . sometimes it seemed to be Mula herself, radiant and glorious in a blue nimbus of Light energy. Sometimes it seemed both . . . or was it always both? Where was the break between deity and avatar? The entry drew her in, past two fidgeting temple guards who did not seem to see her.

She wandered through the open stone halls, her feet crunching on a path made of chipped granite sprinkled with turquoise. Priestesses and shamans shoved past her, heading out into the encampment to heal the wounded and extinguish the fires. Already steam filled the air from water-summoning magic cast by the worshipers of the goddess of fresh water and healing. Kaylana did not notice, but wove her way in through the spider's web of halls, following a summons she would not deny.

Sam managed to stagger back from his attacker and tried to recall the fire . . . but his head was still spinning and he was still exhausted from the long march the day before. His back hit a leather wall, and he scrabbled at it with his hands behind his back, trying to find a way in without taking his eyes off his attacker. The barbarian who had hit him was enraged at the death of his kinsman, and as he raised his huge Plainsman's sword, the assassin saw red flickers in the shafts of obsidian and wondered if he would survive to see the firelight on Kaylana's hair again. Suddenly a hand grabbed the man's weapon from his hand and hit him smartly over the head with it, then smacked him powerfully on the side of his cheek. The barbarian fell, groaning. Only one person Sam knew was strong and tall enough to do that, and he stood up as Blackmail bowed graciously to him. Sam let out a faint sigh of relief.

"Thanks, Blackmail . . . I owe you another one," he said with a faint smile. The knight made a dismissive gesture, and then a shooing motion. Sam took the hint and fled into the shadows, and Blackmail grabbed a support pole from the tent Sam had rested against, and pulled it down. He hefted the Plainsman's sword thoughtfully, giving it a few practice swings, and then headed off purposefully into the confusion.

Creeping through the shadows and smoke, Sam almost bumped into Arcie before he saw him. They quickly ducked down in the shadows for a moment of silent rogue-speak.

"Weapons?" signed Sam.

"Leader/king house, maybe," Arcie replied wordlessly.

"Certain?"

"Nowhere else." Arcie shrugged. Sam sighed, and nodded.

"Lead."

The two rogues crept through the smoke and shadows. Valerie's aim had been excellent. The chief's tent was in flames, and everywhere barbarians went running with buckets of water to try to extinguish the fire. A priestess of Mula had summoned a fountain of water similar to the one the shaman on their march had created, and this was helping somewhat. The main center tent seemed to be a lost cause, but two smaller adjoining were relatively undamaged, and both were guarded. Sam motioned: "You left, I right." They split up, heading for the side rooms.

Sam sneaked around the right building, avoiding the eyes of the guard, and crept through a smoldering corner of the tent. Within were stacks of fine furs, some casks, and, their weapons. Sam hastily rearmed himself, then, slinging Blackmail's sword onto his back and wielding Robin's longsword, he grabbed Arcie's morning star in his off hand and crept out again. As he did so, he looked at the casks and raised an eyebrow. No wonder the Plainsmen were working so hard to keep this tent from going up in flames.

He made his way to the far side of the center of confusion, and soon found Arcie lighting his pipe from a smoldering shelter. The Barigan winked at him as he accepted his morning star back.

"What was in the other tent?" Sam asked curiously. Arcie leered.

"Chief's harem," he answered. "Och! What a fine set of . . . "

"Later, Arcie. Come on, we've got to find Kaylana."

Kaylana walked through the last archway, the most elaborately carved and decorated yet. Here, along with the ever-present turquoise, were set blue topaz and aquamarine stones. She scarcely noticed, however, for before her was the blue pool, glowing bright as the moon and seeming almost as large. There was no one around. She walked up to the edge and stopped. Before her, across the glass-still water, rose the statue of the Goddess Mula, illuminated by the blue light of the pool.

The blue light of the pool seemed to draw her even closer. She looked up, unsure, and into the eyes of the statue. They were two perfect star sapphires, and the six-pointed stars in them seemed real. The blue starlight reflected back in the green depths of the Druid's eyes, back and forth, back and forth, into a flowing, weaving world of aquamarine, and the pool's light grew and grew until it was a pulsing azure sun . . .

Up on the hill, Valerie saw it, and pointed, grabbing Robin's arm.

"Look!" she hissed. "What is the fool tree-wench up to now? That blue light is going to have every barbarian in the place down around her head!"

"Blue?" asked Robin, looking down. "It doesn't look like a flower to me . . . just a lot of white light . . . "

Kaylana stepped forward . . . off the edge of the pool. There was a flash of light . . . but not even a splash. And the pool's radiance again dropped to a dim glow. There was no sign of Kaylana. Valerie and Robin exchanged confused glances.

Kaylana found herself floating in a blue dream. She felt the powerful presence of light all around her, making her uneasy. It was like a wild drug, too out of control, too strong; the sheer power of life seemed almost fatal. She could feel her heart racing and every nerve tingling and each faint breath like pure oxygen . . . This, she realized, was what the sublimation of the world would be like; a glorious but final transcendence, as the world lost its reality to become one with the perfection of Light it had achieved. All boundaries and negatives would be stripped away, all corruptible flesh and minds would give up materiality for pure light energy as the dimension of Light flooded into the world and claimed it for its own, increasing its own infinite size.

But, what if there were other worlds, like their own, such as that which the Elves had traveled to? If they drew on the same dimensions of Light and Darkness as this world, and the dimensions of Light gained in size by claiming this world, then the other worlds would have that much more pressure from the Light. That tiny, tiny amount that would still disrupt the balance of *those* worlds . . .

With a sudden shock, Kaylana realized that the outcome of their quest would affect not only their own world, but possibly infinite numbers of others worlds. The entire scope of a multiverse of creation might be at stake . . .

Poor misinformed child, said a gentle voice in her mind. It was as deep and clear as mountain lakes, and soothed her mind and body even as it terrified her innermost spirit. She knew who the voice was even before the image swirled into shape.

Before her appeared a figure that could only be the Goddess Mula. A woman of unearthly beauty, taller than Blackmail but slender and fair as the most legendary Elf maiden, with long dark hair that shimmered with rainbow mist. She was clad in a long gown made of pure water, clear as snowmelt and yet ever so faintly reflected blue. Her eyes were like star sapphires, but Kaylana could not look directly at them. The Goddess smiled, and it was like the sun on a river at dawn.

The Goddess seemed to recline upon some wave or

shape of the azure dream that surrounded them; she looked at the small, scruffy form of the Druid before her, in her plain dun robes and carrying a staff too big for her. In the blue light, Kaylana's hair had turned an ugly muddy color. But her eyes were still green, still burning.

You came seeking that which might lead to the disruption of the perfect Light we have worked so hard to achieve, said the Goddess sternly. Her words seemed to arrive in Kaylana's mind directly, without hearing, but she could still feel the voice. *So I called you here, as I must.*

"Must?" echoed Kaylana. "Do you mean that this is the Test?"

As you might think of it, came the response, *Yes. Ki'-Kartha knew that no simple preset challenge or battle could test the true faith of a one such as you . . . especially one who knew she was being tested. Therefore, she passed the task to me.*

"But even if I should pass," said Kaylana, "you are of Light and will never give me that which I seek."

As I am of Light, so am I of honesty and truth. And I am bound by the laws of the Test and the Victory. If you are able to convince me of the strength of your misguided, ignorant faith, then I shall give you the Segment that you seek. It is so decreed by the conditions of the Test.

"And death, if I should fail?"

The Goddess laughed, a sound like falling raindrops.

Of course not! I am, after all, of Light and Healing, the infinite mercy of fresh water . . . when you fail, you shall be granted, not death, but new life and new faith in my service. And your companions, as well, shall be saved from darkness. You will be brought into the way of the Light and blessed.

Kaylana squared her shoulders, and stilled her mind. The warm wood of the staff was comforting under her fingers. "Then let the Test begin."

In the encampment, Sam had ducked and weaved his way through the shadows, skillfully avoiding the Plainspeople as they hurried about. The fires were almost all out now, but the smoke was still thick in the night air and reeked of charred leather. He saw barbarians running back and forth with wounded, and the blue-robed priests helping with the injured and the smoulder.

Very well, came the Goddess's voice, with a hint of amusement. *As I understand it, you are a Druidess . . . of the dead religion from the days before the Victory?*

"While one who follows a faith lives, that faith is not dead," replied Kaylana smoothly. "Yes, I am of the sect known as the Druids."

But child, surely you know that your faith is dead? That by its own tenets and beliefs, it is no longer valid?

"I do not understand," Kaylana said, unable to help herself.

I will be happy to explain. Listen closely. Your faith follows, among other things, that the balance of nature and existence is paramount. Conflict allows the strong to survive and continue, while the weak die and provide sustenance . . . am I correct?

"Yes . . . " agreed Kaylana cautiously.

Your people were destroyed in the battles of the War, and the forces of Light, being stronger, came into Victory and dominion. Your people, your faith, being weaker, being less fitting to survive, were destroyed. Was this not, then, the natural outcome? Has not your religion been made extinct by the forces of conflict and survival that it itself held important?

"But your logic is flawed," replied Kaylana, slightly confused. "As I said, my faith is not vanished . . . I survive, and the power of my people survives in me and the staff that was given to me. And while I live, there is hope for the balance. I may teach and gather others to believe, and the ways of Druidism will be known and followed once more."

Your religion was destroyed by destiny and superior power.

"My religion was destroyed by ignorance," said Kaylana. "Because of that ignorance now, this world you fought so hard to save may be destroyed."

* * *

Sam ended up along the outer edge of the camp and here found a trail of prostrate and groaning warriors. He followed these along until he came to Blackmail stalking along the perimeter of the camp, swinging the Plainsman's Sword meaningfully. Several of the sharp obsidian points had broken off the wooden club. He approached the knight, a bit too stealthily, and nearly got a faceful of sword for his troubles. Blackmail hastily checked his blow and touched his helmet in apology; Sam gratefully unslung the huge heavy black sword from his back and gave it to the Knight who took it graciously and dropped the Plainsman's sword with evident disdain.

The fate of the world, came the voice in Kaylana's mind, gentle and patronizing. *How can you, a mere uneducated mortal, think you know more about the fate of the world than the gods?*

"Gods are biased," she answered. "Gods do only what their natures define . . . like animals. If a god is good, it must do good . . . if a god is evil, it will do evil. I cannot even blame you for your ignorance, for you are only doing what your nature defines."

Ignorance? You, who worship such foolish things as trees and the stellar objects, can dare speak to me of ignorance? You do not even know that the sun you worship is only a huge ball of burning chemicals, and the moon only a chunk of cold, dead rock . . . that the solstices and seasons you hold holy are nothing to do with the working of any religion, that they have no power over your prayers, but are simply the effects of logical sciences, orbits, eclipses, physics?

"But I have powers," said Kaylana, confused. What the goddess was saying must be true, she knew, and yet it was as though the divine being spoke another language . . . burning chemicals? Orbits? "I can make the plants grow or die, I can feel the minds of men and beast and plant and stone . . ."

Any wizard or sorcerer could do the same, with study. You, like your people, have certain talents in magical direc-

tions . . . and you yourself know that, without the staff you carry, your powers are curtailed. The staff is a magical focus for your own energy.

"If anything is the focus for my energy, it is my faith," replied Kaylana. "Whether you speak the truth, or simply what you think is the truth . . . I know I have faith in what I believe, and that faith allows me to use my powers. Therefore, as far as I am concerned, my faith is as real and valid as any that your worshipers follow."

Can you understand nothing, child? cried the voice in exasperation. Kaylana felt the hot-cold winds of the Goddess's impatience whip around her, but she stood firm.

"Any sign of Kaylana?" Sam asked Blackmail worriedly. The helmet shook from side to side as the knight flexed his grip on the sword and unslung his shield from his back. The black plumes on the helmet, Sam noticed, had gotten slightly singed in the fires, but seemed to be holding up remarkably well. The knight had already discarded his leather cloak disguise.

"Well, keep going round the edge, I guess . . . and if you find her, get her away . . . It'll be dawn soon." Blackmail nodded, and Sam headed back into the city, searching frantically.

. . . and you have powers of healing, Mula was saying. She seemed to be trying to make a point. Kaylana nodded.

And you have healed people . . . and yet, is healing not an act of good, of Light?

"Yes, normally," said Kaylana, "But I heal only my companions, who are of darkness, who help me on my quest to restore the balance."

Then, if you saw a child injured, dying, would you not heal it?

Kaylana shook her head. "Not now."

If you turn the world back to the "balance," as you call it, there will be wars again, such as your people died in. Your animals that you seem so concerned with, your trees, would be killed and killed again.

"That is the way of things," said the Druid calmly. "The strong will survive, and continue . . . the weak will not. I must heal my companions, despite their weaknesses, because they are vital to the survival of the world as a whole . . ."

The thought that war might kill you as well is no test. Any follower should be glad to give up their lives for their cause . . . as I see you would. But what of others, close to you? Suppose the balance was shifted. Suppose, suddenly, darkness was in power . . . would you then kill your companions, to preserve the balance? The knight, the sorceress, the young centaur, the small thief?

"It would be difficult physically," said the Druid, "but if that was the case, I would have no qualms."

The burning gaze of the Goddess bored into her mind. *And the assassin? The one who gives you wreaths of pixy-clovers . . . would you kill him?*

"Yes." There was no hesitation in Kaylana's voice.

Do you have no caring, no emotion, no soul? Have you no compassion? came the voice, tinged with shock as the Goddess's gaze saw the complete truth of Kaylana's answer.

"I have those. But stronger than those, I have my faith."

Arcie was having worse luck than Sam. He'd managed to hide in a group of Plains children huddled near the center of the camp and watching the fires with wide eyes, but when an adult suddenly appeared to shoo them back to their mothers, Arcie was left standing sheepishly in the open. A barbarian grabbed him with a roar and picked him up by one arm. Arcie tensed himself and muttered quick prayers to Baris and Bella . . . he knew what would follow.

The man swung him around and hurled him into the air, to cheers from watching Plainsfolk. As he flew through the air, he shut his eyes, cursing his small size while blessing his Barigan resilience and rotundity . . . he hit the ground so hard he actually bounced and was immediately grabbed again by another warrior. This man took him by an arm and a leg. As he swung, Arcie could see another Plainsman shouting and motioning, his face in a big grin. *No muscle-balled lot will be playing at catch-the-catty with me,* he thought furiously, and as the barbarian released him he twisted in the man's grasp, sending himself spinning up over the tents instead of across to the waiting Plainsman. He just had time to notice a faint lightening of the sky before he fell heavily onto a tent, bringing it crashing down. Whatever was in it was wriggling and shouting. An obsidian spearhead ripped through the leather next to his ear, and he jumped like a rabbit to take himself away.

"Tell me of the fate of the world, then, Goddess," Kaylana asked. "Tell me, in your omnipotence, what you see in the future."

Mula seemed annoyed at this presumption. *Such knowledge is forbidden to mortals.*

"Speak truth to me as I speak to you . . . can you, in fact, see what will happen in a month's time?"

Mula seemed almost sulky. Her righteous annoyance prickled on Kaylana's skin. *The people of the world were created with free will, and even in this day and age a mortal may have the power to affect all creation . . . even as the Heroes did. Thus, when the future hangs upon a free will . . . the outcome is uncertain.*

"Free will, you say," said Kaylana. "But free will allows the possibility for evil . . . how can you and the other gods, divine beings of Good, allow this potential for evil to exist?"

Your own fellow mortals are dealing with that. Light wizards are removing the desire to do evil while still allowing the people to have free will . . .

"But *is* it free will?" interrupted Kaylana. "If you deprive a man of the potential to do evil, does anything good that he does make any difference? If a contest is set with no way to lose, does winning mean anything?"

This is your Test, not mine. How can your insane, indiscriminate faith make any sense? You would heal one in-

stant and kill the next . . . how can you stand to live with the knowledge that your beliefs will cause so much pain and suffering, so many people, perhaps even yourself, dying? How much ugliness and evil and conflict would be re-released into the world, if you would have your way?

"That is the way of nature," Kaylana explained. "And the way of nature is balance and conflict . . . that is the way of my faith."

Up on their hillside, Robin and Valerie were also noticing the lightening sky.

"Fools," hissed Valerie under her breath. "We can't escape in the daylight! They would be on us in an instant, mounts or no! Where are those idiots?"

Robin, ears flickering, caught a sound. At first he thought it was distant thunder, but the pre-dawn sky was clear all the way to the horizon, and anyway, it was too steady, too even, for thunder. It was a low, growly, rumbling noise that seemed to come . . . his ears turned, pinpointing the sound. From the east. He looked in that direction, but the Plains were still too deep and dark to show their secrets. He was certain, however, that the noise was growing louder.

Angry waves of exasperation and frustration whipped around Kaylana, and she clutched her staff for support.

Your own ignorance and lack of comprehension blind you! You cannot see the truth, see how foolish and useless your faith is . . . I cannot teach you if you do not understand my words, I cannot help you if you will not understand my concepts. You are misguided and uneducated in even the most basic of decent thinking, and will die on your senseless quest . . . and despite my Light, I cannot help but know the world will be well-rid of your callous and blind heart! Take the Segment, and go . . . I tire of your stupidity, and my worshipers need me.

Kaylana was suddenly drowning in icy-blue water . . . she thrashed, choking, and . . .

sprawled out on the edge of the pool. In her hand was

clasped a chunk of crystal, blue as the waters of the pool.

She stood up slowly, her head throbbing from the contact with the deity . . . already the details were swimming, vanishing. Time had been distorted. There was much she could not remember. They had talked for hours, but here, the animals she had called had not even . . .

She froze, her head jerking up, listening. Then, staff in one hand, crystal in the other, she ran.

Grasscut Sundowner, master of the Tantelope herds, was inspecting the cut walls of the pen with ill-concealed rage. His son and apprentice, Dustwind Sundowner, stood beside him with the patching kit.

"Will we have to go and track down the Tantelopes, father?" Dustwind asked; his father sighed.

"With luck, my son, they will return . . . they know that here is good water and plenty of food . . . and they are used to calling our camp their home. Soon, I pray to Mula's mercy, we shall hear their hoofbeats as they return . . . "

"Father! I think I hear the hoofbeats even now!" cried the son. Grasscut stopped, listened, and then with a word that Dustwind had never heard his father use before, scooped up his son and ran.

The villains heard the low rumbling noise about the same time that the barbarians began racing past them, carrying children and valuables, heading west. Some ran into the temple and sheltered in the stone walls, while others tried to get as far away from the camp as possible. Arcie came thumping past Blackmail at one point, following the flow, and the knight grabbed him and hoisted him into the air, his short legs still pumping. Arcie recovered himself and shouted at the knight, "Och, you great armored clod! Lemme down! It's a stampede!"

Sam recognized that accent from two tents away, even though he couldn't make out the words. He ran over and almost bumped into Kaylana as she emerged from a tangle of barbarians trying to push their way into the stone temple sanctuary.

"Kaylana! Where—" began the assassin, very glad to see the Druid. She ignored him, interrupting,

"Get the others! We must get to Valerie and Robin at once!"

They ran, collecting Blackmail, who tucked Arcie under his arm, and ran to the southern edge of the encampment. Dawn was breaking, and the rumbling noise was filling the air like the anger of gods.

They reached it just as Valerie and Robin came running down into the gully. Robin cried out to warn them.

"It's a stampede! Hundred of animals, all kinds, heading this way!" he shouted.

"Do something, Druid!" Valerie snapped. "Animals are your specialty, are they not?" Her raven circled above, calling hoarse warnings. Valerie halted at the group, but Robin ran on, galloping into the encampment, shouting back at them to save themselves. In a few seconds he was lost to view.

"Indeed, I called the animals," Kaylana said, preoccupied for a moment. "We must form a circle, facing inward . . ."

"What good will that do?" demanded Sam, who nevertheless allowed himself to be shoved into position beside Blackmail.

"Trampled flat we'll be," cried Arcie, as the rumbling shook the earth. The bellowing of animals was clear now, mingling with the renewed shouts of the barbarians. "What difference is it what pattern our corpses form in the sand?"

"Silence!" demanded Kaylana, as she took her place in the circle, and, gripping her staff, closed her eyes. The ground trembled so hard they could barely keep their feet.

Sam turned and saw, by the sudden clear light of dawn, a wave of dust and motion and force cresting the hill, sweeping down upon them: hooves and horns, breath steaming, ground rocking, voices honking and bellowing and trumpeting.

Here came familiar Tantelopes, their nostrils flaring

with the effort, necks swaying like masts; the small, lithe prongbucks, running in great, leaping bounds, and the heavy Plains bison, thundering like shaggy stormclouds. There were the ornyx, taller than the prongbucks, with huge, backswept curling horns, and, the huge yellow-gray forms of wheeumps, massive creatures large as a house with white, outswept tusks and a long, curling nose through which they trumpeted their distinctive call. Sam noticed all this, and then they were on him. Dust choked his nostrils as sudden vertigo swept up his body.

. . . legs and hide and horns and the dust and stink in his nostrils, and his hooves pounded the ground flat under them, there were tents, afraid! but no turning, no swerving, he did not stop and the walls fell under his horns and tusks, and he trampled it under his feet, and there a stone wall, people-smell, he leaped over it and the wind of his kind around him as they jumped with him . . . his hooves skidded on leather while his other hooves found purchase, and he fell and could not stop himself from trampling himself flat . . . the smell of his blood made him even more afraid, and his heart wanted to burst as it struggled to keep up, running on and leaping back up the hillside and out into the open plains, crowding himself on all sides and there were fleeing things before him but he could not stop, could not stop, the air was full of fear and blood and he could only run and run and run . . .

As soon as he was out of sight, Robin activated his magic bracelet without bothering to slow down. Thus it was that he appeared suddenly in one of the rooms of the Castle of Diamond Magic, and only the sudden clatter of his hooves on stone made him snap himself to a clumsy halt. He stopped, every muscle quivering, his ears trying to pin themselves back, and looked. Mizzamir stood at one end of the room, regarding him with mild surprise.

"Well, well . . . I was beginning to wonder what had happened to you," said the Arch-Mage. Mizzamir had been in the middle of breakfast, and on the table before him were spread a few small loaves of bread and some fruit, and a clear glass of starwine. "Those villains aren't starting to corrupt you, are they?"

"Me? No! No sir!" stammered Robin. "It was just difficult to get away . . . things happening . . . "

"I understand," interrupted Mizzamir reassuringly. "The whole business while they were here in Natodik . . . most unpleasant."

"Yes, sir," agreed Robin, nodding violently.

"Well, can't be helped . . . what have they done now?"

"We . . . they, were captured by the Plainsmen of Sei'cks," Robin reported, "And they escaped their cell . . . but when I left, a stampede was rushing down upon the camp. I don't know how they will survive that."

"These villains seem extraordinarily adept at surviving, Robin," sighed Mizzamir, taking a sip of wine. They were in a different room than Mizzamir's usual Tower study; Robin wondered if the stained-glass window had been replaced. "Which is well enough, for I still hope that they may be saved . . . And the Key?"

"They weren't sure where to search for the one on Sei'cks," answered the centaur. "And were captured before they could begin to look."

"The Key is important, Robin . . . Do you know where they are keeping the Segments?"

"No, sir, though I think thus far each one has kept the Segment they have discovered . . . except myself, of course."

"Would it be possible, do you think, to . . . *acquire* these Segments?" asked Mizzamir casually. Robin shook his head.

"Even when they assign me to watch, the knight never seems to sleep. He would see if I tried to search for the Segments."

"Ah yes . . . this knight . . . " Mizzamir seemed lost in thought a moment, then asked, "What does he call himself?"

"He doesn't speak, sir . . . we . . . the others call him Blackmail, sir, I think because of his black armor."

"Hmm . . . a play on words . . . " Mizzamir thought a

moment. "Well, keep your eyes open, Robin. If these villains have survived this stampede, you must continue to follow them . . . and if you have the opportunity, capture one of the Segments and return it to me. One Segment will be enough to assure that the world is safe and that will give us time to capture the others, and the villains as well."

"Yes, sir," said Robin. He bowed low.

But he was still jittery, seeing disturbing images of brilliant, blinding light, and rocks and plants vaporizing into pure energy . . .

There was sunlight on his eyelids. His back prickled. He was warm. His mouth had a faint taste of mud. There was the faint sound of wind and rustling, and a ringing in his ears. What was he forgetting? Oh, yes.

He gasped, pulling clean, warm air deep into his lungs. He wheezed, as he gasped again. His chest ached. How long had he forgotten to breathe for, he wondered. Who was he?

He was hooves and horn and speed, the race of the grass below, and . . .

He had two legs, two arms. They ached . . .

He was running and falling and . . .

He had only one heart, beating in his chest . . . he was . . .

He was . . .

He was Sam. The assassin, named Samalander, raised in Bistort . . . kill Mizzamir . . . off on a quest . . . Kaylana, Tests, fate of the world . . . barbarians . . . capture . . . escape . . . stampede . . .

He sat up instantly, eyes flying open. Around him was the infinite expanse of the Plains, chewed up here into a mass of torn grass and earth. He could hear a faint metallic scraping noise. The sky was blue overhead, with a few circling hungry vultures. It was almost noon.

He felt battered all over, but he seemed to be fine. The grass, where it still stood, was about three feet tall. He rose and looked around, his legs shaking. There was no sign of the barbarian camp, the temple, or the gully.

A few yards away he saw Blackmail, who was also sitting up and rubbing his helmet. That was the metallic noise. To one side, a sprawled dark form with a raven sitting atop it—Valerie. She seemed to be breathing, and her raven appeared calm. A groan to his left indicated that somewhere among the grasses, Arcie had regained consciousness. That left two unaccounted for. He staggered about, looking.

At last he found Kaylana, lying on her face in the dirt. Her robes and armor were in disarray, and her breathing very shallow. She did not awaken when Sam shook her shoulders gently.

Arcie and Blackmail came up to them as Sam carefully turned the Druid's still form over. Her head lolled on its pillow of red hair and her arm flopped limply. A shining chunk of blue crystal tumbled out of her nerveless fingers.

Sir Fenwick and Company had ridden since dawn with the guide who had promised to deliver the villains into their hands. As the sun crested the sky, they came upon the gully of the High Temple of Mula, and their guide suddenly cursed and galloped his Tantelope down into the wreckage. Fenwick and his men followed.

The encampment was a shredded, trampled heath of torn leather and animal carcasses. The priestesses and shamans of Mula were walking among the mess, helping the Plainsmen to salvage what they could. Those who had fled from the stampede were slowly returning.

Their guide returned, grim faced. "Was anyone hurt?" asked Fenwick. The barbarian shook his head.

"Several have been hurt, but by the mercy of Mula only a few have gone Beyond . . . and those were killed not by animals, but by the villains when they escaped."

"So the carnage continues," muttered Fenwick, drumming his hands on his saddle. Suddenly, his head snapped up. "Towser! Zanithir! I have messages you must send . . . this violence must end!"

With a dragon to scout for me, and two armies to fence them in . . . there can be no escape, he thought grimly. The smoldering ruins of the Plainsmen's camp steamed under the noonday sun.

IX

"Blackmail? Something wrong?" Sam asked.

They had recovered from the strange occurrences of the stampede and had continued on westward, both to avoid the Plainsfolk to the east and to press on to the land called Ein, the last one of the Six. They still saw a few signs of the Plains barbarians; campfires seen in the distance when they traveled at night. Kaylana, recovered though still weak from the ordeal of the magic needed to allow them to survive and use the stampede, helped hide their presence from the barbarian trackers. She was aided at times by Valerie's spells of darkness and misdirection, and they made good progress under the night sky.

Kaylana would tell nothing of her Test, nor of how she had controlled the stampede. She had hidden the blue crystal in the folds of her robes; Robin's attempts to get it in his hands for just a moment, the split second that would be all he would need to take it to Mizzamir, proved futile. Such an action, he knew, would ruin his place among them, but, he felt, it would at least remove him from their dangerous presence.

Sam found himself thinking about the Tests. Since there were six Segments, and the other five members of his party had each recovered one, it seemed logical that the last one would be his to attempt. He wondered what sort of task he would face . . . The only Hero whose Test had not yet been encountered was that of Lord Tamarne, warrior and king of Light, whose family had ruled Ein for generations, even before the War. Tamarne, it was rumored, had been part godling; the circumstances were uncertain, having to do with his mother being visited by the Thunder God in the guise of a tiger, and indeed, the royal crest bore a white tiger. Ein was a land of rocks and snow and storms and legends of huge serpents, fire giants, dwarves, and similar things. Not a very hospitable place, thought Sam, for a city-bred assassin to try to win the most important contest of all time. He had borrowed a stub of inkwood from Arcie and copied down the pertinent verse from Bhazo's prophecy, under Valerie's supervision.

"How do you spell 'T'krung-Tabak'?" he asked, squinting as he tried to decipher the thin, coiled, Nathauan handwriting.

"It's an Ancient Einian word, I think . . . it has roots in Dwarvish. It means something like 'Sacrifice of Self,' " Valerie explained. "Though the translation of 'self' is a bit hazy. It has connotations with both the soul and the essence of one's being; in a Dwarf's case, family honor and tradition, the background that shapes the individual."

Sam thought about this later as he read and re-read the verse, copied onto a scrap of parchment in his own square letters. Sacrifice himself? In an eagle's claws? He shook his head. T'krung-Tabak, in eagle's claws, where warm blood outlines stony flaws. Blood, stone . . . sounded like a sacrifice, indeed. But that would be a rather pointless thing to do, and his whole reason for being here was for his survival. *If dare to face the inner eye* . . . what was that supposed to mean? he wondered again. The group had all gone over this verse before, as they travelled, but no firm ideas were forthcoming. Sam muttered the line to himself, then, on an impulse, crossed out "eye" and wrote a capital letter "I" over it. Then, shaking his head, he changed it back again. And last . . . *To thy knees, 'neath moonlit sky.* More sacrifice nonsense. He wondered if Kaylana's people had ever practiced human sacrifice, as post-Victory rumors would have it. He doubted it; she seemed to want little or nothing to do with humankind, especially him.

That still ached. He'd tried kind words, flowers . . . was she just not interested, or did she even know? Maybe he would have to be more obvious. If this Test was as gloomy as it sounded, it would be nice to have at least a smile from her to think on before his blood went into some stony flaws somewhere. He resolved to tell her, charmingly but openly, that he thought she was the most courageous and beautiful woman he had ever known, that her strength and spirit had won him even more than her grace and gentle wisdom, and that no one had ever understood him as did she, that no one had ever brought him such fascination and hope and fear and confusion, that he would suffer a thousand painful agonies to see her happy again, and that maybe, when this was all over and assuming they survived, would she like to go out for a drink or a walk or something. But what if she hit him with the staff again? What if he stammered and blushed, and what if Arcie appeared and spoiled it all with some lewd comment?

The very thought made him nervous enough, and when he sensed a similar, but distinctly different feeling radiating from the imperturbable dark figure of Blackmail, he became even more concerned, but about more immediate things than the tangled paths of emotion.

The knight was not sitting down to relax as were the rest of them. He was standing against the dawn sky, facing out toward the west. Sam followed his gaze, but saw nothing save endless prairie and a faint smudge on the horizon that might have been the sea that was the border between Sei'cks and Ein.

"The ocean, silent knight?" asked Sam, looking up at Blackmail's still figure. "Is that what you're looking at?"

The knight made no comment for a long moment, then shook his head in dismissal and sat down with a barrage of creaks and metallic noises. Sam admired the way the knight, strange though he was, was able to move about in that armor. He required no assistance rising or lowering himself to a seated position, and walked as quickly as any of them and with great stamina.

"We'll try to avoid the area to the northwest," Valerie

was saying. "From what I have heard, the Plains barbarians have another main camp there at this time of year. They may have heard of what happened at the other camp and would not be pleased to see us."

"Nary a soul ever is," said Arcie with a sigh.

"Sir Fenwick!" Jason, one of the younger scouts in the Verdant Company, ran into the high-raftered room. Fenwick had taken charge of an abandoned warehouse in Pila'Mab as his temporary headquarters, and was even now discussing spell choices with his mages. He looked up as Jason stumbled into the room and saluted.

"Yes, Jason?" he asked.

"Sir Fenwick, Lord Tasmene to see you," announced Jason importantly. Fenwick grinned in delight.

"Really! Show the clumsy ox in, then," he directed. The mages watched curiously as their leader pressed himself against the side of the doorway, eyes sparkling, and motioned to them to be silent.

A moment later, a ringing of mail sounded, and into the doorway stepped an impressive figure. A handsome man, over six feet tall, with shaggy brown hair and a thick curly beard. He was garbed all in silver chain mail, over which he wore a crimson tunic with a device of a white tiger rampant. Over his shoulders was thrown a red cloak trimmed in white fur, and he carried a helmet inlaid with silver under his arm. This was Lord Tasmene, descendant of the Hero Tamarne. Tasmene was an ex-adventurer, and the King of Ein. His eagle-sharp blue eyes glinted as he looked around the room, stepping through the doorway.

Fenwick reached out from his hiding place and abruptly pounded the man on the shoulder. The two men jerked around and faced each other, then began roaring like bears and cuffing each other around the head and shoulders. Finally Lord Tasmene fetched the smaller, slighter prince a hefty whap across the shoulder blades that knocked him sprawling, and the two burst into laughter.

"Blast it, Fenwick, you're too delicate! Don't they feed

you over there?" roared Tasmene cheerfully.

"And you, old friend, like a great wheeump!" said Fenwick, laughing and leaping to his feet unharmed. His eyes widened, and he reached out and tugged on the man's beard. "And what's this, then? Have you become so clumsy that you feared for your life each day you took up a razor?"

The big man gently picked the ranger up by his collar. "You are but jealous, my old friend, ever since I joshed your little smudge mustache on the Fields of Kalorn." Fenwick laughed, and Tasmene set him down. "Enough of this, Fenwick. What is this missive you have sent me?"

"I really did not expect you to show up in person, Tasmene. I merely asked for your assistance . . . "

"And you have it, of course! Even now my companions . . . you recall them, o great Prince?" asked Tasmene with a smile.

"How could I not? Your little scruffy band of adventurers has both helped and hindered me and mine time and time again. The sturdy Northerman Thurbin, the noble knight Sir Reginald, your scout Dusty, the fair lady warrior Danathala. Your brother; the sly and mysterious mage Tesubar, the mountain barbarian Icecliff Cragland, and the healer, his lady, Waterwind, of these same plains we now look over. And of course your Lady Tilla, a swordswoman in her own right," finished Fenwick with a smile. Tasmene chuckled.

"All correct save the last, Fenny," he began, as Fenwick heard the stifled snickers from the mages behind him at the sound of his nickname. "Lady Tilla waits safely at home in Castle Praust-Palar, expecting our first child." The big warrior's face beamed with smug pride and Fenwick grabbed his hand and shook it.

"My arrows! Congratulations, old friend! This is fine news indeed." Tasmene bowed his head in proud acknowledgment, then continued in a serious tone.

"And in other business, however, my men-at-arms even now move Plainswards to your stated position. Tell me, friend, what is the cause that such a force as you and I together must have to be called out? I was in such curiosity I had Tesubar teleport me to your location at once."

Fenwick too became serious. "A small force of evil, my friend, small, but slippery as quicksilver. My men and I have so far had to use caution in our attempts to capture them, and this has hindered our efforts. But soon the causes of that caution will be removed, and we shall sweep down upon the remainders like hawks."

"Causes of caution?" asked Lord Tasmene, scratching his beard. Fenwick nodded.

"A centaur, who is in the employ of the Arch-Mage Mizzamir, and a young lady with flame-red hair."

"Oho!" exclaimed Tasmene. "A lady? Is it perhaps that my friend tires of heartbreaking and seeks a more permanent companion, as I have done?"

"Perhaps," chuckled Fenwick. "Although a permanence may not work out . . . if it is the case, there is nothing wrong in a bit of heartbreaking." Fenwick winked.

"Well, then," replied Lord Tasmene, "what is your plan?"

Fenwick smiled. "It involves a dragon . . . "

Blackmail remained uneasy, staring with dark visor-slit at the sky and the distant sea while the others ate a leisurely supper and relaxed aching muscles. Their attitude disturbed Robin; surely people on a quest so serious, facing the odds they did, would be more concerned, more dismal? But perhaps that had something to do with their evilness; heroes were concerned for the fate of all, while these people obviously felt that the rest of the world could go hang so long as they themselves were set up comfortably.

They relaxed on the hillside in the heat of the day. The fields were flat and empty, the sky a bright blue, patched here and there with thick white clouds. And yet Blackmail kept raising his dark visor to the sky, and Sam felt the hair on the back of his neck prickling. His star-shaped birthmark seemed to itch, and he rumpled his tunic scratching at it.

They had just drifted off to sleep when suddenly there

was a great clatter of metal as Blackmail lurched to his feet and drew his sword. The others awoke with a start to see a huge shape burst out of the clouds, great bat-wings beating the air as it swooped down on them. Jacinth flames burst from its gullet as they scrambled in terror. Lumathix had found them, and the attack was too sudden to think.

The grass of the campsite exploded in flames. Sam, wakened from a sound sleep but still quick as ever, rolled out of the way and was missed entirely. Robin shied and ran out of the way, but the dragon ignored him. Blackmail raised his shield as the blast hammered down and not a lick of flame touched him. Arcie and Valerie were not so fortunate, caught in the fringes of the blast; smoke billowed up from the grass around them, drowning cries of pain. Kaylana jumped back as the rose-gold dragon landed with a jarring crash on the campsite.

Then all was chaos. Three daggers bounced in quick succession off the dragon's shoulder scales, then Sam was knocked flat by a lash of the great tail. Robin, unsure of what to do, drew his sword, and Arcie staggered coughing from the flames with his morning star; the dragon spoke words in the language of magic, and the centaur abruptly collapsed, dropped by a spell of magical slumber. The tail lashed again, sending Arcie flying.

Blackmail charged forward, his sword swinging, and dealt the great beast a nasty blow to the side. The dragon roared and lunged at him, claws raking on platemail, jaws snapping. But the knight defended himself with sword and shield, and blood flew. Sam appeared again to the side; the dragon lunged with terrifying swiftness and its great teeth clashed together with a spurt of flame an inch from where the assassin had been.

Lumathix roared again and lashed out with his tail; the great muscular tail struck Kaylana before she could move. She flew backward through the air and landed with a jarring thud some yards away, her staff knocked from her hand. She raised her head, shaking it to clear it, and began groping frantically around for the staff. The dragon smacked Blackmail a final time with a huge fore-paw, slapped Sam crushingly across the chest with its huge tail once more, and bounded forward. It seized the oak staff in its huge mouth, then grabbed the Druid in its huge paws.

With a mighty leap it sprang into the air, Kaylana gripped so tightly in the scaly paws she couldn't move, and flew upward and away, heading toward the dim shadow of the distant sea and leaving a battered and bloody group of villains on a broad patch of black and smoking turf.

"Oh, hells," groaned Sam after a moment. Blackmail, his armor scratched and dented by the dragon's claws, wiped his sword on the grass and sheathed it. Sam got unsteadily to his feet. "That was the same one as before, I think," he added. He limped over to where three of his companions lay scattered on the turf. Arcie was blackened and burned, his clothes a mess of charred edges and soot, but he blinked and opened his eyes when Sam shook him, and then began moaning and complaining loudly of the pain from his burns. Robin seemed to be unharmed, and Sam was just about to wake him when a hoarse cawing sound startled them. They looked over to see Nightshade the raven jumping up and down near Valerie's still form. They hurried over, and Arcie winced.

"Baris and Bella," he whispered. "Yon great beast must have trodden upon her."

It did indeed look so . . . the frail Nathauan's body was twisted into the ground, her fair skin charred and crimson-blistered from the dragon's breath. The long black hair was little more than crumpled soot.

"Are she . . . ?" asked Arcie. The sorceress was unmoving. Sam shook his head.

"Her familiar's still alive, so she must be also . . . I don't know for how long though."

Indeed the raven seemed quite frantic, jumping up and down, flapping its wings. And the broken form on the ground made a faint sound of pain. The men exchanged glances. Robin, woken from the magical sleep by the noise, raised his head and pricked his ears to listen to Sam and Arcie as the knight stood silently by.

" 'Tis best we end it," suggested Arcie. "Nought we might do . . . Kaylana might have done, but . . . " He shrugged and winced, cursing, in pain as he was reminded of his injuries.

Sam shook his head again. "We've got to try to save her. There was that tribe of barbarians around, I remember noticing their campfires not too far away. They may have a healer . . . "

"Sam, 'tis a waste of time and dangerous. Best we leave her and press on. I'm in fardlin' agony."

Ah, thought Robin. *So darkness does abandon its own.*

"Arcie, normally I'd say, yes, let's abandon her. She's evil, she's powerful, thus she's dangerous. But also . . . " he began ticking off his fingers. "One, she's saved my life twice at least. Of course, that doesn't really make much difference, and if that was all, I'd just leave her now. But two, she's the only one who knows where we're going, three, she's the only one who knows what we may have to do when we get there, and four, she's the only thing close to a wizard we have in our little band. Without her, we may as well go home and wait to be whitewashed, or for the world to sublimate, or whatever." He began bandaging what he could see of the Nathauan's wounds with scraps torn from her cloak.

"Argh, you do have a point with that," grumped Arcie. "Well enough. To yon bloody barbarian village it are then . . . and we'll surely all be killed."

Sam shrugged. "They're good people . . . we come seeking healing. Maybe it's a good act to heal, even if it's healing evil people."

"Not for the likes of us, I doubt," muttered Arcie, as Sam and the knight began carefully moving Valerie's unconscious form onto Sam's cloak to use as a stretcher. "Blast and bother! This were my best suit, you know, almost mine own armor, and 'tis all ruined, with me skin's all a-blistered, my hair singed unrecognizable . . . " He paused. "Sam? What are that under your tunic, there?"

he asked, puzzled out of his self pity. The assassin glanced down at a large rip in his newly repaired tunic. A broken chunk of white showed. He tsked, and wrapped his scarf around it, covering a bleeding gash. His assassin training was still so strong he scarcely noticed even the fiercest of pain. He had been trained from the earliest age to ignore pain, for one stifled cry could be enough to give one's position away.

"It's just a rib, Arcie. Let's move out. Get up, centaur, and help us carry the sorceress."

They balanced the crumpled form of Valerie on the centaur's back, with Sam and Blackmail on either side to prevent her from falling off, and Arcie hastening ahead to choose the most level ground and scan for danger.

"After this," said the assassin, as they walked along, "we'll have to go after that dragon."

Arcie turned around to stare at him. "Have ye lost what small mind ye had, Sam? Yon great muckle lizard near killed us!"

Sam sighed. He had his own reasons for wanting to rescue Kaylana, if she still lived . . . but once again he was going to have to convince the rest of the party.

Robin flicked his ears. "The Barigan's right. We haven't any idea where it's gone, we don't know if Kaylana's alive anyway, and that dragon will surely slay us all if we encounter it again."

Blackmail, however, looked in the direction the dragon had gone and raised his mailed fist silently, then looked at Sam, who managed a weak smile. His rib was starting to hurt, now that the shock of adrenaline was wearing off . . . There were still limits to assassin stoicism.

"You're all for it, huh? Want to fight the dragon?" he asked. The helmet nodded determinedly. "Thanks, then. But I think we all have to go."

" 'Tis suicide, laddie," insisted Arcie.

"It's suicide if we don't. We're hurt pretty bad now, and we have to go to a bunch of barbarians who probably won't be too pleased to see us anyway. If we survive this, what happens when we get hurt again? Who's healed us, time and time again, as well as being more than a little handy with magic?" retorted Sam. "She's our survival insurance. Maybe heroes can die trying, but I'm an assassin, and I like living."

Arcie sighed. "Fah! As you will . . . you win again. We'll be going to rescue the lassie."

"They won't bother to rescue her, of course," commented Fenwick. He had just received a report from Towser, who had been in magical contact with Lumathix and reported the Druid captured safely and the rest of the party severely injured. "They are evil, who care nothing for their comrades, and will fear to face the dragon. And thus will have to continue on across the Plains as best they can. Which of course will lead them right into the middle of my Company and Lord Tasmene's men, two groups to close like the jaws of a trap . . . the centaur will break and run for it, and we shall scatter the bodies of those villains into bloody fragments strewn about the Plains." Fenwick took out his silver-etched longsword, the magical blade Truelight, Slayer of Darkness, and tested the edge with his thumb. The hilt pulsed in his hand as he thought of cleaving into the forces of darkness with its edge that could break any magical armor, through any spell. "Mindless overkill, some might say . . . but I have already lost too much to these renegades. I will run no risks. Besides, the Company need the exercise." He smiled and sheathed the blade as he stood and went to saddle his warhorse.

They reached the edge of the camp shortly after noon and found it to be settled around a small river. The tall grass provided a good cover as they watched the barbarians below and debated what to do.

"I'm fair exhausted," whispered Arcie. "Why don't this sort of thing not happen in the night, as we're awake?"

"There's no time," hissed Sam. "How's Valerie?" Blackmail put his helmet close to the sorceress's pale face, then made a gesture with his gauntlet, palm down, shaken slightly. Sam translated—"Not good."

"I can see their temple," spoke up Robin. "There, in the center—that well or pool or something, with the carved stones about it, just like in the other camp, but smaller. One of the many founded by Ki'Kartha the Heroine, after her marriage to the tribesman Sungrass and the recovery of the artifact of Mula, the Waterstone." The others looked at him in surprise, and he added, "Like in the 'Canticle of the Water Lily.' I know all the verses."

" 'Ware!" hissed Arcie suddenly. "They're at bringing some fellow to yon pool!"

The others looked and saw the turquoise-robed clerics of the temple escorting a brawny barbarian man into the open-air sanctuary. He held his arm awkwardly, wrapped in bloody bandages—perhaps injured in a hunt. While the silent villains watched from their hillside hideout, one of the priestesses, with much ceremony, dipped a silver ladle into the small pale blue pool, raised it over the man's head a moment, then poured it on his arm. A brief blue shimmer seemed to engulf the wounded limb, then the fellow took off his bandage and flexed his perfectly healed arm. There were appropriate praises to the goddess, and the man strode out again.

"It looks like that water is the stuff we need, then," murmured Sam, wincing slightly; this hunkering in the grass wasn't doing his broken rib a bit of good. He'd probably be dead in a few days from blood loss and infection. But that was for later. "We'll have to get some."

"I don't think they'll just let us have it," said Robin. "We know these folk are very suspicious of outsiders and, being proud of their heritage, would likely consider it their heroic duty to kill us on sight."

"We'll have to steal some, then," decided Sam. Arcie stood up, and tipped what was left of his hat.

"Ye can leave that one to me," he said, with a broad grin.

The thief set off down the hillside, silent and unseen as

only a thief can be. The others watched from the hill.

"He's crazy," muttered Sam after a bit. "That whole pool is in full view, even from here, and there's priestesses everywhere. Even if he was completely magically invisible, they'd see his shadow."

"Should we go after him?" asked Robin nervously. Sam shook his head.

"He's crazy, but he must know what he's up to. I don't want to mess up whatever he has in mind."

Arcie stealthily made his way down to the barbarian encampment. This was tricky, of course; he was quite obviously not a barbarian, not even a young one. Barbarians and Barigans were not on very good terms; and Arcie was still sore from being used as a catty-ball by the Plainsmen in the west. In the past he'd also had a few tankards placed over his head in bars by visiting barbarians of all kinds.

Considering his experiences Arcie can be pardoned for what he did next. He crept carefully to the edge of the sanctuary, hiding under a flap of a tent, and took out his sling. Then from another pouch he extracted the small, red-gold crystal he'd stolen from one of Fenwick's men. The man had said it was a fire-crystal, capable of creating some sort of magical blast; Arcie had heard of such things and seen a few in his time; it would have been nice to ask the man if he knew where to get any more, but at the time, the man was not in a position to tell anyone anything. That was one of the troubles with traveling with inherently violent people, he mused. The fire-crystal had been wrapped well in padding cotton, so Arcie thought it must be fairly fragile.

Fitting the crystal into his sling, he glanced around to be sure no one was watching, then lobbed it as high and far as he could, sending it tumbling silently into one of the largest clusters of tents, the one with the distinctive shape and guards of a storehouse for Barigan whiskey.

Sam, Blackmail, and Robin on their hill had a splendid view of a sudden huge ball of fire that erupted from a corner of the camp, with a deafening double-explosion and a gout of black smoke and crimson flame. Shouts rang out, barbarians ran with their fur garments aflame. Arcie had learned well what sort of tactics worked with the Plainsmen who scorned metal. The priestesses in the open temple reacted in shock, then quickly scooped up dippers of the water and ran to the scene of the holocaust to heal the injured. The instant they had all vanished, a small quick figure scampered into the enclosure, waved up at them, and knelt at the pool, filling a pair of waterskins.

"I told you he was crazy," said Sam. Robin nodded, ears flicking.

Arcie filled the last waterskin, noticing as he did so that the dragonfire burns on his hands cooled and healed instantly when the water splashed on them. He quickly plugged the waterskins and hastened back out of the temple. The camp was in chaos. As he ran, he splashed himself with some of the water, redoubling his speed as his wounds healed.

At last a winded but healthy Barigan tumbled into the grassy hiding place of the four companions. He handed Sam one of the waterskins and tucked the other one into his belt. The assassin unstoppered the skin, splashed a bit on himself, then, scolded by the raven, quickly poured a heavy dose over Valerie's broken body. The water tingled on his skin, and he felt his wound closing, his broken rib moving painlessly back into place and knitting. Despite his loyalty to the Druid, he had to admit that the power of the healing deity was far more impressive than her slower, herbal formulas. A faint blue mist covered both him and Valerie and then vanished; he looked up. "Robin? Blackmail? Either of you hurt?" The two shook their heads, Robin still watching the flames in shock.

"You blew up their tents," he said after a moment. "And they hadn't even done anything to you!"

"Aye, but they would have," Arcie replied, with a wink. Valerie stirred and sat up in a faint cloud of soot that sent her coughing.

"Where am I?" she gasped. The raven flew with relieved clucks and alighted on her shoulder. She ran a hand through her scorched dark hair, and a large swath of it fell away, leaving her with ragged-cropped locks. She stared at the chunk in horror.

"Outside another barbarian encampment," replied Sam tersely. "And if you're feeling all right now, I think we'd better get moving."

Valerie looked down at the milling campsite. "You never said a truer word, assassin."

"I try," he replied modestly. "Let's go . . . toward the sea."

They hurried away from the smoke and screams of the camp and fled across the fields.

When they had come as far as they felt was necessary, they fell exhausted onto the turf. "Rest!" croaked Arcie. "Them mighty feats of daring takes a powerful lot out of a fellow."

"Agreed," said Valerie. "I think it would be best if we slept for a few hours, then continued on in the evening."

"We're going to go get the Druid before we go on," informed Robin, rummaging in his pack for something to eat. Valerie looked like she might argue, but then nodded.

"All right. Blackmail, would you take watch?" she asked. The knight nodded his helm and sat back in the grass, watching the fields and sky as the others rested.

At last evening fell. Valerie looked up at the pale sky and at the moon. "We'll have to hurry," she said nervously. "There isn't a whole lot of time left."

"And where might we be heading?" asked Arcie, looking into the distance at the dark shadow of the sea. "There are a whole range of plains, and, if we follow the beast on to Ein, a haystack of mountains to find a dragon-needle in. Where might we begin to seek?"

"I'll have to work on that," said Valerie with a sigh. "I doubt we'll find the dragon on Sei'cks, there is no cover for it. Dragons like cover. It will have flown on to Ein; there are a lot of places for a dragon to go in that foul land. I shall have to use magic."

"Magic? How?" asked Robin. All he'd seen of Valerie's power had been various blasts of death and destruction, and he was beginning to wonder if she could do any other sort of magic.

"There are various scrying spells, seeking spells . . . I only hope the wench is smart enough or hurt enough that she is unable to use her concealment powers."

"Seems to me that yon great lizard took care that the lassie was unharmed," commented Arcie. "As though she were wanted live." Blackmail nodded in silent agreement.

"She'd better not be hurt, or—" began Sam angrily, but Valerie shushed him.

"There is no time for your romantic heroics, assassin fool. Find me water, preferably old, rank, muddy stale stuff; this magic healing water is useless."

After some clumsy searching in the darkness, a suitable puddle was located, and Valerie filled her silver eating bowl with the brackish water. She then pulled her hood over her face, and knelt in the deepest shadow of a small hill.

"One unfortunate side effect of this spell is it may draw the attention of any other people scrying in the same general area . . . but without the Druid's magic to cover our presence, we show up like coals in the snow as it is. My own concealing magic, dark as it is, is worse than nothing in this Light world. So, be on your guard, and if any mages come teleporting in, I trust you to kill them." She then clasped her hand, with broken fingernails, around the midnight oval of her Darkportal, and gently touched the surface of the water in the bowl with her other hand. She shifted the bowl slightly, and seemed to fall into a deep trace, as the others exchanged nervous glances and took up watchful positions. Nightshade sat on his mistress's shoulder and watched everyone with a beady eye, hissing if they came too close. The air around Valerie tingled slightly, as she softly whispered words of power in the language of Nathauan magic. It was a sound like snakes slowly moving over gravel.

The spell of Seeking was in four parts. Valerie bound

the first quickly, and rather incautiously; it was the ward around the caster's mind and body that shielded from mind or magic while the spell was in progress. She bound her mind with a loose mental tripwire, more energy-conserving than the full wards, and began the second part of the spell.

This magic was to free her consciousness from her body, similar to what Kaylana had done in reaching out to call the stampede. A difficult task, as living beings were usually very concerned with keeping the body and soul together, and much patient meditation had to be done before the spirit could detach. Valerie was out of practice; it took her over half an hour just to relax enough for her mind to begin to slide free, loose and numb in the astral wind. She had long since lost track of where she was or her surroundings, but she could now feel an openness about her, similar to the way Sam felt when the shadows parted for him. The dark bowl of water filled her vision, engulfed it in its swirling shadows. She was ready.

The third part of the spell was second in importance. This was where the location of the sought object would be determined. Valerie concentrated on the Druid, trying to remember everything she could; it was difficult, she'd never paid much attention to the backwoods female, since she was obviously fairly harmless for all her Druidic power. Red hair, yes, green eyes, taller than herself, the dun robes, the imperious voice.

Confused images swirled, her vision wavered wildly across the edges of reality. She began to get angry, then calmed herself. Anger was dangerous at this stage. She must remain calm, retain her concentration. Perhaps she should try a different tack. Instead of seeking the Druid's physical body, Valerie now sought the distinctive pattern of her aura. The only aura in the world with the strange, gyroscopic spinning of a soul struggling for utter balance.

The villains in the real world of crickets and a soft wind watched from a safe distance. It seemed to Arcie, the most intent watcher, that the water in the bowl was moving and shifting and changing, although the sorceress's fingers were still.

The response was instant. A whirling green-brown light was easily resolved into the shape of the Druid. She leaned against a rough stone wall, chained perhaps, very still. Her staff was nowhere to be seen. The image flickered with a faint red-gold light that seemed to shift and flux. Now, to pull out, to back up the distance to see the location . . .

But her astral vision suddenly began to be crowded. As she focused, the picture was interwoven with thousands of indistinct forms, swirling and screaming an endless ancient agony; not ghosts, but the psychic impression of great pain and death so strong that it was burned into the rocks. The confusion sent her reeling back and she faltered, her imperfect concentration shaking—twists and warps of tunnels and stairs and more and more shades of ancient life and death, dwarves and humans and above all the shrill, screaming death-cry of an evil dragon.

Valerie managed to gather in the reins of her sanity and consciousness. She was drifting in the darkness, instinct having pulled her away from the vision. What now, she wondered. She felt confused, and faltered, beginning to lose herself . . .

A distant pain startled her awake, and she looked. A ghostly raven hovered before her, flapping indistinct wings. It flew a short distance, then returned, drawing her forward.

With Nightshade's help she slowly returned to her senses and was able to begin the most important part of the spell—the ending that would bring her spirit back to her body. If it were not for Nightshade's soul-link, she might have been lost forever . . . She slowly pulled herself together, locked her spirit back in her body as she felt Nightshade return to his, and opened her eyes.

"I know where she is," she stated flatly. Her body ached from being still so long, and the wind ruffled her short hair as she poured the flat, dead water out.

"Where? Where? Where!?" demanded Sam, running over.

"You aren't going to like this," said Valerie, standing.

"It doesn't matter! Where?" The others were watching him, Arcie with leering amusement, Robin with his usual confusion, and Blackmail as calm as ever. Sam managed to control himself and look cool and dignified again.

"She is in Putak-Azum," reported Valerie.

There was dead silence. Then Sam spoke up.

"You're right. I don't like it."

"Putak-Azum?" asked Robin. "Where the Heroes searched for and found the fabled Necklace of Calaina? Putak-Azum, the lair of the dark dragon Kazikuckla and her hordes of evil reptile-men?"

"The same, centaur . . . except the Necklace is long gone, Kazikuckla was slain, as you may recall, by the Heroes, and all the reptile-men were defeated with the aid of the Dwarven folk of the mountains. The place is little more than a dusty wreck by now, I should imagine," Valerie said, looking thoughtful.

"Well, if it's got another dragon now, a pinky-gold one for example, I'm all for visiting it," replied Sam, balancing one of his daggers on his fingertip. Blackmail nodded in agreement. "Where do we get in?"

"There is only one entrance, besides the dragon's way," explained Valerie. "The doorway lies in the wall below the Giant's Crag, according to legend."

"Only one way in, hmm?" said Sam, thoughtfully sheathing his dagger. "I don't like the sound of that. What's the dragon's way?"

"A cave in the side of one of the pinnacles, above a thousand-foot vertical climb with an overhang of polished granite two hundred yards long," replied the sorceress. Sam tried to look cool and pensive.

"Well," he said at last, "I could make it, but I imagine the rest of you might have a hard time. All right, the front door it is then."

"Hear, thank you so very much kindly," replied Arcie,

with more than a trace of sarcasm. They gathered themselves together and began the long march to the crossing to Ein.

"Besides," said Robin, picking his way carefully so as not to trip his hooves on anything in the dimness, "how can it be a trap? No one knows we're here." I've told a lie, he thought to himself, with a touch of pride. Maybe he was cut out for this spy business. Now all that would remain would be theft, to steal a Segment . . .

The journey took several days. What was a brief flight for a dragon was a long walk for humans and a centaur. The channel between Ein and Sei'cks was quite narrow, and they boarded a ferry at the small city that flourished at this vital nexus. The flat countryside vanished abruptly as they turned inland into Ein; after but a few miles of farmland the great jagged Svergald Mountains reared up from the landscape, their peaks black and foreboding in the twilight in which the villains traveled.

Sam was reminded of the myths surrounding the creation of the Six Lands: from all the other continents on the world, the gods had taken huge chunks and lumped them together and tossed them into the sea in a rough ring. The Six Lands were the most magical of all the world and were woven through with some sense of cosmic importance; if anything vital happened, it would happen somewhere in the Six Lands. One last Test, less than a month until the end, for good or evil. Sam smiled wryly at the idea. Good and Evil! He no longer knew what to think about the words anymore.

To the south, across a wide sea, was the lazy, foolish land of Dous, his birthplace and where this had all started. He found himself missing his tiny, cramped room in the abandoned Guild, the cool wine served in the Frothing Otter, the twisty rolls that the vendors would sell on Jasper's Feast, to honor the patron Hero who had been of a slightly sneaky nature himself . . . probably why Arcie and I managed to last that long there, he thought. And Kimi, too, had still retained her mind. Sam looked at the remains of his tunic, cut in the same style as the one Jasper had worn all through the War . . . almost as ragged too. What would the Wilderkin Hero do, he wondered, were he alive today? What if he had survived after the War, and become Lord Mayor as they had wanted him too? Would his descendants chase us with horns and hounds?

A lot of organization is needed to move an army around, especially when the terrain is as inhospitable as most of Ein. Tasmene did not have Fenwick's luxury of a stable of mages to help his troop movements. But with stout Northerman guides and much patience, they slowly made their way to the eastern borders of Ein. The only true wizard in Tasmene's employ was his brother, a blue-robe named Tesubar who had accompanied his brother on many adventures, and been changed in the process. Some of his experiences had begun to darken him, but Mizzamir's intercession at the request of Tasmene had left Tesubar with nothing worse than a slight irritability and a tendency, when under stress, to speak with a harsh rasp to his voice.

Tesubar was accompanying his brother now, and using his mental magic to scout the way ahead. It was while drifting in this ethereal state some days ago that his mind brushed against the edges of another, so dark and evil he withdrew, unseen, and had watched in magical silence as the other hand searched, searched for something . . . And then, days later, he sent his own mind out to search for that one again, and found a surprise.

Too haughty to divulge his reasons to his brother and the stupid grunt fighters of the army, Tesubar steered them in the right direction for his purposes, and then, one night as they camped on a high plateau, the mage scornfully separated himself and his brother from the bawdy campfire singing of the ranks. He drew Tasmene aside to the edge of the plateau, where the setting sun cast stark shadows into the valley below.

"What is it, Tesubar?" asked Tasmene, as they came

away. "Having another one of your insights?"

"No more insight than intelligence, brother," said Tesubar softly, drawing his blue robes close about him. "Prince Fenwick is a fine woodsman, but he is a fool to think he can track a Nathauan like a rabbit. If we had continued as he would have us, we should have passed by our target, and been left sitting with the Verdant Company in the middle of empty plains."

"Thunderbolts! I'd thought we were heading in a rather odd direction!" exclaimed Tasmene, rubbing his brow. "We are near Putak-Azum, aren't we? Why ever in the name of Cror did you bring us this way?"

"Because, brother," sighed Tesubar, "our quarry even now prepares to enter into the vaults of Putak-Azum. It is my opinion that, odd as it may seem, they wish to rescue the Druid captured by Prince Fenwick's foolish pink dragon."

Much long travel had brought them deep into the stony heart of Ein. Valerie had saved them much time by locating and navigating old abandoned Dwarven mining trails and the occasional brief tunnel through a cliffside. Robin was a constant liability, either shivering in terror of the heights of mountain trails, or cringing and gasping in claustrophobic tunnels. Fortunately, neither of these proved to last long, and the occasional sharp word from one of the villains would terrify the minstrel into continuing.

He kept up a running string of melodies on his harp. For a long time after, the sound of a harp would bring back memories to Arcie of the torchlight flickering on stone walls, and the centaur's shadow playing and jiggering to the echoing notes, all combined with the terrified reek of horse sweat.

Robin was slowly working his way through his entire repertoire of songs, ballads, jigs, reels, canticles, lays, poems, and poseys, about one quarter of which were the older songs. These were played rather haltingly; he seldom bothered to practice them, and forgot most of the words. The other three-quarters, which he could sing clearly and well despite his shaky voice, were various odes of the Heroes, or songs of the War or the Victory.

It was during one of these latter ballads that a certain phrase caught Sam's attention. Robin sang,

Said, For it must be t'run to back,
On this evil-fated day,
And Tamarne marched into the storm,
To where, he would not say,
Hours then they found him,
Blinded in the flood,
Gone from his eyes was the shining
Of Cror's divinest blood.

"Robin," he asked, stopping the centaur as he was about to blast through the chorus, "what's that ballad about?"

"Why, it's 'Tamarne's Gift,' didn't you know? I'd thought everyone would know that, it's a very popular one, especially down in the Commots, why . . . " stammered Robin, trying to keep his mind off the close passage around them.

"Surely it don't matter, Sam?" complained Arcie, concerned lest the break in the centaur's concentration would send Robin fainting again.

"Tell me, what is it about?" Sam pressed. "I'm afraid I've never been an extended visitor to the Commots . . . "

"Well, um, of course, you know, the Hero Tamarne was half-god, you know, son of Cror, god of thunder?" Robin whickered, his ears flicking.

"I'd heard that, but wasn't sure it was true . . . "

"Oh yes, Tamarne could call the lightning from the skies and he was promised immortality and he could fight like the great god himself," recounted Robin. "And yet at the darkest point in the War he bargained with the gods that if they would save his companions from death at the hands of the Dark Lord, he would give up his right to the immortal blood. And so the gods took his powers and saved his friends, and that's why Tamarne is dead now instead of ruling on forever, as Mizzamir does."

"Mizzamir isn't half-god, is he?" Sam asked, concerned. Robin shook his head, nervously twanging the strings on his harp.

"No, but he is an Elf . . . they live forever, most people say." Robin burst back into another ballad, "The Hawk Lord."

Unless somebody kills them, Sam thought. But he was also thinking of Robin's ballad. The centaur, like most minstrels, had almost certainly learned most of his repertoire from listening to others' songs, and memorizing the words . . . He'd probably seen very few of them ever written down, and a slur here, a foreign accent there . . . T'run to back . . . T'krung-Tabak?

At last they had come into a valley and before them loomed a mountain too proud and huge to be part of any common range. Immense and haughty, it was a range all to itself. Clouds wisped about its peak in the twilight, and plateaus and crags grouped in the distance all around it, as though paying homage. Near the peak, a faint jag could be seen in the profile: the two-hundred-yard overhang outside the ancient Dragon's cave. This was Putak-Azum. Riddled like a termite mound with the halls and passages of Dwarves and men, now long abandoned because of the unspeakable horrors that had happened there in the long dark years before the Victory.

Now, the secretive Dwarves and their half-kin, the Northermen, lived and worked in the other mountains of Ein, and Putak-Azum was left to nothing more than the occasional pillage by brave adventurers, who were quickly disappointed; too many others before them had had the same idea. Still, some would occasionally enter and never return; there was always talk of clearing it out fully once and for all, but nothing was ever done.

It was after midnight when they finally reached the base of the mountains, but the night was no darker than it had been when they started. A bit of searching about and they discovered the entrance, a rough cave near ground level, with a pile of rubble outside it. Arcie looked at it in disgust.

"Fah! Be this it? The way in? The only way in? Where be the fancy doorway, the mystic runes, the secret passwords, the locks and traps and fearsome guardians?" He scooped up a pebble and hurled it into the cave. It bounced in and echoed hollowly. " 'Tis seems as any old mouse-crack in a wall! What sort of fearsome ancient ruin call ye this?"

"As I understand it," spoke up Robin, glad to be out on the ground in the open, and impressed with the sight of this most legendary of mountains, "when the Heroes went in after the Necklace, the forces of evil sealed the other exits behind them, thinking to leave them to be eaten by the dragon Kazikuckla . . . but the Heroes, after destroying the dragon, came back to this place and the wizard Mizzamir blasted their way out with his magic."

"Looks like they were in a hurry," mused Sam, looking at the rubble. Blackmail nodded.

"Oh yes . . . they were retreating from the dragon's death throes as well as the armies of reptile-men," Robin elaborated. "Racing against time to win the War with the forces of darkness."

"What, retreating?" asked Arcie in surprise. "Yet I thought them so powerful as never needed to retreat."

"Oh no," Valerie shook her head. "They only became really powerful after the Victory. Mizzamir especially."

Sam nodded in silent thought, then said, "Well, not doing us any good loitering on the doorstep. Come, we can make a start before it's time to rest again. Arcie?"

"Eh?"

"You go first."

"Why?" Arcie was suspicious. Sam grinned at him.

"It's traditional, you sneakthief! You go in front and open the locks and stuff for us, check for traps, all those thiefy things, and we follow behind and fire spells and arrows over your head at anything that attacks us. You know, like in all the adventuring stories."

"Och, aye, 'tis so . . . " conceded Arcie grumpily. He remembered his father saying something about that, although with the occasional grouchy complaint about being used as a sort of miner's canary. Still, it did make sense. He drew his morning star and settled his hat on his head.

"Right, then, I'll be needing a light . . . " he said, starting for the entrance.

"Must we?" complained Valerie. Arcie sighed.

"I cannot work locks and traps without a bit of illumination, lady . . . and you know how yon centaur behaves in the darken underbelow.

"I wonder, can you look through darkness, silent knight?" Arcie asked Blackmail. The dark figure gave a sort of shrug. Arcie chuckled. "Och, aye . . . real fighters don't need light, eh? But myself does. And should anything find us, I'll want Sam able to aim best as he can, so's I will not finish with a dagger in my neck."

Valerie sighed in exasperation. "All right, have it your way . . . My Darkportal magic is no use for illumination, of course, but we may be able to find some branches around to make torches."

They glanced about, but no branches were forthcoming. Sam looked thoughtful a moment, and pulled something out of one of his tunic pockets.

"Would this help?" he wondered aloud, holding up a thin silver wand with a small round ball set in the end. It glowed faintly.

Valerie raised an eyebrow. "Let me see that!" The assassin handed it to her.

"It was glowing brightly when I picked it up," he explained, "but it faded after awhile."

"And where did you get that stick?" demanded Arcie curiously. Sam looked embarrassed.

"On the white mage's ship, when I was, um, getting a bit shadowy . . . it was in a sconce, like a torch . . . "

"You *stole* it, laddie?!" cried the Barigan. "For shame! That's my department! I rob 'em blind and you kills 'em dead, remember?"

"Well, I couldn't very well go back now and return it, could I?" retorted Sam.

Meanwhile Valerie had been inspecting the wand.

"Yes, actually, assassin, this will do nicely. A wand of focusing magical energy and transforming it into light . . . how vile. Still, I suppose it will work. I shall activate it, thus . . . " She held it away from her face and said, "*Fiat lux.*" The ball on the end suddenly flashed with bright white light, then dimmed to a glow like that of a fine lantern. With an air of disgust, she handed it to the centaur. "You carry this, then. And bring up the rear."

Even as they vanished into the darkness, eyes watched them. Lord Tasmene, waiting and watching in silence with his brother, saw the sudden light flare along the empty hillside. Fenwick's plan had been to trap the villains on the Plains and box them in so that they would be forced to surrender, or, failing that, to apprehend them somewhere in east Ein. But no one but Tesubar had expected the speed and determination with which the villains had headed for Putak-Azum.

Tasmene had agreed that Fenwick's plan was certainly a good plan, bound to meet with success had it not been for this unforeseen happening . . . but he wasn't too sure of the *style* of the thing anyway. He hadn't had his kingdom and men very long and, much of the time, found them more trouble than they were worth. If evil was there to be dealt with, he would so have preferred to make it an actual *adventure,* such as the foray he and his boyhood friend Fenwick had killed their first goblins on. And later, with his little circle of good friends, adventurers, they had raided ancient crypts and suchlike in great fun. They had even explored the tangled vaults of Putak-Azum . . . or part of it, anyway. There wasn't much to kill in there anymore, just a few animals like giant slugs and centipedes, but it had been fun. He was sitting here now, with his group of companions not far off. His old adventuring friends had come with him and his army on this journey, and their company was much more pleasant than a lot of strange men and Northermen bowing at him and calling him "Lord." He'd often longed to go hunting for griffins with his old friends, just like old times, but the duties of command . . . and yet, if that light passing into the mountainside was any clue, there might be a much more enjoyable task coming up.

"Why, by Cror's Hammer! You're right, Tesubar! By Donin, we must stop them!"

He hastened back to his campsite, and prepared a letter to Sir Fenwick. The mage Tesubar watched him in wry amusement.

"What is it now, Tasmene?" asked the dark-haired wizard after a moment of watching the lord struggle with the spellings once or twice. "Are we going to go down after them, or do you plan to stay up here writing ballads all night?"

"No, no! We shall ask Fenwick to send a company of his men to wait at the entrance, whilst we, the White Tigers, venture once more into that dungeon's dark depths, to flush those villains out of there like a cluster of rabbits."

"Is that wise?" the mage asked, adjusting his blue and gold robes. "These people have already thwarted Fenwick . . ."

"Ah, but you forget, he attacked them out in the open. We are adventurers, my friend, and ruined fortresses are our territory. What's more, we've tromped those tunnels before, and will know our way about from the maps Dusty drew last time . . . it will be easy. We may slay them without difficulty in the tunnels anyway."

"I'm not so sure," replied Tesubar, walking back into the circle of the campfire. The Einian army lay in slumber about them, snoring like a herd of cattle. The wizard paused, looking into the embers of the fire. Tasmene's adventurer companions: Thurbin, Sir Reginald, Dusty, and Danathala lounged in slumber in a separate circle, except for the two barbarians Icecliff and Waterwind, who were rolled up in a tangle of buffalo skins. Tesubar averted his eyes. "It sounds unpleasantly like walking into a bear's cave."

"Oh, Tesubar, don't be so ominous . . . " the warrior king's blue eyes blinked pleadingly at him. "It's an adventure, just like old times, my brother. We haven't had an adventure in years . . . It'll be *fun.*"

Tesubar smiled, in spite of his concern, at the big man's childlike hope. "Very well, Tasmene. Do you wish me to send that letter for you?"

"Yes, please," answered Lord Tasmene, and he rolled the scrap of parchment carefully and handed it to the mage. Tesubar passed his hand over it, murmuring words of magic, finishing with a command of "To Sir Fenwick of the Verdant Company!" The scroll vanished in a twinkle of gold smoke.

"Och, what a muddle."

"Well, I didn't expect the Heroes would leave it all nice and tidy. Any traps, short one?"

"None as I'm seeing. Be there any dangers, o ladder-legs?"

"You're still in front of me, so I guess not."

The voices of the two criminals echoed down the hall, bouncing and refracting off the rough walls. The tunnel of rough-blasted brown stone soon emerged into a fairly sizable room, empty save for broken piles of old wood and rubble. Three passages led away, two winding off into the darkness, and one climbing a flight of stairs. Arcie looked at them thoughtfully, then turned around to address the rest of the party.

"Well, what way?"

Valerie looked about. "I've never been here before . . . but if it's the dragon's lair we're after, then I would assume 'up' would be a good start."

"As makes sense," nodded the Barigan. "Well enough . . . No crowding from the back, please," he added and jogged lightly up the stone steps. They followed, Sam keeping up with the Barigan just at the edge of the circle of illumination the magical wand provided. The other three hung back slightly so as not to disturb the two men's stealthy investigations.

"Be like old times, eh, laddie?" asked Arcie, adding, "Don't step upon yon tile there."

The assassin skirted the tile and waited while the Barigan quickly drove a small spike into a crack of the floor, blocking some unseen mechanism. "Yes . . . it's funny, though, I've never had to go up against a dragon knowingly before. But I'm not scared now."

"Ah, the wonders of luuuuv," leered Arcie, making Sam blush. Arcie chortled, and then added, "I'll not be looking forward to meeting yon great wyrm again, natch, yet if it has treasures to steal . . . och, it may be worth it."

"There's no way in the world we're going to be able to kill it," Sam said as they walked on down the hall. Arcie nodded, poking meditatively at a crack in one wall. "I mean, the best we can hope for is to get Kaylana out and get away."

"Well, perhaps we can do that, and we can be robbing it skint at the same time," answered the thief. "I know *I'm* game to try."

The hallway curved. Now and again they passed doorways with the shattered remains of doors in them. Arcie and Sam peered into the rooms as they passed.

"Och, living quarters, living quarters, prolly a guardroom, empty, empty, empty," the Barigan noted as he walked along. "Seems to me as quite a few people as were here before us. The place are all looted and trashed."

"I imagine so," replied Sam. "Through this part, at any rate."

"How much are there, do ye reckon?" Arcie wondered. He paused a moment, and turned to peer back at where Valerie walked behind the protection of the armored knight. "Ho, Valerie! How big is the place, anyway?"

"The ruins of Putak-Azum are far older than most men know, Barigan . . . it is believed by some that they may extend throughout the entire mountain and down below into others," was the cool response. Arcie whistled softly.

"That's pretty fair vast! We'll not be going through all of that, then," he decided, setting off again.

After they'd gotten used to it, it was actually not a bad place. Arcie was delighted to be following in his father's footsteps, as it were. Sam was glad to have surfaces all around him, and when his ears had at last adjusted to the echoes, he took comfort in the feel of the shapes all around him, tunnels and corridors to lurk in should enemies approach, even (he suppressed a slight shudder) shadows to hide in. Blackmail seemed to be quite assured, marching along the stone floor with a gentle chiming of platemail, looking about him through his dark viewslit. Valerie, born and raised in the twilight underground, enjoyed the comforting feel of thousands of tons of rock protecting her from the vicious sunlight.

Robin was the only one truly ill at ease; he was sweating and trying to keep his hooves from prancing. His eyes rolled, his ears shot back and forth widely, and his tail swished. Valerie could not ignore his obvious distress and turned around to face him. The others, finding the progress of their illumination had stopped, halted and turned around to see what was the matter.

"What *is* the matter with you, centaur?" she snapped. Robin scuffed his hooves nervously.

"It's stuffy, the walls . . . it feels like they're pressing in on me . . . I can't breathe . . . " he quavered, panting. Valerie rolled her large purple eyes in exasperation.

"Wonderful. He's going cave-crazy again."

"Play your harp, minstrel!" barked Arcie. But Robin was unnerved by the strange air of ancient menace that hung in the very stone of the ruins.

"It's crushing me!" whinnied the minstrel, eyes darting about at the walls. "I've got to get out . . . "

"Stop it . . . " began Valerie, but she saw her words were not reaching the centaur. She grabbed him by the belt. He froze in fear.

"Look, Robin of Avensdale. You aren't going anywhere. I'll expend a bit of my awesome magic to protect you from the crushing of the walls, all right?"

"You can do that?" asked Robin. Valerie nodded.

"It will not be easy, but I shall. Wait for just a moment." She turned loose his belt and rummaged in her pouches. At last she came up with a silver chain and lay it down on her palm in a spiral pattern. Then she took out a tiny glass flask, and very carefully let fall a single clear drop onto the chain. The air was filled with a sweet-sour smell. Then she waved her other hand in mystic passes over the chain, reciting words of power: *"Remedius fabulum equus placebo!"* There was a sudden flash of dark purple, and the chain shimmered a minute in the radiance. Then Valerie solemnly shook the chain out into her other hand and offered it to Robin.

"Wear that around your neck, centaur, and even if you walk the darkest, closest tunnels, you shall be safe."

"Gosh!" gasped Robin, swiftly pulling the thin chain over his head, pausing to disentangle it when it hung up on his ears. "Thanks!"

Valerie turned back around, and after a moment the party started on again, Robin now striding along confidently. Blackmail turned to look at her, his mailed shoulders shaking slightly in what they could now recognize as laughter. Valerie smiled at the knight's silent amusement. "Well, it worked, didn't it?" she whispered.

They wandered ever deeper into the complex of tunnels. Perhaps at one time, back in the mists of history, Putak-Azum had been full of life, a city, a castle, a temple, a whole world. Now it was a great sprawling emptiness, like an abandoned badger set. Most of the rooms and passages they passed through had been built with humans in mind, with wide hallways and arched ceilings now filled with cobwebs and mildew. But much of the stonework appeared to be Dwarven work, and in places it was easy to see where older, smaller tunnels had been enlarged to form human-sized passageways.

Putak-Azum had had many inhabitants. The original caverns, perhaps hollowed out by mountainous forces, had been the home of creatures from the dawn of time. Then, perhaps, the unpleasant humanoids of darkness had made their homes here—the goblins and Groinks, the rock-trolls and ogres, until they were driven back into the far depths by the Dwarvenkind. The Dwarvenkind had perhaps lived here many centuries, in a state of intermittent war with the humanoids. They had then vanished, for some unknown reason, or moved away or down into the depths, seeking further wealth to mine from the bones of the mountains. Then the lords of man, seeing in the vaults of Putak-Azum a secure stronghold, had taken over the upper levels. Then the forces of darkness had encroached, and the great evil things from the bowels of the mountains swept up, slaying the humans and taking their treasures for their own. The great black dragon Kazikuckla came to rest in the upper vaults, guarding that most priceless object, the Necklace of Calaina. And the War had raged on until the Heroes had raided Putak-Azum, mortally wounded the dragon, battled strange and evil creatures in the depths of the mountains, escaped, and moved on. After the Victory, Putak-Azum had been a target for adventurers, who battled the few remaining reptile-men until they had been exterminated. Then they could switch to the occasional party of goblins or rock-trolls that would venture to the surface in hopes of gathering food. For with the closing of the Gate and the destruction of the Darkportals, the forces of darkness, though they hid in the depths of the tunnels, grew weak and feeble, and slowly expired in the cold depths. From then on the Ruins of Putak-Azum could offer the hopeful adventurer nothing more than the occasional giant slug, bat, spider or other such unintelligent creatures that lurked in the cool caves and fed off their own slow ecosystem, without benefit of the sun or rain.

The little group of unlikely Druid-rescuers knew little of this, however. They could only conjecture on the nature of the place, aided by Valerie's knowledge and Robin's store of ballad lore as they wandered through the halls.

"I think we're lost," said Sam, after a few hours.

"Nay, we are not," snapped Arcie. "We Barigans can always tell wherever we be anywhere in the underground."

"That's Dwarves that can do that."

"I can do anything what some smelly dwarf can." Arcie looked affronted.

"Where are we, then?" asked Sam, folding his arms. Arcie looked around.

"We're in a hallway, say five paces far from that arched doorway and yon side passage," he replied confidently.

"Wonderful," said Sam sarcastically, as the Barigan continued to look about him in slight puzzlement.

"Hmm, perhaps it does only apply to Dwarves," Arcie admitted after a moment.

"Fear not," said Valerie, coming up with Blackmail behind them. "I have been marking the way as we travel, and my magic will lead us safely out as soon as we need."

"Och," commented Arcie, "I were just at wondering, now as you've your Darkportal back, why don't you just poof-appear us to yon dragon's lair, or just right away to the Labyrinth thingy? One's always hearing of mages and things teleporting all over the place, in stories," he added to Sam.

Valerie shook her head. Her hair had been severely cropped in the dragon's attack, and now was almost as short as Sam's, hanging in uneven locks just above her shoulders. Nightshade examined them with a beady eye. "It's not that simple, you uneducated Barigan. My powers are still quite limited . . . the Darkportal I wear is only a small one, after all. I cannot teleport to a place I have never seen, which includes both the dragon's lair and the Labyrinth. Even if I was to try to get us to the lair, I'd run the risk of materializing us all into solid rock or empty air outside the mountains. And as for the Labyrinth . . . " she shook her head, then continued, "And lastly, I don't think my magic is strong enough to teleport us all safely. Transportation isn't my field of expertise. I'm better at hurting people."

"Aye well," said Arcie with a shrug. "I was but asking."

"It's getting late," mused Sam, looking about. "Or early, rather."

"How can you tell?" asked Robin. The assassin didn't bother to look at him and poked at one of the walls with a frown.

"I've got a good time sense . . . comes in useful in my line of work, to know how long you have before a poison works, or when to come out of hiding."

"Oh," said Robin in a small voice. "At any rate, it's time we started looking for a secure place to camp and get some rest at before going on."

"Aye, and eat," added Arcie enthusiastically. Sam shook his head in amusement.

"If we keep you hungry long enough I think you'd eat that dragon raw and roaring, Arcie," he joked.

"I've had dragon before," mused Valerie to herself. "At my brother's wedding . . . It's kind of strong, but very good with cave-rose sauce and apples. We had his mother-in-law as a side dish."

They moved on again.

Arcie peeped his head into a large hall, spotting a small doorway at the far end. The room was full of rubble and wood, as well as what appeared to be the mortal remains of a good number of creatures. Old rusted armor hung from whitened bones, the etched remains of swords were gripped in bony fingers. Arcie warily walked into the room and up to one of the skeletons. Nothing happened. He kicked it. An arm snapped off and skittered across the room. He sighed in relief.

"What are you playing at, Arcie?" asked Sam, entering the room after him.

"Dead things . . . " explained Arcie. "My father told me . . . "

"Undead? Don't be stupid, half-pint. There haven't been any undead for ages. There's no power source for them, remember?" scoffed Sam, as the other three stepped cautiously into the room behind them. As the pale light of the wand reached into the darker corners of the room, there came a sound like a tumble of sticks and coins. The skeletons, long dead remains of reptile-men, rose to their taloned feet in clattering ranks, their sharp rotted teeth grinning with malice from beyond the grave.

* * *

"Well, Dusty, which way?" asked Tasmene. The White Tigers stood in the first main hall at the end of the entry tunnel in Putak-Azum. Three passages offered themselves: two winding away into the darkness and one leading up a stairway.

Dusty Corners, a small, sprightly Wilderkin, with long brown hair and bright blue eyes, peered about. He was a "locksmith," the term applied to those who had the somewhat suspicious talent of opening locks and defeating traps. Dusty was something of a black sheep among his people. He loved adventuring, and despite being a fierce fighter in a pinch, was quite frivolous—doubtless a side-effect of his companionship with humans. It was frivolity now that ruled him as he inspected the tracks in the dust on the floor.

It seemed to his quick brain that the tracks led more or less in the direction of the stairway . . . but when his party had been in here before, they had gone that way and found it just kind of wound up connecting with the other two passages after going through a lot of rooms. The other passage, however, led not only to where the other two would meet, but also past several areas he hadn't been able to explore thoroughly last time. Curiosity won over.

"This way!" he piped cheerfully and bounded down one of the tunnels. The rest followed, wielding torches of magical light provided by the mage Tesubar.

"I don't know if we should trust that Wilderkin and his maps," rasped the mage as he marched along, his glowing staff held in one hand. Tasmene turned around and eyed the mage in concern.

"Something the matter with your throat, my brother?" he asked in concern. "Don't tell me your cough is coming back . . . " Tesubar cleared his throat and looked embarrassed.

"Um, no. It's fine now," he said in his normal voice.

"That's good," muttered Thurbin. "You used to drive me half out of my skull with all your blasted rasping and coughing."

* * *

"Bleeding Tharzak," cursed Sam, drawing a dagger, then thinking better of it, swapping it for his shortsword.

"By Baris and Bella!" yelled Arcie in surprise, as he jumped back. He drew his morning star and swung wildly at one of the skeletons. The blow caught the leader of the reptile skeletons, shattering a kneecap. It fell on one knee, slashing at him with a broken sword and lashing its clattering tail.

"What's happening?" cried Robin, drawing his sword uncertainly. "Why are they attacking?!"

"Don't talk, fight!" grunted Sam, slashing at one of the rattling warriors. His blade clattered between the ribs without effect, and he ducked as the creature opened its long jaws in a silent warcry and swung at him with its rusty sword.

Valerie quickly began chanting a spell. Blackmail swiftly drew his huge sword and dealt a charging trio of the skeletons a blow with the flat of it that sent them scattering. A moment later, Valerie completed her spell, and a wave of crushing force lashed out, hurling several of the undead warriors against a wall. The others halted a moment, then attacked with renewed vigor as the sorceress stared at her fingertips in puzzlement.

"That spell should have disintegrated the bony bastards . . . what went wrong?" she hissed.

"Ha!" yelled Arcie, and swung his weapon again at the skeleton before him. "Bang thy head!" The heavy spiked ball crashed into the skull, shattering it and sending the rest of the bones clattering in unorganized attack. "Sam! You'll need a piece of wood, or something else blunt!"

Sam had other plans. He grabbed one of the skeletons by its ribcage and swept it off its feet, avoided its sword and lashing tail, swung it over his head, and hurled it through the air. It crashed into some of its fellows and they shattered and collapsed. He spun around in pain as one of them landed an awkward blow on his shoulder with its sword. He kicked it mightily in the sternum, sending it stumbling backward across the stone floor.

Robin, terrified, lashed about with his sword. The

blade seemed to have no effect upon the creatures, rattling harmlessly off the smooth bones.

"Use your hooves, idiot!" Valerie yelled. Robin shuddered at the thought, but then one of the skeletons made a mistake. Trying to grab at the centaur's arm, it instead wrenched the harp from his back and held it as though to smash it. Robin gave a squeal of pure rage, and turned into a whirling bronco. He reared and pawed, then turned and kicked. The skeletons shattered under his hoofblows like kindling, but still more kept coming even as he grabbed his harp and tucked it safely under his arm, panting with exertion.

Blackmail swept a swath clear with a blow from his sword. "Why are his sword working?" mused Arcie, from where he busily broke the ribs off another foe and dodged its rotting spear as best he could. *Och, sure it must be magical . . .*

"What's causing them?" roared Sam, flipping another one over his shoulder and smashing it against a wall. Valerie gasped in sudden realization.

"It must be my Darkportal amulet! They're drawing power from it!" she cried. One of them charged her, but the dark knight deftly interceded with the point of his sword, catching the creature through the reptilian pelvis, hurling it up into the air, and smashing it against the far wall with his incredible strength.

"Well do something!" whinnied Robin, squealing in pain as one scored a hit on his haunch. He reared up and stomped it through the shoulders.

Arcie had found that a swift smack to the vertebrae was the best way to deal with them; if you were lucky, the shock sent the whole rest of the skeleton tumbling down in disarray or at least in two halves. He leaped about in delight, sending bones flying, and ducked as Sam hurled another one over his head. Blackmail waded through them, defending Valerie and mowing the bones down like a harvestman.

"Nothing I can do!" replied Valerie. "We'll have to run for it!"

"No need!" yelled Arcie back. "We'll be taking care of

these!" He smashed through another, then darted about the floor, reducing the few still-thrashing bone torsos and legs into shards. Sam threw the lightweight figures into each other, and left the broken struggling bits to Robin's hooves and Arcie's morning star. Blackmail, swift, silent, and methodical, sent the bones shattering and cracking. Finally the last twitching fragment was ground to powder, and the room was silent save for the panting of the living.

"Whew!" said Arcie cheerfully, pulling out a blue handkerchief and mopping his brow. "What a grand mix-em-up!"

"I don't approve," muttered Sam, rubbing his hands off on his tunic; the rotten dead things had the chill of the grave about them. "Live things becoming dead, that I'm used to, not the other way around." His fingers felt frostbitten.

"Oh dear," Robin said, inspecting his hooves to make sure they weren't damaged. "I hope we don't have to do that again."

"Don't count on it, centaur," said Valerie with a sigh. "I think we're going to have to be extremely careful from now on."

"I don't suppose you'd leave that amulet behind?" asked Robin wistfully. Valerie clutched it firmly.

"You'd have to kill me first," she retorted coldly.

"Here, Arcie, I'm thirsty . . . got anything to drink?" asked Sam. "Especially since you stole my waterskin to fill up at that temple."

Arcie replied, "Sure enough," and went for his waterskin. "This is the stuff from the temple . . . " Sam waved it away.

"No, don't waste that. I'm fine, we may need it later. Anything else?"

"Aye, sure," replied the Barigan, handing him another waterskin offhandedly as he began poking about in the bones to see if there was anything worth stealing. Sam unplugged the skin and tilted his head back, pouring the liquid into his mouth and swallowing in great gulps. As he lowered the skin he smacked his lips thoughtfully. *Wait, that wasn't . . .*

"How are it?" Arcie asked, watching him. The assassin, having just downed perhaps three cups of Barigan whiskey, solemnly handed the skin back, turned around, and took almost three steps before he fell over.

Sam woke some time later and wished he hadn't. As he whimpered slightly, there was a too-loud scuffing sound near him, and Arcie's voice said, "Here, laddie, drink o' this."

Sam squeezed his face shut and muttered through clenched teeth, "I'm not going to drink anything, you poisoner."

"Och, pot and kettle, laddie. Trust me, drink it."

"No."

Something abruptly jumped on his stomach with heavy booted feet. As he opened his mouth to gasp a splash of cool water landed in it, and he had barely time to notice his gut-wrenching head-splitting hangover dissipating as his reflexes threw the Barigan across the room. Arcie landed on his feet, having expected the move, and looked hurt as Sam slowly sat up, shaking his head.

"Just a tad of Mula's magic cure-all," he told Sam. "There were no need to get so cross."

"My apologies then, Arcie." Sam looked around. They were in another room they had passed earlier, one with enough space for them all to rest comfortably. The others were preparing to move on, nodding a greeting to him. "How long have I been out?" Sam asked.

"A wee few hours," answered Arcie. "You fell over in yon hall . . ."

"I remember that," agreed Sam.

"And then ye got up, and started walking about on yer hands," continued Arcie cheerfully. "Ye showed us as ye could balance a dagger on yer nose, and ye almost went putting yer eye out. Ye got amain cross, and then started singing 'Pixie-Clover Wine' up and down the hall. Robin tried to settle ye, and ye went and tried to throw him over yer shoulder, and close almost gave yerself the muscle-wrench. Ye went at shouting about what ye were meaning to do to Mizzamir, then ye puked up all over the skeletons and ye passed out, so we went and dragged you back here."

Sam stared at Arcie. "You're joking!"

Arcie grinned through the smoke of his lit pipe. "Aye, yer right, I am. Ye was out perhaps four, say five hours. Ye snored, but 'tis all. We ourselfs ate and slept."

"That's more like it," said the assassin. "But I don't snore. Give me my birchwood throwing knife, Arcie."

The Barigan sighed and passed it over. Sam's diligent efforts had managed to get most of the Groink residue off, and it was once again a fine blade worth stealing. "Were hoping you wouldn't notice," he murmured. Sam managed a smile at his incorrigible old friend.

"When we get out of this, I'll buy you one of your own. Let's get started."

Sam munched a few dried rations for a breakfast and made a mental note to keep an eye out for a well or something else that might provide water for him to refill his empty waterskin.

The tunnels wound ever further into the depths of Putak-Azum. The band of villains walked on through the halls, wandering more or less aimlessly but ever seeking further upward passages that might take them to the dragon's lair. Here, further in, past where so many had gone before, the rooms and tunnels were in better condition, holding more of the glory of their former years.

In one room, a circular chamber, was a large round well or shaft. Arcie, curious, looked into it; it was empty, just a straight shaft extending into the depths. On a whim, he threw a pebble down it; the sound of the fragment bouncing and clattering its way down echoed so loudly that it prompted Valerie to shush him severely.

One room, with its door ajar, prompted a look-in; rows and rows of sarcophagi lay therein, many with the lids broken open and strange corpses in rotting garments lying within. Arcie was all for a bit of grave-robbing, but when they moved to step closer, eerie black shrouds of vapor seemed to coalesce about the tombs, hungrily searching for the stone at Valerie's neck. Unnerved, the party quickly backed out and slammed the door, then hastened with all speed away down the hall.

They then came onto a large eight-sided room, which was worked with frescoes so elaborate they had to stop and inspect them. The carvings took the form of a rich mural going all around the room, including the ceiling, and weaving over the arch of the door.

"What do you suppose this is?" wondered Sam, looking at the mural. There were knights and dragons and men on horseback, mountains and ships and cities.

"It seems to be a story-mural of some sort," replied Valerie. "Robin? Does any of this look familiar?"

The centaur shook his head. "No . . . This is all much older than anything I know of."

"Hmmph," sniffed Valerie. "A bard would know."

"What *is* a bard?" asked Robin, a little testily.

"It's hard to say . . . you'll have to ask Kaylana," replied the sorceress.

Meanwhile, Arcie had been discovering mechanisms in the stonework. He almost alerted the party, but then he realized the devices weren't traps. They just seemed to be sections of the mural that would sink down when pressed. Here a helmet, here a sheaf of grain, here a sword, here a section of hill; tiny chunks of the carving so intricately worked into the rest of the design that the lines of their borders were almost invisible. He pressed down a few in curiosity.

They sank with a faint clicking noise, but no secret panel opened, no chest of jewels spilled out from any concealed vaults. He pressed quite a few of them, then, discouraged, gave the border around the base a kick. The section his foot hit sank with a definite snap, and suddenly the mountain began to tremble.

"Tharzak's blades! Arcie, what did you do?!" yelled Sam, trying to keep his balance on the trembling floor.

"I didn't!" Arcie shouted back, as a sudden tremor knocked him on his back.

"Get out before the whole room caves in!" cried Valerie, suiting action to word. They ran after her and into a large hallway beyond.

Valerie ran five steps and a pit opened underneath her. She fell with a scream, her raven flapping and cawing. Robin, close behind, leaped over the pit and turned down into another passage, just as it tilted up at a steep angle and slid him down its length to deeper parts of the mountain, his hooves skidding on the stone. Sam came next, as a section of floor snapped up and shot him through the air to a chute that conveniently opened in one wall, closing behind him. Blackmail and Arcie, hastening out the doorway and looking at the confusion of moving stonework all around them, had barely time to exchange shocked looks when a spring in the floor catapulted the Barigan through a just-opened hole in the ceiling and a section of hallway abruptly elongated itself and engulfed the knight like a giant worm.

In another part of Putak-Azum, the White Tigers, just beginning to be ready for the day's hunting, felt the shaking.

"What is that?!" roared Tasmene.

"Someone must have triggered the Dwarven mechanic defenses of Putak-Azum!" yelled Thurbin the Northerman in surprise.

"Haha! This is fun!" cheered Dusty, as the room suddenly split like a pie. The triangular sections tilted upward and sent the heroes rolling to opening chutes in the walls.

"Blast Dwarven mechanics!" cursed Danathala the archer, as she and her pack went tumbling. They heard the mage Tesubar beginning a spell as he fell into the depths.

"Pheythar—"

"Arrgh!" bellowed the noble paladin, Sir Reginald, as he fell with a great clatter of plate-mail. Muffled cries marked the passage of the barbarian priestess Waterwind and the barbarian named Icecliff as they fell down a chute together.

"We shall die together, my beloved!"

"Yes, my darling of the snows!"

The moving stonework ground to a halt, finally, and all was silent in the rearranged vaults of Putak-Azum.

X

Sam fell for quite a long way. He hadn't lived to the age of thirty-some summers by not keeping a clear head, however. He dragged his heels on the chute, trying to slow his passage, grabbing with his hands at cracks that shot by too fast, and was just debating whether to risk ruining a dagger on stopping himself when he shot out of the chute, did a double back somersault in mid-air, and landed with a splash in an icy pool.

He surfaced, spluttering. It was pitch dark. His assassin's vision swiftly adapted; there was no light whatsoever to make distant shapes, but he could sense the air and the echoes . . . In the distance was the reflective echo of a wall. Trying not to think about what things might lurk in the dark water around him, he struck out for shore, swimming strongly.

Arcie shot up out of the hallway and immediately fell down another as it tilted swiftly. *Why didn't I see all these traps?* he cursed himself as he fell. *The whole damn place are a trap!*

Abruptly the hallway began to level off, and the Barigan's descent went from a plummet to a bounce to a tumble to a roll, at last letting him crumple to a stop against a wall. Arcie lay very still for a long moment. The air was cold, and smelled stale. He seemed to be alive. It was very dark. He could tell he was up against a wall, and there seemed to be floor underneath him, but other than that even his pride had to admit he was lost. Well, no sense lying about feeling sorry for yourself, he thought firmly, and got to his feet. Other than a few scratches and bruises he seemed to be all right. The others might scoff at his chubbiness, but a bit of padding was really sometimes the best friend a fellow could have.

A good smoke would be most welcome now, he decided, while he figured out his next move. He fumbled his tobacco things out blindly. After filling his pipe and getting it going, he tried to find something else that would burn long enough to make a suitable light. There didn't seem to be anything. With a shrug and a quick readjustment of his battered hat, he set off down the passageway he'd been dumped into.

Robin, skittering as he fell, had only one panicked thought. He gripped the bracelet and activated it. With a flux of power he found himself in the Diamond Tower once more . . .

Valerie muttered a quick spell as she saw she was approaching the bottom of the pit. A bubble of force caught and supported her and Nightshade, and they drifted down. The sorceress carefully avoided the two-foot long rusty spikes as she landed gently and looked around.

She seemed to be in the bottom of a ten-by-ten square pit. There were no exits to be seen by most, but Valerie was a Nathauan. Born in darkness, raised in darkness, in a world of underground passages and secret tunnels. As her large purple eyes widened, she noted the rough stonework, the barbs on the spikes, and a thin crack of a concealed doorway in one wall. At least the mountain seemed to have stopped shaking. She pushed on the door gently with a graceful hand, and smiled as it slid open with a faint grating noise.

Sir Reginald clattered to a halt on his armored rump, after a most unsporting tumble down a steep chute. He raised his visor, his long mustache twitching; it seemed to be dark. Well, that was easily remedied, certain. The paladin drew his great sword, the magical silver-worked blade Starstrike, and held it aloft with a word of command: *"Forte!"*

White light coruscated from the blade and filled the chamber with radiance. He lowered the blade and looked around. Abruptly there was the sound of a mailed footstep, and he turned to face it. A tall, dark figure, all armored in black plate-mail, stepped through a doorway at the far end of the chamber.

"What ho!" cried Sir Reginald. "The black knight of the villains! I challenge you to combat!" he roared, snapping his visor down. "Draw your sword!"

The dark knight drew a sword black as ebony, and raised a mailed fist in acceptance of the challenge. With a ringing clatter of metal, the two combatants charged each other.

Sam climbed out of the pool onto a slimy, pebbly beach. He couldn't see the water clearly, but he had tasted it, and it seemed fresh enough . . . he filled his waterskin. Hanging it on his belt, he looked around. There was the echo of a passageway there, and if he was not mistaken, there was a twinkle of light at the far end. He took off his sodden tunic and squidged down the hallway.

He at last stepped out into an open room and found he was not alone. He tensed. A female figure, holding a glowing magical torch that was the source of the light, turned to face him, and gasped.

Danathala, Dana for short, saw where there had been nothing before, a very interesting looking person. A man, about her age, maybe a bit younger, with wet blond hair. He was wearing black silk. Wet black silk, that clung in very interesting ways to a lean, strong body, with a broad muscular chest, nice legs and . . . she noted, as he gave a quick half-turn to check behind him, cute buns.

"Hey, handsome," she said, in her most charming voice, as the vision whipped out a dagger and assumed a ready stance, "Calm down . . . you're much too good looking to fight with. Let's chat for awhile instead, hmmm?"

Sam didn't much care for either the look in her eyes or the tone of her voice, but forced himself to think clearly. She did have a large sword, a magical torch, a bow, a quiver of arrows, and was standing in front of the only non-swimming exit. Maybe she knew the way out. He forced himself out of his alert crouch and managed a winning smile. The woman was attractive, though not a patch on Kaylana or Cata, with curly dark hair and predatory eyes. She had the set and tack of an archer or woodsman, but, fortunately, she didn't seem to be wearing Fenwick's colors . . . in fact, she was wearing normal brown leathers. Tasmene's companions, despite the name White Tigers, did not share his heraldic crest. But Sam didn't know this. What a lady archer was doing down in the depths of an abandoned mountain fortress, Sam also didn't know, but she might be useful.

"Well, all right," he purred. "Since the company is so attractive."

Tasmene and Fenwick can kill the rest, thought Dana smugly. *I'm going to* **keep** *this one.*

Dusty landed cheerfully on a pile of moss and jumped up.

"Wow! That was fun!" He looked back up the chute that had dumped him, wondering if it would be worthwhile to climb back up it and slide down again. He decided against it, after some thought, instead deciding to explore his surroundings. He trotted down a passageway, magic torch held high, long hair flapping.

The Wilderkin peeked into all the side passages he went by. Down one of them he thought he saw a flicker of movement. He hurriedly covered his torch. Far down the passage was a faint reddish glow and a faint smell of smoke reached the Wilderkin's sensitive nostrils.

"A dragon!" whispered Dusty to himself. "Maybe a big huge evil one! All sitting on a pile of coins and gems!" Keeping his torch snuffed, he scampered silently down the hall, almost panting in excitement.

He reached the reddish glow long before he should have. It hovered in the air just about five feet from him, on a level with his chin.

"That's odd," he muttered, and took out his torch. Light flared, illuminating and revealing the source of the red glow and the smell of smoke as a gray clay pipe held in the teeth of a person about the same size as himself. A very short little man, of older middle age and Barigan by his build, with wide blue eyes and a battered hat that he raised in greeting.

"Hullo!" said the Barigan.

"Hello!" replied Dusty. "Hey, I thought you were a dragon but I guess you aren't because you're a Barigan, right? I fell down a big tunnel when the floor opened up and everyone else fell down too but I don't know where they are now. Here, are you one of the villains?"

"Me?" replied the Barigan. "O'course not, laddie! What villains? I but live here."

"You live here?" asked Dusty in amazement.

"Aye, o'course. I'm from Bariga. Barigans live underground, you know *that* . . . "

"Oh yes!" replied Dusty hurriedly. "I always wondered about that, I mean, we Wilderkin live in trees mostly, at least the wild ones do, and they have foxdogs and things but I don't have one, I had a hamster for awhile but Tesubar made me get rid of it. He made me get rid of the sparrow too, and I had a goldfish for awhile but one day he was talking about doing a spell and then I couldn't find my goldfish so I guess he got rid of that too. My name's Dusty Corners, what's yours?" finished the Wilderkin happily, extending a small hand. Arcie took it and shook it in a friendly manner.

"Timlin Marzipan, at yer service," replied Arcie cheerfully. "So ye fell down a tunnel, then?"

"Oh yes, it was such fun! I fell and slid for soooo long, and then I fell out—boom!—onto this big pile of moss. I was going to climb back up but I didn't. We could go back there now and play on the slide; see, I drew a map so I'd know the way . . . " The Wilderkin briefly displayed a pen-and-ink sketch of tunnels drawn on a scrap of paper, over the words "Eggs, soap, bread, 2 spools white yarn," then continued: "Unless, of course, you have a better idea . . . "

"Och, I'm far too old to play on slides," chuckled the Barigan richly. "But I can teach you a new game, if you like."

"Really, Marzipan? A new game! Tell me tell me," enthused the Wilderkin, setting his torch down and sitting on the floor with the Barigan, who winked at him from a bright eye.

"O'course! Yon's a game my father taught me, and his father before him, and his before . . . "

"What's it called?" asked Dusty. The Barigan smiled, and reached into one of his pouches.

" 'Tis called, 'Riddles,' laddie," he replied mysteriously.

"Oh wonderful!" chirped Dusty. "Great! I know lots of riddles!"

"So do I," said Arcie, with a grin.

In another chamber, the two barbarians huddled together for warmth in the cold dampness of the dungeon. They had survived the fall quite well, and, there being no immediate danger present, were enjoying the time away from the eyes of their companions.

"I will never leave you, my skybird."

"I love you forever, my frost-eagle."

Valerie marched softly down the tunnel. She came to a large open room, and started across it . . . then broke into a run as hideous deformed creatures, like walking corpses, rose up from the piles of rubble and shambled in pursuit of her and the amulet she wore.

Tesubar stomped along a corridor crossly. He hated it when this happened. Dumped unceremoniously down tunnels and left to find one's own way out. Well, he wasn't going to stand for it. He was a mage, by the Pentacles, and he wasn't going to stand for it. He was going to teleport back to clearer ground. He stopped, raised his arms, and began to chant.

"*Alau kubrek tsthiran malesta feiana* . . . Oooof!" he

finished as something crashed into him from behind. Valerie, looking over her shoulder to check on the progress of the undead, suddenly ran into the blue-robed mage. A flood of magic whirled around the two of them and shot them through inter-dimensional space. The fiends collapsed into inertness as their power source fled.

The two magic-users materialized in another room that Valerie didn't recognize. They sprang apart and faced each other. Tesubar knew a dark sorceress when he saw one. Valerie was keyed-up enough to blast anything that moved. The two began chanting simultaneously, finishing on almost the same breath.

A wave of frost leapt from the black fingernails of the Nathauan into a sheet of flame generated by the human mage. Steam hissed, and the two combatants, unharmed, glared at each other an instant, then tried again. Words of magic rang through the air. Then two blots of power flashed and bounced across the room in sizzling smoke. One section of wall turned into a small startled chicken, and a large chunk of the opposite wall shattered into gravel. They tried again. And again.

Steel rang on steel as the two armored knights circled each other, raining blows. Sir Reginald found himself sweating mightily inside his armor. This dark fellow was incredibly skilled, parrying most of the paladin's blows easily with sword and shield. It was all Reginald could do to defend himself equally. They circled the floor, weapons crashing and clanging, the bright-burning blade of the paladin sparking against the deep black sword of the dark knight.

With a sudden blow, Reginald found himself disarmed. The black sword knocked Starstrike from his hands, sending it skittering across the rubble-strewn room. *Oh blast,* he thought, and grabbed for his secondary weapon, a heavy mace. It was gone. *I must have dropped it in the fall!* he thought distractedly. *I'm in for it now . . .*

But the knight stopped his attack and backed off, motioning to the sword. Sir Reginald stood up in surprise.

"By the Shield! You follow the Code! A dark villain like yourself follows the lawful Code . . . This is odd," he said, half to the knight and half to himself, as he wonderingly went over to retrieve his still-shining sword. He picked it up, and turned to the knight. "I would know the name of such a man who would do this, sir!" he called.

The knight made no sound. "Ha! Snub me, will you?" roared Sir Reginald and charged back into the fray, blows once more ringing through the hall.

"So," asked Sam, "what's a nice girl like you doing in a dungeon like this?" He smiled his most charming smile and got a coy look in return.

"Well, I think we're looking for you and your friends," Dana purred, her hand on his thigh. Sam carefully put an arm around her waist, and she snuggled against him.

"You've caught me," he said. "But I don't know where the rest of my group are, and I've seen no signs of yours . . . do you know the way out of here?"

"No," replied the lady, running her hands over his body through the black silk. "And I certainly hope they don't show up anytime soon." She looked into his eyes seductively.

Dana had both the self-confidence to be certain she could handle (in more ways than one) this good-looking assassin and the ego to feel that that was all men were for anyway. She gripped the man tightly and smothered his lips in a kiss so passionate she didn't even notice the stab of a tiny needle run through her elbow. Her consciousness dissolved in a warm pink mist.

Sam caught his breath and disentangled himself from the lady archer's powerful embrace, letting her slump gently to the floor. He scooped up Dana's dropped torch and hastened away, not stealing anything else from her out of force of habit. He walked quickly through the tunnels, looking for his companions or a way out . . . she'd be waking up in a few hours, and he wasn't looking forward to encountering her again.

* * *

"All right, I've got another one, I've got another one," enthused Dusty. "Here, match this," he said, digging around in his pocket and hauling out a small sapphire. Arcie appraised it thoughtfully, then took out of his own pouch an incredibly garish belt buckle, etched in bronze with dragons and pegusi. The Wilderkin's eyes widened in admiration. They put the stakes on the floor between them, and the Wilderkin closed his eyes to think better, and recited:

Never have I been seen before
Soon never to be seen a-more
A rainbow caught in a dome of sky
In air I am born, to air I die.

"Hmm, tricky," admitted Arcie, rubbing his chin in thought.

"You'll never guess it," chirped Dusty gleefully. Arcie thought for a long moment, his auburn-and-silver eyebrows knitting, then snapped his fingers in delight.

"Pop! Soap bubbles!" he exclaimed. The Wilderkin laughed in admiration.

"That's right! You're good at this!" he said with a grin, pushing the stakes over to Arcie's side. "Your turn again."

"Och aye," Arcie replied, and lapsed into thought. "Well enough, I have got one." He put the belt buckle back into the stakes, and the Wilderkin thought for a moment, then put one of his embroidered cloth pouches in. Arcie nodded and sat back. He raised a hand for emphasis, and recited:

Wizards and warriors, dragons and kings
Flying forever on vast midnight wings
Larger than worlds beyond mankind's sight
Yet small as a pinprick that lets in the light.

"Wow, that's a hard one too," commented Dusty, twirling a strand of his long hair as he mused. "Hm, let's see, large, small, forever . . . "

" 'Tis really quite easy," apologized Arcie.

"Don't tell me, don't tell me!" squeaked Dusty. "I'm thinking . . . I've almost . . . Ha! Constellations, right, Marzipan?" He grinned at the Barigan confidently.

Arcie nodded with a wide-eyed smile. "And so it is! You've really now got the way of it!"

"My turn again!"

In another room, many tunnels away, two magic users faced each other. Frost and soot covered the walls. Several patches of dissipating noxious gases drifted about in the corners. A few uneasy newts padded about on the floor. A large chunk of ceiling had fallen in. A huge block of stone stood in one corner, and a wall of ice was melting on its side on the floor. Purple goo dripped from one wall, and the battered remains of a few magically summoned creatures littered the room.

"Well," said Tesubar after a moment. "I am about done. How about you?"

"Quite," replied Valerie. "The only spell I have left is False Magical Aura."

"I've got Wizard's Logo," offered Tesubar. They looked at each other.

"All right then," said Valerie, and hoarse voices changed, tired hands traced patterns in the air. Valerie caused a perfectly normal tile of the floor to show as magical to those with the sight to see it, and Tesubar left a runic "T_r" etched in soft magical letters on the wall near him. The two mages inspected each other's work, and nodded to each other politely. Then they turned around and walked away in opposite directions down the halls of Putak-Azum.

Elsewhere, the clatter and crash of armor and sword was drawing to a close. Sir Reginald had fought long and hard, but the great black knight seemed tireless, beating him back, blow for blow. He feared not death at the hands of this creature, but dishonor should the knight defeat him and leave him alive to face the humiliation.

His fierce chivalric pride roared in his heart, and he attacked with renewed vigor, battling the dark knight around the room.

The villain countered with blows and defended himself with his magical shield against the flashing sword, and Sir Reginald uttered a silent prayer to the Hero of all paladins, the great Hero Sir Pryse who had defeated so many of the dark forces in the War at the risk of his own life. *Save me from dishonor!* he thought.

Strength flowed through his arm, and he struck a mighty blow across the other knight's breastplate. The dark figure staggered backward a step, backing heavily into a corner . . . and the whole corner flipped open into a dark chasm. With a great clattering, the silent knight slid down into the darkness as Sir Reginald slashed triumphantly at the air where he had been.

"Ha! Coward!" he roared. "Come back and fight, you spawn of darkness! Come back and fight!" The trap slid shut as swiftly as it had opened, and Sir Reginald, flushed with success, flipped up his faceplate and sat down, panting for breath. As he sat there, thinking on his victory and murmuring prayers of thanks to his deities, soft footsteps made him look up, gripping his sword in apprehension. But it was only the blue-robed mage Tesubar, who looked mildly surprised to see him.

Sam ducked into a side tunnel as he heard loud footsteps approaching. A quick glance soon allayed his fears though, and he stepped out to greet Blackmail as the knight wandered down the hallway. "Ho there, Blackmail," he said. "Where have you been?" The mailed shoulders shrugged. Sam noticed that the dark armor had a number of scratches and here and there a dent or two. "Hey, big guy, you look kind of scuffed . . . get in a fight?"

The helmet nodded. Sam grinned. It must have been someone either very strong, or wielding something magical, to have damaged that dark armor. "Did you win?" The black gauntlet waggled in a non-committal sort of way. "Was it somebody from a bunch of adventurers out looking for us?" he asked. The helmet seemed to think for a moment, then nodded. Sam nodded also. "Yeah, I met one too. A lady . . . well, a woman, at any rate. Seen any signs of the others?" The helmet shook no. "Well, let's go look for them, then." They set off down the hall.

"Well, that was a lot of fun," enthused Dusty, collecting his treasures and getting to his feet. "I'll have to teach that to Thurbin and Tasmene and the others," he added.

"Well, 'twas certainly fine meeting ye, Dusty," replied Arcie with a smile, getting up and shaking the Wilderkin by the hand. "If you ever find yourself down in Putak-Azum again, stop yourself by an' have a cuppa tea."

"Why, thank you, Marzipan," answered Dusty happily, "I will!"

"And o'course feel free to bring your friends," added Arcie. "Sure you can find the ways back well enough?"

"Oh sure," answered Dusty confidently. "I've got all the maps."

"Well, good luck to you, then," said Arcie, as the Wilderkin began bouncing back up the hallway.

The Wilderkin, with his spare torch held aloft, vanished into the tunnels. Arcie had the other torch, as well as a good number of small precious stones. The Wilderkin had swapped them in stakes for a lot of near-worthless items Arcie had been carrying around. They were both quite happy with the trade, and Arcie had even snagged one of Dusty's pouches. He laughed to himself, chuckling in the dim tunnels of Putak-Azum. He turned and wandered down the halls, until he heard a faint cawing noise. Quickly hurrying to the spot, he found Valerie sitting against a wall, feeding her raven.

"Well, took you long enough," she greeted. "Where have you been?"

"Playing at riddles with a Wilderkin," answered Arcie. "And yourself?"

"Spellfighting with a very nice young man in blue robes. Do you have a bit of cord, Barigan? I used the last scrap for one of my spell components, and I want some to have in case I need to cast that spell again," she explained.

"Cord? Aye, I've some right in here, in the pouch with my repair kit and . . . um . . . " Arcie fumbled around. "Here! My pouch are gone!" Arcie slapped at the place where his pouch had hung, eyes wide in surprise. "That Wilderkin . . . "

"Oh well, never mind . . . " began Valerie, then frowned. "What are you laughing at, Barigan?"

Sam and Blackmail walked down the halls, looking about. The strange confusing tunnels seemed to go on forever. Suddenly the assassin saw something out of the corner of his eye and motioned to Blackmail to hide, snuffing his magical torch as he did so. The knight ducked into a side passage and pulled the assassin in after him.

Another torch like the one he held was coming down the hallway. Assassin and knight waited in silence as the torchlight drew closer, and soon voices could be heard.

"And I were thinking you said the magic could find the ways out," said a familiar voice with just a trace of skepticism. Another familiar voice, colder, answered haughtily,

"It could have, if you hadn't completely rearranged the entire complex with your bungling."

"Here! Arcie! Valerie!" called Sam, stepping out of hiding with his torch. The other two started in surprise. "Great to see you again! I've found Blackmail . . . any sign of that idiot centaur or any dragons or Druids?" he asked.

"Nae luck," reported Arcie. "I did find a Wilderkin though. He knew some fair good riddles, too. Bet you canna get this, Sammy my lad, it goes—"

"Not now, Arcie. Those goodys are still crawling around here somewhere. We've got to put some distance between us and them."

"Very true," agreed Valerie. "And as soon as we have, I've got to recover my power."

They set off together down the halls.

About an hour later, they stopped to rest.

"Yon place is fair regular maze!" gasped Arcie, sitting down on a stairstep.

"Wait until we enter the Labyrinth, Barigan," retorted Valerie ominously. Sam looked around, but saw no indication of any way to go other than further corridors. Even Blackmail seemed to be getting tired. His great shoulders gave a sigh, and he leaned back against a wall . . . and fell through it with a clatter. The others stared.

"Baris and Bella! An illusory secret door!" gasped Arcie in surprise.

"Come on, let's go after him," suggested Sam, and they quickly hurried through the section of wall.

A few minutes later, the sound of voices drifted into the room. The White Tigers, all together once more, walked past, comparing notes.

"You say you fought with a black sorceress?" asked Lord Tasmene of his brother. Tesubar nodded. "And she got away?" Tesubar scowled.

"I fought her with all my powers, to my last atom of energy, to my last spell . . . but she was most foul and devious and escaped," he rasped.

"You're rasping again," complained Thurbin.

"I've been chanting all afternoon, Northerman," retorted the blue-robed mage.

Dusty had found the pair of barbarians curled up in each others arms and had woken them with a shrill blast on his shiny new whistle won from that nice Marzipan. The two lovers were now back into public behavior mode, pretending to be aloof from one another. Later he'd found Dana and Thurbin, the lady archer looking rather woozy and cross, and neither of them seemed to want to hear his newly learned riddles, so he was trying them out on the two brothers as they walked down the hall arguing.

"Hear, hear, Tesubar, I've got a riddle . . . why is a raven like a writing desk?"

His cheerful voice and the mage's snarled reply drifted away into the dark tunnels as the heroes moved on.

* * *

The rooms the villains were traversing now were far different than those they had walked before. Whereas the previous tunnels, halls, and chambers had shown signs of much looting and combat, these seemed to still have much of the grandeur and glory that had once graced them. Carvings and murals decorated the walls, mosaics still showed through the dust of the floor.

"Will you gander at this place!" enthused Arcie, holding his torch aloft and looking about in delight. "Now *this* are real adventuring!" They were walking through what must at one time have been a great hall, with a great pavilion at one end and a huge arc-shaped open fireplace at the other. A great stone table spanned the length of the room. Thick cobwebs hung in the shadows of the arched ceiling and its buttresses.

"Careful, Arcie," warned Sam, as the Barigan hopped up onto the table and ran its length. "This is the kind of place where people get attacked without warning."

"I know what I'm about, blondie!" the Barigan assured him. He hopped down off the table at the far end and padded over to the fireplace, looked up the chimney, and a large hairy spider fell on him.

"Eeeyuk!" he yelled, shaking it off in a panic and then bashing it repeatedly with his morning star as it attempted to scurry away. Sam snickered.

"If you two are *quite* done playing around," interrupted Valerie coolly, "May I suggest we find a place to camp?"

"Aye, aye, right enough," answered Arcie with a shudder, rubbing his face. He came out of the treacherous fireplace and led the way down into the ancient glories of Putak-Azum.

"This must be stuff left over from about the time of the War," mused Sam, touching a rotting tapestry that hung on one wall. It puffed into dust.

"That could be," agreed Valerie. "The Heroes probably weren't interested in looting the place, and though it could be some other people have come through here since, either they didn't do much or they didn't get very far."

"And such would be depending upon the presence of unpleasant monsters as roam the halls and eats unwary adventurers, eh?" added Arcie a bit nervously.

"Well, just be wary, then," said Sam.

They found a large room that might once have served as a mage's study. There were shelves with old, moldering non-magical books, and a lot of glassware, jars of antiquated spell components, and the remains of a stuffed alligator hanging from the ceiling. Best of all, it had a secure door.

"We can camp here," insisted Valerie. "I can see if some of these spell components are useful, and look through those books for a map or something. The rest of you can loot the place or whatever you want."

"Aye, well enough," agreed Arcie. "Me, I'm going to eat." He sat down and pulled out his rations.

"I'll scout around and make sure there aren't any nasty monsters in the general vicinity," offered Sam, walking back out the door. He was feeling restless, uneasy. "If you hear me screaming, run away," he advised.

"You never scream, Sam," corrected the Barigan, his mouth full. Sam smiled.

"That's why you'd run away. You want to come along, knight?" he asked Blackmail. The knight gave a nod and followed him as he walked out the door.

They searched the surrounding rooms. One appeared to be a sitting room of some sort, with another fireplace; Sam wondered where it led to, but decided not to stick his head up it. Another was a bathroom, dry and empty but with a sunken pool in the floor and tilework over all the surfaces.

The last room was a bedchamber of sorts. There was a large old full length mirror on one wall, rimmed in patina brass and set flush with the wall. Sam, like many assassins, had a bit of a fondness for his appearance, and looked at himself in this mirror. His scruffiness disgruntled him slightly; he adjusted his collar and cloak and felt a bit better. He looked about the room again.

A small desk and chair stood in one corner. Here, the furniture was well-preserved by the cold, dry air of the fortress. Small things scuttled away from the light of the magical torch. A large bed sat in another corner, with a chest nearby; Sam investigated it, but the lock was open and the container held nothing more than a carefully folded set of robes and a wizard's pointy hat of a sort that had been out of style for centuries. In a spark of whimsey, Sam picked up the hat. It was conical, blue satin stitched with moons and stars, and empty. He showed it to Blackmail, who nodded politely. Sam put the hat on. It fitted pretty well, except for his ears, which stuck out slightly. He went to check himself in the mirror. Well, how about that, he looked ridiculous. Playfully he struck a wizardly pose, and cackled at his reflection:

Mirror, Mirror, on the wall,
Bronze is green and glass is clear,
Mirror, Mirror, hear my call
And show me Arch-Mage Mizzamir!

Sam jumped as his reflection suddenly vanished in a swirl of cloud within the mirror. He and Blackmail stared in mute astonishment as the image suddenly cleared, showing a blurred picture of the inside of a white room. Within that image Sam saw Mizzamir, in all his resplendent whiteness. Although no sound filtered through the glass, Mizzamir was obviously in deep discussion with a familiar gray centaur, who was bowing and scraping with all the respect and admiration in the world.

The image vanished. He and Blackmail stared silently at each other a long moment, then they raced out and back to the study where they had left Arcie and Valerie.

"Robin's a spy!" panted Sam, bursting into the room. "We saw him on a magic mirror! He's talking to Mizzamir right now!"

"Sam, laddie . . . " said Arcie, shaking his head, "I were thinking you said you were going to lay off the booze."

"Dammit, Arcie, I'm serious and sober!"

"Then why the blazes are you wearing that stupid hat?" retorted the Barigan. Sam reached up, discovering to his chagrin he was indeed still topped by the ridiculous headgear. He ripped it off his head and threw it on the ground. It rolled in a small circle. Valerie, meanwhile, had turned to Blackmail.

"Knight, is what this assassin says true?" she asked, raising an elegant eyebrow. The helmet nodded solemnly. Valerie picked up the hat and rolled it thoughtfully in her hands.

"Show me this mirror," she commanded.

Soon they were standing back in front of the mirror, which, through Valerie's careful magical ministrations, gave a clear picture of the conversation between the archmage and centaur, as well as a fragment of sound, distorted over distance.

Valerie gave a final invoking wave to the mirror, and the image stabilized.

"That's as clear as I can get it without risking that white-robe's attention," she said. The four villains watched and listened to the conversation in the mirror's depths.

"And I know not where they are now," the centaur was finishing, "but the last Segment, I believe, is still their goal. Assuming they get out of Putak-Azum, whether they rescue the Druid or not, I think that's where they'll head . . . wherever it is."

"Very good," Mizzamir said, nodding his head. "Well, keep up the good work, then." Robin looked startled.

"You mean I can't quit now?" he quavered. Mizzamir shook his head.

"No, Robin of Avensdale. Your work is proving far too valuable. Besides, I still need a Segment! It is very, very possible they will not survive long in Putak-Azum, in which case we will be spared the trouble of confronting them. And, as you know, it is not so far a remote contingency that the villains will turn instead to another goal, or that they have other, deeper plans that they may not have told you. So return, Robin, and continue your heroic mission."

The centaur sighed, his equine sides and human chest heaving in unison. "Yes, Arch-Mage Mizzamir."

Valerie dismissed the image with a wave of her hand. The company exchanged glances.

"Can we kill him now?" asked Arcie angrily.

"I could use a bit of fresh meat," agreed Valerie.

"Wait a minute," broke in Sam. "I've got an idea."

"Enough with ideas, Sammy," said Arcie. "Let's us just be sharpening up our weapons, aye?"

"No, really. Look, the problem now is Mizzamir knows where we're going, right? We know that, but neither Robin nor he knows that we know, so if we were to tell him something new, a change in plans, for example, and he tells Mizzamir, then they won't know any better, get it?"

"I think that yon pointy hat squeezeled yer brains a bit, old chum," answered Arcie doubtfully, but Valerie nodded.

"I see what you're saying," she said. "We give them a red herring, let Robin report it, then snuff the centaur and Mizzamir won't have any further news to go on. He'll be confused, at least."

"Yes, close enough," answered Sam. "What shall we tell him, then?"

" 'Tis an opportunity for some supreme lying," said Arcie gleefully. "Let's us make it a right doozy."

Robin appeared in a hallway of Putak-Azum. He had no idea where the others were, or even where he was for that matter . . . Mizzamir had been able to send him back to a safe open area in the tunnels, dredged from his memory of the time he himself had walked those halls during the War. "If you do not find them after a few hours," he had said, "return, and I shall send you to another area."

Robin still had his glowing wand to light his way, and Valerie's magic necklace to keep the walls from crushing him, so he managed to keep a fairly brave pair of hearts (like all centaurs, he had two hearts and four lungs) as he trotted down the halls.

He was just negotiating a flight of stairs when a voice spoke out of the shadows, "Here, Robin!"

Robin shied, then recovered himself when he saw it was only Sam waiting at the top of the stairs.

"Oh, it's you," the minstrel gasped thankfully, his ears flicking. "My hooves, I've been looking all over for you . . . where are the others?"

"Waiting for you," answered Sam in a voice so pleasant that the centaur felt a faint prickle of unease ripple across his hide. "We've been finding out a few things about this place and were just waiting for you to turn up. I was sent to look for you."

"Oh, thanks," replied Robin. "Where do we go, then?"

"Ah, follow me, minstrel," answered the assassin with an oily smile.

He led the centaur up the rest of the stairs and into another hall. They wound through a number of galleries and rooms until Sam finally walked directly into a wall and vanished with a faint shimmer. Robin balked. After a moment Sam stuck his head out through the wall with another shimmer. He looked annoyed.

"Come on, ponyboy, it's perfectly safe," he snapped. The head vanished again, and Robin, ears up in caution, stepped carefully to the wall. He extended a hand, touched it; his hand passed through the brown stone as though it was not there. It isn't there, he told himself firmly. I just saw Sam walk through it. Nervously, feeling his way with his forehooves, he stepped through, to find himself in a room with the assassin waiting impatiently. He looked behind him quickly as the assassin led on; the way he had come looked like another blank wall.

"We're going in circles, dammit," cursed Thurbin, as they wandered into another room. "I swear by the bones of Rockhead we've been here before."

"No, we haven't," corrected Dusty cheerfully, holding up a map. "We were in a room *like* this, but that one had just a bunch of footprints in the dust. This room has footprints *and hoofprints.* See? They go right up to that wall there," he added, pointing.

"Right up to the . . . " began Dana in surprise. Tesubar hurried forward and examined the wall. He reached out to touch it, and his hand moved through the solid stone with a faint shimmer.

"It's an illusion!" he gasped. "A passageway!"

"They must have gone that way!" cried Tasmene, gripping his sword.

"Well then, let's follow, what?" answered Sir Reginald boldly, and he started for the wall. Lord Tasmene gripped him by his armored arm and held him back.

"No, good sir knight," he said firmly. "We have done much today, and my brother is weakened from his spell-casting. We will rest and recover, and then follow. After all, some of Fenwick's finest men now guard the only exit of Putak-Azum."

Sir Reginald sighed. "Very well . . . But *I* shall guard this passage so that the villains do not sneak up upon us and cut our throats as we rest!" he asserted. He sat back against the solid part of the wall, and the others went about setting up camp in the room.

"The great forgotten Fangclaw Army of Darkness?" asked Robin doubtfully, as he sat with the others in the ancient alchemical lab. Valerie nodded solemnly.

"When Light began to grow in power, many of the forces of Darkness hid in the depths of the very mountain we now sit in. Like clockwork unwound, they gradually fell into stasis . . . but they are still there. Ice trolls and goblins and demons, vampires and demons, even a number of the great evil dragons . . . "

"Like Kazikuckla?" asked Robin, eyes wide in fear.

"Kazikuckla would be a mere lizard compared to these wyrms. In addition, the war machines of the great Dark Lord, and his mighty armies of lizard-men and evil warriors. All lie in slumber, waiting for the night when I bring *this.*" Valerie touched her amulet with her jet fingernails. Nightshade croaked softly.

"But how . . . ?" began Robin.

"Robin, you remember when those reptile-men skeletons attacked us, right?" interrupted Sam. "Valerie's a Nathauan . . . they know about things of darkness way down in the earth."

"The shark bitch 'as been leading us the way all along," muttered Arcie, his voice resentful. "She were just waiting for Sam to be *stupid* enough to give her back the amulet . . . "

"You shut up!" barked Sam crossly. Arcie glared at him and went on, "And all the pretending to have but weak magic were just a front . . . she's prolly about so powerful as, say, Mizzamir."

"And now you must all do as I say," purred Valerie evilly. "With my amulet, I can destroy you all. Your lives hang by a thread, and I hold the shears." Her teeth flashed in the dim light, deadly sharp points. "Especially you, centaur . . . You've been gaining weight, haven't you? That's nice . . . I'll have enough for breakfast, should you cross me." Robin gulped, his ears quivering in terror.

"Now then," said the sorceress, "there will be no more talk of rescuing that blasted Druid. We rest now, but tomorrow we plunge straight down into the bowels of Putak-Azum, to wake the sleeping armies. If you behave, I may keep the forces of darkness from ripping you to bloody shreds." Her teeth flashed again, and the companions moved off into various corners to settle down to rest. Nightshade watched with a beady eye from his mistress's shoulder as Robin pretended to sleep. As soon as the centaur judged everyone else had fallen into slumber, he rose as swiftly and as silently as he could. He looked closely; even Blackmail was still, and looking the other way. Was this the time to steal one of the Segments? But he couldn't begin to guess where to look, and to try fumbling around in the villains' pockets would be suicide . . . He would make his report now, and hope that Mizzamir would find that sufficient.

He left the room as quietly as possible, not noticing the smiles in the darkness behind him as he left.

* * *

"Slumbering forces, eh?" asked Mizzamir, rubbing his hairless Elven chin. Robin nodded.

"You can't send me back there . . . That sorceress wants to eat me!" he whinnied. Mizzamir patted him gently on the shoulder.

"Don't worry, Robin . . . the bracelet will get you out of there just ahead of one of her spells. And think of what a song it will make!" he said, cajolingly. Robin looked doubtful, as Mizzamir paced the floor of the Tower. The stained-glass window was gone, not yet replaced, and a warm breeze blew in, scented with jasmine.

"H'mm, that is a difficulty . . . I've not heard of slumbering forces in Putak-Azum before, but I'm sure if there are any, that's likely where they would be . . . and no one would be more likely to know than a Nathauan. Well, you must keep us informed of further developments, Robin."

The renegades, watching in the magic mirror, nodded to themselves. Without the power of his scrying font, Mizzamir could not notice the faint prickle of another scrying power watching him in his preoccupied state. They quickly hurried back to be looking innocent when Robin returned . . . except for Sam, who lingered by the mirror, which had dulled into stillness again.

He stepped up to it, a bit fearful of what it might show, and whispered:

"Mirror, Mirror, on the wall,
Where's the last Druid of them all?"

The mirror swirled in smoke, then finally cleared to show Kaylana, apparently chained to a stone wall. Her face was pale, her eyes closed, her form still. Asleep? Or dead? He couldn't say . . . but in the image was a vague flickering light, a pulsing orangeness that seemed to ebb and flow like huge breathing—dragonfire.

Sam stood in the dim room a long moment, gazing at

the graceful lines of that still face, the soft lips, the rich coppery hair falling in soft waves over the shoulders, until the image faded.

"Be you following, Sam?" asked Arcie, sticking his head back in the room.

Sam shook his head and sighed. "Yes, be right there," he answered and plodded out of the room softly.

Robin showed up in the room a few minutes after they had all gotten settled again. They pretended not to notice his absence, and he settled down sleepily. But when the centaur at last drifted into slumber, small Barigan fingers gently slid the silver and gemstone bracelet off his wrist. A deft hand pried loose the two pale blue stones, and they popped out with a shower of pale sparks as the magic was canceled. A moment's quiet tinkering, then two other stones, pale lime-green stones, won from a Wilderkin's purse, were pressed in the empty sockets, the tiny silver prongs bent to hold them in place. Then the bracelet was returned with utmost care to the sleeping centaur's wrist.

"Sure he willna notice?" whispered Arcie, as he gently set Robin's limp arm back down.

Sam shook his head. "Centaurs are colorblind to blue and green. He won't notice until he tries to use it. Let's get some sleep."

They curled up as best they could on the dusty-carpeted floor, and allowed the aches of travel to slip from their bodies. Blackmail's dark unmoving figure sat in a corner and watched over them silently.

After about eight hours they were up and moving again. As they wandered down a hallway Arcie spotted a small niche in the wall. Set into the niche was a largish wooden chest, bound in brass, with a large lock.

"Here!" he paused, stopping at it. "Look on this!"

"We're not here to loot the place, Barigan," snapped Valerie sharply. Arcie looked defiant.

"But perhaps it are full o' gold, or muchly powerful magical items . . . " he pleaded, moving over to it. Sam's eyes widened. Was the chest quivering slightly? His danger sense tingled faintly.

" . . . just a wee quick look," the Barigan went on, reaching for the lock.

"Arcie! Look out!" cried Sam, too late, as the chest suddenly snapped open and leaped out of its niche, snapping like a giant clam around the Barigan's head and torso. Arcie's booted feet kicked outside in panic as the companions rushed to his aid.

Sam drew his dagger, and jumped ahead of Blackmail and Robin as they drew their swords. "Stop, you two! You want to cut him in half!?" he snapped.

"An Aydaptor!" breathed Valerie. "Well, I can handle that. Move, assassin," she commanded. Sam backed to one side as Valerie began to chant. Ending on a final word, she made as if to fling an invisible object at the rocking chest, with its lid chomping down on the thief. The results were dramatic.

"Ptoo!" the creature spat, and Arcie tumbled out onto the floor, gasping for breath. Sam raised his dagger to strike the quivering creature, but Valerie called, "Don't waste your blade, assassin, those creatures have blood like acid."

The Aydaptor meanwhile had dissolved into an amorphous sort of blob, its color changing to blend perfectly with the stonework. It was making an odd thrumming noise, like a lute, Robin thought, and they were suddenly startled to hear the humming form into words.

"Ooowow! No more, stop it, stop it!" it whirred, in a slightly petulant tone. "A poor Aydaptor has a hard enough time as it is, trying to find rats and bats enough to eat, without people running up and down throwing spells at it, and dragons stomping all over the place and . . . "

"Dragons?" broke in Sam, staring at the creature. It formed a trio of large, multifaceted eyes and peered at him. "You've seen a dragon?"

"Well of course, I see just about anything," it purred, growing another eye. Its texture changed to that of soft cloth, so that it looked like an old velvet robe crumpled on the floor, with rainbow-faceted eyes watching from its folds. "I see you, certainly, you scruffy human."

"Where be the dragon?" asked Arcie. One of the eyes turned to look at him.

"Well now, well now, so you want to know, eh, morsel? I'll tell you if you feed me."

"I'll not!" Arcie backed off. The blob burbled and formed itself into a perfect cube.

"We've got a centaur here . . . " began Sam, and the cube shuddered and turned its texture to that of sand.

"Ugh, no thanks. Horsemeat gives me a bellyache."

"Well you can't eat any of the rest of us," argued Sam.

"I'll take the kind of dull dead food you people eat, if that's all you have," and a slot appeared in its "lid." It shifted into a globe shape. "Then I'll tell you where the dragon is. Fair enough?"

Sam looked at Valerie. The sorceress sighed. "Go ahead, fool sunlander, if you must. My magic will work as well a second time if it double-crosses us."

Sam dug a day's worth of beef jerky out of his pouch, and gingerly dropped it into the proffered slot. There were the sounds of munching, then a belch.

"Straight on, third left, fourth right, up the staircase and through the second door by the wall-fountain. Can't miss it," it hiccuped, and turned into a small pile of gold coins. Arcie looked at it wistfully, but the eyes were still watching from the faces of the coins.

"All right," said Valerie. "Come on."

"We're going to find the dragon?" asked Robin uncertainly. "But I thought you said . . . "

"Shut up, centaur," growled Valerie.

It was not long (all too soon for some) before they found themselves huddled in a narrow hallway that was nothing more than a gash in the rock. It narrowed down to a space that Robin, by dropping onto his knees and wriggling, could possibly just make it through. And on the other side, through the small opening, gleamed a red-gold light—dragonfire.

Arcie and Sam, self-appointed scouts, scrambled up the tunnel to peer into the room beyond. Robin, decidedly ill at ease in the change in attitude of the group, tried to back down the passage, hoping to make a report to Mizzamir. "I'll just go guard the rear, shall I?" he began, and backed into the shield of the silent knight. He looked over his shoulder, saw Blackmail standing there with his hand on the pommel of his sword, and heard Valerie speak.

"No, why don't you just stay here with us, dearie?" she hissed softly. Robin froze, trembling.

Meanwhile, two faces peered out from a dark crack into a huge open cavern. The air was thick and musty with the smell of dragon, both the fresh scent of the huge rose-gold that rested among the rocks, and the ancient slow reek that harkened back to the days when black Kazikuckla had tortured her kills to death in the cavern.

Lumathix lay curled up with his tail to the exit, a semi-circular entrance that showed only blue sky beyond. His wings were folded demurely, and his head rested atop a pile of broken stone. Kaylana's staff lay across two tall stalagmites, and one huge white claw curved over the top of it. The far wall of the room displayed many sets of manacles, from which the reptile-men used to hang their human sacrifices to Kazikuckla. In the most complete and comfortable of these was Kaylana, awake now, to Sam's relief, and stirring slightly in her chains. The half-eaten carcass of a doe lay on the floor near the tunnel. The wind was in their favor, luckily, blowing from the mouth of the cave down into the tunnel.

Sam looked at Arcie. "How sneaky can you be?" he whispered.

Arcie tipped his hat. "Fair plentiful sneaky. What are your plan?" he asked.

In reply, Sam took out a glass flask he'd swiped from the mage's room and began rummaging in his pockets. Into the flask went a splash of plain water, a bagful of gray powder, the contents of three different colored vials, three white pills, and a final pinch of dried herbs. Sam shook the mixture gently, spat in it for good luck, and handed it to Arcie.

"Dose the doe," he whispered, pointing to the deer. "I

don't know quite what that'll do to a dragon, but it may give us a bit of an edge."

"Right," whispered the Barigan in return, and, silent as a mouse, he crept out into the open.

I wonder if dad ever had to do such a thing, he wondered, as he made his way along the loose pebbles, careful not to make the slightest crunch under his soft feet.

Thirty feet, twenty feet, ten . . . fates, the dragon was huge. Don't look at it, look at the deer. Disemboweled. Remains of another lying nearby, and a third. Blood on the rocks, slippery . . . a stumble . . .

The dragon snorted softly. Arcie froze and wished the gods of thieves and rogues were still around so he'd have someone to pray to. He whipped off a quick promise to the memory of Baris and Bella, twin gods of thieves and dark mischief, just in case. The dragon's huge eyelids twitched, dreaming . . . then its slow heavy breathing resumed. Arcie took a deep breath himself, and carefully but quickly covered the remaining distance to the deer. He swiftly poured the contents of the flask over the raw flesh, nodded in satisfaction as he saw it mingle with the blood and meat and become undetectable. Sam was a bother at times, but he certainly knew his business.

The thief carefully turned around on the loose shingle and made his way back to the tunnel. He had been so quiet, so cautious, that not even the Druid had seen him.

"Now what?" hissed Valerie, as Arcie tumbled back into the safety of the tunnel.

"Now we wait," answered Sam. Arcie looked out at the dragon again. Where was its treasure? he wondered. Not here, certainly. It must have another lair, elsewhere; thievish interests thwarted again. He'd have to watch for another chance to grab some dragon gold.

A short way away, a Wilderkin also thought of gold. A nice pile of it seemed to have been left in this niche, and he was just reaching for it when it opened a sparkling eye and looked at him. "Whez, what is it with all these people today? You want the dragon too? Straight, third left, fourth right, up stairs, second door by the wall fountain," the coins thrummed.

"Stars!" gasped Dusty. "Talking money!"

"People?" asked Tesubar, looking at the Aydaptor. "Speak, Aydaptor, what people?"

"Oh, a short guy and a scruffy guy and a black-robed sorceress and a centaur and a person who didn't talk much," it purred. "Friends of yours?"

"The villains!" cried Tasmene, drawing his sword. "Come on!"

"Oh Tesubar!" piped Dusty. "Isn't it neat! Can I have it for a pet?"

Tesubar shrugged, and said, "Well, if it will hush your prattling . . . " He swiftly incanted a spell as the rest of the party of heroes hurried past up the passage, following the Aydaptor's instructions. *"Kindafar mimicant domesticallin inerticus!"*

"No!" wailed the Aydaptor in anguish as it felt its attack capability thwarted, and was scooped up into the delighted Wilderkin's arms.

"I'm gonna call you George," Dusty told it happily, as he hurried after Tesubar and the others. It moaned softly, and turned into a small box of wood in despair.

They had waited, it seemed, for far too long. At last the dragon snorted again and opened its huge golden eyes. Its scaly brow wrinkled a moment, and it sniffed the air; Lumathix could smell something not quite right . . . but the foul dragon reek of Kazikuckla still lingered too strong, and of course there was this human female as well. Hard to tell anything. He turned his great head toward her and coughed a puff of smoke.

"Well, Druid," he trilled, in his shrill voice, "had any second thoughts yet?" He tapped his claw on the staff meaningfully. The wood flexed slightly under the pressure, and Kaylana winced. One good swat would snap her staff like a toothpick and . . . she forced herself to glare at the dragon, avoiding its eyes.

"Never."

"Come now, your band of villains has abandoned you, and your misguided way of life vanished forever. Why don't you come around to the Light?" fluted Lumathix.

"Because this world is mine and I am going to save it," snapped Kaylana defiantly.

Lumathix sighed and began tidying up, raking up the leftover bones with his claws and shoving them behind an outcropping, where they vanished down a deep shaft. "I do wish you'd see reason," he shrilled petulantly, extending his long neck to pick up his half-finished deer. "Are you hungry?"

"I will not eat that rotting flesh," snarled Kaylana.

Thank Hruul for that, thought Sam to himself, relieved.

The dragon seemed miffed. "Well, fine," it sniffed, crunching down the deer with huge bites of its sharp teeth. "I'm going to go pick up some more food from Sir Fenwick's men," it said, licking its chops. Sam began counting silently, more for curiosity's sake than expectation. *One . . . two . . .*

"Shall I bring you something?" Lumathix asked. Kaylana rattled slightly in her chains.

"Do me no favors, lizard," she growled.

Six . . . seven . . .

"Going to go see Fenwick . . . right after . . . " the dragon's eyes began to glaze. "Right after a li'l nappy-nap." It sank with a sigh back into its nest and began snoring softly. Kaylana stared at it in surprise.

"Come on," said Sam, scrambling up out of the hole. "We've got to work fast," he added, pulling Arcie out after him. They hurried over to where Kaylana was imprisoned. She was mildly surprised to see them.

"Well, it took you a long while," she commented, as they reached her. "You are going to need Valerie, if you intend to release me . . . these chains are magical."

"I'll get the dark lass," said Arcie, hurrying back to the tunnel while Sam gave Kaylana an odd look.

"What do you mean, if we intend to release you?" he asked.

Kaylana looked down at her sandaled feet idly. "I was not sure," she answered. "I knew you all were of evil when I met you, and I am afraid I have not treated you too well on this quest . . . I thought you might welcome the chance to be rid of me."

"Well," said Sam with a faint smile, "they're doing it because they need a healer . . . But I . . . "

"Here's Valerie," announced Arcie, running up with the sorceress following just behind. Sam looked back at the tunnel and saw that Blackmail and the centaur, his knees scraped, had also emerged, Blackmail holding the centaur close by with a drawn blade. "What did they do that for?" he asked Arcie, as Valerie began inspecting the chains.

"Hostage," explained Arcie briefly, as Valerie began to chant. "In the case the dragon should wake up. As Robin are a good fellow, yon dragon will hopefully not kill us do we have Robin's life in our hands."

"Good thinking," nodded Sam. There was a crackling behind them, and Kaylana stepped away from the wall, free and rubbing her wrists.

"I shall need my staff," she announced. They looked over to where it was. Lumathix had taken his claw off it, but it was still uncomfortably close to the huge bulk of the dragon. It stretched like a fragile bridge across the tops of two tall, water-smoothed stalagmites.

"I canna climb those pillars," muttered Arcie.

"I can," answered Sam softly, and he was off across the lair like a lanky shadow.

"He's crazy, that one," Arcie informed Valerie, jerking a thumb in Sam's direction. "Utterly mad."

Sam had no idea how long the dragon would rest in its drugged slumber. He thought if no loud noise woke it, it might sleep almost a quarter of an hour. He ran on quiet feet to the nearest stalagmite, rubbed his palms, and began climbing.

The surface was slippery from eons of water dripping from the cavern ceiling, and the rounded edges provided few handholds. But he persevered, and soon a grasping hand closed around oakwood that tingled faintly in his grasp. He gripped it tightly and slid down, and made his way quickly and quietly back to Kaylana. She met him halfway, with what might almost have been a trace of a smile of thanks. He handed her the staff with a bow and was about to say something witty and charming when a commotion near the tunnel entrance jerked him back to reality.

Blackmail and Robin jumped away from the tunnel just in time to avoid a huge ball of fire that came rushing out of the hole and exploded with a boom. Following close behind was a sword-wielding, war-cry-shouting band of heroes. Lumathix jerked his head up at the sudden noise, his huge vertical pupils dilated from the drug, and roared with a depth and timbre that surprised everyone, including himself.

The villains were outnumbered, the way they had come in barred by heroes, the only other way out guarded by an intoxicated dragon and, in any case, a sheer drop through a thousands of feet of empty space.

"Run!" shouted Kaylana, pushing Sam toward the corner. "He has a dump-chute in the corner!" They ran.

But things were happening too fast. Arrows whizzed around their heads, and another fireball crashed so close behind the fleeing figures of Blackmail and Robin that part of the centaur's tail sizzled off. And then the dragon pounced, its huge head inhaling for the fieriest, fiercest blast of flame of its whole career.

We are not going to make it! thought Kaylana, as they ran. *There is no time!* The staff was warm under her hand, and she could feel it suddenly swirling with a suggestion of a powerful spell, under the guidance of centuries of Druidic wisdom. *Yes, that would work, but I do not have the focuses, the components . . . I should need fireblooms and saxifrage and a dozen different kinds of rare plants . . . Especially the magical pixy-clovers . . .* But maybe she *did* have those! Kaylana grabbed her belt, snapping loose the dried and tattered wreath of flowers Sam had woven. She called up the power, throwing the blooms into the air as the focus. And there were the shimmering fibers of seconds, woven through like the stems of dried blossoms . . . The staff prickled in her grasp as a surge of power coursed through it. She grabbed hold of reality and twisted.

Druids were the priests and magicians of nature and

the elements. Kaylana, with her staff of distilled wisdom and power, could exercise control over air, fire, water and earth, could help life to flourish or set it to wilt. Her magic could make sun out of rain, and even make summer follow autumn in a small area, had she willed it hard enough. And thus it was she twisted one of the most tricky elements in existence—time.

Arrows slowed in midair, the shouts of the heroes crawling to a blur of noise. The dragon flamed in slow-motion, a great puff of crimson fire bursting from its gullet; they dodged the crawling flames as easily as they outran the arrows. A lightning bolt, fired by Tesubar, headed at a slightly faster pace for Blackmail, but he dodged around a clump of rocks and the bolt flashed with a slow shower of blue and purple sparks. The scrambling of their running feet sounded loud in the slowed cavern. Then the chute showed ahead, and one by one they flung themselves down it, a moment before the creeping yet still deadly flames of the dragon washed over the entrance. As the villains slid down the slick, none-too-clean tunnel, they heard the dragon's roar suddenly snap back into full speed, and a barely tolerable wave of heat reached them. There was a clattering, crashing sound as the rock wall snapped, melted, and broke outside the tunnel, huge molten chunks bouncing down after them as the entrance caved in from the heat of the dragon's breath.

To the heroes and dragon the villains they had been pursuing seemed to suddenly vanish in a blur; the heroes exchanged confused glances as the dragon clawed at the chute's entrance in a rage, burying it still further.

"We must follow!" roared Sir Reginald, brandishing his huge sword.

"Don't be a fool!" countered Tesubar haughtily. "We have no idea where that chute leads . . . it may dump them out into the Abyss for all we know!"

"No! Don't *go* down there!" shrilled the dragon. "It ends in a sheer plummet into the chasm . . . they'll all be smashed. Oh, my aching head . . . " he moaned, pressing his paws to the sides of his huge skull.

"No more running away!" vowed Sam at the top of his lungs as they tumbled end over end down the chute, sometimes banging against the sides.

"Baris's balls! It just go on and on!" cried Arcie, as he dropped like a stone. "Most curiouser and curiouser!"

Robin had just discovered his bracelet was no longer functioning.

"Aaaaaaahheeeeeeeeeeeeehiiiiiiihhhihhhhhihhhhhih-hhhhhi!!!!!"

"Silence, you imbecile centaur! Bad enough we have to die without listening to you screaming!" shouted Valerie. The raven cawed in fury and fear, plummeting with its mistress, its soul-link too strong to abandon her.

"Aaaaaaaaaaaaaiiiihiiiii—" There was the sudden whacking sound of a mailed gauntlet knocking a centaur upside the head, and the noise stopped.

"Do something, Valerie!" Kaylana requested loudly.

"Any suggestions?! There's too many of us to levitate!"

"Slow us down, then! I shall handle the landing!"

"Postulum momentum entropicus descendus—" Valerie squeezed her eyes shut as she hurriedly wove a spell.

The air seemed to thicken around them, just as the chute suddenly did a slick curve and shot them out into the air and sunlight, with craggy mountains all around and a very rocky bottom looming below them. They swooped up into the air and then began to fall, slower, but not slow enough.

"Hahoo!" cried a voice. There was a faint crackle around them as a swirl of energy plummeted past them, toward the rocks below . . .

The jagged stones racing up to meet them abruptly seemed to blur and run . . .

There was a series of loud splocking noises as a Barigan, an assassin, a sorceress, a Druid, a centaur and a knight fell one by one into a deep pool of soft mud.

"Effective," commented Valerie, as they scrambled out. "Messy, but effective."

"I am so glad you approve," muttered Kaylana.

"Sanitarius," muttered Valerie, and a shower of shimmering purple-black lights enveloped her. The coat of mud fell away, and her clothes, hair, and skin were clean once more.

Kaylana found a large boulder as the others were trying to brush the mud off as best they could. Blackmail, for reasons best known to himself, was dragging the unconscious centaur out of the thick mud. The others didn't give the minstrel a second thought. Kaylana spoke a few words of magic and tapped the stone lightly with the point of her staff. A gush of clear water fountained from the bare rock. Sam was uncomfortably reminded of the shamans of Mula.

"Wash yourselves off," she recommended, as the party hastened over. "It will not last long."

Soon, damp but clean, with the magical spring depleted, they contemplated their next move.

"Well, where are we?" asked Sam. He glanced over at the centaur, who was still out cold. "By the way, Kaylana, I've got to bring you up to date on our four-legged fink over there . . . " he moved over to talk to her as Arcie answered his question.

"I've gotten a map," volunteered Arcie, taking out a folded piece of paper. Valerie eyed it suspiciously as the Barigan unfolded it.

"That looks like a Wilderkin drew it," she said.

"Well, perhaps so," admitted Arcie. "But it's still a map."

"Are you a Wilderkin?" Valerie asked rhetorically. Arcie shook his curly head. "Then it won't help us." The thief snorted and consulted the map.

"Horsefeathers! 'Tis perfectly simple, see you, here's the mountains, there are the ocean. Nay, I'm mistook, 'tis a desert. I'm sorry . . . wait, nay, that's a . . . west is . . . um . . . " His eyebrows curled up in confusion like dying caterpillars. "Um. Well, we're at in a gorge of mountains, 'tis obvious enough." He quickly folded the map and put it away in his tobacco pouch.

"Ohhoooyy," came a quavering moan, and Robin slowly staggered to his hooves, rubbing his head. Finding himself muddy, he set his hooves and shook himself, nearly splattering the others, then pulled his bedraggled hat out of the mud, and put it on. Robin looked at the knight accusingly. "You hit me," he grumbled. Blackmail nodded his head; Robin decided not to press the issue, but nervously took out his harp, making sure it was undamaged.

"What time are it?" asked Arcie.

"Two of your clock, after noon," answered Kaylana.

"Six o'clock," said Sam.

They looked at each other. "It is two by the sun," asserted Kaylana.

"It's six by my timesense," answered Sam.

"Whatever it be, it's light out," said Arcie. "Plenty of time to be making a start out of here . . . "

They began to make their laborious way through the crags of the mountains. The chute had dropped them on the far side of Putak-Azum, where foothills and crags they had not seen in their earlier approach nuzzled against the side of the huge central mountain. A small path, perhaps used by the ancient Dwarves, availed itself, and they followed it.

It led them up among the rocks and boulders. They had to scramble along in silence in several places, and Robin had more than a little difficulty. None of them spoke to him. If Robin suspected that they had found him out, he gave no sign. Unable to report to Mizzamir, he was harmless. They could easily have killed him, but there didn't seem to be much point; he was rather a pitiful figure, a little difficult to just slay in cold blood. Sam could have done it, but not without payment; Valerie could have also, but felt it was a waste of her power. They were content, for now, to let him tag along, as a possible hostage or bait.

A narrow cliff-ledge almost solved their problem for

them. Robin, bringing up the rear, began trembling uncontrollably as he looked over the edge. The ground seemed to spin and swoop far, far below him. His legs began to shake like leaves.

Robin shared with most centaurs, those of the Commots in particular, a fear of heights. Now, the dizziness caused by his recent head-wound, the terror of the previous fall, the sudden danger of the hostile villains, and the vertiginous drop below the pass all struck him at once.

Robin's blood ran cold as he imagined a terrible crashing fall, snapping bones . . . and as he shook in nameless fear, frozen on the ledge, afraid to move, pebbles rattled down from his hooves. The others, hearing the noise, turned around just in time to see him suddenly slide down the cliff as the path gave way under him. He was too terrified to even make a sound, hooves backpedalling in fear until at last he came to a halt again on a tiny ledge on the rocky slope, half-sitting on his haunches, a few inches away from the sheer drop.

"Och, that takes care of the spy, then," snorted Arcie softly.

"Help." Robin's voice drifted up to them, very small, very scared, very young-sounding. He was past screaming, past scrambling or fainting, just locked into that paralyzed animal fear that sends creatures into frozen deafness, unable to move, or think, or run, as their death approaches. Valerie smiled down at him, but he didn't see her.

"Well, centaur. It looks like your friend Mizzamir isn't going to help you now, eh?" she purred. Robin's ears didn't even twitch. They were laid back flat against his skull, hidden in his thick gray mane. A whimsical wind whipped his plumed hat off his head and sent it spinning away into the chasm.

"Might we give him a wee push, or just let him fall when his legs gets woozy?" asked Arcie, looking down at the stricken centaur.

Sam looked away. He'd seen enough of death in his time. He didn't enjoy it, but he didn't hate it either. It was just something that happened, something he did, as a farmer would slaughter hogs. But when death came, he felt, it should be swift and sudden, unforeseen, unsuffered. He didn't like to see this lingering misery, fear . . . He shook his blowgun out of his sleeve and snapped it together.

A quick spot of sleeping toxin would send the minstrel tumbling unaware into the depths, to die in his sleep. He glanced up at Kaylana. She stood back, not looking at the centaur, not looking at them. He wondered what she was thinking. By her stance on good and evil, he would imagine she expected this sort of thing from the group of evildoers, and because of the great imbalance, would condone the act. But how she felt personally about the whole thing was another matter; the green eyes, the stern face told nothing.

"Help." The voice floated up to them again. There was no hope in it, not even any pleading now; it was simply the only word his frozen voice could produce.

"A pity," mused Valerie. "We won't even get so much as a steak off him now."

She was enjoying the spectacle. Sam shook his head slightly. She must have an awful lot of bitterness inside somewhere to act like that . . . but, of course, she was evil. They all were, even Kaylana by association. He fitted a needle into his gun, raised, aimed . . . and was stopped by a hand on his shoulder. A gauntlet, to be precise. He lowered the blowgun and looked quizzically up into the dark visor of Blackmail.

The knight shook his head slightly, pulled a coil of rope from the shoulder pack Kaylana had given him, and handed it to Sam. "What?" he asked. The knight indicated the centaur, made a scooping gesture, and then indicated Sam. Sam shook his head. The others didn't seem to notice their quiet one-sided conversation. "Save him? No. He's a spy. He's a liability. Besides, that's not my business."

"Help," said Robin again, softer now.

Blackmail then reached inside the wrist joint of a

gauntlet, and drew out a tiny black leather pouch in his mailed fingers. He handed it to Sam. Sam took it, puzzled, opened it, and shook the contents out into his hand. And caught his breath in wonder.

In his palm sparkled a perfectly faceted stone, spherical, slightly larger than a cherry-pit. It was clear, but with radiance unlike anything so common as a diamond. It picked up the colors of Sam's hair and eyes and clothing, and sent glittering flashes of black and hazel and gold dancing in its depths. He'd never seen one before, but he knew, by legend and rumor, what it was. It tingled slightly against his skin.

He looked up at the still and silent figure of the knight, reverently placed the stone back into its pouch, tucked the pouch into his tunic, shouldered the rope, and smiled.

"Well, Blackmail, it just so happens that the price of a one-assignment mid-hire complete reversal of my profession is one, count 'em, one, Heartstone." He stepped to the edge of the cliff and looked down, motioning to Arcie to step back.

"Move, old chum. I'm hired to get that centaur to safety," he explained cheerfully. He looked over the side. The ledge the centaur was huddled on was already crumbling around the edges. It probably wouldn't take his weight in addition. Have to come at it from the side.

"Hired to save him?" hissed Valerie sharply. "Who by?"

Sam refused to answer; no assassin would answer such a question about an assignment, but Blackmail raised a mailed hand. Valerie stared at him. The two matched gazes a long moment, then the sorceress backed down from that inscrutable black visor. "I assume you have a reason, strange one," she muttered. The helmet nodded. "Well, it had better be a good one."

"Here now, laddie," complained Arcie, moving out of his way. "Ye bein't whitewashing, now are ye?" Sam shook his head as he checked his boots carefully.

"Nope, just greed, old chum. Perfectly acceptable motive."

"Ye'll be risking yer life, ye great clommox!"

"Aren't we all? Now don't drop pebbles on me." Sam swung himself over the side. The group watched in silence.

Sam crawled down the ledge like a spider. It was obvious what would have to be done: get Robin to tie the rope around himself, or tie it around him by hand, then hope that Blackmail could pull hard enough and that Robin would snap out of his fear enough to scramble back to the ledge. Robin was obviously in no state to get the rope on himself, the others didn't seem willing to assist; hence the need for Sam. And he felt great. He hadn't liked having to see the poor colt get snuffed, and with this unexpected sparkling bonus . . . The cliff wasn't too bad, vertical, sure, but plenty of handholds. His legs swung out over a three-hundred-foot drop, and he looked down at an eagle flying below. He almost laughed in delight. Sam liked heights.

"Och, I told you he were crazy," Arcie said to Valerie. "A whatsit, splitten personality."

Sam worked his way hand over hand to where Robin sat. The centaur's eyes were open, staring, and focused only on the empty space below. Sam could almost hear the double-thumping of the centaur's two hearts. The human grinned.

"Hi, ponybutt," he greeted Robin, fixing his feet and one hand into holds on the wall while he unslung the coil of rope from his shoulder. "Gonna get you out."

"Help," whispered Robin.

Fates, he looks just like a kid, thought Sam. *Did I ever look like that?* He whipped the rope around the centaur's human waist, over the shoulders and withers in a harness, and secured the whole with a knot he painstakingly tied with his free hand. Then he gave a shrill whistle, and Blackmail appeared on the ledge above.

He threw the other end of the rope, and the knight caught it. Sam pulled his old black scarf out of his tunic, and whipped it around the minstrel's staring eyes, tying it in a blindfold, blocking out the view of certain death. After a moment, the centaur's trembling eased.

"Help?" he asked, with a little more interest this time.

"Right," agreed Sam. "We're going to pull you, but you have to back up and out as best you can, all right?"

"Up, out," agreed Robin shakily. "All right."

"Now, Blackmail!" called Sam, and he quickly climbed up and away as the rope pulled taut. Robin began painstakingly backing his way up the steep rocky ledge, his hooves slipping on the loose stones but still making progress. Sam threw one leg over the edge onto the path and hauled himself up to safety. Blackmail stood on the path, his armored feet set, pulling hand over hand on the rope. And soon up over the edge came Robin's gray hindquarters and singed tail, and finally with a clatter of hooves he scrambled back onto the path, still wearing his blindfold, feeling his way with his hooves.

"Don't take the blindfold off," cautioned Sam, as he got to his feet.

"Well, you were lucky this time, minstrel," Valerie said, as Robin panted with exertion and clung to the path. The centaur gulped and nodded.

"You know about Mizzamir," he said.

"Aye," agreed Arcie.

"And yet you saved me . . . Why?" His covered face looked at Sam and Blackmail, his furry ears swiveling to pinpoint them. Sam spread his palms.

"I was paid. Ask him," he answered, jerking a thumb in Blackmail's direction. Blackmail just stood still and silent.

Robin dropped his head. "Mizzamir told me you were all evil . . . "

"That's right," said Valerie. "Except for Kaylana, of course."

"Druids dinna count," put in Arcie.

"No," agreed Kaylana. "That does seem to be the case, at times."

"And yet you let them save me . . . " argued Robin.

"Here, would you wish to be crossin' Blackmail and that great muckle sword of his?" asked Arcie, raising an eyebrow.

"And you work together . . . "

"Better than dying," commented Sam.

"And you haven't been fighting or stabbing each other in the back or even abandoning each other anymore!" exclaimed the minstrel. "I don't understand it! Why? Why are you acting this way? You aren't acting like evil people!"

"Oh pshaw, the whole good/evil lot again," grumbled the Barigan scornfully.

"Look," began Sam, but Valerie broke smoothly over him.

"Centaur, an evil person can do all the things a good person can do and still be what they are. The only difference is motive."

"And a good person can do some incredibly evil things, with the right motive," added Kaylana softly. "For instance, is it evil to kill sentient beings?"

"Um, yes?" hazarded Robin.

"But Fenwick and his men are good, and they want to kill us. That doesn't make them evil."

"And we destroyed those skeletons," put in Valerie, "which were creatures of darkness . . . but that doesn't make us good."

"This fool Sam went an' killed a rapist off in Martogon," said Arcie, as he took out his pipe. "What do that make him? Hero, for saving the lassie, or villain, for killing the man?"

"Yes," added Sam. "And Arcie risked his hide to steal healing for us . . . is he evil, then, for stealing and hurting all those barbarians, or good, because he helped us?"

"We are evil because we help each other for selfish motives," admitted Valerie. "We have realized that without all of our help, without working together, our quest will die, and we and the world with it."

"If it were anything smaller, less important, this

group would not last five minutes," said Kaylana solemnly. "An ordinary 'adventure' would have us cutting each other's throats over who got all the treasure . . . but when this much is at stake, the choice is work together or die . . . and we are far too self-centered to want to die."

"There's more to people than some definded label," said Arcie. "There are more than straight good and evil, aye, even more than law or disorders or fence-sittin'. There's prejudice, whimsey, affection, superstition, habit, upbringing, alliance, pride, society, morals, animosity, preference, values, religion, circumstance, humor, perversity, honor, vengeance, jealousy, frustration . . . hundreds o' factors, from the past and in every present moment, as decides what some one person'll do in an individious situation."

"You have a good vocabulary for a shire-peasant, Barigan," Valerie commented. Arcie squirmed slightly.

"Och, well, you picks up things in the trade and like that . . . " he muttered.

"Sometimes there's other reasons for helping, other than personal gain or benefit," added Sam softly. "Friendship, companionship, trust and love are not confined to light alone . . . they are harder won, fewer seen . . . but no less real." His eyes were looking wistfully at Kaylana as he spoke, but no one noticed. Robin raised his blindfolded head.

"You really believe the world will be destroyed if your quest fails?" he asked. There were general sounds of agreement, ranging from Kaylana's "definitely" to Arcie's "Aye, why not?"

Robin thought for a long moment, his ears twitching, then he appeared to reach a decision.

"Then I have a motive to join you, a selfish motive. I don't want to die, and I don't want the world to be destroyed either. *And* you have saved my life. I owe you, Blackmail in particular, my life. By my culture and society, I owe you a life-debt. What you seek to do may be dark, but the alternative is far worse, and the motive, surprisingly, is right. It may be good, it may be evil, I can't say, but it is right. I will help you to the ends of my strength."

He pulled the defunct silver bracelet off his wrist and threw it into the chasm. It made a sound like the breaking of a chain.

"He speaks the truth," Kaylana said, quietly. The Druid took Robin's hand and led him along the edge, and they walked on through the mountains. Sam looked up at Blackmail, and the knight nodded slightly.

XI

"Tasmene, I trust you as my own brother, but I know these villains. If ever there was an escape from death at the other end of that chute, they'll have found it." Fenwick bent over his arrows, fletching them in green and yellow feathers.

Tasmene blinked in bewilderment. "But where can they go?" he inquired. "There's nothing on that side of the mountains but . . . well, more mountains."

"It doesn't matter," stated Fenwick. "I've chased them across half of the Six Lands already, and I'm not going to give up now. I want them brought to justice, and the centaur and Druid saved from their clutches. And I do hope, Lord Tasmene, that you won't give up on me."

"No, of course not, Fenwick . . . but, really . . . what harm can they do?"

Fenwick looked up, his eyes cold.

"All the harm in the world, my friend. All the harm in the world."

The woodsman looked out at the dim shadows of the mountains. "We shall have to move quickly; we don't know where they've come out. Send your men through the north pass, Tasmene, and my company shall move in from the south."

In a makeshift scrying mirror, borrowed from the store of the Castle's magical treasures, Arch-Mage Mizzamir looked thoughtful as he listened to the conversation between the two heroes. It would take some time to complete the enchantments on his new scrying font; the loss of both water and enchanted gems had caused difficulties. He dismissed the image, and stared into his dusty reflection thoughtfully.

"Well, perhaps I had better attempt to see how my agent is doing," he mused, and concentrated on the bracelet he had given the young centaur. The magic of Druid and Nathauan had thwarted many of his attempts to espy the location of the bracelet, but it was not so now. He saw it quite clearly, lying broken on the bottom of a gorge, its stones missing. The sight caused the mage to raise one fine silver eyebrow in surprise.

"Hmm, it seems the young fellow has turncoated . . . or been found out and slain. Well, if it is the first, then I shall use my magic to bring him back to the light with the others . . . and if it is the last . . . well, revenge is a nasty thing. I'll just do my best to find his body and restore him."

He tapped the glass of the mirror in thought, then turned away. He walked away from it and looked out the newly repaired window.

"But first things first," he said to himself. "They are obviously not delving into Putak-Azum any longer, so the other alternative, as we presumed before . . . Somewhere, the last Segment of the Key . . . and then, to the Labyrinth? With the Key assembled, it is easily possible . . . even the Nathauan would likely know that. The Labyrinth's magic, my magic and that of others, would prevent me from journeying there by magical means while it is still unriddled . . . But should those villains solve it, the magic will weaken, and I will meet them at its center. And should they fail . . . " He sighed sadly.

"A tragedy, but as I have said, the problem would be solved." He turned and strode from the room in a swirl of silver-white hair and robes, sending the dustmotes swirling past him like a host of fairies.

* * *

They tumbled down the last of the scree slopes of the Durdrudin Mountains and found themselves standing on low hills at the edge of what was known as the Frozen Waste. It was cool, but not cold, yet the ground seemed to be rimmed with frost. Arcie kicked at it, puzzled, then scooped some up in his hand. It was dry and not frozen.

"Salts," explained Valerie, noting his confused expression. "Leached out of the ground from the blood of a thousand fiends, some say."

"So it's not really frozen?" asked Robin, yawning. He was brushing at his singed tail with a comb, trying to get the mud and char out of the silky gray plume he was so proud of.

"It will get very cold at night," said Kaylana, frowning up at the sky. The sun was certainly taking its time about setting. "Whenever that is."

"Told you it was six o'clock," Sam commented with a trace of smugness. "Of course, now it's more like eleven at night."

Kaylana continued to glare at the sun. Her people had raised vast stone monuments to its orderly rise and fall and turn of the seasons, and she didn't like what it was doing now at all. It was just skirting the horizon, going to shortcut around the edge of the world and come up on the other side.

"The time are out of joint," muttered Arcie, scooping up some of the larger salt crystals into his pouch, out of idle interest. "And I'm dead beat and half-starved. Night, morning, noon, whatever, I say we'd best snooze and snack and be headin' out when we're ready."

"I like that idea." Robin yawned again and pawed at the salt-frosted ground with a hoof.

Valerie nodded. "All right . . . here in the lee of the mountains we should be fairly well sheltered from the scouring winds at any rate."

"And the rain, when it comes," added Kaylana, looking up thoughtfully at the clear sky. The others secretly sighed at the thought of cold Einian rains.

They settled down to rest, yanking loose a few tufts of dried heather from the sides of the mountain to make into a small fire. Under Valerie's direction, they built the fire up in the rocks of the mountains; when Arcie asked why, she scooped up a handful of salt-crystals and threw them into the flames. They exploded with a hot blue fire.

"Flammable chemical compounds," she explained. "Alchemists have tried for years to unlock their secret. One of my tutors lost his sight when a beaker of these exploded in his face."

The few smoky flames were small comfort against the bitter chill that settled over them when at last the shadow of the mountain fell long across the Waste. Clouds began to gather, blotting out the stars, and there was a smell of thunder.

In another part of the mountain's feet Fenwick was addressing a small band of the members of his Company.

"All right, I know it is past your bedtime, but we must to do some scouting. There is a good moon tonight, until the clouds get thicker, and I don't want to waste it. There's going to be a storm later, and if we don't find them before the rain washes away their tracks, we will be in dire straits. We must search now. If they're moving by night, we shall see them; if they're camping, we'll look for a campfire or other signs."

Tasmene, visiting his friend's camp, had decided to go along on the hunting party. He tugged at his beard in thought, and, as the rest of the scouts and the wizard Towser hastened off to saddle their horses, he addressed Sir Fenwick dubiously.

"Fenwick, I've been wondering . . . these people, you said there weren't more than six of them at full strength? One of those being the centaur, harmless?"

"That's right," answered the young hero, stringing his bow.

"Then . . . I mean, do we really need all these people? All these men? It doesn't seem, I don't know, *fair* somehow. Like hunting ducks with a catapult." The big man's brows crinkled in uncertainty. Fenwick peered up at him from under his traditional plumed cap.

"My friend, you have not personally encountered these villains before, I gather?"

"Well, no," admitted Lord Tasmene.

"Then trust me on this. These people are cunning, crafty, cruel, and desperate. They killed quite a number of my best men in the Fens of Friat by means I know not. These are ducks who are capable of dodging anything less than a catapult. I don't like to see my men killed. Now, if we outnumber them by enough, casualties will be minimized. Simple strategy . . . and we'll likely be able to take the . . . *important* ones . . . alive." Fenwick's eyes flickered briefly with lustful thoughts of the red-haired Druid.

Tasmene sighed. "All right . . . I suppose you know what you're doing."

"Of course," replied Fenwick, with a smile. "I'm doing what I do best."

They rode out with thirty men and women of the Company across the salt-rimmed plains, into an icy scouring wind that blew stinging lashes of salt-laden mist into their eyes and skin. In the half-light of the setting sun and the large moon overhead, the ground gleamed like frost and their shadows jumped over the plains, occasionally blotted out by the larger shadows of passing clouds. But all was dead, lifeless . . . they were about to turn back when Fenwick suddenly called the company to a halt and pointed.

In the shadows of the mountains gleamed a tiny distant flicker of a campfire.

"Towser," whispered Fenwick, "your spell of secrecy would avail us well now."

The mage nodded and began weaving the magic with words and hands, the strength of Light in the world lending strength to his magic. A mist of vagueness seemed to settle over the company of mounted persons, muting the sounds of hoof and harness, blurring the outlines of horse and rider. Fenwick gave the silent command, and they approached the flickering campfire with weapons drawn.

Sam awoke with a start at the sound of a fully armored knight leaping to his feet. A last word of a magic spell clicked into place, and suddenly every limb was filled with aching weariness and weakness. All around him his companions jerked awake, bleary-eyed, and were struck with the same debilitating spell. They managed to look around, to see themselves surrounded in a complete circle by men and women in green and yellow tunics with fully drawn longbows.

"Right," said their leader, a familiar face under a peaked and feathered woodsman's hat. "Good work, Towser, and the rest of you. Don't any of you villains move, or you will die. Except you, Robin, you can get out of here."

Robin shook his head solemnly, his hand on his swordhilt. "No, Fenwick. I've changed sides."

"Oh, Baris's balls," muttered Arcie, putting his face in his hand. If the centaur had remained free he might have worked an escape . . . instead, there was this, a noble gesture, but a stupid one. Fenwick seemed to agree.

"A turncoat, eh?" he scoffed. "Then you shall die too." He addressed his band. "If anyone hits the red-haired woman, I will be exceedingly cross. All right, on my signal . . . "

"Wait!" spoke a deep voice. Tasmene was scowling at Fenwick. The woodsman sighed and loosened his draw a bit to look at his friend.

"What is it now?" he asked petulantly.

"You can't do this. It isn't right. We've got them outnumbered, surrounded, helpless. I say, capture them and take them back for justice."

"I'd rather be shot, thanks," said Sam brightly. Arcie shushed him. Valerie started to speak, and a single bowstring twanged. She cried out in pain and sat down suddenly, clutching her arm. Deep magenta blood welled against the white skin in the moonlight.

"We know of your tricks, Nathauan," shouted Fenwick. "You shall die as all your vile kin did, at my hands!"

"Steady on, Fenny," spoke Tasmene. He addressed the renegades. "We have twenty-two fully armed and armored fighting men on horseback here, as well as a green-robed mage. If you surrender, you shall be taken as prisoners, but no harm shall come to you."

"And how d'you define harm," snapped Arcie, while Kaylana quickly bandaged Valerie's wound. Fenwick watched Kaylana with open lust in his eyes. Sam seethed. Robin fretted. Blackmail stayed still and silent. Tasmene ignored all of them, and said,

"It is your choice . . . surrender yourselves, or Fenwick and his company will cut you down dead where you stand."

"We'll take some of you with us," growled Sam dangerously, stepping between Kaylana and Fenwick. Another bowstring twanged. Sam dodged ever so slightly, to save his vitals, then stood unmoving, an arrow in his shoulder. The fire was leaping in Sam's eyes, even through Towser's magic, and Fenwick found he had to look away from that cold gaze. The salty ground cackled at the blood dripping onto it, and Arcie staggered to his feet.

"Och, we surrender," he gasped, raising his pudgy but nimble hands above his head. "Halt your arrows . . . Bring on the chains."

"Well, now what?" muttered Sam disconsolately. They sat in a wagon-cage of iron bars. Their weapons had been taken. Kaylana was nowhere to be seen. The sky was at its darkest now, but still not very dark; about the depth of early morning. Sam had begun to get slightly dizzy with blood loss by the time they had finished searching him, leaving him with nothing more to wear than his patched and faded leggings. He hung his bare feet out the bars, waving them in the night air. The fawn-color mark on his shoulder was clearly visible, and he rubbed at it with weak annoyance. After the Company had disarmed the renegades, the two healers of the abbreviated Company healed Sam and Valerie with curt apologies for the rough treatment. Valerie had tried to bite one of them, and Robin had managed a half-hearted kick. Blackmail's sword and shield had been removed, and he sat in silent dignity in one corner of the cage.

The Company had been unable to find either Valerie's amulet or her raven, and had settled on posting a warrior-wizard guard named Zanithir outside the cage. Robin, shackled on all four hooves and both hands, stood tethered disconsolately nearby. The clouds were thick now, and the feeling of thunder in the air was sticky and oppressive. Occasionally a faint rumble could be heard, but the clouds retained their heavy burden stubbornly.

At last Arcie sighed and muttered in the language of rogues:

"Time for escape."

Sam sighed, and answered in the same language. "Escape? Guards, bars, locks, no weapons. No way."

"You get guard."

"No weapons," repeated Sam in a gesture of futility.

"Since when do you need those?" snapped Arcie in exasperation in his normal language. The guard glanced their way suspiciously, and Arcie pretended to be fascinated by something under his thumbnail. Sam stiffened. True, he didn't need weapons . . . the only weapon he needed was the fire that danced in his blood.

"I do lock," offered Arcie, in cant again, with a trace of a smile. Sam shook his head doubtfully. Arcie was a very skilled thief, but to try to unlock the padlock on their cage door with only his bare pudgy hands was ridiculous.

Arcie of course realized this. He had a much better idea. Wincing, he yanked a long tuft of his curly auburn hair out and twisted it straight. The hair-twist was far too flexible for a lockpick, of course . . . but not after he'd picked up Valerie's discarded bandage and soaked the hair in the thick Nathauan blood congealing there. *Papa might be proud of me,* he thought, as he waited patiently for it to dry. *If he wouldn't of been so ashamed of me for getting caught in the first place.* Of course, the improvised pick wouldn't stand up to repeated work . . . one shot or nothing. And he wouldn't want the guard to see him at it.

At last he tested the point. Stiff. He nodded to Sam and casually went over to lean against the door of the cage near the lock. Sam put on his best dead-dog face and looked out of the cage.

"You there, guard," he called in a raspy voice, dangling his hands through the bars with every sign of extreme weakness. "Could you . . . possibly . . . get me . . . water?" he croaked, wheezing. "Please?" he added in a desperate tone.

The guard came over to see what was wrong with the assassin. He didn't get quite close enough for a killing attack, Sam noted, clever cautious bastard . . . but he did get close enough for Sam to kick him extremely hard in the groin with one of his dangling feet. As the guard folded, there was a sudden extended clicking sound and the cage swung open. Sam jumped to the ground and put the struggling guard down for a nice nap.

"Robin! Horses!" hissed Arcie, jumping out, and he grabbed a ring of keys off the guard's belt and freed the centaur. Robin lifted his feet free of the chains and galloped away swiftly and silently. As Valerie and Blackmail escaped to freedom, there was a sudden shout and the sounds of running footsteps coming closer. The renegades scattered.

In the well-appointed tent of Sir Fenwick, the prince looked up from his glass of wine across the small table at the Druid. She said no word, just looked at him with those impossible green eyes. She hadn't touched her aphrodisiac-spiked wine. She hadn't responded to his winsome words and seductive charms . . . He'd let her keep her staff, confident that he could block any blow from it or stop her in the process of any spell. But now, Fenwick was wondering . . . perhaps she would be more tractable without it. He knew Druids had some powers to resist charms and magics. Perhaps something of that was caught up in the staff.

"Don't you think you'd be more comfortable setting that stick aside for a moment?" he asked reasonably. She blinked coldly at him.

Suddenly the hue and cry reached their ears. Fenwick raised his handsome eyebrows, and stood up, flashing her a smile.

"Well, duty calls . . . don't go anywhere, lovely one . . . this tent is surrounded by my men at arms, and they sometimes get a bit rough. I wouldn't want you to have to face them without me there to protect you."

With a last sly grin, he vanished out the door, warning the guards as he did so to keep close watch on the tent. They did so, very carefully. But they did not look inside as Kaylana, gently resting on her staff, closed her eyes. Slow, easy magic parted the salty soil as easily as water, and Kaylana slipped down through the floor like a dignified upright mole.

She rose up from the earth again some yards away, out of sight behind a cooking tent. But there were too many people around . . . it would be best to continue on in a form that would attract less attention.

Valerie heard a welcome sound of flapping wings amidst the chaos as she hid under a wagon. Nightshade dropped down with a satisfied croak, her amulet dangling from his beak. She took it gratefully and hung it around her neck, cold power thrilling through her once more. "Wonderful, precious, fluffykins Nightshade," she muttered evilly, "let's do something nasty." She flexed her fingers.

Sam ducked and rolled as a sudden explosion echoed behind him, then another and another. *Valerie must have found her amulet,* he thought distractedly as he dodged into one of the tents. A series of female curses greeted him as a number of lady warriors and archers drew their swords and came at him, and he jumped back out and ran away. A sudden foot stuck out and tripped him, and he fell sprawling to see Arcie hiding under another wagon. The Barigan grinned at him.

"This'n has our weapons," whispered the Barigan. They scrambled up into the wagon and quickly recovered their weapons. Sam's were still in their places in his confiscated clothing, and he slipped his shirt, belt, boots, and tunic on in relief, adding the few extra knives and suchlike to their loops in the folded seams of his leggings. As he was doing so, Sam saw Blackmail laying about him with a tent pole amidst a group of warriors. He picked up the knight's sword and black shield and hurled both as hard as he could in the knight's direction. They were dreadfully heavy, and never should have sailed more than a few feet, but they crossed the distance easily. Blackmail raised a hand without looking up and caught the heavy blade easily by the hilt, even as it spun and knocked down a member of the Company. The shield also scythed into the ranks, propelled by Sam's curse/blessing of never-miss, and the warriors fled in terror, allowing Blackmail to scoop up the shield.

But Sam had been seen; he and Arcie had to jump away as a shower of arrows rattled into the wagon.

Sam ran down through an alley of tents, suffering vivid flashbacks of the battle in the Plainsmen's camp, found himself cornered, and feet coming his way. He prepared to fight, then saw Valerie's head appear in the air a few feet away.

"Get in here, fool!" she hissed. Sam didn't bother to question the logic, but ducked behind Valerie into the magical invisible space surrounding her. Valerie, concentrating on her spell, was bleeding slightly from a few sword slashes. She closed the shimmering curtain of invisibility behind him.

"Where's Kaylana?" asked Sam; Valerie shook her head.

Fenwick saw the chaos, figured that the villains must be escaping, and saw the need for speed. He threw himself onto the back of the nearest horse, a chestnut mare, and gripping its mane, clapped his heels to its sides. He could ride bareback without any reins as well as most men could ride with full tack. But the mare refused to move. He kicked it again, harder, and suddenly it reared and twisted, smashing sideways into a tent. Fenwick fell off as the mare galloped away. He barely had time to wonder why the horse would behave like that, and why it should have such strange greenish eyes.

"Come on!" cried a panicked voice near Arcie, and an arm scooped him up from the ground at a full canter. Robin dropped the Barigan onto his back and started to run. Ripping through another section of crowd was Blackmail, mounted on Lord Tasmene's huge roan warhorse. The knight's sword was swinging like a scythe, and arrows rained off his armor and the horse's chain barding. Arcie would have sworn the fellow was having the best time he'd had since they'd fought the dragon in the flood-canyon.

Valerie and Sam crept from their hiding place. With a quick slash of a dagger, Sam knocked a Verdant guard off his horse, and boosted the sorceress into the saddle. She grabbed the reins and motioned for Sam to join her on the prancing animal. He shook his head.

"Got to find Kaylana," he gasped. "If Fenwick's hurt her . . . " he ran off into the chaos, daggers whirling and slashing as he cut his way through the crowd. Valerie didn't stay to wait for that crowd, but spurred her horse and took off, Nightshade flapping in the air after her.

Sam did not escape unscathed through the army of the Verdant Company. Arrows and swords and hand axes pressed him on all sides however he ran, dodged, and hid. By the time he finally tumbled up over another wagon, he was just about done for. He rolled off the wagon and onto the neck of a large animal. Horse? Yes, a horse. Before he could move, the animal bolted, and out of instinct he clung to its long mane. It wasn't wearing a saddle, but he held on as best he could. Through whipping chestnut strands he saw himself break away from the camp and head out across the frosty plains. Just ahead were three running figures that he hoped were his companions . . . He risked a look behind him. Coming up fast were the forces of the Verdant Company, with a figure in a plumed hat leading the charge. Sam shut his eyes tight and hoped the horse knew enough to follow the others in front of it.

Someone blew a hunting horn, and the dogs began to

bugle and bay. The noise woke Lumathix from his sleep at the Einian camp, and his keen dragon eyes saw the running figures. With a roar he took to the cloudy, turgid skies.

Hooves pounded on packed earth and salt, and shouts rang out in the dim light. A huge shape blotted out the moon for an instant, too fast for a cloud, then again, circling. It swooped down, and Sam tensed as he waited for the horse to bolt and run as the reek of dragon washed over them. But the animal held a straight course, even when the dragon came in at a low dive toward them from the front, illuminated awesomely by a brief flicker of lightning.

Fenwick heard Towser shout, "No!" as there was a sudden burst of flame in the twilight. Lumathix blasted fire into the path of the fleeing renegades, and they would surely have been finished had it not been for the properties of the salts. Lumathix, who made his home in the secret high wild places of Goodness, had never seen a salt-desert before, and did not know why Tasmene and Fenwick had carefully kept their fires small, and lit only on large slabs of stone.

Ignited by the exploding-hot dragonfire, the complex chemicals burst into wild blue flames, sweeping across the sands. Lumathix shrilled as the unnatural flames singed even his fireproof skin, and jumped into the air with a great downrush of wings. The fire licked and roared about the hooves of horses and centaur, going too fast to burn yet, then swept back, growing in strength, to threaten the charge of the Company.

The Company tumbled to a halt, and then was in full retreat. The flames licked out in a wide, sweeping path, blown on the scouring winds back toward the camp at incredible speed. Any rider who tried to outflank the flames would be caught in the superhot fire. The fire would exhaust itself explosively soon, but they must retreat now, or suffer a death of horrible agony.

The villains knew that any gods they might have had in their favor had vanished long ago, so it was only pure luck and chance that let them pass through and away from the flames with only mild scorches and the painful burning of ammonia-like fumes in their eyes.

"Where be we runnin'?" shouted Arcie, the wind slashing his words.

"Away!" Valerie cried back. "No time to look for the last Test . . . we've got to put some distance between ourselves and them!"

"We can't leave Kaylana!" Sam shouted, still wrenching at the horse's mane, trying to get it to turn. It was ignoring him, even though he pulled out a great hank of its chestnut hair in his frustration. As he raised a hand to try to knock it across the cheek, in the hopes of shocking it out of its mad dash, it angled its head back and looked at him, without slowing down. Sam froze, barely remembering to keep his seat. The horse's eyes were green, a very familiar green.

"Mountains . . . ahead!" called Robin, gasping with the effort of his gallop. He normally wore horseshoes, to protect his hooves from cobblestones, but the long journey over the rocky terrain had loosened them, and in this mad dash he'd thrown both of the shoes on his left side, and was beginning to feel the bruises as he ran unbalanced.

The mountains sloped up in jagged, rocky crags, so battered by storm and wind that they had taken on strange shapes; here a dragon sprawled, there a rabbit seemed to hunker, an eagle with its wings outspread, and a twisted human face. The shapes leered from the pinnacles of the stony gate to the mountain gorges beyond. The figures were silhouetted in brief, painful contrast in sporadic flashes of lightning, and the smell of storm in the air was even stronger.

"Robin! Can you make it up the hills?" called Valerie.

"I think so! I'm game to try!"

They thundered to a halt as they reached the first scree, the riders dismounting. Blackmail's borrowed roan horse turned and trotted away, but when Sam slid off the back of the chestnut mare, the animal seemed to waver slightly and then shrank itself into a familiar Druid with tousled hair. Arcie reacted in surprise.

"Och! How did you do that, lassie?" he demanded.

"Kaylana! How . . . where . . . " began Sam, but the Druid pointed back across the desert, and Valerie, following her gaze, cursed.

The fires had died down, whether by natural means or some action by the Company, and Fenwick's army was coming up fast again, so close they could see the leading figure. He was waving a sword that glowed with its own shining white fire, and Sam shuddered as he looked at it.

"Up the hills!" commanded Kaylana. "We must get to safety before the storm breaks!"

"We canna find safety in some bloody rocks," snapped Arcie. "They'll catch us up like rabbits!"

"Leave that to me! Go!" she insisted. And so, skittering and stumbling, they clambered up the rough slope. Robin stumbled and staggered, but his human intellect helped him find the best pathway, and the occasional helpful shove from Blackmail allowed him to scramble on.

Sam was the last to begin the climb into the rocks. A few fat drops of ice-cold rain spattered him. As he looked out at their pursuers, he realized that though the Company may not have been able to see the precise point where they entered the mountains, they could surely find the trail . . . unless could distract them until the rain could muddy and confuse the path.

Sam jumped down from the slope and began to run along the edge of the mountains, running open and visible, keeping an eye on the pursuers. The rain suddenly exploded, pounding down around him, soaking him in seconds. He looked to the pursuers . . . closer, closer, maybe three hundred yards? Less? And here was another pass through the mountains, already running with a trickle of water. He began scrambling up, climbing openly and obviously, and looked back.

They saw him all right. He saw them converge, come flooding up to him like waves as he abandoned the pass and strove for height alone, like a treed animal.

* * *

As they scrambled down into the gully and ran along the bottom, Robin jumping and tumbling over the huge rocks, the rain was already making the gully-bottom ripple and run with water. Light-suffused the world might be, but rain was still as plentiful as flowers. Arcie was the first to try to make a headcount, as a lightning flash and immediate explosion of thunder turned the gully into a blast of light and noise.

"Where's that assassin?" he shouted, over the storm. Kaylana stopped, turning to look, but Valerie grabbed her by the arm and dragged her along through the wet.

"We wouldn't stop for you, we can't stop for him! Come on!" shrieked the sorceress, and Kaylana, gripping her staff, tumbled on.

"We must find a dry cave," she explained, trying to be heard through the storm. "These canyons will flood very soon, when the rain comes off the mountains."

"What's a dry cave?" shouted Robin, and then cried out suddenly as a treacherous rock twisted under him. He fell hard, in a tangle of legs, into the muddy gully. Blackmail pointed upstream, even as he moved to assist the centaur.

There, tucked under an outcropping on which grew a few scraggled pines, was a dark shadow above the slicked line of a high-water mark. The others scrambled toward it as Kaylana and Blackmail helped the centaur stand. Robin was hopping on three legs awkwardly.

"Nothing broken," said Kaylana tersely. "Still, a sprain. Come, we will get you to safety."

"I can make it." Robin gritted his teeth and began clawing his way with all six limbs along the rocks. When his leg would fail him, he would push himself along by his arms. The rain made the rocks slippery and sharp, and by the time they reached the bottom of the dry cave, Robin was cut and bloody, and Kaylana and Blackmail were bruised and mud-covered. The water in the gully was a respectable creek now.

Arcie and Valerie had already climbed up the rough rocks to the cave, and lowered a rope that was tied to protruding tree roots within. Kaylana ascended, and then Blackmail. The knight braced his mailed feet against the lip of the cave, and hauled on the rope, dragging Robin slowly up the wall. The centaur scrambled and kicked his way along, and finally tumbled into the safety of the cave, blood and rain plastering his mane to his face and shoulders. Only then did his strength fail him, and he collapsed on the rough uneven floor.

Unbeknownst to either heroes or villains, a set of Elven eyes were watching the proceedings with interest. Mizzamir had managed, by dint of scrying on Sir Fenwick, to get a good all-around view of the scene. He'd watched as Sam led the pursuit off, and tsked to himself. He pulled up a large chair and sat down to watch. The party with the Druid soon slipped from view, hidden by the Druid's magic and the help of the storm and other elements that favored her. But he could watch the area of Fenwick's attention, and did so, holding his chin thoughtfully.

Sam scrambled up the tower of stone until there wasn't any more, just slick steep rock and a tiny ledge just big enough for him to stand on. He looked down.

Sir Fenwick, Lord Tasmene, and the rest came up to the bottom of the stone, and stopped, looking up at him. He thought he recognized, what was her name, Dana?, from Putak-Azum down there. Fenwick shouted an order, and men in green and yellow tunics dismounted and ran through the rain to surround his stony pinnacle, which was barely the height and size of an average castle tower. Sam looked up at the rest of it, through the driving rain, and in the dim twilight of the storm saw its shape loom above him, like a bird with a great streamlined head and hooked beak, wide raptor's wings uneven but outspread, and its shanks driving down to surround his ledge like a nest, or like great claws.

In his mirror, Mizzamir saw the strange rock-shape as well. He frowned. It seemed somehow familiar . . . years ago, in the War and storm and rain, and the ever-gloomy Tamarne stomping off to bargain with the gods, or so he'd said . . .

Fenwick sighed and put Truelight, the glowing sword, Slayer of Darkness, into its scabbard. It seemed to hum in disappointment. He unslung his bow instead.

"Well, we've treed one of them."

"It would be deadly to follow the others into the pass," agreed Lord Tasmene. "I've been in those passes before . . . in storms they are full of floods and rockslides . . . impossible to travel."

"We will have to continue the search as soon as possible," said Fenwick. "But, in the meantime, we can at least get rid of this one."

"Shall I send someone up after him?" offered Lord Tasmene. Fenwick shook his head.

"No, that would be a waste . . . besides . . . this one . . ." Fenwick squinted up at the figure. The assassin. It could only be. Without moving his gaze, he took out one of his best hunting arrows, with the wide, razor-sharp double blades, set at right angles so there was a pointed cross of steel to cut into flesh and organs. "This one . . . is mine."

He nocked the arrow, drew back, pointed the bow high. The figure under the eagle-shaped rock seemed to be watching him. He almost chuckled. The rain ran down the arrow and onto his hand, but his bow was of Troisian make and never felt the weather.

"Nowhere to dodge, scorpion. For all your cleverness, I doubt you can learn to fly faster than my arrows."

The arrow leaped from the bow, and the figure on the ledge stumbled.

The arrow had hit Sam in the hip. It had been aimed for his gut, he knew: a slow, painful death that he had only barely avoided. He could feel the point grating against bone as he leaned against the rock wall, vowing to meet death on his feet.

"Ooh, you missed his vitals, Fenny," commented Tasmene. "Your aim is slipping."

"No it isn't." Another shaft hissed through the rain.

Sam was luckier at dodging this one; but it skimmed across his arm and tore open some important veins before it stuck in his shoulder. Again he'd been lucky; that one had been meant for a lung. The pain was intense, as the salty dust washed off the rock and into his wounds. His blood was warm on his arm, and he looked down at Fenwick, a dagger in his hand. Bad angle, and Fenwick was coping with it well . . . however, of course, Fenwick could miss. Sam never did.

"Bastard," hissed Sam silently to the figure below. "Let's see how well your Company can track with you undergoing resurrection?" If only the woodsman would step out just a bit more . . .

"Fenny, don't be cruel . . . finish the poor man. After all, he's human, just like you and I." Tasmene looked concerned. The figure was slumping. Sir Fenwick sighed.

"Very well. I'll get in from the front—clearer shot there." Fenwick urged his horse forward a few paces, and somewhat to the side, drawing a last arrow.

There was a sudden movement, and Fenwick jerked back. The horse, already upset, reared as something hit the ground with a metallic sound, and leaped up again, spinning. A curse from one of the company to his left reported minor damage. Fenwick steadied his horse and looked up at the figure on the ledge, which had almost fallen in the effort of throwing the dagger.

"Some sting left, scorpion? Try this." Fenwick drew back his bow as the figure slowly collapsed, still visible. At that moment, as though to help his aim, the roiling sea of stormcloud above broke open just enough to let a shaft of moonlight down, spotlighting the pinnacle. He fired.

With the failed attack Sam felt his strength leave him, too much of his blood gone for the fire to burn strong enough. He slumped onto his knees, blood running down his legs and arms from his wounds and mixing with the rainwater in puddles on the ledge, but mostly blood, red blood, seeping into the stone and filling up cracks in the ledge . . . funny how you notice these things, he thought, even as he felt the arrow heading toward him, toward his heart and too fast to dodge, how one looks at cracks and they almost look deliberate, kneeling here like this and you wonder what they looked like before wind and rain got them, a hundred and fifty years ago and . . . glowing?

There was a faint puff of crimson light, and the ledge was empty. Only Fenwick's keen ears heard the splintering noise of the arrow hitting the stone. Tasmene's eyebrows flew up in surprise.

"Cror's blood, Fenny, good shot! You vaporized him! Magical arrow, eh?"

Sir Fenwick said nothing, but stared at the blank rocky ledge, his expression unreadable. The stone eagle seemed to look back down at him with the same face.

Mizzamir sat bolt upright in his chair. Tamarne's Test! The last Test . . . the last chance. He had to do something. He quickly collected some of his strongest magics and watched the mirror carefully.

The waters had reached a point about three feet below the entrance to their cramped hideout. The dry cave was very shallow, with barely enough room for all of them. The wind blew the rain straight in, and they were chilled and wet through. Robin lapsed into the sick slumber of exhaustion, his injured leg swelling painfully. Kaylana cleaned and bound his wounds and those of Arcie and Valerie and herself as best she could, and they huddled together in the uncomfortable shelter. Robin was useful here, at least; his large bulk provided warmth and some protection from the wind and the rain, and Arcie and Valerie took full advantage of this, huddling behind him and slipping into cramped slumber. Blackmail watched at the entrance, also providing something of a windbreak, and Kaylana curled herself up against Robin's side, with the knight's broad armored back shielding her from the weather, and fell asleep, her thoughts troubled with the black-garbed figure that had run away from them in the storm.

Sam collapsed onto a cold stone floor, his vision dissolving in a swirl of red and black mist, the arrows grinding in his flesh. There was no sense of danger, just a slow fatalistic gloom. He would die now, and at the hands of some stupid pompous prince, of Trois no less, bloody Elf-huggers, and he would have to spend his time in the special hell for assassins who died before completing their mission, and what a long and painful way to go, too . . . arrows, why couldn't it have been a good clean sword blow, or dragon breath, or something . . . his consciousness fled.

When he woke again, his first thought was pain, the next, anger. The arrows still cut him, and his wounds were aching from the infection and salt. He wasn't even dead yet! Stupid Fenwick couldn't even kill him when Sam gave up. *Azel, blast you, dark lord whom I've served so long, where is your release? Do even you abandon me?* Sam rolled onto his back, gasping and choking with nausea. He couldn't see, but his assassin senses again felt no danger. He gripped the shaft of the arrow that grated in his hip, and worked at it. Barbed? No. Good. Trust a hero . . . He slowly and carefully pulled it out and passed out silently from the pain.

When he came round again, a few minutes later, he pushed the arrow in his shoulder straight out the other side, just as he had been taught. He managed to stuff some of the crenelations of his tunic into the wounds, and then went down for another nap.

When he woke again, about a half-hour later, his mind was beginning to clear, although his wounds were swelling. He finally began to wonder where he was, and what he could do about it. He managed to open his crusted eyes and looked blearily around. All was whiteness that hurt his eyes and made it hard to see anything. He squinted, tried to focus.

The first thing he saw was himself, pale, bloody, and battered. His zombie-like self-care had probably saved his life; the bloody arrows lying beside him were tipped with lethal blades, the first of which would surely have punctured his vital organs had he moved about much more. But he would still be dead soon if he couldn't find some way to clean himself, and get food and water. Water . . . there was a possibility. He could sense a faint dripping noise, and the room he was in . . . a room, yes. White marble. Large room, perhaps . . . he shifted a bit, listened to the echoes . . . fifty or sixty feet square? Neutral air, no smells but his own salty reek. Light, no source. And a dripping sound.

He rolled onto his good side and looked about. The sound came from the center of the room, where a large white marble fountain of simple design rose from the floor. It was in the shape of two bowls, one about twelve feet in diameter supported on a short column above another that was slightly larger. The water dripped slowly from the top level to the one below. On one leg and one arm, Sam dragged himself to the fountain. The lower level, he noted with cynical satisfaction, was only damp, steeply sloped so that the drops ran down to the base and whatever pumping mechanism lay within. He'd have to stand up to get the water, typical. As he paused for breath, he noticed something odd about the rhythmic fall of water. It took him a moment to figure it out; it was a beat quite similar to that of a human heart . . . it perfectly matched his own, slow, stumbling pulse, in fact.

He pulled himself into a semi-upright position by the rim of the upper level of the fountain, and scooped a few mouthfuls of cold water from the top level. It didn't much matter if it was poisoned or not; there were no exits out of this room and he'd die soon anyway without water. The liquid was cool and good, however, and helped ease his burning throat. A few splashes made his wounds sting, but further cleansing would be necessary. He slowly pulled himself into a standing position, and looked down at the upper bowl of the fountain, which reached his waist. The water was clear and still, and some trick of the light showed a very sharp reflection, fully colored down to his bloodshot hazel eyes and sodden tunic, torn and twisted so that it revealed the birthmark on his shoulder. The sight was rather unpleasant, and Sam reached into the bowl to stir the water and break up the image, but as his hand touched the surface, the hand of his reflection seemed to come loose from the water, and grab his wrist. With a snarl, Sam's reflection yanked him into the pool.

"Well, they can't be allowed to just slip away! Towser, get your mages together and get rid of this storm." Fenwick was back in control, ordering his Company to begin sweeping the unflooded passes for signs of the renegades. Lumathix took to the air on his scorched wings to try to spy them out from above, while Fenwick, Tasmene, and their retinues took shelter under a ledge.

Soon after the Company had abandoned the eagle-shaped tower, a faint flash of white appeared where the assassin had vanished. Mizzamir stood there and looked up at the rain, frowning. With a wave of his hand, the drops suddenly parted, falling past as though an invisible umbrella protected the mage. Satisfied, Mizzamir stooped, and looked carefully at the inscriptions in the stone. They were still glowing slightly. He couldn't enter the Test through the normal way, that was certain . . . but perhaps he could open it, briefly? He could open portals between worlds, after all. He was the most powerful wizard in existence; made even more so in these glorious days, when the power of Good was so strong that even novice mages of Light could cast spells that once were much beyond them. Certainly this ancient magic Test must have loopholes somewhere. All it would take would be a brief open and twist, to expel the magic and "real" contents from the magical fabric of the Test; the assassin, and the Segment. Then he could rescue both. Well worth the effort, he decided and he began to lay out the runes and objects needed for the spell, weaving a circle of power around the faintly glowing entrance to the Test.

Sam's footing was bad, and he was weakened from his wounds. He fell into the bowl. Instead of falling into water and landing on the stone bottom, he fell on top of something that fought and kicked. The water seemed to cool his wounds somewhat and gave him an extra burst of energy. He fought back, the water in his eyes. At last he and his opponent separated and surfaced. The water was about three or four feet deep, with an oddly flat bottom.

He viewed his opponent with surprise and amazement. Instead of a water-monster that had, through his feverish hallucinations, seemed to take on the form of his reflection, what was standing in the pool and facing him now, panting and dripping, was a mirror image of himself. The image was cast in solid reality, right down to the clothing and the wounds . . . except that both his own wounds and those of his opposite seemed to be somewhat healed . . . as though the damage he had originally sustained had been divided equally between them when the image had come into being.

He had only a moment to marvel at this before the image drew a dagger, identical to one of his own LiteFlite Shadrezarian blades, and lunged at him. Sam did not wait for the attack, but back-flipped out of the pool, stumbling slightly but recovering. The image climbed cautiously out of the fountain and approached him.

"Who are you, and what the shades is going on?" Sam asked, watching warily as the other Sam shifted his grip on the dagger.

"I suppose you'd call me your darker side," said the figure, "except that you and I both know there isn't much else to you. So, I'm just another you . . . what better opponent to test your fighting skills?" The blond man had Sam's own voice, and the strangeness of it gave him chills. However, it was the words that made his eyes open wide.

"Test me? Am I in one of the Tests?"

"That's right. Surprised?" The figure almost grinned at him. "And I'm just as strong as you, just as fast, just as deadly . . . I wield the fire too, as you've probably guessed . . . " Sam had indeed; the way the other moved was distinctive; "Except darker. I'm everything you should be . . . "

With a motion too fast to follow, the other threw his

dagger. Sam dodged, but the blade flew up, hit a pillar, flashed back, and before Sam could move it had sunk deep into his calf, making his dodge turn into a roll.

" . . . and," said the other, drawing another blade, "I never miss, either."

Sam dodged the next blade, and its rebound, and it went purring off into the rafters. Then he threw one himself, the one with a carnelian in the pommel. The other dodged it easily, having almost second-guessed where he would aim. *Got to watch that,* Sam noted. Sam dodged again as one of the daggers came back at him, and his opponent ducked behind a pillar. Sam realized that missile combat would be futile, so, a dagger in each hand, he leaped after his identical self.

The other tried to duck, but Sam had been expecting that, and grabbed accordingly. They went down in a tangle of black cloth, silently struggling. Sam sensed something, and wrenched the other over just as the other tried to do the same. Sam had a pillar to brace against, though, so he won, flipping the other over on top of him. He heard the faint thunk as one of the flying daggers took the other in the shoulder. The other then used this position of leverage to knee him very hard in the groin.

His reaction threw the other about ten feet to land rather awkwardly on the wet slippery marble around the pool. Sam spent an instant curled up, breathing fast to flood himself with fire and adrenaline to block the pain. When the footsteps came closer he jumped up like a startled cat, and just managed to dodge the second airborne dagger. The other had apparently had time to draw and poison a third dagger; a faint sheen of blue oil glistened on the blade. Sam looked at it.

"We're immune to blue poxwort toxin, darker self," he admonished. His darker self looked at the blade and sighed.

"Right, I'd forgotten."

"It's all right . . . I would have done the same thing."

"Of course. Well, maybe the poison's no good, but I don't recall as we're immune to steel, anyway." So saying, he flung the blade. Sam tried to dodge, but his already wounded calf betrayed him, and he took the blade in the foot. The poison stung briefly, but he'd spent years adapting his body to all the toxins he'd ever use, carry, or encounter. The other was on him in an instant, a birchwood dagger going for his neck. Sam grabbed the arm and wrestled with it.

"Two hits for one, Sam . . . I seem to be winning," said his other self.

"Game's not over yet, Sam," grunted Sam, and with a mighty twist he sent the dagger twisting out of the other's hand. He then grabbed for the neck, but the other jerked out of his way and they both rolled to the left as the carnelian dagger *spanged* off the floor where they had been. The exertion widened recent wounds, and they both became bloodstained. There was no time to draw weapons in this close combat, but there was no need; every assassin spends the entire first few years of training learning nothing but body combat, long before ever being allowed to pick up a weapon. Sam, realizing he was in a fight for his life, opened his heart and blood and will to the fire, letting the flames take him and lift him to ride where he would. His last clear image was of the sudden dilation and burning of the other's hazel eyes, and a sudden hardness come into the face . . . *Is that what it looks like?* he wondered, and then he was gone.

They sprang apart and drew weapons, the other moving slightly to avoid the returning flash of the thrown dagger. They circled, wary as cats, a stab here, a jump there, never a connection. It seemed to Sam that his opponent knew what he would do before he did it . . . at one point Sam thought of feinting to the left and then coming in with the right, and then as his opponent slashed for his left Sam turned and countered as the blade suddenly changed hands and lunged for his right. He jumped away as the flying dagger flicked past once again. The two men circled each other.

We're cautious, Sam thought, through the fire. *I'm cautious. We're too alike . . . but we must be different somehow*

. . . he is my dark side . . . what would my dark side be least likely to do? Or most likely to do? He didn't get a chance to think—his dark side lunged at him, daggers flashing. Sam ducked under and came up with his own, managed to get in a lucky jab in the shoulder, and grabbed at the other by a leg, tossing him aside. The other Sam landed oddly, and there was a splash of blood. Sam's hunter instincts saw it and tensed. He'd managed to widen the wound in his enemy's hip with that wrenching throw.

Mizzamir looked at his preparations with satisfaction. A ring of glowing stones outlined the Test gateway, and a few candles burned under his rain-shield. With a pleased nod, the Arch-Mage raised his arms, called up his mighty magic, and began to chant in a deep, powerful voice.

His opponent was up in an instant, and ready for what would have been Sam's killing blow. He slashed expertly with his shortsword and cut a large gash across Sam's chest. Only Sam's quick turn saved his jugular. Sam staggering back from the blow, leaned against a pillar, clutching at his chest and making bubbling noises. The flying dagger came at him again, and he ducked to avoid it; it clattered off the pillar and flew away into the rafters. Sam opened one eye slightly; his opponent, he knew, had run out of good throwing daggers, and Sam was exhibiting all the characteristics of a lung wound, an easy kill. So easy, in fact, that it would be best and most satisfying to his darkest killing instincts to stick the wide long blade of the shortsword in from close range, to watch the face twist in the rictus of death and feel the satisfaction of a kill. The other Sam approached carefully, sword at the ready, as Sam gasped and gurgled and spat, his legs shaking, strength apparently failing.

The other approached to close range—Sam could smell the sourness of his own familiar blood and sweat—and with the fire dancing in his eyes, raised the blade to strike . . .

Sam grabbed the sword with one hand, twisting it

away, and with the other he jabbed his flattened hand up and in, like a blade itself, through the hip wound on his opponent's side, breaking through flesh and membrane and closing at last upon a mess of slimy intestines . . . and froze.

They looked into each other's eyes. Sam saw in the other's expression that realization of death, with his own eyes showing the same look he had seen so many times before; not even a fear, just a sudden knowing, like looking into the world beyond that of the living. The intestines and blood vessels in his grip trembled slightly. Sam stood there, with his hand inside his own belly, as it were, and looking into his own fire-lit eyes, and holding his own life in his hands.

"You sly bastard," said the other, with his voice. "Do it."

To thine own self be true, Sam thought, recalling the words of an ancient play . . . but which is my own self? He hesitated, the fire burning but held as though frozen at the instant of the kill . . .

There was a sudden peripheral flash and a meaty noise. The familiar face he stared into suddenly took on a strange, puzzled expression, the eyes unfocusing . . . and the body fell down on top of him, knocking them both to the ground. Sam recovered his hand from its gory grip and wriggled free and looked down. Sunk into the back of his darker self's skull was the carnelian-pommeled dagger that had flown through the air for so long.

He recovered the dagger, wiping it clean, then turned the body over, and stared at his own face, pale and twisted in the rictus of death. He stared at it a long time, the fire slowly calming.

Then pillars and walls and pool and corpse became hazy, and blew away on a white mist. He looked up, but there was nothing there. Just white, on all sides. And hanging in midair, a ruby crystal segment.

He reached for it, but an invisible force blocked his way. A voice boomed out of nowhere.

"If you would pass the Test of Tamarne, you must make

a sacrifice, as he did. You must give up that which makes you special, that which is your greatest power."

"I just killed myself, dammit," Sam snapped, aching from his wounds. "What more do you want?"

"You must give up that which makes you what you are, that which is your source of pride and identity, as Tamarne did. This must be your sacrifice, for the Segment of the Spectrum Key."

"I'm no demigod!" cried Sam, feeling like an idiot for talking to empty space.

"You have the means. Have you the will? Only for this price will you gain the last Segment." The voice fell silent.

"The means . . . ?" asked Sam, thinking.

Legend . . . he took out a tiny black pouch he'd had tucked in his pants lining, and shook the glittering Heartstone, which Blackmail had given him for Robin's life, into his hand. Legend had it that those with strong enough will could use the power of a Heartstone to drain the very essence of their enemies. That was why they were so valuable, said to be tears of the gods, gems of rarity, magic and beauty so strong they could only be destroyed by the deliberate actions of a true and mighty Hero. Perhaps he could . . .

No. He couldn't. He knew what the Test wanted him to give up. Not his soul, maybe, but almost . . . There was only one thing he had close to the vitality and power of a demigod's immortality. But give it up . . . never. Without it, he'd die. He'd be worse than whitewashed. He'd be useless.

But without the Segment, they couldn't open the DarkGate . . . and then where would they be?

Sam stared into the Heartstone, lost in desperate thought. Maybe it wouldn't be so bad. Maybe he could make it. After all, he did have training, thirty-some years of experience, plenty of weapons . . . it was only a bit of an unusual mindset he was being asked to give up, just a sort of magic "gone awry." He pictured his companions; the incorrigible Barigan, the beautiful aloof Druid, the sly Nathauan, the mysterious knight, the young centaur, saw them waiting helplessly as the Light poured through the world and the trees and rocks blew away on a brilliant wind and all was sublimated into a featureless, blinding emptiness of pure positive energy . . . and, for those allied with evil, an agonizing, torturous death . . . he saw the flesh charring away from the bones in the shining light, heard the dying cries of pain and despair . . . he saw Kaylana's tears.

He gripped the stone in his hand and closed his eyes, his brow wrinkling with concentration, summoning the fire for what he knew was the last time.

Sam sent the fire rushing up in his blood, swirling higher and higher, his breath getting shallow, his heart pounding. What the strange power might be, whether insanity, talent, or inherent magic gone strange and dark, had never been explored. Sam recalled all the times he'd felt that instinctive, rushing, endless strength, from the faintest glow to the steady raging flame that drove him from within beyond the bounds of his flesh and bone. He called the fire and it filled him with tension and glory and power . . .

. . . and then forced it out with a supreme effort of will that brought tears to his eyes from more than exhaustion and pain. It was like breathing a last breath, like feeling his soul ripped raw. The feeling was worse than any wound, any hurt, as the flames swirling in his body were slowly sucked out, drained into the sparkling depths of the Heartstone and leaving aching weakness in their place.

The fire rushed out and away, leaving a strange, empty ache in every vein. Sam felt himself being sucked dry, helpless, the warm pride he'd always had around his heart torn away in bloody shreds.

The last glowing flickers ripped themselves free of the assassin's soul and spiraled away into sparkling crystal. Sam opened his eyes and hand . . .

Mizzamir began to near the completion of his spell and readied himself for the final burst of energy aimed at the Test, his power cresting.

* * *

The Heartstone sparkled in his palm with new unearthly beauty, crimson and jacinth and soft blackness, like a drop of blood, shadow, and flame. He only saw it for a moment before it vanished, snatched away by the magic of the Test, and Sam crumpled slowly to the floor . . .

. . . And Mizzamir released the spell.

As his magical force wrenched open a gate that was being exploded outward anyway, the effect was rather like a geyser of magic. The candles blew out and the glowing stones skittered away. The ledge exploded like a fountain of fireworks, red and white and silver. Mizzamir stumbled backward as the explosion crashed into him and fell off the ledge. There was a spurt like a volcano that decapitated the eagle-rock and sent an indistinct figure sailing high away over the mountains. The area lit up like noontime, and the people of Fenwick's Company and the Einian army exclaimed at the fiery burning farther down the mountain range.

Mizzamir caught himself by magic long before hitting the ground. As the explosion died away, he hovered back up the pinnacle and examined the ledge hopefully. Nothing was there but a charred patch of stone. He thought of the indistinct figure he had seen go sailing away.

"Bother," he said to himself. "The Segment and that assassin must have been blown into who-knows-where." He sighed. "I'll have to go looking." So saying, he teleported back to his Tower to his magic scrying mirror.

The Segment sailed into the air. It described a graceful arc, then tumbled down. It smacked into a rock outcropping, striking sparks, and then bounced its way down along the jagged outjuttings and ledges. It glittered dancing in the raindrops, then hit a rock midstream and clattered down a steep hill, finally coming to rest, an impossible treasure, on a pile of rough stones in the bottom of a dry gully.

Sam was mercifully unconscious for his airborne journey. He flew through the rain and air and wind, tumbling limply, spattering the ground below with drops of blood. Some tiny last bit of his luck held out, and he splashed down in a deep, fast-flowing river.

The Heartstone glittered in the night, a fire-sparkle among the raindrops. It was so light that the winds scooped it up and played with it, tossing it from side to side and across the distances like a hailstone. Finally they tired of the bauble and let it drop. It fell, and landed lightly in a tiny crevice high up a mountainside, hidden away forever from the sight of mankind.

The shock of the water woke Sam, sort of; he barely had the strength to cling on to a passing log, like a drowning kitten. Working his failing hands around the trunk, he locked his fingers together and concentrated on keeping his head above water. At least the cold numbed his wounds. A short while later, a change made him open his eyes; the rain was stopping, and the river slowing. The sky was different—lighter. It was dawn. He drifted down the current, uncaring as to where it might take him.

The rain stopped, the sun came out, and soon the unpleasantness of the night was dissolved away as swiftly as the mist. The rivers slowed and drained down, falling back into their normal courses as they emptied themselves into the Western Sea. Fenwick and Tasmene and their men prepared themselves for the hunt, and began making their cautious way into the mountain passes, hounds and guides leading the way.

As soon as the flood had ebbed enough, Blackmail woke his sleeping companions and they all edged cautiously out of the cave and made their way along the steep banks of the river. As soon as they could, they moved away from the water and continued to make their way through the mountains, wanting to put as much distance as possible between them and their pursuers. They had suffered a crushing capture and defeat, and lost one of their number, and were still in great danger. All agreed that a strategic retreat was in order. The day was bright and cheerful, Kaylana noticed; and in the light she could see tiny flowers sprouting from cracks in the bare rock, where no flowers should grow. The Light was getting stronger . . . she judged they had less than a week before the world finally tipped from balance far enough, and began its rapid slide into burning light.

"Trust that fool Sam to go and get himself losted," snapped Arcie. "There'll be no finding him in all this rock."

"We shall find him . . . or he will find us," Kaylana said, with more certainty than she felt. They were passing by another fast-flowing river; the slippery rocks made the going treacherous. Nightshade had abandoned his mistress's shoulder and had gone off scouting along the river's edge, poking at twigs and debris.

"I hardly expect him to just turn up under a rock or something," scoffed Valerie.

Robin was walking more slowly, closer to the edge of the river where the rocks were flatter and the going a bit smoother. Nightshade had landed ahead of him, and was busy pecking at something dead that had been washed into a crack of the rock. Robin averted his eyes in disgust at the carrion-eater's habits, but suddenly something odd in the scene made him look again. What the raven was tearing and stabbing at was a human hand, still attached to an arm, still attached to . . .

Robin gasped and stumbled, almost falling into the current. He ran up to the object, startling Nightshade into flight, and looked, going pale.

"I found him!" he cried, motioning the company to the water's edge.

Wedged in a crack between two rocks, the detritus of the ebbing river, was Sam. His hand, pecked and gouged by Nightshade, scarcely bled. Kaylana checked his pulse, and then, between worried muttered spells, ordered Robin and Blackmail to extricate him from the rocks. Arcie sat on a nearby rock and lit up his pipe, glad of the rest, while Valerie soothed the grumbling Nightshade, and fed him with scraps from her few remaining provisions.

It took them upwards of a quarter hour to work Sam free. Blood loss and exposure had left him in a deep coma, and something had charred his clothing badly. Kaylana, going about the meticulous job of healing the many wounds and abrasions, was shocked to see the network of scars covering the assassin's skin. Scarcely a handspan anywhere was lacking the pale tracks of old battles, or the darker red scars and scabs of more recent ones gained on their journey. On his torso and arms there were so many scars they often overlapped. Only his face was unmarred; for that was the only wound an assassin would bother to have magically healed—a facial scar would be far too easily recognized.

At length, Kaylana sat back and shook her head. "The exposure has taken too great a toll," she said grimly. "He will not wake to see another dawn."

"Oh, bugger," sighed Arcie. "Well, I'd guess you'd better be giving him some of this, then," he added, and passed over a wineskin.

"What's that? More Barigan whiskey?" sneered Valerie. Arcie looked affronted.

"Nay, 'tis some o' Mula's magic water . . . I were saving it for an emergency."

"This is one," Kaylana snapped, taking the waterskin. She quickly poured a few shimmering drops over the pale, dead-looking fresh wounds in Sam's flesh, and then forced some down his throat.

The color slowly began to return to Sam's face, and his breathing steadied. He heaved a deep sigh and opened his eyes.

"Cold," he muttered. Then he tensed.

"Test! I was in the Test . . . fought . . . me. Got the rock . . . red rock. Segment. Where is it?" He sat up and then woozily sank back down. Kaylana and the others exchanged glances.

"You went through the last Test?" snapped Valerie. "And won? Where is the Segment?"

"Explosion," gasped Sam. "Blew up into the air, fell in the river."

"It could be anywhere!" whinnied Robin in exasperation. Blackmail nodded assent.

"I'll get Nightshade to look for it . . . Will you do that, my pet?" she crooned to her raven. "Find mommy the big pretty red rock, won't you please? I'm sorry if the nasty man woke up and wouldn't let you eat him," she added, glaring at Sam. Nightshade clucked happily, and then took off.

"What happened to you in there, Sam?" asked Arcie, as Blackmail helped Sam to his feet. Sam shook his head and pulled his sodden cloak close.

"More than I like to say, Arcie . . . maybe too much."

Sam was so tired . . . despite the healing water, his whole body ached. He looked around and was stunned at what he was seeing.

The shadows were dark and frightening. Superstition warned him away from them. The people around him seemed strangely different; he realized, suddenly, that their movements ceased to catch his eye, that he no longer noted their vital spots. He tried to think of Mizzamir, but the image of the wizard just made him frightened and tired, and the thought of sticking a knife into flesh turned his stomach. He felt slow, weak, and tired.

As he stood, he put out a hand for support, and leaned heavily on a sharp rock. He reacted, and twisted an ankle as he tried to move.

"Ouch!" he yelped loudly, jerking back. He froze in horror, and his gaze caught and echoed Arcie's look of shock.

"Laddie . . . you cried out!" gasped the thief. "In all of our years of knowing you I've never heard you do that. What happened in there?"

"I . . . " Sam hopped around on one foot, trying to take the weight off his ankle. "Ouch! Ow! Shi–" Then he fell over. Blackmail and Robin caught him.

"And yer clumsy as a pup, ye lummox!" Arcie jumped down from his rock as Blackmail carefully helped the shaking assassin upright. "Speak!"

"I . . . I guess you could say I sacrificed my assassiness," answered Sam softly. "I had a Heartstone . . . it was the only way . . . "

"Sam? Is this true?" Kaylana stared at him with those impossible green eyes and he felt something in his guts flutter. Maybe now that he was no longer an evil death-dealer, but just a normal man, maybe she would see him differently. He tried to deny to himself that such thoughts had crossed his mind before he accepted the terms of the final Test. She was about to speak again when a voice called out.

"Come on! We must get moving! Nightshade just came back to tell me that as yet there's no sign of the Segment, but there *are* a number of men heading this way." Valerie motioned to them from where she had already begun to press on through the passes. Nightshade circled above, and then swooped off again, searching. They pressed on, Sam picking his way through the rocks with a pitiful mockery of his former grace.

In his Tower, Mizzamir finished his few preparations to scry for the Segment. He'd needed to change clothes and compose himself a bit. He set up the mirror and began his incantations, safe in his Castle on the far eastern edge of the Six Lands.

Nightshade was also looking for the Segment. He flew high over the rocky crags, turning and soaring in the thermals. He took a moment to harass an owl that was trying to sleep in the shelter of a tree trunk, then sailed on his way, scanning the ground below with sharp black eyes. In the distance he could just see the bright colors of the people who pursued his mistress; the rocks hid her and her party. A red glitter caught his eye, far below; the pretty red rock! He swooped down to get a better look.

But when he landed, he was disappointed. It wasn't a big pretty red rock, like the other big pretty rocks. It was a little rock, red and sparkly and pretty, yes, but only small, the size of squirrel's eyeball. It was just sitting up here, in a crack of the mountain.

The raven liked sparkly things. And this was, even if not what was wanted, a very nice sparkly thing, just the size to pick up and carry in one's beak. He scooped it up, and tucked it under his tongue for safekeeping. A lovely sparkly for him! He shuffled his feathers smugly, and then took to the air again, searching for the rock his mistress wanted.

* * *

Mizzamir had no trouble locating the stone. An artifact of that much power is easy to find in a barren land like Ein. A few minutes concentration soon showed the chunk of ruby-red crystal resting atop a pile of similar-sized stones, at the bottom of a gully. Mizzamir smiled in satisfaction. There was no one around the stone. He concentrated on the picture, getting a firmer fix on the location; he meant to travel through the mirror and emerge at the other side. He had never been to that location, thus he could not teleport himself straight there. Such were the few limitations of his power.

It was difficult to dodge the pursuing heroes. The terrain was cruel, and Sam and Robin both were hindered by it. Arcie, as well, was soon panting from exertion; his small size necessitated climbing up and down rocks that the others could step up upon. They all wanted to know about Sam's experience, and why he now seemed so stumbling and helpless; but the need for silence and speed damped conversation and curiosity. Finally, both to throw the pursuers off the trail and to make going easier, they waded into the shallows of the river and trudged along through knee-deep water. There was no sign of Nightshade, and Valerie in exasperation hit upon an idea. They stopped for a short rest, and she tested it.

She reached into a carefully constructed black pouch in the lining of her robe, made from the mysterious dweomer-worm silk that holds more than it should, and withdrew the shining chunk of yellow crystal she had won from the Test in the Castle of Diamond Magic. Holding it gently in her hands, she focused her mind upon it.

Like calls to like, as power to power. Each one is part of a whole, and all seek at last the eventual rejoining. What calls to thee?

At first, nothing. Then a strange warmth seemed to spread from the stone. It was magic, power, not good nor evil, simply a preset strength and purpose. On the inside of her vision, lights and sounds flared into being.

Golden light rippled before her, a high fluting. A cool blue tone pulsed to her left, where Kaylana startled, noticing the blue crystal in her cloth backpack beginning to glow. A rich purple bass thrummed from Blackmail's satchel, and a double note, of a warm, brassy orange and a bold green fluttered from Arcie's laden knapsack; the thief, in his usual way, had stolen the green Segment Sam had taken from Robin so long ago. Then, in the distance, seen and heard only by Valerie, a strong red blared its slow presence. Valerie looked up, the colors still dancing in her eyes.

"That way," she said, pointing. They abandoned the riverside at once and headed in that direction.

Mizzamir stepped through the portal and walked over to where the Segment rested atop the pile. He reached for it; but as he did so, it did something that startled him. It began to glow, a warm ruby light that pulsed slightly. It also seemed to be making a noise, reminiscent of a horn or perhaps a huge violin. Mizzamir furrowed his brow thoughtfully, but the noise and glow did not seem to be concerned with him. He picked the Segment up carefully. It did not change, but simply sat in his hands glowing.

At last! A Segment! Now the fate of the world was assured. The sheer power of the stone thrilled him; he ran his fingers over it gently. True, he had helped to design the original Key; but the reality, created by the gods themselves, was so marvelous and rich he could not help but admire it.

Thus it was that he was still admiring the glowing stone when a scramble of shale made him look up in surprise. Down a scree slope tumbled the villains he'd had so many unpleasant dealings with, all apparently still alive. They stopped dead at the bottom of the slope. Remembering the assassin and his daggers, he quickly put up an invisible magical wall of minor protection and faced them.

The lead figure, the sorceress dressed in black, was holding the yellow Segment; it was glowing as was the red one he carried. She instantly ducked behind the others; the Druid, warily gripping her staff, the centaur shuffling his feet, and the strange knight whose presence disturbed him so. The knight, silent as shadow, drew his sword, but did not approach. They remained in a frozen tableau.

Arcie, next to Sam, tugged on the tall man's belt. "There he are, Sammy my lad! Quick! Draw your dagger and let him have it! I'm paying you for this!" he hissed.

"I . . . " Sam started to fumble a dagger out of his belt.

Mizzamir smiled and said, "Well, so we meet all together at last. Please, drop the other Segments that I know you carry, and I promise you, no harm shall come to you."

"We will not," stated Kaylana firmly and Blackmail gave a faint nod. The motion made Mizzamir stare at the dark knight for a thoughtful second; and Sam got his dagger out of the sheath, and, gripping it awkwardly, drew back and threw.

It flipped through the air, and Mizzamir reacted instinctively, jerking back even though the dagger went past him and hit a nearby boulder. It clattered to the ground. Arcie swore an incredulous oath.

Sam's jaw dropped. He'd missed. He'd *missed.* And as fear struck him deep and strong, he saw the fate of death and felt gravity and pain and weakness and fear all dragging at him, and he felt his knees begin to buckle as he realized what he'd sacrificed. Mizzamir sighed and raised a hand. With a sudden wave, the villains felt a sudden cold stillness settle over them. Mizzamir took a breath, ready to complete the spell that would root them to the spot until he decided otherwise.

But, so used was he to the centaur's allegiance, he had excluded Robin from the spell. Even if the centaur were a turncoat, Mizzamir knew that Robin was far too timid to attempt any attack. Robin, he knew, had a lot of respect for him and his power. Robin could wait, while Mizzamir finished dealing with the real villains . . .

A gray flash zipped through the space between them, with a rapid drumming of hooves.

Robin, his ears pinned back, fists clenched, sprinted

forward. His hooves clattered on the stone, and then he crashed, full on, into the Arch-Mage. Mizzamir's protective shield, designed to stop small objects, was no match for the heavy bulk of the centaur, and it exploded in a flash of orange-silver shards. The Segment went flying.

As Mizzamir fell, his concentration failed, and the spell of holding vanished. The villains sprang into action. Robin, using frantic blows of hooves and fists, prevented the Arch-Mage from being able to concentrate long enough to complete a spell, but flashes of incomplete magics zipped and zinged around the two, and the smell of scorched hair was strong.

Arcie ran forward, grabbed the red Segment, and they ran out of the area along one of the passes. As Sam, in the rear, made his stumbling way through, Kaylana shouted back to Robin—

"Hurry, centaur! You journey with us!"

Robin jumped away from Mizzamir, with a final hind-leg kick, and galloped after them. As he swept past the Druid at the far end of the pass, Kaylana touched her staff to the rock wall and sent a burst of sheer power and command through the ancient stone.

The mountainside cracked with a sound like lightning and burst outward, shuddering and sundering all around its faults and fissures. Thousands of tons of rock tumbled down to where Mizzamir was regaining his feet. With a faint noise of annoyance, Mizzamir vanished from view, an instant before the rocks smashed into the small gully where he had been.

"Och we've . . . got all the bits," wheezed Arcie, as they ran. "Now what?"

"I don't know!" replied Valerie, with the same difficulty, as she scrambled over the rocks. "Bhazo said . . . "

"The way should be open ahead!" gasped Robin, his ears flickering. "I can hear the noise of the river!" Sam and Blackmail stumbled on in silence.

Suddenly, a black shape came winging down from the clouds, fluttering frantically. Kaylana looked up in annoyance.

"Well, your raven has decided to return, despite his

lack of success," she began, when Valerie, listening to the raven's muffled cries, suddenly stopped, and turned to run back.

"We've come the wrong way!" she shouted. "Fenwick and his men—"

An arrow thudded into the ground before her, cutting her words short. They looked up in despair as dozens of green-and-yellow and blue-and-white garbed men came pouring down from the rocks on all sides. The villains froze for a moment, and Sam had a desperate hope that they could surrender and just give up, rest and sleep and maybe die, anything to stop moving . . . but it was not to be.

Blackmail drew his sword, as did Robin. But Arcie had a much better idea. He bolted, running as fast as his short legs would carry him down the pass. Without hesitation, the others followed him, Robin and Blackmail bringing up the rear and cleaving their way through the first ranks of the attackers. Arrows hailed around them and splattered off the dark knight's platemail. More thudded into Robin's flanks, making him whinny and squeal with pain, until the cover of the rocks made accurate aim impossible.

They ran down the pass, the slope adding to their speed. Suddenly, the pass opened up, tumbling down a steep, muddy slope that had recently served as a floodwash. They slid down this, their pursuers close at their heels. As they fell, Valerie's voice could be heard over the muffled curses scrambling.

"Quickly! Assemble the Segments! Our only possible escape is into the Labyrinth!"

"Where is the entrance?" Kaylana called back. "Is it here on Ein?"

"It's wherever it needs to be!" the sorceress shouted. "All we need is the Key and fast-moving water, if legend serves!"

"There's a waterfall up ahead!" Robin announced. His four-legged gallop, though treacherous in the slope and mud, was carrying him along at a fast clip.

"Perfect!"

They landed at the base of the slope and turned, running as best they could upstream through the cold shallows. The rushing noise of water filled the air and before them, they could see the waterfall—a forty-foot straight fall, sending crashing cascades of mist and foam swirling about in a deep pool. The mist formed a huge rainbow that danced in the sunlight; a wide indistinct arch that hovered between air, land, and water, spun of the firelight of the sun. The sun had shifted little from its high place in the sky; the Light of the world showed strong. Little time was left.

They reached the edge and halted; there was nowhere else to go with steep cliffs to all sides but one. From behind them, the shouts of pursuit came ever closer. Arcie fumbled the three Segments he carried out of his pockets. Kaylana, Valerie, and Blackmail quickly added theirs, and there was a scramble to fit them together.

"Hurry!" whinnied Robin, looking ahead; more of Tasmene's men had cut around and were sliding down the cliffs, swords drawn. Others had begun firing arrows from the clifftops.

Sam screamed suddenly, and fell as an arrow stabbed into his back, and another one into his leg. Pain! Agonizing pain! It ripped through him and made him curl up, crying and retching. The sounds of his agony were more terrifying than his usual silence; his voice, always so calm and controlled, twisted in high, helpless anguish.

Valerie and Arcie, working on the Segments, were protected by Blackmail's upraised shield. The knight moved and twisted to block the arrows as the two fumbled with the Segments.

"You Barigan fool!" shouted Valerie. "The spectrum! Put them in order of the spectrum! Like the rainbow!"

"Och, Richard-Oversees-Ye-Great-Battle-Plans," Arcie's voice recited indistinctly. "Red-orange-yeller . . ."

Kaylana did not seem to be a target of the bowmen; she used this to her advantage, causing the rocks that many stood upon to turn to loose mud, tumbling the archers to their deaths. Robin grabbed a dropped longbow and arrows from one of the bodies, and, taking partial cover behind a rock, returned their fire with legendary centaur accuracy. The air was full of shouted orders and screams and the zip and hiss of arrows. Sam, looking up through pain-wracked vision, saw Lord Tasmene running back and forth at the top of the cliff, giving orders, and up the path they had come charged a second group, led by Fenwick. Sir Fenwick wasn't waving his sword now; he had it drawn, but he was holding it sensibly and advancing in deadly earnest. It was just as they were about to close ranks that a shout rang out.

" . . . Purple!" finished Arcie's voice triumphantly. There was a very loud *click* noise, as the last Segment snapped into place.

Arcie and Valerie fell back as a sudden burst of white light exploded outward from a single, shining star. The Spectrum Key, perfectly round now that all its Segments had been joined, hung in midair, a burning too bright to look at that flashed in its whiteness all colors of the rainbow. And as it pulsed, waves of pure magic fluxed out, warping reality around them.

The air thickened, and the ground warped; the sky seemed to ripple and shift. Everyone fell, disoriented, as the very nature of reality twisted, changed, making allowances for something very vast to exist. The Key called to the Lock, and the Lock came, bearing with it the Labyrinth. The Labyrinth was everywhere and nowhere; a continuous thread through the fabric of the world that lay flat and unseen, but present at every point; unseen until the right hook dragged it up from the surrounding cloth. And as it was dragged, it caused space around it to crinkle up.

The rainbow of the waterfall, the link of all the elements, was the focus and the door. As the light of the Key fell upon it, it thickened and widened and became a full arch, solidifying into a multicolored construct no thicker than soap bubbles but real as ice. Around this, behind the shimmering space beneath its arch, white whorls swirled up, rippling themselves over the mountains and water without regard for gravity, spiralling high into the bright air, diving through the earth in tunneling coils.

Lumathix the dragon, who had just taken off to begin scouting from the air after a short rest, had the best view as the Labyrinth solidified. Twisting white marble passages finally settled into full existence, and he spent much time later trying to describe it fully. But when people would ask the great rose-gold, "Yes, but what did it *look* like?", the best Lumathix could do was blurt that it seemed as though some god had taken a huge potful of pure-white noodles and dumped them over a large part of the Einian scenery.

Luckily, as the world ceased its strange magical upheaval, and the Labyrinth stood, sparkling in the clear sunshine, the villains who had caused its summoning were the first to recover. The Spectrum Key abruptly ceased its brilliant glare and fell to earth with a gentle thud. Arcie grabbed it, and kicked Sam back to consciousness as the others got to their feet, looking about in awe. The men of Ein and the Verdant Company were also recovering fast. The villains ran into the shimmering, rainbow-marked archway, and before anyone could shout or fire a spell or arrow, the last one, a limping, bleeding man dressed all in black, had disappeared.

Fenwick and Company, along with a large section of the Einian army, slowed their charge and stopped before the entrance, uncertain. The Labyrinth, bathed in the light of the high bright sun, hulked there like a great sand-sculpture, its shimmering magic casting strange colors over faces and clothing.

The men of the Einian army backed off, muttering among themselves. In the Einian culture, a rainbow was a gateway to the world of the dead; a place of feasting and happiness, perhaps, but still not a place any living soul wished to venture too soon. They looked to their leader, Lord Tasmene. He viewed the archway with suspicion and motioned to his men to stay back.

But Fenwick scowled, hefted his sword, and marched to the entrance. He turned around to face his men.

The members of the Verdant Company, the finest elite fighting force assembled in the Six Lands . . . avoided his piercing glance. He addressed them.

"Well? Come on! Follow them! Follow me!" he roared.

There was a long moment of silence, broken only by the panting of the men and dogs, their breath steaming in the mountain air. Armor jingled.

The men looked away, fidgeted with their weapons, looked at the Einians, looked at each other. Then Towser spoke for all of them, in a young, frightened voice.

"Sir, we follow you. To the depths of the earth, to the peaks of the mountains. We've followed you through fen and fire, forest and flood, across the entire chain of the Six Lands . . . but we will not follow you into the Labyrinth." The young heroic prince glared at him, but Towser, with the air of one who has greater things to fear, met the gaze and continued.

"If you pass through that portal now, sir, you go alone."

Fenwick stood unmoving a long moment, his eyes glinting in the sunlight. Then he spoke sharply, decisively.

"All right! We camp here for one week. If nothing has happened in that time, we go home. The villains will be as good as dead. But, should they manage by the greatest of miracles to survive once more, and even solve the mystery of the Labyrinth . . . "

Sounds of scoffing came from the ranks. Fenwick ignored them.

"Then we will be ready. We will track them to the center of the maze if the magic is removed, and meet them for the final battle there. Towser, I'll want you and your colleagues to keep a twenty-four-hour-a-day watch on the magical field of this place, and notify me of any changes. The rest of you, bring the rest of the troops here, and call the clerics in from Clairlune Castle to heal the injured and raise the dead. We will not fail again." The sun burned at its high apex over the mountains, bathing the Labyrinth in golden light.

XII

It seemed they ran through solid walls of twisting stone, and the stones fell away; and then there came a twisting and a falling and time and distance were stretched away into past and future. They tried to keep together but the turning passages were alive and wriggled like snakes, spinning them down into emptiness and then . . .

"Oh *no,*" groaned the thief. In all directions, white marble passageways stretched, slanted, twisted, and curved. The air was still and cool, and eye-tricking lilac light filled everything. They had no idea how they had gotten there, but it didn't seem to be important. Their wounds were healed, or perhaps they had never been. All that they could focus on was a shallow impression of some vague past, a familiarity with each other, and a vague sense of purpose. They were there, and they had to find their way out.

"Very well, who wants to map the way?" asked Valerie.

"What about your magic?" asked Robin doubtfully. The Nathauan shook her head.

"Magical mapping would be useless in this place."

"I don't see as even a written map will be much good," commented Sam, looking around. "I mean, which way is north? And where did we come in from?"

There was much looking around. In all directions stretched the passageways, but not a one of them looked like the one they had started to walk down.

"Maybe we could . . . " began Robin, trying to scratch

the marble with his hoof. Nothing happened. He gave up. Arcie fumbled in his pockets and pulled out a piece of charcoal. He made a mark on the floor with it. But a moment later the mark faded and vanished.

"Well, bugger," whistled Arcie softly.

"It is simple," said Kaylana calmly. "There is no need for a map, because there is no way out but the solving of the Labyrinth of Dreams."

And was it waking or dreaming? The mind played tricks, and when the eyes were closed things happened. And what was past and now and waking and dreaming and all was spinning . . .

"Oh, you'll like being a good person," assured Oarf. "Everyone does." The dungeon was filled with flickering shadows, and Arcie struggled in iron bonds, but his fingers and toes were numb, frozen, and wouldn't work right.

"Yes, and you'll forget I even did this, once it's over . . . your past of darkness and fear will just seem like a bad dream, long ago . . . " Mizzamir smiled, displaying a dagger that was like a shaft of pure white light. Arcie held his breath. Grains of sand were starting to fall away from the wall bolts of Sam's right-hand manacle. Then the assassin seemed to shiver and melt into the shadows, and Arcie was alone in the cell, with Mizzamir standing over him, smiling, the shining dagger held high. "I just use this, you see," the Arch-Mage explained patiently, "and cut out your soul. It won't hurt a bit." The knife descended . . .

"Is there a trap, old chum?" Sam asked, looking around. The Barigan nodded, and pulled out his tools from an embroidered pouch with a large "R" on it.

"Aye, a trap. Big one, too. Don't move, now, or that large tile in the ceiling will open up and no doubt spill something nasty down on you."

Sam slumped against a wall. "We are going in circles," he muttered in a low monotone. "We are trapped in here, the last of our kind, in the last days of the world. We will all die, whether we move on or stay in this room forever. We will languish here until the walls burst into pure white light and ascend into utter unbearable brightness and the very earth shatters with perfection, and our souls will not even have a hell to flee to for their eternal damnation."

He put his head on his hands, and the light on his eyelids shifted and changed.

Kaylana walked through fields of blood, confused; everything was the same color, and it was hard to see. There were men, with strange devices of cold metal that fired tiny arrows of lead and slew things at a great distance. Smoke was in the air, and it was hard to breathe. Something was coming, something dangerous, and no matter how fast she tried to run it was always gaining . . .

Robin's voice sang, in gentle cadences, the strains of a song he had learned well. Around him it seemed as though he and an indistinct other walked through white passages, and the song had some connection to it . . .

And darkness was swept from the world forever,
For the Light formed a maze of white
Hidden within the keys of the Heroes
To be won again should the need arise,
In the lock that saved the world,
And all to reach within the mind,
And find the true and hardest test.
The darkness was swept from the world forever
And the last remains were sealed in the fabric of stone.

"That's one of your new-modern free-form thingies," Sam muttered. "No rhyme, no rhythm, typical minstrel stuff."

"I don't know," said Valerie. "It's sort of tolerable in an artsy-smartsy sort of way."

"It's just a translation," apologized Robin, a bit stiffly.

Sam, after a moment to lift his head again, picked a

dart up off a side table. It was made of a carved bone, and the fletchings were carnelian. The bar was full of vague shadows, watching and laughing in distant voices . . . Sam looked at them, trying to find faces—faces half-familiar, half-forgotten. A slow fear turned in his stomach when he suddenly realized that each and every one of the patrons had met death at Sam's hands. A half-formed, stinking, sneering face, seen through blood and flickering fire, chilled his blood with memories over thirty years old . . . and chuckling merchants, and laughing Plainsmen, and snickering woodsmen, and last of all his own face that smiled with his mouth and raised a glass of blood-red wine to his health. Sam felt a searing pain in his hand, and looked; the dart had turned into a tiny lizard, all colors and glowing like flame, that had sunk its venomous teeth into his finger. He could feel the poison rushing up his arm, and felt his heart tremble, and fail . . .

Valerie stumbled through whiteness that burned into her eyelids, making them close in pain. Burning, searing light . . . she couldn't see. Outside, in the heat, sand blowing, under her fingers, choking her throat. A pile of feathers under fingers . . . She knew, without needing to look, without daring to look. Nightshade, his blood soaking into the sand, and the cold emptiness at her throat where the Darkportal had once hung. The sand stripped her clothes away and the sun attacked her skin, worse than dragon fire, blistering and burning until the skin was slowly peeling away, not even hurting very much, but she could feel bits of her flesh dropping off. She crawled forward, trying to get to shelter. The sand and sun scoured her of flesh and skin and blood and then she was a skeleton, crawling blind over the sand, and the wind felt strange blowing through her rib cage, like a mockery of breath. She slipped into the cool shade, of a rock cleft, stone, caves, underground. The cool darkest deepest caves where the Nathauan would place their dead to age for a few days before eating. But she had no skin, no flesh, and no one would even know her. Her empty eye sockets wept tears of sand.

* * *

Robin felt his feet trapped in the mud turned to stone, caught! With the villains approaching! But, wait . . . were they villains? He shook his head. All around him were clouds. On his wrist was a silver bracelet; it was very tight, but he knew better than to touch it. There was a strange wind, blowing up around him from below. He looked down as the wind blew the mist away and saw the jagged rocks of the mountains of Ein rushing up at him as he fell . . . he screamed and passed out.

When he woke, he was on a hill at sunset. Mountains ranged in the distance, outlined by the setting sun; they seemed familiar somehow, but he could not say why. There was a tree at the top of the hill—huge and old and gnarled, a great oak thrown into stark relief by the sunset. He walked up to it and lay down under it. As he rested his head against the trunk, he froze. Thrumming through the wood he could hear music! A strange and ancient music, filled with such grief and sorrow he could not move or think. He sat where he was, listening to the tree. He could almost make out words.

"Adventure?!" Sam shouted incredulously. "Where do you get the idea that this is anything more than a wild goose-chase through the most hellish parts of the world with everything in existence trying to kill us!" A stinking fog whipped through the Fens, chased by ghosts and half-seen vegetables. The rain poured. They had to shout to be heard over the storm. It was raining drops of light, pure light like fireflies.

"All this were never to happen had we but stayed in Dous enjoying the laxity of the lawfolk, instead of trying to make trouble," grumbled Arcie hotly. "We might have had food and horses to spare if you hadn't wanted to chase dreams!" The rain of lights lashed in his face and tossed his words like whips.

Arcie sighed. "I dinna expect to find it easy," he said, half to himself. "Yet it are so alone . . . In th' stories about adventurers, ye always hear of them as being captured by goblins, then rescued by Elves, meeting strange old wizards, enjoying the hospitality of fairies, sailing on ships with strange companions, meeting interesting people from yon days past . . . but such them things are for heroes, I warrant. There's but the few of us against a world as hates us, and even those we meet as thinks the same wants to kill us." He ran a hand, stiff with arthritis, through his hair thoughtfully, and many of the strands came loose. He looked at them, all of them silver-gray, thinning. He sighed. "Yet I would no' trade myself as I am for anything. I doubt but anyone would."

The room was white and lilac-lit again, and it seemed as though they had been there a long time, but none could say how they had gotten there. But Arcie, why he could not say even to himself, was rummaging in a small crevice in the white stone wall.

"What is it, old chum?" asked Sam. "Gold, so you can pay me back the deposit you stole?"

"Nay!" The Barigan was almost crowing in excitement. "Some such much *better!*"

Arcie stood there with a wine bottle in each hand and a huge grin on his face. The bottles held a pale golden-pink liquid.

"Pixy-Clover Wine!" crowed Arcie.

"Oh, get off your sky-horse," snorted Sam. "There is no such thing."

Arcie looked hurt. "There *are so,* Sam, and I have got two bottles right here to be proof of it. Has anyone got any goblets?"

"Right here," announced Robin, digging in his saddle-pouches and pulling six fine glass and silver drinking cups. Where he got them from, he couldn't say, but he knew they were there. Arcie was rummaging in his pockets for a corkscrew.

" 'Tis late, I'm fair parched and away hungry—"

"What else is new?" broke in Sam. Arcie ignored him.

"And by greatest of serendipity we has two bottles of Pixy-Clover Wine. Don't ask how, say when."

"Very well, then," decided Kaylana, looking about with suspicion. The walls were very white. "We shall camp here."

Arcie had dug out a small folding corkscrew and was working the cork out of one of the bottles. Sam wrinkled his lip in mild disdain and sat down, at least glad for the opportunity to rest. He felt tired and drained, though what he had been doing that had caused him to feel so he could not say. The fire was gone, gone forever, and he was a useless waste of flesh . . . what did it matter what Arcie did?

The Barigan quickly filled the six glasses with sparkling amber liquid, and passed them around. Sam looked at his when Arcie pushed it toward him, and looked away.

"No, you aren't going to get me drunk again, short one," he said sternly.

"Alcohol is a poison and rots the body," said Kaylana virtuously, ignoring her glass.

"This isn't bad, Sam, really," Robin commented, taking a cautious sip. The liquid flew into his veins like a bird, and he giggled and drank the rest of his glass.

Arcie, meanwhile, was looking back and forth between Kaylana and Sam. "Come on, you two lumps. 'Tis nay harmful, I swear."

"And where are you such an expert?" asked Sam.

"I will drink it if you will stop babbling," Kaylana sighed, picking up her glass.

"Babble all you want, Arcie," retorted Sam. "You won't get me a second time."

"Sam, here, at least smell it . . . " Arcie held the glass under his nose. "You really ought to try it by rights . . . too many people die without ever having tasted Pixy-Clover Wine."

Sam sniffed involuntarily and was surprised. The smell was familiar, though he didn't remember it from any place or time . . . but it was a beautiful smell of flowers and sunshine and lazy times lying on the roof of the Guild in summer with the clouds sweeping past in a blue sky and the laughter of his assassin friends below in the training halls . . . he took the glass.

"Well, just a taste," he relented. Arcie grinned. "Good boy!"

Sam took a mouthful. It made his eyes open wide and he banged his head against the wall behind him. The stuff was magical, obviously—it brought back memories of every good thing that had ever happened to him, all the times he'd felt happy, or proud, or cheerful, or just content with the world. There was the euphoria of the Shadowrealm and the comforting security of his old room at the Guild when he was just about ten, a young boy whose only family and friends were black-clad killers. There was the time he had spent on Grozzle's farm in the summer, learning the alchemy of the thousands of poisons and antidotes Grozzle grew there. He had wandered in the blooming gardens till his head swam from the scents and he laughed in the sun. It reminded him of warm summer evenings, walking along in the streetlights with Cata, arms linked. It was the smell of a thousand intoxicating perfumes, from strawberry pie to the faint scent of Kaylana's hair when she had bent over him to heal his wounds. It almost made the ache of the missing fire go away . . .

Kaylana had half-finished her glass and appeared to be staring into the depths of the clear liquid. She was thinking of green summer fields, the flight of birds, the running of deer. She remembered, so many years ago, the summer festivals when the Druids would gather great wreaths of fragrant blooms and strew them about for the great rituals, when the bards would come to gather and play their songs from faraway lands. She fumbled and took hold of her staff. The images drifted away. Puzzled, she released the staff, and the feeling of joy and happiness returned. She sighed and held the staff, letting the images vanish, and sipped the rest of her wine. Her staff protected her from its intoxicating magic, and she pondered on the nature of the beverage while trying to ignore the general frivolity of the others.

The Pixy-Clover was one of a small number of rare plants with inherent magic. The small, fragrant fairy bloom had a power to twist time around itself so that it lived in a continual state of summer, vanishing into the timestreams for the other seasons and emerging into temporal reality only in the warm months. Fresh or distilled, this power was a vital component of most spells that involved changes in time, such as freezing a person in time or Kaylana's speed-slowing of time. If the distilled potion was drunk, much of the magic went instead into the associated intoxication, as well as reminding the brain of cheerful times, particularly in summer months past. Mages had scorned this practice of consumption, which they regarded as a waste of valuable magical extracts. The wine could only be brewed by the Fair Folk of the Hills, it was said, a race of beings older than the Elves, who had fled from the land in the destruction of the War. Now the pale amber liquid was worth far more than liquid gold, but what was money, or time, or even reality? The dreams of summer were no stranger than the other dreams that flickered in the corners of her vision.

Arcie was looking at Robin.

"Minstrel," he said owlishly, "mayhaps you can give us the music as goesh with this."

Robin snorted and started giggling at the sound. "Of course I know it," he scoffed. "Doesn't everyone?" He hauled out his harp, buffed the wood tenderly with his sleeve, and began to play and sing in his clear voice.

Of all the nectars in the fields,
None are quite so fine,
As the Fair Folk's brew of summer's dew,
Pixy-Clover Wine!

The sprightly tune made Sam look up and smile. He knew the words too. This was a very old song, and a very well known one.

Sweeter far than all the fruit,
That grows on branch or vine
Of time-twist power or fragrant flower
Pixy-Clover Wine!

Arcie scooped up three empty glasses and juggled them in a brief circle before setting them down again and refilling them. Sam found his glass full again, and drank some more, enjoying himself. Kaylana watched Arcie fill her glass and gave a smile. *You would never think these people were hardened villains,* she thought. Look at them, listen. Even without the effects of the wine, she couldn't resist singing along. This was an old song, older even than the War and all it had brought.

Let your sorrows drift away
Summers past are yours and mine
Glass to the sky, your spirit high
On Pixy-Clover Wine!

Sam stood up and said, "Here, Arcie, did I ever show you how I can balance a dagger on the end of my nose?"

"Nay, Sammy, dinna try it now," spoke Arcie in a brave attempt at seriousness. "You canna do that sort of thing nay more, recall you?" Undaunted, the wine fizzing in his brain, making him feel like he was sixteen again and immortal, Sam shook out a dagger and tried to flip it in midair, but the Barigan jumped up and caught it. "Nay, you'll put your eyes out."

"Just one," insisted Sam.

Robin had got his fingers tangled in the harp strings and was doing his best to recover. He finally yanked his fingers free with a twanging sound, flexed them and began the next verse.

Sam bowed to Kaylana, putting his glass down. "May I have this dance?" he asked solemnly. Kaylana regarded him thoughtfully. He looked so happy, his eyes sparkling with the wine, that she didn't have the heart to refuse him.

"All right," she said condescendingly, standing up, and before she knew what she was doing, she set the staff aside, leaning it against the wall. Instantly the effects of two glasses of aged Pixy-Clover Wine crashed into her, and she half-fell sideways into the ex-assassin's arms with the faintest suspicion of a giggle.

Futures are a mystery
But you'll always find a sign,
Of times to come in summer's sun
With Pixy-Clover Wine!

Sam whirled Kaylana in his arms. He was happy and sad and confused and old and young and lost all at the same time. But clearer than anything else was the strange ache in his heart, not of loss, but somehow connected intricately with the beautiful woman before him who had impressed herself into his soul as no one else had ever done. Kaylana danced like a dryad in the wind, and his vision was full of flowing copper hair and a flash of green eyes. She might be formal and distant, but underneath all of that was a woman of courage, strength, and intellect. He'd never felt quite this way about anyone before, not even Cata . . . he knew he'd never feel this way again.

Joy is free the wide lands over
From desert to the frothy brine
Let a year pass way in a single day
By Pixy-Clover Wine!

He spun her close, and she turned her face toward him, the wine shining in her eyes. He almost gasped, she was so beautiful. Her cheeks were flushed ever so delicately, her hair tangled around her face. And she was smiling! A beautiful, wide, joyous smile, and she gave a little laugh of delight at the wonder of it all, a laugh that struck the poor ex-assassin like a blow to his heart. She looked into his eyes, and he lost himself. He folded her into his arms and kissed her.

As past and future meet in now
So take my hand in thine,
Distill a flower to a joyous hour,
Pixy-Clover Wine!

For an instant she was uncertain, then her lips responded warmly to his. He held her close. Kaylana felt the pounding of his heart, felt weak for a moment, and reached out to the wall for support, her fingers closing around the staff.

Sam felt the change instantly, and threw himself away as the Druid suddenly sobered. The others didn't seem to have noticed; Arcie was trying to play the other strings of the centaur's harp. Kaylana looked at him out of hard green eyes. She pulled a lock of hair out of her eyes.

"Do not do that again," she told him sternly.

He sat up, shaking his head to dispel the images. Kaylana looked coldly at him a moment, then vanished into a cloudbank before he could call out.

In the outside world, Sir Fenwick relaxed in the shade of great fruitbearing trees that had sprung up from the ground and bare rocks of Ein. All around was emerald green grass, filled with multicolored wildflowers. The men and women of the Company laughed and chatted and enjoyed the long, sunlit days and the slightly softer dusky times of what had once been darkest night. The Einian army had been sent home to be with their families, but Lord Tasmene and his adventuring companions remained, keeping company with Fenwick and his men in the strange new spring that had fallen on Ein.

In the Silver Tower, the radiance shining into the rooms through the stained-glass windows was almost too bright to bear. Mizzamir moved in patient waiting, polishing his magic stones, enjoying the music of the world as it soared to perfection.

She gripped the staff tight. Things were confusing. She was not in control. She didn't like that. With all her will she forced her mind to see what was there, instead of what it chose. Illusions began to fall away, slowly but surely, like earth eroding under the steady rain of her strength . . .

Sam followed and came out into a wide area where a huge structure loomed, like a massive black vertical hole twice as tall as a man, ringed with a crackling field of light . . . the DarkGate!

Even as he strode forward, there was the sudden shouting of men, and the Verdant Company, set to charge now that the magic of the Labyrinth had vanished, came running in, and he drew a weapon and prepared to fight for his life, as the others did the same . . .

It was some weeks later. The journey home, with the battle won, the darkness restored, had been quite peaceful. He and Arcie had obtained passage on a ship back to Dous and rode horses home. Since Sam was no longer an assassin, Arcie had agreed that the contract on the ArchMage was expired, and Mizzamir could be allowed to live, his power curtailed now, of course. Sam and Arcie had gone to the Frothing Otter first thing, back in Bistort, and ordered a pint each of the fine brown ale. They sat back in a dark table in the far corner, relaxing for the first time in months.

"Well, it were quite a tussle-up there, eh?" Arcie remembered, chuckling at how the sudden opening of the DarkGate had sent the Verdant Company fleeing in terror. Sam nodded.

"Yes indeed . . . pity Kaylana had to go home after we'd won, though," he sighed wistfully.

"Och, you'd never have brought her back into another town anyway," said Arcie. "Anyway, what's for you now? Back to assassining?"

Sam shook his head. "No, that's gone forever . . . I don't really know. I suppose I can learn a trade . . . the others did."

"Ah, but them were whitewashed," the thief pointed out. Sam nodded.

"I thought, perhaps, of trying to find Valerie. She vanished about the same time Kaylana did . . . heading home. She said I might have some magical talent . . . maybe I'd make a good sorcerer."

"You looked mighty farce in the hat," replied Arcie doubtfully. Sam smiled.

"It's pleasant to be able to just relax and look back on it all," he said, with a sigh. "It seems so far away now. Everything, after we got into the Labyrinth, until we got out and came all this way home. It seems so distant . . . like a . . . "

Two mugs of ale froze halfway to two mouths. Arcie and Sam stared at each other with eyes suddenly full of shock and realization.

" . . . dream," they said, simultaneously.

"I'm picking up some fluctuations in the field, Sir Fenwick!" called Towser. Fenwick looked through a cloud of scintillating butterflies to where the mage sat. The sky was blue, the sun was bright, a very pleasant eleven o'clock in the evening. The grass and wildflowers were lush and thick, songbirds sang continually in the trees. There was no trace of the barren, rocky land that had bred the hardened Einian people since the beginnings of time. Reports came in that in the areas around the mountain Putak-Azum, there were lush green fields and no trace of the barren, salt-poisoned plain that had once been the Frozen Waste. The very air seemed to shiver with perfect light. Troubles with the Labyrinth seemed a distant memory. Though it still sprawled in white coils across the valleys, it had sat there without change or danger for almost a full week now and seemed to be harmless, though the wildflowers which grew everywhere would not root in its smooth marble surface. It was truly an enigma . . . but soon, perhaps . . .

"Well, keep an eye on it," Fenwick instructed with a smile. *Soon, soon,* he thought. *Soon there will be nothing more to worry about, ever.*

* * *

Sam and Arcie sat frozen, ice flooding into their stomachs as they realized the narrow escape they'd had. Around them, burning off under their lucidity, the warm familiarity of the Frothing Otter melted away, leaving behind icy white marble walls, smooth and featureless but swirling faintly with half-images. If Sam closed his eyes, or looked out of the corners, he could see faint dreams—faces, places, shadows. It was a similar experience to days past when he'd been deprived of sleep during finals week, back in the Guild in studies, and would start seeing things . . .

"Wake up! Sam, wake up!" Hands shook his shoulders and he sat up, warm bedsheets tumbling around him. Tousle-haired, he looked up into a pair of rich azure eyes, framed by black curly hair and a worried face. He smiled, and the face smiled back at him. Around him, the warm shapes of his bedroom resolved themselves. Sunlight was pouring through the window behind Cata, helping to outline her nimble figure dressed all in tight-fitting black silk. She must have just come back from an assignment. It was good to see her, especially dressed so provocatively.

"Cata," he said with a sigh, reaching out to stroke her cheek. She sat on the bed, winking at him. "Was I having a nightmare?"

"Yes indeed, and darker than any of Hruul's adventures it sounded, too," Cata replied, running her long fingers through his hair. He took her hand and kissed the fingertips gently, as he had done so many times before. She smiled. "You were yelling about a labyrinth and someone named Kaylana . . . "

"Kaylana . . . " Sam looked up, unsure. Kaylana. The name was vaguely familiar, but . . .

"Sam! Wake up! Wake up!" Hands shook him and his eyes flew open into a world of white marble. Blue eyes and black hair blew away and were replaced by impossible green and red. The green eyes bored into his mind, his soul; once, guarded by the fire, his spirit could have withstood almost anything. Now, dream-dizzy and powerless, Kaylana's Druidic strength reached in, took hold of his will, and shook it.

You will stay awake. You will stay aware. We are in the Labyrinth of Dreams. We are searching for the DarkGate. You must concentrate on that and let nothing else distract you, or we shall all die. The commanding presence finished with a shot of strength to his will that helped clear his head some. Kaylana dropped her fixing gaze and lifted his hand to place it on her staff, and he looked around for the first time clearly, the oak wood tingling under his fingers.

Next to Kaylana, also with a hand on the staff, was Arcie. Blackmail stood in a corner, his sword out, slashing at nothing. Robin sat some distance away, his ears up as if listening, his eyes open but unseeing. Valerie walked in a small circle, and Nightshade fluttered around on the floor, as if wounded.

"The dreams of the Labyrinth have caught them," Kaylana said sternly, "as you yourselves were caught. I myself only managed to escape by the power of my staff."

"How long have we been wandering about this place?" asked Arcie. Kaylana shook her head. Sam looked down. He, too, had no idea, his timesense having vanished with the fire. Kaylana, leading the two rogues by her staff, managed to wake the others out of their dream-trances. They were able to keep their concentration by holding hands, as long as the end of the chain was in contact with Kaylana's magical staff. Robin was the hardest to waken; even after he had been shaken into consciousness and made to understand the situation, he seemed vague, as though trying to remember some lost knowledge. Blackmail was difficult as well; it took some quick maneuvering by Kaylana to duck his wildly swinging sword so that she could make contact with him, and of course, being unable to see his eyes, she could not reach into his mind to pull him into waking life. But his strange will was strong in its own way, and even as she touched him he seemed to recover, shaking his helmet and then looking around.

"We may have been out for days," grumbled Valerie. "And we have no way of knowing how far the sublimation has progressed outside the Labyrinth. That at least is a small mercy—the magic of the Labyrinth protects us, at least until the final destruction of the world."

"Och, such a mercy," grumbled Arcie. "I'm half wanting to give up and go back to my dreams here!"

"But are we awake now?" Robin asked, looking worried. "What if this is just another dream?"

"We cannot attempt to puzzle that further," snapped Kaylana. "We have come this far and must press on. We must find our way through the Labyrinth."

"That will take until the end of the world!" exclaimed Valerie in annoyance. "Literally!"

Blackmail rapped on one of the walls; it seemed solid, though its exact shape and dimensions seemed unclear due to the ghostly images surrounding it and the eerie light that shone from every surface. Passages twisted off in all directions, unpleasantly organic-looking, like the intestines of some huge beast.

"If it's all dreams," put in Sam, "shouldn't we just be able to walk through it?"

"Some people can control their dreams," Valerie said thoughtfully, gently scratching Nightshade as he sat on her wrist. "Perhaps by lucid thinking we can determine where we go in this mess of a maze."

"And how are we to do that?" demanded Arcie.

"If all the Labyrinth is a dream, then all space and time are no thicker than a thought," stated Kaylana. "And once the destination is known, the journey is no more than a single step." She strode forward, dragging the others with her . . .

And as it turned out, by her own backward, stubborn will, she was right.

The floor trembled beneath their feet as the icy whiteness shivered and began to melt into faded half-images, the Labyrinth losing power now that they no longer believed its dreams to be reality. The world seemed to spin, and there was the sensation of movement, and that feeling again of great energies being expended into the fabric of existence itself. As strangely as it had appeared, the Labyrinth of Dreams was dissolving.

The whiteness fell away, leaving them atop a flat plateau of rock of no kind natural to Ein; a red-brown, burnt-looking stone, a broad table left behind by the slowly vanishing Labyrinth like a fossil frozen in ice. Even now the white dome over the center was creaking open, and brilliant light burst in upon them.

The sun and moon shone together in the sky, moving slowly in an impossible conjunction. The sight twisted Kaylana's soul with fear, as these figures of vital importance to the Druids moved in terrible, unbalanced, unnatural ways.

The light flowed in, burning white, and, as the Labyrinth's protective magic slipped away, they were struck with the full force of a world on the brink of utter goodness. The air was strained and warped, even stronger than the Labyrinth's magic; the twisting of the world's existence could be felt in every motion, thrumming from every stone, like a glorious but demented music.

Around them, the light burst into everything. The red-brown stones suddenly flashed into soft blue-gray, and everything, everything of colors of shadow and darkness faded. Valerie's hair fugued into a soft shade of brown, and Nightshade turned a brilliant blue while the sorceress's clothes melted into a cheerful yellow color. Sam's tattered clothing lost ink and dye in a rush, leaving him wearing tattered creamy-colored silk and cotton decorated with bright patches of other colors put there by a Martogon tailor. Even the blackness of the silent knight began to shade into a mouse gray, the heavy shield dull with layers of fading paint.

At the camp of Sir Fenwick, the more gradual buildup of light energy had been hailed as a glorious sign from the gods that all was well; the men and women of the Company had never been better. Towser and his mages had power they had never dreamed of, everyone was healthy and strong and never felt fatigue. The countryside of Ein was thick with flowers, and reports came in everywhere of similar wonders that had been occurring all over the world. For the triumph of energy, evil or good, is similar to any fall; the object may teeter on the brink of falling for a long time with little change, but once that final plummet begins, it accelerates.

Fenwick and his companions knew nothing of this. All they knew was that the Labyrinth seemed to be disintegrating; barely visible at what once had been its highest point was a strange chunk of rock that could be seen jutting from the frothy white remains, with several indistinct figures atop it.

"Towser! Summon your mages and begin the charge!" shouted Sir Fenwick in sheer joy, as he drew his sword Truelight and raised it above his head. It glowed like a stab of lightning as Tasmene and his men came to rally with him, and the mages appeared . . .

Everything was shifting; it was as though the world suddenly became a flat, artificial picture, with no more depth than a child's drawing. It took them a minute in baffled shock before they realized that almost all the shadows had vanished. Everything was illuminated equally, even the insides of their mouths as they gaped in astonishment.

The light picked out in vivid detail a crater of jagged stone. At the bottom was a circular area, perhaps fifteen feet across, covered by a mesh of glowing magical cords, forming a shield over whatever lay beneath. A double arch stretched over this area, the two spans meeting at right angles and dropping from their intersection a long needle of stone, with a hole straight through, about three feet from the spear-sharp tip. The hole shimmered with magical workings, and was just about the size of a large apple, or the size of the glowing composite gemstone Arcie now held in his hands.

"The Key!" cried Valerie, looking at the gemstone, her eyes squinting as she fought the burning light. Yet her joy gave her strength to endure the all-pervading force of Good. "And the Lock on the DarkGate . . . by all the dark dead gods, I never thought I should live to see this place . . . "

"So all as we has to do is put it into yon hole?" asked Arcie, ignoring the metaphysics.

"Not quite," said Valerie with sudden deathly seriousness. "The DarkGate is evil . . . many lives were sacrificed to seal it. From what I was able to learn from my tomes, it will take at least one more life to open it."

"That's why you dragged us all up here?" gasped Sam, shocked out of his self-pity. "For Gatefodder?"

"Not all of you," said the sorceress pleasantly. "Just one."

Things might have gotten very nasty at this point had it not been for a series of sudden soft explosions as air was displaced in teleportation. There in a flash stood Sir Fenwick, at the head of thirty of the Verdant Company. Another, and there appeared Lord Tasmene and his powerful adventuring companions. A swooping shadow overhead told them that Lumathix the dragon as well was on call.

"Get to work, Sam!" Arcie hissed, as the party drew weapons. The Labyrinth was already closing behind them, sliding down away from the crater on the summit. Its magic fading, it sank slowly under its own weight into the solid dark stone. There was no retreat. Sam shook his tousled head.

"I can't," he whispered. He willed his muscles to draw, to throw, to kill . . . but he couldn't.

"Then open the Gate," urged Kaylana, snatching the Key from Arcie and pressing it into his hands. "You are the only one who can climb there anyway."

"She's right," Arcie muttered, hefting his morning star. "No way in hells are you getting *me* up them arches carrying yon rock."

"But I don't want to die!" protested Sam. He felt so lost. His patched gaudy clothing hurt his eyes and made him feel like a jester in motley.

"Don't worry, old chum," said Arcie, as he started forward. "We should be able to throw but one of these bastards in there."

Arrows suddenly hailed around them, Valerie fired a spell of flaming fire, and the battle for the DarkGate had begun.

Sam tucked the Spectrum Key under his arm and ran forward, trying to keep out of sight but knowing himself hopelessly visible, and too slow. His companions spread out and met the attackers face on, Blackmail, Arcie, and Robin in front, hewing at those who came within range, and Kaylana and Valerie staying just behind, hurling spells into the oncoming ranks.

Arcie wasn't cut out for this kind of fighting. He contented himself with thwacking his morning star into the shins of any who looked like they were moving to intercept the ex-assassin as he ran. Blackmail charged into the thick of Fenwick's warriors and the fighters of Tasmene's company and did great damage with his huge sword. Robin fought with the panicked desperation of a wild horse, his sword swinging and his wicked hooves lashing out in all directions. Words of chanting rang out, and a number of longbowmen vanished in a puff of dry dust under Valerie's power. Though her magic was puny compared to the incredible power of Light, she fought for her life, and the nearby presence of the DarkGate gave her courage, if not support. Kaylana gripped her staff and whispered words of magic, and from the hard rock grew wicked long spikes of stone that tripped and caught the troops of Light.

But the forces of good were certainly in the majority. The mages of the Verdant Company threw spells that forced the renegades to dodge and fumble. Gouts of flame burst, arrows of light were fired, and wounds bled.

Fenwick, shouting his men on, saw the running figure of the ex-assassin and swiftly nocked an arrow to his Troisian bow, drew and fired. He didn't know what the villain was up to, but it was bound to be no good.

A cloth-yard arrow buried itself in Sam's side, and he stumbled. Pain! Pain that wracked his limbs in stabbing agony, tearing into his nerves no longer shielded by the fire of assassin determination. An assassin never screamed in pain, it would give his position away . . . but

Sam heard his voice cry out, a hoarse scream of agony. He saw Fenwick draw his glowing, magical sword and begin to approach him. Shaking with crippling agony, he drew a dagger from his boot, panic and fear giving him strength, and threw it in desperate self-defense.

Fenwick dodged easily, and the dagger's arc of flight completed with a clatter to the floor.

Valerie drew back in agony as a blast of lightning from Tesubar crackled into her arm. Nightshade croaked in rage and flew in a flurry of feathers and hoarse cries at the blue-robed mage. Something flew from his beak and sparkled in the air as Tesubar cursed and flailed at the raven.

Robin crashed his sword against the Dwarven blade of Lord Tasmene, and the centaur's weapon shattered. He spun and kicked the man as hard as he could in the chest. "Ooof!" exploded Tasmene, unbalanced, as he stumbled backward a step. Robin scooped up a sheaf of arrows from those fallen on the ground and pulled forth the bow he'd taken from the combat outside the Labyrinth.

Fenwick, about to skewer the helpless, bleeding villain on the point of his sword, suddenly found himself in a swarm of stinging bees conjured up by the Druid. As he tried to shake free of them, a painful spiky object crashed into the back of his legs. He jumped away, and Arcie, bleeding heavily, threw an almost-empty wineskin at Sam, the stopper removed. The last of the cool liquid poured out, splashing over the ex-assassin's bleeding side, dissolving the arrow away, healing his wounds.

"Run, you daft idiot!" Arcie yelled, and plunged back into the fray, running from Fenwick's slashing sword, as Sam scrambled to his feet and ran on.

Sam reached the place where one of the arches joined the stone, and tried his best to scramble up it, to climb out to where the Key must fit. But his hands slipped helplessly on the stone; a surface that once would have held a thousand handholds was impassible to him now.

Arcie saw something sparkle on the ground amongst the trampling feet and spattering blood. A red gem, not a ruby, but . . . he was a good enough thief to recognize a Heartstone when he saw it. And Sam had said . . . Suddenly all was made clear.

"Sam!" he yelled, scooping up the stone and throwing it as hard as he could toward the assassin. A flash of metal to his side made him leap away, barely avoiding the slashing blade of a snarling Verdant Company warrior.

Something fell with a faint noise near Sam, and he scooped it up in amazement as he huddled behind the grounding of the arch. The Heartstone, glowing ruby-orange from his stored powers within . . . How, where, why it had returned, he couldn't guess . . . but it was useless, unless a Hero could destroy it, and set free the fire to fly back to him. He gripped it, felt the trembling flame trapped within. The success of his Test had been worth it, but he knew now what he knew before—the nature of a person, good or bad, is central to existence. He could no longer even think of himself as Samalander . . . even the inborn magical talents that Valerie and the Guildsmen had seen in him had been linked to the fire, and his weapons now flew according to the laws of nature, not of magic.

"Well, well," said Mizzamir to himself, in the Silver Tower, as the image in his newly repaired scrying font resolved with a flash into a scene of battle around a shining pit. Around him, the room blazed with shafts of color as the stained-glass windows threatened to melt under the powerful light of the sublimation conjunction. "So they made it? Quite amazing . . . Well, best go to meet them before things get out of hand." He took hold of his staff and teleported with a mere thought; his was a magical strength now rivaling the gods, and he no longer had any need for words for such trivial spells.

Sam looked up in shock as there was a sudden shimmer in the air across the pit from him, and he gasped as Mizzamir appeared in all his radiant glory.

The mage seemed to smile at him benevolently and shook his head in pity. He reached into his belt pockets for spell components. What Mizzamir had in mind would take a bit of finesse . . . a job begun long ago that would now, finally, be completed. He would use his magic to turn all these villains to the path of Light, and all would be well forever.

Robin fired shaft after shaft into the ranks, until a returned bolt punched right through his upper biceps, preventing him from drawing his bow. He scooped up a sword from one of the fallen and continued to battle, his legs and sides raked with cuts.

Kaylana shouted words of power, gripping her staff tight. A wall of thorns sprung up from the rocky ground, writhing and twisting in sudden growth. The hedge wrapped up and around the emerging forces of the second group of the Verdant Company as they teleported in.

Sam jerked in fear as Mizzamir raised his hands and began casting a spell. Sam thought frantically, *I've got to break his concentration!* He couldn't let Mizzamir trap and whitewash him even further, even if he hadn't the will or the skill or the strength to kill the Elven wizard Hero. He hurled the first thing that came to hand: the small but heavy magical Heartstone. The mage saw it coming and halted his spellcasting to catch it. The power of his spell hovered in the air as he inspected the red gem.

"But this is used, silly lad," he admonished gently. "It won't work on me." He pressed it tightly in his fingers, about to crush it in contempt. Sam caught his breath. But then the mage seemed to change his mind.

"Perhaps . . . no," he said with a smile, and tossed it over his shoulder. Sam scrambled to his feet, ready to run, attack perhaps, anything, as Mizzamir raised his hands to complete the spell. The stone twinkled in the dust . . . and, out of the fray, a grayish-armored foot reached out and stomped on it, crushing it to powder.

Brilliant crimson and orange darkness leaped up, flashing in beautiful, terrible power. Sam caught his breath in wonder at the fire, unleashed, wild and glorious in its might, loosed from the confines of the crystal or his humble flesh. The fighting men cringed away from it, crying out in terror as its touch sent shooting agony through them. But it bathed a solitary, tall, armored figure in its flames an instant, burning away grey-faded paint with its power before it relented and spiraled free in the air.

Sam raised his arm in joy, like a falconer calling to his hawk. The cloak of flaming power slashed through the air to him and plunged into the pale blue veins of his wrist, driving home like a bloody lightning bolt, vanishing into his body.

Mizzamir was staring in shock at the figure that had crushed the Heartstone.

Blackmail's armor had been scoured clean and shone brilliant silver. The layers of faded black paint over the large shield had been stripped away, and the object now bore a device, in blazing color, of a golden griffin rampant on a field of crimson. The knight gripped his helmet with one gauntleted hand, and tore it off, the welds snapping in the after-heat of the firebath. A human head, stern and mighty of face, with long mustaches only just silvering with age, piercing gray eyes and a handsome countenance that were unmistakable from murals and paintings and tapestries and legends. A chorus of astonishment rose from the ranks.

"Sir Pryse!"

"Correct!" shouted the Hero-turned-villain. His voice was deep and powerful, his eyes flashed around the battered multitude, and suddenly glittered in fury as he noticed the stunned Arch-Mage. "I watched what you led the land into, Mizzamir! The land I nearly died for! Light is a choice, you old fool, not something that you must force on all those you do not approve of! Everywhere, hundreds of thousands of men and women have been brought by your magic into near-mindless slavery, and creatures who did none any harm were slain without mercy. When my own brother turned to darkness, and you went after him, I begged you spare his life and soul. In your *mercy,* you turned him into a warhorse! Perhaps you thought that funny, Mizzamir. But even I, once a paladin, would never stoop to such self-righteous tyranny." He paused a moment. "These villains you pursue are the world's last hope of salvation, and I am with them!" He roared an ancient battle-cry and swung his great black sword back into the fray as the combatants suddenly remembered where they were.

Sam, meanwhile, had undergone a resurrection, scarcely noticing the unmasking of the knight. Sheer glory and power lifted him off his feet, drove the pain away, snapped the world back into perfect perspective. Mizzamir. The Key.

A single motion drew and flung a dagger with lightning speed and perfect precision, without the burden of thought, only the being-ness of weapon and target.

The blade flew, spinning, and struck Mizzamir in the chest. The mage gasped and gripped at the dagger, blood staining white robes. Sam, having now bought some time, gripped the Key in his free hand and scrambled up the archway.

Fenwick's archers cursed and swore as their light armor was invaded by swarms of stinging, clinging ants that rushed up their boots and into their breeches. Valerie fired spell after spell, her amulet burning cold against her skin as she strove to draw enough of its power to survive. The burning light of an over-illuminated world singed her skin and blinded her.

Arcie crashed into her, knocking her aside to safety as one of Towser's fireballs smashed into the place where she had stood. Arcie jumped up, flailing about in pain as his clothing burned yet again.

Robin, almost purple from blood on his gray hide, panted and gasped in exhaustion. His ears were pinned back in fighting fury, and a bleeding stub of a tail lashed; the long gray plume, severed by a blow from Tasmene's sword, lay trampled in the bloody dirt and stone.

Sam slid down the needle and held fast as he tried to maneuver the Key into its slot without falling into the shimmering pit of the DarkGate and its silvery Lock field. Someone would have to get thrown in there for the Lock to open, but Sam didn't feel like volunteering.

Just then that Sir Fenwick looked up, saw what Sam was doing, saw the staggering form of Mizzamir trying to wrest the dagger free. With a howl of pure rage Sir Fenwick threw at Sam the first thing he had to hand; the magical sword Truelight Slayer of Darkness.

A longsword was certainly not meant to be hurled, but Fenwick was driven by anger and power, and the magical sword knew to speed to its target like a bolt of vengeance.

Sam saw the spinning weapon, ducked his head behind the pillar, but misjudged, and there was a stab of pain and his grip fumbled. He wrapped his arms and legs as tight as he could around the end of the pillar. His left biceps seemed to have been chopped clean through, and blood was starting to fountain. The sword was stuck into a crack in the stone, humming in anger because it had not killed him.

He clutched the Key against his chest, and he clamped his gory arm into a fold of his tunic to keep the blood from spoiling his grip. He looked up to see Arch-Mage Mizzamir set down a bottle of magical healing potion and face him.

"Get down from there," said the mage gently but firmly.

"Go to the Abyss," hissed Sam, trying to work his way downward to where he could install the Key. The magical sword spat a shower of sparks down at the assassin.

"You are a brave man," Mizzamir said. "Come down from there. Come join the Light. Goodness is the only path to happiness."

Sam could hear Blackmail—or Sir Pryse the Hero—roaring in the background. The stalactite was already getting slippery, and the arteries and veins in his arm were spurting blood.

"Please, come over to the Light side," urged the wizard, stealthily drawing forth spell components. "I don't want you to get hurt . . . Join the side of good and live in happiness."

"Give it up, Mizzamir!" shouted Sir Pryse, hurling a Verdant warrior away with a slap of his magical shield.

"He's stubborn, just like his father. Yes, just like you."

"What did you say?" gasped the Arch-Mage in shock. Even Sam looked up, wide-eyed, from his bloodstained perch.

"I should have thought it would be obvious," growled the knight, never pausing in his relentless battle. He knew he had only a short while before the powerful enchantments woven into his armor gave out. "Look at him. Your hair, before it silvered from the War. Your eyes, your Elven blood refining human features. Your inherent magical ability. You know me, Mizzamir, as I know you, and what you've done. You know I'm not lying."

Sam felt his jaw drop. The image of his mother's dying face swam before him, her mind suddenly clear in approaching death, her eyes showing sanity and remembrance before they dimmed and dulled. Remembering pains and humiliation endured long in the past, that had left her confused and broken, trying to raise a bastard son in a cold world. Saw in that son's features, even then, the face that had set her on the road to despair and death.

"But I . . . " stammered Mizzamir, shocked. "She was . . . No! Impossible!"

"And you confused her mind with your magic, so she wouldn't spoil your reputation," scoffed Sir Pryse. "That was all that ever mattered to you—your glory, your power, your image. And when you suffered a moment of weakness, you refused to pay the price for it."

Mizzamir stared at Sam, and Sam stared back. Each now saw the truth behind the strange unease they felt when facing each other; the face that looked back was like a distorting mirror, each showing what the other wished never to be, but over the same blood and bone.

And Sam's eyes widened. In the chaos of battle and the removal of Sam's thrown dagger, the Arch-Mage's white robes had gone somewhat askew, pulling down slightly from the left shoulder. Nestled against the pale almond-colored Elven skin, in the fragile hollow between neck and collarbone, was a familiar, pale brown, asymetrical starburst birthmark.

The voice of Sir Pryse the Hero boomed in the background.

"Almost a hundred and fifty years in a suit of magical darkened-armor gives a fellow plenty of time for thought, and I saw your features in that assassin's face the moment I saw him. You gave him a life he didn't ask for, but with your blood he's got the power to kill even you."

Sam lunged suddenly, tearing his gaze away from the eyes of the mage, and shoved the Key into the hole in the rock. Anger over thirty years old burned in his soul, but he remembered his mission, and the quest he and his friends had risked their lives for.

The huge gemstone Key flashed in brilliant light, sending sparks coruscating along the Lock. There was a creaking, grating noise, as of magic under great stress. All the Lock needed now was a life to open it, the ultimate sacrifice that would fulfil the conditions of the magic. Sam was convenient . . . but he had other business first.

"No!" shouted Mizzamir. He was a kindly wizard of Light, but he knew destiny when he saw it flashing in the eyes of a trained assassin hanging in front of him. Sam no longer looked foolish in his rainbow garb; his eyes burned with a light that was pure shadow.

Panicked, Mizzamir shouted a spell, fired. A lightning bolt tore through the air and crashed into the assassin, burning skin, boiling blood, searing flesh. Sam ignored it.

In chess, someone has to take the black pieces, he thought. Checkmate.

With his free hand, Sam wrenched the magical sword free of the stone above him. It burned in his grasp, searing his flesh in its anger at being touched, but he only held it an instant, then threw. And he *had* learned how to properly throw a weapon of that sort. It flashed in a shining, spinning arc. A blade, even a magical blade, is designed to kill. That is its ultimate function, for good or evil, it kills whom it is wielded against . . . like an assassin. It scythed through the air, and struck, thrown harder and faster than any blade should have been, strong enough to slay even a Hero.

The Arch-Mage Mizzamir's head flew off his staggering body, and rolled across the ground to come to a halt near Arcie's feet. The Barigan gasped in shock as the dead face of the Hero gazed up at him in a twisted leer, blood drizzling.

Sam sagged, pain ripping through his body from the hole torn in his torso by Mizzamir's lightning bolt. He was dying. His grip was slipping. Mizzamir was gone, Sam's last job was finished. He felt himself pulling away from the needle of stone.

Sir Pryse saw Mizzamir fall, saw Sam sliding helplessly. He shook his noble head.

"The world has had enough of Heroes," he said softly to himself. "I will not continue as the last."

The tall armored knight rushed forward and threw himself headlong into the crackling light of the Lock, even as Sam's grip failed. The knight reached the mesh of light an instant before the assassin, and the glowing screen burst into sparks that vanished, destroying themselves and the Hero with them. Sam shouted aloud as he fell, what he chose as his dying words, the last thing he had to say. Sparks flashed around him.

"Kaylana! I love you!"

The words struck like arrows into the Druid's heart; she felt the truth of them as clearly as she felt the sudden snapping of the tension of the Balance, and the Dark-Gate opened.

Sam was suddenly falling into darkness, wonderful, cool, deliciously dangerous darkness, darker than night, than death, blackness so deep it was full of shadows thick as cotton. So thick, so deep, like a great ocean of liquid onyx power that reached up a whirlwind of slashing claws. It turned his clothes back to their jet darkness and made his skin shiver. Darkness and dark magic . . . The shadows were like cool water, diving into cool water. The darkness was full of rising shapes that grabbed for his falling body to rend and tear in the wild rush of freedom and didn't even notice as they passed instead through dark empty air.

An explosion of night burst from the DarkGate, a rushing torrent of shadows and blackness and half-seen nightmare shapes. A burst of icy force sent the combatants tumbling like autumn leaves. The air was rent by the shrieking of a thousand fiends as they shot from their prison and dissipated in the light of the goodness-filled air. With them came the dark power, and the fabric of the world creaked and trembled as the pressure of light began to ease.

Shadows returned to perspective in a rush, and the sun fled from its out-of-place position in the night sky. Evil and darkness flowed into the world like fresh water. The plummet of the world into Light was halted, turned. Slowly, the effects of evil power began to return. And still the flood of darkness continued.

Slowly, undead in the vaults of Putak-Azum and a thousand other crypts of legend raised their bony heads once more. The fox stalked in the woods, and killed, and the falcon dropped from the sky, and killed.

In the towns, men and women suddenly saw with eyes of reality, and some men would soon think ill of their fellows, fight in anger, or squabble, or take wealth for themselves, in accordance with human nature. Noblemen, suddenly shocked into realizing how lazy their soldiers had become, would soon begin stockpiling weapons against what the neighboring lords might be doing, and heroes suddenly looked up from their lazy retirement to think perhaps they were needed once more. Conflict, the driving, pounding force of life, whirred into action and existence once more.

As the world tilted slowly back to normal, the shapes flying out of the DarkGate kept their forms in shadowy substance as they fled back to their lairs. Shaggy, red-eyed werewolves, snapping kobolds, floating gornabar, snake-fiends, shouting bandits and hobgoblins and strange-shaped creatures from the depths of night whirled in hideous shapes against the sky. A rush of wind sent thirteen huge dark dragons wheeling into the night on vast wings, and Lumathix spun away in terror, but the beasts merely turned and fled to the corners of the lands to spread themselves out once again in a balanced play of life and death, good and evil.

The warriors in the battle for the DarkGate fell down the smooth, vast slope of the roof of the still-dissolving Labyrinth, rolling and stumbling. Kaylana grabbed the Barigan and Robin scooped up Valerie, and they jumped onto the smooth plain of the roof on the opposite side and began to slide down at rapid speed. The Frozen Waste, littered with dead flowers, rushed up to meet them.

They hit the ground heavily and rolled to their feet. Kaylana gripped her staff and once more transformed into a chestnut horse, while Robin hoisted a bleeding and exhausted Arcie onto his back. Valerie, at a nudge from the mare, climbed onto Kaylana's back, and they galloped away from the white marble of the Labyrinth as it began to crash and crumble.

Fenwick and his men, landing on the other side, didn't see them go. They rolled in the cracking of dying flowers, looked up into a night sky at the towering smoky column of released fiends. They panted, staggered to their feet, and muttered among themselves.

"Damn," cursed Fenwick. He got to his feet, and looked around for his hat, his eyes stinging with rage. A gentle hand was laid on his shoulder, and he looked up to see Lord Tasmene standing nearby. Behind the warrior's head, stars flickered with the drifting passage of evil beasts.

"You did the best you could, Fenny," said the big warrior gently. "No one can say that isn't good enough." Tasmene looked out across the land. It was dark now, but the stars were out, and a moon almost full. He knew dawn would come in due time, that despite the horror of the things they had seen, the battle was far from lost. "I'm not happy about this either, but we did have over a century of purification of the world before this happened.

It will be many, many years until darkness can threaten us as it did in the War. In the meantime . . . " Fenwick looked up at his friend, and the big warrior smiled. "Look on the bright side. At least we still have jobs. This world needs heroes again . . . the minstrels will soon be singing your praises as never before."

"And what of those villains? They must have escaped," muttered the ranger, still not quite comforted.

"Our children's children will curse their names," said Tasmene cheerfully, "for bringing the darkness back. But in the meantime, let's leave this part of my realm, before it becomes too bare to support us. We shall return to my castle, for a fine meal and singing."

"You are right, old friend," nodded Fenwick. He went to gather his troops for departure, his mind already working out plans to track down and destroy the creatures of evil that had been released. A good hunt, like he hadn't had in a long time . . . he'd need a new suit, and maybe a new hunting horn as well . . . Maybe this wouldn't be so bad after all. A pity about the sword, though . . . and Mizzamir . . .

In a sparsely wooded valley in the foothills at the southeastern edge of the Waste, a small band of renegades, minus two, collapsed in the green cover and watched the dawn rise over the hills in gentle harmony with the night.

Arcie, his wounds healed by Kaylana's strengthened magic, looked at the sun in silence, tears running down his small face. Poor old Sam. And all that time they'd been traveling with a Hero . . . He'd never really known the knight, and still couldn't believe what had happened, but the death of his lanky, insane friend hurt him deeply.

Sam had never asked for anything more than to live the way he was born to, in a world where he was needed. Now that things were back in balance, there would be evil men as well as good men, darkness as well as light, and a whole variety of color and shades of person that he still couldn't fit into Mizzamir's theory of good and evil. In a way, Sam had been like the clothes he'd worn; all one color on the surface, pure evil at first glance . . . but that shadow was supported and held together by a thousand other patches that made him what he was, more than an assassin, more than a man, but a sentient being, with opinions, desires, laughter and tears, three-dimensional and multicolored, a thousand shades of gray and a cluster of patches of rainbow covered unfairly by the blanket definition of evil.

Robin was stroking his harp gently. There were a lot of words to write . . . maybe Fenwick and company would try to hunt him down, but he had lived through the salvation of a world, and he was going to tell his stories as he'd lived them. He looked back at the bandaged stub of his tail, the gray waterfall that had once been his pride and joy, gone. A good thing no other centaurs were here to see him like this. And there was still that strange song from the tree in his dream, going through his head. *I would write and play music like that,* he thought. *I will.*

Valerie looked up at the leaves on the tree, her hood pulled over her face once more in the dawning sunlight. But there would be night again, blessed coolness. Someday, perhaps, revenge . . . when she was stronger, and Fenwick weaker. She could wait. For now, imagining his anguish at the return of evil was enough. She had used her magic to color her robes and hair black once more. Nightshade, glossy jet again, perched on a stump nearby and preened solemnly.

Far away, the last trickling scraps of darkness needed for the balancing flew free, and the DarkGate stilled in its silent, salt-wind-scoured hilltop. Then, suddenly, it vanished, rock and all. For like the Labyrinth and the LightGate, the DarkGate was everywhere and nowhere, a common thread through all existence that now at last could run along correctly over the mesh of reality, adding its own steady balance to the force of the LightGate. The last few grains of white marble from the Labyrinth vanished, and the great magical construction of the gods was no more.

Unseen, as the pressure eased, a million tiny holes appeared in the fabric of the universe, falling to earth like onyx gems of many sizes, gently sprinkling negative energy of darkness and evil, a slow welling that began throughout the world, countering the influx of Light from the Lightportals scattered across the lands. The balance stabilized as the new Darkportals glittered, in seas, in deserts, in farmers' fields and mountain caves. Some would be found by young wizards, seeking a way of power without the scruples of the white robes; some would lie undiscovered, keeping the balance, weaving darkness as their diametric oppositions poured light.

In the divine realms, beyond the eyes of man, even the heavens tilted into balance as ancient gods of darkness and evil returned, cautiously, taking their places in opposition to the gods of goodness and light. Hruul watched from the shadows, his eyes glinting, and Tharzak, with his collection of blades, walked the sharp edges of existence. Baris and Bella came sneaking back, grinning and poking each other, and thought up new mischief. Azal, Lord of Death, far beyond the lesser gods, had never truly been away, and only smiled softly as the world shifted back to normal. The divine beings circled each other warily. Slowly, men and women who, for their own reasons, turned from the light, or reverted to their old ways as some of the whitewashing magic slowly faded, would turn to these gods and begin to build temples and relearn old rituals.

Kaylana sat against a large boulder torn free of the mountain, her staff across her knees. The world was back in balance, she could feel its gentle turning beneath her like a wooden bowl, spinning gently and evenly. A War as great as that that had led to this might never happen again . . . but once more there was the conflict, the battle between good and evil, life and death, that let the seasons turn, that let existence continue. She would have to go back to her forest, or another forest . . . sooner or later, some people would turn their backs on both good and evil and seek to learn the ancient ways of balance, and Kaylana would be there to instruct them. It might be lonely, though . . . she'd never thought of being lonely before. An image of blond hair and laughing hazel eyes drifted across her thoughts, and she shook her head, trying to forget, to remain aloof and away from such emotions . . . but it was not easy. She almost sighed.

Suddenly her head jerked up. Something out of the corner of her eye . . . she sprang to her feet and the others spun around to see what had alarmed her.

With a stumble, a figure in patched black silk fell out of a flat shadow on the rock and collapsed on the grass, face pale, clothes bloodstained.

"Sam!" Arcie shouted, as Kaylana dropped to her knees and touched his chest, gripping her staff and reciting words of power. Slowly the color returned to the assassin's face as his wounds healed. His hazel eyes blinked, opened, and looked around with a cool sparkle.

"Hello," he said. "I swear, I think I've passed out more times these past few weeks than ever in all my life. By the way, if the situation should arise again, don't run so damn fast. Even through Shadow I had a hell of a time tracking you down."

"We thought you were dead," stammered Robin. Sam shook his head.

"Takes more than that to kill an assassin . . . speaking of which . . . "

"Here," Arcie said, in relief, tossing a small sack of gemstones to him. "By rights there must be more than some thousand gold worth in there . . . plus this." He dug around in a pocket and pulled out a large, red-gold coin; a blood-coin, carried for many years. He handed it to the assassin, who took it respectfully, bowing his head as tradition demanded, accepting the stigma of the kill with the coin. "A fine job, laddie."

Valerie shook her head. "I must admit, I'm amazed we made it . . . "

"But Blackmail . . . " began Sam.

"It was his choice, at the end," said Kaylana gently. "I heard him say as much."

Sam nodded. He sat up. "That's a lot better, thanks . . . So we won?"

"Yes," a new yet familiar voice said, **"You did. But then, I knew that."**

They looked up, startled, to see a tall figure sitting on the rock before them. He was dressed in loose, rippling garments of some strange substance that shifted and changed colors like a soap bubble. His eyes, still shivering with knowledge like a rushing flame, were truly insane, but with a calm, self-assured madness that was different than the wildness they had seen before.

"Bhazo!" exclaimed Arcie, taking a few steps backward, in case the freed semi-deity decided to lunge for him, while at the same time being unsure whether to run for it or bow in respect. The others reacted instinctively; Sam tensed, Kaylana gripped her staff. Robin, caught lying down, froze as the others did, though he had never seen the figure before. Valerie inched back slightly, her hand holding her Darkportal. But Bhazo simply sat and watched them, a faint insane smile playing across his lips.

"Don't worry," he said, **"I just came by to thank you."**

"Thank us?" asked Kaylana. "But we left you trapped!"

Bhazo smiled. **"Ah, but when you brought the darkness back, there was enough negative energy at last for the necessary to happen . . . for a divine being to die."**

"You mean you're . . . dead?" stammered Arcie. Sam's professional opinion was that Bhazo didn't *look* dead, but one never could tell with deities . . .

Valerie stammered, "Sorry about that whole thing with the Darkportal and all, I was really not . . . "

Bhazo waved a hand genially. They could see around his neck a large scar from where the dragonfire noose had burned so long.

"I've gotten what I wanted, and it's you five, plus the knight, who helped me. By the way, remember what I said about the fruits, it's very important. Any by the how-what-why, I'm glad things worked out as they did. You know, the Tests were designed so that only the one person who was fated to do so could win it . . . It's nice how Fate can sometimes come through."

"We didn't need to work so hard? We'd have passed

the Tests anyway?" Robin gasped. "But that can't be! The Tests were designed by Heroes, for heroes . . . "

"Heroes are what you make them, and where you find them. No, neither gods nor Heroes knew who the people that could pass the Tests would be; that was left up to the workings of Fate, who isn't a deity, by the way. Even I didn't know if you'd make it . . . but, as I said, I'm glad you did. And if you hadn't worked hard, Robin of Avensdale, you might not have been the precise person needed to pass the Test."

"Very strange," said Sam, shaking his head. "And what happened to the DarkGate?"

"Gone but still here, in everything without being anywhere. Sort of like shadows, and you know what I mean, assassin." Bhazo winked. **"You'd have to be mad to understand it . . . "**

"So what happens to you, now that you're dead?" Valerie asked.

"That I can't tell you. By the small singing turtles, it's confusing enough in my head with getting metaphysical! I suppose I'll have to wait and see. But first, a final parting gift of some last mad wisdom." Bhazo raised a finger, his eyes glittering. **"Centaur; remember this. Thirty north, forty west. You'll understand one day."** Robin seemed confused, but dutifully wrote the words down on a scrap of paper. **"Valeriana Ebonstar. Replace wormroot with greenweed some time in casting the Elder Nine Seeking spell. I think you'll find the results interesting. You, Kaylana Nathalorial . . . "** Bhazo paused, thinking a moment, occasionally flinching as some particularly powerful burst of knowledge thumped through his brain. Being dead, however, seemed to have helped calm his madness somewhat. He smiled. **"There's nothing really I can tell you that you'd need to know . . . except a bit of advice. You're very good at following your will . . . Take a rest, young one; and yes, you are young, though you and I have seen not too different a number of summers."** There were a few startled exclamations; though they had had their suspicions, none had really been able to believe that

Kaylana was, in fact, one of the original Druids, over a century and a half old. Bhazo continued. **"Let your heart off the short leash you keep it on, for a change. As the world fully balances, and your people return under your guidance, Time will begin to notice you once again. You will have a lifespan. Use it to the fullest."** He turned from the thoughtful Druid to the Barigan, with a grin. **"Ah, Reinhart Corallis MacRory."** Arcie yelped, and waved his hands, trying to deny the words.

"Nay! Nay! Argh, blast your mad eyes, you fool's god!" He pulled his hat over his face, hiding in shame.

"Reinhart?" Sam exclaimed in shock. "Reinhart *Corallis?* And you teased *me* about *my* name?"

"That's not important," said Bhazo, waving a hand. **"Anyway, dragon gold you were after, right? I've got something better. Your father has a map of the Triangle Isles, but he's read it wrong all these years. Get it, fold the corners inward. Then it should show you something worth seeing."**

"Cor!" exclaimed Arcie, or rather, R.C., as he peered over the edge of his battered hat.

"And the assassin they call Sam," said Bhazo at last, thoughtfully. **"I could tell you your true name, but I don't think it would serve any purpose. You are what you are, and you have always known that."**

"Yes," admitted Sam. "I guess so. These past weeks have brought that home fairly strongly.

"And you also are content in yourself . . . Therefore, simple advice. Don't change . . . unless you want to. And in response to your other difficulties . . . that sort of thing has troubled men and gods for all eternity. All I can suggest is patience, persistence, and being yourself. Nothing else will work in the long run. Just like an assignment." Bhazo stood up on the rock, stretching, and they backed off slightly, in respect. **"Time to go . . . by the way, now that Mizzamir is dead, some of his spells may be wearing off. Things may be getting interesting in your home Lands. But, after all, that was what you wanted. Anything but boredom."** There was a last chuckle, ever so slightly insane, and a shimmer, and the Mad Godling, free at last of his mortal coil, vanished.

"Is he gone?" Robin asked after a moment, looking around.

"Looks as that way," Arcie said, still surprised both at the assassin's miraculous escape from death and the strange visitation by the Mad Godling. "You know, Sam, there's bound to be work opening up for you soon . . . and all your whitewashed friends may as be needing refresher courses. Are you going to go back to Bistort?"

"I don't know," answered the assassin thoughtfully. There was much to think about. "Where are you all going to go?"

"Back to the tunnels," answered Valerie with a sharp smile. "To continue my research and occasionally wreak terrible villainy on surface dwellers when I get bored. You may hear of me, but don't come looking . . . or I may invite you to dinner."

"I'm going to continue my wanderings as a minstrel," said Robin.

"You should become a bard," Kaylana told him.

Robin stamped a hoof and wagged his docked tail. "But you've never told me what one is!"

"Then you can begin your training by looking," answered the Druid with a cool smile.

Robin waggled his ears in thought at this. He might just know of a place to start . . .

"I were thinking of going to see my father," Arcie said thoughtfully. "Take it easy for awhile. I'm not gettin' any younger . . . You could be Guildmaster of your own Guild, you know, Sam my lad," he added.

"Well . . . " mused the assassin. He looked at Kaylana shyly. *Patience, persistence,* he thought. "Where are you going, Druid?" he asked softly. Kaylana looked down, a bit of a smile on her face. She too was remembering Bhazo's words.

"Back to the woods, wandering on the way . . . to see if there are any who might choose to take up Druidism," she answered. Sam raised his eyebrows.

"Wandering . . . it may be dangerous."

"That is true," conceded Kaylana with a faint smile.

"You might need someone along, just for backup."

"That is possible," she replied.

"Even if he isn't a Druid, I know someone who'd be more than willing to wander with you." Sam smiled as he spoke. Kaylana returned the gaze and expression.

"I think that would be quite acceptable," she said.

"Och, now it starts," muttered Arcie, rolling his eyes and pulling out his pipe. Valerie chuckled to herself, and Robin smiled at his harp, thinking of lands to visit in search of the mysteries of the bards. Sam whispered something to Kaylana, and she laughed, and the stars moved in their courses, and the sun moved across the sky, and the world turned through its delicate balance, a game of chess, a set of scales, a spinning bowl, a drifting dream of a thousand thousand possible combinations spun from two extremes.